The Portable

Mark Twain

Edited by
BERNARD DE VOTO

PENGUIN BOOKS

PENGUIN BOOKS
Published by the Penguin Group
Penguin Books USA Inc.,
375 Hudson Street, New York, New York 10014, U.S.A.
Penguin Books Ltd, 27 Wrights Lane, London W8 5TZ, England
Penguin Books Australia Ltd, Ringwood, Victoria Australia
Penguin Books Canada Ltd, 10 Alcorn Avenue,
Toronto, Ontario, Canada M4V 3B2
Penguin Books (N.Z.) Ltd, 182-190 Wairau Road, Auckland 10, New Zealand

Penguin Books Ltd, Registered Offices:
Harmondsworth, Middlesex, England

First published in the United States of America
by Viking Penguin Inc. 1946
Paperbound edition published 1955
Reprinted 1956 (twice), 1957 (twice), 1958 (twice),
1959 (twice), 1960 (twice), 1961 (twice), 1962 (twice),
1963, 1964 (twice), 1965 (twice), 1966 (twice), 1967 (twice),
1968 (twice), 1969 (three times), 1970 (twice), 1971 (twice),
1972 (twice), 1973 (twice), 1974 (twice), 1975, 1976
Published by Penguin Books 1977

27 29 30 28 26

LIBRARY OF CONGRESS CATALOGING IN PUBLICATION DATA
Clemens, Samuel Langhorne, 1835–1910.
The portable Mark Twain.
Reprint of the 1946 ed. published by The Viking Press, New York.
I. De Voto, Bernard Augustine, 1897–1955.   II. Title.
ps1302.D4   1977   818'.4'09   76-48900
ISBN 0 14 015.020 X

Printed in the United States of America
Set in Caledonia, Barnum and Beton

CONTENTS

v

INTRODUCTION
BY BERNARD DeVoto

THE first truly American literature grew out of the tidewater culture of the early republic. It was the culture of a people who, whatever their diversity, were more homogeneous in feeling and belief than Americans as a people have ever been since them. We have come to think of the literature whose greatest names are Emerson and Poe, Thoreau and Melville, Hawthorne and Whitman, as our classic period, and in a very real sense the republic that shaped their mind was classical. It felt a strong affinity for the Roman Republic, it believed that Roman virtues and ideas had been expressed in the Constitution, it gave us a great architectural style because it identified its own emotions in the classic style. When Horatio Greenough let a toga fall from Washington's naked shoulders he was not out of tune with contemporary taste: Washington seemed a kind of consul, so did Jefferson, and in the portraits of them which our stamps and coins preserve they have a Roman look. This classical republican culture was at its most vigorous when our classic writers were growing up. But there is an element of anachronism in all literature, and while these men were themselves in full vigor American culture entered a new phase.

The culture of the early republic crossed the Alleghenies in two streams, one Southern, the other mainly New England; but they were more like each other than either was like the one which their mingling presently helped to produce. For beyond the mountains people found different landscapes, different river courses, different relationships of sky and wind and water, different conceptions of space and distance, different soils and climates—different conditions of life. Beyond still farther mountains lay Oregon and California—and they were implicit in the expanding nation as soon as the treaty that gave us Louisiana was signed—but first the United States had to incorporate the vast expanse between the eastern and the western heights of land. That area is the American heartland. Its greatest son was to call it the Egypt of the West because nature had organized it round a central river and it touched no ocean, but it came into the American consciousness as the Great Valley. When the tidewater culture came to the Great Valley it necessarily broke down: new conditions demanded adaptations, innovations, new combinations and amplifications. The new way of life that began to develop there had a different organization of feeling, a different metabolism of thought. It was no more native, no more "American," than that of the first republic, but it was different and it began to react on it.

The heartland was midcontinental and its energies were oriented toward the river at its center—and were therefore turned away from Europe, which had been a frontier of the early republic. And life in the heartland, with its mingling of stocks, its constant shifting of population, and its tremendous distances, led people in always increasing numbers to think continentally. Both facts were fundamental in the thought and feeling of the new culture.

The American littoral came only slowly, with greater slowness than the fact demanded, to realize that the nation's center of gravity was shifting westward. It tragically failed to understand one consequence of that shift, thirty years of contention between the Northeast and the South to dominate the Great Valley or at least achieve a preferential linkage with it. The failure to understand was in great part a failure to think continentally—as was made clear at last when the Civil War demonstrated that no peaceful way of resolving the contention had been found. Even now too many Americans fail to understand that the war, the resolution by force, only made explicit the organization of our national life that is implicit in the geography which the Great Valley binds together. Abraham Lincoln understood our continental unity; he argued it persistently down to the outbreak of the war and from then on. And Lincoln was a distillation of the heartland culture.

Lincoln's feeling for the continentalism of the American nation was so intense that it almost transcended the transcendent facts. It was a deposit in the very cells of his bones from the soil of the Great Valley. He was, Herndon rightly says, one of the limestone men, the tall, gaunt, powerful, sallow, saturnine men who appear in quantity enough to constitute a type when the wilderness on both sides of the Ohio comes under the plow. His radical democracy was wrought from the experience of the Great Valley. In his ideas and beliefs as in the shadowed depths of his personality there is apparent a new articulation of American life. His very lineaments show it. When you turn from the Jefferson nickel to the Lincoln penny as when you turn from Jefferson's first inaugural address to any of Lincoln's state papers, in the flash of a total and immediate response you understand that you have turned from one era to a later one. You have turned from the tidewater republic to the continental empire.

Lincoln expressed a culture and brought a type to climax. Similarly, when that culture found major literary expression it did so from a rich and various, if humble, literary tradition. As always, the literary expression was the later one; the economic, social, and political impact was felt much earlier. The lag, however, was not so great as Walt Whitman thought. Whitman was sixty when in 1879 he traveled across the Great Valley to its western limit, where the Front Range walls it off. He traversed it with a steadily growing conviction that here in the flesh were the people whose society he had envisioned in so many rhapsodies, Americans who had been fused, annealed, compacted (those are his words) into a new identity. He felt that literature had not yet spoken to these prairie people, "this continental inland West," that it had not yet spoken for them, that it had not made images for their spirit.

The poet supposed that he was speaking of things still to come but he was already wrong by a full ten years. The thing had happened. And the first notification that it had happened can be dated with an exactness not often possible in the history of literature. That notification came in 1869 with the appearance of a book of humorous travel sketches by Samuel Langhorne Clemens, who, faithful to the established tradition, signed it with a pen name, Mark Twain.

Innocents Abroad was greeted with an enthusiasm that made Mark Twain a celebrity overnight, and with too much misunderstanding of a kind that was to persist throughout his career. It was a funny book and a cardinal part of its fun was its disdain of European culture. This disdain, the mere fact of making humor of such disdain, and its frequent exaggeration into burlesque all produced an effect of shock—in most ways a delightful shock but in some ways an uneasy one. Yet the point was not the provinciality of such humor, though it was frequently provincial, and not its uncouthness, though it was sometimes uncouth, but the kind of consciousness it implied. Again it is absurd to speak of this as the first American literature that was independent of European influences, for our literature had obediently divorced itself from Europe as soon as Emerson ordered it to. The humorous core of *Innocents Abroad* was not independence of Europe, but indifference to it. Thoreau and Emerson and Poe were detached from Europe but completely aware of being heirs to it, but here was a literature which had grown up in disregard of Europe—which had looked inward toward the Mississippi and not outward beyond the Atlantic. Failure to appreciate the implications of this difference was one reason, no doubt the weightiest one, why for two full generations literary critics thought of Mark Twain as no more than a clown. But the same identity, the same organization of personality, that made Lincoln the artificer of our continental unity was what made Mark Twain a great writer.

There are striking affinities between Lincoln and Mark Twain. Both spent their boyhoods in a society that was still essentially frontier; both were rivermen. Both absorbed the midcontinental heritage: fiercely equalitarian democracy, hatred of injustice and oppression, the man-to-man individualism of an expanding society. Both were deeply acquainted with melancholy and despair; both were fatalists. On the other hand, both were instinct with the humor of the common life and from their earliest years made fables of it. As humorists, both felt the basic gravity of humor; with both it was an adaptation of the mind, a reflex of the struggle to be sane; both knew, and Mark Twain said, that there is no humor in heaven. It was of such resemblances that William Dean Howells was thinking when he called Mark Twain "the Lincoln of our literature."

II

Samuel Clemens was born at Florida, Monroe County, Missouri, on November 30, 1835, a few months after his parents reached the village from Tennessee. His father was a Virginian, his mother a Kentuckian, and as a family they had made three moves before this one. Florida was a handful of log cabins only two hundred miles east of the Indian Country and in the earliest stage of frontier economy. Though he could have only a generalized memory of it, Sam's earliest years were thus spent in the "Sweet Betsy from Pike" society which has contributed a color and a flavor of its own to American legendry. More: the town was located at the forks of that Salt Creek which figures in the folk proverbs. He could retain little conscious memory of the chinked-log, open-fireplace hamlet with its woods-runners and movers; mostly it would mean the immediacy of nature, the infinity of the forest, the ease of escape into solitude and an all-encompassing freedom. He was still short of four when the Clemenses made their last move, this time eastward. They seem to have been movers by force of circumstance, not instinct; it was always the pressure of poverty and the hope of betterment that impelled them on. But they bequeathed restlessness to their son.

The final move brought them to Hannibal, an older settlement than Florida and perhaps four times as large but still short of five hundred inhabitants. Hannibal is the most important single fact in the life of Samuel Clemens the person and Mark Twain the writer. It too was lapped round by forest; it maintained the romantic mystery, the subliminal dread, and the intimacy with nature that he had been born to; but it had passed the pioneering stage. It must be seen as a later stage that characterized all our frontiers east of the great plains, after the actual frontier of settlement had pushed westward, after the farms had been brought in and functional communities had been established, but while the frontier crafts and values and ways of thinking lingered on, a little mannered perhaps, a little nostalgic, but still vital. The frontier thugs had passed to other fields or degenerated to village loafers and bullies. There were a few Indians near by and sizable numbers not too far away but they were a spectacle, not a threat. A few hunters and trappers ranged the woods but they were relics, brush folk, not of the great race. There were as many frame houses as log cabins; if the schoolhouse had a puncheon floor, the squire's wife had a silk dress from St. Louis. Caste lines were almost nonexistent. Hannibal was a farmers' market village. More than half of its inhabitants were Southerners, but Southerners modified by the Great Valley. Its slaves were servants, not gang laborers.

But also Hannibal was on the Mississippi. Here enters the thread of cosmopolitanism that is so paradoxically interwoven with the extreme provincialism of this society. Steamboats bore the travelers and commerce of half a continent past the town wharf. Great rafts of logs and lumber—it was the latter kind that Huck and Jim traveled on—came down from Wisconsin. A population of freighters, movers, and mere drifters in shanty boats, keelboats, broadhorns, mackinaws, and scows added pageantry. Other types and other costumery came down from the lakes and northern rivers: voyageurs, trappers, winterers, Indians of the wilderness tribes always seen in ceremonial garments on their way to make treaties or collect annuities. All these belonged to the rapidly widening movement of the expanding nation. Moreover, Hannibal was within the aura of St. Louis, eighty miles away, and St. Louis was the port through which the energies of a truly imperial expansion were moving toward Santa Fe, Oregon, and California. Perhaps dimly but quite permanently any river town so near St. Louis would give even the most local mind an awareness of the continental divide, the Columbia, the Pacific, the Southwest. A town that may have never heard of Zebulon Pike or John Ledyard or Jonathan Carver nevertheless felt the national will that had turned them westward. The year of Mark's birth, 1835, may properly be taken as the year when the final phase of our continental expansion began. And the fruitfulness of Hannibal for Mark's imagination may reasonably be said to have stopped with his tenth year, just before that final phase raised up the irrepressible conflict.

For two things remain to be said of the society that shaped Sam Clemens's mind and feelings: that its post-pioneer, frontier stage stops short of the industrial revolution, and that the sectional conflict which produced the Civil War has not yet shown itself. The life which is always most desirable in Mark's thinking is the pre-industrial society of a little river town; it is a specific identification of Hannibal. Whereas the evils of life are the eternal cruelties, hypocrisies, and stupidities of mankind which have nothing to do with time or place but result from Our Heavenly Father's haste in experimenting when He grew dissatisfied with the monkey.

As the St. Petersburg of *Tom Sawyer*, Hannibal is one of the superb idyls of American literature, perhaps the supreme one. A town of sun, forest shade, drowsy peace, limpid emotions, simple humanity—and eternity going by on the majestic river. Even here, however, a mood of melancholy is seldom far away: a melancholy of the river itself, of our westering people who had always known solitude, and of a child's feeling, which was to grow through the years, that he was a stranger and a mysterious one under the stars. And below the melancholy there is a deeper stratum, a terror or disgust that may break through in a graveyard at midnight or at the sound of unidentified voices whispering above the water. This is in part fantasy, but in part also it is the weary knowledge of evil that paints Hannibal in far different colors in *Pudd'nhead Wilson* or *Huckleberry Finn*.

Almost as soon as he begins to write, Mark Twain is a citizen of the world, but he is always a citizen of Hannibal too. He frequently misunderstood himself, but he knew that quite clearly. In a postscript to the fragment of a letter "to an unidentified person," printed on page 773 (omitted in the text because Mark himself crossed it out), he says:

And yet I can't go away from the boyhood period & write novels because *capital* [that is, personal experience] is not sufficient by itself & I lack the other essential: interest in handling the men & experiences of later times.

While still a boy, he was apprenticed to a printer and so got the education that served more nineteenth-century American writers than any other. (It was a surprisingly extensive education. By twenty he knew the English classics thoroughly, was an inveterate reader of history, and had begun to cultivate his linguistic bent.) The trade eventually led him to newspaper reporting but first it took him on a series of *Wanderjahre* toward which heredity may have impelled him. At eighteen he went to St. Louis and on to New York. Philadelphia followed, Muscatine, St. Louis again, Keokuk (where he began to write humorous newspaper sketches), and Cincinnati, always setting type on a newspaper or in a job shop. He was twenty-two years old (and, if his memory can be trusted, ripe with a characteristic fan-

tasy of South American adventure) when the American
spectacle caught him up. In 1857 he began his apprenticeship to a Mississippi pilot.

Little need be said about his piloting in a book that
includes "Old Times on the Mississippi," a study in pure
ecstasy. The book is of course stamped from his memory, which was always nostalgic, and from the ro-
mancing half of his twinned talent. It records a supreme
experience about whose delight there can be no doubt
whatever, and it testifies to Mark's admiration of all
skills and his mastery of one of the most difficult. But
piloting gave him more than ever got into "Old Times"
or its enlargement, *Life on the Mississippi.* "Flush
Times" would have done as well as "Old Times" to
describe the climactic years of the prewar Mississippi
Valley, with the rush and fever of the expanding nation.
Those years vastly widened Mark's knowledge of America and fed his insatiable enjoyment of men, his absorbed observation of man's depravity, and his delight
in spectacle.

The Civil War put an end to piloting. Mark has
described his experience and that of many others in
that war, in all wars, in a sketch which is one of the
best things he ever wrote. "The Private History of a
Campaign That Failed" could not be spared from the
mosaic of our national catastrophe; it is one of the contexts in which Mark Twain has perfectly refracted a
national experience through a personal one. When his
military career petered out in absurdity, he joined the
great national movement which even civil war could
not halt. His older brother, the gentle zany Orion, was
made Secretary of the Territory of Nevada and, paying
the Secretary's passage west, Mark went along. In
Nevada he found another national retort, another mixed
and violent society, another speculative flush times. He

became a drunkard of speculation, a prospector, a hunter of phantasmal mines, a silver miner, a laborer in a stamp mill, and at last a newspaperman. He went to work for that fabulous paper *The Territorial Enterprise* of Virginia City as an "editor," that is to say a reporter. And it was here that he took his immortal *nom de plume*, a phrase from the pilot's mystery. "Mark Twain" was signed to a species of humor in which Sam Clemens had been immersed ever since his apprenticeship, the newspaper humor of the Great Valley, which was in turn a development of the pungent oral humor he had heard from childhood on. Far from establishing a literary tradition, Mark Twain brought one to culmination.

After less than two years on the *Enterprise* he went to California, in 1864. He had met Artemus Ward in Nevada; now he joined the transient, bright Bohemia of the Golden Gate: Bret Harte, Prentice Mulford, Charles Warren Stoddard, Charles H. Webb, Ada Clare, Ina Coolbrith, still slighter and more forgotten names. He got a new kind of companionship and his first experience of literary sophistication. After a short time as a reporter he began to write humor for the Coast's literary papers, the *Californian* and the *Golden Era*. Promptly his work developed a strain of political and ethical satire which it never lost: the humorist was seldom separable from the satirist from this year on. That is to say, the individual humor of Mark Twain with its overtones of extravaganza and its undercurrent of misanthropy was, however crude and elliptical, fully formed by the end of 1864. He had not yet revealed the novelist's power to endow character with life, but it— together with a memorable talent for the vernacular— was made clear to anyone with eyes on December 16, 1865, when the New York *Saturday Press* published "Jim Smiley and His Jumping Frog."

The immortal story derived from still another Western experience, one which had made Mark, however lackadaisically, a pocket miner. He had sent it east at Artemus Ward's suggestion, but only an accident got it into type. It was a momentary smash hit, and so Mark was not altogether an unknown when he went to New York in 1867. Before he went there, however, he had reached the farthest limit of the expansionist dream, having gone to the Sandwich Islands as a newspaper correspondent. That voyage in turn had initiated his career as a lecturer. He had a marked histrionic talent; for years he barnstormed or made occasional appearances as a public "reader" and story-teller; all his life was making the after-dinner appearances of that vanished age, which pleased his vanity and gratified the longings of an actor *manqué*. But he went to New York as a correspondent: he had arranged to travel to Europe and the Holy Land with a conducted tour. In 1867 he published his first book, a collection of sketches called *The Celebrated Jumping Frog of Calaveras County* after the best of them, but the year is more notable for the travel letters he wrote for the *Alta California* and the New York *Tribune*. He made a book of them after his return, meanwhile writing free-lance humor and Washington correspondence. The book, *Innocents Abroad,* was published in 1869.

All this has been detailed to show how deep and various an experience of American life Mark Twain had had when he began to write. The rest of his biography is also strikingly typical of nineteenth-century America, but the seed-time has now been accounted for. It is not too much to say that he had seen more of the United States, met more kinds and castes and conditions of Americans, observed the American in more occupations and moods and tempers—in a word had intimately shared a greater variety of the characteristic experiences of his countrymen—than any other major American writer. The selections printed in this book have been chosen to show, as well as may be, the richness of that variety. Mark Twain's work is almost as diverse as his experience, and no selection can justly represent it in a single volume. The decision has been to sacrifice first of all the funny man, the professional joker working at his trade from day to day. Not the humorist, for Mark's humor is as much style as joke and is more personality than style, and he could not write about even death or man's depravity without infusing them with the humor that kept him sane. The fabulist of *Tom Sawyer* is also unrepresented: the reader must accept that greater fable, *Adventures of Huckleberry Finn*, and for the idyl of St. Petersburg is referred to John Quarles's farm. The most serious distortion is that our selections hardly even suggest the extent of Mark's *ad hoc* satire. It would have been obligatory, if it had been possible, to include much from his forty years of tireless castigation of American society, government, morals, and manners, and more than appears here of his quarrel with France, the German language, and literary sentimentality. The decision has been to hold to the more general and more profound satire, which becomes misanthropic in his last fifteen years and, after transformation, reaches a climax in *The Mysterious Stranger*. The hope is that enough else has been exhibited to lead anyone who needs leading to the rich remainder.

III

Mark Twain was a man of moods, of the extreme of moods. He had a buoyancy which, twinned as it was with gentleness and intuition and wit, gave him a per-

sonal magnetism which his friends did not hesitate to
call enchantment. Yet it alternated with an anger that
readily became fury and was rooted in a revulsion between disgust and despair. The alternation suggests a
basic split; it is clearly marked in his personality and
equally evident in his books. The splendor his friends
felt, his kindness to the unfortunate and the lowly and
the oppressed, his generosity, his sensitiveness unite in
a singular luminosity of spirit. Yet he was capable of
savage vindictiveness, he exaggerated small or imaginary grievances out of all reason, and on little or no
provocation he repeatedly believed himself misrepre-
sented or betrayed. One doubts if any other American
writer was ever so publicly beloved or privately adored;
one is certain that no other was involved in so many
lawsuits. "I am full of malice, saturated with malignity,"
he wrote eight months before his death. His malice and
malignity of that moment were for the damned human
race, but he could feel them in his private life whenever
he thought he had been wronged. When *A Connecticut
Yankee* was finished he wrote Howells that if he could
write it over again "there wouldn't be so many things
left out. They burn in me and they keep multiplying and
multiplying, but now they can't even be said. And besides they would require a library—and a pen warmed
up in hell." With a pen warmed up in hell he did fill a
library and an extraordinary bulk of letters too. If it
was sometimes avenging personal, usually imaginary
wrongs, that private activity was only a reflex of the
public function. For what burned in him was hatred of
cruelty and injustice, a deep sense of human evil, and a
recurrent accusation of himself. Like Swift he found
himself despising man while loving Tom, Dick, and
Harry so warmly that he had no proper defense against
the anguish of human relationships. The trouble was

that in terms of either earth or heaven he was never sure what to make of Samuel L. Clemens and so is recorded on both sides.

He is usually to be found on both sides of any question he argues. His intelligence was intuitive, not analytical. He reasoned fluently, with an avidity that touched most of the surface flow of his time, but superficially and with habitual contradictions. He had little capacity for sustained thought and to get to the heart of a question had to abandon analysis and rely on feeling. The philosophy which he spent years refining and supposed he had perfected is a sophomoric determinism. Even so, it is less a philosophy than a symbol or a rationalization; the perceptions it stood for are expressed at the level of genius in his fiction—not as idea but in terms of human life. Most of the nineteenth century's optimisms were his also. He fiercely championed the democratic axioms; they are the ether of his fiction and the fulcrum of his satire. He thought too that the nineteenth century, especially as Progress, and more especially as Progress in the United States, was the happiest estate of man; he believed that it was bringing on a future of greater freedom and greater happiness. This was basic and spontaneous in his mind, but at the same time he felt something profoundly wrong. There seemed to be some limitation to freedom, some frustration of happiness. He never really came to grips with the conflict. Only in the last fifteen years of his life did he ascribe any part of what might be wrong to any but superficial injustices in American life or any but slight dislocations in our system. By the time he became aware of serious threats to freedom they did not seem to matter much: he was so absorbed in the natural depravity of man that the collapse or frustration of democracy, which he was by then taking for granted, seemed only

an unimportant detail. Ideally, his last years would
have been spent in more rigorous analysis—if not of
the objective data, then of his intuitive awareness of
them. They were not and so his judgments remained
confused—and his principal importance in our literature
belongs to his middle years, the period when his mind
and feelings are in healthy equilibrium. It is an importance of his perceptions, not his thinking, and it
exists primarily in his fiction, most purely in *Huckleberry Finn*. The best of Mark Twain's fiction is, historically, the first mature realization in our literature
of a conflict between the assumptions of democracy and
the limitations on democracy. Between the ideal of freedom and the nature of man.

Not less important is the fact that there is a reconcili-
ation, even an affirmation. Detachment could be no
greater but it is still somehow compassionate; condem-
nation could be no more complete, but it is somehow
magnanimous. The damned human race is displayed
with derision and abhorrence, yet this is on the ground
that it has fallen short of its own decencies. Moreover
at least *Huckleberry Finn* has a hero, the only heroic
character (apart from Joan of Arc, a debauch of gyn-
eolatry) he ever drew, and it is the essence of what
Mark Twain had to say that the hero is a Negro slave.
It has also a vindication not only of freedom, but of
loyalty and decency, kindness and courage; and it is
the essence of Mark Twain that this vindication is made
by means of a boy who is a spokesman of the folk mind
and whom experience has taught wariness and skepti-
cism. Like all great novels *Huckleberry Finn* moves on
many levels of significance, but it describes a flight and
a struggle for freedom, and the question it turns on is
a moral question.

Mark found zest and gusto—nouns that do not de-

scribe very much American literature of the first rank—
in whatsoever was alive. He liked few novels except
those of his intimate friends. What he praised in the
ones he did like was reality of behavior, speech, or
motive; his notebooks are sulphurous with comments on
merely literary, that is false, characters. His taste was
for biography, autobiography, history—life direct, men
revealing themselves. No doubt the race was damned
but it was fascinating. And that was proper for if his
fiction is the best of his work, his most salient talent as a
novelist is the life giving power. It is a careless and
prodigal fecundity, but nevertheless remarkably con-
centrated. Old Man Finn, for instance, is greatly
imagined and he seems to fill the first half of the book,
yet he appears in only a few pages. Mrs. Judith Loftus
lives completely in a single chapter. A mere passer-by,
a casual of the river or a thug heard talking in a frowzy
town, may reveal a whole personality in a few paragraphs. Nor is this fecundity confined to Mark's fiction,
for the framework of all his books is anecdotal and all
the people in them are dramatized. The whole population of his principal books, nine-tenths of the population of all his books, has the same vividness. Boys, villagers, the rivermen, the Negroes, Colonel Sellers, the
two great vagabonds—there is nothing quite like the
Mark Twain gallery elsewhere in American literature.

But there is a striking limitation: nowhere in that
gallery are there women of marriageable age. No white
women, that is, for the slave Roxana in *Pudd'nhead
Wilson* lives as vividly as Old Man Finn himself. It
must be significant that the only credible woman of an
age that might sanction desire is withdrawn from desire
behind the barrier of race. None of Mark Twain's nubile
girls, young women, or young matrons are believable;
they are all bisque, saccharine, or tears. He will do girl

children in the romantic convention of boys' books and he is magnificent with the sisterhood of worn frontier wives whom Aunt Polly climaxes, but something like a taboo drains reality from any woman who might trouble the heart or the flesh. There is no love story in Mark Twain, there is no love at all beyond an occasional admission, for purposes of plot only, that someone is married or is going to be. Women seldom have husbands and men seldom have wives unless they are beyond middle age. Mark's endless absorption in human motives did not, for literary purposes at least, extend to sexual motives. Sex seems to be forbidden unless it can be treated mawkishly, and this writer of great prose who habitually flouted the genteel proprieties of language was more prudish than the most tremulous of his friends in regard to language that might suggest either desire or its gratification. So there is a sizable gap in the world he created. That gap has never been accounted for. Certainly there was nothing bloodless about Mark Twain; and his marriage, one of the happiest of literary marriages, was clearly passionate. Yet he did not marry till he was thirty-five (1870), and there may have been something permissive—to a man whose characters have usually lost a father if not both parents—in the fact that he married an invalid.

Few Americans have written as much as Mark Twain. His published works are not much greater in bulk than his unpublished manuscripts, the books he finished fewer than the ones he broke off and abandoned. He wrote on impulse and enthusiasm and while they lasted he wrote easily, but he wrote as needs must, for he had little faculty of self-criticism and but small ability to sustain or elaborate an idea. He was best at the short haul. Not only his fiction but the personalized narrative that is the vehicle of *Innocents Abroad, A Tramp*

Abroad, Life on the Mississippi, and much else is episodic. When what he was writing was in circuit with his deepest perceptions he was superb. The breaking of the circuit always threw him into extemporization, which meant that fiction fell away into extravaganza and satire into burlesque. At such times he did not know that he was flatting; the serious artist could become a vaudeville monologuist in a single page without being aware that the tone had changed. That such a well-imagined novel as *Pudd'nhead Wilson* was written round the grotesque joke called "Those Extraordinary Twins" would be incredible if the same tone-deafness were not plentifully evident elsewhere. He thought the mawkish *Joan of Arc* and the second-rate *The Prince and the Pauper* his best work. He interrupted his masterpiece before it was half-finished, liking it so little that he threatened to burn it, and ignored it for six years during which, though he wrote constantly, he wrote nothing of importance. Then he finished it almost as casually as he had begun it. There is no greater book in American literature, but critics agree that the last quarter of it is impaired by the extravaganza that begins when Huck gets to Uncle Silas's farm. It is typical of Mark Twain that he felt no difference in kind or key between this admittedly superb extravaganza and the searching of American society and human experience that precedes it. In fact, the delivery of Jim from the dungeon was one of Mark's favorite platform readings.

Furthermore, he lacked the attribute of the artist—whatever it may be—that enables him to think a novel through till its content has found its own inherent form. Of his novels only *Joan of Arc, The Prince and the Pauper,* and *Tom Sawyer* have structures that have developed from within; significantly, all are simple and only one is first-rate. Mark lived with his material for a long time, sometimes for many years, but not consciously, not with critical or searching dissatisfaction. A book must come of its own momentum from the unconscious impulse, be it as a whole, as a fragment, or as something that hardly got started before it broke off. This is to say that he had no conscious esthetic. He stood at the opposite pole from Henry James, with the other great contemporary of both, Howells, in between but nearer to James. Yet he had as large a share as either of them in creating the modern American novel.

The explanation for his lack of self-criticism and for his innocence of esthetics is not to be found in the supposed naïveté of the society that bore him. In the first place, that society was far from naïve; in the second place, not only did the fine artist Howells come from it, but Mark himself raised its native tale-telling to a fine art, which surely establishes a discipline. He had, besides, two other disciplines: that of the daily job, which he observed as faithfully as any writer who ever lived, and the taskmastership of a great style. Nor can Mark's own explanation, which he pleads so earnestly in the letter to Andrew Lang, be supported: that he wrote for the belly and members only. *Huckleberry Finn* is no more written for the belly and members only than *War and Peace* is or *Recherche du Temps Perdu*. But it is written at the behest of an instinctive drive, and explanation need go no farther if it could, for this time at least Mark's whole personality was behind it. In short, he wrote trivially or splendidly or magnificently as what appears to have been little more than chance might determine: he was not a fully self-conscious artist. But when he wrote greatly he was writing from an inner harmony of desire and will. Or call it a harmony of his deepest self and his inheritance from the Great Valley. Only that harmony, seen in relation to time and history, can explain him. For no man ever became a great writer more inadvertently than Mark Twain. He first became famous as a superior Artemus Ward, and that corresponded to his idea of himself. A long time passed before he had any desire to be more. He exploited a joke-maker's talent as systematically as a production manager could have done it for him, delighted by the discovery that he could raise his status, prestige, and income beyond Tom Sawyer's dreams. Nevertheless there is the paradox that almost from the beginning the attack of the funny man had been supported by that of a serious artist. Already in "The Jumping Frog" mastery of fictional character is clearly presaged, and the prophecy is fulfilled as early as *The Gilded Age* (1874). By *The Gilded Age* also a satirist is dealing maturely with a wide expanse of American life. From this composite the funny man cannot be separated out for a long time, and during that time there are only sporadic indications that Mark saw either the novelist or the satirist as more than instrumentalities of the humorist. The paradox resists criticism. One can only repeat that Mark Twain's greatness developed because the time and the continent had shaped him at their core.

This representative centrality goes on undiminished after the establishment of his fame. Following his marriage he was briefly a newspaper owner in Buffalo but abandoned that career to move to a provincial New England city, Hartford, and set up as a professional writer. His periodic restlessness continued; he never spent the full year in Hartford, he made at least twelve trips abroad, and he once expatriated himself for nine years. The Hartford period, 1874–1891, covered his greatest happiness and the beginning of his catastrophe. His was an unusually happy family life, and he was the center of an always widening circle. Howells and the Rev. Joseph Twichell were his closest friends; Cable, Aldrich, most of the leading writers of his generation were of the circle, and it widened to include the rich, the famous, the powerful, and the great. Mark ruled it by divine right: there have always been conflicting opinions about his books, but only one has ever been possible about his dominion over men's affections. He seemed alien to mortality. A fantasy of his childhood is frequently set down in notes and fragments of manuscript: the child had identified himself with a romantic stranger in Hannibal, a mysterious, perhaps supernatural visitor from Elsewhere. As the one-gallus village boy came to be a world figure, that fantasy seemed on the way to being confirmed. There was further confirmation as the author of *The Gilded Age* entered with a blithe and innocent heart on another career as a speculator, and the stamp-mill operator and tramp printer, who sincerely believed all his life that he was a member of the laboring class, undertook with the same innocence to be an industrial promoter.

Always convinced that his publishers were defrauding him, Mark had established his own firm to publish his books. The expansion it underwent in order to handle the bestseller of the generation, *Personal Memoirs of U. S. Grant,* could not be sustained. The firm sank into insolvency and finally went bankrupt. It could probably have been saved except that the most fantastic of Mark's promotions failed at the same time and left him bankrupt. For years he had been pouring his earnings and his wife's fortune into a mechanical typesetter which would indeed have made him a multimillionaire if it had succeeded. Its failure and that of the publishing firm were only the beginning of a series of disasters on the same scale as his fantastic rise. He paid off his indebtedness by a heroic lecture tour that took him round the world but his health broke. The oldest of his three daughters, the one who seemed most like him in temperament and talent, died during his absence. An agonizing personality change in his youngest daughter was finally diagnosed as epilepsy. Mrs. Clemens declined into permanent invalidism and in 1904 died.

This prolonged catastrophe brought Mark's misanthropy out of equilibrium; it dominated the rest of his life. The disasters were, of course, personal and yet it is hardly straining the facts to find him here also representative of the nineteenth-century America that had already found so much expression in him. As the century neared its end there was a good deal of pessimism and disenchantment in the United States. A wave of doubt and questioning swept many minds. The people who began an imperialistic adventure in the Pacific with the same naïve enthusiasm that had taken Mark Twain into the industrial life were widely, at the very time they stepped out on the world stage, beginning to be troubled about themselves. The nineteenth century, looking back on its course, found cause to be dismayed. Was the democratic dream being served as well as the nation had assumed? Had the United States gone wrong somewhere during the avalanche of expansion? Were there, then, limits to what democracy could do, or flaws or contradictions in its theses, or impassable barriers in its path? Was the good time ending, were the vigorous years running out under a gathering shadow?

However deep or shallow this *fin de siècle* weariness may have been in the United States at large, Mark Twain's last fifteen years must be seen as related to it, if only distantly. During this period he wrote as much as in any similar length of time in his life, perhaps more, but most of it is fragmentary, unfinished.[1] Almost all of it deals with the nature of man, man's fate, and man's conceptions of honor and morality. There are fables, dialogues, diatribes—sometimes cold, sometimes passionate, derisive, withering, savage. Mark sees the American republic perishing, like republics before it, through the ineradicable cowardice, corruption, and mere baseness of mankind. He elaborates theories, which he embodies in imaginary histories of the world (and sometimes of extra-mundane societies) to support his prophecy, and yet he cannot be much troubled by the going-down of this western land, for year by year he is writing a general apocalypse. The Old Testament fables had always served him for humorous derision of man's gullibility, but now he uses them as missiles in a ferocious attack on human stupidity and cruelty. Man is compact of malignity, cowardice, weakness, and absurdity, a diseased organism, a parasite on nature, a foolish but murderous animal much lower than the swine.

Yet *What Is Man?* (published anonymously in 1906 but written before the turn of the century), the fullest of many developments of these themes, cannot be seen solely as a document in anthropophobia. It is also in complex ways a justification, even a self-justification. Its fixed universe, with an endless chain of cause and effect from the beginning of time, permits Mark to compose many variations on the theme of human pettiness, but also it serves to free man of blame—and thus satis-

---

[1] This period of Mark Twain's work has been studied only once and in part. See "The Symbols of Despair," in Bernard DeVoto, *Mark Twain at Work*, 1942. Note that even Mark Twain's Autobiography was not finished; in fact it was not meant to be. *What Is Man?* consists of a series of dialogues selected from a much larger number more or less loosely related. The chapter here referred to discusses various states of *The Mysterious Stranger*.

fies a need deeply buried in Mark's personal remorse. To this period also belongs *Mark Twain's Autobiography,* which serves him as an escape into the security of the boyhood idyl he had made immortal in *Tom Sawyer.* The need to escape is significant, but the release is even more so, for it breaks the obsession signified by *What Is Man?* But a much truer release and a fulfillment as well came, as always, when Mark turned from reasoning to the instinctual portions of his mind. The highest reach of his last period is *The Mysterious Stranger.* It is an almost perfect book—perfect in expression of his final drive, in imaginative projection of himself, in tone and tune, in final judgment on the nature of man and the experience of Mark Twain. It is on a humbler level than his great books. More than any of them it is Mark Twain somewhat in disregard of America. It is not, finally, a major work; but in its small way it is a masterpiece. Those who know and love Mark Twain will always find it as revealing as *Huckleberry Finn.*

IV

Mark Twain died in 1910 with, as he had foretold, the return of the mysterious visitor from beyond the solar system under whose sign he had been born, Halley's comet. His last years had been as full of honors as his middle years had been of fame. Even so, in 1910 it was hardly possible to define his importance in American literature as clearly as we can after another generation.

No doubt his first importance in that literature is the democratizing effect of his work. It is a concretely liberating effect, and therefore different in kind from Whitman's vision of democracy, which can hardly be said to have been understood by or to have found a response among any considerable number of Americans. Mark Twain was the first great American writer who was also a popular writer, and that in itself is important. Much more important is the implicit and explicit democracy of his books. They are the first American literature of the highest rank which portrays the ordinary bulk of Americans, expresses them, accepts their values, and delineates their hopes, fears, decencies, and indecencies as from within. The area proper to serious literature in the United States was enormously widened by them, in fact widened to the boundaries it still observes today. There have been no acknowledged priorities of caste in American writing since Mark Twain. Moreover, in his native equalitarian point of view, in his assertion of the basic democratic axioms, in his onslaught on privilege, injustice, vested power, political pretense, and economic exploitation (much of it admittedly superficial or confused, though much else is the most vigorous satire we have), in his transmutation of the town-meeting or country-store sharpness of judgment into a fine art—he is midnineteenth-century American democracy finding its first major voice in literature, ultimately its strongest voice. In him the literature of democracy becomes more robust than it had been before, such part of that literature, at least, as may be said to contain multitudes and speak to them. And this, to return to our starting point, embodies the transforming experience of the American people as they occupied the Great Valley and pushed beyond it, on the way forging the continental mind.

The nature of his writing is hardly less important. Mark Twain wrote one of the great styles of American literature, he helped develop the modern American style, he was the first writer who ever used the American vernacular at the level of art. There has been some failure to understand this achievement. Shortly before this Introduction was written, the most pontifical American critic guessed that Mark must have turned to the vernacular of *Huckleberry Finn* because he lacked education, was unacquainted with literary traditions, and therefore wrote thin or awkward prose. That absurdity disregards Mark's life and his books as well. The reader may determine herein whether the style of *The Mysterious Stranger* lacks strength or subtlety, lacks any quality whatever for the effects required of it, or if that represents too late a period, may turn to "Old Times on the Mississippi," which was written before *Huckleberry Finn*, or "The Private History of a Campaign That Failed," which was written while *Huck* was still half finished. Mark Twain wrote English of a remarkable simplicity and clarity, and of singular sensitiveness, flexibility, and beauty as well. Its simplicity might deceive a patronizing reader for the sentence structure is not involved, usually consisting of short elements in natural sequence, and in order to understand without analysis how much art has gone into it one must have an ear for the tones and accents of speech as well as some feeling for the vigor of words. It is so lucid that it seems effortless—but just what is style?

Now, it is important that Mark made the American vernacular the medium of a great novel. Even before that he had used local, class, and racial dialects with immeasurably greater skill than anyone before him in our literature. "The Jumping Frog" raised such dialects above the merely humorous use which was the only one they had previously had and gave them a function in the writing of fiction. And the first two chapters of *The Gilded Age* bring to American literature genuine Negro speech and a rural dialect that are both genuine and an instrument of art—literally for the first time.

In the rendition of Negro speech he may have had one equal, though there are those who will not grant that Harris is an equal; but it is doubtful if anyone has used the dialects of the middle South, or for that matter any other American dialect, as well as he. This on the basis of *The Gilded Age* and its immediate successors: the achievement of *Huckleberry Finn* is greater still. Huck's style, which is the spoken language of the untutored American of his place and time, differentiates the most subtle meanings and emphases and proves capable of the most difficult psychological effects. In a single step it made a literary medium of the American language; the liberating effect on American writing could hardly be overstated. Since *Huckleberry Finn* the well of American undefiled has flowed confidently.

Nevertheless, Mark's principal service to the American language was not Huck's vernacular: it lay within the recognized limits of literary prose. Within those limits he was a radical innovator, a prime mover who changed the medium by incorporating in it the syntax, the idioms, and especially the vocabulary of the common life. The vigor of his prose comes directly from the speech of the Great Valley and the Far West. A superlative may be ventured: that Mark Twain had a greater effect than any other writer on the evolution of American prose.

His place in that evolution cannot be analyzed or even illustrated here. He is in the direct succession and he powerfully accelerates the movement. The evolution is of course older than our independence, even older than our nationality—which it helped to produce. Only an American could have said, "We must all hang together, or assuredly we shall all hang separately" in the traditional context. Only an American could have written, "It is not necessary that a man should earn his living by the sweat of his brow unless he sweats easier than I do." Only an American could have written, "the calm confidence of a Christian with four aces." The sequence is Franklin, Thoreau, Mark Twain; and the point here made lightly can be made with as profound a search into the fusion of thought, expression, and nationality as anyone may care to undertake. But before Mark Twain no American, no one writing in English, could have launched a novel into the movement of fiction with such a passage as:

> At the end of an hour we saw a far-away town sleeping in a valley by a winding river, and beyond it on a hill, a vast gray fortress with towers and turrets, the first I had ever seen out of a picture.
> "Bridgeport?" said I, pointing.
> "Camelot," said he.

Such questions as these, however, interest the historian of literature more than the general reader. The general reader who, it may be worth reminding you, continues to read Mark Twain, here and in Europe, more often by far than any other of our great dead. It is not difficult to say why.

The Americanism just mentioned is part of it. Any unidentified quotation from Mark Twain will be recognized at sight as American. It is, furthermore, a national Americanism; his great books are set along the Mississippi, but no one can think of them as local or regional. But there is also a kind of centripetal Americanism, so that he seems frequently to speak for the nation. The character of national spokesman is in his work as early as *Innocents Abroad;* by *Huckleberry Finn* it is self-evident. Fifteen years before he died it was generally acknowledged—so that if the nation's

mood changed or its honor came in peril, the newspapers could hardly be put to bed till Mark Twain had
spoken.

But there is something more basic. What the millions
who have gone on reading Mark Twain since 1869 have
chiefly wanted and received from him is precisely those
images which, three years after *Tom Sawyer* and four
years after "Old Times on the Mississippi" had been
published, Walt Whitman was still hoping someone
would forge from the new national life.

So long as anyone may be interested in our past there
will be readers for the books in which Mark embodied
his plentiful share of it. These are chiefly *Life on the
Mississippi, Roughing It,* and the *Autobiography.* But he
is so persistently an autobiographer that the same lens
repeatedly refracts something deeply American and
casual contexts suddenly rise to the level of his better
books. It may be a lynching in Marion County, a
reminiscence of General Grant, a pocket-miner's tom-
cat, Harriet Beecher Stowe in her dotage fetching a
warwhoop behind someone's ear—but it is more likely
to be a page or two of dialogue which make a society
transparent and register a true perception forever.
This more than the verbal humor is likely to preserve
some of the lesser books, perhaps even *Following the
Equator,* though the always painful burlesque that is
now intolerable predominates in others. The humor
that was the essential Mark Twain remains; it is inter-
stitial, it is the breathing of his mind. Whether it be
exuberance, an individual way of letting light in, the
passion of a man hardly able to contain his wrath, or
the deadlier laughter in suspension that means a tortured mind's adaptation to reality, it is the fundamental
attribute of Mark Twain. The critic who for a moment
forgets that Mark was a humorist is betrayed.

In the end, however, Mark's fiction is the best part of him. *The Prince and the Pauper* and *Joan of Arc* have already lost their luster, though the first still charms children as it once charmed Victorian adults. A middle group which lost their audience for a while have begun to regain it, books with great qualities in them but marred by the improvisation or the failure of artistic intelligence that have been described above. *Pudd'n-head Wilson*, the most courageous of Mark's books, has a fine verve, a theme he never dared to face outside it, the magnificent Roxana, and a certain historical importance as one of the few serious treatments in American fiction of any aspect of slavery. It is a matter of some regret that Mark began writing fiction with *The Gilded Age*, for he was still inexpert at narrative and in fact hardly in earnest as a novelist, and the exceedingly serious book suffers in consequence. It is also too bad that he wrote it with a collaborator, for Mark would have contributed enough mistakes by himself, whereas Charles Dudley Warner quadruples them, adding the melodrama of the wronged girl for good measure. Nevertheless *The Gilded Age* named an era for all American thinking since it and remains one of the very few contemporary attacks on that venal period. Finally, it has Colonel Sellers in it and so is immortal.

Shorter pieces range from the fathomlessly mawkish "Horse's Tale" and "Dog's Tale" (a similar and worse one of the same kind remains unpublished) to "The Man Who Corrupted Hadleyburg" and "Captain Stormfield's Visit to Heaven," which are part of the Mark Twain canon and contain essential portions of his quarrel with mankind. The best of his shorter pieces however, is "Tom Sawyer Abroad." Presumably because the setting (a navigable balloon) makes it look like burlesque, most critics have ignored it. It is a deliberate exploration of the provincial mind and its prejudices, ignorances, assumptions, wisdoms, cunning. It memorably differentiates three stages of that mind, by way of the familiar Tom, Huck, and Nigger Jim. It is among the very best of Mark's work, frequently on a level with *Huckleberry Finn* itself, and must eventually be recognized as what it is.

A Connecticut Yankee in King Arthur's Court is the most tragically marred of Mark's books. It might have been a masterpiece, it repeatedly flashes to greatness, some of its satire is Mark Twain at his most serene or most savage; but nothing is sustained, tinny extravaganza or burlesque sooner or later spoils every clearly sounded note, and in short the book is at war with itself. Within a single set of covers Mark repeated every error of judgment that can be found in the Collected Works. Probably it will always be read for its fine moments but no one will ever name it among his great books.

Those are *The Adventures of Tom Sawyer* and *Adventures of Huckleberry Finn.* Here the images Walt Whitman desired of and for the new society are actually forged. They are the America of their time speaking with many voices—and the sharp difference between them corresponds not only to the dichotomy in Mark's mind but to one that is basic in our thinking about ourselves. Between them the idyllic *Tom* and the corrosive *Huck* express most of the American consciousness. Forgetting that he himself had made several plays of it, Mark once refused to let an applicant dramatize *Tom Sawyer* because you cannot make a hymn into a play. It is a hymn: to boyhood, to the fantasies of boyhood, to the richness and security of the child's world, to a phase of American society now vanished altogether, to the loveliness of woods and prairies that were the

Great Valley, to the river, to many other things in which millions of readers have recognized themselves and their inheritance. It is wrought out of beauty and nostalgia. Yet Mark is nowhere truer to us, to himself, or to childhood than in the dread which holds this idyl inclosed. The book so superbly brings the reader within its enchantment that some reflection is required before he can realize of what ghastly stuff it is made—murder and starvation, grave-robbery and revenge, terror and panic, some of the darkest emotions of men, some of the most terrible fears of children, and the ghosts and demons and death portents of the slaves. The book could have been written nowhere but in America and by no American but Mark Twain, but it has passed out of our keeping. It is the fantasy of boyhood in world literature.

Huckleberry Finn also has become a universal possession. It is a much deeper book than *Tom Sawyer*—deeper as of Mark Twain, of America, and of humanity. When after some stumbling it finds its purpose, it becomes an exploration of an entire society, the middle South along the river. In accomplishing this purpose it maintains at the level of genius Mark's judgment in full on the human race. It is well to remember that no one had spoken so witheringly to Americans about themselves before Huck raised his voice. But the book is not only the judgment on the damned human race which the much later *What Is Man?* only tried to be, it is also incomparably rich with the swarming life that so absorbed Mark Twain—and contains a forthright assertion of the inalienable dignity of man. It is the most complete expression of Mark Twain.

Like *Tom* and in much greater measure it has a mythic quality. This is in part the river itself, the Mississippi which had dominion over Mark's imagination and here becomes a truly great symbol. It is in part the symbol of the downriver journey—made the more momentous by a boy's bewilderment and a slave's flight for freedom. But in greater part it is the developing pageantry which becomes ecstatic when two vagabonds join Jim and Huck, and the Duke of Bilgewater and the "pore disappeared Dauphin, Looy the Seventeen," take their place in a small company of literature's immortals.

Thus realism, fantasy, satire, mythology, and the tragic knowledge of man, all of them a good many layers deep, united in Mark Twain's masterpiece. It is the book he was meant to write. A book of itself alone, unlike any other, unique, essentially Mark Twain, essentially America, it also has transcended our national literature. Every new generation of readers discovers that it belongs to mankind.

THE
Notorious Jumping Frog
of Calaveras County

*This famous yarn, which first made Mark Twain
known outside of California, has had various forms and
titles. It is most often published in the version used here
but called "The Celebrated Jumping Frog of Calaveras
County." It was originally published as "Jim Smiley and
His Jumping Frog" and in the form of a letter to Artemus Ward.*

IN COMPLIANCE with the request of a friend of
mine who wrote me from the East, I called on good-
natured, garrulous old Simon Wheeler and inquired
after my friend's friend, Leonidas W. Smiley, as requested to do, and I hereunto append the result. I have
a lurking suspicion that *Leonidas W.* Smiley is a myth,
that my friend never knew such a personage, and that
he only conjectured that if I asked old Wheeler about
him, it would remind him of his infamous *Jim* Smiley
and he would go to work and bore me to death with
some exasperating reminiscence of him as long and as
tedious as it should be useless to me. If that was the
design, it succeeded.

I found Simon Wheeler dozing comfortably by the
barroom stove of the dilapidated tavern in the decayed
mining camp of Angel's, and I noticed that he was fat

and bald-headed and had an expression of winning
gentleness and simplicity upon his tranquil countenance.
He roused up and gave me good day. I told him that a
friend of mine had commissioned me to make some inquiries about a cherished companion of his boyhood
named *Leonidas W.* Smiley—*Rev. Leonidas W.* Smiley,
a young minister of the Gospel, who he had heard was
at one time a resident of Angel's Camp. I added that if
Mr. Wheeler could tell me anything about this Rev.
Leonidas W. Smiley, I would feel under many obligations to him.

Simon Wheeler backed me into a corner and block-
aded me there with his chair, and then sat down and
reeled off the monotonous narrative which follows this
paragraph. He never smiled, he never frowned, he
never changed his voice from the gentle-flowing key to
which he tuned his initial sentence, he never betrayed
the slightest suspicion of enthusiasm, but all through
the interminable narrative there ran a vein of impressive earnestness and sincerity which showed me plainly
that, so far from his imagining that there was anything
ridiculous or funny about his story, he regarded it as a
really important matter and admired its two heroes as
men of transcendent genius in *finesse*. I let him go on
in his own way and never interrupted him once.

"Rev. Leonidas W. H'm, Reverend Le—— Well,
there was a feller here once by the name of *Jim* Smiley,
in the winter of '49—or maybe it was the spring of '50—
I don't recollect exactly, somehow, though what makes
me think it was one or the other is because I remember
the big flume warn't finished when he first come to the
camp; but anyway, he was the curiousest man about
always betting on anything that turned up you ever see,
if he could get anybody to bet on the other side, and if
he couldn't he'd change sides. Any way that suited the

other man would suit *him*—any way just so's he got a bet, *he* was satisfied. But still he was lucky, uncommon lucky; he most always come out winner. He was always ready and laying for a chance; there couldn't be no solit'ry thing mentioned but that feller'd offer to bet on it and take ary side you please, as I was just telling you. If there was a horse-race, you'd find him flush or you'd find him busted at the end of it; if there was a dog-fight, he'd bet on it; if there was a cat-fight, he'd bet on it; if there was a chicken-fight, he'd bet on it; why, if there was two birds setting on a fence, he would bet you which one would fly first; or if there was a camp-meeting, he would be there reg'lar to bet on Parson Walker, which he judged to be the best exhorter about here, and so he was too, and a good man. If he even see a straddle-bug start to go anywheres, he would bet you how long it would take him to get to—to wherever he was going to, and if you took him up, he would foller that straddle-bug to Mexico but what he would find out where he was bound for and how long he was on the road. Lots of the boys here has seen that Smiley and can tell you about him. Why, it never made no difference to *him*—he'd bet on *any* thing—the dangdest feller. Parson Walker's wife laid very sick once for a good while, and it seemed as if they warn't going to save her; but one morning he come in and Smiley up and asked him how she was, and he said she was considerable better—thank the Lord for his inf'nite mercy—and coming on so smart that with the blessing of Prov'dence she'd get well yet; and Smiley, before he thought, says, 'Well, I'll resk two-and-a-half she don't anyway.'

"Thish-yer Smiley had a mare—the boys called her the fifteen-minute nag but that was only in fun, you know, because of course she was faster than that—and

he used to win money on that horse, for all she was so
slow and always had the asthma, or the distemper, or
the consumption, or something of that kind. They used
to give her two or three hundred yards' start and then
pass her under way, but always at the fag end of the
race she'd get excited and desperate like, and come
cavorting and straddling up and scattering her legs
around limber, sometimes in the air and sometimes out
to one side among the fences, and kicking up m-o-r-e
dust and raising m-o-r-e racket with her coughing and
sneezing and blowing her nose—and *always* fetch up at
the stand just about a neck ahead, as near as you could
cipher it down.

"And he had a little small bull-pup, that to look at
him you'd think he warn't worth a cent but to set around
and look ornery and lay for a chance to steal something.
But as soon as money was up on him he was a different
dog; his under-jaw'd begin to stick out like the fo'castle
of a steamboat and his teeth would uncover and shine
like the furnaces. And a dog might tackle him and
bully-rag him, and bite him and throw him over his
shoulder two or three times, and Andrew Jackson—
which was the name of the pup—Andrew Jackson
would never let on but what *he* was satisfied and hadn't
expected nothing else—and the bets being doubled and
doubled on the other side all the time, till the money
was all up; and then all of a sudden he would grab that
other dog jest by the j'int of his hind leg and freeze to
it—not chaw, you understand, but only just grip and
hang on till they throwed up the sponge, if it was a
year. Smiley always come out winner on that pup till
he harnessed a dog once that didn't have no hind legs,
because they'd been sawed off in a circular saw, and
when the thing had gone along far enough and the
money was all up and he come to make a snatch for his

pet holt, he see in a minute how he'd been imposed on and how the other dog had him in the door, so to speak, and he 'peared surprised, and then he looked sorter discouraged-like and didn't try no more to win the fight, and so he got shucked out bad. He give Smiley a look, as much as to say his heart was broke, and it was *his* fault for putting up a dog that hadn't no hind legs for him to take holt of, which was his main dependence in a fight, and then he limped off a piece and laid down and died. It was a good pup, was that Andrew Jackson, and would have made a name for hisself if he'd lived, for the stuff was in him and he had genius—I know it, because he hadn't no opportunities to speak of, and it don't stand to reason that a dog could make such a fight as he could under them circumstances if he hadn't no talent. It always makes me feel sorry when I think of that last fight of his'n and the way it turned out.

"Well, thish-yer Smiley had rat-tarriers, and chicken cocks, and tomcats and all them kind of things till you couldn't rest, and you couldn't fetch nothing for him to bet on but he'd match you. He ketched a frog one day and took him home, and said he cal'lated to educate him; and so he never done nothing for three months but set in his back yard and learn that frog to jump. And you bet you he *did* learn him, too. He'd give him a little punch behind, and the next minute you'd see that frog whirling in the air like a doughnut—see him turn one summerset, or maybe a couple if he got a good start, and come down flat-footed and all right, like a cat. He got him up so in the matter of ketching flies, and kep' him in practice so constant, that he'd nail a fly every time as fur as he could see him. Smiley said all a frog wanted was education and he could do 'most anything —and I believe him. Why, I've seen him set Dan'l Webster down here on this floor—Dan'l Webster was

the name of the frog—and sing out, 'Flies, Dan'l, flies!'
and quicker'n you could wink he'd spring straight up
and snake a fly off'n the counter there, and flop down
on the floor ag'in as solid as a gob of mud, and fall to
scratching the side of his head with his hind foot as
indifferent as if he hadn't no idea he'd been doin' any
more'n any frog might do. You never see a frog so
modest and straight-for'ard as he was, for all he was so
gifted. And when it come to fair and square jumping
on a dead level, he could get over more ground at one
straddle than any animal of his breed you ever see.
Jumping on a dead level was his strong suit, you understand; and when it come to that, Smiley would ante up
money on him as long as he had a red. Smiley was
monstrous proud of his frog, and well he might be for
fellers that had traveled and been everywheres all said
he laid over any frog that ever *they* see.

"Well, Smiley kep' the beast in a little lattice box,
and he used to fetch him down-town sometimes and lay
for a bet. One day a feller—a stranger in the camp, he
was—come acrost him with his box and says:

" 'What might it be that you've got in the box?'

"And Smiley says, sorter indifferent-like, 'It might be
a parrot, or it might be a canary, maybe, but it ain't—
it's only just a frog.'

"And the feller took it and looked at it careful, and
turned it round this way and that, and says, 'H'm—so
'tis. Well, what's *he* good for?'

" 'Well,' Smiley says, easy and careless, 'he's good
enough for *one* thing, I should judge—he can outjump
any frog in Calaveras County.'

"The feller took the box again and took another long,
particular look, and give it back to Smiley and says, very
deliberate, 'Well,' he says, 'I don't see no p'ints about
that frog that's any better'n any other frog.'

" 'Maybe you don't,' Smiley says. 'Maybe you understand frogs and maybe you don't understand 'em; maybe you've had experience and maybe you ain't only a amature, as it were. Anyways, I've got *my* opinion, and I'll resk forty dollars that he can outjump any frog in Calaveras County.'

"And the feller studied a minute and then says, kinder sad-like, 'Well, I'm only a stranger here and I ain't got no frog; but if I had a frog, I'd bet you.'

"And then Smiley says, 'That's all right—that's all right—if you'll hold my box a minute, I'll go and get you a frog.' And so the feller took the box and put up his forty dollars along with Smiley's, and set down to wait.

"So he set there a good while thinking and thinking to himself, and then he got the frog out and prized his mouth open and took a teaspoon and filled him full of quail-shot—filled him pretty near up to his chin—and set him on the floor. Smiley he went to the swamp and slopped around in the mud for a long time, and finally he ketched a frog and fetched him in and give him to this feller, and says:

" 'Now, if you're ready, set him alongside of Dan'l, with his forepaws just even with Dan'l's, and I'll give the word.' Then he says, 'One—two—three—*git!*' and him and the feller touched up the frogs from behind, and the new frog hopped off lively, but Dan'l give a heave and hysted up his shoulders—so—like a Frenchman, but it warn't no use—he couldn't budge; he was planted as solid as a church, and he couldn't no more stir than if he was anchored out. Smiley was a good deal surprised, and he was disgusted too, but he didn't have no idea what the matter was, of course.

"The feller took the money and started away, and when he was going out at the door, he sorter jerked his thumb over his shoulder—so—at Dan'l and says again, very deliberate, 'Well,' he says, '*I* don't see no p'ints about that frog that's any better'n any other frog.'

"Smiley he stood scratching his head and looking down at Dan'l a long time, and at last he says, 'I do wonder what in the nation that frog throw'd off for—I wonder if there ain't something the matter with him— he 'pears to look mighty baggy, somehow.' And he ketched Dan'l by the nap of the neck and hefted him, and says, 'Why, blame my cats if he don't weigh five pound!' and turned him upside down and he belched out a double handful of shot. And then he see how it was, and he was the maddest man—he set the frog down and took out after that feller, but he never ketched him. And—"

[Here Simon Wheeler heard his name called from the front yard and got up to see what was wanted.] And turning to me as he moved away, he said: "Just set where you are, stranger, and rest easy—I ain't going to be gone a second."

But, by your leave, I did not think that a continuation of the history of the enterprising vagabond *Jim* Smiley would be likely to afford me much information concerning the Rev. *Leonidas* W. Smiley and so I started away.

At the door I met the sociable Wheeler returning, and he buttonholed me and recommenced:

"Well, thish-yer Smiley had a yaller one-eyed cow that didn't have no tail, only just a short stump like a bannanner, and—"

However, lacking both time and inclination, I did not wait to hear about the afflicted cow but took my leave.

FROM
A Tramp Abroad

JIM BAKER'S BLUEJAY YARN

ANIMALS talk to each other, of course. There can
be no question about that, but I suppose there are
very few people who can understand them. I never
knew but one man who could. I knew he could, however, because he told me so himself. He was a middle-
aged, simple-hearted miner who had lived in a lonely
corner of California among the woods and mountains a
good many years, and had studied the ways of his only
neighbors, the beasts and the birds, until he believed
he could accurately translate any remark which they
made. This was Jim Baker. According to Jim Baker,
some animals have only a limited education and use
only very simple words, and scarcely ever a comparison
or a flowery figure; whereas certain other animals have
a large vocabulary, a fine command of language and a
ready and fluent delivery; consequently these latter talk
a great deal; they like it, they are conscious of their
talent, and they enjoy "showing off." Baker said that
after long and careful observation, he had come to the
conclusion that the bluejays were the best talkers he
had found among birds and beasts. Said he:

"There's more *to* a bluejay than any other creature.
He has got more moods, and more different kinds of
feelings than other creatures; and, mind you, whatever a
bluejay feels, he can put into language. And no mere
commonplace language, either, but rattling, out-and-out
book-talk—and bristling with metaphor too—just bristling! And as for command of language—why *you*

43

never see a bluejay get stuck for a word. No man ever did. They just boil out of him! And another thing: I've noticed a good deal and there's no bird, or cow, or anything that uses as good grammar as a bluejay. You may say a cat uses good grammar. Well, a cat does—but you let a cat get excited once; you let a cat get to pulling fur with another cat on a shed, nights, and you'll hear grammar that will give you the lockjaw. Ignorant people think it's the *noise* which fighting cats make that is so aggravating but it ain't so; it's the sickening grammar they use. Now I've never heard a jay use bad grammar but very seldom, and when they do, they are as ashamed as a human, they shut right down and leave.

"You may call a jay a bird. Well, so he is, in a measure —because he's got feathers on him, and don't belong to no church, perhaps, but otherwise he is just as much a human as you be. And I'll tell you for why. A jay's gifts and instincts and feelings and interests cover the whole ground. A jay hasn't got any more principle than a Congressman. A jay will lie, a jay will steal, a jay will deceive, a jay will betray; and four times out of five, a jay will go back on his solemnest promise. The sacredness of an obligation is a thing which you can't cram into no bluejay's head. Now on top of all this there's another thing, a jay can outswear any gentleman in the mines. You think a cat can swear. Well, a cat can, but you give a bluejay a subject that calls for his reserve-powers and where is your cat? Don't talk to *me*—I know too much about this thing. And there's yet another thing, in the one little particular of scolding—just good, clean, out-and-out scolding—a bluejay can lay over anything, human or divine. Yes, sir, a jay is everything that a man is. A jay can cry, a jay can laugh, a jay can feel shame, a jay can reason and plan and discuss, a jay likes gossip and scandal, a jay has got a sense of humor, a jay knows

when he is an ass just as well as you do—maybe better.
If a jay ain't human, he better take in his sign, that's all.
Now I'm going to tell you a perfectly true fact about
some bluejays.

"When I first begun to understand jay language correctly, there was a little incident happened here. Seven
years ago, the last man in this region but me moved
away. There stands his house—been empty ever since,
a log house with a plank roof—just one big room and
no more, no ceiling, nothing between the rafters and the
floor. Well, one Sunday morning I was sitting out here
in front of my cabin with my cat, taking the sun and
looking at the blue hills and listening to the leaves
rustling so lonely in the trees, and thinking of the home
away yonder in the states that I hadn't heard from in
thirteen years, when a bluejay lit on that house, with
an acorn in his mouth, and says, 'Hello, I reckon I've
struck something.' When he spoke the acorn dropped
out of his mouth and rolled down the roof, of course,
but he didn't care; his mind was all on the thing he had
struck. It was a knot-hole in the roof. He cocked his
head to one side, shut one eye and put the other one to
the hole, like a possum looking down a jug, then he
glanced up with his bright eyes, gave a wink or two
with his wings—which signifies gratification, you understand—and says, 'It looks like a hole, it's located like a
hole—blamed if I don't believe it *is* a hole!'

"Then he cocked his head down and took another
look; he glances up perfectly joyful this time, winks his
wings and his tail both, and says, 'Oh, no, this ain't no
fat thing, I reckon! If I ain't in luck!—why it's a perfectly elegant hole!' So he flew down and got that acorn
and fetched it up and dropped it in, and was just tilting
his head back with the heavenliest smile on his face,
when all of a sudden he was paralyzed into a listening

attitude and that smile faded gradually out of his countenance like breath off'n a razor, and the queerest look of surprise took its place. Then he says, 'Why, I didn't hear it fall!' He cocked his eye at the hole again and took a long look; raised up and shook his head; stepped around to the other side of the hole and took another look from that side; shook his head again. He studied a while, then he just went into the *details*— walked round and round the hole and spied into it from every point of the compass. No use. Now he took a thinking attitude on the comb of the roof and scratched the back of his head with his right foot a minute, and finally says, 'Well, it's too many for *me*, that's certain; must be a mighty long hole; however, I ain't got no time to fool around here, I got to 'tend to business; I reckon it's all right—chance it, anyway.'

"So he flew off and fetched another acorn and dropped it in, and tried to flirt his eye to the hole quick enough to see what become of it but he was too late. He held his eye there as much as a minute; then he raised up and sighed, and says, 'Confound it, I don't seem to understand this thing, no way; however, I'll tackle her again.' He fetched another acorn, and done his level best to see what become of it, but he couldn't. He says, 'Well, I never struck no such a hole as this before; I'm of the opinion it's a totally new kind of a hole.' Then he begun to get mad. He held in for a spell, walking up and down the comb of the roof and shaking his head and muttering to himself; but his feelings got the upper hand of him presently and he broke loose and cussed himself black in the face. I never see a bird take on so about a little thing. When he got through he walks to the hole and looks in again for half a minute; then he says, 'Well, you're a long hole, and a deep hole, and a mighty singular hole altogether—but

I've started in to fill you and I'm d—d if I *don't* fill you,
if it takes a hundred years!'

"And with that, away he went. You never see a bird
work so since you was born. He laid into his work like
a nigger and the way he hove acorns into that hole for
about two hours and a half was one of the most exciting and astonishing spectacles I ever struck. He never
stopped to take a look any more—he just hove 'em in
and went for more. Well, at last he could hardly flop his
wings, he was so tuckered out. He comes a-drooping
down, once more, sweating like an ice-pitcher, drops
his acorn in and says, '*Now* I guess I've got the bulge on
you by this time!' So he bent down for a look. If you'll
believe me, when his head come up again he was just
pale with rage. He says, 'I've shoveled acorns enough
in there to keep the family thirty years, and if I can see
a sign of one of 'em I wish I may land in a museum with
a belly full of sawdust in two minutes!'

"He just had strength enough to crawl up on to the
comb and lean his back agin the chimbly, and then he
collected his impressions and begun to free his mind. I
see in a second that what I had mistook for profanity
in the mines was only just the rudiments, as you may
say.

"Another jay was going by and heard him doing his
devotions, and stops to inquire what was up. The sufferer told him the whole circumstance, and says, 'Now
yonder's the hole, and if you don't believe me, go and
look for yourself.' So this fellow went and looked, and
comes back and says, 'How many did you say you put
in there?' 'Not any less than two tons,' says the sufferer.
The other jay went and looked again. He couldn't seem
to make it out, so he raised a yell and three more jays
come. They all examined the hole, they all made the
sufferer tell it over again, then they all discussed it and

got off as many leather-headed opinions about it as an average crowd of humans could have done.

"They called in more jays; then more and more, till pretty soon this whole region 'peared to have a blue flush about it. There must have been five thousand of them, and such another jawing and disputing and ripping and cussing, you never heard. Every jay in the whole lot put his eye to the hole and delivered a more chuckle-headed opinion about the mystery than the jay that went there before him. They examined the house all over, too. The door was standing half open and at last one old jay happened to go and light on it and look in. Of course, that knocked the mystery galley-west in a second. There lay the acorns, scattered all over the floor. He flopped his wings and raised a whoop. 'Come here!' he says, 'Come here, everybody; hang'd if this fool hasn't been trying to fill up a house with acorns!' They all came a-swooping down like a blue cloud, and as each fellow lit on the door and took a glance, the whole absurdity of the contract that that first jay had tackled hit him home and he fell over backward suffocating with laughter, and the next jay took his place and done the same.

"Well, sir, they roosted around here on the housetop and the trees for an hour, and guffawed over that thing like human beings. It ain't any use to tell me a bluejay hasn't got a sense of humor, because I know better. And memory, too. They brought jays here from all over the United States to look down that hole, every summer for three years. Other birds, too. And they could all see the point, except an owl that come from Nova Scotia to visit the Yosemite, and he took this thing in on his way back. He said he couldn't see anything funny in it. But then he was a good deal disappointed about Yosemite, too."

FROM
Old Times on the Mississippi

I. "Cub" Wants to Be a Pilot

WHEN I was a boy there was but one permanent ambition among my comrades in our village[1] on the west bank of the Mississippi River. That was to be a steamboatman. We had transient ambitions of other sorts but they were only transient. When a circus came and went, it left us all burning to become clowns; the first Negro minstrel show that ever came to our section left us all suffering to try that kind of life; now and then we had a hope that, if we lived and were good, God would permit us to be pirates. These ambitions faded out, each in its turn; but the ambition to be a steamboatman always remained.

Once a day a cheap, gaudy packet arrived upward from St. Louis, and another downward from Keokuk. Before these events, the day was glorious with expectancy; after them, the day was a dead and empty thing. Not only the boys but the whole village felt this. After all these years I can picture that old time to myself now, just as it was then: the white town drowsing in the sunshine of a summer's morning; the streets empty or pretty nearly so; one or two clerks sitting in front of the Water Street stores, with their splint-bottomed chairs tilted back against the walls, chins on breasts,

---

[1] *Hannibal, Missouri.*

hats slouched over their faces, asleep—with shingle-shavings enough around to show what broke them down; a sow and a litter of pigs loafing along the side-walk, doing a good business in watermelon rinds and seeds; two or three lonely little freight piles scattered about the "levee"; a pile of "skids" on the slope of the stone-paved wharf, and the fragrant town drunkard asleep in the shadow of them; two or three wood flats at the head of the wharf but nobody to listen to the peaceful lapping of the wavelets against them; the great Mississippi, the majestic, the magnificent Mississippi, rolling its mile-wide tide along, shining in the sun; the dense forest away on the other side; the "point" above the town, and the "point" below, bounding the river-glimpse and turning it into a sort of sea, and withal a very still and brilliant and lonely one. Presently a film of dark smoke appears above one of those remote "points"; instantly a Negro drayman, famous for his quick eye and prodigious voice, lifts up the cry, "S-t-e-a-m-boat a-comin'!" and the scene changes! The town drunkard stirs, the clerks wake up, a furious clat-ter of drays follows, every house and store pours out a human contribution, and all in a twinkling the dead town is alive and moving. Drays, carts, men, boys, all go hurrying from many quarters to a common center, the wharf. Assembled there, the people fasten their eyes upon the coming boat as upon a wonder they are seeing for the first time. And the boat *is* rather a handsome sight, too. She is long and sharp and trim and pretty; she has two tall, fancy-topped chimneys, with a gilded device of some kind swung between them; a fanciful pilot-house, all glass and "gingerbread," perched on top of the "texas" deck behind them; the paddle-boxes are gorgeous with a picture or with gilded rays above the boat's name; the boiler-deck, the hurricane-deck, and the texas deck are fenced and ornamented with clean white railings; there is a flag gallantly flying from the jack-staff; the furnace doors are open and the fires glaring bravely; the upper decks are black with passengers; the captain stands by the big bell, calm, imposing, the envy of all; great volumes of the blackest smoke are rolling and tumbling out of the chimneys—a husbanded grandeur created with a bit of pitch-pine just before arriving at a town; the crew are grouped on the forecastle; the broad stage is run far out over the port bow and an envied deck-hand stands picturesquely on the end of it with a coil of rope in his hand; the pent steam is screaming through the gauge-cocks; the captain lifts his hand, a bell rings, the wheels stop; then they turn back, churning the water to foam, and the steamer is at rest. Then such a scramble as there is to get aboard and to get ashore, and to take in freight and to discharge freight, all at one and the same time; and such a yelling and cursing as the mates facilitate it all with! Ten minutes later the steamer is under way again, with no flag on the jack-staff and no black smoke issuing from the chimneys. After ten more minutes the town is dead again and the town drunkard asleep by the skids once more.

My father was a justice of the peace and I supposed he possessed the power of life and death over all men and could hang anybody that offended him. This was distinction enough for me as a general thing, but the desire to be a steamboatman kept intruding nevertheless. I first wanted to be a cabin-boy, so that I could come out with a white apron on and shake a table-cloth over the side, where all my old comrades could see me; later I thought I would rather be the deck-hand who stood on the end of the stage-plank with the coil of rope in his hand, because he was particularly conspicuous. But these were only day-dreams—they were too heavenly to be contemplated as real possibilities. By and by one of our boys went away. He was not heard of for a long time. At last he turned up as apprentice engineer or "striker" on a steamboat. This thing shook the bottom out of all my Sunday-school teachings. That boy had been notoriously worldly and I just the reverse; yet he was exalted to this eminence and I left in obscurity and misery. There was nothing generous about this fellow in his greatness. He would always manage to have a rusty bolt to scrub while his boat tarried at our town, and he would sit on the inside guard and scrub it, where we all could see him and envy him and loathe him. And whenever his boat was laid up he would come home and swell around the town in his blackest and greasiest clothes, so that nobody could help remembering that he was a steamboatman; and he used all sorts of steamboat technicalities in his talk, as if he were so used to them that he forgot common people could not understand them. He would speak of the "labboard" side of a horse in an easy, natural way that would make one wish he was dead. And he was always talking about "St. Looy" like an old citizen; he would refer casually to occasions when he was "coming down Fourth Street," or when he was "passing by the Planter's House," or when there was a fire and he took a turn on the brakes of "the old Big Missouri"; and then he would go on and lie about how many towns the size of ours were burned down there that day. Two or three of the boys had long been persons of consideration among us because they had been to St. Louis once and had a vague general knowledge of its wonders, but the day of their glory was over now. They lapsed into a humble silence and learned to disappear when the ruthless "cub"-engineer approached. This fellow had money, too, and hair-oil. Also an ignorant silver watch and a showy brass watch-chain. He wore a leather belt and used no suspenders. If ever a youth was cordially admired and hated by his comrades, this one was. No girl could withstand his charms. He "cut out" every boy in the village. When his boat blew up at last, it diffused a tranquil contentment among us such as we had not known for months. But when he came home the next week, alive, renowned, and appeared in church all battered up and bandaged, a shining hero, stared at and wondered over by everybody, it seemed to us that the partiality of Providence for an undeserving reptile had reached a point where it was open to criticism.

This creature's career could produce but one result, and it speedily followed. Boy after boy managed to get on the river. The minister's son became an engineer. The doctor's and the postmaster's sons became "mud clerks"; the wholesale liquor dealer's son became a barkeeper on a boat; four sons of the chief merchant and two sons of the county judge became pilots. Pilot was the grandest position of all. The pilot, even in those days of trivial wages, had a princely salary—from a hundred and fifty to two hundred and fifty dollars a month, and no board to pay. Two months of his wages would pay a preacher's salary for a year. Now some of us were left disconsolate. We could not get on the river—at least our parents would not let us.

So, by and by, I ran away. I said I would never come home again till I was a pilot and could come in glory. But somehow I could not manage it. I went meekly aboard a few of the boats that lay packed together like sardines at the long St. Louis wharf, and humbly inquired for the pilots, but got only a cold shoulder and short words from mates and clerks. I had to make the best of this sort of treatment for the time being, but I had comforting day-dreams of a future when I should be a great and honored pilot, with plenty of money, and could kill some of these mates and clerks and pay for them.

Months afterward the hope within me struggled to a reluctant death, and I found myself without an ambition. But I was ashamed to go home. I was in Cincinnati, and I set to work to map out a new career. I had been reading about the recent exploration of the river Amazon by an expedition sent out by our government. It was said that the expedition, owing to difficulties, had not thoroughly explored a part of the country lying about the headwaters, some four thousand miles from the mouth of the river. It was only about fifteen hundred miles from Cincinnati to New Orleans, where I could doubtless get a ship. I had thirty dollars left; I would go and complete the exploration of the Amazon. This was all the thought I gave to the subject. I never was great in matters of detail. I packed my valise, and took passage on an ancient tub called the *Paul Jones*, for New Orleans. For the sum of sixteen dollars I had the scarred and tarnished splendors of "her" main saloon principally to myself, for she was not a creature to attract the eye of wiser travelers.

When we presently got under way and went poking down the broad Ohio, I became a new being and the subject of my own admiration. I was a traveler! A word never had tasted so good in my mouth before. I had an exultant sense of being bound for mysterious lands and distant climes which I never have felt in so uplifting a degree since. I was in such a glorified condition that all ignoble feelings departed out of me, and I was able to look down and pity the untraveled with a compassion that had hardly a trace of contempt in it. Still, when we stopped at villages and wood-yards, I could not help lolling carelessly upon the railings of the boiler-deck to enjoy the envy of the country boys on the bank. If they did not seem to discover me, I presently sneezed to attract their attention, or moved to a position where they could not help seeing me. And as soon as I knew they saw me I gaped and stretched, and gave other signs of being mightily bored with traveling.

I kept my hat off all the time, and stayed where the wind and the sun could strike me, because I wanted to get the bronzed and weather-beaten look of an old traveler. Before the second day was half gone I experienced a joy which filled me with the purest gratitude, for I saw that the skin had begun to blister and peel off my face and neck. I wished that the boys and girls at home could see me now.

We reached Louisville in time—at least the neighborhood of it. We stuck hard and fast on the rocks in the middle of the river and lay there four days. I was now beginning to feel a strong sense of being a part of the boat's family, a sort of infant son to the captain and younger brother to the officers. There is no estimating the pride I took in this grandeur or the affection that began to swell and grow in me for those people. I could not know how the lordly steamboatman scorns that sort of presumption in a mere landsman. I particularly longed to acquire the least trifle of notice from the big stormy mate, and I was on the alert for an opportunity to do him a service to that end. It came at last. The riotous pow-wow of setting a spar was going on down on the forecastle, and I went down there and stood around in the way—or mostly skipping out of it—till the mate suddenly roared a general order for somebody to bring him a capstan bar. I sprang to his side and said: "Tell me where it is—I'll fetch it!"

If a rag-picker had offered to do a diplomatic service

for the Emperor of Russia, the monarch could not have been more astounded than the mate was. He even stopped swearing. He stood and stared down at me. It took him ten seconds to scrape his disjointed remains together again. Then he said impressively, "Well, if this don't beat h——ll!," and turned to his work with the air of a man who had been confronted with a problem too abstruse for solution.

I crept away and courted solitude for the rest of the day. I did not go to dinner, I stayed away from supper until everybody else had finished. I did not feel so much like a member of the boat's family now as before. However, my spirits returned, in instalments, as we pursued our way down the river. I was sorry I hated the mate so, because it was not in (young) human nature not to admire him. He was huge and muscular, his face was bearded and whiskered all over, he had a red woman and a blue woman tattooed on his right arm—one on each side of a blue anchor with a red rope to it—and in the matter of profanity he was sublime. When he was getting out cargo at a landing, I was always where I could see and hear. He felt all the majesty of his great position and made the world feel it too. When he gave even the simplest order, he discharged it like a blast of lightning and sent a long, reverberating peal of profanity thundering after it. I could not help contrasting the way in which the average landsman would give an order with the mate's way of doing it. If the landsman should wish the gang-plank moved a foot farther forward, he would probably say, "James, or William, one of you push that plank forward, please," but put the mate in his place, and he would roar out, "Here, now, start that gang-plank for'ard! Lively, now! *What* 're you about! Snatch it! *snatch* it! There! there! aft again! aft again! Don't you hear me? Dash it to dash! are you going to *sleep* over it! 'Vast heaving. 'Vast heaving, I tell you! Going to heave it clear astern? WHERE 're you going with that barrel! *for'ard* with it 'fore I make you swallow it, you dash-dash-dash-*dashed* split between a tired mud-turtle and a crippled hearse-horse!"

I wished I could talk like that.

When the soreness of my adventure with the mate had somewhat worn off, I began timidly to make up to the humblest official connected with the boat—the night watchman. He snubbed my advances at first, but I presently ventured to offer him a new chalk pipe, and that softened him. So he allowed me to sit with him by the big bell on the hurricane-deck, and in time he melted into conversation. He could not well have helped it, I hung with such homage on his words and so plainly showed that I felt honored by his notice. He told me the names of dim capes and shadowy islands as we glided by them in the solemnity of the night under the winking stars, and by and by got to talking about himself. He seemed over-sentimental for a man whose salary was six dollars a week—or rather he might have seemed so to an older person than I. But I drank in his words hungrily and with a faith that might have moved mountains if it had been applied judiciously. What was it to me that he was soiled and seedy and fragrant with gin? What was it to me that his grammar was bad, his construction worse, and his profanity so void of art that it was an element of weakness rather than strength in his conversation? He was a wronged man, a man who had seen trouble, and that was enough for me. As he mellowed into his plaintive history his tears dripped upon the lantern in his lap, and I cried too from sympathy. He said he was the son of an English nobleman, either an earl or an alderman, he could not remember which, but believed was both; his father, the nobleman, loved him but his mother hated him from the cradle; and so while he was still a little boy he was sent to "one of them old, ancient colleges," he couldn't remember which; and by and by his father died and his mother seized the property and "shook" him, as he phrased it. After his mother shook him, members of the nobility with whom he was acquainted used their influence to get him the position of "loblolly-boy in a ship," and from that point my watchman threw off all trammels of date and locality and branched out into a narrative that bristled all along with incredible adventures, a narrative that was so reeking with bloodshed and so crammed with hair-breadth escapes and the most engaging and unconscious personal villainies that I sat speechless, enjoying, shuddering, wondering, worshiping.

It was a sore blight to find out afterward that he was a low, vulgar, ignorant, sentimental, half-witted humbug, an untraveled native of the wilds of Illinois, who had absorbed wildcat literature and appropriated its marvels, until in time he had woven odds and ends of the mess into this yarn and then gone on telling it to fledglings like me until he had come to believe it himself.

ii. A "Cub" Pilot's Experience; or; Learning the River.

What with lying on the rocks four days at Louisville and some other delays, the poor old *Paul Jones* fooled away about two weeks in making the voyage from Cincinnati to New Orleans. This gave me a chance to get acquainted with one of the pilots, and he taught me how to steer the boat, and thus made the fascination of river life more potent than ever for me.

It also gave me a chance to get acquainted with a

youth who had taken deck passage[1]—more's the pity, for he easily borrowed six dollars of me on a promise to return to the boat and pay it back to me the day after we should arrive. But he probably died or forgot, for he never came. It was doubtless the former, since he had said his parents were wealthy and he only traveled deck passage because it was cooler.

I soon discovered two things. One was that a vessel would not be likely to sail for the mouth of the Amazon under ten or twelve years, and the other was that the nine or ten dollars still left in my pocket would not suffice for so impossible an exploration as I had planned, even if I could afford to wait for a ship. Therefore it followed that I must contrive a new career. The *Paul Jones* was now bound for St. Louis. I planned a siege against my pilot, and at the end of three hard days he surrendered. He agreed to teach me the Mississippi River from New Orleans to St. Louis for five hundred dollars, payable out of the first wages I should receive after graduating. I entered upon the small enterprise of "learning" twelve or thirteen hundred miles of the great Mississippi River with the easy confidence of my time of life. If I had really known what I was about to require of my faculties, I should not have had the courage to begin. I supposed that all a pilot had to do was to keep his boat in the river, and I did not consider that that could be much of a trick, since it was so wide.

The boat backed out from New Orleans at four in the afternoon, and it was "our watch" until eight. Mr. Bixby, my chief, "straightened her up," plowed her along past the sterns of the other boats that lay at the Levee, and then said, "Here, take her; shave those steamships as close as you'd peel an apple." I took the wheel and my heart went down into my boots; for

[1] *"Deck" passage i.e. steerage passage.*

it seemed to me that we were about to scrape the side off every ship in the line, we were so close. I held my breath and began to claw the boat away from the danger, and I had my own opinion of the pilot who had known no better than to get us into such peril, but I was too wise to express it. In half a minute I had a wide margin of safety intervening between the *Paul Jones* and the ships, and within ten seconds more I was set aside in disgrace and Mr. Bixby was going into danger again and flaying me alive with abuse of my cowardice. I was stung but I was obliged to admire the easy confidence with which my chief loafed from side to side of his wheel and trimmed the ships so closely that disaster seemed ceaselessly imminent. When he had cooled a little he told me that the easy water was close ashore and the current outside, and therefore we must hug the bank up-stream, to get the benefit of the former, and stay well out down-stream, to take advantage of the latter. In my own mind I resolved to be a down-stream pilot and leave the up-streaming to people dead to prudence.

Now and then Mr. Bixby called my attention to certain things. Said he, "This is Six-Mile Point." I assented. It was pleasant enough information but I could not see the bearing of it. I was not conscious that it was a matter of any interest to me. Another time he said, "This is Nine-Mile Point." Later he said, "This is Twelve-Mile Point." They were all about level with the water's edge; they all looked about alike to me; they were monotonously unpicturesque. I hoped Mr. Bixby would change the subject. But no, he would crowd up around a point, hugging the shore with affection, and then say: "The slack water ends here, abreast this bunch of China trees; now we cross over." So he crossed over. He gave me the wheel once or twice but I had no luck. I either came near chipping off the edge of a sugar-plantation, or I yawed too far from shore and so dropped back into disgrace again and got abused.

The watch was ended at last, and we took supper and went to bed. At midnight the glare of a lantern shone in my eyes, and the night watchman said:

"Come, turn out!"

And then he left. I could not understand this extraordinary procedure; so I presently gave up trying to and dozed off to sleep. Pretty soon the watchman was back again, and this time he was gruff. I was annoyed. I said:

"What do you want to come bothering around here in the middle of the night for? Now, as like as not, I'll not get to sleep again to-night."

The watchman said:

"Well, if this ain't good, I'm blessed."

The "off-watch" was just turning in and I heard some brutal laughter from them, and such remarks as "Hello, watchman! ain't the new cub turned out yet? He's delicate, likely. Give him some sugar in a rag and send for the chambermaid to sing 'Rock-a-by Baby,' to him."

About this time Mr. Bixby appeared on the scene. Something like a minute later I was climbing the pilot-house steps with some of my clothes on and the rest in my arms. Mr. Bixby was close behind, commenting. Here was something fresh—this thing of getting up in the middle of the night to go to work. It was a detail in piloting that had never occurred to me at all. I knew that boats ran all night but somehow I had never happened to reflect that somebody had to get up out of a warm bed to run them. I began to fear that piloting was not quite so romantic as I had imagined it was; there was something very real and worklike about this new phase of it.

It was a rather dingy night, although a fair number of stars were out. The big mate was at the wheel and he had the old tub pointed at a star and was holding her straight up the middle of the river. The shores on either hand were not much more than half a mile apart, but they seemed wonderfully far away and ever so vague and indistinct. The mate said:

"We've got to land at Jones's plantation, sir."

The vengeful spirit in me exulted. I said to myself, "I wish you joy of your job, Mr. Bixby; you'll have a good time finding Mr. Jones's plantation such a night as this, and I hope you never *will* find it as long as you live."

Mr. Bixby said to the mate:

"Upper end of the plantation, or the lower?"

"Upper."

"I can't do it. The stumps there are out of water at this stage. It's no great distance to the lower and you'll have to get along with that."

"All right, sir. If Jones don't like it, he'll have to lump it, I reckon."

And then the mate left. My exultation began to cool and my wonder to come up. Here was a man who not only proposed to find this plantation on such a night but to find either end of it you preferred. I dreadfully wanted to ask a question, but I was carrying about as many short answers as my cargo-room would admit of, so I held my peace. All I desired to ask Mr. Bixby was the simple question whether he was ass enough to really imagine he was going to find that plantation on a night when all plantations were exactly alike and all of the same color. But I held in. I used to have fine inspirations of prudence in those days.

Mr. Bixby made for the shore and soon was scraping it, just the same as if it had been daylight. And not only that but singing:

"Father in heaven, the day is declining," etc.

It seemed to me that I had put my life in the keeping of a peculiarly reckless outcast. Presently he turned on me and said:

"What's the name of the first point above New Orleans?"

I was gratified to be able to answer promptly, and I did. I said I didn't know.

"Don't *know?*"

This manner jolted me. I was down at the foot again, in a moment. But I had to say just what I had said before.

"Well, you're a smart one!" said Mr. Bixby. "What's the name of the *next* point?"

Once more I didn't know.

"Well, this beats anything. Tell me the name of *any* point or place I told you."

I studied awhile and decided that I couldn't.

"Look here! What do you start out from, above Twelve-Mile Point, to cross over?"

"I—I—don't know."

"You—you—don't know?" mimicking my drawling manner of speech. "What *do* you know?"

"I—I—nothing, for certain."

"By the great Cæsar's ghost, I believe you! You're the stupidest dunderhead I ever saw or ever heard of, so help me Moses! The idea of *you* being a pilot—*you!* Why, you don't know enough to pilot a cow down a lane."

Oh, but his wrath was up! He was a nervous man, and he shuffled from one side of his wheel to the other as if the floor was hot. He would boil awhile to himself and then overflow and scald me again.

"Look here! What do you suppose I told you the names of those points for?"

I tremblingly considered a moment and then the devil of temptation provoked me to say:

"Well to—to—be entertaining, I thought."

This was a red rag to the bull. He raged and stormed so (he was crossing the river at the time) that I judged it made him blind, because he ran over the steering-oar of a trading-scow. Of course the traders sent up a volley of red-hot profanity. Never was a man so grateful as Mr. Bixby was, because he was brimful and here were subjects who could *talk back*. He threw open a window, thrust his head out, and such an irruption followed as I never had heard before. The fainter and farther away the scowmen's curses drifted, the higher Mr. Bixby lifted his voice and the weightier his adjectives grew. When he closed the window he was empty. You could have drawn a seine through his system and not caught curses enough to disturb your mother with. Presently he said to me in the gentlest way:

"My boy, you must get a little memorandum-book, and every time I tell you a thing, put it down right away. There's only one way to be a pilot and that is to get this entire river by heart. You have to know it just like ABC."

That was a dismal revelation to me, for my memory was never loaded with anything but blank cartridges. However, I did not feel discouraged long. I judged that it was best to make some allowances, for doubtless Mr. Bixby was "stretching". Presently he pulled a rope and struck a few strokes on the big bell. The stars were all gone now and the night was as black as ink. I could hear the wheels churn along the bank but I was not entirely certain that I could see the shore. The voice of the invisible watchman called up from the hurricane-deck:

"What's this, sir?"

"Jones's plantation."

I said to myself, "I wish I might venture to offer a
small bet that it isn't." But I did not chirp. I only waited
to see. Mr. Bixby handled the engine-bells and in due
time the boat's nose came to the land, a torch glowed
from the forecastle, a man skipped ashore, a darky's
voice on the bank said: "Gimme de k'yarpet-bag, Mass'
Jones," and the next moment we were standing up the
river again, all serene. I reflected deeply awhile, and
then said—but not aloud—"Well, the finding of that
plantation was the luckiest accident that ever happened, but it couldn't happen again in a hundred years."
And I fully believed it *was* an accident, too.

By the time we had gone seven or eight hundred
miles up the river, I had learned to be a tolerably plucky
up-stream steersman, in daylight, and before we reached
St. Louis I had made a trifle of progress in night work,
but only a trifle. I had a note-book that fairly bristled
with the names of towns, "points," bars, islands, bends,
reaches, etc., but the information was to be found only
in the note-book—none of it was in my head. It made
my heart ache to think I had only got half of the river
set down, for as our watch was four hours off and four
hours on, day and night, there was a long four-hour
gap in my book for every time I had slept since the
voyage began.

My chief was presently hired to go on a big New
Orleans boat and I packed my satchel and went with
him. She was a grand affair. When I stood in her pilot-
house I was so far above the water that I seemed
perched on a mountain, and her decks stretched so far
away, fore and aft, below me, that I wondered how I
could ever have considered the little *Paul Jones* a large
craft. There were other differences too. The *Paul Jones's*
pilot-house was a cheap, dingy, battered rattletrap,

cramped for room, but here was a sumptuous glass
temple: room enough to have a dance in, showy red
and gold window-curtains, an imposing sofa, leather
cushions and a back to the high bench where visiting
pilots sit to spin yarns and "look at the river," bright,
fanciful "cuspidores" instead of a broad wooden box
filled with sawdust, nice new oilcloth on the floor, a
hospitable big stove for winter, a wheel as high as my
head costly with inlaid work, a wire tiller-rope, bright
brass knobs for the bells, and a tidy, white-aproned,
black "texas-tender," to bring up tarts and ices and coffee during mid-watch, day and night. Now this was
"something like," and so I began to take heart once
more to believe that piloting was a romantic sort of
occupation after all. The moment we were under way
I began to prowl about the great steamer and fill myself
with joy. She was as clean and as dainty as a drawing-
room; when I looked down her long, gilded saloon, it
was like gazing through a splendid tunnel; she had an
oil-picture, by some gifted sign-painter, on every stateroom door; she glittered with no end of prism-fringed
chandeliers; the clerk's office was elegant, the bar was
marvelous, and the barkeeper had been barbered and
upholstered at incredible cost. The boiler-deck (*i.e.*,
the second story of the boat, so to speak) was as spacious as a church, it seemed to me, so with the forecastle, and there was no pitiful handful of deck-hands,
firemen, and roustabouts down there but a whole battalion of men. The fires were fiercely glaring from a
long row of furnaces and over them were eight huge
boilers! This was unutterable pomp. The mighty engines—but enough of this. I had never felt so fine before. And when I found that the regiment of natty
servants respectfully "sir'd" me, my satisfaction was
complete.

When I returned to the pilot-house St. Louis was gone and I was lost. Here was a piece of river which was all down in my book but I could make neither head nor tail of it: you understand, it was turned around. I had seen it when coming up-stream but I had never faced about to see how it looked when it was behind me. My heart broke again, for it was plain that I had got to learn this troublesome river *both ways.*

The pilot-house was full of pilots, going down to "look at the river." What is called the "upper river" (the two hundred miles between St. Louis and Cairo, where the Ohio comes in) was low, and the Mississippi changes its channel so constantly that the pilots used to always find it necessary to run down to Cairo to take a fresh look when their boats were to lie in port a week, that is, when the water was at a low stage. A deal of this "looking at the river" was done by poor fellows who seldom had a berth and whose only hope of getting one lay in their being always freshly posted and therefore ready to drop into the shoes of some reputable pilot for a single trip, on account of such pilot's sudden illness or some other necessity. And a good many of them constantly ran up and down inspecting the river, not because they ever really hoped to get a berth but because (they being guests of the boat) it was cheaper to "look at the river" than stay ashore and pay board. In time these fellows grew dainty in their tastes and only infested boats that had an established reputation for setting good tables. All visiting pilots were useful, for they were always ready and willing, winter or summer, night or day, to go out in the yawl and help buoy the channel or assist the boat's pilots in any way they could. They were likewise welcomed because all pilots are tireless talkers when gathered together, and as they talk only about the river they are always understood and are always interesting. Your true pilot cares nothing about anything on earth but the river, and his pride in his occupation surpasses the pride of kings.

We had a fine company of these river inspectors along this trip. There were eight or ten, and there was abundance of room for them in our great pilot-house. Two or three of them wore polished silk hats, elaborate shirt-fronts, diamond breastpins, kid gloves, and patent-leather boots. They were choice in their English, and bore themselves with a dignity proper to men of solid means and prodigious reputation as pilots. The others were more or less loosely clad, and wore upon their heads tall felt cones that were suggestive of the days of the Commonwealth.

I was a cipher in this august company and felt sub-dued, not to say torpid. I was not even of sufficient consequence to assist at the wheel when it was neces-sary to put the tiller hard down in a hurry; the guest that stood nearest did that when occasion required—and this was pretty much all the time, because of the crookedness of the channel and the scant water. I stood in a corner, and the talk I listened to took the hope all out of me. One visitor said to another:

"Jim, how did you run Plum Point, coming up?"

"It was in the night there, and I ran it the way one of the boys on the *Diana* told me; started out about fifty yards above the wood-pile on the false point and held on the cabin under Plum Point till I raised the reef—quarter less twain—then straightened up for the middle bar till I got well abreast the old one-limbed cottonwood in the bend, then got my stern on the cottonwood and head on the low place above the point, and came through a-booming—nine and a half."

"Pretty square crossing, ain't it?"

"Yes, but the upper bar's working down fast."

Another pilot spoke up and said:

"I had better water than that and ran it lower down; started out from the false point—mark twain—raised the second reef abreast the big snag in the bend and had quarter less twain."

One of the gorgeous ones remarked:

"I don't want to find fault with your leadsmen but that's a good deal of water for Plum Point, it seems to me."

There was an approving nod all around as this quiet snub dropped on the boaster and "settled" him. And so they went on talk-talk-talking. Meantime, the thing that was running in my mind was, "Now, if my ears hear aright, I have not only to get the names of all the towns and islands and bends, and so on by heart, but I must even get up a warm personal acquaintanceship with every old snag and one-limbed cottonwood and obscure wood-pile that ornaments the banks of this river for twelve hundred miles; and more than that, I must actually know where these things are in the dark, unless these guests are gifted with eyes that can pierce through two miles of solid blackness. I wish the piloting business was in Jericho and I had never thought of it."

At dusk Mr. Bixby tapped the big bell three times (the signal to land) and the captain emerged from his drawing-room in the forward end of the "texas," and looked up inquiringly. Mr. Bixby said:

"We will lay up here all night, captain."

"Very well, sir."

That was all. The boat came to shore and was tied up for the night. It seemed to me a fine thing that the pilot could do as he pleased, without asking so grand a captain's permission. I took my supper and went immediately to bed, discouraged by my day's observations and experiences. My late voyage's note-booking was but a confusion of meaningless names. It had tangled me all up in a knot every time I had looked at it in the daytime. I now hoped for respite in sleep, but no, it reveled all through my head till sunrise again, a frantic and tireless nightmare.

Next morning I felt pretty rusty and low-spirited. We went booming along, taking a good many chances, for we were anxious to "get out of the river" (as getting out to Cairo was called) before night should overtake us. But Mr. Bixby's partner, the other pilot, presently grounded the boat and we lost so much time getting her off that it was plain the darkness would overtake us a good long way above the mouth. This was a great misfortune, especially to certain of our visiting pilots, whose boats would have to wait for their return, no matter how long that might be. It sobered the pilot-house talk a good deal. Coming up-stream, pilots did not mind low water or any kind of darkness; nothing stopped them but fog. But down-stream work was different; a boat was too nearly helpless with a stiff current pushing behind her, so it was not customary to run down-stream at night in low water.

There seemed to be one small hope, however: if we could get through the intricate and dangerous Hat Island crossing before night, we could venture the rest, for we would have plainer sailing and better water. But it would be insanity to attempt Hat Island at night. So there was a deal of looking at watches all the rest of the day and a constant ciphering upon the speed we were making; Hat Island was the eternal subject; sometimes hope was high and sometimes we were delayed in a bad crossing and down it went again. For hours all hands lay under the burden of this suppressed excitement; it was even communicated to me and I got to feeling so solicitous about Hat Island, and under such an awful pressure of responsibility, that I wished I might have five minutes on shore to draw a good, full, relieving breath and start over again. We were standing no regular watches. Each of our pilots ran such portions of the river as he had run when coming up-stream, because of his greater familiarity with it, but both remained in the pilot-house constantly.

An hour before sunset Mr. Bixby took the wheel and Mr. W. stepped aside. For the next thirty minutes every man held his watch in his hand and was restless, silent, and uneasy. At last somebody said, with a doomful sigh:

"Well, yonder's Hat Island—and we can't make it."

All the watches closed with a snap, everybody sighed and muttered something about its being "too bad, too bad—ah, if we could *only* have got here half an hour sooner!" and the place was thick with the atmosphere of disappointment. Some started to go out but loitered, hearing no bell-tap to land. The sun dipped behind the horizon, the boat went on. Inquiring looks passed from one guest to another, and one who had his hand on the door-knob and had turned it, waited, then presently took away his hand and let the knob turn back again. We bore steadily down the bend. More looks were exchanged and nods of surprised admiration—but no words. Insensibly the men drew together behind Mr. Bixby, as the sky darkened and one or two dim stars came out. The dead silence and sense of waiting became oppressive. Mr. Bixby pulled the cord and two deep, mellow notes from the big bell floated off on the night. Then a pause, and one more note was struck. The watchman's voice followed, from the hurricane-deck:

"Labboard lead, there! Stabboard lead!"

The cries of the leadsmen began to rise out of the distance and were gruffly repeated by the word-passers on the hurricane-deck.

"M-a-r-k three! M-a-r-k three! Quarter-less-three! Half twain! Quarter twain! M-a-r-k twain! Quarter-less—"

Mr. Bixby pulled two bell-ropes and was answered by faint jinglings far below in the engine-room, and our speed slackened. The steam began to whistle through the gauge-cocks. The cries of the leadsmen went on—and it is a weird sound, always, in the night. Every pilot in the lot was watching now, with fixed eyes, and talking under his breath. Nobody was calm and easy but Mr. Bixby. He would put his wheel down and stand on a spoke, and as the steamer swung into her (to me) utterly invisible marks—for we seemed to be in the midst of a wide and gloomy sea—he would meet and fasten her there. Out of the murmur of half-audible talk one caught a coherent sentence now and then—such as:

"There; she's over the first reef all right!"

After a pause, another subdued voice:

"Her stern's coming down just *exactly* right, by *George!* Now she's in the marks; over she goes!"

Somebody else muttered:

"Oh, it was done beautiful—*beautiful!*"

Now the engines were stopped altogether and we drifted with the current. Not that I could see the boat drift, for I could not, the stars being all gone by this time. This drifting was the dismalest work; it held one's heart still. Presently I discovered a blacker gloom than that which surrounded us. It was the head of the island. We were closing right down upon it. We entered its deeper shadow, and so imminent seemed the peril that I was likely to suffocate, and I had the strongest impulse to do *something,* anything, to save the vessel. But still Mr. Bixby stood by his wheel, silent, intent as a cat, and all the pilots stood shoulder to shoulder at his back.

"She'll not make it!" somebody whispered.

The water grew shoaler and shoaler by the leadsman's cries, till it was down to:

"Eight-and-a-half! E-i-g-h-t feet! E-i-g-h-t feet! Seven-and—"

Mr. Bixby said warningly through his speaking-tube to the engineer:

"Stand by, now!"

"Ay, ay, sir!"

"Seven-and-a-half! Seven feet! Six-and—"

We touched bottom! Instantly Mr. Bixby set a lot of bells ringing, shouted through the tube, "*Now,* let her have it—every ounce you've got!" then to his partner, "Put her hard down! snatch her! snatch her!" The boat rasped and ground her way through the sand, hung upon the apex of disaster a single tremendous instant, and then over she went! And such a shout as went up at Mr. Bixby's back never loosened the roof of a pilot-house before!

There was no more trouble after that. Mr. Bixby was a hero that night, and it was some little time, too, before his exploit ceased to be talked about by river-men.

Fully to realize the marvelous precision required in laying the great steamer in her marks in that murky waste of water, one should know that not only must she pick her intricate way through snags and blind reefs, and then shave the head of the island so closely as to brush the overhanging foliage with her stern, but at one place she must pass almost within arm's reach of a sunken and invisible wreck that would snatch the hull timbers from under her if she should strike it—and destroy a quarter of a million dollars' worth of steam-boat and cargo in five minutes, and maybe a hundred and fifty human lives into the bargain.

The last remark I heard that night was a compliment

to Mr. Bixby, uttered in soliloquy and with unction by one of our guests. He said:

"By the Shadow of Death, but he's a lightning pilot!"

III. The Continued Perplexities of Cub Piloting

At the end of what seemed a tedious while, I had managed to pack my head full of islands, towns, bars, "points," and bends, and a curiously inanimate mass of lumber it was, too. However, inasmuch as I could shut my eyes and reel off a good long string of these names without leaving out more than ten miles of river in every fifty, I began to feel that I could take a boat down to New Orleans if I could make her skip those little gaps. But of course my complacency could hardly get start enough to lift my nose a trifle into the air, before Mr. Bixby would think of something to fetch it down again. One day he turned on me suddenly with this settler:

"What is the shape of Walnut Bend?"

He might as well have asked me my grandmother's opinion of protoplasm. I reflected respectfully and then said I didn't know it had any particular shape. My gunpowdery chief went off with a bang, of course, and then went on loading and firing until he was out of adjectives.

I had learned long ago that he only carried just so many rounds of ammunition and was sure to subside into a very placable and even remorseful old smoothbore as soon as they were all gone. That word "old" is merely affectionate; he was not more than thirty-four. I waited. By and by he said:

"My boy, you've got to know the *shape* of the river perfectly. It is all there is left to steer by on a very dark night. Everything else is blotted out and gone. But mind you, it hasn't the same shape in the night that it has in the daytime."

"How on earth am I ever going to learn it, then?"

"How do you follow a hall at home in the dark? Because you know the shape of it. You can't see it."

"Do you mean to say that I've got to know all the million trifling variations of shape in the banks of this interminable river as well as I know the shape of the front hall at home?"

"On my honor, you've got to know them *better* than any man ever did know the shapes of the halls in his own house."

"I wish I was dead!"

"Now I don't want to discourage you, but—"

"Well, pile it on me; I might as well have it now as another time."

"You see, this has got to be learned, there isn't any getting around it. A clear starlight night throws such heavy shadows that, if you didn't know the shape of a shore perfectly, you would claw away from every bunch of timber, because you would take the black shadow of it for a solid cape, and you see you would be getting scared to death every fifteen minutes by the watch. You would be fifty yards from shore all the time when you ought to be within fifty feet of it. You can't see a snag in one of those shadows but you know exactly where it is, and the shape of the river tells you when you are coming to it. Then there's your pitch-dark night; the river is a very different shape on a pitch-dark night from what it is on a star-light night. All shores seem to be straight lines then, and mighty dim ones too, and you'd *run* them for straight lines, only you know better. You boldly drive your boat right into what seems to be a solid, straight wall (you knowing very well that in

reality there is a curve there) and that wall falls back
and makes way for you. Then there's your gray mist.
You take a night when there's one of these grisly,
drizzly, gray mists, and then there isn't *any* particular
shape to a shore. A gray mist would tangle the head of
the oldest man that ever lived. Well, then, different
kinds of *moonlight* change the shape of the river in
different ways. You see—"

"Oh, don't say any more, please! Have I got to learn
the shape of the river according to all these five hundred
thousand different ways? If I tried to carry all that
cargo in my head it would make me stoop-shouldered."

"*No!* you only learn *the* shape of the river, and you
learn it with such absolute certainty that you can always
steer by the shape that's *in your head* and never mind
the one that's before your eyes."

"Very well, I'll try it; but, after I have learned it,
can I depend on it? Will it keep the same form and not
go fooling around?"

Before Mr. Bixby could answer, Mr. W. came in to
take the watch, and he said:

"Bixby, you'll have to look out for President's Island
and all that country clear away up above the Old Hen
and Chickens. The banks are caving and the shap⸗ of
the shores changing like everything. Why, you wouldn't
know the point above 40. You can go up inside the old
sycamore snag, now." [1]

So that question was answered. Here were leagues
of shore changing shape. My spirits were down in the
mud again. Two things seemed pretty apparent to me.
One was that in order to be a pilot a man had got to
learn more than any one man ought to be allowed to

---

[1] It may not be necessary but still it can do no harm to explain
that "inside" means between the snag and the shore.—M. T.

know, and the other was that he must learn it all over again in a different way every twenty-four hours.

That night we had the watch until twelve. Now it was an ancient river custom for the two pilots to chat a bit when the watch changed. While the relieving pilot put on his gloves and lit his cigar, his partner, the retiring pilot, would say something like this:

"I judge the upper bar is making down a little at Hale's Point; had quarter twain with the lower lead and mark twain[1] with the other."

"Yes, I thought it was making down a little, last trip. Meet any boats?"

"Met one abreast the head of 21 but she was away over hugging the bar, and I couldn't make her out entirely. I took her for the *Sunny South*—hadn't any skylights forward of the chimneys."

And so on. And as the relieving pilot took the wheel his partner[2] would mention that we were in such-and-such a bend, and say we were abreast of such-and-such a man's wood-yard or plantation. This was courtesy; I supposed it was *necessity*. But Mr. W. came on watch full twelve minutes late on this particular night, a tremendous breach of etiquette; in fact, it is the unpardonable sin among pilots. So Mr. Bixby gave him no greeting whatever but simply surrendered the wheel and marched out of the pilot-house without a word. I was appalled; it was a villainous night for blackness, we were in a particularly wide and blind part of the river where there was no shape or substance to anything, and it seemed incredible that Mr. Bixby should have left that poor fellow to kill the boat, trying to find out where

---

[1] *Two fathoms. Quarter twain is 2¼ fathoms, 13½ feet. Mark three is three fathoms.*

[2] *"Partner" is technical for "the other pilot."*

he was. But I resolved that I would stand by him anyway. He should find that he was not wholly friendless. So I stood around and waited to be asked where we were. But Mr. W. plunged on serenely through the solid firmament of black cats that stood for an atmosphere, and never opened his mouth. "Here is a proud devil!" thought I, "here is a limb of Satan that would rather send us all to destruction than put himself under obligations to me, because I am not yet one of the salt of the earth and privileged to snub captains and lord it over everything dead and alive in a steamboat." I presently climbed up on the bench; I did not think it was safe to go to sleep while this lunatic was on watch.

However, I must have gone to sleep in the course of time, because the next thing I was aware of was the fact that day was breaking, Mr. W. gone, and Mr. Bixby at the wheel again. So it was four o'clock and all well— but me; I felt like a skinful of dry bones, and all of them trying to ache at once.

Mr. Bixby asked me what I had stayed up there for. I confessed that it was to do Mr. W. a benevolence— tell him where he was. It took five minutes for the entire preposterousness of the thing to filter into Mr. Bixby's system, and then I judge it filled him nearly up to the chin; because he paid me a compliment, and not much of a one either. He said:

"Well, taking you by and large, you do seem to be more different kinds of an ass than any creature I ever saw before. What did you suppose he wanted to know for?"

I said I thought it might be a convenience to him.

"Convenience! D——nation! Didn't I tell you that a man's got to know the river in the night the same as he'd know his own front hall?"

"Well, I can follow the front hall in the dark if I

know it *is* the front hall, but suppose you set me down in the middle of it in the dark and not tell me which hall it is, how am *I* to know?"

"Well, you've *got* to, on the river!"

"All right. Then I'm glad I never said anything to Mr. W."

"I should say so! Why, he'd have slammed you through the window and utterly ruined a hundred dollars' worth of window-sash and stuff."

I was glad this damage had been saved, for it would have made me unpopular with the owners. They always hated anybody who had the name of being careless and injuring things.

I went to work now to learn the shape of the river, and of all the eluding and ungraspable objects that ever I tried to get mind or hands on, that was the chief. I would fasten my eyes upon a sharp, wooded point that projected far into the river some miles ahead of me and go to laboriously photographing its shape upon my brain, and just as I was beginning to succeed to my satisfaction, we would draw up toward it and the exasperating thing would begin to melt away and fold back into the bank! If there had been a conspicuous dead tree standing upon the very point of the cape, I would find that tree inconspicuously merged into the general forest and occupying the middle of a straight shore, when I got abreast of it! No prominent hill would stick to its shape long enough for me to make up my mind what its form really was, but it was as dissolving and changeful as if it had been a mountain of butter in the hottest corner of the tropics. Nothing ever had the same shape when I was coming down-stream that it had borne when I went up. I mentioned these little difficulties to Mr. Bixby. He said:

"That's the very main virtue of the thing. If the

shapes didn't change every three seconds they wouldn't be of any use. Take this place where we are now, for instance. As long as that hill over yonder is only one hill, I can boom right along the way I'm going, but the moment it splits at the top and forms a V, I know I've got to scratch to starboard in a hurry or I'll bang this boat's brains out against a rock, and then the moment one of the prongs of the V swings behind the other, I've got to waltz to larboard again or I'll have a misunderstanding with a snag that would snatch the keelson out of this steamboat as neatly as if it were a sliver in your hand. If that hill didn't change its shape on bad nights there would be an awful steamboat graveyard around here inside of a year."

It was plain that I had got to learn the shape of the river in all the different ways that could be thought of —upside down, wrong end first, inside out, fore-and-aft, and "thort-ships"—and then know what to do on gray nights when it hadn't any shape at all. So I set about it. In the course of time I began to get the best of this knotty lesson and my self-complacency moved to the front once more. Mr. Bixby was all fixed and ready to start it to the rear again. He opened on me after this fashion:

"How much water did we have in the middle crossing at Hole-in-the-Wall, trip before last?"

I considered this an outrage. I said:

"Every trip, down and up, the leadsmen are singing through that tangled place for three-quarters of an hour on a stretch. How do you reckon I can remember such a mess as that?"

"My boy, you've got to remember it. You've got to remember the exact spot and the exact marks the boat lay in when we had the shoalest water, in every one of the five hundred shoal places between St. Louis and

New Orleans, and you mustn't get the shoal soundings and marks of one trip mixed up with the shoal soundings and marks of another, either, for they're not often twice alike. You must keep them separate."

When I came to myself again, I said:

"When I get so that I can do that, I'll be able to raise the dead, and then I won't have to pilot a steamboat to make a living. I want to retire from this business. I want a slush-bucket and a brush, I'm only fit for a roustabout. I haven't got brains enough to be a pilot, and if I had I wouldn't have strength enough to carry them around, unless I went on crutches."

"Now drop that! When I say I'll learn[1] a man the river, I mean it. And you can depend on it, I'll learn him or kill him."

There was no use in arguing with a person like this. I promptly put such a strain on my memory that by and by even the shoal water and the countless crossing-marks began to stay with me. But the result was just the same. I never could more than get one knotty thing learned before another presented itself. Now I had often seen pilots gazing at the water and pretending to read it as if it were a book, but it was a book that told me nothing. A time came at last, however, when Mr. Bixby seemed to think me far enough advanced to bear a lesson on water-reading. So he began:

"Do you see that long, slanting line on the face of the water? Now, that's a reef. Moreover, it's a bluff reef. There is a solid sand-bar under it that is nearly as straight up and down as the side of a house. There is plenty of water close up to it, but mighty little on top of it. If you were to hit it you would knock the boat's brains out. Do you see where the line fringes out at the upper end and begins to fade away?"

---

[1] "Teach" is not in the river vocabulary.

"Yes, sir."

"Well, that is a low place; that is the head of the reef. You can climb over there and not hurt anything. Cross over, now, and follow along close under the reef —easy water there—not much current."

I followed the reef along till I approached the fringed end. Then Mr. Bixby said:

"Now get ready. Wait till I give the word. She won't want to mount the reef; a boat hates shoal water. Stand by—wait—*wait*—keep her well in hand. *Now* cramp her down! Snatch her! snatch her!"

He seized the other side of the wheel and helped to spin it around until it was hard down, and then we held it so. The boat resisted and refused to answer for a while, and next she came surging to starboard, mounted the reef, and sent a long angry ridge of water foaming away from her bows.

"Now watch her, watch her like a cat, or she'll get away from you. When she fights strong and the tiller slips a little, in a jerky, greasy sort of way, let up on her a trifle; it is the way she tells you at night that the water is too shoal; but keep edging her up, little by little, toward the point. You are well up on the bar now; there is a bar under every point, because the water that comes down around it forms an eddy and allows the sediment to sink. Do you see those fine lines on the face of the water that branch out like the ribs of a fan? Well, those are little reefs; you want to just miss the ends of them but run them pretty close. Now look out—look out! Don't you crowd that slick, greasy-looking place, there ain't nine feet there, she won't stand it. She begins to smell it; look sharp, I tell you! Oh, blazes, there you go! Stop the starboard wheel! Quick! Ship up to back! Set her back!"

The engine bells jingled and the engines answered

promptly, shooting white columns of steam far aloft out of the 'scape-pipes, but it was too late. The boat had "smelt" the bar in good earnest; the foamy ridges that radiated from her bows suddenly disappeared, a great dead swell came rolling forward, and swept ahead of her, she careened far over to larboard and went tearing away toward the shore as if she were about scared to death. We were a good mile from where we ought to have been when we finally got the upper hand of her again.

During the afternoon watch the next day, Mr. Bixby asked me if I knew how to run the next few miles. I said:

"Go inside the first snag above the point, outside the next one, start out from the lower end of Higgins's wood-yard, make a square crossing, and—"

"That's all right. I'll be back before you close up on the next point."

But he wasn't. He was still below when I rounded it and entered upon a piece of the river which I had some misgivings about. I did not know that he was hiding behind a chimney to see how I would perform. I went gaily along, getting prouder and prouder, for he had never left the boat in my sole charge such a length of time before. I even got to "setting" her and letting the wheel go entirely, while I vaingloriously turned my back and inspected the stern marks and hummed a tune, a sort of easy indifference which I had prodigiously admired in Bixby and other great pilots. Once I inspected rather long, and when I faced to the front again my heart flew into my mouth so suddenly that if I hadn't clapped my teeth together I should have lost it. One of those frightful bluff reefs was stretching its deadly length right across our bows! My head was gone in a moment; I did not know which end I stood on; I gasped and could not get my breath; I spun the wheel down with such rapidity that it wove itself together like a spider's web; the boat answered and turned square away from the reef, but the reef followed her! I fled but still it followed, still it kept—right across my bows! I never looked to see where I was going, I only fled. The awful crash was imminent. Why didn't that villain come? If I committed the crime of ringing a bell I might get thrown overboard. But better that than kill the boat. So in blind desperation, I started such a rattling "shivaree" down below as never had astounded an engineer in this world before, I fancy. Amidst the frenzy of the bells the engines began to back and fill in a curious way and my reason forsook its throne—we were about to crash into the woods on the other side of the river. Just then Mr. Bixby stepped calmly into view on the hurricane-deck. My soul went out to him in gratitude. My distress vanished; I would have felt safe on the brink of Niagara with Mr. Bixby on the hurricane-deck. He blandly and sweetly took his toothpick out of his mouth between his fingers, as if it were a cigar—we were just in the act of climbing an overhanging big tree and the passengers were scudding astern like rats—and lifted up these commands to me ever so gently:

"Stop the starboard! Stop the larboard! Set her back on both!"

The boat hesitated, halted, pressed her nose among the boughs a critical instant, then reluctantly began to back away.

"Stop the larboard! Come ahead on it! Stop the starboard! Come ahead on it! Point her for the bar!"

I sailed away as serenely as a summer's morning. Mr. Bixby came in and said, with mock simplicity:

"When you have a hail, my boy, you ought to tap the big bell three times before you land, so that the engineers can get ready."

I blushed under the sarcasm and said I hadn't had any hail.

"Ah! Then it was for wood, I suppose. The officer of the watch will tell you when he wants to wood up."

I went on consuming and said I wasn't after wood.

"Indeed? Why, what could you want over here in the bend, then? Did you ever know of a boat following a bend up-stream at this stage of the river?"

"No, sir—and I wasn't trying to follow it. I was getting away from a bluff reef."

"No, it wasn't a bluff reef; there isn't one within three miles of where you were."

"But I saw it. It was as bluff as that one yonder."

"Just about. Run over it!"

"Do you give it as an order?"

"Yes. Run over it!"

"If I don't, I wish I may die."

"All right; I am taking the responsibility."

I was just as anxious to kill the boat, now, as I had been to save it before. I impressed my orders upon my memory, to be used at the inquest, and made a straight break for the reef. As it disappeared under our bows I held my breath, but we slid over it like oil.

"Now, don't you see the difference? It wasn't anything but a *wind* reef. The wind does that."

"So I see. But it is exactly like a bluff reef. How am I ever going to tell them apart?"

"I can't tell you. It is an instinct. By and by you will just naturally *know* one from the other, but you never will be able to explain why or how you know them apart."

It turned out to be true. The face of the water in time became a wonderful book—a book that was a dead language to the uneducated passenger but which told its mind to me without reserve, delivering its most cherished secrets as clearly as if it uttered them with a voice. And it was not a book to be read once and thrown aside, for it had a new story to tell every day. Throughout the long twelve hundred miles there was never a page that was void of interest, never one that you could leave unread without loss, never one that you would want to skip, thinking you could find higher enjoyment in some other thing. There never was so wonderful a book written by man, never one whose interest was so absorbing, so unflagging, so sparklingly renewed with every reperusal. The passenger who could not read it was charmed with a peculiar sort of faint dimple on its surface (on the rare occasions when he did not overlook it altogether) but to the pilot that was an *italicized* passage; indeed it was more than that, it was a legend of the largest capitals with a string of shouting exclamation-points at the end of it, for it meant that a wreck or a rock was buried there that could tear the life out of the strongest vessel that ever floated. It is the faintest and simplest expression the water ever makes, and the most hideous to a pilot's eye. In truth, the passenger who could not read this book saw nothing but all manner of pretty pictures in it, painted by the sun and shaded by the clouds, whereas to the trained eye these were not pictures at all, but the grimmest and most dead-earnest of reading-matter.

Now when I had mastered the language of this water and had come to know every trifling feature that bordered the great river as familiarly as I knew the letters of the alphabet, I had made a valuable acquisition. But I had lost something, too. I had lost something which could never be restored to me while I lived. All the grace, the beauty, the poetry, had gone out of the majestic river! I still kept in mind a certain wonderful sunset which I witnessed when steamboating was new to me. A broad expanse of the river was turned to blood; in the middle distance the red hue brightened into gold, through which a solitary log came floating, black and conspicuous; in one place a long, slanting mark lay sparkling upon the water; in another the surface was broken by boiling, tumbling rings, that were as many-tinted as an opal; where the ruddy flush was faintest, was a smooth spot that was covered with graceful circles and radiating lines, ever so delicately traced; the shore on our left was densely wooded and the somber shadow that fell from this forest was broken in one place by a long, ruffled trail that shone like silver; and high above the forest wall a clean-stemmed dead tree waved a single leafy bough that glowed like a flame in the un-obstructed splendor that was flowing from the sun. There were graceful curves, reflected images, woody heights, soft distances, and over the whole scene, far and near, the dissolving lights drifted steadily, enriching it every passing moment with new marvels of coloring.

I stood like one bewitched. I drank it in, in a speech-less rapture. The world was new to me and I had never seen anything like this at home. But as I have said, a day came when I began to cease from noting the glories and the charms which the moon and the sun and the twilight wrought upon the river's face; another day came when I ceased altogether to note them. Then, if that sunset scene had been repeated, I should have looked upon it without rapture, and should have com-mented upon it inwardly after this fashion: "This sun means that we are going to have wind to-morrow; that floating log means that the river is rising, small thanks to it; that slanting mark on the water refers to a bluff reef which is going to kill somebody's steamboat one of these nights, if it keeps on stretching out like that; those tumbling 'boils' show a dissolving bar and a changing channel there; the lines and circles in the slick water over yonder are a warning that that troublesome place is shoaling up dangerously; that silver streak in the shadow of the forest is the 'break' from a new snag and he has located himself in the very best place he could have found to fish for steamboats; that tall dead tree, with a single living branch, is not going to last long, and then how is a body ever going to get through this blind place at night without the friendly old landmark?"

No, the romance and beauty were all gone from the river. All the value any feature of it had for me now was the amount of usefulness it could furnish toward compassing the safe piloting of a steamboat. Since those days, I have pitied doctors from my heart. What does the lovely flush in a beauty's cheek mean to a doctor but a "break" that ripples above some deadly disease? Are not all her visible charms sown thick with what are to him the signs and symbols of hidden decay? Does he ever see her beauty at all, or doesn't he simply view her professionally and comment upon her unwholesome condition all to himself? And doesn't he sometimes wonder whether he has gained most or lost most by learning his trade?

iv. The "Cub" Pilot's Education Nearly Completed

Whosoever has done me the courtesy to read my chapters which have preceded this may possibly wonder that I deal so minutely with piloting as a science. It was the prime purpose of those chapters, and I am not quite done yet. I wish to show in the most patient and painstaking way what a wonderful science it is. Ship-channels are buoyed and lighted, and therefore it is a comparatively easy undertaking to learn to run them;

clear-water rivers with gravel bottoms change their channels very gradually, and therefore one needs to learn them but once; but piloting becomes another matter when you apply it to vast streams like the Mississippi and the Missouri, whose alluvial banks cave and change constantly, whose snags are always hunting up new quarters, whose sand-bars are never at rest, whose channels are forever dodging and shirking, and whose obstructions must be confronted in all nights and all weathers without the aid of a single lighthouse or a single buoy, for there is neither light nor buoy to be found anywhere in all this three or four thousand miles of villainous river.[1] I feel justified in enlarging upon this great science for the reason that I feel sure no one has ever yet written a paragraph about it who had piloted a steamboat himself and so had a practical knowledge of the subject. If the theme was hackneyed, I should be obliged to deal gently with the reader, but since it is wholly new, I have felt at liberty to take up a considerable degree of room with it.

When I had learned the name and position of every visible feature of the river, when I had so mastered its shape that I could shut my eyes and trace it from St. Louis to New Orleans, when I had learned to read the face of the water as one would cull the news from the morning paper, and finally when I had trained my dull memory to treasure up an endless array of soundings and crossing-marks, and keep fast hold of them, I judged that my education was complete; so I got to tilting my cap to the side of my head and wearing a toothpick in my mouth at the wheel. Mr. Bixby had his eye on these airs. One day he said:

"What is the height of that bank yonder, at Burgess's?"

---

[1] *True at the time referred to; not true now (1882).*

"How can I tell, sir? It is three-quarters of a mile away."

"Very poor eye—very poor. Take the glass."

I took the glass and presently said:

"I can't tell. I suppose that that bank is about a foot and a half high."

"Foot and a half! That's a six-foot bank. How high was the bank along here last trip?"

"I don't know; I never noticed."

"You didn't? Well, you must always do it hereafter."

"Why?"

"Because you'll have to know a good many things that it tells you. For one thing, it tells you the stage of the river—tells you whether there's more water or less in the river along here than there was last trip."

"The leads tell me that." I rather thought I had the advantage of him there.

"Yes, but suppose the leads lie? The bank would tell you so and then you would stir those leadsmen up a bit. There was a ten-foot bank here last trip, and there is only a six-foot bank now. What does that signify?"

"That the river is four feet higher than it was last trip."

"Very good. Is the river rising or falling?"

"Rising."

"No, it ain't."

"I guess I am right, sir. Yonder is some driftwood floating down the stream."

"A rise *starts* the driftwood but then it keeps on floating awhile after the river is done rising. Now the bank will tell you about this. Wait till you come to a place where it shelves a little. Now here: do you see this narrow belt of fine sediment? That was deposited while the water was higher. You see the driftwood begins to strand, too. The bank helps in other ways. Do you see that stump on the false point?"

"Ay, ay, sir."

"Well, the water is just up to the roots of it. You must make a note of that."

"Why?"

"Because that means that there's seven feet in the chute of 103."

"But 103 is a long way up the river yet."

"That's where the benefit of the bank comes in. There is water enough in 103 *now,* yet there may not be by the time we get there, but the bank will keep us posted all along. You don't run close chutes on a falling river up-stream, and there are precious few of them that you are allowed to run at all down-stream. There's a law of the United States against it. The river may be rising by the time we get to 103 and in that case we'll run it. We are drawing—how much?"

"Six feet aft—six and a half forward."

"Well, you do seem to know something."

"But what I particularly want to know is, if I have got to keep up an everlasting measuring of the banks of this river, twelve hundred miles, month in and month out?"

"Of course!"

My emotions were too deep for words for a while. Presently I said:

"And how about these chutes? Are there many of them?"

"I should say so! I fancy we sha'n't run any of the river this trip as you've ever seen it run before—so to speak. If the river begins to rise again, we'll go up behind bars that you've always seen standing out of the river high and dry, like a roof of a house; we'll cut across low places that you've never noticed at all, right through the middle of bars that cover three hundred acres of river; we'll creep through cracks where you've always thought was solid land; we'll dart through the woods and leave twenty-five miles of river off to one side; we'll see the hind side of every island between New Orleans and Cairo."

"Then I've got to go to work and learn just as much more river as I already know."

"Just about twice as much more, as near as you can come at it."

"Well, one lives to find out. I think I was a fool when I went into this business."

"Yes, that is true. And you are yet. But you'll not be when you've learned it."

"Ah, I never can learn it!"

"I will see that you *do*."

By and by I ventured again:

"Have I got to learn all this thing just as I know the rest of the river—shapes and all—and so I can run it at night?"

"Yes. And you've got to have good fair marks from one end of the river to the other, that will help the bank tell you when there is water enough in each of these countless places—like that stump, you know. When the river first begins to rise, you can run half a dozen of the deepest of them; when it rises a foot more you can run another dozen; the next foot will add a couple of dozen, and so on: so you see you have to know your banks and marks to a dead moral certainty and never get them mixed, for when you start through one of those cracks, there's no backing out again, as there is in the big river; you've got to go through or stay there six months if you get caught on a falling river. There are about fifty of these cracks which you can't run at all except when the river is brimful and over the banks."

"This new lesson is a cheerful prospect."

"Cheerful enough. And mind what I've just told you, when you start into one of those places you've got to go through. They are too narrow to turn around in, too crooked to back out of, and the shoal water is always *up at the head*, never elsewhere. And the head of them is always likely to be filling up little by little, so that the marks you reckon their depth by this season may not answer for next."

"Learn a new set, then, every year?"

"Exactly. Cramp her up to the bar! What are you standing up through the middle of the river for?"

The next few months showed me strange things. On the same day that we held the conversation above narrated we met a great rise coming down the river. The whole vast face of the stream was black with drifting dead logs, broken boughs, and great trees that had caved in and been washed away. It required the nicest steering to pick one's way through this rushing raft even in the daytime, when crossing from point to point; and at night the difficulty was mightily increased; every now and then a huge log, lying deep in the water, would suddenly appear right under our bows, coming head-on; no use to try to avoid it then; we could only stop the engines, and one wheel would walk over that log from one end to the other, keeping up a thundering racket and careening the boat in a way that was very uncomfortable to passengers. Now and then we would hit one of these sunken logs a rattling bang, dead in the center, with a full head of steam, and it would stun the boat as if she had hit a continent. Sometimes this log would lodge and stay right across our nose and back the Mississippi up before it; we would have to do a little crawfishing then, to get away from the obstruction. We often hit *white* logs in the dark, for we could not see

them until we were right on them, but a black log is a
pretty distinct object at night. A white snag is an ugly
customer when the daylight is gone.

Of course, on the great rise down came a swarm of
prodigious timber-rafts from the headwaters of the Mississippi, coal-barges from Pittsburgh, little trading-scows
from everywhere, and broadhorns from "Posey County,"
Indiana, freighted with "fruit and furniture"—the usual
term for describing it, though in plain English the
freight thus aggrandized was hoop-poles and pumpkins.
Pilots bore a mortal hatred to these craft and it was
returned with usury. The law required all such helpless
traders to keep a light burning but it was a law that was
often broken. All of a sudden on a murky night, a light
would hop up right under our bows, almost, and an
agonized voice with the backwoods "whang" to it would
wail out:

"Whar'n the —— you goin' to! Cain't you see nothin',
you dash-dashed aig-suckin', sheep-stealin', one-eyed
son of a stuffed monkey!"

Then for an instant as we whistled by, the red glare
from our furnaces would reveal the scow and the form
of the gesticulating orator, as if under a lightning flash,
and in that instant our firemen and deck-hands would
send and receive a tempest of missiles and profanity, one
of our wheels would walk off with the crashing fragments of a steering-oar, and down the dead blackness
would shut again. And that flatboatman would be sure
to go into New Orleans and sue our boat, swearing
stoutly that he had a light burning all the time, when in
truth his gang had the lantern down below to sing and
lie and drink and gamble by, and no watch on deck.
Once at night, in one of those forest-bordered crevices
(behind an island) which steamboatmen intensely describe with the phrase "as dark as the inside of a cow,"

we should have eaten up a Posey County family, fruit, furniture, and all, but that they happened to be fiddling down below and we just caught the sound of the music in time to sheer off, doing no serious damage, unfortunately, but coming so near it that we had good hopes for a moment. These people brought up their lantern, then, of course, and as we backed and filled to get away, the precious family stood in the light of it—both sexes and various ages—and cursed us till everything turned blue. Once a coal-boatman sent a bullet through our pilot-house when we borrowed a steering-oar of him in a very narrow place.

During this big rise these small-fry craft were an intolerable nuisance. We were running chute after chute —a new world to me—and if there was a particularly cramped place in a chute, we would be pretty sure to meet a broadhorn there, and if he failed to be there we would find him in a still worse locality, namely, the head of the chute, on the shoal water. And then there would be no end of profane cordialities exchanged.

Sometimes in the big river, when we would be feeling our way cautiously along through a fog, the deep hush would suddenly be broken by yells and a clamor of tin pans, and all in an instant a log raft would appear vaguely through the webby veil, close upon us, and then we did not wait to swap knives, but snatched our engine-bells out by the roots and piled on all the steam we had, to scramble out of the way! One doesn't hit a rock or a solid log raft with a steamboat when he can get excused.

You will hardly believe it, but many steamboat clerks always carried a large assortment of religious tracts with them in those old departed steamboating days. Indeed they did! Twenty times a day we would be cramping up around a bar, while a string of these small-fry rascals were drifting down into the head of the bend away above and beyond us a couple of miles. Now a skiff would dart away from one of them and come fighting its laborious way across the desert of water. It would "ease all" in the shadow of our forecastle and the panting oarsmen would shout, "Gimme a pa-a-per!" as the skiff drifted swiftly astern. The clerk would throw over a file of New Orleans journals. If these were picked up *without comment,* you might notice that now a dozen other skiffs had been drifting down upon us without saying anything. You understand, they had been waiting to see how No. 1 was going to fare. No. 1 making no comment, all the rest would bend to their oars and come on now, and as fast as they came the clerk would heave over neat bundles of religious tracts, tied to shingles. The amount of hard swearing which twelve packages of religious literature will command when impartially divided up among twelve raftsmen's crews, who have pulled a heavy skiff two miles on a hot day to get them, is simply incredible.

As I have said, the big rise brought a new world under my vision. By the time the river was over its banks we had forsaken our old paths and were hourly climbing over bars that had stood ten feet out of water before; we were shaving stumpy shores like that at the foot of Madrid Bend, which I had always seen avoided before; we were clattering through chutes like that of 82, where the opening at the foot was an unbroken wall of timber till our nose was almost at the very spot. Some of these chutes were utter solitudes. The dense, untouched forest overhung both banks of the crooked little crack and one could believe that human creatures had never intruded there before. The swinging grape-vines, the grassy nooks and vistas glimpsed as we swept by, the flowering creepers waving their red blossoms from the tops of dead trunks, and all the spendthrift richness of the forest foliage were wasted and thrown away there. The chutes were lovely places to steer in; they were deep except at the head, the current was gentle, under the "points" the water was absolutely dead and the invisible banks so bluff that where the tender willow thickets projected you could bury your boat's broadside in them as you tore along, and then you seemed fairly to fly.

Behind other islands we found wretched little farms and wretcheder little log cabins; there were crazy rail fences sticking a foot or two above the water, with one or two jeans-clad, chills-racked, yellow-faced male miserables roosting on the top rail, elbows on knees, jaws in hands, grinding tobacco and discharging the result at floating chips through crevices left by lost teeth; while the rest of the family and the few farm animals were huddled together in an empty wood-flat riding at her moorings close at hand. In this flatboat the family would have to cook and eat and sleep for a lesser or greater number of days (or possibly weeks) until the river should fall two or three feet and let them get back to their log cabins and their chills again—chills being a merciful provision of an all-wise Providence to enable them to take exercise without exertion. And this sort of watery camping out was a thing which these people were rather liable to be treated to a couple of times a year: by the December rise out of the Ohio and the June rise out of the Mississippi. And yet these were kindly dispensations, for they at least enabled the poor things to rise from the dead now and then and look upon life when a steamboat went by. They appreciated the blessing, too, for they spread their mouths and eyes wide open and made the most of these occasions. Now what *could* these banished creatures find to do to keep from dying of the blues during the low-water season!

Once, in one of these lovely island chutes, we found

our course completely bridged by a great fallen tree. This will serve to show how narrow some of the chutes were. The passengers had an hour's recreation in a virgin wilderness while the boat-hands chopped the bridge away, for there was no such thing as turning back, you comprehend.

From Cairo to Baton Rouge, when the river is over its banks you have no particular trouble in the night, for the thousand-mile wall of dense forest that guards the two banks all the way is only gapped with a farm or woodyard opening at intervals, and so you can't "get out of the river" much easier than you could get out of a fenced lane; but from Baton Rouge to New Orleans it is a different matter. The river is more than a mile wide and very deep—as much as two hundred feet in places. Both banks, for a good deal over a hundred miles, are shorn of their timber and bordered by continuous sugar-plantations, with only here and there a scattering sapling or row of ornamental China trees. The timber is shorn off clear to the rear of the plantations, from two to four miles. When the first frost threatens to come, the planters snatch off their crops in a hurry. When they have finished grinding the cane, they form the refuse of the stalks (which they call *bagasse*) into great piles and set fire to them, though in other sugar countries the bagasse is used for fuel in the furnaces of the sugar-mills. Now the piles of damp bagasse burn slowly and smoke like Satan's own kitchen.

An embankment ten or fifteen feet high guards both banks of the Mississippi all the way down that lower end of the river, and this embankment is set back from the edge of the shore from ten to perhaps a hundred feet, according to circumstances, say thirty or forty feet as a general thing. Fill that whole region with an impenetrable gloom of smoke from a hundred miles of burning bagasse piles, when the river is over the banks, and turn a steamboat loose along there at midnight and see how she will feel. And see how you will feel, too! You find yourself away out in the midst of a vague, dim sea that is shoreless, that fades out and loses itself in the murky distances, for you cannot discern the thin rib of embankment and you are always imagining you see a straggling tree when you don't. The plantations themselves are transformed by the smoke and look like a part of the sea. All through your watch you are tortured with the exquisite misery of uncertainty. You hope you are keeping in the river but you do not know. All that you are sure about is that you are likely to be within six feet of the bank *and* destruction when you think you are a good half-mile from shore. And you are sure also that if you chance suddenly to fetch up against the embankment and topple your chimneys overboard, you will have the small comfort of knowing that it is about what you were expecting to do. One of the great Vicksburg packets darted out into a sugar-plantation one night at such a time, and had to stay there a week. But there was no novelty about it; it had often been done before.

I thought I had finished this chapter, but I wish to add a curious thing, while it is in my mind. It is only relevant in that it is connected with piloting. There used to be an excellent pilot on the river, a Mr. X, who was a somnambulist. It was said that if his mind was troubled about a bad piece of river, he was pretty sure to get up and walk in his sleep and do strange things. He was once fellow-pilot for a trip or two with George Ealer, on a great New Orleans passenger-packet. During a considerable part of the first trip George was uneasy but got over it by and by, as X seemed content to stay in his bed when asleep. Late one night the boat was approaching Helena, Ark.; the water was low and the crossing above the town in a very blind and tangled condition. X had seen the crossing since Ealer had and as the night was particularly drizzly, sullen, and dark, Ealer was considering whether he had not better have X called to assist in running the place, when the door opened and X walked in. Now, on very dark nights light is a deadly enemy to piloting; you are aware that if you stand in a lighted room, on such a night, you cannot see things in the street to any purpose, but if you put out the lights and stand in the gloom you can make out objects in the street pretty well. So, on very dark nights pilots do not smoke, they allow no fire in the pilot-house stove if there is a crack which can allow the least ray to escape, they order the furnaces to be curtained with huge tarpaulins and the skylights to be closely blinded. Then no light whatever issues from the boat. The undefinable shape that now entered the pilot-house had Mr. X's voice. This said:

"Let me take her, George; I've seen this place since you have and it is so crooked that I reckon I can run it myself easier than I could tell you how to do it."

"It is kind of you and I swear *I* am willing. I haven't got another drop of perspiration left in me. I have been spinning around and around the wheel like a squirrel. It is so dark I can't tell which way she is swinging till she is coming around like a whirligig."

So Ealer took a seat on the bench, panting and breathless. The black phantom assumed the wheel without saying anything, steadied the waltzing steamer with a turn or two, and then stood at ease, coaxing her a little to this side and then to that, as gently and as sweetly as if the time had been noonday. When Ealer observed this marvel of steering, he wished he had not confessed! He stared and wondered, and finally said:

"Well, I thought I knew how to steer a steamboat but that was another mistake of mine."

X said nothing but went serenely on with his work. He rang for the leads; he rang to slow down the steam; he worked the boat carefully and neatly into invisible marks, then stood at the center of the wheel and peered blandly out into the blackness, fore and aft, to verify his position; as the leads shoaled more and more he stopped the engines entirely, and the dead silence and suspense of "drifting" followed; when the shoalest water was struck, he cracked on the steam, carried her handsomely over, and then began to work her warily into the next system of shoal-marks; the same patient, heedful use of leads and engines followed, the boat slipped through without touching bottom, and entered upon the third and last intricacy of the crossing; imperceptibly she moved through the gloom, crept by inches into her marks, drifted tediously till the shoalest water was cried, and then, under a tremendous head of steam, went swinging over the reef and away into deep water and safety!

Ealer let his long-pent breath pour in a great relieving sigh, and said:

"That's the sweetest piece of piloting that was ever done on the Mississippi River! I wouldn't believe it could be done, if I hadn't seen it."

There was no reply, and he added:

"Just hold her five minutes longer, partner, and let me run down and get a cup of coffee."

A minute later Ealer was biting into a pie, down in the "texas," and comforting himself with coffee. Just then the night watchman happened in, and was about to happen out again when he noticed Ealer and exclaimed:

"Who is at the wheel, sir?"

"X."

"Dart for the pilot-house, quicker than lightning!"

The next moment both men were flying up the pilot-house companionway, three steps at a jump! Nobody there! The great steamer was whistling down the middle of the river at her own sweet will! The watchman shot out of the place again; Ealer seized the wheel, set an engine back with power, and held his breath while the boat reluctantly swung away from a "towhead" which she was about to knock into the middle of the Gulf of Mexico!

By and by the watchman came back and said:

"Didn't that lunatic tell you he was asleep, when he first came up here?"

"No."

"Well, he was. I found him walking along on top of the railings, just as unconcerned as another man would walk a pavement, and I put him to bed; now just this minute there he was again, away astern, going through that sort of tight-rope deviltry the same as before."

"Well, I think I'll stay by next time he has one of those fits. But I hope he'll have them often. You just ought to have seen him take this boat through Helena crossing. *I* never saw anything so gaudy before. And if he can do such gold-leaf, kid-glove, diamond-breastpin piloting when he is sound asleep, what *couldn't* he do if he was dead!"

v. "Sounding". Faculties Peculiarly Necessary
to a Pilot

When the river is very low and one's steamboat is "drawing all the water" there is in the channel—or a few inches more, as was often the case in the old times

—one must be painfully circumspect in his piloting. We used to have to "sound" a number of particularly bad places almost every trip when the river was at a very low stage.

Sounding is done in this way: The boat ties up at the shore, just above the shoal crossing; the pilot not on watch takes his "cub" or steersman and a picked crew of men (sometimes an officer also), and goes out in the yawl—provided the boat has not that rare and sumptuous luxury, a regularly devised "sounding-boat"—and proceeds to hunt for the best water, the pilot on duty watching his movements through a spy-glass, meantime, and in some instances assisting by signals of the boat's whistle, signifying "try higher up" or "try lower down"; for the surface of the water, like an oil-painting, is more expressive and intelligible when inspected from a little distance than very close at hand. The whistle signals are seldom necessary, however; never, perhaps, except when the wind confuses the significant ripples upon the water's surface. When the yawl has reached the shoal place, the speed is slackened, the pilot begins to sound the depth with a pole ten or twelve feet long, and the steersman at the tiller obeys the order to "hold her up to starboard" or "let her fall off to larboard" [1] or "steady —steady as you go."

When the measurements indicate that the yawl is approaching the shoalest part of the reef, the command is given to "Ease all!" Then the men stop rowing and the yawl drifts with the current. The next order is, "Stand by with the buoy!" The moment the shallowest point is reached, the pilot delivers the order, "Let go the buoy!" and over she goes. If the pilot is not satisfied, he sounds the place again; if he finds better water higher up or

---

[1] The term "larboard" is never used at sea, now, to signify the left hand; but was always used on the river in my time.

lower down, he removes the buoy to that place. Being finally satisfied, he gives the order and all the men stand their oars straight up in the air, in line; a blast from the boat's whistle indicates that the signal has been seen; then the men "give way" on their oars and lay the yawl alongside the buoy; the steamer comes creeping carefully down, is pointed straight at the buoy, husbands her power for the coming struggle, and presently, at the critical moment, turns on all her steam and goes grinding and wallowing over the buoy and the sand, and gains the deep water beyond. Or maybe she doesn't, maybe she "strikes and swings." Then she has to while away several hours (or days) sparring herself off.

Sometimes a buoy is not laid at all but the yawl goes ahead, hunting the best water, and the steamer follows along in its wake. Often there is a deal of fun and excitement about sounding, especially if it is a glorious summer day or a blustering night. But in winter the cold and the peril take most of the fun out of it.

A buoy is nothing but a board four or five feet long with one end turned up, it is a reversed schoolhouse bench with one of the supports left and the other removed. It is anchored on the shoalest part of the reef by a rope with a heavy stone made fast to the end of it. But for the resistance of the turned-up end of the reversed bench, the current would pull the buoy under water. At night, a paper lantern with a candle in it is fastened on top of the buoy and this can be seen a mile or more, a little glimmering spark in the waste of blackness.

Nothing delights a cub so much as an opportunity to go out sounding. There is such an air of adventure about it; often there is danger; it is so gaudy and man-of-war like to sit up in the stern-sheets and steer a swift yawl; there is something fine about the exultant spring of the boat when an experienced old sailor crew throw their souls into the oars; it is lovely to see the white foam stream away from the bows; there is music in the rush of the water; it is deliciously exhilarating, in summer, to go speeding over the breezy expanses of the river when the world of wavelets is dancing in the sun. It is such grandeur, too, to the cub, to get a chance to give an order; for often the pilot will simply say, "Let her go about!" and leave the rest to the cub, who instantly cries in his sternest tone of command, "Ease, starboard! Strong on the larboard! Starboard, give way! With a will, men!" The cub enjoys sounding for the further reason that the eyes of the passengers are watching all the yawl's movements with absorbing interest, if the time be daylight, and if it be night he knows that those same wondering eyes are fastened upon the yawl's lantern as it glides out into the gloom and dims away in the remote distance.

One trip a pretty girl of sixteen spent her time in our pilot-house with her uncle and aunt, every day and all day long. I fell in love with her. So did Mr. Thornburg's cub, Tom G. Tom and I had been bosom friends until this time, but now a coolness began to arise. I told the girl a good many of my river adventures, and made myself out a good deal of a hero; Tom tried to make himself appear to be a hero, too, and succeeded to some extent, but then he always had a way of embroidering. However, virtue is its own reward, so I was a barely perceptible trifle ahead in the contest. About this time something happened which promised handsomely for me: the pilots decided to sound the crossing at the head of 21. This would occur about nine or ten o'clock at night, when the passengers would be still up; it would be Mr. Thornburg's watch, therefore my chief would have to do the sounding. We had a perfect love of a sounding-boat, long, trim, graceful, and as fleet as a greyhound; her thwarts were cushioned; she carried twelve oarsmen; one of the mates was always sent in her to transmit orders to her crew, for ours was a steamer where no end of "style" was put on.

We tied up at the shore above 21 and got ready. It was a foul night, and the river was so wide there that a landsman's uneducated eyes could discern no opposite shore through such a gloom. The passengers were alert and interested; everything was satisfactory. As I hurried through the engine-room, picturesquely gotten up in storm toggery, I met Tom, and could not forbear delivering myself of a mean speech:

"Ain't you glad *you* don't have to go out sounding?"

Tom was passing on, but he quickly turned, and said:

"Now just for that, you can go and get the sounding-pole yourself. I was going after it, but I'd see you in Halifax, now, before I'd do it."

"Who wants you to get it? *I* don't. It's in the sounding-boat."

"It ain't, either. It's been new-painted, and it's been up on the ladies' cabin-guards two days, drying."

I flew back and shortly arrived among the crowd of watching and wondering ladies just in time to hear the command:

"Give way, men!"

I looked over, and there was the gallant sounding-boat booming away, the unprincipled Tom presiding at the tiller and my chief sitting by him with the sounding-pole which I had been sent on a fool's errand to fetch. Then that young girl said to me:

"Oh, how awful to have to go out in that little boat on such a night! Do you think there is any danger?"

I would rather have been stabbed. I went off, full of venom, to help in the pilot-house. By and by the boat's lantern disappeared, and after an interval a wee spark glimmered upon the face of the water a mile away. Mr. Thornburg blew the whistle in acknowledgment, backed the steamer out, and made for it. We flew along for a while, then slackened steam and went cautiously gliding toward the spark. Presently Mr. Thornburg exclaimed:

"Hello, the buoy lantern's out!"

He stopped the engines. A moment or two later he said:

"Why, there it is again!"

So he came ahead on the engines once more, and rang for the leads. Gradually the water shoaled up, and then began to deepen again! Mr. Thornburg muttered:

"Well, I don't understand this. I believe that buoy has drifted off the reef. Seems to be a little too far to the left. No matter, it is safest to run over it, anyhow."

So, in that solid world of darkness we went creeping down on the light. Just as our bows were in the act of plowing over it, Mr. Thornburg seized the bell-ropes, rang a startling peal, and exclaimed:

"My soul, it's the sounding-boat!"

A sudden chorus of wild alarms burst out far below— a pause—and then a sound of grinding and crashing followed. Mr. Thornburg exclaimed:

"There! the paddle-wheel has ground the sounding-boat to lucifer matches! Run! See who is killed!"

I was on the main-deck in the twinkling of an eye. My chief and the third mate and nearly all the men were safe. They had discovered their danger when it was too late to pull out of the way; then when the great guards overshadowed them a moment later, they were prepared and knew what to do; at my chief's order they sprang at the right instant, seized the guard, and were hauled aboard. The next moment the sounding-yawl

swept aft to the wheel and was struck and splintered to
atoms. Two of the men and the cub Tom were missing
—a fact which spread like wildfire over the boat. The
passengers came flocking to the forward gangway, ladies
and all, anxious-eyed, white-faced, and talked in awed
voices of the dreadful thing. And often and again I
heard them say, "Poor fellows! poor boy, poor boy!"

By this time the boat's yawl was manned and away,
to search for the missing. Now a faint call was heard, off
to the left. The yawl had disappeared in the other direction. Half the people rushed to one side to encourage
the swimmer with their shouts; the other half rushed
the other way to shriek to the yawl to turn about. By
the callings the swimmer was approaching, but some
said the sound showed failing strength. The crowd
massed themselves against the boiler-deck railings, leaning over and staring into the gloom, and every faint and
fainter cry wrung from them such words as "Ah, poor
fellow, poor fellow! is there *no* way to save him?"

But still the cries held out, and drew nearer, and
presently the voice said pluckily:

"I can make it! Stand by with a rope!"

What a rousing cheer they gave him! The chief mate
took his stand in the glare of a torch-basket, a coil of
rope in his hand, and his men grouped about him. The
next moment the swimmer's face appeared in the circle
of light, and in another one the owner of it was hauled
aboard, limp and drenched, while cheer on cheer went
up. It was that devil Tom.

The yawl crew searched everywhere, but found no
sign of the two men. They probably failed to catch the
guard, tumbled back, and were struck by the wheel and
killed. Tom had never jumped for the guard at all, but
had plunged head first into the river and dived under
the wheel. It was nothing; I could have done it easy

enough, and I said so; but everybody went on just the same, making a wonderful to-do over that ass, as if he had done something great. That girl couldn't seem to have enough of that pitiful "hero" the rest of the trip; but little I cared; I loathed her, anyway.

The way we came to mistake the sounding-boat's lantern for the buoy light was this: My chief said that after laying the buoy he fell away and watched it till it seemed to be secure; then he took up a position a hundred yards below it and a little to one side of the steamer's course, headed the sounding-boat up-stream, and waited. Having to wait some time, he and the officer got to talking; he looked up when he judged that the steamer was about on the reef, saw that the buoy was gone but supposed that the steamer had already run over it; he went on with his talk; he noticed that the steamer was getting very close down to him but that was the correct thing; it was her business to shave him closely for convenience in taking him aboard; he was expecting her to sheer off, until the last moment; then it flashed upon him that she was trying to run him down, mistaking his lantern for the buoy light; so he sang out, "Stand by to spring for the guard, men!" and the next instant the jump was made.

But I am wandering from what I was intending to do, that is, make plainer than perhaps appears in the previous chapters some of the peculiar requirements of the science of piloting. First of all, there is one faculty which a pilot must incessantly cultivate until he has brought it to absolute perfection. Nothing short of perfection will do. That faculty is memory. He cannot stop with merely thinking a thing is so and so, he must *know* it, for this is eminently one of the "exact" sciences. With what scorn a pilot was looked upon in the old times, if he ever ventured to deal in that feeble phrase "I think," instead of the vigorous one, "I know!" One cannot easily realize what a tremendous thing it is to know every trivial detail of twelve hundred miles of river and know it with absolute exactness. If you will take the longest street in New York and travel up and down it, conning its features patiently until you know every house and window and lamppost and big and little sign by heart, and know them so accurately that you can instantly name the one you are abreast of when you are set down at random in that street in the middle of an inky black night, you will then have a tolerable notion of the amount and the exactness of a pilot's knowledge who carries the Mississippi River in his head. And then, if you will go on until you know every street-crossing, the character, size, and position of the crossing-stones, and the varying depth of mud in each of these numberless places, you will have some idea of what the pilot must know in order to keep a Mississippi steamer out of trouble. Next, if you will take half of the signs in that long street and *change their places* once a month, and still manage to know their new positions accurately on dark nights, and keep up with these repeated changes without making any mistakes, you will understand what is required of a pilot's peerless memory by the fickle Mississippi.

I think a pilot's memory is about the most wonderful thing in the world. To know the Old and New Testaments by heart and be able to recite them glibly, forward or backward, or begin at random anywhere in the book and recite both ways and never trip or make a mistake, is no extravagant mass of knowledge and no marvelous facility, compared to a pilot's massed knowledge of the Mississippi and his marvelous facility in the handling of it. I make this comparison deliberately, and believe I am not expanding the truth when I do it.

Many will think my figure too strong but pilots will not.

And how easily and comfortably the pilot's memory does its work, how placidly effortless is its way, how *unconsciously* it lays up its vast stores, hour by hour, day by day, and never loses or mislays a single valuable package of them all! Take an instance. Let a leadsman cry, "Half twain! half twain! half twain! half twain! half twain!" until it becomes as monotonous as the ticking of a clock; let conversation be going on all the time, and the pilot be doing his share of the talking, and no longer consciously listening to the leadsman; and in the midst of this endless string of half twains let a single "quarter twain!" be interjected without emphasis, and then the half-twain cry go on again just as before: two or three weeks later that pilot can describe with precision the boat's position in the river when that quarter twain was uttered and give you such a lot of headmarks, stern-marks, and side-marks to guide you, that you ought to be able to take the boat there and put her in that same spot again yourself! The cry of "quarter twain" did not really take his mind from his talk but his trained faculties instantly photographed the bearings, noted the change of depth, and laid up the important details for future reference without requiring any assistance from *him* in the matter. If you were walking and talking with a friend, and another friend at your side kept up a monotonous repetition of the vowel sound A, for a couple of blocks, and then in the midst interjected an R, thus, A, A, A, A, A, R, A, A, A, etc., and gave the R no emphasis, you would not be able to state, two or three weeks afterward, that the R had been put in, nor be able to tell what objects you were passing at the moment it was done. But you could if your memory had been patiently and laboriously trained to do that sort of thing mechanically.

Give a man a tolerably fair memory to start with, and piloting will develop it into a very colossus of capability. But *only in the matters it is daily drilled in.* A time would come when the man's faculties could not help noticing landmarks and soundings, and his memory could not help holding on to them with the grip of a vise, but if you asked that same man at noon what he had had for breakfast, it would be ten chances to one that he could not tell you. Astonishing things can be done with the human memory if you will devote it faithfully to one particular line of business.

At the time that wages soared so high on the Missouri River, my chief, Mr. Bixby, went up there and learned more than a thousand miles of that stream with an ease and rapidity that were astonishing. When he had seen each division *once* in the daytime and *once* at night, his education was so nearly complete that he took out a "daylight" license; a few trips later he took out a full license and went to piloting day and night—and he ranked A 1, too.

Mr. Bixby placed me as steersman for a while under a pilot whose feats of memory were a constant marvel to me. However, his memory was born in him, I think, not built. For instance, somebody would mention a name. Instantly Mr. Brown would break in:

"Oh, I knew *him.* Sallow-faced, red-headed fellow, with a little scar on the side of his throat, like a splinter under the flesh. He was only in the Southern trade six months. That was thirteen years ago. I made a trip with him. There was five feet in the upper river then; the *Henry Blake* grounded at the foot of Tower Island drawing four and a half; the *George Elliott* unshipped her rudder on the wreck of the *Sunflower*—"

"Why, the *Sunflower* didn't sink until—"

"*I* know when she sunk; it was three years before

that, on the 2d of December; Asa Hardy was captain of her and his brother John was first clerk; and it was his first trip in her, too; Tom Jones told me these things a week afterward in New Orleans; he was first mate of the *Sunflower*. Captain Hardy stuck a nail in his foot the 6th of July of the next year and died of the lockjaw on the 15th. His brother John died two years after—3d of March—erysipelas. I never saw either of the Hardys —they were Alleghany River men—but people who knew them told me all these things. And they said Captain Hardy wore yarn socks winter and summer just the same, and his first wife's name was Jane Shook—she was from New England—and his second one died in a lunatic asylum. It was in the blood. She was from Lexington, Kentucky. Name was Horton before she was married."

And so on, by the hour, the man's tongue would go. He could *not* forget anything. It was simply impossible. The most trivial details remained as distinct and luminous in his head, after they had lain there for years, as the most memorable events. His was not simply a pilot's memory; its grasp was universal. If he were talking about a trifling letter he had received seven years before, he was pretty sure to deliver you the entire screed from memory. And then, without observing that he was departing from the true line of his talk, he was more than likely to hurl in a long-drawn parenthetical biography of the writer of that letter, and you were lucky indeed if he did not take up that writer's relatives, one by one, and give you their biographies, too.

Such a memory as that is a great misfortune. To it, all occurrences are of the same size. Its possessor cannot distinguish an interesting circumstance from an uninteresting one. As a talker, he is bound to clog his narrative with tiresome details and make himself an

insufferable bore. Moreover, he cannot stick to his subject. He picks up every little grain of memory he dis-
cerns in his way, and so is led aside. Mr. Brown would
start out with the honest intention of telling you a vastly
funny anecdote about a dog. He would be "so full of
laugh" that he could hardly begin; then his memory
would start with the dog's breed and personal appearance; drift into a history of his owner; of his owner's
family, with descriptions of weddings and burials that
had occurred in it, together with recitals of congratu-
latory verses and obituary poetry provoked by the same;
then this memory would recollect that one of these
events occurred during the celebrated "hard winter" of
such-and-such a year, and a minute description of that
winter would follow, along with the names of people
who were frozen to death, and statistics showing the
high figures which pork and hay went up to. Pork and
hay would suggest corn and fodder; corn and fodder
would suggest cows and horses; cows and horses would
suggest the circus and certain celebrated bare-back
riders; the transition from the circus to the menagerie
was easy and natural; from the elephant to equatorial
Africa was but a step; then of course the heathen savages would suggest religion; and at the end of three or
four hours' tedious jaw, the watch would change, and
Brown would go out of the pilot-house muttering ex-
tracts from sermons he had heard years before about
the efficacy of prayer as a means of grace. And the
original first mention would be all you had learned about
that dog, after all this waiting and hungering.

A pilot must have a memory, but there are two higher
qualities which he must also have. He must have good
and quick judgment and decision, and a cool, calm
courage that no peril can shake. Give a man the merest
trifle of pluck to start with and by the time he has be-

come a pilot he cannot be unmanned by any danger a steamboat can get into, but one cannot quite say the same for judgment. Judgment is a matter of brains and a man must *start* with a good stock of that article or he will never succeed as a pilot.

The growth of courage in the pilot-house is steady all the time but it does not reach a high and satisfactory condition until some time after the young pilot has been "standing his own watch" alone and under the staggering weight of all the responsibilities connected with the position. When the apprentice has become pretty thoroughly acquainted with the river, he goes clattering along so fearlessly with his steamboat, night or day, that he presently begins to imagine that it is *his* courage that animates him, but the first time the pilot steps out and leaves him to his own devices he finds out it was the other man's. He discovers that the article has been left out of his own cargo altogether. The whole river is bristling with exigencies in a moment, he is not prepared for them, he does not know how to meet them; all his knowledge forsakes him, and within fifteen minutes he is as white as a sheet and scared almost to death. Therefore pilots wisely train these cubs by various strategic tricks to look danger in the face a little more calmly. A favorite way of theirs is to play a friendly swindle upon the candidate.

Mr. Bixby served me in this fashion once and for years afterward I used to blush, even in my sleep, when I thought of it. I had become a good steersman; so good, indeed, that I had all the work to do on our watch, night and day. Mr. Bixby seldom made a suggestion to me; all he ever did was to take the wheel on particularly bad nights or in particularly bad crossings, land the boat when she needed to be landed, play gentleman of leisure nine-tenths of the watch, and collect the wages.

The lower river was about bank-full and if anybody had questioned my ability to run any crossing between Cairo and New Orleans without help or instruction, I should have felt irreparably hurt. The idea of being afraid of any crossing in the lot, in the *daytime,* was a thing too preposterous for contemplation. Well, one matchless summer's day I was bowling down the bend above Island 66, brimful of self-conceit and carrying my nose as high as a giraffe's, when Mr. Bixby said:

"I am going below awhile. I suppose you know the next crossing?"

This was almost an affront. It was about the plainest and simplest crossing in the whole river. One couldn't come to any harm whether he ran it right or not, and as for depth, there never had been any bottom there. I knew all this, perfectly well.

"Know how to *run* it? Why, I can run it with my eyes shut."

"How much water is there in it?"

"Well, that is an odd question. I couldn't get bottom there with a church steeple."

"You think so, do you?"

The very tone of the question shook my confidence. That was what Mr. Bixby was expecting. He left, without saying anything more. I began to imagine all sorts of things. Mr. Bixby, unknown to me, of course, sent somebody down to the forecastle with some mysterious instructions to the leadsmen, another messenger was sent to whisper among the officers, and then Mr. Bixby went into hiding behind a smoke-stack where he could observe results. Presently the captain stepped out on the hurricane-deck; next the chief mate appeared; then a clerk. Every moment or two a straggler was added to my audience, and before I got to the head of the island I had fifteen or twenty people assembled down there under my nose. I began to wonder what the trouble was. As I started across, the captain glanced aloft at me and said, with a sham uneasiness in his voice:

"Where is Mr. Bixby?"

"Gone below, sir."

But that did the business for me. My imagination began to construct dangers out of nothing, and they multiplied faster than I could keep the run of them. All at once I imagined I saw shoal water ahead! The wave of coward agony that surged through me then came near dislocating every joint in me. All my confidence in that crossing vanished. I seized the bell-rope; dropped it, ashamed; seized it again; dropped it once more; clutched it tremblingly once again, and pulled it so feebly that I could hardly hear the stroke myself. Captain and mate sang out instantly, and both together:

"Starboard lead there! and quick about it!"

This was another shock. I began to climb the wheel like a squirrel, but I would hardly get the boat started to port before I would see new dangers on that side and away I would spin to the other, only to find perils accumulating to starboard and be crazy to get to port again. Then came the leadsman's sepulchral cry:

"D-e-e-p four!"

Deep four in a bottomless crossing! The terror of it took my breath away.

"M-a-r-k three! M-a-r-k three! Quarter-less-three! Half twain!"

This was frightful! I seized the bell-ropes and stopped the engines.

"Quarter twain! Quarter twain! *Mark* twain!"

I was helpless. I did not know what in the world to do. I was quaking from head to foot and I could have hung my hat on my eyes, they stuck out so far.

"Quarter-*less*-twain! Nine-and-a-*half!*"

We were *drawing* nine! My hands were in a nerveless flutter. I could not ring a bell intelligibly with them. I flew to the speaking-tube and shouted to the engineer:

"Oh, Ben, if you love me, *back* her! Quick, Ben! Oh, back the immortal *soul* out of her!"

I heard the door close gently. I looked around, and there stood Mr. Bixby, smiling a bland, sweet smile. Then the audience on the hurricane-deck sent up a thundergust of humiliating laughter. I saw it all, now, and I felt meaner than the meanest man in human history. I laid in the lead, set the boat in her marks, came ahead on the engines, and said:

"It was a fine trick to play on an orphan, *wasn't* it? I suppose I'll never hear the last of how I was ass enough to heave the lead at the head of 66."

"Well, no, you won't, maybe. In fact I hope you won't, for I want you to learn something by that experience. Didn't you *know* there was no bottom in that crossing?"

"Yes, sir, I did."

"Very well, then. You shouldn't have allowed me or anybody else to shake your confidence in that knowledge. Try to remember that. And another thing, when you get into a dangerous place, don't turn coward. That isn't going to help matters any."

It was a good enough lesson but pretty hardly learned. Yet about the hardest part of it was that for months I so often had to hear a phrase which I had conceived a particular distaste for. It was, "Oh, Ben, if you love me, back her!"

The Private History of
a Campaign that Failed

YOU have heard from a great many people who did something in the war,[1] is it not fair and right that you listen a little moment to one who started out to do something in it, but didn't? Thousands entered the war, got just a taste of it, and then stepped out again permanently. These, by their very numbers, are respectable and are therefore entitled to a sort of a voice—not a loud one but a modest one, not a boastful one but an apologetic one. They ought not to be allowed much space among better people—people who did something. I grant that, but they ought at least to be allowed to state why they didn't do anything and also to explain the process by which they didn't do anything. Surely this kind of light must have a sort of value.

Out West there was a good deal of confusion in men's minds during the first months of the great trouble—a good deal of unsettledness, of leaning first this way, then that, then the other way. It was hard for us to get our bearings. I call to mind an instance of this. I was piloting on the Mississippi when the news came that South Carolina had gone out of the Union on the 20th of December, 1860. My pilot mate was a New Yorker. He was strong for the Union; so was I. But he would not listen to me with any patience; my loyalty was smirched, to his eye, because my father had owned slaves. I said

[1] *In "Battles and Leaders of the Civil War," then running in the Century.—Ed.*

119

in palliation of this dark fact that I had heard my father say, some years before he died, that slavery was a great wrong and that he would free the solitary Negro he then owned if he could think it right to give away the property of the family when he was so straitened in means. My mate retorted that a mere impulse was nothing—anybody could pretend to a good impulse, and went on decrying my Unionism and libeling my ancestry. A month later the secession atmosphere had considerably thickened on the Lower Mississippi and I became a rebel; so did he. We were together in New Orleans the 26th of January, when Louisiana went out of the Union. He did his full share of the rebel shouting but was bitterly opposed to letting me do mine. He said that I came of bad stock—of a father who had been willing to set slaves free. In the following summer he was piloting a Federal gunboat and shouting for the Union again and I was in the Confederate army. I held his note for some borrowed money. He was one of the most upright men I ever knew but he repudiated that note without hesitation because I was a rebel and the son of a man who owned slaves.

In that summer of 1861 the first wash of the wave of war broke upon the shores of Missouri. Our state was invaded by the Union forces. They took possession of St. Louis, Jefferson Barracks, and some other points. The Governor, Claib Jackson, issued his proclamation calling out fifty thousand militia to repel the invader.

I was visiting in the small town where my boyhood had been spent, Hannibal, Marion County. Several of us got together in a secret place by night and formed ourselves into a military company. One Tom Lyman, a young fellow of a good deal of spirit but of no military experience, was made captain; I was made second lieutenant. We had no first lieutenant; I do not know why;

it was long ago. There were fifteen of us. By the advice of an innocent connected with the organization we called ourselves the Marion Rangers. I do not remember that any one found fault with the name. I did not; I thought it sounded quite well. The young fellow who proposed this title was perhaps a fair sample of the kind of stuff we were made of. He was young, ignorant, good-natured, well-meaning, trivial, full of romance, and given to reading chivalric novels and singing forlorn love-ditties. He had some pathetic little nickel-plated aristocratic instincts and detested his name, which was Dunlap; detested it partly because it was nearly as common in that region as Smith but mainly because it had a plebeian sound to his ear. So he tried to ennoble it by writing it in this way: *d'Unlap*. That contented his eye but left his ear unsatisfied, for people gave the new name the same old pronunciation—emphasis on the front end of it. He then did the bravest thing that can be imagined, a thing to make one shiver when one remembers how the world is given to resenting shams and affectations, he began to write his name so: *d'Un ·Lap*. And he waited patiently through the long storm of mud that was flung at this work of art and he had his reward at last, for he lived to see that name accepted and the emphasis put where he wanted it by people who had known him all his life, and to whom the tribe of Dunlaps had been as familiar as the rain and the sunshine for forty years. So sure of victory at last is the courage that can wait. He said he had found by consulting some ancient French chronicles that the name was rightly and originally written d'Un Lap, and said that if it were translated into English it would mean Peterson: *Lap*, Latin or Greek, he said, for stone or rock, same as the French *pierre*, that is to say, Peter: *d'*, of or from; *un*, a or one; hence, d'Un Lap, of or from a stone or a Peter; that is to say, one who is the son of a stone, the son of a Peter—Peterson. Our militia company were not learned and the explanation confused them; so they called him Peterson Dunlap. He proved useful to us in his way; he named our camps for us and he generally struck a name that was "no slouch," as the boys said.

That is one sample of us. Another was Ed Stevens, son of the town jeweler, trim-built, handsome, graceful, neat as a cat; bright, educated, but given over entirely to fun. There was nothing serious in life to him. As far as he was concerned, this military expedition of ours was simply a holiday. I should say that about half of us looked upon it in the same way; not consciously, per- haps, but unconsciously. We did not think; we were not capable of it. As for myself, I was full of unreasoning joy to be done with turning out of bed at midnight and four in the morning for a while, grateful to have a change, new scenes, new occupations, a new interest. In my thoughts that was as far as I went; I did not go into the details; as a rule one doesn't at twenty-four.

Another sample was Smith, the blacksmith's appren- tice. This vast donkey had some pluck, of a slow and sluggish nature, but a soft heart; at one time he would knock a horse down for some impropriety and at another he would get homesick and cry. However, he had one ultimate credit to his account which some of us hadn't; he stuck to the war and was killed in battle at last.

Jo Bowers, another sample, was a huge, good-natured, flax-headed lubber, lazy, sentimental, full of harmless brag, a grumbler by nature; an experienced, industrious, ambitious, and often quite picturesque liar and yet not a successful one, for he had had no intelligent training but was allowed to come up just any way. This life was serious enough to him, and seldom satisfactory. But he

was a good fellow, anyway, and the boys all liked him.
He was made orderly sergeant; Stevens was made corporal.

These samples will answer—and they are quite fair
ones. Well, this herd of cattle started for the war. What
could you expect of them? They did as well as they
knew how but, really, what was justly to be expected
of them? Nothing, I should say. That is what they did.

We waited for a dark night, for caution and secrecy
were necessary; then toward midnight we stole in
couples and from various directions to the Griffith place,
beyond the town; from that point we set out together
on foot. Hannibal lies at the extreme southeastern corner
of Marion County, on the Mississippi River; our objective point was the hamlet of New London, ten miles
away, in Ralls County.

The first hour was all fun, all idle nonsense and laughter. But that could not be kept up. The steady trudging
came to be like work, the play had somehow oozed out
of it, the stillness of the woods and the somberness of the
night began to throw a depressing influence over the
spirits of the boys, and presently the talking died out
and each person shut himself up in his own thoughts.
During the last half of the second hour nobody said a
word.

Now we approached a log farm-house where, according to report, there was a guard of five Union soldiers. Lyman called a halt and there, in the deep gloom
of the overhanging branches, he began to whisper a plan
of assault upon that house, which made the gloom more
depressing than it was before. It was a crucial moment;
we realized with a cold suddenness that here was no
jest—we were standing face to face with actual war.
We were equal to the occasion. In our response there
was no hesitation, no indecision: we said that if Lyman

wanted to meddle with those soldiers, he could go ahead and do it, but if he waited for us to follow him, he would wait a long time.

Lyman urged, pleaded, tried to shame us, but it had no effect. Our course was plain, our minds were made up: we would flank the farm-house—go out around. And that was what we did.

We struck into the woods and entered upon a rough time, stumbling over roots, getting tangled in vines and torn by briers. At last we reached an open place in a safe region and sat down, blown and hot, to cool off and nurse our scratches and bruises. Lyman was annoyed but the rest of us were cheerful; we had flanked the farm-house, we had made our first military movement and it was a success; we had nothing to fret about, we were feeling just the other way. Horse-play and laughing began again; the expedition was become a holiday frolic once more.

Then we had two more hours of dull trudging and ultimate silence and depression; then about dawn we straggled into New London, soiled, heel-blistered, fagged with our little march, and all of us except Stevens in a sour and raspy humor and privately down on the war. We stacked our shabby old shotguns in Colonel Ralls's barn and then went in a body and breakfasted with that veteran of the Mexican War. Afterward he took us to a distant meadow, and there in the shade of a tree we listened to an old-fashioned speech from him, full of gunpowder and glory, full of that adjective-piling, mixed metaphor and windy declamation which were regarded as eloquence in that ancient time and that remote region; and then he swore us on the Bible to be faithful to the State of Missouri and drive all invaders from her soil, no matter whence they might come or under what flag they might march. This mixed us considerably and we could not make out just what service we were embarked in, but Colonel Ralls, the practised politician and phrase-juggler, was not similarly in doubt; he knew quite clearly that he had invested us in the cause of the Southern Confederacy. He closed the solemnities by belting around me the sword which his neighbor, Colonel Brown, had worn at Buena Vista and Molino del Rey; and he accompanied this act with another impressive blast.

Then we formed in line of battle and marched four miles to a shady and pleasant piece of woods on the border of the far-reaching expanses of a flowery prairie. It was an enchanting region for war—our kind of war.

We pierced the forest about half a mile and took up a strong position, with some low, rocky, and wooded hills behind us and a purling, limpid creek in front. Straightway half the command were in swimming and the other half fishing. The ass with the French name gave this position a romantic title but it was too long, so the boys shortened and simplified it to Camp Ralls.

We occupied an old maple-sugar camp, whose half-rotted troughs were still propped against the trees. A long corn-crib served for sleeping-quarters for the battalion. On our left, half a mile away, were Mason's farm and house, and he was a friend to the cause. Shortly after noon the farmers began to arrive from several directions with mules and horses for our use, and these they lent us for as long as the war might last, which they judged would be about three months. The animals were of all sizes, all colors, and all breeds. They were mainly young and frisky, and nobody in the command could stay on them long at a time, for we were town boys and ignorant of horsemanship. The creature that fell to my share was a very small mule, and yet so quick and active that it could throw me without difficulty, and

it did this whenever I got on it. Then it would bray—
stretching its neck out, laying its ears back, and spreading its jaws till you could see down to its works. It was a
disagreeable animal in every way. If I took it by the
bridle and tried to lead it off the grounds, it would sit
down and brace back and no one could budge it. However, I was not entirely destitute of military resources
and I did presently manage to spoil this game, for I had
seen many a steamboat aground in my time and knew a
trick or two which even a grounded mule would be
obliged to respect. There was a well by the corn-crib;
so I substituted thirty fathom of rope for the bridle, and
fetched him home with the windlass.

I will anticipate here sufficiently to say that we did
learn to ride after some days' practice, but never well.
We could not learn to like our animals; they were not
choice ones and most of them had annoying peculiarities
of one kind or another. Stevens's horse would carry him,
when he was not noticing, under the huge excrescences
which form on the trunks of oak-trees, and wipe him
out of the saddle; in this way Stevens got several bad
hurts. Sergeant Bowers's horse was very large and tall,
with slim, long legs, and looked like a railroad bridge.
His size enabled him to reach all about, and as far as
he wanted to, with his head; so he was always biting
Bowers's legs. On the march, in the sun, Bowers slept a
good deal, and as soon as the horse recognized that he
was asleep he would reach around and bite him on the
leg. His legs were black and blue with bites. This was
the only thing that could ever make him swear but this
always did; whenever his horse bit him he always swore,
and of course Stevens, who laughed at everything,
laughed at this and would even get into such convul-
sions over it as to lose his balance and fall off his horse;
and then Bowers, already irritated by the pain of the

horse-bite, would resent the laughter with hard language, and there would be a quarrel; so that horse made no end of trouble and bad blood in the command.

However, I will get back to where I was—our first afternoon in the sugar-camp. The sugar-troughs came very handy as horse-troughs and we had plenty of corn to fill them with. I ordered Sergeant Bowers to feed my mule, but he said that if I reckoned he went to war to be a dry-nurse to a mule it wouldn't take me very long to find out my mistake. I believed that this was insubordination but I was full of uncertainties about everything military, and so I let the thing pass and went and ordered Smith, the blacksmith's apprentice, to feed the mule; but he merely gave me a large, cold, sarcastic grin, such as an ostensibly seven-year-old horse gives you when you lift his lip and find he is fourteen, and turned his back on me. I then went to the captain and asked if it were not right and proper and military for me to have an orderly. He said it was but as there was only one orderly in the corps, it was but right that he himself should have Bowers on his staff. Bowers said he wouldn't serve on anybody's staff, and if anybody thought he could make him, let him try it. So, of course, the thing had to be dropped; there was no other way.

Next, nobody would cook; it was considered a degradation; so we had no dinner. We lazied the rest of the pleasant afternoon away, some dozing under the trees, some smoking cob-pipes and talking sweethearts and war, some playing games. By late supper-time all hands were famished and to meet the difficulty all hands turned to on an equal footing, and gathered wood, built fires, and cooked the meal. Afterward everything was smooth for a while; then trouble broke out between the corporal and the sergeant, each claiming to rank the other. Nobody knew which was the higher office; so

Lyman had to settle the matter by making the rank of both officers equal. The commander of an ignorant crew like that has many troubles and vexations which probably do not occur in the regular army at all. However, with the song-singing and yarn-spinning around the camp-fire, everything presently became serene again, and by and by we raked the corn down level in one end of the crib and all went to bed on it, tying a horse to the door, so that he would neigh if any one tried to get in.[1]

We had some horsemanship drill every forenoon; then, afternoons, we rode off here and there in squads a few miles and visited the farmers' girls, and had a youthful good time and got an honest good dinner or supper, and then home again to camp, happy and content.

For a time life was idly delicious, it was perfect; there was nothing to mar it. Then came some farmers with an alarm one day. They said it was rumored that the enemy were advancing in our direction from over Hyde's prairie. The result was a sharp stir among us, and general consternation. It was a rude awakening from our pleasant trance. The rumor was but a rumor—nothing definite about it; so in the confusion we did not know which way to retreat. Lyman was for not retreating at all in these uncertain circumstances, but he found that if he tried to maintain that attitude he would fare badly,

---

[1] It was always my impression that that was what the horse was there for and I know that it was also the impression of at least one other of the command, for we talked about it at the time and admired the military ingenuity of the device; but when I was out West three years ago, I was told by Mr. A. G. Fuqua, a member of our company, that the horse was his, that the leaving him tied at the door was a matter of mere forgetfulness, and that to attribute it to intelligent invention was to give him quite too much credit. In support of his position he called my attention to the suggestive fact that the artifice was not employed again. I had not thought of that before.

for the command were in no humor to put up with insubordination. So he yielded the point and called a council of war, to consist of himself and the three other officers; but the privates made such a fuss about being left out that we had to allow them to remain, for they were already present and doing the most of the talking too. The question was, which way to retreat; but all were so flurried that nobody seemed to have even a guess to offer. Except Lyman. He explained in a few calm words that, inasmuch as the enemy were approaching from over Hyde's prairie, our course was simple: all we had to do was not to retreat *toward* him; any other direction would answer our needs perfectly. Everybody saw in a moment how true this was, and how wise, so Lyman got a great many compliments. It was now decided that we should fall back on Mason's farm.

It was after dark by this time and as we could not know how soon the enemy might arrive, it did not seem best to try to take the horses and things with us; so we only took the guns and ammunition, and started at once. The route was very rough and hilly and rocky, and presently the night grew very black and rain began to fall; so we had a troublesome time of it, struggling and stumbling along in the dark, and soon some person slipped and fell, and then the next person behind stumbled over him and fell, and so did the rest, one after the other; and then Bowers came, with the keg of powder in his arms, while the command were all mixed together, arms and legs, on the muddy slope, and so he fell, of course, with the keg, and this started the whole detachment down the hill in a body, and they landed in the brook at the bottom in a pile, and each that was undermost pulling the hair and scratching and biting those that were on top of him, and those that were being scratched and bitten scratching and biting the rest in their turn, and all saying they would die before they would ever go to war again if they ever got out of this brook this time and the invader might rot for all they cared, and the country along with him—and all such talk as that, which was dismal to hear and take part in, in such smothered, low voices, and such a grisly dark place and so wet, and the enemy, maybe, coming any moment.

The keg of powder was lost, and the guns too; so the growling and complaining continued straight along while the brigade pawed around the pasty hillside and slopped around in the brook hunting for these things; consequently we lost considerable time at this, and then we heard a sound and held our breath and listened, and it seemed to be the enemy coming, though it could have been a cow, for it had a cough like a cow; but we did not wait but left a couple of guns behind and struck out for Mason's again as briskly as we could scramble along in the dark. But we got lost presently among the rugged little ravines and wasted a deal of time finding the way again, so it was after nine when we reached Mason's stile at last; and then before we could open our mouths to give the countersign several dogs came bounding over the fence with great riot and noise, and each of them took a soldier by the slack of his trousers and began to back away with him. We could not shoot the dogs without endangering the persons they were attached to; so we had to look on helpless at what was perhaps the most mortifying spectacle of the Civil War. There was light enough and to spare, for the Masons had now run out on the porch with candles in their hands. The old man and his son came and undid the dogs without difficulty, all but Bowers's; but they couldn't undo his dog, they didn't know his combination; he was of the bull kind and seemed to be set with a Yale time-lock, but they got him loose at last with some scalding water, of which Bowers got his share and returned thanks. Peterson Dunlap afterward made up a fine name for this engagement, and also for the night march which preceded it, but both have long ago faded out of my memory.

We now went into the house and they began to ask us a world of questions, whereby it presently came out that we did not know anything concerning who or what we were running from; so the old gentleman made himself very frank and said we were a curious breed of soldiers and guessed we could be depended on to end up the war in time, because no government could stand the expense of the shoe-leather we should cost it trying to follow us around. "Marion *Rangers!* good name, b'gosh!" said he. And wanted to know why we hadn't had a picket-guard at the place where the road entered the prairie, and why we hadn't sent out a scouting party to spy out the enemy and bring us an account of his strength, and so on, before jumping up and stampeding out of a strong position upon a mere vague rumor— and so on, and so forth, till he made us all feel shabbier than the dogs had done, not half so enthusiastically welcome. So we went to bed shamed and low-spirited, except Stevens. Soon Stevens began to devise a garment for Bowers which could be made to automatically display his battle-scars to the grateful or conceal them from the envious, according to his occasions, but Bowers was in no humor for this, so there was a fight and when it was over Stevens had some battle-scars of his own to think about.

Then we got a little sleep. But after all we had gone through, our activities were not over for the night, for about two o'clock in the morning we heard a shout of warning from down the lane, accompanied by a chorus from all the dogs, and in a moment everybody was up

and flying around to find out what the alarm was about.
The alarmist was a horseman who gave notice that a
detachment of Union soldiers was on its way from Hannibal with orders to capture and hang any bands like
ours which it could find, and said we had no time to
lose. Farmer Mason was in a flurry this time himself.
He hurried us out of the house with all haste, and sent
one of his Negroes with us to show us where to hide ourselves and our telltale guns among the ravines half a
mile away. It was raining heavily.

We struck down the lane, then across some rocky
pasture-land which offered good advantages for stumbling; consequently we were down in the mud most of
the time, and every time a man went down he black-
guarded the war and the people that started it and
everybody connected with it, and gave himself the master dose of all for being so foolish as to go into it. At
last we reached the wooded mouth of a ravine, and
there we huddled ourselves under the streaming trees
and sent the Negro back home. It was a dismal and
heart-breaking time. We were like to be drowned with
the rain, deafened with the howling wind and the booming thunder, and blinded by the lightning. It was indeed
a wild night. The drenching we were getting was misery
enough, but a deeper misery still was the reflection that
the halter might end us before we were a day older. A
death of this shameful sort had not occurred to us as
being among the possibilities of war. It took the romance
all out of the campaign and turned our dreams of glory
into a repulsive nightmare. As for doubting that so bar-
barous an order had been given, not one of us did that.

The long night wore itself out at last, and then the
Negro came to us with the news that the alarm had
manifestly been a false one and that breakfast would
soon be ready. Straightway we were light-hearted again,

and the world was bright and life as full of hope and promise as ever—for we were young then. How long ago that was! Twenty-four years.

The mongrel child of philology named the night's refuge Camp Devastation and no soul objected. The Masons gave us a Missouri country breakfast in Missourian abundance, and we needed it: hot biscuits, hot "wheat bread," prettily criss-crossed in a lattice pattern on top, hot corn-pone, fried chicken, bacon, coffee, eggs, milk, buttermilk, etc., and the world may be confidently challenged to furnish the equal of such a breakfast, as it is cooked in the South.

We stayed several days at Mason's, and after all these years the memory of the dullness and stillness and life-lessness of that slumberous farm-house still oppresses my spirit as with a sense of the presence of death and mourning. There was nothing to do, nothing to think about; there was no interest in life. The male part of the household were away in the fields all day, the women were busy and out of our sight; there was no sound but the plaintive wailing of a spinning-wheel, forever moaning out from some distant room, the most lonesome sound in nature, a sound steeped and sodden with homesickness and the emptiness of life. The family went to bed about dark every night, and as we were not invited to intrude any new customs we naturally followed theirs. Those nights were a hundred years long to youths accustomed to being up till twelve. We lay awake and miserable till that hour every time, and grew old and decrepit waiting through the still eternities for the clock-strikes. This was no place for town boys. So at last it was with something very like joy that we received news that the enemy were on our track again. With a new birth of the old warrior spirit we sprang to our places in line of battle and fell back on Camp Ralls.

Captain Lyman had taken a hint from Mason's talk, and he now gave orders that our camp should be guarded against surprise by the posting of pickets. I was ordered to place a picket at the forks of the road in Hyde's prairie. Night shut down black and threatening. I told Sergeant Bowers to go out to that place and stay till midnight and, just as I was expecting, he said he wouldn't do it. I tried to get others to go but all refused. Some excused themselves on account of the weather, but the rest were frank enough to say they wouldn't go in any kind of weather. This kind of thing sounds odd now, and impossible, but there was no surprise in it at the time. On the contrary, it seemed a perfectly natural thing to do. There were scores of little camps scattered over Missouri where the same thing was happening. These camps were composed of young men who had been born and reared to a sturdy independence, and who did not know what it meant to be ordered around by Tom, Dick, and Harry, whom they had known familiarly all their lives in the village or on the farm. It is quite within the probabilities that this same thing was happening all over the South. James Redpath recognized the justice of this assumption and furnished the following instance in support of it. During a short stay in East Tennessee he was in a citizen colonel's tent one day talking, when a big private appeared at the door and, without salute or other circumlocution, said to the colonel:

"Say, Jim, I'm a-goin' home for a few days."

"What for?"

"Well, I hain't b'en there for a right smart while and I'd like to see how things is comin' on."

"How long are you going to be gone?"

" 'Bout two weeks."

"Well, don't be gone longer than that, and get back sooner if you can."

That was all, and the citizen officer resumed his conversation where the private had broken it off. This was in the first months of the war, of course. The camps in our part of Missouri were under Brigadier-General Thomas H. Harris. He was a townsman of ours, a first-rate fellow and well liked, but we had all familiarly known him as the sole and modest-salaried operator in our telegraph-office, where he had to send about one despatch a week in ordinary times and two when there was a rush of business; consequently, when he appeared in our midst one day on the wing, and delivered a military command of some sort in a large military fashion, nobody was surprised at the response which he got from the assembled soldiery:

"Oh, now, what 'll you take to *don't*, Tom Harris?"

It was quite the natural thing. One might justly imagine that we were hopeless material for war. And so we seemed in our ignorant state, but there were those among us who afterward learned the grim trade, learned to obey like machines, became valuable soldiers; fought all through the war, and came out at the end with excellent records. One of the very boys who refused to go out on picket duty that night and called me an ass for thinking he would expose himself to danger in such a foolhardy way, had become distinguished for intrepidity before he was a year older.

I did secure my picket that night, not by authority but by diplomacy. I got Bowers to go by agreeing to exchange ranks with him for the time being, and go along and stand the watch with him as his subordinate. We stayed out there a couple of dreary hours in the pitchy darkness and the rain, with nothing to modify the dreariness but Bowers's monotonous growlings at the war and the weather; then we began to nod and presently found it next to impossible to stay in the saddle, so we gave up the tedious job and went back to the camp without waiting for the relief guard. We rode into camp without interruption or objection from anybody and the enemy could have done the same, for there were no sentries. Everybody was asleep; at midnight there was nobody to send out another picket, so none was sent. We never tried to establish a watch at night again, as far as I remember, but we generally kept a picket out in the daytime.

In that camp the whole command slept on the corn in the big corn-crib and there was usually a general row before morning, for the place was full of rats and they would scramble over the boys' bodies and faces, annoying and irritating everybody, and now and then they would bite some one's toe, and the person who owned the toe would start up and magnify his English and begin to throw corn in the dark. The ears were half as heavy as bricks and when they struck they hurt. The persons struck would respond and inside of five minutes every man would be locked in a death-grip with his neighbor. There was a grievous deal of blood shed in the corn-crib but this was all that was spilt while I was in the war. No, that is not quite true. But for one circumstance it would have been all. I will come to that now.

Our scares were frequent. Every few days rumors would come that the enemy were approaching. In these cases we always fell back on some other camp of ours; we never stayed where we were. But the rumors always turned out to be false, so at last even we began to grow indifferent to them. One night a Negro was sent to our corn-crib with the same old warning, the enemy was hovering in our neighborhood. We all said let him hover. We resolved to stay still and be comfortable. It was a fine warlike resolution, and no doubt we all felt the stir of it in our veins—for a moment. We had been having a very jolly time, that was full of horse-play and school-boy hilarity, but that cooled down now and presently the fast-waning fire of forced jokes and forced laughs died out altogether and the company became silent. Silent and nervous. And soon uneasy—worried—apprehensive. We had said we would stay and we were committed. We could have been persuaded to go but there was nobody brave enough to suggest it. An almost noiseless movement presently began in the dark by a general but unvoiced impulse. When the movement was completed each man knew that he was not the only person who had crept to the front wall and had his eye at a crack between the logs. No, we were all there, all there with our hearts in our throats and staring out toward the sugar-troughs where the forest footpath came through. It was late and there was a deep woodsy stillness everywhere. There was a veiled moonlight, which was only just strong enough to enable us to mark the general shape of objects. Presently a muffled sound caught our ears and we recognized it as the hoof-beats of a horse or horses. And right away a figure appeared in the forest path; it could have been made of smoke, its mass had so little sharpness of outline. It was a man on horseback and it seemed to me that there were others behind him. I got hold of a gun in the dark, and pushed it through a crack between the logs, hardly knowing what I was doing, I was so dazed with fright. Somebody said "Fire!" I pulled the trigger. I seemed to see a hundred flashes and hear a hundred reports; then I saw the man fall down out of the saddle. My first feeling was of surprised gratification; my first impulse was an apprentice-sportsman's impulse to run and pick up his game. Somebody said, hardly audibly, "Good—we've got him!—wait for the rest." But the rest did not come. We waited—listened—still no more came. There was not a sound, not the whisper of a leaf; just perfect stillness, an uncanny kind of stillness which was all the more uncanny on account of the damp, earthy, late-night smells now rising and pervading it. Then, wondering, we crept stealthily out and approached the man. When we got to him the moon revealed him distinctly. He was lying on his back with his arms abroad, his mouth was open and his chest heaving with long gasps, and his white shirt-front was all splashed with blood. The thought shot through me that I was a murderer, that I had killed a man, a man who had never done me any harm. That was the coldest sensation that ever went through my marrow. I was down by him in a moment, helplessly stroking his forehead, and I would have given anything then—my own life freely—to make him again what he had been five minutes before. And all the boys seemed to be feeling in the same way; they hung over him, full of pitying interest, and tried all they could to help him and said all sorts of regretful things. They had forgotten all about the enemy, they thought only of this one forlorn unit of the foe. Once my imagination persuaded me that the dying man gave me a reproachful look out of his shadowy eyes, and it seemed to me that I could rather he had stabbed me than done that. He muttered and mumbled like a dreamer in his sleep about his wife and his child, and I thought with a new despair, "This thing that I have done does not end with him; it falls upon *them* too, and they never did me any harm, any more than he."

In a little while the man was dead. He was killed in

war, killed in fair and legitimate war, killed in battle, as you may say, and yet he was as sincerely mourned by the opposing force as if he had been their brother. The boys stood there a half-hour sorrowing over him and recalling the details of the tragedy, and wondering who he might be and if he were a spy, and saying that if it were to do over again they would not hurt him unless he attacked them first. It soon came out that mine was not the only shot fired; there were five others, a division of the guilt which was a great relief to me since it in some degree lightened and diminished the burden I was carrying. There were six shots fired at once but I was not in my right mind at the time, and my heated imagination had magnified my one shot into a volley.

The man was not in uniform and was not armed. He was a stranger in the country, that was all we ever found out about him. The thought of him got to preying upon me every night; I could not get rid of it. I could not drive it away, the taking of that unoffending life seemed such a wanton thing. And it seemed an epitome of war, that all war must be just that the killing of strangers against whom you feel no personal animosity, strangers whom in other circumstances you would help if you found them in trouble, and who would help you if you needed it. My campaign was spoiled. It seemed to me that I was not rightly equipped for this awful business, that war was intended for men and I for a child's nurse. I resolved to retire from this avocation of sham soldiership while I could save some remnant of my self-respect. These morbid thoughts clung to me against reason, for at bottom I did not believe I had touched that man. The law of probabilities decreed me guiltless of his blood for in all my small experience with guns I had never hit anything I had tried to hit and I knew I had done my best to hit him. Yet there was no solace in the thought. Against a diseased imagination demonstration goes for nothing.

The rest of my war experience was of a piece with what I have already told of it. We kept monotonously falling back upon one camp or another and eating up the farmers and their families. They ought to have shot us; on the contrary, they were as hospitably kind and courteous to us as if we had deserved it. In one of these camps we found Ab Grimes, an Upper Mississippi pilot who afterward became famous as a dare-devil rebel spy, whose career bristled with desperate adventures. The look and style of his comrades suggested that they had not come into the war to play and their deeds made good the conjecture later. They were fine horsemen and good revolver shots, but their favorite arm was the lasso. Each had one at his pommel and could snatch a man out of the saddle with it every time, on a full gallop, at any reasonable distance.

In another camp the chief was a fierce and profane old blacksmith of sixty and he had furnished his twenty recruits with gigantic home-made bowie-knives, to be swung with two hands like the *machetes* of the Isthmus. It was a grisly spectacle to see that earnest band practising their murderous cuts and slashes under the eye of that remorseless old fanatic.

The last camp which we fell back upon was in a hollow near the village of Florida where I was born, in Monroe County. Here we were warned one day that a Union colonel was sweeping down on us with a whole regiment at his heel. This looked decidedly serious. Our boys went apart and consulted; then we went back and told the other companies present that the war was a disappointment to us and we were going to disband. They were getting ready themselves to fall back on some place or other, and we were only waiting for General Tom Harris, who was expected to arrive at any moment, so they tried to persuade us to wait a little while but the majority of us said no, we were accustomed to falling back and didn't need any of Tom Harris's help, we could get along perfectly well without him and save time, too. So about half of our fifteen, including myself, mounted and left on the instant; the others yielded to persuasion and stayed—stayed through the war.

An hour later we met General Harris on the road, with two or three people in his company, his staff probably, but we could not tell; none of them were in uniform; uniforms had not come into vogue among us yet. Harris ordered us back but we told him there was a Union colonel coming with a whole regiment in his wake and it looked as if there was going to be a disturbance, so we had concluded to go home. He raged a little but it was of no use, our minds were made up. We had done our share, had killed one man, exterminated one army, such as it was; let him go and kill the rest and that would end the war. I did not see that brisk young general again until last year; then he was wearing white hair and whiskers.

In time I came to know that Union colonel whose coming frightened me out of the war and crippled the Southern cause to that extent—General Grant. I came within a few hours of seeing him when he was as unknown as I was myself; at a time when anybody could have said, "Grant?—Ulysses S. Grant? I do not remember hearing the name before." It seems difficult to realize that there was once a time when such a remark could be rationally made but there *was*, and I was within a few miles of the place and the occasion too, though proceeding in the other direction.

The thoughtful will not throw this war paper of mine lightly aside as being valueless. It has this value: it is a not unfair picture of what went on in many and many a militia camp in the first months of the rebellion, when the green recruits were without discipline, without the steadying and heartening influence of trained leaders, when all their circumstances were new and strange and charged with exaggerated terrors, and before the invaluable experience of actual collision in the field had turned them from rabbits into soldiers. If this side of the picture of that early day has not before been put into history, then history has been to that degree incomplete, for it had and has its rightful place there. There was more Bull Run material scattered through the early camps of this country than exhibited itself at Bull Run. And yet it learned its trade presently and helped to fight the great battles later. I could have become a soldier myself if I had waited. I had got part of it learned, I knew more about retreating than the man that invented retreating.

A Connecticut Yankee in King Arthur's Court

FREEMEN

YES, it is strange how little a while at a time a person can be contented. Only a little while back, when I was riding and suffering, what a heaven this peace, this rest, this sweet serenity in this secluded shady nook by this purling stream would have seemed, where I could keep perfectly comfortable all the time by pouring a dipper of water into my armor now and then; yet already I was getting dissatisfied, partly because I could not light my pipe—for although I had long ago started a match factory, I had forgotten to bring matches with me—and partly because we had nothing to eat. Here was another illustration of the childlike improvidence of this age and people. A man in armor always trusted to chance for his food on a journey, and would have been scandalized at the idea of hanging a basket of sandwiches on his spear. There was probably not a knight of all the Round Table combination who would not rather have died than been caught carrying such a thing as that on his flagstaff. And yet there could not be anything more sensible. It had been my intention to smuggle a couple of sandwiches into my helmet, but I was interrupted in the act and had to make an excuse and lay them aside, and a dog got them.

Night approached and with it a storm. The darkness come on fast. We must camp, of course. I found a good

shelter for the demoiselle under a rock, and went off
and found another for myself. But I was obliged to
remain in my armor, because I could not get it off by
myself and yet could not allow Alisande to help, because it would have seemed so like undressing before
folk. It would not have amounted to that in reality, because I had clothes on underneath, but the prejudices
of one's breeding are not gotten rid of just at a jump
and I knew that when it came to stripping off that bob-
tailed iron petticoat I should be embarrassed.

With the storm came a change of weather, and the
stronger the wind blew and the wilder the rain lashed
around, the colder and colder it got. Pretty soon various
kinds of bugs and ants and worms and things began to
flock in out of the wet and crawl down inside my armor
to get warm, and while some of them behaved well
enough and snuggled up amongst my clothes and got
quiet, the majority were of a restless, uncomfortable
sort, and never stayed still but went on prowling and
hunting for they did not know what; especially the ants,
which went tickling along in wearisome procession from
one end of me to the other by the hour and are a kind
of creatures which I never wish to sleep with again. It
would be my advice to persons situated in this way, to
not roll or thrash around, because this excites the interest of all the different sorts of animals and makes
every last one of them want to turn out and see what is
going on, and this makes things worse than they were
before and of course makes you objurgate harder, too,
if you can. Still, if one did not roll and thrash around
he would die, so perhaps it is as well to do one way as
the other; there is no real choice. Even after I was
frozen solid I could still distinguish that tickling, just as
a corpse does when he is taking electric treatment. I
said I would never wear armor after this trip.

All those trying hours whilst I was frozen and yet was in a living fire, as you may say, on account of that swarm of crawlers, that same unanswerable question kept circling and circling through my tired head: How do people stand this miserable armor? How have they managed to stand it all these generations? How can they sleep at night for dreading the tortures of next day?

When the morning came at last I was in a bad enough plight: seedy, drowsy, fagged from want of sleep, weary from thrashing around, famished from long fasting, pining for a bath and to get rid of the animals, and crippled with rheumatism. And how had it fared with the nobly born, the titled aristocrat, the Demoiselle Alisande la Carteloise? Why, she was as fresh as a squirrel; she had slept like the dead; and as for a bath, probably neither she nor any other noble in the land had ever had one, and so she was not missing it. Measured by modern standards they were merely modified savages, those people. This noble lady showed no impatience to get to breakfast—and that smacks of the savage too. On their journeys those Britons were used to long fasts, and knew how to bear them and also how to freight up against probable fasts before starting, after the style of the Indian and the anaconda. As like as not, Sandy was loaded for a three-day stretch.

We were off before sunrise, Sandy riding and I limping along behind. In half an hour we came upon a group of ragged poor creatures who had assembled to mend the thing which was regarded as a road. They were as humble as animals to me, and when I proposed to breakfast with them, they were so flattered, so overwhelmed by this extraordinary condescension of mine that at first they were not able to believe that I was in earnest. My lady put up her scornful lip and withdrew to one side; she said in their hearing that she would as soon think of eating with the other cattle—a remark which embarrassed these poor devils merely because it referred to them and not because it insulted or offended them, for it didn't. And yet they were not slaves, not chattels. By a sarcasm of law and phrase they were freemen. Seven-tenths of the free population of the country were of just their class and degree: small "independent" farmers, artisans, etc., which is to say they were the nation, the actual Nation; they were about all of it that was useful or worth saving or really respectworthy, and to subtract them would have been to subtract the Nation and leave behind some dregs, some refuse, in the shape of a king, nobility and gentry, idle, unproductive, acquainted mainly with the arts of wasting and destroying and of no sort of use or value in any rationally constructed world. And yet by ingenious contrivance, this gilded minority, instead of being in the tail of the procession where it belonged, was marching head up and banners flying at the other end of it; had elected itself to be the Nation, and these innumerable clams had permitted it so long that they had come at last to accept it as a truth, and not only that but to believe it right and as it should be. The priests had told their fathers and themselves that this ironical state of things was ordained of God, and so, not reflecting upon how unlike God it would be to amuse himself with sarcasms, and especially such poor transparent ones as this, they had dropped the matter there and become respectfully quiet.

The talk of these meek people had a strange enough sound in a formerly American ear. They were freemen but they could not leave the estates of their lord or their bishop without his permission; they could not prepare their own bread but must have their corn ground and their bread baked at his mill and his bakery, and pay roundly for the same; they could not sell a piece of their

own property without paying him a handsome per-
centage of the proceeds nor buy a piece of somebody
else's without remembering him in cash for the privilege;
they had to harvest his grain for him gratis and be ready
to come at a moment's notice, leaving their own crop to
destruction by the threatened storm; they had to let
him plant fruit trees in their fields and then keep their
indignation to themselves when his heedless fruit-
gatherers trampled the grain around the trees; they had
to smother their anger when his hunting-parties galloped
through their fields laying waste the result of their patient toil; they were not allowed to keep doves themselves and when the swarms from my lord's dovecote
settled on their crops they must not lose their temper
and kill a bird, for awful would the penalty be; when
the harvest was at last gathered, then came the procession of robbers to levy their blackmail upon it: first the
Church carted off its fat tenth, then the king's commis-
sioner took his twentieth, then my lord's people made
a mighty inroad upon the remainder; after which the
skinned freeman had liberty to bestow the remnant in
his barn, in case it was worth the trouble; there were
taxes, and taxes, and taxes, and more taxes, and taxes
again, and yet other taxes—upon this free and independent pauper, but none upon his lord the baron or
the bishop, none upon the wasteful nobility or the all-
devouring Church; if the baron would sleep unvexed,
the freeman must sit up all night after his day's work
and whip the ponds to keep the frogs quiet; if the freeman's daughter—but no, that last infamy of mon-
archical government is unprintable; and finally, if the
freeman, grown desperate with his tortures, found his
life unendurable under such conditions and sacrificed
it and fled to death for mercy and refuge, the gentle
Church condemned him to eternal fire, the gentle law

buried him at midnight at the crossroads with a stake through his back, and his master the baron or the bishop confiscated all his property and turned his widow and his orphans out of doors.

And here were these freemen assembled in the early morning to work on their lord the bishop's road three days each—gratis, every head of a family, and every son of a family, three days each, gratis, and a day or so added for their servants. Why, it was like reading about France and the French before the ever memorable and blessed Revolution, which swept a thousand years of such villainy away in one swift tidal wave of blood— one: a settlement of that hoary debt in the proportion of half a drop of blood for each hogshead of it that had been pressed by slow tortures out of that people in the weary stretch of ten centuries of wrong and shame and misery the like of which was not to be mated but in hell. There were two "Reigns of Terror," if we would but remember it and consider it; the one wrought murder in hot passion, the other in heartless cold blood; the one lasted mere months, the other had lasted a thousand years; the one inflicted death upon ten thousand persons, the other upon a hundred millions; but our shudders are all for the "horrors" of the minor Terror, the momentary Terror, so to speak, whereas what is the horror of swift death by the ax compared with life-long death from hunger, cold, insult, cruelty, and heartbreak? What is swift death by lightning compared with death by slow fire at the stake? A city cemetery could contain the coffins filled by that brief Terror which we have all been so diligently taught to shiver at and mourn over, but all France could hardly contain the coffins filled by that older and real Terror—that unspeakably bitter and awful Terror which none of us has been taught to see in its vastness or pity as it deserves.

These poor ostensible freemen who were sharing their breakfast and their talk with me were as full of humble reverence for their king and Church and nobility as their worst enemy could desire. There was something pitifully ludicrous about it. I asked them if they supposed a nation of people ever existed, who, with a free vote in every man's hand, would elect that a single family and its descendants should reign over it forever, whether gifted or boobies, to the exclusion of all other families—including the voter's—and would also elect that a certain hundred families should be raised to dizzy summits of rank and clothed on with offensive transmissible glories and privileges to the exclusion of the rest of the nation's families—*including his own.*

They all looked unhit and said they didn't know, that they had never thought about it before, and it hadn't ever occurred to them that a nation could be so situated that every man *could* have a say in the government. I said I had seen one—and that it would last until it had an Established Church. Again they were all unhit—at first. But presently one man looked up and asked me to state that proposition again and state it slowly, so it could soak into his understanding. I did it, and after a little he had the idea, and he brought his fist down and said *he* didn't believe a nation where every man had a vote would voluntarily get down in the mud and dirt in any such way, and that to steal from a nation its will and preference must be a crime and the first of all crimes. I said to myself:

"This one's a man. If I were backed by enough of his sort, I would make a strike for the welfare of this country and try to prove myself its loyalest citizen by making a wholesome change in its system of government."

You see my kind of loyalty was loyalty to one's country, not to its institutions or its office-holders. The country is the real thing, the substantial thing, the eternal thing; it is the thing to watch over and care for and be loyal to; institutions are extraneous, they are its mere clothing, and clothing can wear out, become ragged, cease to be comfortable, cease to protect the body from winter, disease, and death. To be loyal to rags, to shout for rags, to worship rags, to die for rags—that is a loyalty of unreason, it is pure animal; it belongs to monarchy, was invented by monarchy; let monarchy keep it. I was from Connecticut, whose Constitution declares "that all political power is inherent in the people, and all free governments are founded on their authority and instituted for their benefit; and that they have *at all times* an undeniable and indefeasible right to *alter their form of government* in such a manner as they may think expedient."

Under that gospel, the citizen who thinks he sees that the commonwealth's political clothes are worn out, and yet holds his peace and does not agitate for a new suit, is disloyal; he is a traitor. That he may be the only one who thinks he sees this decay, does not excuse him; it is his duty to agitate anyway, and it is the duty of the others to vote him down if they do not see the matter as he does.

And now here I was, in a country where a right to say how the country should be governed was restricted to six persons in each thousand of its population. For the nine hundred and ninety-four to express dissatisfaction with the regnant system and propose to change it would have made the whole six shudder as one man, it would have been so disloyal, so dishonorable, such putrid black treason. So to speak, I was become a stockholder in a corporation where nine hundred and ninety-four of the members furnished all the money and did all the work, and the other six elected themselves a

permanent board of direction and took all the dividends.
It seemed to me that what the nine hundred and ninety-
four dupes needed was a new deal. The thing that would
have best suited the circus side of my nature would have
been to resign the Boss-ship and get up an insurrection
and turn it into a revolution, but I knew that the Jack
Cade or the Wat Tyler who tries such a thing without
first educating his materials up to revolution grade is
almost absolutely certain to get left. I had never been
accustomed to getttng left, even if I do say it myself.
Wherefore, the "deal" which had been for some time
working into shape in my mind was of a quite different
pattern from the Cade-Tyler sort.

So I did not talk blood and insurrection to that man
there who sat munching black bread with that abused
and mistaught herd of human sheep, but took him aside
and talked matter of another sort to him. After I had
finished, I got him to lend me a little ink from his veins,
and with this and a sliver I wrote on a piece of bark—

Put him in the Man-factory—

and gave it to him, and said:

"Take it to the palace at Camelot and give it into the
hands of Amyas le Poulet, whom I call Clarence, and
he will understand."

"He is a priest, then," said the man, and some of the
enthusiasm went out of his face.

"How—a priest? Didn't I tell you that no chattel of
the Church, no bond-slave of pope or bishop can enter
my Man-factory? Didn't I tell you that *you* couldn't
enter unless your religion, whatever it might be, was
your own free property?"

"Marry, it is so and for that I was glad; wherefore it
liked me not, and bred in me a cold doubt, to hear of
this priest being there."

"But he isn't a priest, I tell you."

The man looked far from satisfied. He said:

"He is not a priest and yet can read?"

"He is not a priest and yet can read—yes, and write, too, for that matter. I taught him myself." The man's face cleared. "And it is the first thing that you yourself will be taught in that Factory—"

"I? I would give blood out of my heart to know that art. Why, I will be your slave, your—"

"No you won't, you won't be anybody's slave. Take your family and go along. Your lord the bishop will confiscate your small property but no matter. Clarence will fix you all right."

A ROYAL BANQUET

Madame, seeing me pacific and unresentful, no doubt judged that I was deceived by her excuse, for her fright dissolved away and she was soon so importunate to have me give an exhibition and kill somebody that the thing grew to be embarrassing. However, to my relief she was presently interrupted by the call to prayers. I will say this much for the nobility: that, tyrannical, murderous, rapacious, and morally rotten as they were, they were deeply and enthusiastically religious. Nothing could divert them from the regular and faithful performance of the pieties enjoined by the Church. More than once I had seen a noble who had gotten his enemy at a disadvantage stop to pray before cutting his throat; more than once I had seen a noble, after ambushing and despatching his enemy, retire to the nearest wayside shrine and humbly give thanks, without even waiting to rob the body. There was to be nothing finer or sweeter in the life of even Benvenuto Cellini, that rough-hewn saint, ten centuries later. All the nobles of Britain, with their families, attended divine service morning and night daily in their private chapels, and even the worst of them had family worship five or six times a day besides. The credit of this belonged entirely to the Church. Although I was no friend to that Catholic Church, I was obliged to admit this. And often, in spite of me, I found myself saying, "What would this country be without the Church?"

After prayers we had dinner in a great banqueting-hall which was lighted by hundreds of grease-jets, and everything was as fine and lavish and rudely splendid as might become the royal degree of the hosts. At the head of the hall, on a dais, was the table of the king, queen, and their son, Prince Uwaine. Stretching down the hall from this was the general table, on the floor. At this, above the salt, sat the visiting nobles and the grown members of their families, of both sexes, the resident Court in effect, sixty-one persons; below the salt sat minor officers of the household, with their principal subordinates: altogether a hundred and eighteen persons sitting, and about as many liveried servants standing behind their chairs or serving in one capacity or another. It was a very fine show. In a gallery a band with cymbals, horns, harps, and other horrors, opened the proceedings with what seemed to be the crude first-draft or original agony of the wail known to later centuries as "In the Sweet Bye and Bye." It was new, and ought to have been rehearsed a little more. For some reason or other the queen had the composer hanged, after dinner.

After this music the priest who stood behind the royal table said a noble long grace in ostensible Latin. Then the battalion of waiters broke away from their posts and darted, rushed, flew, fetched and carried, and the mighty feeding began; no words anywhere but absorbing attention to business. The rows of chops opened and shut in vast unison, and the sound of it was like to the muffled burr of subterranean machinery.

The havoc continued an hour and a half, and unimaginable was the destruction of substantials. Of the chief feature of the feast, the huge wild boar that lay stretched out so portly and imposing at the start, nothing was left but the semblance of a hoop-skirt, and he was but the type and symbol of what had happened to all the other dishes.

With the pastries and so on, the heavy drinking began—and the talk. Gallon after gallon of wine and mead disappeared, and everybody got comfortable, then happy, then sparklingly joyous—both sexes—and by and by pretty noisy. Men told anecdotes that were terrific to hear but nobody blushed, and when the nub was sprung the assemblage let go with a horse-laugh that shook the fortress. Ladies answered back with historiettes that would almost have made Queen Margaret of Navarre or even the great Elizabeth of England hide behind a handkerchief, but nobody hid here, but only laughed—howled, you may say. In pretty much all of these dreadful stories ecclesiastics were the hardy heroes, but that didn't worry the chaplain any, he had his laugh with the rest; more than that, upon invitation he roared out a song which was of as daring a sort as any that was sung that night.

By midnight everybody was fagged out and sore with laughing, and, as a rule, drunk: some weepingly, some affectionately, some hilariously, some quarrelsomely, some dead and under the table. Of the ladies, the worst spectacle was a lovely young duchess whose wedding-eve this was, and indeed she was a spectacle, sure enough. Just as she was she could have sat in advance

for the portrait of the young daughter of the Regent
d'Orleans, at the famous dinner whence she was carried,
foul-mouthed, intoxicated, and helpless, to her bed, in
the lost and lamented days of the Ancient Régime.

Suddenly, even while the priest was lifting his hands,
and all conscious heads were bowed in reverent expec-
tation of the coming blessing, there appeared under the
arch of the far-off door at the bottom of the hall an old
and bent and white-haired lady, leaning upon a crutch-
stick, and she lifted the stick and pointed it toward the
queen and cried out:

"The wrath and curse of God fall upon you, woman
without pity, who have slain mine innocent grandchild
and made desolate this old heart that had nor chick, nor
friend nor stay nor comfort in all this world but him!"

Everybody crossed himself in a grisly fright, for a
curse was an awful thing to those people, but the queen
rose up majestic, with the death-light in her eye, and
flung back this ruthless command:

"Lay hands on her! To the stake with her!"

The guards left their posts to obey. It was a shame;
it was a cruel thing to see. What could be done? Sandy
gave me a look; I knew she had another inspiration. I
said:

"Do what you choose."

She was up and facing toward the queen in a moment. She indicated me and said:

"Madame, *he* saith this may not be. Recall the commandment, or he will dissolve the castle and it shall
vanish away like the instable fabric of a dream!"

Confound it, what a crazy contract to pledge a person
to! What if the queen—

But my consternation subsided there and my panic
passed off, for the queen, all in a collapse, made no show
of resistance but gave a countermanding sign and sunk

into her seat. When she reached it she was sober. So were many of the others. The assemblage rose, whiffed ceremony to the winds, and rushed for the door like a mob, overturning chairs, smashing crockery, tugging, struggling, shouldering, crowding—anything to get out before I should change my mind and puff the castle into the measureless dim vacancies of space. Well, well, well, they *were* a superstitious lot. It is all a body can do to conceive of it.

The poor queen was so scared and humbled that she was even afraid to hang the composer without first consulting me. I was very sorry for her—indeed any one would have been, for she was really suffering; so I was willing to do anything that was reasonable and had no desire to carry things to wanton extremities. I therefore considered the matter thoughtfully and ended by having the musicians ordered into our presence to play that "Sweet Bye and Bye" again, which they did. Then I saw that she was right and gave her permission to hang the whole band. This little relaxation of sternness had a good effect upon the queen. A statesman gains little by the arbitrary exercise of iron-clad authority upon all occasions that offer, for this wounds the just pride of his subordinates and thus tends to undermine his strength. A little concession now and then, where it can do no harm, is the wiser policy.

Now that the queen was at ease in her mind once more and measurably happy, her wine naturally began to assert itself again and it got a little the start of her. I mean it set her music going—her silver bell of a tongue. Dear me, she was a master talker. It would not become me to suggest that it was pretty late and that I was a tired man and very sleepy. I wished I had gone off to bed when I had the chance. Now I must stick it out; there was no other way. So she tinkled along and along

in the otherwise profound and ghostly hush of the
sleeping castle, until by and by there came, as if from
deep down under us, a far-away sound, as of a muffled
shriek—with an expression of agony about it that made
my flesh crawl. The queen stopped and her eyes lighted
with pleasure; she tilted her graceful head as a bird does
when it listens. The sound bored its way up through the
stillness again.

"What is it?" I said.

"It is truly a stubborn soul, and endureth long. It is
many hours now."

"Endureth what?"

"The rack. Come—ye shall see a blithe sight. An he
yield not his secret now, ye shall see him torn asunder."

What a silky smooth hellion she was, and so composed and serene when the cords all down my legs were
hurting in sympathy with that man's pain. Conducted
by mailed guards bearing flaring torches, we tramped
along echoing corridors and down stone stairways dank
and dripping and smelling of mold and ages of impris-
oned night—a chill, uncanny journey and a long one,
and not made the shorter or the cheerier by the sor-
ceress's talk, which was about this sufferer and his crime.
He had been accused by an anonymous informer of
having killed a stag in the royal preserves. I said:

"Anonymous testimony isn't just the right thing, your
Highness. It were fairer to confront the accused with
the accuser."

"I had not thought of that, it being but of small consequence. But an I would, I could not, for that the
accuser came masked by night, and told the forester,
and straightway got him hence again, and so the forester
knoweth him not."

"Then is this Unknown the only person who saw the
stag killed?"

"Marry, *no* man *saw* the killing but this Unknown saw this hardy wretch near to the spot where the stag lay, and came with right loyal zeal and betrayed him to the forester."

"So the Unknown was near the dead stag, too? Isn't it just possible that he did the killing himself? His loyal zeal—in a mask—looks just a shade suspicious. But what is your Highness's idea for racking the prisoner? Where is the profit?"

"He will not confess, else; and then were his soul lost. For his crime his life is forfeited by the law—and of a surety will I see that he payeth it!—but it were peril to my own soul to let him die unconfessed and unabsolved. Nay, I were a fool to fling me into hell for *his* accommodation."

"But, your Highness, suppose he has nothing to confess?"

"As to that, we shall see, anon. An I rack him to death and he confess not, it will peradventure show that he had indeed naught to confess—ye will grant that that is sooth? Then shall I not be damned for an unconfessed man that had naught to confess—wherefore, I shall be safe."

It was the stubborn unreasoning of the time. It was useless to argue with her. Arguments have no chance against petrified training; they wear it as little as the waves wear a cliff. And her training was everybody's. The brightest intellect in the land would not have been able to see that her position was defective.

As we entered the rack-cell I caught a picture that will not go from me; I wish it would. A native young giant of thirty or thereabouts lay stretched upon the frame on his back, with his wrists and ankles tied to ropes which led over windlasses at either end. There was no color in him, his features were contorted and set, and sweat-drops stood upon his forehead. A priest bent over him on each side; the executioner stood by; guards were on duty; smoking torches stood in sockets along the walls; in a corner crouched a poor young creature, her face drawn with anguish, a half-wild and hunted look in her eyes, and in her lap lay a little child asleep. Just as we stepped across the threshold the executioner gave his machine a slight turn, which wrung a cry from both the prisoner and the woman, but I shouted, and the executioner released the strain without waiting to see who spoke. I could not let this horror go on; it would have killed me to see it. I asked the queen to let me clear the place and speak to the prisoner privately, and when she was going to object I spoke in a low voice and said I did not want to make a scene before her servants but I must have my way, for I was King Arthur's representative, and was speaking in his name. She saw she had to yield. I asked her to indorse me to these people, and then leave me. It was not pleasant for her, but she took the pill, and even went further than I was meaning to require. I only wanted the backing of her own authority, but she said:

"Ye will do in all things as this lord shall command. It is The Boss."

It was certainly a good word to conjure with: you could see it by the squirming of these rats. The queen's guards fell into line, and she and they marched away with their torch-bearers, and woke the echoes of the cavernous tunnels with the measured beat of their retreating footfalls. I had the prisoner taken from the rack and placed upon his bed, and medicaments applied to his hurts, and wine given him to drink. The woman crept near and looked on, eagerly, lovingly, but timorously— like one who fears a repulse; indeed, she tried furtively to touch the man's forehead and jumped back, the picture of fright, when I turned unconsciously toward her. It was pitiful to see.

"Lord," I said, "stroke him, lass, if you want to. Do anything you're a mind to; don't mind me."

Why, her eyes were as grateful as an animal's when you do it a kindness that it understands. The baby was out of her way and she had her cheek against the man's in a minute, and her hands fondling his hair and her happy tears running down. The man revived and caressed his wife with his eyes, which was all he could do. I judged I might clear the den now, and I did, cleared it of all but the family and myself. Then I said:

"Now, my friend, tell me your side of this matter; I know the other side."

The man moved his head in sign of refusal. But the woman looked pleased—as it seemed to me—pleased with my suggestion. I went on:

"You know of me?"

"Yes. All do, in Arthur's realms."

"If my reputation has come to you right and straight, you should not be afraid to speak."

The woman broke in, eagerly:

"Ah, fair my lord, do thou persuade him! Thou canst an thou wilt. Ah, he suffereth so; and it is for me—for me! And how can I bear it? I would I might see him die—a sweet, swift death; oh, my Hugo, I cannot bear this one!"

And she fell to sobbing and groveling about my feet, and still imploring. Imploring what? The man's death? I could not quite get the bearings of the thing. But Hugo interrupted her and said:

"Peace! Ye wit not what ye ask. Shall I starve whom I love, to win a gentle death? I wend thou knewest me better."

"Well," I said, "I can't quite make this out. It is a puzzle. Now—"

"Ah, dear my lord, an ye will but persuade him! Consider how these his tortures wound me! Oh, and he will not speak!—whereas, the healing, the solace that lie in a blessed swift death—"

"What *are* you maundering about? He's going out from here a free man and whole—he's not going to die."

The man's white face lit up, and the woman flung herself at me in a most surprising explosion of joy, and cried out:

"He is saved!—for it is the king's word by the mouth of the king's servant—Arthur, the king whose word is gold!"

"Well, then you do believe I can be trusted, after all. Why didn't you before?"

"Who doubted? Not I indeed, and not she."

"Well, why wouldn't you tell me your story, then?"

"Ye had made no promise; else had it been otherwise."

"I see, I see. . . . And yet I believe I don't quite see, after all. You stood the torture and refused to confess; which shows plain enough to even the dullest understanding that you had nothing to confess—"

"*I*, my lord? How so? It was I that killed the deer!"

"You *did?* Oh, dear, this is the most mixed-up business that ever—"

"Dear lord, I begged him on my knees to confess, but—"

"You *did!* It gets thicker and thicker. What did you want him to do that for?"

"Sith it would bring him a quick death and save him all this cruel pain."

"Well—yes, there is reason in that. But *he* didn't want the quick death."

"He? Why, of a surety he *did*."

"Well, then, why in the world *didn't* he confess?"

"Ah, sweet sir, and leave my wife and chick without bread and shelter?"

"Oh, heart of gold, now I see it! The bitter law takes the convicted man's estate and beggars his widow and his orphans. They could torture you to death, but without conviction or confession they could not rob your wife and baby. You stood by them like a man, and *you* —true wife and true woman that you are—you would have bought him release from torture at cost to yourself of slow starvation and death—well, it humbles a body to think what your sex can do when it comes to self-sacrifice. I'll book you both for my colony; you'll like it there, it's a Factory where I'm going to turn groping and grubbing automata into *men*."

THE HOLY FOUNTAIN

The pilgrims were human beings. Otherwise they would have acted differently. They had come a long and difficult journey and now when the journey was nearly finished, and they learned that the main thing they had come for had ceased to exist, they didn't do as horses or cats or angle-worms would probably have done—turn back and get at something profitable—no, anxious as they had before been to see the miraculous fountain, they were as much as forty times as anxious now to see the place where it had used to be. There is no accounting for human beings.

We made good time and a couple of hours before sunset we stood upon the high confines of the Valley of Holiness, and our eyes swept it from end to end and noted its features. That is, its large features. These were the three masses of buildings. They were distant and isolated temporalities shrunken to toy constructions in the lonely waste of what seemed a desert—and was. Such a scene is always mournful, it is so impressively still and looks so steeped in death. But there was a sound here which interrupted the stillness only to add to its mournfulness; this was the faint far sound of tolling bells which floated fitfully to us on the passing breeze, and so faintly, so softly that we hardly knew whether we heard it with our ears or with our spirits.

We reached the monastery before dark, and there the males were given lodging but the women were sent over to the nunnery. The bells were close at hand now and their solemn booming smote upon the ear like a message of doom. A superstitious despair possessed the heart of every monk and published itself in his ghastly face. Everywhere, these black-robed, soft-sandaled, tallow-visaged specters appeared, flitted about and disappeared, noiseless as the creatures of a troubled dream and as uncanny.

The old abbot's joy to see me was pathetic. Even to tears; but he did the shedding himself. He said:

"Delay not, son, but get to thy saving work. An we bring not the water back again, and soon, we are ruined and the good work of two hundred years must end. And see thou do it with enchantments that be holy, for the Church will not endure that work in her cause be done by devil's magic."

"When I work, Father, be sure there will be no devil's work connected with it. I shall use no arts that come of the devil and no elements not created by the hand of God. But is Merlin working strictly on pious lines?"

"Ah, he said he would, my son, he said he would, and took oath to make his promise good."

"Well, in that case, let him proceed."

"But surely you will not sit idle by, but help?"

"It will not answer to mix methods, Father, neither would it be professional courtesy. Two of a trade must not underbid each other. We might as well cut rates and be done with it; it would arrive at that in the end. Merlin has the contract; no other magician can touch it till he throws it up."

"But I will take it from him; it is a terrible emergency and the act is thereby justified. And if it were not so, who will give law to the Church? The Church giveth law to all; and what she wills to do, that she may do, hurt whom it may. I will take it from him; you shall begin upon the moment."

"It may not be, Father. No doubt, as you say, where power is supreme one can do as one likes and suffer no injury, but we poor magicians are not so situated. Merlin is a very good magician in a small way and has quite a neat provincial reputation. He is struggling along doing the best he can, and it would not be etiquette for me to take his job until he himself abandons it."

The abbot's face lighted.

"Ah, that is simple. There are ways to persuade him to abandon it."

"No-no, Father, it skills not, as these people say. If he were persuaded against his will, he would load that well with a malicious enchantment which would balk me until I found out its secret. It might take a month. I could set up a little enchantment of mine which I call the telephone, and he could not find out its secret in a hundred years. Yes, you perceive, he might block me for a month. Would you like to risk a month in a dry time like this?"

"A month! The mere thought of it maketh me to shudder. Have it thy way, my son. But my heart is heavy with this disappointment. Leave me, and let me wear my spirit with weariness and waiting, even as I have done these ten long days, counterfeiting thus the thing that is called rest, the prone body making outward sign of repose where inwardly is none."

Of course, it would have been best all round for Merlin to waive etiquette and quit and call it half a day, since he would never be able to start that water, for he was a true magician of the time; which is to say, the big miracles, the ones that gave him his reputation, always had the luck to be performed when nobody but Merlin was present; he couldn't start this well with all this crowd around to see; a crowd was as bad for a magician's miracle in that day as it was for a spiritualist's miracle in mine; there was sure to be some skeptic on hand to turn up the gas at the crucial moment and spoil everything. But I did not want Merlin to retire from the job until I was ready to take hold of it effectively myself, and I could not do that until I got my things from Camelot, and that would take two or three days.

My presence gave the monks hope and cheered them up a good deal; insomuch that they ate a square meal that night for the first time in ten days. As soon as their stomachs had been properly reinforced with food, their spirits began to rise fast; when the mead began to go round they rose faster. By the time everybody was half-seas over, the holy community was in good shape to make a night of it; so we stayed by the board and put it through on that line. Matters got to be very jolly. Good old questionable stories were told that made the tears run down and cavernous mouths stand wide and the round bellies shake with laughter, and questionable songs were bellowed out in a mighty chorus that drowned the boom of the tolling bells.

At last I ventured a story myself, and vast was the success of it. Not right off, of course, for the native of

those islands does not as a rule dissolve upon the early
applications of a humorous thing; but the fifth time I
told it, they began to crack in places; the eighth time I
told it, they began to crumble; at the twelfth repetition
they fell apart in chunks; and at the fifteenth they dis-
integrated and I got a broom and swept them up. This
language is figurative. Those islanders—well, they are
slow pay at first, in the matter of return for your investment of effort, but in the end they make the pay of all
other nations poor and small by contrast.

I was at the well next day betimes. Merlin was there,
enchanting away like a beaver but not raising the mois-
ture. He was not in a pleasant humor, and every time I
hinted that perhaps this contract was a shade too hefty
for a novice he unlimbered his tongue and cursed like a
bishop—French bishop of the Regency days, I mean.

Matters were about as I expected to find them. The
"fountain" was an ordinary well, it had been dug in the
ordinary way and stoned up in the ordinary way. There
was no miracle about it. Even the lie that had created
its reputation was not miraculous; I could have told it
myself, with one hand tied behind me. The well was in
a dark chamber which stood in the center of a cut-
stone chapel, whose walls were hung with pious pictures
of a workmanship that would have made a chromo feel
good, pictures historically commemorative of curative
miracles which had been achieved by the waters when
nobody was looking. That is, nobody but angels; they
are always on deck when there is a miracle to the fore—
so as to get put in the picture, perhaps. Angels are as
fond of that as a fire company; look at the old masters.

The well-chamber was dimly lighted by lamps; the
water was drawn with a windlass and chain by monks,
and poured into troughs which delivered it into stone
reservoirs outside in the chapel—when there was water

to draw, I mean—and none but monks could enter the well-chamber. I entered it for I had temporary authority to do so, by courtesy of my professional brother and subordinate. But he hadn't entered it himself. He did everything by incantations; he never worked his intellect. If he had stepped in there and used his eyes instead of his disordered mind, he could have cured the well by natural means and then turned it into a miracle in the customary way; but no, he was an old numskull, a magician who believed in his own magic, and no magician can thrive who is handicapped with a superstition like that.

I had an idea that the well had sprung a leak, that some of the wall stones near the bottom had fallen and exposed fissures that allowed the water to escape. I measured the chain—ninety-eight feet. Then I called in a couple of monks, locked the door, took a candle, and made them lower me in the bucket. When the chain was all paid out, the candle confirmed my suspicion; a considerable section of the wall was gone, exposing a good big fissure.

I almost regretted that my theory about the well's trouble was correct, because I had another one that had a showy point or two about it for a miracle. I remembered that in America, many centuries later, when an oil-well ceased to flow, they used to blast it out with a dynamite torpedo. If I should find this well dry and no explanation of it, I could astonish these people most nobly by having a person of no especial value drop a dynamite bomb into it. It was my idea to appoint Merlin. However, it was plain that there was no occasion for the bomb. One cannot have everything the way he would like it. A man has no business to be depressed by a disappointment, anyway; he ought to make up his mind to get even. That is what I did. I said to myself, I am in no hurry, I can wait; that bomb will come good yet. And it did, too.

When I was above ground again, I turned out the monks and let down a fish-line; the well was a hundred and fifty feet deep, and there was forty-one feet of water in it! I called in a monk and asked:

"How deep is the well?"

"That, sir, I wit not, having never been told."

"How does the water usually stand in it?"

"Near to the top, these two centuries, as the testimony goeth, brought down to us through our predecessors."

It was true—as to recent times at least—for there was witness to it, and better witness than a monk; only about twenty or thirty feet of the chain showed wear and use, the rest of it was unworn and rusty. What had happened when the well gave out that other time? Without doubt some practical person had come along and mended the leak, and then had come up and told the abbot he had discovered by divination that if the sinful bath were destroyed the well would flow again. The leak had befallen again now, and these children would have prayed and processioned and tolled their bells for heavenly succor till they all dried up and blew away, and no innocent of them all would ever have thought to drop a fishline into the well or go down in it and find out what was really the matter. Old habit of mind is one of the toughest things to get away from in the world. It transmits itself like physical form and feature; and for a man in those days to have had an idea that his ancestors hadn't had, would have brought him under suspicion of being illegitimate. I said to the monk:

"It is a difficult miracle to restore water in a dry well but we will try, if my brother Merlin fails. Brother Merlin is a very passable artist but only in the parlor-magic line, and he may not succeed; in fact, is not likely to succeed. But that should be nothing to his discredit; the man that can do *this* kind of miracle knows enough to keep hotel."

"Hotel? I mind not to have heard—"

"Of hotel? It's what you call hostel. The man that can do this miracle can keep hostel. I can do this miracle; I shall do this miracle; yet I do not try to conceal from you that it is a miracle to tax the occult powers to the last strain."

"None knoweth that truth better than the brotherhood, indeed; for it is of record that aforetime it was parlous difficult and took a year. Natheless, God send you good success, and to that end will we pray."

As a matter of business it was a good idea to get the notion around that the thing was difficult. Many a small thing has been made large by the right kind of advertising. That monk was filled up with the difficulty of this enterprise; he would fill up the others. In two days the solicitude would be booming.

On my way home at noon I met Sandy. She had been sampling the hermits. I said:

"I would like to do that myself. This is Wednesday. Is there a matinée?"

"A which, please you, sir?"

"Matinée. Do they keep open afternoons?"

"Who?"

"The hermits, of course."

"Keep open?"

"Yes, keep open. Isn't that plain enough? Do they knock off at noon?"

"Knock off?"

"Knock off?—yes, knock off. What is the matter with knock off? I never saw such a dunderhead; can't you understand anything at all? In plain terms, do they shut up shop, draw the game, bank the fires—"

"Shut up shop, draw—"

"There, never mind, let it go; you make me tired. You can't seem to understand the simplest thing."

"I would I might please thee, sir, and it is to me dole and sorrow that I fail, albeit sith I am but a simple damsel and taught of none, being from the cradle un-baptized in those deep waters of learning that do anoint with a sovereignty him that partaketh of that most noble sacrament, investing him with reverend state to the mental eye of the humble mortal, who by bar and lack of that great consecration seeth in his own unlearned estate but a symbol of that other sort of lack and loss which men do publish to the pitying eye with sackcloth trappings whereon the ashes of grief do lie bepowdered and bestrewn, and so, when such shall in the darkness of his mind encounter these golden phrases of high mys-tery, these shut-up-shops, and draw-the-game, and bank-the-fires, it is but by the grace of God that he burst not for envy of the mind that can beget, and tongue that can deliver so great and mellow-sounding miracles of speech, and if there do ensue confusion in that humbler mind, and failure to divine the meanings of these wonders, then if so be this miscomprehension is not vain but sooth and true, wit ye well it is the very substance of wor-shipful dear homage and may not lightly be misprized, nor had been, an ye had noted this complexion of mood and mind and understood that that I would I could not, and that I could not I might not, nor yet nor might *nor* could, nor might-not nor could-not, might be by ad-vantage turned to the desired *would*, and so I pray you mercy of my fault, and that ye will of your kindness and your charity forgive it, good my master and most dear lord."

I couldn't make it all out—that is, the details—but I

got the general idea, and enough of it too to be ashamed. It was not fair to spring those ninteenth-century technicalities upon the untutored infant of the sixth and then rail at her because she couldn't get their drift, and when she was making the honest best drive at it she could too, and no fault of hers that she couldn't fetch the home plate; and so I apologized. Then we meandered pleasantly away toward the hermit holes in sociable converse together, and better friends than ever.

I was gradually coming to have a mysterious and shuddery reverence for this girl; nowadays whenever she pulled out from the station and got her train fairly started on one of those horizonless transcontinental sentences of hers, it was borne in upon me that I was standing in the awful presence of the Mother of the German Language. I was so impressed with this that sometimes when she began to empty one of these sentences on me I unconsciously took the very attitude of reverence and stood uncovered, and if words had been water, I had been drowned sure. She had exactly the German way; whatever was in her mind to be delivered, whether a mere remark, or a sermon, or a cyclopedia, or the history of a war, she would get it into a single sentence or die. Whenever the literary German dives into a sentence, that is the last you are going to see of him till he emerges on the other side of his Atlantic with his verb in his mouth.

We drifted from hermit to hermit all the afternoon. It was a most strange menagerie. The chief emulation among them seemed to be to see which could manage to be the uncleanest and most prosperous with vermin. Their manner and attitudes were the last expression of complacent self-righteousness. It was one anchorite's pride to lie naked in the mud and let the insects bite him and blister him unmolested; it was another's to lean against a rock all day long, conspicuous to the admiration of the throng of pilgrims and pray; it was another's to go naked and crawl around on all fours; it was another's to drag about with him, year in and year out, eighty pounds of iron; it was another's to never lie down when he slept but to stand among the thorn-bushes and snore when there were pilgrims around to look; a woman who had the white hair of age, and no other apparel, was black from crown to heel with forty-seven years of holy abstinence from water. Groups of gazing pilgrims stood around all and every of these strange objects, lost in reverent wonder, and envious of the fleckless sanctity which these pious austerities had won for them from an exacting heaven.

By and by we went to see one of the supremely great ones. He was a mighty celebrity, his fame had penetrated all Christendom, the noble and the renowned journeyed from the remotest lands on the globe to pay him reverence. His stand was in the center of the widest part of the valley, and it took all that space to hold his crowds.

His stand was a pillar sixty feet high, with a broad platform on the top of it. He was now doing what he had been doing every day for twenty years up there— bowing his body ceaselessly and rapidly almost to his feet. It was his way of praying. I timed him with a stop-watch, and he made twelve hundred and forty-four revolutions in twenty-four minutes and forty-six seconds. It seemed a pity to have all this power going to waste. It was one of the most useful motions in mechanics, the pedal movement; so I made a note in my memorandum-book, purposing some day to apply a system of elastic cords to him and run a sewing-machine with it. I afterward carried out that scheme, and got five years' good service out of him; in which time he turned out upward

of eighteen thousand first-rate tow-linen shirts, which
was ten a day. I worked him Sundays and all; he was
going, Sundays the same as week-days, and it was no
use to waste the power. These shirts cost me nothing but
just the mere trifle for the materials—I furnished those
myself, it would not have been right to make him do
that—and they sold like smoke to pilgrims at a dollar
and a half apiece, which was the price of fifty cows or
a blooded race-horse in Arthurdom. They were regarded
as a perfect protection against sin, and advertised as
such by my knights everywhere with the paint-pot and
stencil-plate, insomuch that there was not a cliff or a
boulder or a dead wall in England but you could read
on it at a mile distance:

*"Buy the only genuine St. Stylite; patronized by the
Nobility. Patent applied for."*

There was more money in the business than one knew
what to do with. As it extended, I brought out a line of
goods suitable for kings, and a nobby thing for duchesses
and that sort, with ruffles down the fore-hatch and the
running-gear clewed up with a feather-stitch to leeward
and then hauled aft with a backstay and triced up with
a half-turn in the standing rigging forward of the
weather-gaskets. Yes, it was a daisy.

But about that time I noticed that the motive power
had taken to standing on one leg and I found that there
was something the matter with the other one; so I
stocked the business and unloaded, taking Sir Bors de
Ganis into camp financially along with certain of his
friends, for the works stopped within a year, and the
good saint got him to his rest. But he had earned it. I
can say that for him.

When I saw him that first time—however, his personal condition will not quite bear description here.
You can read it in the *Lives of the Saints*.

Saturday noon I went to the well and looked on awhile. Merlin was still burning smoke-powders and pawing the air and muttering gibberish as hard as ever, but looking pretty downhearted, for of course he had not started even a perspiration in that well yet. Finally I said:

"How does the thing promise by this time, partner?"

"Behold, I am even now busied with trial of the powerfulest enchantment known to the princes of the occult arts in the lands of the East; an it fail me, naught can avail. Peace, until I finish."

He raised a smoke this time that darkened all the region and must have made matters uncomfortable for the hermits, for the wind was their way and it rolled down over their dens in a dense and billowy fog. He poured out volumes of speech to match and contorted his body and sawed the air with his hands in a most extraordinary way. At the end of twenty minutes he dropped down, panting and about exhausted. Now arrived the abbot and several hundred monks and nuns, and behind them a multitude of pilgrims and a couple of acres of foundlings, all drawn by the prodigious smoke and all in a grand state of excitement. The abbot inquired anxiously for results. Merlin said:

"If any labor of mortal might break the spell that binds these waters, this which I have but just essayed had done it. It has failed, whereby I do now know that that which I had feared is a truth established; the sign of this failure is that the most potent spirit known to the magicians of the East, and whose name none may utter and live, has laid his spell upon this well. The mortal does not breathe, nor ever will, who can penetrate the secret of that spell, and without that secret none can

174

break it. The water will flow no more forever, good Father. I have done what man could. Suffer me to go."

Of course this threw the abbot into a good deal of a consternation. He turned to me with the signs of it in his face, and said:

"Ye have heard him. Is it true?"

"Part of it is."

"Not all, then, not all! What part is true?"

"That that spirit with the Russian name has put his spell upon the well."

"God's wownds, then are we ruined!"

"Possibly."

"But not certainly? Ye mean, not certainly?"

"That is it."

"Wherefore, ye also mean that when he saith none can break the spell—"

"Yes, when he says that, he says what isn't necessarily true. There are conditions under which an effort to break it may have some chance—that is, some small, some trifling chance—of success."

"The conditions—"

"Oh, they are nothing difficult. Only these: I want the well and the surroundings for the space of half a mile entirely to myself from sunset to-day until I remove the ban, and nobody allowed to cross the ground but by my authority."

"Are these all?"

"Yes."

"And you have no fear to try?"

"Oh, none. One may fail, of course; and one may also succeed. One can try and I am ready to chance it. I have my conditions?"

"These and all others ye may name. I will issue commandment to that effect."

"Wait," said Merlin, with an evil smile. "Ye wit that

he that would break this spell must know that spirit's name?"

"Yes, I know his name."

"And wit you also that to know it skills not of itself, but ye must likewise pronounce it? Ha-ha! Knew ye that?"

"Yes, I knew that, too."

"You had that knowledge! Art a fool? Are ye minded to utter that name and die?"

"Utter it? Why certainly. I would utter it if it was Welsh."

"Ye are even a dead man, then, and I go to tell Arthur."

"That's all right. Take your gripsack and get along. The thing for *you* to do is to go home and work the weather, John W. Merlin."

It was a home shot and it made him wince, for he was the worst weather failure in the kingdom. Whenever he ordered up the danger-signals along the coast there was a week's dead calm, sure, and every time he prophesied fair weather it rained brickbats. But I kept him in the weather bureau right along, to undermine his reputation. However, that shot raised his bile and instead of starting home to report my death, he said he would remain and enjoy it.

My two experts arrived in the evening, and pretty well fagged for they had traveled double tides. They had pack-mules along and had brought everything I needed, tools, pump, lead pipe, Greek fire, sheaves of big rockets, roman candles, colored fire sprays, electric apparatus, and a lot of sundries—everything necessary for the stateliest kind of a miracle. They got their supper and a nap, and about midnight we sallied out through a solitude so wholly vacant and complete that

it quite overpassed the required conditions. We took
possession of the well and its surroundings. My boys
were experts in all sorts of things, from the stoning-up
of a well to the constructing of a mathematical instrument. An hour before sunrise we had that leak mended
in shipshape fashion and the water began to rise. Then
we stowed our fireworks in the chapel, locked up the
place, and went home to bed.

Before the noon mass was over, we were at the well
again, for there was a deal to do yet and I was determined to spring the miracle before midnight for business reasons: for whereas a miracle worked for the
Church on a week-day is worth a good deal, it is worth
six times as much if you get it in on a Sunday. In nine
hours the water had risen to its customary level; that
is to say, it was within twenty-three feet of the top. We
put in a little iron pump, one of the first turned out by
my works near the capital; we bored into a stone reser-
voir which stood against the outer wall of the well-
chamber and inserted a section of lead pipe that was
long enough to reach to the door of the chapel and
project beyond the threshold, where the gushing water
would be visible to the two hundred and fifty acres of
people I was intending should be present on the flat
plain in front of this little holy hillock at the proper time.

We knocked the head out of an empty hogshead and
hoisted this hogshead to the flat roof of the chapel,
where we clamped it down fast, poured in gunpowder
till it lay loosely an inch deep on the bottom, then we
stood up rockets in the hogshead as thick as they could
loosely stand, all the different breeds of rockets there
are, and they made a portly and imposing sheaf, I can
tell you. We grounded the wire of a pocket electrical
battery in that powder, we placed a whole magazine of

Greek fire on each corner of the roof—blue on one corner, green on another, red on another, and purple on the last—and grounded a wire in each.

About two hundred yards off in the flat, we built a pen of scantlings about four feet high, and laid planks on it and so made a platform. We covered it with swell tapestries borrowed for the occasion and topped it off with the abbot's own throne. When you are going to do a miracle for an ignorant race, you want to get in every detail that will count; you want to make all the properties impressive to the public eye; you want to make matters comfortable for your head guest, then you can turn yourself loose and play your effects for all they are worth. I know the value of these things, for I know human nature. You can't throw too much style into a miracle. It costs trouble and work and sometimes money, but it pays in the end. Well, we brought the wires to the ground at the chapel and then brought them under the ground to the platform, and hid the batteries there. We put a rope fence a hundred feet square around the platform to keep off the common multitude, and that finished the work. My idea was, doors open at ten-thirty, performance to begin at eleven-twenty-five sharp. I wished I could charge admission but of course that wouldn't answer. I instructed my boys to be in the chapel as early as ten, before anybody was around, and be ready to man the pumps at the proper time and make the fur fly. Then we went home to supper.

The news of the disaster to the well had traveled far by this time, and now for two or three days a steady avalanche of people had been pouring into the valley. The lower end of the valley was become one huge camp; we should have a good house, no question about that. Criers went the rounds early in the evening and announced the coming attempt, which put every pulse up to fever-heat. They gave notice that the abbot and his official suite would move in state and occupy the platform at ten-thirty, up to which time all the region which was under my ban must be clear; the bells would then cease from tolling, and this sign should be permission to the multitudes to close in and take their places.

I was at the platform and all ready to do the honors when the abbot's solemn procession hove in sight, which it did not do till it was nearly to the rope fence, because it was a starless black night and no torches permitted. With it came Merlin and took a front seat on the platform; he was as good as his word for once. One could not see the multitudes banked together beyond the ban but they were there, just the same. The moment the bells stopped, those banked masses broke and poured over the line like a vast black wave and for as much as a half-hour it continued to flow, and then it solidified itself and you could have walked upon a pavement of human heads to—well, miles.

We had a solemn stage-wait now for about twenty minutes, a thing I had counted on for effect; it is always good to let your audience have a chance to work up its expectancy. At length, out of the silence a noble Latin chant—men's voices—broke and swelled up and rolled away into the night, a majestic tide of melody. I had put that up too, and it was one of the best effects I ever invented. When it was finished I stood up on the platform and extended my hands abroad for two minutes, with my face uplifted—that always produces a dead hush—and then slowly pronounced this ghastly word with a kind of awfulness which caused hundreds to tremble, and many women to faint:

"𝕮𝖔𝖓𝖘𝖙𝖆𝖓𝖙𝖎𝖓𝖔𝖕𝖔𝖑𝖎𝖙𝖆𝖓𝖎𝖘𝖈𝖍𝖊𝖗𝖉𝖚𝖉𝖊𝖑𝖘𝖆𝖈𝖐𝖘𝖕𝖋𝖊𝖎𝖋𝖊𝖓𝖒𝖆𝖈𝖍-𝖊𝖗𝖘𝖌𝖊𝖘𝖊𝖑𝖑𝖘𝖈𝖍𝖆𝖋𝖙!"

Just as I was moaning out the closing hunks of that word I touched off one of my electric connections, and all that murky world of people stood revealed in a hideous blue glare! It was immense—that effect! Lots of people shrieked, women curled up and quit in every direction, foundlings collapsed by platoons. The abbot and the monks crossed themselves nimbly and their lips fluttered with agitated prayers. Merlin held his grip but he was astonished clear down to his corns; he had never seen anything to begin with that before. Now was the time to pile in the effects. I lifted my hands and groaned out this word—as it were in agony:

"Nihilistendynamittheaterkaestchenssprengungsattentaetsuersuchungen!"

—and turned on the red fire! You should have heard that Atlantic of people moan and howl when that crimson hell joined the blue! After sixty seconds I shouted:

"Transvaaltruppentropentransporttrampelthiertreibertrauungsthraenentragoedie!"

—and lit up the green fire! After waiting only forty seconds this time, I spread my arms abroad and thundered out the devastating syllables of this word of words:

"Mekkamuselmannenmassenmenchenmoerdermohrenmuttermarmormonumentenmacher!"

—and whirled on the purple glare! There they were, all going at once, red, blue, green, purple!—four furious volcanoes pouring vast clouds of radiant smoke aloft and spreading a blinding rainbowed noonday to the furthest confines of that valley. In the distance one could see that fellow on the pillar standing rigid against the background of sky, his seesaw stopped for the first time in twenty years. I knew the boys were at the pump now and ready. So I said to the abbot:

"The time is come, Father. I am about to pronounce the dread name and command the spell to dissolve. You want to brace up and take hold of something." Then I shouted to the people: "Behold, in another minute the spell will be broken, or no mortal can break it. If it break, all will know it, for you will see the sacred water gush from the chapel door!"

I stood a few moments, to let the hearers have a chance to spread my announcement to those who couldn't hear and so convey it to the furthest ranks, then I made a grand exhibition of extra posturing and gesturing, and shouted:

"Lo, I command the fell spirit that possesses the holy fountain to now disgorge into the skies all the infernal fires that still remain in him, and straightway dissolve his spell and flee hence to the pit, there to lie bound a thousand years. By his own dread name I command it— BGWJJILLIGKKK!"

Then I touched off the hogshead of rockets, and a vast fountain of dazzling lances of fire vomited itself toward the zenith with a hissing rush and burst in mid-sky into a storm of flashing jewels! One mighty groan of terror started up from the massed people, then suddenly broke into a wild hosannah of joy, for there, fair and plain in the uncanny glare, they saw the freed water leaping forth! The old abbot could not speak a word, for tears and the chokings in his throat; without utterance of any sort, he folded me in his arms and mashed me. It was more eloquent than speech. And harder to get over too, in a country where there were really no doctors that were worth a damaged nickel.

You should have seen those acres of people throw themselves down in that water and kiss it; kiss it, and pet it, and fondle it, and talk to it as if it were alive, and welcome it back with the dear names they gave their darlings, just as if it had been a friend who was long gone away and lost, and was come home again. Yes, it was pretty to see and made me think more of them than I had done before.

I sent Merlin home on a shutter. He had caved in and gone down like a landslide when I pronounced that fearful name, and had never come to since. He never had heard that name before—neither had I—but to him it was the right one. Any jumble would have been the right one. He admitted afterward that that spirit's own mother could not have pronounced that name better than I did. He never could understand how I survived it, and I didn't tell him. It is only young magicians that give away a secret like that. Merlin spent three months working enchantments to try to find out the deep trick of how to pronounce that name and outlive it. But he didn't arrive.

When I started to the chapel, the populace uncovered and fell back reverently to make a wide way for me, as if I had been some kind of a superior being— and I was. I was aware of that. I took along a night shift of monks and taught them the mystery of the pump and set them to work, for it was plain that a good part of the people out there were going to sit up with the water all night, consequently it was but right that they should have all they wanted of it. To those monks that pump was a good deal of a miracle itself and they were full of wonder over it, and of admiration too, of the exceeding effectiveness of its performance.

It was a great night, an immense night. There was reputation in it. I could hardly get to sleep for glorying over it.

THE YANKEE'S FIGHT WITH THE KNIGHTS

Up to the day set, there was no talk in all Britain of anything but this combat. All other topics sank into insignificance and passed out of men's thoughts and interest. It was not because a tournament was a great matter; it was not because Sir Sagramor had found the Holy Grail, for he had not but had failed; it was not because the second (official) personage in the kingdom was one of the duelists; no, all these features were commonplace. Yet there was abundant reason for the extraordinary interest which this coming fight was creating. It was born of the fact that all the nation knew that this was not to be a duel between mere men, so to speak, but a duel between two mighty magicians; a duel not of muscle but of mind, not of human skill but of superhuman art and craft, a final struggle for supremacy between the two master enchanters of the age. It was realized that the most prodigious achievements of the most renowned knights could not be worthy of comparison with a spectacle like this; they could be but child's play, contrasted with this mysterious and awful battle of the gods. Yes, all the world knew it was going to be in reality a duel between Merlin and me, a measuring of his magic powers against mine. It was known that Merlin had been busy whole days and nights together, imbuing Sir Sagramor's arms and armor with supernal

powers of offense and defense, and that he had procured for him from the spirits of the air a fleecy veil
which would render the wearer invisible to his an-
tagonist while still visible to other men. Against Sir
Sagramor, so weaponed and protected, a thousand
knights could accomplish nothing; against him no known
enchantments could prevail. These facts were sure; re-
garding them there was no doubt, no reason for doubt.
There was but one question: might there be still other
enchantments, *unknown* to Merlin, which could render
Sir Sagramor's veil transparent to me and make his enchanted mail vulnerable to my weapons? This was the
one thing to be decided in the lists. Until then the world
must remain in suspense.

So the world thought there was a vast matter at stake
here, and the world was right, but it was not the one
they had in their minds. No, a far vaster one was upon
the cast of this die: *the life of knight-errantry.* I was a
champion, it was true, but not the champion of the
frivolous black arts, I was the champion of hard unsenti-
mental common sense and reason. I was entering the
lists to either destroy knight-errantry or be its victim.

Vast as the show-grounds were, there were no vacant
spaces in them outside of the lists at ten o'clock on the
morning of the 16th. The mammoth grand-stand was
clothed in flags, streamers, and rich tapestries and
packed with several acres of small-fry tributary kings,
their suites, and the British aristocracy; with our own
royal gang in the chief place, and each and every individual a flashing prism of gaudy silks and velvets—
well, I never saw anything to begin with it but a fight
between an Upper Mississippi sunset and the aurora
borealis. The huge camp of beflagged and gay-colored
tents at one end of the lists, with a stiff-standing senti-
nel at every door and a shining shield hanging by him

for challenge, was another fine sight. You see, every knight was there who had any ambition or any caste feeling, for my feeling toward their order was not much of a secret and so here was their chance. If I won my fight with Sir Sagramor, others would have the right to call me out as long as I might be willing to respond.

Down at our end there were but two tents, one for me and another for my servants. At the appointed hour the king made a sign and the heralds, in their tabards, appeared and made proclamation, naming the combatants and stating the cause of quarrel. There was a pause, then a ringing bugle-blast, which was the signal for us to come forth. All the multitude caught their breath and an eager curiosity flashed into every face.

Out from his tent rode great Sir Sagramor, an imposing tower of iron, stately and rigid, his huge spear standing upright in its socket and grasped in his strong hand, his grand horse's face and breast cased in steel, his body clothed in rich trappings that almost dragged the ground —oh, a most noble picture. A great shout went up, of welcome and admiration.

And then out I came. But I didn't get any shout. There was a wondering and eloquent silence for a moment, then a great wave of laughter began to sweep along that human sea but a warning bugle-blast cut its career short. I was in the simplest and comfortablest of gymnast costumes—flesh-colored tights from neck to heel, with blue silk puffings about my loins, and bareheaded. My horse was not above medium size but he was alert, slender-limbed, muscled with watch-springs, and just a greyhound to go. He was a beauty, glossy as silk, and naked as he was when he was born, except for bridle and ranger-saddle.

The iron tower and the gorgeous bed-quilt came cumbrously but gracefully pirouetting down the lists, and we tripped lightly up to meet them. We halted; the tower saluted, I responded; then we wheeled and rode side by side to the grand-stand and faced our king and queen, to whom we made obeisance. The queen exclaimed:

"Alack, Sir Boss, wilt fight naked, and without lance or sword or—"

But the king checked her and made her understand, with a polite phrase or two, that this was none of her business. The bugles rang again and we separated and rode to the ends of the lists and took position. Now old Merlin stepped into view and cast a dainty web of gossamer threads over Sir Sagramor which turned him into Hamlet's ghost; the king made a sign, the bugles blew, Sir Sagramor laid his great lance in rest, and the next moment here he came thundering down the course with his veil flying out behind, and I went whistling through the air like an arrow to meet him—cocking my ear the while, as if noting the invisible knight's position and progress by hearing, not sight. A chorus of encouraging shouts burst out for him, and one brave voice flung out a heartening word for me—said:

"Go it, slim Jim!"

It was an even bet that Clarence had procured that favor for me—and furnished the language, too. When that formidable lance-point was within a yard and a half of my breast I twitched my horse aside without an effort, and the big knight swept by, scoring a blank. I got plenty of applause that time. We turned, braced up, and down we came again. Another blank for the knight, a roar of applause for me. This same thing was repeated once more, and it fetched such a whirlwind of applause that Sir Sagramor lost his temper and at once changed his tactics and set himself the task of chasing me down. Why, he hadn't any show in the world at that; it was a game of tag with all the advantage on my side; I whirled out of his path with ease whenever I chose and once I slapped him on the back as I went to the rear. Finally I took the chase into my own hands; and after that, turn, or twist, or do what he would, he was never able to get behind me again; he found himself always in front at the end of his manœuver. So he gave up that business and retired to his end of the lists. His temper was clear gone now and he forgot himself and flung an insult at me which disposed of mine. I slipped my lasso from the horn of my saddle and grasped the coil in my right hand. This time you should have seen him come!—it was a business trip, sure; by his gait there was blood in his eye. I was sitting my horse at ease and swinging the great loop of my lasso in wide circles about my head; the moment he was under way, I started for him; when the space between us had narrowed to forty feet, I sent the snaky spirals of the rope a-cleaving through the air, then darted aside and faced about and brought my trained animal to a halt with all his feet braced under him for a surge. The next moment the rope sprang taut and yanked Sir Sagramor out of the saddle! Great Scott, but there was a sensation!

Unquestionably, the popular thing in this world is novelty. These people had never seen anything of that cowboy business before and it carried them clear off their feet with delight. From all around and everywhere, the shout went up:

"Encore! encore!"

I wondered where they got the word but there was no time to cipher on philological matters, because the whole knight-errantry hive was just humming now and my prospect for trade couldn't have been better. The moment my lasso was released and Sir Sagramor had been assisted to his tent, I hauled in the slack, took my

station and began to swing my loop around my head
again. I was sure to have use for it as soon as they could
elect a successor for Sir Sagramor, and that couldn't
take long where there were so many hungry candidates.
Indeed, they elected one straight off—Sir Hervis de
Revel.

Bzz! Here he came, like a house afire; I dodged: he
passed like a flash, with my horse-hair coils settling
around his neck; a second or so later, *fst!* his saddle was
empty.

I got another encore; and another, and another, and
still another. When I had snaked five men out, things
began to look serious to the ironclads, and they stopped
and consulted together. As a result, they decided that it
was time to waive etiquette and send their greatest and
best against me. To the astonishment of that little world,
I lassoed Sir Lamorak de Galis and after him Sir Gala-
had. So you see there was simply nothing to be done
now but play their right bower—bring out the superbest
of the superb, the mightiest of the mighty, the great Sir
Launcelot himself!

A proud moment for me? I should think so. Yonder
was Arthur, King of Britain; yonder was Guinever; yes,
and whole tribes of little provincial kings and kinglets;
and in the tented camp yonder, renowned knights from
many lands; and likewise the selectest body known to
chivalry, the Knights of the Table Round, the most illustrious in Christendom; and biggest fact of all, the very
sun of their shining system was yonder couching his
lance, the focal point of forty thousand adoring eyes;
and all by myself, here was I laying for him. Across my
mind flitted the dear image of a certain hello-girl of
West Hartford and I wished she could see me now. In
that moment, down came the Invincible with the rush of
a whirlwind—the courtly world rose to its feet and bent

forward—the fateful coils went circling through the air, and before you could wink I was towing Sir Launcelot across the field on his back, and kissing my hand to the storm of waving kerchiefs and the thunder-crash of applause that greeted me!

Said I to myself, as I coiled my lariat and hung it on my saddle-horn and sat there drunk with glory, "The victory is perfect—no other will venture against me—knight-errantry is dead." Now imagine my astonishment—and everybody else's, too—to hear the peculiar bugle-call which announces that another competitor is about to enter the lists! There was a mystery here; I couldn't account for this thing. Next, I noticed Merlin gliding away from me; and then I noticed that my lasso was gone! The old sleight-of-hand expert had stolen it, sure, and slipped it under his robe.

The bugle blew again. I looked, and down came Sagramor riding again, with his dust brushed off and his veil nicely rearranged. I trotted up to meet him, and pretended to find him by the sound of his horse's hoofs. He said:

"Thou'rt quick of ear, but it will not save thee from this!" and he touched the hilt of his great sword. "An ye are not able to see it, because of the influence of the veil, know that it is no cumbrous lance, but a sword—and I ween ye will not be able to avoid it."

His visor was up; there was death in his smile. I should never be able to dodge his sword, that was plain. Somebody was going to die this time. If he got the drop on me, I could name the corpse. We rode forward together and saluted the royalties. This time the king was disturbed. He said:

"Where is thy strange weapon?"

"It is stolen, sire."

"Hast another at hand?"

"No, sire, I brought only the one."

Then Merlin mixed in:

"He brought but the one because there was but the one to bring. There exists none other but that one. It belongeth to the king of the Demons of the Sea. This man is a pretender, and ignorant; else he had known that that weapon can be used in but eight bouts only, and then it vanisheth away to its home under the sea."

"Then is he weaponless," said the king. "Sir Sagramor, ye will grant him leave to borrow."

"And I will lend!" said Sir Launcelot, limping up. "He is as brave a knight of his hands as any that be on live, and he shall have mine."

He put his hand on his sword to draw it but Sir Sagramor said:

"Stay, it may not be. He shall fight with his own weapons; it was his privilege to choose them and bring them. If he has erred, on his head be it."

"Knight!" said the king. "Thou'rt overwrought with passion; it disorders thy mind. Wouldst kill a naked man?"

"An he do it, he shall answer it to me," said Sir Launcelot.

"I will answer it to any he that desireth!" retorted Sir Sagramor hotly.

Merlin broke in, rubbing his hands and smiling his low-downest smile of malicious gratification:

"'Tis well said, right well said! And 'tis enough of parleying, let my lord the king deliver the battle signal."

The king had to yield. The bugle made proclamation, and we turned apart and rode to our stations. There we stood, a hundred yards apart, facing each other, rigid and motionless, like horsed statues. And so we remained, in a soundless hush, as much as a full minute, everybody gazing, nobody stirring. It seemed as if the king could not take heart to give the signal. But at last he lifted his hand, the clear note of a bugle followed, Sir Sagramor's long blade described a flashing curve in the air, and it was superb to see him come. I sat still. On he came. I did not move. People got so excited that they shouted to me:

"Fly, fly! Save thyself! This is murther!"

I never budged so much as an inch till that thundering apparition had got within fifteen paces of me; then I snatched a dragoon revolver out of my holster, there was a flash and a roar, and the revolver was back in the holster before anybody could tell what had happened.

Here was a riderless horse plunging by and yonder lay Sir Sagramor, stone dead.

The people that ran to him were stricken dumb to find that the life was actually gone out of the man and no reason for it visible, no hurt upon his body, nothing like a wound. There was a hole through the breast of his chain-mail, but they attached no importance to a little thing like that; and as a bullet-wound there produces but little blood, none came in sight because of the clothing and swaddlings under the armor. The body was dragged over to let the king and the swells look down upon it. They were stupefied with astonishment naturally. I was requested to come and explain the miracle. But I remained in my tracks like a statue, and said:

"If it is a command, I will come, but my lord the king knows that I am where the laws of combat require me to remain while any desire to come against me."

I waited. Nobody challenged. Then I said:

"If there are any who doubt that this field is well and fairly won, I do not wait for them to challenge me, I challenge them."

"It is a gallant offer," said the king, "and well beseems you. Whom will you name first?"

"I name none, I challenge all! Here I stand, and dare the chivalry of England to come against me—not by individuals, but in mass!"

"What!" shouted a score of knights.

"You have heard the challenge. Take it, or I proclaim you recreant knights and vanquished, every one!"

It was a "bluff" you know. At such a time it is sound judgment to put on a bold face and play your hand for a hundred times what it is worth; forty-nine times out of fifty nobody dares to "call" and you rake in the chips. But just this once—well, things looked squally! In just no time, five hundred knights were scrambling into their saddles and before you could wink a widely scattering drove were under way and clattering down upon me. I snatched both revolvers from the holsters and began to measure distances and calculate chances.

Bang! One saddle empty. Bang! another one. Bang—bang, and I bagged two. Well, it was nip and tuck with us and I knew it. If I spent the eleventh shot without convincing these people, the twelfth man would kill me, sure. And so I never did feel so happy as I did when my ninth downed its man and I detected the wavering in the crowd which is premonitory of panic. An instant lost now could knock out my last chance. But I didn't lose it. I raised both revolvers and pointed them—the halted host stood their ground just about one good square moment, then broke and fled.

The day was mine. Knight-errantry was a doomed institution. The march of civilization was begun. How did I feel? Ah, you never could imagine it.

And Brer Merlin? His stock was flat again. Somehow, every time the magic of fol-de-rol tried conclusions with the magic of science, the magic of fol-de-rol got left.

Adventures of Huckleberry Finn

NOTICE

Persons attempting to find a motive in this narrative will be prosecuted; persons attempting to find a moral in it will be banished; persons attempting to find a plot in it will be shot.

BY ORDER OF THE AUTHOR,
Per G. G., Chief of Ordnance.

EXPLANATORY

In this book a number of dialects are used, to wit: the Missouri Negro dialect, the extremest form of the backwoods Southwestern dialect, the ordinary "Pike County" dialect, and four modified varieties of this last. The shadings have not been done in a haphazard fashion or by guesswork, but painstakingly and with the trustworthy guidance and support of personal familiarity with these several forms of speech.

I make this explanation for the reason that without it many readers would suppose that all these characters were trying to talk alike and not succeeding.

THE AUTHOR.

I. I DISCOVER MOSES AND THE BULRUSHERS

YOU don't know about me without you have read a book by the name of *The Adventures of Tom Sawyer,* but that ain't no matter. That book was made by Mr. Mark Twain and he told the truth, mainly. There was things which he stretched, but mainly he told the truth. That is nothing. I never seen anybody but lied one time or another, without it was Aunt Polly or the widow, or maybe Mary. Aunt Polly—Tom's Aunt Polly, she is—and Mary and the Widow Douglas is all told about in that book, which is mostly a true book, with some stretchers as I said before.

Now the way that the book winds up is this: Tom and me found the money that the robbers hid in the cave and it made us rich. We got six thousand dollars apiece—all gold. It was an awful sight of money when it was piled up. Well, Judge Thatcher he took it and put it out at interest, and it fetched us a dollar a day apiece all the year round—more than a body could tell what to do with. The Widow Douglas she took me for her son and allowed she would sivilize me; but it was rough living in the house all the time, considering how dismal regular and decent the widow was in all her ways, and so when I couldn't stand it no longer I lit out. I got into my old rags and my sugar-hogshead again, and was free and satisfied. But Tom Sawyer he hunted me up and said he was going to start a band of robbers, and I might join if I would go back to the widow and be respectable. So I went back.

The widow she cried over me and called me a poor lost lamb, and she called me a lot of other names, too, but she never meant no harm by it. She put me in them new clothes again, and I couldn't do nothing but sweat and sweat and feel all cramped up. Well, then, the old thing commenced again. The widow rung a bell for supper and you had to come to time. When you got to the table you couldn't go right to eating but you had to wait for the widow to tuck down her head and grumble a little over the victuals, though there warn't really anything the matter with them—that is, nothing only everything was cooked by itself. In a barrel of odds and ends it is different; things get mixed up and the juice kind of swaps around and the things go better.

After supper she got out her book and learned me about Moses and the Bulrushers and I was in a sweat to find out all about him; but by and by she let it out that Moses had been dead a considerable long time; so then I didn't care no more about him, because I don't take no stock in dead people.

Pretty soon I wanted to smoke and asked the widow to let me. But she wouldn't. She said it was a mean practice and wasn't clean, and I must try to not do it any more. That is just the way with some people. They get down on a thing when they don't know nothing about it. Here she was a-bothering about Moses, which was no kin to her and no use to anybody, being gone, you see, yet finding a power of fault with me for doing a thing that had some good in it. And she took snuff, too; of course that was all right, because she done it herself.

Her sister, Miss Watson, a tolerable slim old maid with goggles on, had just come to live with her, and took a set at me now with a spelling-book. She worked me middling hard for about an hour and then the widow made her ease up. I couldn't stood it much longer. Then for an hour it was deadly dull, and I was fidgety. Miss Watson would say, "Don't put your feet up there, Huckleberry"; and "Don't scrunch up like that, Huckle-berry—set up straight"; and pretty soon she would say, "Don't gap and stretch like that, Huckleberry—why don't you try to behave?" Then she told me all about the bad place and I said I wished I was there. She got mad then but I didn't mean no harm. All I wanted was to go somewheres; all I wanted was a change, I warn't particular. She said it was wicked to say what I said,

said she wouldn't say it for the whole world, *she* was going to live so as to go to the good place. Well, I couldn't see no advantage in going where she was going, so I made up my mind I wouldn't try for it. But I never said so, because it would only make trouble and wouldn't do no good.

Now she had got a start and she went on and told me all about the good place. She said all a body would have to do there was to go around all day long with a harp and sing, forever and ever. So I didn't think much of it. But I never said so. I asked her if she reckoned Tom Sawyer would go there and she said not by a considerable sight. I was glad about that, because I wanted him and me to be together.

Miss Watson she kept pecking at me and it got tiresome and lonesome. By and by they fetched the niggers in and had prayers and then everybody was off to bed. I went up to my room with a piece of candle and put it on the table. Then I set down in a chair by the window and tried to think of something cheerful, but it warn't no use. I felt so lonesome I most wished I was dead. The stars were shining and the leaves rustled in the woods ever so mournful; and I heard an owl, away off, who-whooing about somebody that was dead, and a whippowill and a dog crying about somebody that was going to die; and the wind was trying to whisper something to me and I couldn't make out what it was, and so it made the cold shivers run over me. Then away out in the woods I heard that kind of a sound that a ghost makes when it wants to tell about something that's on its mind and can't make itself understood, and so can't rest easy in its grave and has to go about that way every night grieving. I got so downhearted and scared I did wish I had some company. Pretty soon a spider went crawling up my shoulder and I flipped it off and it lit in the candle, and before I could budge it was all shriveled up. I didn't need anybody to tell me that that was an awful bad sign and would fetch me some bad luck, so I was scared and most shook the clothes off of me. I got up and turned around in my tracks three times and crossed my breast every time, and then I tied up a little lock of my hair with a thread to keep witches away. But I hadn't no confidence. You do that when you've lost a horseshoe that you've found, instead of nailing it up over the door, but I hadn't ever heard anybody say it was any way to keep off bad luck when you'd killed a spider.

I set down again, a-shaking all over, and got out my pipe for a smoke, for the house was all as still as death now and so the widow wouldn't know. Well, after a long time I heard the clock away off in the town go boom—boom—boom—twelve licks, and all still again—stiller than ever. Pretty soon I heard a twig snap down in the dark amongst the trees—something was a-stirring. I set still and listened. Directly I could just barely hear a *"me-yow! me-yow!"* down there. That was good! Says I, *"me-yow! me-yow!"* as soft as I could, and then I put out the light and scrambled out of the window on to the shed. Then I slipped down to the ground and crawled in among the trees, and sure enough there was Tom Sawyer waiting for me.

II. Our Gang's Dark Oath

We went tiptoeing along a path amongst the trees back towards the end of the widow's garden, stooping down so as the branches wouldn't scrape our heads. When we was passing by the kitchen I fell over a root and made a noise. We scrouched down and laid still.

Miss Watson's big nigger, named Jim, was setting in the kitchen door; we could see him pretty clear, because there was a light behind him. He got up and stretched his neck out about a minute, listening. Then he says:

"Who dah?"

He listened some more; then he came tiptoeing down and stood right between us; we could 'a' touched him, nearly. Well, likely it was minutes and minutes that there warn't a sound, and we all there so close together. There was a place on my ankle that got to itching but I dasn't scratch it; and then my ear begun to itch; and next my back, right between my shoulders. Seemed like I'd die if I couldn't scratch. Well, I've noticed that thing plenty times since. If you are with the quality, or at a funeral, or trying to go to sleep when you ain't sleepy— if you are anywheres where it won't do for you to scratch, why you will itch all over in upwards of a thousand places. Pretty soon Jim says:

"Say, who is you? Whar is you? Dog my cats ef I didn' hear sumf'n. Well, I knows what I's gwyne to do: I's gwyne to set down here and listen tell I hears it agin."

So he set down on the ground betwixt me and Tom. He leaned his back up against a tree, and stretched his legs out till one of them most touched one of mine. My nose begun to itch. It itched till the tears come into my eyes. But I dasn't scratch. Then it begun to itch on the inside. Next I got to itching underneath. I didn't know how I was going to set still. This miserableness went on as much as six or seven minutes, but it seemed a sight longer than that. I was itching in eleven different places now. I reckoned I couldn't stand it more'n a minute longer, but I set my teeth hard and got ready to try. Just then Jim begun to breathe heavy, next he begun to snore—and then I was pretty soon comfortable again.

Tom he made a sign to me—kind of a little noise with
his mouth—and we went creeping away on our hands
and knees. When we was ten foot off Tom whispered
to me, and wanted to tie Jim to the tree for fun. But I
said no; he might wake and make a disturbance, and
then they'd find out I warn't in. Then Tom said he
hadn't got candles enough and he would slip in the
kitchen and get some more. I didn't want him to try. I
said Jim might wake up and come. But Tom wanted to
resk it; so we slid in there and got three candles and
Tom laid five cents on the table for pay. Then we got
out and I was in a sweat to get away; but nothing would
do Tom but he must crawl to where Jim was, on his
hands and knees, and play something on him. I waited
and it seemed a good while, everything was so still and
lonesome.

As soon as Tom was back we cut along the path,
around the garden fence, and by and by fetched up on
the steep top of the hill the other side of the house. Tom
said he slipped Jim's hat off of his head and hung it on
a limb right over him, and Jim stirred a little but he
didn't wake. Afterwards Jim said the witches bewitched
him and put him in a trance and rode him all over the
state, and then set him under the trees again and hung
his hat on a limb to show who done it. And next time
Jim told it he said they rode him down to New Orleans;
and after that every time he told it he spread it more
and more, till by and by he said they rode him all over
the world and tired him most to death and his back was
all over saddle-boils. Jim was monstrous proud about it
and he got so he wouldn't hardly notice the other niggers. Niggers would come miles to hear Jim tell about it
and he was more looked up to than any nigger in that
country. Strange niggers would stand with their mouths
open and look him all over, same as if he was a wonder.

Niggers is always talking about witches in the dark by the kitchen fire, but whenever one was talking and letting on to know all about such things, Jim would happen in and say, "Hm! What you know 'bout witches?" and that nigger was corked up and had to take a back seat. Jim always kept that five-center piece round his neck with a string, and said it was a charm the devil give to him with his own hands and told him he could cure anybody with it and fetch witches whenever he wanted to just by saying something to it; but he never told what it was he said to it. Niggers would come from all around there and give Jim anything they had, just for a sight of that five-center piece, but they wouldn't touch it because the devil had had his hands on it. Jim was most ruined for a servant, because he got so stuck up on account of having seen the devil and been rode by witches.

Well, when Tom and me got to the edge of the hilltop we looked away down into the village and could see three or four lights twinkling, where there was sick folks, maybe, and the stars over us was sparkling ever so fine, and down by the village was the river, a whole mile broad and awful still and grand. We went down the hill and found Joe Harper and Ben Rogers, and two or three more of the boys, hid in the old tanyard. So we unhitched a skiff and pulled down the river two mile and a half, to the big scar on the hillside, and went ashore.

We went to a clump of bushes and Tom made everybody swear to keep the secret and then showed them a hole in the hill, right in the thickest part of the bushes. Then we lit the candles and crawled in on our hands and knees. We went about two hundred yards and then the cave opened up. Tom poked about amongst the passages and pretty soon ducked under a wall where

you wouldn't 'a' noticed that there was a hole. We went
along a narrow place and got into a kind of room, all
damp and sweaty and cold, and there we stopped. Tom
says:

"Now, we'll start this band of robbers and call it Tom
Sawyer's Gang. Everybody that wants to join has got to
take an oath and write his name in blood."

Everybody was willing. So Tom got out a sheet of
paper that he had wrote the oath on, and read it. It
swore every boy to stick to the band and never tell any
of the secrets, and if anybody done anything to any boy
in the band, whichever boy was ordered to kill that
person and his family must do it, and he mustn't eat and
he mustn't sleep till he had killed them and hacked a
cross in their breast, which was the sign of the band.
And nobody that didn't belong to the band could use
that mark, and if he did he must be sued, and if he done
it again he must be killed. And if anybody that belonged
to the band told the secrets, he must have his throat cut
and then have his carcass burnt up and the ashes scattered all around and his name blotted off the list with
blood and never mentioned again by the gang, but have
a curse put on it and be forgot forever.

Everybody said it was a real beautiful oath and asked
Tom if he got it out of his own head. He said some of it,
but the rest was out of pirate-books and robber-books
and every gang that was high-toned had it.

Some thought it would be good to kill the *families* of
boys that told the secrets. Tom said it was a good idea,
so he took a pencil and wrote it in. Then Ben Rogers
says:

"Here's Huck Finn, he hain't got no family; what you
going to do 'bout him?"

"Well, hain't he got a father?" says Tom Sawyer.

"Yes, he's got a father but you can't never find him

these days. He used to lay drunk with the hogs in the tanyard but he hain't been seen in these parts for a year or more."

They talked it over and they was going to rule me out, because they said every boy must have a family or somebody to kill, or else it wouldn't be fair and square for the others. Well, nobody could think of anything to do—everybody was stumped, and set still. I was most ready to cry, but all at once I thought of a way and so I offered them Miss Watson—they could kill her. Everybody said:

"Oh, she'll do. That's all right. Huck can come in."

Then they all stuck a pin in their fingers to get blood to sign with, and I made my mark on the paper.

"Now," says Ben Rogers, "what's the line of business of this Gang?"

"Nothing only robbery and murder," Tom said.

"But who are we going to rob?—houses, or cattle, or—"

"Stuff! stealing cattle and such things ain't robbery, it's burglary," says Tom Sawyer. "We ain't burglars. That ain't no sort of style. We are highwaymen. We stop stages and carriages on the road, with masks on, and kill the people and take their watches and money."

"Must we always kill the people?"

"Oh, certainly. It's best. Some authorities think different but mostly it's considered best to kill them—except some that you bring to the cave here, and keep them till they're ransomed."

"Ransomed? What's that?"

"I don't know. But that's what they do. I've seen it in books, and so of course that's what we've got to do."

"But how can we do it if we don't know what it is?"

"Why, blame it all, we've *got* to do it. Don't I tell you it's in the books? Do you want to go to doing dif-

ferent from what's in the books, and get things all
muddled up?"

"Oh, that's all very fine to *say*, Tom Sawyer, but how
in the nation are these fellows going to be ransomed if
we don't know how to do it to them?—that's the thing
I want to get at. Now, what do you *reckon* it is?"

"Well, I don't know. But per'aps if we keep them till
they're ransomed, it means that we keep them till
they're dead."

"Now, that's something *like*. That'll answer. Why
couldn't you said that before? We'll keep them till
they're ransomed to death, and a bothersome lot they'll
be, too—eating up everything, and always trying to get
loose."

"How you talk, Ben Rogers. How can they get loose
when there's a guard over them, ready to shoot them
down if they move a peg?"

"A guard! Well, that *is* good. So somebody's got to
set up all night and never get any sleep, just so as
to watch them. I think that's foolishness. Why can't a
body take a club and ransom them as soon as they get
here?"

"Because it ain't in the books so—that's why. Now,
Ben Rogers, do you want to do things regular, or don't
you?—that's the idea. Don't you reckon that the people
that made the books knows what's the correct thing to
do? Do you reckon *you* can learn 'em anything? Not by a
good deal. No, sir, we'll just go on and ransom them in
the regular way."

"All right. I don't mind; but I say it's a fool way,
anyhow. Say, do we kill the women, too?"

"Well, Ben Rogers, if I was as ignorant as you I
wouldn't let on. Kill the women? No; nobody ever saw
anything in the books like that. You fetch them to the
cave, and you're always as polite as pie to them, and by

and by they fall in love with you and never want to go home any more."

"Well, if that's the way I'm agreed, but I don't take no stock in it. Mighty soon we'll have the cave so cluttered up with women and fellows waiting to be ransomed that there won't be no place for the robbers. But go ahead, I ain't got nothing to say."

Little Tommy Barnes was asleep now, and when they waked him up he was scared, and cried and said he wanted to go home to his ma and didn't want to be a robber any more.

So they all made fun of him and called him cry-baby, and that made him mad and he said he would go straight and tell all the secrets. But Tom give him five cents to keep quiet and said we would all go home and meet next week and rob somebody and kill some people.

Ben Rogers said he couldn't get out much, only Sundays, and so he wanted to begin next Sunday, but all the boys said it would be wicked to do it on Sunday and that settled the thing. They agreed to get together and fix a day as soon as they could, and then we elected Tom Sawyer first captain and Joe Harper second captain of the Gang, and so started home.

I clumb up the shed and crept into my window just before day was breaking. My new clothes was all greased up and clayey and I was dog-tired.

III. WE AMBUSCADE THE A-RABS

Well, I got a good going-over in the morning from old Miss Watson on account of my clothes, but the widow she didn't scold, but only cleaned off the grease and clay and looked so sorry that I thought I would behave awhile if I could. Then Miss Watson she took

me in the closet and prayed, but nothing come of it.
She told me to pray every day and whatever I asked for
I would get it. But it warn't so. I tried it. Once I got a
fish-line but no hooks. It warn't any good to me without
hooks. I tried for the hooks three or four times but somehow I couldn't make it work. By and by, one day I
asked Miss Watson to try for me, but she said I was a
fool. She never told me why and I couldn't make it out
no way.

I set down one time back in the woods and had a
long think about it. I says to myself, if a body can get
anything they pray for, why don't Deacon Winn get
back the money he lost on pork? Why can't the widow
get back her silver snuff-box that was stole? Why can't
Miss Watson fat up? No, says I to myself, there ain't
nothing in it. I went and told the widow about it and
she said the thing a body could get by praying for it
was "spiritual gifts." This was too many for me, but
she told me what she meant—I must help other people
and do everything I could for other people and look out
for them all the time and never think about myself.
This was including Miss Watson, as I took it. I went out
in the woods and turned it over in my mind a long time,
but I couldn't see no advantage about it—except for the
other people; so at last I reckoned I wouldn't worry
about it any more but just let it go. Sometimes the
widow would take me one side and talk about Providence in a way to make a body's mouth water; but
maybe next day Miss Watson would take hold and knock
it all down again. I judged I could see that there was
two Providences and a poor chap would stand considerable show with the widow's Providence, but if Miss
Watson's got him there warn't no help for him any more.
I thought it all out and reckoned I would belong to the
widow's if he wanted me, though I couldn't make out

how he was a-going to be any better off then than what
he was before, seeing I was so ignorant and so kind of
low-down and ornery.

Pap he hadn't been seen for more than a year and
that was comfortable for me; I didn't want to see him
no more. He used to always whale me when he was
sober and could get his hands on me; though I used to
take to the woods most of the time when he was around.
Well, about this time he was found in the river
drownded, about twelve mile above town, so people
said. They judged it was him, anyway; said this
drownded man was just his size and was ragged, and
had uncommon long hair, which was all like pap, but
they couldn't make nothing out of the face, because it
had been in the water so long it warn't much like a face
at all. They said he was floating on his back in the water.
They took him and buried him on the bank. But I
warn't comfortable long, because I happened to think of
something. I knowed mighty well that a drownded man
don't float on his back but on his face. So I knowed,
then, that this warn't pap but a woman dressed up in a
man's clothes. So I was uncomfortable again. I judged
the old man would turn up again by and by, though I
wished he wouldn't.

We played robber now and then about a month, and
then I resigned. All the boys did. We hadn't robbed
nobody, hadn't killed any people, but only just pretended. We used to hop out of the woods and go
charging down on hog-drivers and women in carts taking garden stuff to market, but we never hived any of
them. Tom Sawyer called the hogs "ingots," and he
called the turnips and stuff "julery," and we would go
to the cave and powwow over what we had done and
how many people we had killed and marked. But I
couldn't see no profit in it. One time Tom sent a boy to

run about town with a blazing stick, which he called a
slogan (which was the sign for the Gang to get together) and then he said he had got secret news by his
spies that next day a whole parcel of Spanish merchants
and rich A-rabs was going to camp in Cave Hollow
with two hundred elephants and six hundred camels
and over a thousand "sumter" mules, all loaded down
with di'monds, and they didn't have only a guard of
four hundred soldiers and so we would lay in ambuscade, as he called it, and kill the lot and scoop the
things. He said we must slick up our swords and guns
and get ready. He never could go after even a turnip-
cart but he must have the swords and guns all scoured
up for it, though they was only lath and broomsticks
and you might scour at them till you rotted and then
they warn't worth a mouthful of ashes more than what
they was before. I didn't believe we could lick such a
crowd of Spaniards and A-rabs but I wanted to see the
camels and elephants, so I was on hand next day, Saturday, in the ambuscade, and when we got the word we
rushed out of the woods and down the hill. But there
warn't no Spaniards and A-rabs and there warn't no
camels nor no elephants. It warn't anything but a Sunday-school picnic, and only a primer class at that. We
busted it up and chased the children up the hollow, but
we never got anything but some doughnuts and jam,
though Ben Rogers got a rag doll and Joe Harper got a
hymn-book and a tract, and then the teacher charged
in and made us drop everything and cut. I didn't see no
di'monds, and I told Tom Sawyer so. He said there was
loads of them there, anyway, and he said there was
A-rabs there, too, and elephants and things. I said, why
couldn't we see them, then? He said if I warn't so ignorant but had read a book called *Don Quixote,* I would
know without asking. He said it was all done by en-

chantment. He said there was hundreds of soldiers there, and elephants and treasure and so on, but we had enemies which he called magicians and they had turned the whole thing into an infant Sunday-school, just out of spite. I said, all right; then the thing for us to do was to go for the magicians. Tom Sawyer said I was a num-skull.

"Why," says he, "a magician could call up a lot of genies and they would hash you up like nothing before you could say Jack Robinson. They are as tall as a tree and as big around as a church."

"Well," I says, "s'pose we got some genies to help *us* —can't we lick the other crowd then?"

"How you going to get them?"

"I don't know. How do *they* get them?"

"Why, they rub an old tin lamp or an iron ring and then the genies come tearing in, with the thunder and lightning a-ripping around and the smoke a-rolling, and everything they're told to do they up and do it. They don't think nothing of pulling a shot-tower up by the roots and belting a Sunday-school superintendent over the head with it—or any other man."

"Who makes them tear around so?"

"Why, whoever rubs the lamp or the ring. They belong to whoever rubs the lamp or the ring and they've got to do whatever he says. If he tells them to build a palace forty miles long out of di'monds and fill it full of chewing-gum, or whatever you want, and fetch an emperor's daughter from China for you to marry, they've got to do it—and they've got to do it before sun-up next morning, too. And more: they've got to waltz that palace around over the country wherever you want it, you understand."

"Well," says I, "I think they are a pack of flatheads for not keeping the palace themselves 'stead of fooling them away like that. And what's more—if I was one of them I would see a man in Jericho before I would drop my business and come to him for the rubbing of an old tin lamp."

"How you talk, Huck Finn. Why, you'd *have* to come when he rubbed it, whether you wanted to or not."

"What! and I as high as a tree and as big as a church? All right, then; I *would* come; but I lay I'd make that man climb the highest tree there was in the country."

"Shucks, it ain't no use to talk to you, Huck Finn. You don't seem to know anything, somehow—perfect saphead."

I thought all this over for two or three days, and then I reckoned I would see if there was anything in it. I got an old tin lamp and an iron ring and went out in the woods and rubbed and rubbed till I sweat like an Injun, calculating to build a palace and sell it, but it warn't no use, none of the genies come. So then I judged that all that stuff was only just one of Tom Sawyer's lies. I reckoned he believed in the A-rabs and the elephants, but as for me I think different. It had all the marks of a Sunday-school.

IV. The Hair-Ball Oracle

Well, three or four months run along and it was well into the winter now. I had been to school most all the time and could spell and read and write just a little, and could say the multiplication table up to six times seven is thirty-five, and I don't reckon I could ever get any further than that if I was to live forever. I don't take no stock in mathematics, anyway.

At first I hated the school, but by and by I got so I could stand it. Whenever I got uncommon tired I played hookey, and the hiding I got next day done me good and cheered me up. So the longer I went to school the easier it got to be. I was getting sort of used to the widow's ways, too, and they warn't so raspy on me. Living in a house and sleeping in a bed pulled on me pretty tight mostly, but before the cold weather I used to slide out and sleep in the woods sometimes, and so that was a rest to me. I liked the old ways best but I was getting so I liked the new ones, too, a little bit. The widow said I was coming along slow but sure and doing very satisfactory. She said she warn't ashamed of me.

One morning I happened to turn over the salt-cellar at breakfast. I reached for some of it as quick as I could to throw over my left shoulder and keep off the bad luck, but Miss Watson was in ahead of me and crossed me off. She says, "Take your hands away, Huckleberry; what a mess you are always making!" The widow put in a good word for me but that warn't going to keep off the bad luck, I knowed that well enough. I started out after breakfast, feeling worried and shaky, and wondering where it was going to fall on me and what it was going to be. There is ways to keep off some kinds of bad luck, but this wasn't one of them kind; so I never tried to do anything but just poked along low-spirited and on the watch-out.

I went down to the front garden and clumb over the stile where you go through the high board fence. There was an inch of new snow on the ground and I seen somebody's tracks. They had come up from the quarry and stood around the stile awhile and then went on around the garden fence. It was funny they hadn't come in, after standing around so. I couldn't make it out. It was very curious, somehow. I was going to follow around but I stooped down to look at the tracks first. I didn't notice anything at first but next I did. There was a cross in the left boot-heel made with big nails, to keep off the devil.

I was up in a second and shinning down the hill. I looked over my shoulder every now and then, but I didn't see nobody. I was at Judge Thatcher's as quick as I could get there. He said:

"Why, my boy, you are all out of breath. Did you come for your interest?"

"No, sir," I says; "is there some for me?"

"Oh, yes, a half-yearly is in last night—over a hundred and fifty dollars. Quite a fortune for you. You better let me invest it along with your six thousand, because if you take it you'll spend it."

"No, sir," I says, "I don't want to spend it. I don't want it at all—nor the six thousand, nuther. I want you to take it; I want to give it to you—the six thousand and all."

He looked surprised. He couldn't seem to make it out. He says:

"Why, what can you mean, my boy?"

I says, "Don't you ask me no questions about it, please. You'll take it—won't you?"

He says:

"Well, I'm puzzled. Is something the matter?"

"Please take it," says I, "and don't ask me nothing—then I won't have to tell no lies."

He studied awhile, and then he says:

"Oho-o! I think I see. You want to *sell* all your property to me—not give it. That's the correct idea."

Then he wrote something on a paper and read it over, and says:

"There; you see it says 'for a consideration.' That means I have bought it of you and paid you for it. Here's a dollar for you. Now you sign it."

So I signed it and left.

Miss Watson's nigger, Jim, had a hair-ball as big as your fist, which had been took out of the fourth stomach of an ox, and he used to do magic with it. He said there was a spirit inside of it and it knowed everything. So I went to him that night and told him pap was here again, for I found his tracks in the snow. What I wanted to know was, what he was going to do and was he going to stay? Jim got out his hair-ball and said something over it, and then he held it up and dropped it on the floor. It fell pretty solid and only rolled about an inch. Jim tried it again and then another time, and it acted just the same. Jim got down on his knees and put his ear against it and listened. But it warn't no use; he said it wouldn't talk. He said sometimes it wouldn't talk without money. I told him I had an old slick counterfeit quarter that warn't no good because the brass showed through the silver a little and it wouldn't pass nohow, even if the brass didn't show, because it was so slick it felt greasy and so that would tell on it every time. (I reckoned I wouldn't say nothing about the dollar I got from the judge.) I said it was pretty bad money but maybe the hair-ball would take it, because maybe it wouldn't know the difference. Jim smelt it and bit it and rubbed it, and said he would manage so the hair-ball would think it was good. He said he would split open a raw Irish potato and stick the quarter in between and keep it there all night, and next morning you couldn't see no brass and it wouldn't feel greasy no more, and so anybody in town would take it in a minute, let alone a hair-ball. Well, I knowed a potato would do that before but I had forgot it.

Jim put the quarter under the hair-ball and got down and listened again. This time he said the hair-ball was all right. He said it would tell my whole fortune if I wanted it to. I says, go on. So the hair-ball talked to Jim, and Jim told it to me. He says:

"Yo' ole father doan' know yit what he's a-gwyne to do. Sometimes he spec he'll go 'way, en den agin he spec he'll stay. De bes' way is to res' easy en let de ole man take his own way. Dey's two angels hoverin' roun' 'bout him. One uv 'em is white en shiny, en t'other one is black. De white one gits him to go right a little while, den de black one sail in en bust it all up. A body can't tell yit which one gwyne to fetch him at de las'. But you is all right. You gwyne to have considable trouble in yo' life, en considable joy. Sometimes you gwyne to git hurt, en sometimes you gwyne to git sick, but every time you's gwyne to git well agin. Dey's two gals flyin' 'bout you in yo' life. One uv 'em's light en t'other one is dark. One is rich en t'other is po'. You's gwyne to marry de po' one fust en de rich one by en by. You wants to keep 'way fum de water as much as you kin, en don't run no resk, 'kase it's down in de bills dat you's gwyne to git hung."

When I lit my candle and went up to my room that night there set pap—his own self!

v. PAP STARTS IN ON A NEW LIFE

I had shut the door to. Then I turned around, and there he was. I used to be scared of him all the time, he tanned me so much. I reckoned I was scared now, too; but in a minute I see I was mistaken—that is, after the first jolt, as you may say, when my breath sort of hitched, he being so unexpected; but right away after, I see I warn't scared of him worth bothring about.

He was most fifty, and he looked it. His hair was long and tangled and greasy and hung down, and you

could see his eyes shining through like he was behind
vines. It was all black, no gray; so was his long,
mixed-up whiskers. There warn't no color in his face,
where his face showed; it was white, not like another
man's white but a white to make a body sick, a white to
make a body's flesh crawl—a tree-toad white, a fish-belly
white. As for his clothes—just rags, that was all. He had
one ankle resting on t'other knee; the boot on that foot
was busted and two of his toes stuck through, and he
worked them now and then. His hat was laying on the
floor—an old black slouch with the top caved in, like
a lid.

I stood a-looking at him; he set there a-looking at me,
with his chair tilted back a little. I set the candle down.
I noticed the window was up; so he had clumb in by
the shed. He kept a-looking me all over. By and by he
says:

"Starchy clothes—very. You think you're a good deal
of a big-bug, *don't* you?"

"Maybe I am, maybe I ain't," I says.

"Don't you give me none o' your lip," says he. "You've
put on considerable many frills since I been away. I'll
take you down a peg before I get done with you. You're
educated, too, they say—can read and write. You think
you're better'n your father, now, don't you, because he
can't? *I'll* take it out of you. Who told you you might
meddle with such hifalut'n foolishness, hey?—who told
you you could?"

"The widow. She told me."

"The widow, hey?—and who told the widow she
could put in her shovel about a thing that ain't none of
her business?"

"Nobody never told her."

"Well, I'll learn her how to meddle. And looky here—
you drop that school, you hear? I'll learn people to bring

up a boy to put on airs over his own father and let on
to be better'n what *he* is. You lemme catch you fooling around that school again, you hear? Your mother
couldn't read, and she couldn't write, nuther, before she
died. None of the family couldn't before *they* died. *I*
can't; and here you're a-swelling yourself up like this. I
ain't the man to stand it—you hear? Say, lemme hear
you read."

I took up a book and begun something about General
Washington and the wars. When I'd read about a half
a minute, he fetched the book a whack with his hand
and knocked it across the house. He says:

"It's so. You can do it. I had my doubts when they
told me. Now looky here; you stop that putting on frills.
I won't have it. I'll lay for you, my smarty, and if I
catch you about that school I'll tan you good. First you
know you'll get religion, too. I never see such a son."

He took up a little blue and yaller picture of some
cows and a boy, and says:

"What's this?"

"It's something they give me for learning my lessons
good."

He tore it up, and says:

"I'll give you something better—I'll give you a cowhide."

He set there a-mumbling and a-growling a minute,
and then he says:

"*Ain't* you a sweet-scented dandy, though? A bed,
and bedclothes, and a look'n'-glass, and a piece of carpet
on the floor—and your own father got to sleep with the
hogs in the tanyard. I never see such a son. I bet I'll
take some o' these frills out o' you before I'm done with
you. Why, there ain't no end to your airs—they say
you're rich. Hey?—how's that?"

"They lie—that's how."

"Looky here—mind how you talk to me; I'm a-standing about all I can stand now—so don't gimme no sass. I've been in town two days and I hain't heard nothing but about you bein' rich. I heard about it away down the river, too. That's why I come. You git me that money to-morrow—I want it."

"I hain't got no money."

"It's a lie. Judge Thatcher's got it. You git it. I want it."

"I hain't got no money, I tell you. You ask Judge Thatcher; he'll tell you the same."

"All right. I'll ask him; and I'll make him pungle, too, or I'll know the reason why. Say, how much you got in your pocket? I want it."

"I hain't got only a dollar, and I want that to—"

"It don't make no difference what you want it for—you just shell it out."

He took it and bit it to see if it was good, and then he said he was going down-town to get some whisky; said he hadn't had a drink all day. When he had got out on the shed he put his head in again and cussed me for putting on frills and trying to be better than him, and when I reckoned he was gone he come back and put his head in again and told me to mind about that school, because he was going to lay for me and lick me if I didn't drop that.

Next day he was drunk, and he went to Judge Thatcher's and bullyragged him and tried to make him give up the money, but he couldn't, and then he swore he'd make the law force him.

The judge and the widow went to law to get the court to take me away from him and let one of them be my guardian, but it was a new judge that had just come and he didn't know the old man; so he said courts mustn't interfere and separate families if they could help it, said he'd druther not take a child away from its father. So Judge Thatcher and the widow had to quit on the business.

That pleased the old man till he couldn't rest. He said he'd cowhide me till I was black and blue if I didn't raise some money for him. I borrowed three dollars from Judge Thatcher and pap took it and got drunk and went a-blowing around and cussing and whooping and carrying on, and he kept it up all over town, with a tin pan, till most midnight; then they jailed him and next day they had him before court and jailed him again for a week. But he said *he* was satisfied; said he was boss of his son and he'd make it warm for *him*.

When he got out the new judge said he was a-going to make a man of him. So he took him to his own house, and dressed him up clean and nice, and had him to breakfast and dinner and supper with the family, and was just old pie to him, so to speak. And after supper he talked to him about temperance and such things till the old man cried and said he'd been a fool and fooled away his life but now he was a-going to turn over a new leaf and be a man nobody wouldn't be ashamed of, and he hoped the judge would help him and not look down on him. The judge said he could hug him for them words; so *he* cried and his wife she cried too; pap said he'd been a man that had always been misunderstood before and the judge said he believed it. The old man said that what a man wanted that was down was sympathy and the judge said it was so; so they cried again. And when it was bedtime the old man rose up and held out his hand, and says:

"Look at it, gentlemen and ladies all; take a-hold of it; shake it. There's a hand that was the hand of a hog; but it ain't so no more; it's the hand of a man that's started in on a new life and'll die before he'll go back.

You mark them words—don't forget I said them. It's a clean hand now; shake it—don't be afeard."

So they shook it, one after the other, all around, and cried. The judge's wife she kissed it. Then the old man he signed a pledge—made his mark. The judge said it was the holiest time on record, or something like that. Then they tucked the old man into a beautiful room, which was the spare room, and in the night some time he got powerful thirsty and clumb out on to the porch-roof and slid down a stanchion and traded his new coat for a jug of forty-rod, and clumb back again and had a good old time; and towards daylight he crawled out again, drunk as a fiddler, and rolled off the porch and broke his left arm in two places and was most froze to death when somebody found him after sun-up. And when they come to look at that spare room they had to take soundings before they could navigate it.

The judge he felt kind of sore. He said he reckoned a body could reform the old man with a shotgun, maybe, but he didn't know no other way.

VI. PAP STRUGGLES WITH THE DEATH ANGEL

Well, pretty soon the old man was up and around again, and then he went for Judge Thatcher in the courts to make him give up that money, and he went for me, too, for not stopping school. He catched me a couple of times and thrashed me, but I went to school just the same, and dodged him or outrun him most of the time. I didn't want to go to school much before but I reckoned I'd go now to spite pap. That law trial was a slow business—appeared like they warn't ever going to get started on it; so every now and then I'd borrow two or three dollars off of the judge for him, to keep from getting a cowhiding. Every time he got money he got drunk, and every time he got drunk he raised Cain around town, and every time he raised Cain he got jailed. He was just suited—this kind of thing was right in his line.

He got to hanging around the widow's too much, and so she told him at last that if he didn't quit using around there she would make trouble for him. Well, *wasn't* he mad? He said he would show who was Huck Finn's boss. So he watched out for me one day in the spring and catched me and took me up the river about three mile in a skiff, and crossed over to the Illinois shore where it was woody and there warn't no houses but an old log hut in a place where the timber was so thick you couldn't find it if you didn't know where it was.

He kept me with him all the time and I never got a chance to run off. We lived in that old cabin and he always locked the door and put the key under his head nights. He had a gun which he had stole, I reckon, and we fished and hunted, and that was what we lived on. Every little while he locked me in and went down to the store, three miles, to the ferry, and traded fish and game for whisky and fetched it home and got drunk and had a good time and licked me. The widow she found out where I was by and by and she sent a man over to try to get hold of me, but pap drove him off with the gun and it warn't long after that till I was used to being where I was and liked it—all but the cowhide part.

It was kind of lazy and jolly, laying off comfortable all day, smoking and fishing, and no books nor study. Two months or more run along and my clothes got to be all rags and dirt, and I didn't see how I'd ever got to like it so well at the widow's, where you had to wash and eat on a plate and comb up and go to bed and get up regular, and be forever bothering over a book and

have old Miss Watson pecking at you all the time. I
didn't want to go back no more. I had stopped cussing
because the widow didn't like it, but now I took to it
again because pap hadn't no objections. It was pretty
good times up in the woods there, take it all around.

But by and by pap got too handy with his hick'ry and
I couldn't stand it. I was all over welts. He got to going
away so much, too, and locking me in. Once he locked
me in and was gone three days. It was dreadful lonesome. I judged he had got drownded and I wasn't ever
going to get out any more. I was scared. I made up my
mind I would fix up some way to leave there. I had
tried to get out of that cabin many a time but I couldn't
find no way. There warn't a window to it big enough for
a dog to get through. I couldn't get up the chimbly; it
was too narrow. The door was thick, solid oak slabs.
Pap was pretty careful not to leave a knife or anything
in the cabin when he was away; I reckon I had hunted
the place over as much as a hundred times; well, I was
most all the time at it, because it was about the only
way to put in the time. But this time I found something
at last; I found an old rusty wood-saw without any
handle; it was laid in between a rafter and the clap-
boards of the roof. I greased it up and went to work.
There was an old horse-blanket nailed against the logs
at the far end of the cabin behind the table, to keep the
wind from blowing through the chinks and putting the
candle out. I got under the table and raised the blanket,
and went to work to saw a section of the big bottom log
out—big enough to let me through. Well, it was a good
long job but I was getting towards the end of it when
I heard pap's gun in the woods. I got rid of the signs of
my work and dropped the blanket and hid my saw, and
pretty soon pap come in.

Pap warn't in a good humor—so he was his natural

self. He said he was down to town and everything was going wrong. His lawyer said he reckoned he would win his lawsuit and get the money if they ever got started on the trial, but then there was ways to put it off a long time and Judge Thatcher knowed how to do it. And he said people allowed there'd be another trial to get me away from him and give me to the widow for my guardian, and they guessed it would win this time. This shook me up considerable because I didn't want to go back to the widow's any more and be so cramped up and sivilized, as they called it. Then the old man got to cussing and cussed everything and everybody he could think of, and then cussed them all over again to make sure he hadn't skipped any, and after that he polished off with a kind of a general cuss all round, including a considerable parcel of people which he didn't know the names of and so called them what's-his-name when he got to them and went right along with his cussing.

He said he would like to see the widow get me. He said he would watch out and if they tried to come any such game on him he knowed of a place six or seven mile off to stow me in, where they might hunt till they dropped and they couldn't find me. That made me pretty uneasy again but only for a minute; I reckoned I wouldn't stay on hand till he got that chance.

The old man made me go to the skiff and fetch the things he had got. There was a fifty-pound sack of corn meal and a side of bacon, ammunition, and a four-gallon jug of whisky and an old book and two newspapers for wadding, besides some tow. I toted up a load, and went back and set down on the bow of the skiff to rest. I thought it all over and I reckoned I would walk off with the gun and some lines and take to the woods, when I run away. I guessed I wouldn't stay in one place but just tramp right across the country, mostly night-times, and hunt and fish to keep alive and so get so far away that the old man nor the widow couldn't ever find me any more. I judged I would saw out and leave that night if pap got drunk enough, and I reckoned he would. I got so full of it I didn't notice how long I was staying till the old man hollered and asked me whether I was asleep or drownded.

I got the things all up to the cabin, and then it was about dark. While I was cooking supper the old man took a swig or two and got sort of warmed up and went to ripping again. He had been drunk over in town and laid in the gutter all night, and he was a sight to look at. A body would 'a' thought he was Adam—he was just all mud. Whenever his liquor begun to work he most always went for the govment. This time he says:

"Call this a govment! why, just look at it and see what it's like. Here's the law a-standing ready to take a man's son away from him—a man's own son, which he has had all the trouble and all the anxiety and all the expense of raising. Yes, just as that man has got that son raised at last, and ready to go to work and begin to do suthin' for *him* and give him a rest, the law up and goes for him. And they call *that* govment! That ain't all, nuther. The law backs that old Judge Thatcher up and helps him to keep me out o' my property. Here's what the law does: The law takes a man worth six thousand dollars and up'ards and jams him into an old trap of a cabin like this, and lets him go round in clothes that ain't fitten for a hog. They call that govment! A man can't get his rights in a govment like this. Sometimes I've a mighty notion to just leave the country for good and all. Yes, and I *told* 'em so; I told old Thatcher so to his face. Lots of 'em heard me and can tell what I said. Says I, for two cents I'd leave the blamed country and never

come a-near it agin. Them's the very words. I says, look
at my hat—if you call it a hat—but the lid raises up
and the rest of it goes down till it's below my chin, and
then it ain't rightly a hat at all but more like my head
was shoved up through a jint o' stove-pipe. Look at it,
says I—such a hat for me to wear—one of the wealthiest
men in this town if I could git my rights.

"Oh, yes, this is a wonderful govment, wonderful.
Why, looky here. There was a free nigger there from
Ohio—a mulatter, most as white as a white man. He
had the whitest shirt on you ever see, too, and the
shiniest hat, and there ain't a man in that town that's got
as fine clothes as what he had, and he had a gold watch
and chain and a silver-headed cane—the awfulest old
gray-headed nabob in the state. And what do you think?
They said he was a p'fessor in a college and could talk
all kinds of languages and knowed everything. And that
ain't the wust. They said he could *vote* when he was at
home. Well, that let me out. Thinks I, what is the country a-coming to? It was 'lection day and I was just about
to go and vote myself if I warn't too drunk to get there,
but when they told me there was a state in this country
where they'd let that nigger vote, I drawed out. I says
I'll never vote agin. Them's the very words I said, they
all heard me, and the country may rot for all me—I'll
never vote agin as long as I live. And to see the cool
way of that nigger—why, he wouldn't 'a' give me the
road if I hadn't shoved him out o' the way. I says to the
people, why ain't this nigger put up at auction and sold?
—that's what I want to know. And what do you reckon
they said? Why, they said he couldn't be sold till he'd
been in the state six months, and he hadn't been there
that long yet. There, now—that's a specimen. They call
that a govment that can't sell a free nigger till he's been
in the state six months. Here's a govment that calls itself

a govment and lets on to be a govment, and thinks it is
a govment, and yet's got to set stock-still for six whole
months before it can take a-hold of a prowling, thieving,
infernal, white-shirted free nigger, and—"

Pap was a-going on so he never noticed where his old
limber legs was taking him to, so he went head over
heels over the tub of salt pork and barked both shins,
and the rest of his speech was all the hottest kind of
language—mostly hove at the nigger and the govment,
though he give the tub some, too, all along, here and
there. He hopped around the cabin considerable, first
on one leg and then on the other, holding first one shin
and then the other one, and at last he let out with his
left foot all of a sudden and fetched the tub a rattling
kick. But it warn't good judgment because that was the
boot that had a couple of his toes leaking out of the
front end of it; so now he raised a howl that fairly made
a body's hair raise and down he went in the dirt and
rolled there and held his toes, and the cussing he done
then laid over anything he had ever done previous. He
said so his own self afterwards. He had heard old Sow-
berry Hagan in his best days and he said it laid over
him, too, but I reckon that was sort of piling it on,
maybe.

After supper pap took the jug, and said he had enough
whisky there for two drunks and one delirium tremens.
That was always his word. I judged he would be blind
drunk in about an hour, and then I would steal the
key, or saw myself out, one or t'other. He drank and
drank and tumbled down on his blankets by and by, but
luck didn't run my way. He didn't go sound asleep but
was uneasy. He groaned and moaned and thrashed
around this way and that for a long time. At last I got
so sleepy I couldn't keep my eyes open, and so before I

knowed what I was about I was sound asleep, and the candle burning.

I don't know how long I was asleep but all of a sudden there was an awful scream and I was up. There was pap looking wild and skipping around every which way and yelling about snakes. He said they was crawling up his legs, and then he would give a jump and scream and say one had bit him on the cheek—but I couldn't see no snakes. He started and run round and round the cabin, hollering "Take him off! take him off! he's biting me on the neck!" I never see a man look so wild in the eyes. Pretty soon he was all fagged out and fell down panting, then he rolled over and over wonderful fast, kicking things every which way and striking and grabbing at the air with his hands and screaming and saying there was devils a-hold of him. He wore out by and by and laid still awhile, moaning. Then he laid stiller and didn't make a sound. I could hear the owls and the wolves away off in the woods, and it seemed terrible still. He was laying over by the corner. By and by he raised up part way and listened, with his head to one side. He says, very low:

"Tramp—tramp—tramp; that's the dead; tramp—tramp—tramp; they're coming after me; but I won't go. Oh, they're here! don't touch me—don't! hands off—they're cold; let go. Oh, let a poor devil alone!"

Then he went down on all fours and crawled off, begging them to let him alone, and he rolled himself up in his blanket and wallowed in under the old pine table, still a-begging; and then he went to crying. I could hear him through the blanket.

By and by he rolled out and jumped up on his feet looking wild, and he see me and went for me. He chased me round and round the place with a clasp-knife, calling me the Angel of Death, and saying he would kill me and then I couldn't come for him no more. I begged, and told him I was only Huck, but he laughed *such* a screechy laugh and roared and cussed and kept on chasing me up. Once when I turned short and dodged under his arm he made a grab and got me by the jacket between my shoulders and I thought I was gone, but I slid out of the jacket quick as lightning and saved myself. Pretty soon he was all tired out and dropped down with his back against the door and said he would rest a minute and then kill me. He put his knife under him, and said he would sleep and get strong and then he would see who was who.

So he dozed off pretty soon. By and by I got the old split-bottom chair and clumb up as easy as I could, not to make any noise, and got down the gun. I slipped the ramrod down it to make sure it was loaded, and then I laid it across the turnip-barrel, pointing towards pap, and set down behind it to wait for him to stir. And how slow and still the time did drag along.

VII. I FOOL PAP AND GET AWAY

"Git up! What you 'bout?"

I opened my eyes and looked around, trying to make out where I was. It was after sun-up, and I had been sound asleep. Pap was standing over me looking sour—and sick, too. He says:

"What you doin' with this gun?"

I judged he didn't know nothing about what he had been doing, so I says:

"Somebody tried to get in, so I was laying for him."

"Why didn't you roust me out?"

"Well, I tried to but I couldn't; I couldn't budge you."

"Well, all right. Don't stand there palavering all day, but out with you and see if there's a fish on the lines for breakfast. I'll be along in a minute."

He unlocked the door and I cleared out up the river-bank. I noticed some pieces of limbs and such things floating down, and a sprinkling of bark; so I knowed the river had begun to rise. I reckoned I would have great times now if I was over at the town. The June rise used to be always luck for me, because as soon as that rise begins here comes cordwood floating down, and pieces of log rafts—sometimes a dozen logs together, so all you have to do is to catch them and sell them to the woodyards and the sawmill.

I went along up the bank with one eye out for pap and t'other one out for what the rise might fetch along. Well, all at once here comes a canoe; just a beauty, too, about thirteen or fourteen foot long, riding high like a duck. I shot head-first off of the bank like a frog, clothes and all on, and struck out for the canoe. I just expected there'd be somebody laying down in it, because people often done that to fool folks, and when a chap had pulled a skiff out most to it they'd raise up and laugh at him. But it warn't so this time. It was a drift-canoe sure enough, and I clumb in and paddled her ashore. Thinks I, the old man will be glad when he sees this—she's worth ten dollars. But when I got to shore pap wasn't in sight yet, and as I was running her into a little creek like a gully, all hung over with vines and willows, I struck another idea: I judged I'd hide her good and then, 'stead of taking to the woods when I run off, I'd go down the river about fifty mile and camp in one place for good and not have such a rough time tramping on foot.

It was pretty close to the shanty and I thought I heard the old man coming all the time, but I got her hid, and then I out and looked around a bunch of willows and there was the old man down the path a piece just drawing a bead on a bird with his gun. So he hadn't seen anything.

When he got along I was hard at it taking up a "trot" line. He abused me a little for being so slow, but I told him I fell in the river and that was what made me so long. I knowed he would see I was wet, and then he would be asking questions. We got five catfish off the lines and went home.

While we laid off after breakfast to sleep up, both of us being about wore out, I got to thinking that if I could fix up some way to keep pap and the widow from trying to follow me, it would be a certainer thing than trusting to luck to get far enough off before they missed me; you see, all kinds of things might happen. Well, I didn't see no way for a while but by and by pap raised up a minute to drink another barrel of water, and he says:

"Another time a man comes a-prowling round here you roust me out, you hear? That man warn't here for no good. I'd 'a' shot him. Next time you roust me out, you hear?"

Then he dropped down and went to sleep again; what he had been saying give me the very idea I wanted. I says to myself, I can fix it now so nobody won't think of following me.

About twelve o'clock we turned out and went along up the bank. The river was coming up pretty fast, and lots of driftwood going by on the rise. By and by along comes part of a log raft—nine logs fast together. We went out with the skiff and towed it ashore. Then we had dinner. Anybody but pap would 'a' waited and seen the day through, so as to catch more stuff, but that warn't pap's style. Nine logs was enough for one time; he must shove right over to town and sell. So he locked

me in and took the skiff and started off towing the raft
about half past three. I judged he wouldn't come back
that night. I waited till I reckoned he had got a good
start, then I out with my saw and went to work on that
log again. Before he was t'other side of the river I was
out of the hole; him and his raft was just a speck on the
water away off yonder.

I took the sack of corn meal and took it to where the
canoe was hid and shoved the vines and branches apart
and put it in; then I done the same with the side of
bacon, then the whisky-jug. I took all the coffee and
sugar there was and all the ammunition; I took the wadding; I took the bucket and gourd; took a dipper and a
tin cup and my old saw and two blankets and the skillet
and the coffee-pot. I took fish-lines and matches and
other things—everything that was worth a cent. I
cleaned out the place. I wanted an ax but there wasn't
any, only the one out at the woodpile, and I knowed
why I was going to leave that. I fetched out the gun and
now I was done.

I had wore the ground a good deal crawling out of the
hole and dragging out so many things. So I fixed that as
good as I could from the outside by scattering dust on
the place, which covered up the smoothness and the
sawdust. Then I fixed the piece of log back into its place
and put two rocks under it and one against it to hold it
there, for it was bent up at that place and didn't quite
touch ground. If you stood four or five foot away and
didn't know it was sawed, you wouldn't never notice it;
and besides, this was the back of the cabin and it warn't
likely anybody would go fooling around there.

It was all grass clear to the canoe, so I hadn't left a
track. I followed around to see. I stood on the bank and
looked out over the river. All safe. So I took the gun
and went up a piece into the woods and was hunting

around for some birds when I see a wild pig; hogs soon
went wild in them bottoms after they had got away
from the prairie farms. I shot this fellow and took him
into camp.

I took the ax and smashed in the door. I beat it and
hacked it considerable a-doing it. I fetched the pig in
and took him back nearly to the table and hacked into
his throat with the ax and laid him down on the ground
to bleed; I say ground because it *was* ground—hard
packed and no boards. Well, next I took an old sack
and put a lot of big rocks in it—all I could drag—and I
started it from the pig and dragged it to the door and
through the woods down to the river and dumped it in,
and down it sunk, out of sight. You could easy see that
something had been dragged over the ground. I did
wish Tom Sawyer was there; I knowed he would take an
interest in this kind of business and throw in the fancy
touches. Nobody could spread himself like Tom Sawyer
in such a thing as that.

Well, last I pulled out some of my hair and blooded
the ax good, and stuck it on the back side and slung the
ax in the corner. Then I took up the pig and held him
to my breast with my jacket (so he couldn't drip) till I
got a good piece below the house and then dumped him
into the river. Now I thought of something else. So I
went and got the bag of meal and my old saw out of the
canoe and fetched them to the house. I took the bag to
where it used to stand and ripped a hole in the bottom
of it with the saw, for there warn't no knives and forks
on the place—pap done everything with his clasp-knife
about the cooking. Then I carried the sack about a hundred yards across the grass and through the willows
east of the house, to a shallow lake that was five mile
wide and full of rushes—and ducks too, you might say,
in the season. There was a slough or a creek leading out

of it on the other side that went miles away, I don't know where, but it didn't go to the river. The meal sifted out and made a little track all the way to the lake. I dropped pap's whetstone there too, so as to look like it had been done by accident. Then I tied up the rip in the meal-sack with a string, so it wouldn't leak no more, and took it and my saw to the canoe again.

It was about dark now; so I dropped the canoe down the river under some willows that hung over the bank and waited for the moon to rise. I made fast to a willow; then I took a bite to eat and by and by laid down in the canoe to smoke a pipe and lay out a plan. I says to my-self, they'll follow the track of that sackful of rocks to the shore and then drag the river for me. And they'll follow that meal track to the lake and go browsing down the creek that leads out of it to find the robbers that killed me and took the things. They won't ever hunt the river for anything but my dead carcass. They'll soon get tired of that and won't bother no more about me. All right; I can stop anywhere I want to. Jackson's Island is good enough for me; I know that island pretty well and nobody ever comes there. And then I can paddle over to town, nights, and slink around and pick up things I want. Jackson's Island's the place.

I was pretty tired and the first thing I knowed I was asleep. When I woke up I didn't know where I was for a minute. I set up and looked around, a little scared. Then I remembered. The river looked miles and miles across. The moon was so bright I could 'a' counted the drift-logs that went a-slipping along, black and still, hun-dreds of yards out from shore. Everything was dead quiet, and it looked late and *smelt* late. You know what I mean—I don't know the words to put it in.

I took a good gap and a stretch, and was just going to unhitch and start when I heard a sound away over the

water. I listened. Pretty soon I made it out. It was that
dull kind of a regular sound that comes from oars working in rowlocks when it's a still night. I peeped out
through the willow branches, and there it was—a skiff,
away across the water. I couldn't tell how many was in
it. It kept a-coming, and when it was abreast of me I
see there warn't but one man in it. Thinks I, maybe it's
pap, though I warn't expecting him. He dropped below
me with the current, and by and by he come a-swinging
up shore in the easy water, and he went by so close I
could 'a' reached out the gun and touched him. Well, it
was pap, sure enough—and sober, too, by the way he
laid to his oars.

I didn't lose no time. The next minute I was a-spin-
ning down-stream, soft but quick, in the shade of the
bank. I made two mile and a half and then struck out a
quarter of a mile or more towards the middle of the
river, because pretty soon I would be passing the ferry-
landing and people might see me and hail me. I got out
amongst the driftwood and then laid down in the bottom
of the canoe and let her float. I laid there and had a
good rest and a smoke out of my pipe, looking away
into the sky; not a cloud in it. The sky looks ever so
deep when you lay down on your back in the moonshine; I never knowed it before. And how far a body
can hear on the water such nights! I heard people talking at the ferry-landing. I heard what they said, too—
every word of it. One man said it was getting towards
the long days and the short nights now. T'other one said
this warn't one of the short ones, he reckoned—and then
they laughed, and he said it over again and they laughed
again; then they waked up another fellow and told him
and laughed; but he didn't laugh, he ripped out something brisk and said let him alone. The first fellow said
he 'lowed to tell it to his old woman—she would think

it was pretty good; but he said that warn't nothing to
some things he had said in his time. I heard one man
say it was nearly three o'clock and he hoped daylight
wouldn't wait more than about a week longer. After that
the talk got further and further away and I couldn't
make out the words any more, but I could hear the
mumble and now and then a laugh, too, but it seemed
a long ways off.

I was away below the ferry now. I rose up, and there
was Jackson's Island, about two mile and a half down-
stream, heavy-timbered and standing up out of the middle of the river, big and dark and solid, like a steamboat
without any lights. There warn't any signs of the bar
at the head—it was all under water now.

It didn't take me long to get there. I shot past the
head at a ripping rate, the current was so swift, and
then I got into the dead water and landed on the side
towards the Illinois shore. I run the canoe into a deep
dent in the bank that I knowed about; I had to part the
willow branches to get in, and when I made fast nobody
could 'a' seen the canoe from the outside.

I went up and set down on a log at the head of the
island and looked out on the big river and the black
driftwood and away over to the town, three mile away,
where there was three or four lights twinkling. A monstrous big lumber-raft was about a mile up-stream, coming along down, with a lantern in the middle of it. I
watched it come creeping down, and when it was most
abreast of where I stood I heard a man say, "Stern oars,
there! heave her head to stabboard!" I heard that just
as plain as if the man was by my side.

There was a little gray in the sky now; so I stepped
into the woods, and laid down for a nap before breakfast.

The sun was up so high when I waked that I judged it was after eight o'clock. I laid there in the grass and the cool shade, thinking about things and feeling rested and ruther comfortable and satisfied. I could see the sun out at one or two holes, but mostly it was big trees all about, and gloomy in there amongst them. There was freckled places on the ground where the light sifted down through the leaves, and the freckled places swapped about a little, showing there was a little breeze up there. A couple of squirrels set on a limb and jabbered at me very friendly.

I was powerful lazy and comfortable—didn't want to get up and cook breakfast. Well, I was dozing off again when I thinks I hears a deep sound of "boom!" away up the river. I rouses up and rests on my elbow and listens; pretty soon I hears it again. I hopped, and went and looked out at a hole in the leaves, and I see a bunch of smoke laying on the water a long ways up—about abreast the ferry. And there was the ferryboat full of people floating along down. I knowed what was the matter now. "Boom!" I see the white smoke squirt out of the ferryboat's side. You see, they was firing cannon over the water, trying to make my carcass come to the top.

I was pretty hungry but it warn't going to do for me to start a fire, because they might see the smoke. So I set there and watched the cannon-smoke and listened to the boom. The river was a mile wide there and it always looks pretty on a summer morning—so I was having a good enough time seeing them hunt for my remainders if I only had a bite to eat. Well, then I happened to think how they always put quicksilver in loaves of bread and float them off, because they always go right to the drownded carcass and stop there. So, says I, I'll keep a lookout and if any of them's floating around after me I'll give them a show. I changed to the Illinois edge of the island to see what luck I could have, and I warn't disappointed. A big double loaf come along and I most got it with a long stick, but my foot slipped and she floated out further. Of course I was where the current set in the closest to the shore—I knowed enough for that. But by and by along comes another one and this time I won. I took out the plug and shook out the little dab of quicksilver, and set my teeth in. It was "baker's bread"—what the quality eat, none of your lowdown corn-pone.

I got a good place amongst the leaves and set there on a log, munching the bread and watching the ferryboat and very well satisfied. And then something struck me. I says, now I reckon the widow or the parson or somebody prayed that this bread would find me, and here it has gone and done it. So there ain't no doubt but there is something in that thing—that is, there's something in it when a body like the widow or the parson prays but it don't work for me, and I reckon it don't work for only just the right kind.

I lit a pipe and had a good long smoke and went on watching. The ferryboat was floating with the current and I allowed I'd have a chance to see who was aboard when she come along, because she would come in close, where the bread did. When she'd got pretty well along down towards me, I put out my pipe and went to where I fished out the bread and laid down behind a log on the bank in a little open place. Where the log forked I could peep through.

By and by she come along, and she drifted in so close that they could 'a' run out a plank and walked ashore. Most everybody was on the boat. Pap, and Judge Thatcher, and Bessie Thatcher, and Joe Harper, and

Tom Sawyer, and his old Aunt Polly, and Sid and Mary, and plenty more. Everybody was talking about the murder but the captain broke in and says:

"Look sharp, now; the current sets in the closest here and maybe he's washed ashore and got tangled amongst the brush at the water's edge. I hope so, anyway."

I didn't hope so. They all crowded up and leaned over the rails, nearly in my face, and kept still, watching with all their might. I could see them first-rate but they couldn't see me. Then the captain sung out, "Stand away!" and the cannon let off such a blast right before me that it made me deef with the noise and pretty near blind with the smoke, and I judged I was gone. If they'd 'a' had some bullets in, I reckon they'd 'a' got the corpse they was after. Well, I see I warn't hurt, thanks to goodness. The boat floated on and went out of sight around the shoulder of the island. I could hear the booming now and then, further and further off, and by and by, after an hour, I didn't hear it no more. The island was three mile long. I judged they had got to the foot and was giving it up. But they didn't yet awhile. They turned around the foot of the island and started up the channel on the Missouri side, under steam, and booming once in a while as they went. I crossed over to that side and watched them. When they got abreast the head of the island they quit shooting and dropped over to the Missouri shore and went home to the town.

I knowed I was all right now. Nobody else would come a-hunting after me. I got my traps out of the canoe and made me a nice camp in the thick woods. I made a kind of a tent out of my blankets to put my things under so the rain couldn't get at them. I catched a catfish and haggled him open with my saw, and towards sundown I started my camp-fire and had supper.

Then I set out a line to catch some fish for breakfast.

When it was dark I set by my camp-fire smoking and feeling pretty satisfied, but by and by it got sort of lonesome, and so I went and set on the bank and listened to the current swashing along and counted the stars and drift-logs and rafts that come down and then went to bed; there ain't no better way to put in time when you are lonesome; you can't stay so, you soon get over it.

And so for three days and nights. No difference—just the same thing. But the next day I went exploring around down through the island. I was boss of it; it all belonged to me, so to say, and I wanted to know all about it, but mainly I wanted to put in the time. I found plenty strawberries, ripe and prime, and green summer grapes and green razberries; and the green blackberries was just beginning to show. They would all come handy by and by, I judged.

Well, I went fooling along in the deep woods till I judged I warn't far from the foot of the island. I had my gun along but I hadn't shot nothing, it was for protection; thought I would kill some game nigh home. About this time I mighty near stepped on a good-sized snake and it went sliding off through the grass and flowers, and I after it, trying to get a shot at it. I clipped along, and all of a sudden I bounded right on to the ashes of a camp-fire that was still smoking.

My heart jumped up amongst my lungs. I never waited for to look further, but uncocked my gun and went sneaking back on my tiptoes as fast as ever I could. Every now and then I stopped a second amongst the thick leaves and listened, but my breath come so hard I couldn't hear nothing else. I slunk along another piece further, then listened again, and so on and so on. If I see a stump, I took it for a man; if I trod on a stick and broke it, it made me feel like a person had cut one of my breaths in two and I only got half, and the short half, too.

When I got to camp I warn't feeling very brash, there warn't much sand in my craw, but I says, this ain't no time to be fooling around. So I got all my traps into my canoe again so as to have them out of sight, and I put out the fire and scattered the ashes around to look like an old last-year's camp, and then clumb a tree.

I reckon I was up in the tree two hours, but I didn't see nothing, I didn't hear nothing—I only *thought* I heard and seen as much as a thousand things. Well, I couldn't stay up there forever; so at last I got down, but I kept in the thick woods and on the lookout all the time. All I could get to eat was berries and what was left over from breakfast.

By the time it was night I was pretty hungry. So when it was good and dark I slid out from shore before moonrise and paddled over to the Illinois bank—about a quarter of a mile. I went out in the woods and cooked a supper, and I had about made up my mind I would stay there all night when I hear a *plunkety-plunk, plunkety-plunk,* and says to myself, horses coming, and next I hear people's voices. I got everything into the canoe as quick as I could, and then went creeping through the woods to see what I could find out. I hadn't got far when I hear a man say:

"We better camp here if we can find a good place; the horses is about beat out. Let's look around."

I didn't wait but shoved out and paddled away easy. I tied up in the old place, and reckoned I would sleep in the canoe.

I didn't sleep much. I couldn't, somehow, for thinking. And every time I waked up I thought somebody had me by the neck. So the sleep didn't do me no good.

By and by I says to myself, I can't live this way; I'm
a-going to find out who it is that's here on the island
with me; I'll find it out or bust. Well, I felt better right
off.

So I took my paddle and slid out from shore just a
step or two, and then let the canoe drop along down
amongst the shadows. The moon was shining, and outside of the shadows it made it most as light as day. I
poked along well on to an hour, everything still as rocks
and sound asleep. Well, by this time I was most down
to the foot of the island. A little ripply, cool breeze begun to blow, and that was as good as saying the night
was about done. I give her a turn with the paddle and
brung her nose to shore; then I got my gun and slipped
out and into the edge of the woods. I set down there on
a log and looked out through the leaves. I see the moon
go off watch and the darkness begin to blanket the river.
But in a little while I see a pale streak over the treetops
and knowed the day was coming. So I took my gun and
slipped off towards where I had run across that camp-
fire, stopping every minute or two to listen. But I hadn't
no luck somehow; I couldn't seem to find the place. But
by and by, sure enough, I catched a glimpse of fire
away through the trees. I went for it, cautious and slow.
By and by I was close enough to have a look, and there
laid a man on the ground. It most give me the fantods.
He had a blanket around his head, and his head was
nearly in the fire. I set there behind a clump of bushes
within about six foot of him and kept my eyes on him
steady. It was getting gray daylight now. Pretty soon he
gapped and stretched himself and hove off the blanket—
and it was Miss Watson's Jim! I bet I was glad to see
him. I says:

"Hello, Jim!" and skipped out.

He bounced up and stared at me wild. Then he drops

down on his knees and puts his hands together and says:

"Doan' hurt me—don't! I hain't ever done no harm to a ghos'. I alwuz liked dead people, en done all I could for 'em. You go en git in de river agin, whah you b'longs, en doan' do nufin to Ole Jim, 'at 'uz alwuz yo' fren'.' "

Well, I warn't long making him understand I warn't dead. I was ever so glad to see Jim. I warn't lonesome now. I told him I warn't afraid of *him* telling the people where I was. I talked along but he only set there and looked at me, never said nothing. Then I says:

"It's good daylight. Le's get breakfast. Make up your camp-fire good."

"What's de use er makin' up de camp-fire to cook strawbries en sich truck? But you got a gun, hain't you? Den we kin git sumfn better den strawbries."

"Strawberries and such truck," I says. "Is that what you live on?"

"I couldn' git nuffn else," he says.

"Why, how long you been on the island, Jim?"

"I come heah de night arter you's killed."

"What, all that time?"

"Yes-indeedy."

"And ain't you had nothing but that kind of rubbage to eat?"

"No, sah—nuffn else."

"Well, you must be most starved, ain't you?"

"I reck'n I could eat a hoss. I think I could. How long you ben on de islan'?"

"Since the night I got killed."

"No! W'y, what has you lived on? But you got a gun. Oh, yes, you got a gun. Dat's good. Now you kill sumfn en I'll make up de fire."

So we went over to where the canoe was and while he built a fire in a grassy open place amongst the trees, I fetched meal and bacon and coffee and coffee-pot and frying-pan and sugar and tin cups, and the nigger was set back considerable, because he reckoned it was all done with witchcraft. I catched a good big catfish, too, and Jim cleaned him with his knife and fried him.

When breakfast was ready we lolled on the grass and eat it smoking hot. Jim laid it in with all his might, for he was most about starved. Then when we had got pretty well stuffed, we laid off and lazied.

By and by Jim says:

"But looky here, Huck, who wuz it dat 'uz killed in dat shanty ef it warn't you?"

Then I told him the whole thing, and he said it was smart. He said Tom Sawyer couldn't get up no better plan than what I had. Then I says:

"How do you come to be here, Jim, and how'd you get here?"

He looked pretty uneasy, and didn't say nothing for a minute. Then he says:

"Maybe I better not tell."

"Why, Jim?"

"Well, dey's reasons. But you wouldn' tell on me ef I 'uz to tell you, would you, Huck?"

"Blamed if I would, Jim."

"Well, I b'lieve you, Huck. I—I *run off*."

"Jim!"

"But mind, you said you wouldn' tell—you know you said you wouldn' tell, Huck."

"Well, I did. I said I wouldn't and I'll stick to it. Honest *injun*, I will. People would call me a low-down Abolitionist and despise me for keeping mum—but that don't make no difference. I ain't a-going to tell, and I ain't a-going back there, anyways. So, now, le's know all about it."

"Well, you see, it 'uz dis way. Ole missus—dat's Miss Watson—she pecks on me all de time, en treats me

pooty rough, but she alwuz said she wouldn' sell me
down to Orleans. But I noticed dey wuz a nigger trader
roun' de place considable lately, en I begin to git oneasy. Well, one night I creeps to de do' pooty late, en de
do' warn't quite shet, en I hear ole missus tell de widder
she gwyne to sell me down to Orleans, but she didn'
want to, but she could git eight hund'd dollars for me,
en it 'uz sich a big stack o' money she couldn' resis'. De
widder she try to git her to say she wouldn' do it, but I
never waited to hear de res'. I lit out mighty quick, I
tell you.

"I tuck out en shin down de hill, en 'spec to steal a
skift 'long de sho' som'ers 'bove de town, but dey wuz
people a-stirring yit, so I hid in de ole tumbledown
cooper shop on de bank to wait for everybody to go
'way. Well, I wuz dah all night. Dey wuz somebody
roun' all de time. 'Long 'bout six in de mawnin' skifts
begin to go by, en 'bout eight er nine every skift dat
went 'long wuz talkin' 'bout how yo' pap come over to
de town en say you's killed. Dese las' skifts wuz full o'
ladies en genlmen a-goin' over for to see de place. Sometimes dey'd pull up at de sho' en take a res' b'fo' dey
started acrost, so by de talk I got to know all 'bout de
killin'. I 'uz powerful sorry you's killed, Huck, but I
ain't no mo' now.

"I laid dah under de shavin's all day. I 'uz hungry but
I warn't afeard; bekase I knowed ole missus en de widder wuz goin' to start to de camp-meet'n' right arter
breakfas' en be gone all day, en dey knows I goes off
wid de cattle 'bout daylight, so dey wouldn' 'spec to see
me roun' de place, en so dey wouldn' miss me tell arter
dark in de evenin'. De yuther servants wouldn' miss me,
kase dey'd shin out en take holiday soon as de ole folks
'uz out'n de way.

"Well, when it come dark I tuck out up de river road, en went 'bout two mile er more to whah dey warn't no houses. I'd made up my mine 'bout what I's a-gwyne to do. You see, ef I kep' on tryin' to git away afoot, de dogs 'ud track me; ef I stole a skift to cross over, dey'd miss dat skift, you see, en dey'd know 'bout whah I'd lan' on de yuther side, en whah to pick up my track. So I says, a raff is what I's arter; it doan' *make* no track.

"I see a light a-comin' roun' de p'int bymeby, so I wade' in en shove' a log ahead o' me en swum more'n half-way acrost de river, en got in 'mongst de driftwood, en kep' my head down low, en kinder swum agin de current tell de raff come along. Den I swum to de stern uv it en tuck a-holt. It clouded up en 'uz pooty dark for a little while. So I clumb up en laid down on de planks. De men 'uz all 'way yonder in de middle, whah de lantern wuz. De river wuz a-risin', en dey wuz a good current; so I reck'n'd 'at by fo' in de mawnin' I'd be twenty-five mile down de river, en den I'd slip in jis b'fo' daylight en swim asho', en take to de woods on de Illinois side.

"But I didn' have no luck. When we 'uz mos' down to de head er de islan' a man begin to come aft wid de lantern. I see it warn't no use fer to wait, so I slid over-board en struck out fer de islan'. Well, I had a notion I could lan' mos' anywhers, but I couldn'—bank too bluff. I 'uz mos' to de foot er de islan' b'fo' I foun' a good place. I went into de woods en jedged I wouldn' fool wid raffs no mo', long as dey move de lantern roun' so. I had my pipe en a plug er dog-leg en some matches in my cap, en dey warn't wet, so I 'uz all right."

"And so you ain't had no meat nor bread to eat all this time? Why didn't you get mud-turkles?"

"How you gwyne to git 'm? You can't slip up on um

en grab um; en how's a body gwyne to hit um wid a
rock? How could a body do it in de night? En I warn't
gwyne to show myself on de bank in de daytime."

"Well, that's so. You've had to keep in the woods all
the time, of course. Did you hear 'em shooting the
cannon?"

"Oh, yes. I knowed dey was arter you. I see um go
by heah—watched um thoo de bushes."

Some young birds come along, flying a yard or two
at a time and lighting. Jim said it was a sign it was going
to rain. He said it was a sign when young chickens flew
that way, and so he reckoned it was the same way when
young birds done it. I was going to catch some of them
but Jim wouldn't let me. He said it was death. He said
his father laid mighty sick once and some of them
catched a bird, and his old granny said his father would
die, and he did.

And Jim said you mustn't count the things you are
going to cook for dinner, because that would bring bad
luck. The same if you shook the tablecloth after sundown. And he said if a man owned a beehive and that
man died, the bees must be told about it before sun-up
next morning, or else the bees would all weaken down
and quit work and die. Jim said bees wouldn't sting
idiots; but I didn't believe that, because I had tried them
lots of times myself, and they wouldn't sting me.

I had heard about some of these things before, but
not all of them. Jim knowed all kinds of signs. He said
he knowed most everything. I said it looked to me like
all the signs was about bad luck, and so I asked him if
there warn't any good-luck signs. He says:

"Mighty few—an' *dey* ain't no use to a body. What
you want to know when good luck's a-comin' for? Want
to keep it off?" And he said: "Ef you's got hairy arms
en a hairy breas', it's a sign dat you's a-gwyne to be

rich. Well, dey's some use in a sign like dat, 'kase it's so fur ahead. You see, maybe you's got to be po' a long time fust, en so you might git discourage' en kill yo'sef 'f you didn' know by de sign dat you gwyne to be rich bymeby."

"Have you got hairy arms and a hairy breast, Jim?"

"What's de use to ax dat question? Doan' you see I has?"

"Well, are you rich?"

"No, but I ben rich wunst, and gwyne to be rich agin. Wunst I had fo'teen dollars, but I tuck to specalat'n', en got busted out."

"What did you speculate in, Jim?"

"Well, fust I tackled stock."

"What kind of stock?"

"Why, live stock—cattle, you know. I put ten dollars in a cow. But I ain' gwyne to resk no mo' money in stock. De cow up 'n' died on my han's."

"So you lost the ten dollars."

"No, I didn' lose it all. I on'y los' 'bout nine of it. I sole de hide en taller for a dollar en ten cents."

"You had five dollars and ten cents left. Did you speculate any more?"

"Yes. You know dat one-laigged nigger dat b'longs to old Misto Bradish? Well, he sot up a bank, en say anybody dat put in a dollar would git fo' dollars mo' at de en' er de year. Well, all de niggers went in but dey didn' have much. I wuz de on'y one dat had much. So I stuck out for mo' dan fo' dollars, en I said 'f I didn' git it I'd start a bank mysef. Well, o' course dat nigger want' to keep me out er de business, bekase he says dey warn't business 'nough for two banks, so he say I could put in my five dollars en he pay me thirty-five at de en' er de year.

"So I done it. Den I reck'n'd I'd inves' de thirty-five

dollars right off en keep things a-movin'. Dey wuz a nigger name' Bob, dat had ketched a wood-flat, en his marster didn' know it; en I bought it off'n him en told him to take de thirty-five dollars when de en' er de year come; but somebody stole de wood-flat dat night, en nex' day de one-laigged nigger say de bank's busted. So dey didn' none uv us git no money."

"What did you do with the ten cents, Jim?"

"Well, I 'uz gwyne to spen' it but I had a dream, en de dream tole me to give it to a nigger name' Balum— Balum's Ass dey call him for short; he's one er dem chuckleheads, you know. But he's lucky, dey say, en I see I warn't lucky. De dream say let Balum inves' de ten cents en he'd make a raise for me. Well, Balum he tuck de money, en when he wuz in church he hear de preacher say dat whoever give to de po' len' to de Lord, en boun' to git his money back a hund'd times. So Balum he tuck en give de ten cents to de po', en laid low to see what wuz gwyne to come of it."

"Well, what did come of it, Jim?"

"Nuffn never come of it. I couldn' manage to k'lect dat money no way; en Balum he couldn'. I ain' gwyne to len' no mo' money 'dout I see de security. Boun' to git yo' money back a hund'd times, de preacher says! Ef I could git de ten cents back, I'd call it squah, en be glad er de chanst."

"Well, it's all right anyway, Jim, long as you're going to be rich again some time or other."

"Yes; en I's rich now, come to look at it. I owns mysef, en I's wuth eight hund'd dollars. I wisht I had de money, I wouldn' want no mo'."

I wanted to go and look at a place right about the middle of the island that I'd found when I was exploring; so we started and soon got to it, because the island was only three miles long and a quarter of a mile wide.

This place was a tolerable long, steep hill or ridge about forty foot high. We had a rough time getting to the top, the sides was so steep and the bushes so thick. We tramped and clumb around all over it and by and by found a good big cavern in the rock, most up to the top on the side towards Illinois. The cavern was as big as two or three rooms bunched together and Jim could stand up straight in it. It was cool in there. Jim was for putting our traps in there right away but I said we didn't want to be climbing up and down there all the time.

Jim said if we had the canoe hid in a good place and had all the traps in the cavern, we could rush there if anybody was to come to the island and they would never find us without dogs. And, besides, he said them little birds had said it was going to rain, and did I want the things to get wet?

So we went back and got the canoe and paddled up abreast the cavern, and lugged all the traps up there. Then we hunted up a place close by to hide the canoe in, amongst the thick willows. We took some fish off of the lines and set them again and begun to get ready for dinner.

The door of the cavern was big enough to roll a hogshead in, and on one side of the door the floor stuck out a little bit and was flat and a good place to build a fire on. So we built it there and cooked dinner.

We spread the blankets inside for a carpet, and eat our dinner in there. We put all the other things handy

at the back of the cavern. Pretty soon it darkened up
and begun to thunder and lighten; so the birds was right
about it. Directly it begun to rain and it rained like all
fury, too, and I never see the wind blow so. It was one
of these regular summer storms. It would get so dark
that it looked all blue-black outside, and lovely; and the
rain would thrash along by so thick that the trees off a
little ways looked dim and spider-webby; and here
would come a blast of wind that would bend the trees
down and turn up the pale underside of the leaves; and
then a perfect ripper of a gust would follow along and
set the branches to tossing their arms as if they was just
wild; and next, when it was just about the bluest and
blackest—*fst!* it was as bright as glory and you'd have a
little glimpse of tree-tops a-plunging about away off
yonder in the storm, hundreds of yards further than you
could see before; dark as sin again in a second and now
you'd hear the thunder let go with an awful crash and
then go rumbling, grumbling, tumbling down the sky
towards the under side of the world, like rolling empty
barrels down-stairs—where it's long stairs and they
bounce a good deal, you know.

"Jim, this is nice," I says. "I wouldn't want to be nowhere else but here. Pass me along another hunk of fish
and some hot corn-bread."

"Well, you wouldn' 'a' ben here 'f it hadn't 'a' ben for
Jim. You'd 'a' ben down dah in de woods widout any
dinner, en gittin' mos' drownded, too; dat you would,
honey. Chickens knows when it's gwyne to rain, en so
do de birds, chile."

The river went on raising and raising for ten or twelve
days, till at last it was over the banks. The water was
three or four foot deep on the island in the low places
and on the Illinois bottom. On that side it was a good
many miles wide but on the Missouri side it was' the

same old distance across—a half a mile—because the
Missouri shore was just a wall of high bluffs.

Daytimes we paddled all over the island in the canoe.
It was mighty cool and shady in the deep woods, even
if the sun was blazing outside. We went winding in and
out amongst the trees and sometimes the vines hung so
thick we had to back away and go some other way.
Well, on every old broken-down tree you could see rabbits and snakes and such things, and when the island
had been over-flowed a day or two they got so tame, on
account of being hungry, that you could paddle right
up and put your hand on them if you wanted to, but
not the snakes and turtles—they would slide off in the
water. The ridge our cavern was in was full of them.
We could 'a' had pets enough if we'd wanted them.

One night we catched a little section of a lumber-raft
—nice pine planks. It was twelve foot wide and about
fifteen or sixteen foot long, and the top stood above
water six or seven inches—a solid, level floor. We could
see saw-logs go by in the daylight sometimes but we let
them go; we didn't show ourselves in daylight.

Another night when we was up at the head of the
island just before daylight, here comes a frame house
down, on the west side. She was a two-story, and tilted
over considerable. We paddled out and got aboard—
clumb in at an up-stairs window. But it was too dark to
see yet, so we made the canoe fast and set in her to wait
for daylight.

The light begun to come before we got to the foot of
the island. Then we looked in at the window. We could
make out a bed and a table and two old chairs and lots
of things around about on the floor, and there was
clothes hanging against the wall. There was something
laying on the floor in the far corner that looked like a
man. So Jim says:

"Hello, you!"

But it didn't budge. So I hollered again, and then Jim
says:

"De man ain't asleep—he's dead. You hold still—I'll
go en see."

He went and bent down and looked, and says:

"It's a dead man. Yes, indeedy; naked, too. He's ben
shot in de back. I reck'n he's ben dead two er three days.
Come in, Huck, but doan' look at his face—it's too
gashly."

I didn't look at him at all. Jim throwed some old rags
over him, but he needn't done it; I didn't want to see
him. There was heaps of old greasy cards scattered
around over the floor and old whisky-bottles and a
couple of masks made out of black cloth; and all over
the walls was the ignorantest kind of words and pictures
made with charcoal. There was two old dirty calico
dresses and a sun-bonnet and some women's under-
clothes hanging against the wall, and some men's clothing, too. We put the lot into the canoe; it might come
good. There was a boy's old speckled straw hat on the
floor; I took that, too. And there was a bottle that had
had milk in it and it had a rag stopper for a baby to
suck. We would 'a' took the bottle but it was broke.
There was a seedy old chest and an old hair trunk with
the hinges broke. They stood open but there warn't
nothing left in them that was any account. The way
things was scattered about we reckoned the people left
in a hurry and warn't fixed so as to carry off most of
their stuff.

We got an old tin lantern, and a butcher-knife without
any handle, and a bran-new Barlow knife worth two bits
in any store, and a lot of tallow candles, and a tin candlestick, and a gourd, and a tin cup, and a ratty old bed-
quilt off the bed, and a reticule with needles and pins

and beeswax and buttons and thread and all such truck
in it, and a hatchet and some nails, and a fish-line as
thick as my little finger with some monstrous hooks on
it, and a roll of buckskin, and a leather dog-collar, and
a horseshoe, and some vials of medicine that didn't have
no label on them; and just as we was leaving I found a
tolerable good currycomb and Jim he found a ratty old
fiddle-bow and a wooden leg. The straps was broke off
of it but, barring that, it was a good enough leg, though
it was too long for me and not long enough for Jim, and
we couldn't find the other one, though we hunted all
around.

And so, take it all around, we made a good haul.
When we was ready to shove off we was a quarter of a
mile below the island and it was pretty broad day; so I
made Jim lay down in the canoe and cover up with the
quilt, because if he set up people could tell he was a
nigger a good ways off. I paddled over to the Illinois
shore and drifted down most a half a mile doing it. I
crept up the dead water under the bank and hadn't no
accidents and didn't see nobody. We got home all safe.

x. WHAT COMES OF HANDLIN' SNAKE-SKIN

After breakfast I wanted to talk about the dead man
and guess out how he come to be killed but Jim didn't
want to. He said it would fetch bad luck and besides, he
said, he might come and ha'nt us; he said a man that
warn't buried was more likely to go a-ha'nting around
than one that was planted and comfortable. That
sounded pretty reasonable, so I didn't say no more; but
I couldn't keep from studying over it and wishing I
knowed who shot the man and what they done it for.

We rummaged the clothes we'd got and found eight

dollars in silver sewed up in the lining of an old blanket
overcoat. Jim said he reckoned the people in that house
stole the coat, because if they'd 'a' knowed the money
was there they wouldn't 'a' left it. I said I reckoned they
killed him, too, but Jim didn't want to talk about that.
I says:

"Now you think it's bad luck; but what did you say
when I fetched in the snake-skin that I found on the top
of the ridge day before yesterday? You said it was the
worst bad luck in the world to touch a snake-skin with
my hands. Well, here's your bad luck! We've raked in
all this truck and eight dollars besides. I wish we could
have some bad luck like this every day, Jim."

"Never you mind, honey, never you mind. Don't you
git too peart. It's a-comin'. Mind I tell you, it's a-comin'."

It did come, too. It was a Tuesday that we had that
talk. Well, after dinner Friday we was laying around in
the grass at the upper end of the ridge, and got out of
tobacco. I went to the cavern to get some and found a
rattlesnake in there. I killed him and curled him up on
the foot of Jim's blanket, ever so natural, thinking there'd
be some fun when Jim found him there. Well, by night
I forgot all about the snake, and when Jim flung himself
down on the blanket while I struck a light the snake's
mate was there, and bit him.

He jumped up yelling, and the first thing the light
showed was the varmint curled up and ready for another spring. I laid him out in a second with a stick, and
Jim grabbed pap's whisky-jug and begun to pour it
down.

He was barefooted and the snake bit him right on the
heel. That all comes of my being such a fool as to not
remember that wherever you leave a dead snake its
mate always comes there and curls around it. Jim told
me to chop off the snake's head and throw it away and

then skin the body and roast a piece of it. I done it, and he eat it and said it would help cure him. He made me take off the rattles and tie them around his wrist, too. He said that that would help. Then I slid out quiet and throwed the snakes clear away amongst the bushes; for I warn't going to let Jim find out it was all my fault, not if I could help it.

Jim sucked and sucked at the jug and now and then he got out of his head and pitched around and yelled, but every time he come to himself he went to sucking at the jug again. His foot swelled up pretty big and so did his leg but by and by the drunk begun to come and so I judged he was all right, but I'd druther been bit with a snake than pap's whisky.

Jim was laid up for four days and nights. Then the swelling was all gone and he was around again. I made up my mind I wouldn't ever take a-holt of a snake-skin again with my hands, now that I see what had come of it. Jim said he reckoned I would believe him next time. And he said that handling a snake-skin was such awful bad luck that maybe we hadn't got to the end of it yet. He said he druther see the new moon over his left shoulder as much as a thousand times than take up a snake-skin in his hand. Well, I was getting to feel that way myself, though I've always reckoned that looking at the new moon over your left shoulder is one of the carelessest and foolishest things a body can do. Old Hank Bunker done it once, and bragged about it, and in less than two years he got drunk and fell off of the shot-tower and spread himself out so that he was just a kind of a layer, as you may say, and they slid him edgeways between two barn doors for a coffin and buried him so, so they say, but I didn't see it. Pap told me. But anyway it all come of looking at the moon that way, like a fool.

Well, the days went along, and the river went down

between its banks again, and about the first thing we
done was to bait one of the big hooks with a skinned
rabbit and set it and catch a catfish that was as big as a
man, being six foot two inches long, and weighed over
two hundred pounds. We couldn't handle him, of
course; he would 'a' flung us into Illinois. We just set
there and watched him rip and tear around till he
drownded. We found a brass button in his stomach and
a round ball and lots of rubbage. We split the ball open
with the hatchet and there was a spool in it. Jim said
he'd had it there a long time, to coat it over so and make
a ball of it. It was as big a fish as was ever catched in
the Mississippi, I reckon. Jim said he hadn't ever seen a
bigger one. He would 'a' been worth a good deal over
at the village. They peddle out such a fish as that by the
pound in the market-house there; everybody buys some
of him; his meat's as white as snow and makes a good
fry.

Next morning I said it was getting slow and dull, and
I wanted to get a stirring-up some way. I said I reckoned
I would slip over the river and find out what was going
on. Jim liked that notion, but he said I must go in the
dark and look sharp. Then he studied it over and said,
couldn't I put on some of them old things and dress up
like a girl? That was a good notion, too. So we shortened
up one of the calico gowns and I turned up my trouser-
legs to my knees and got into it. Jim hitched it behind
with the hooks and it was a fair fit. I put on the sun-
bonnet and tied it under my chin, and then for a body
to look in and see my face was like looking down a joint
of stove-pipe. Jim said nobody would know me, even in
the daytime, hardly. I practised around all day to get the
hang of the things, and by and by I could do pretty
well in them, only Jim said I didn't walk like a girl, and

he said I must quit pulling up my gown to get at my britches-pocket. I took notice and done better.

I started up the Illinois shore in the canoe just after dark.

I started across to the town from a little below the ferry-landing, and the drift of the current fetched me in at the bottom of the town. I tied up and started along the bank. There was a light burning in a little shanty that hadn't been lived in for a long time, and I wondered who had took up quarters there. I slipped up and peeped in at the window. There was a woman about forty year old in there knitting by a candle that was on a pine table. I didn't know her face; she was a stranger, for you couldn't start a face in that town that I didn't know. Now this was lucky, because I was weakening; I was getting afraid people might know my voice and find me out. But if this woman had been in such a little town two days she could tell me all I wanted to know; so I knocked at the door, and made up my mind I wouldn't forget I was a girl.

XI. They're After Us!

"Come in," says the woman, and I did. She says: "Take a cheer."

I done it. She looked me all over with her little shiny eyes, and says:

"What might your name be?"

"Sarah Williams."

"Where'bouts do you live? In this neighborhood?"

"No'm. In Hookerville, seven mile below. I've walked all the way and I'm all tired out."

"Hungry, too, I reckon. I'll find you something."

"No'm, I ain't hungry. I was so hungry I had to stop two mile below here at a farm; so I ain't hungry no more. It's what makes me so late. My mother's down sick and out of money and everything, and I come to tell my uncle Abner Moore. He lives at the upper end of the town, she says. I hain't ever been here before. Do you know him?"

"No; but I don't know everybody yet. I haven't lived here quite two weeks. It's a considerable ways to the upper end of the town. You better stay here all night. Take off your bonnet."

"No," I says; "I'll rest awhile, I reckon, and go on. I ain't afeard of the dark."

She said she wouldn't let me go by myself, but her husband would be in by and by, maybe in a hour and a half, and she'd send him along with me. Then she got to talking about her husband, and about her relations up the river, and her relations down the river, and about how much better off they used to was, and how they didn't know but they'd made a mistake coming to our town, instead of letting well alone—and so on and so on, till I was afeard I had made a mistake coming to her to find out what was going on in the town; but by and by she dropped on to pap and the murder and then I was pretty willing to let her clatter right along. She told about me and Tom Sawyer finding the twelve thousand dollars (only she got it twenty) and all about pap and what a hard lot he was, and what a hard lot I was, and at last she got down to where I was murdered. I says:

"Who done it? We've heard considerable about these goings-on down in Hookerville, but we don't know who 'twas that killed Huck Finn."

"Well, I reckon there's a right smart chance of people *here* that 'd like to know who killed him. Some thinks old Finn done it himself "

"No—is that so?"

"Most everybody thought it at first. He'll never know how nigh he come to getting lynched. But before night they changed around and judged it was done by a runaway nigger named Jim."

"Why *he*—"

I stopped. I reckoned I better keep still. She run on, and never noticed I had put in at all:

"The nigger run off the very night Huck Finn was killed. So there's a reward out for him—three hundred dollars. And there's a reward out for old Finn, too—two hundred dollars. You see, he come to town the morning after the murder and told about it, and was out with 'em on the ferryboat hunt, and right away after he up and left. Before night they wanted to lynch him but he was gone, you see. Well, next day they found out the nigger was gone; they found out he hadn't ben seen sence ten o'clock the night the murder was done. So then they put it on him, you see; and while they was full of it, next day, back comes old Finn, and went boohooing to Judge Thatcher to get money to hunt for the nigger all over Illinois with. The judge give him some, and that evening he got drunk and was around till after midnight with a couple of mighty hard-looking strangers, and then went off with them. Well, he hain't come back sence and they ain't looking for him back till this thing blows over a little, for people thinks now that he killed his boy and fixed things so folks would think robbers done it, and then he'd get Huck's money without having to bother a long time with a lawsuit. People do say he warn't any too good to do it. Oh, he's sly, I reckon. If he don't come back for a year he'll be all right. You can't prove anything on him, you know; everything will be quieted down then, and he'll walk into Huck's money as easy as nothing."

"Yes, I reckon so, 'm. I don't see nothing in the way of it. Has everybody quit thinking the nigger done it?"

"Oh, no, not everybody. A good many thinks he done it. But they'll get the nigger pretty soon now, and maybe they can scare it out of him."

"Why, are they after him yet?"

"Well, you're innocent, ain't you! Does three hundred dollars lay around every day for people to pick up? Some folks think the nigger ain't far from here. I'm one of them—but I hain't talked it around. A few days ago I was talking with an old couple that lives next door in the log shanty, and they happened to say hardly anybody ever goes to that island over yonder that they call Jackson's Island. Don't anybody live there? says I. No, nobody, says they. I didn't say any more but I done some thinking. I was pretty near certain I'd seen smoke over there, about the head of the island, a day or two before that, so I says to myself, like as not that nigger's hiding over there; anyway, says I, it's worth the trouble to give the place a hunt. I hain't seen any smoke sence, so I reckon maybe he's gone, if it was him; but husband's going over to see—him and another man. He was gone up the river; but he got back to-day, and I told him as soon as he got here two hours ago."

I had got so uneasy I couldn't set still. I had to do something with my hands; so I took up a needle off of the table and went to threading it. My hands shook and I was making a bad job of it. When the woman stopped talking I looked up, and she was looking at me pretty curious and smiling a little. I put down the needle and thread and let on to be interested—and I was, too—and says:

"Three hundred dollars is a power of money. I wish my mother could get it. Is your husband going over there to-night?"

"Oh, yes. He went up-town with the man I was telling you of, to get a boat and see if they could borrow another gun. They'll go over after midnight."

"Couldn't they see better if they was to wait till daytime?"

"Yes. And couldn't the nigger see better, too? After midnight he'll likely be asleep and they can slip around through the woods and hunt up his camp-fire all the better for the dark, if he's got one."

"I didn't think of that."

The woman kept looking at me pretty curious, and I didn't feel a bit comfortable. Pretty soon she says:

"What did you say your name was, honey?"

"M—Mary Williams."

Somehow it didn't seem to me that I said it was Mary before, so I didn't look up—seemed to me I said it was Sarah; so I felt sort of cornered and was afeard maybe I was looking it, too. I wished the woman would say something more; the longer she set still the uneasier I was. But now she says:

"Honey, I thought you said it was Sarah when you first come in?"

"Oh, yes'm, I did. Sarah Mary Williams. Sarah's my first name. Some calls me Sarah, some calls me Mary."

"Oh, that's the way of it?"

"Yes'm."

I was feeling better then but I wished I was out of there, anyway. I couldn't look up yet.

Well, the woman fell to talking about how hard times was, and how poor they had to live, and how the rats was as free as if they owned the place, and so forth and so on, and then I got easy again. She was right about the rats. You'd see one stick his nose out of a hole in the corner every little while. She said she had to have things handy to throw at them when she was alone, or they

wouldn't give her no peace. She showed me a bar of
lead twisted up into a knot and said she was a good
shot with it generly, but she'd wrenched her arm a day
or two ago and didn't know whether she could throw
true now. But she watched for a chance and directly
banged away at a rat, but she missed him wide and
said, "Ouch!" it hurt her arm so. Then she told me to
try for the next one. I wanted to be getting away before
the old man got back, but of course I didn't let on. I got
the thing, and the first rat that showed his nose I let
drive, and if he'd 'a' stayed where he was he'd 'a' been
a tolerable sick rat. She said that was first-rate and she
reckoned I would hive the next one. She went and got
the lump of lead and fetched it back, and brought along
a hank of yarn which she wanted me to help her with. I
held up my two hands and she put the hank over them,
and went on talking about her and her husband's matters. But she broke off to say:

"Keep your eye on the rats. You better have the lead
in your lap, handy."

So she dropped the lump into my lap just at that moment, and I clapped my legs together on it and she went
on talking. But only about a minute. Then she took off
the hank and looked me straight in the face, but very
pleasant, and says:

"Come, now, what's your real name?"

"Wh-what, mum?"

"What's your real name? Is it Bill, or Tom, or Bob?—
or what is it?"

I reckon I shook like a leaf and I didn't know hardly
what to do. But I says:

"Please to don't poke fun at a poor girl like me, mum.
If I'm in the way here, I'll—"

"No, you won't. Set down and stay where you are. I
ain't going to hurt you and I ain't going to tell on you,

nuther. You just tell me your secret, and trust me. I'll
keep it; and, what's more, I'll help you. So'll my old man
if you want him to. You see, you're a runaway 'prentice,
that's all. It ain't anything. There ain't no harm in it.
You've been treated bad and you made up your mind to
cut. Bless you, child, I wouldn't tell on you. Tell me all
about it now, that's a good boy."

So I said it wouldn't be no use to try to play it any
longer, and I would just make a clean breast and tell her
everything but she mustn't go back on her promise.
Then I told her my father and mother was dead and the
law had bound me out to a mean old farmer in the country thirty mile back from the river, and he treated me so
bad I couldn't stand it no longer; he went away to be
gone a couple of days and so I took my chance and stole
some of his daughter's old clothes and cleared out, and I
had been three nights coming the thirty miles. I traveled nights and hid daytimes and slept, and the bag of
bread and meat I carried from home lasted me all the
way, and I had a-plenty. I said I believed my uncle
Abner Moore would take care of me, and so that was
why I struck out for this town of Goshen.

"Goshen, child? This ain't Goshen. This is St. Petersburg. Goshen's ten mile further up the river. Who told
you this was Goshen?"

"Why, a man I met at daybreak this morning, just as
I was going to turn into the woods for my regular sleep.
He told me when the roads forked I must take the right
hand, and five mile would fetch me to Goshen."

"He was drunk, I reckon. He told you just exactly
wrong."

"Well, he did act like he was drunk but it ain't no matter now. I got to be moving along. I'll fetch Goshen before daylight."

"Hold on a minute. I'll put you up a snack to eat. You might want it."

So she put me up a snack, and says:

"Say, when a cow's laying down, which end of her gets up first? Answer up prompt now—don't stop to study over it. Which end gets up first?"

"The hind end, mum."

"Well, then, a horse?"

"The for'rard end, mum."

"Which side of a tree does the moss grow on?"

"North side."

"If fifteen cows is browsing on a hillside, how many of them eats with their heads pointed the same direction?"

"The whole fifteen, mum."

"Well, I reckon you *have* lived in the country. I thought maybe you was trying to hocus me again. What's your real name, now?"

"George Peters, mum."

"Well, try to remember it, George. Don't forget and tell me it's Elexander before you go, and then get out by saying it's George Elexander when I catch you. And don't go about women in that old calico. You do a girl tolerable poor but you might fool men, maybe. Bless you, child, when you set out to thread a needle don't hold the thread still and fetch the needle up to it; hold the needle still and poke the thread at it; that's the way a woman most always does but a man always does t'other way. And when you throw at a rat or anything, hitch yourself up a-tiptoe and fetch your hand up over your head as awkward as you can and miss your rat about six or seven foot. Throw stiffarmed from the shoulder, like there was a pivot there for it to turn on, like a girl, not from the wrist and elbow, with your arm out to one side, like a boy. And, mind you, when a girl tries to

catch anything in her lap she throws her knees apart;
she don't clap them together, the way you did when
you catched the lump of lead. Why, I spotted you for a
boy when you was threading the needle and I contrived
the other things just to make certain. Now trot along
to your uncle, Sarah Mary Williams George Elexander
Peters, and if you get into trouble you send word to
Mrs. Judith Loftus, which is me, and I'll do what I can
to get you out of it. Keep the river road all the way and
next time you tramp take shoes and socks with you. The
river road's a rocky one, and your feet'll be in a condition when you get to Goshen, I reckon."

I went up the bank about fifty yards, and then I
doubled on my tracks and slipped back to where my
canoe was, a good piece below the house. I jumped in
and was off in a hurry. I went up-stream far enough to
make the head of the island, and then started across. I
took off the sun-bonnet, for I didn't want no blinders on
then. When I was about the middle I heard the clock
begin to strike, so I stops and listens; the sound come
faint over the water but clear—eleven. When I struck
the head of the island I never waited to blow, though I
was most winded, but I shoved right into the timber
where my old camp used to be, and started a good fire
there on a high and dry spot.

Then I jumped in the canoe and dug out for our place,
a mile and a half below, as hard as I could go. I landed,
and slopped through the timber and up the ridge and
into the cavern. There Jim laid, sound asleep on the
ground. I roused him out and says:

"Git up and hump yourself, Jim! There ain't a minute
to lose. They're after us!"

Jim never asked no questions, he never said a word,
but the way he worked for the next half an hour showed
about how he was scared. By that time everything we

had in the world was on our raft and she was ready to be shoved out from the willow cove where she was hid. We put out the camp-fire at the cavern the first thing, and didn't show a candle outside after that.

I took the canoe out from the shore a little piece and took a look; but if there was a boat around I couldn't see it, for stars and shadows ain't good to see by. Then we got out the raft and slipped along down in the shade, past the foot of the island dead still—never saying a word.

XII. "BETTER LET BLAME' WELL ALONE."

It must 'a' been close on to one o'clock when we got below the island at last, and the raft did seem to go mighty slow. If a boat was to come along we was going to take to the canoe and break for the Illinois shore; and it was well a boat didn't come, for we hadn't ever thought to put the gun in the canoe, or a fishing-line, or anything to eat. We was in ruther too much of a sweat to think of so many things. It warn't good judgment to put *everything* on the raft.

If the men went to the island I just expect they found the camp-fire I built and watched it all night for Jim to come. Anyways, they stayed away from us, and if my building the fire never fooled them it warn't no fault of mine. I played it as low-down on them as I could.

When the first streak of day begun to show we tied up to a towhead in a big bend on the Illinois side, and hacked off cottonwood branches with the hatchet, and covered up the raft with them so she looked like there had been a cave-in in the bank there. A towhead is a sand-bar that has cottonwoods on it as thick as harrow-teeth.

We had mountains on the Missouri shore and heavy
timber on the Illinois side, and the channel was down
the Missouri shore at that place, so we warn't afraid of
anybody running across us. We laid there all day, and
watched the rafts and steamboats spin down the Missouri shore, and up-bound steamboats fight the big river
in the middle. I told Jim all about the time I had jabber-
ing with that woman; and Jim said she was a smart one,
and if she was to start after us herself *she* wouldn't set
down and watch a camp-fire—no, sir, she'd fetch a dog.
Well, then, I said, why couldn't she tell her husband to
fetch a dog? Jim said he bet she did think of it by the
time the men was ready to start, and he believed they
must 'a' gone up-town to get a dog and so they lost all
that time, or else we wouldn't be here on a towhead
sixteen or seventeen mile below the village—no, indeedy, we would be in that same old town again. So I
said I didn't care what was the reason they didn't get
us as long as they didn't.

When it was beginning to come on dark we poked
our heads out of the cottonwood thicket, and looked up
and down and across; nothing in sight; so Jim took up
some of the top planks of the raft and built a snug wigwam to get under in blazing weather and rainy, and to
keep the things dry. Jim made a floor for the wigwam
and raised it a foot or more above the level of the raft,
so now the blankets and all the traps was out of reach
of steamboat waves. Right in the middle of the wigwam
we made a layer of dirt about five or six inches deep
with a frame around it for to hold it to its place; this
was to build a fire on in sloppy weather or chilly; the
wigwam would keep it from being seen. We made an
extra steering-oar, too, because one of the others might
get broke on a snag or something. We fixed up a short
forked stick to hang the old lantern on, because we must

always light the lantern whenever we see a steamboat coming down-stream, to keep from getting run over; but we wouldn't have to light it for up-stream boats unless we see we was in what they call a "crossing"; for the river was pretty high yet, very low banks being still a little under water, so up-bound boats didn't always run the channel but hunted easy water.

This second night we run between seven and eight hours, with a current that was making over four mile an hour. We catched fish and talked, and we took a swim now and then to keep off sleepiness. It was kind of solemn, drifting down the big, still river, laying on our backs looking up at the stars, and we didn't ever feel like talking loud and it warn't often that we laughed— only a little kind of a low chuckle. We had mighty good weather as a general thing and nothing ever happened to us at all—that night, nor the next, nor the next.

Every night we passed towns, some of them away up on black hillsides, nothing but just a shiny bed of lights; not a house could you see. The fifth night we passed St. Louis and it was like the whole world lit up. In St. Petersburg they used to say there was twenty or thirty thousand people in St. Louis, but I never believed it till I see that wonderful spread of lights at two o'clock that still night. There warn't a sound there; everybody was asleep.

Every night now I used to slip ashore towards ten o'clock at some little village, and buy ten or fifteen cents' worth of meal or bacon or other stuff to eat; and some-times I lifted a chicken that warn't roosting comfortable and took him along. Pap always said, take a chicken when you get a chance, because if you don't want him yourself you can easy find somebody that does, and a good deed ain't ever forgot. I never see pap when he didn't want the chicken himself but that is what he used to say, anyway.

Mornings before daylight I slipped into corn-fields and borrowed a watermelon or a mushmelon or a pun-kin, or some new corn or things of that kind. Pap always said it warn't no harm to borrow things if you was mean-ing to pay them back some time, but the widow said it warn't anything but a soft name for stealing and no de-cent body would do it. Jim said he reckoned the widow was partly right and pap was partly right, so the best way would be for us to pick out two or three things from the list and say we wouldn't borrow them any more—then he reckoned it wouldn't be no harm to borrow the others. So we talked it over all one night, drifting along down the river, trying to make up our minds whether to drop the watermelons or the cantelopes or the mush-melons, or what. But towards daylight we got it all set-tled satisfactory and concluded to drop crabapples and p'simmons. We warn't feeling just right before that but it was all comfortable now. I was glad the way it come out, too, because crabapples ain't ever good and the p'simmons wouldn't be ripe for two or three months yet.

We shot a water-fowl now and then that got up too early in the morning or didn't go to bed early enough in the evening. Take it all around, we lived pretty high.

The fifth night below St. Louis we had a big storm after midnight, with a power of thunder and lightning, and the rain poured down in a solid sheet. We stayed in the wigwam and let the raft take care of itself. When the lightning glared out we could see a big straight river ahead, and high, rocky bluffs on both sides. By and by says I, "Hel-*lo*, Jim, looky yonder!" It was a steamboat that had killed herself on a rock. We was drifting straight down for her. The lightning showed her very distinct. She was leaning over, with part of her upper deck above water, and you could see every little chimbly-guy clean and clear, and a chair by the big bell, with an old slouch hat hanging on the back of it, when the flashes come.

Well, it being away in the night and stormy and all so mysterious-like, I felt just the way any other boy would 'a' felt when I seen that wreck laying there so mournful and lonesome in the middle of the river. I wanted to get aboard of her and slink around a little, and see what there was there. So I says:

"Le's land on her, Jim."

But Jim was dead against it at first. He says:

"I doan' want to go fool'n' 'long er no wrack. We's doin' blame' well, en we better let blame' well alone, as de good book says. Like as not dey's a watchman on dat wrack."

"Watchman your grandmother," I says; "there ain't nothing to watch but the texas and the pilot-house, and do you reckon anybody's going to resk his life for a texas and a pilot-house such a night as this, when it's likely to break up and wash off down the river any minute?" Jim couldn't say nothing to that, so he didn't try. "And besides," I says, "we might borrow something worth having out of the captain's stateroom. Seegars, I bet you—and cost five cents apiece, solid cash. Steamboat captains is always rich and get sixty dollars a month, and *they* don't care a cent what a thing costs, you know, long as they want it. Stick a candle in your pocket; I can't rest, Jim, till we give her a rummaging. Do you reckon Tom Sawyer would ever go by this thing? Not for pie, he wouldn't. He'd call it an adventure—that's what he'd call it, and he'd land on that wreck if it was his last act. And wouldn't he throw style into it?—wouldn't he spread himself, nor nothing? Why, you'd

think it was Christopher C'lumbus discovering Kingdom
Come. I wish Tom Sawyer *was* here."

Jim he grumbled a little but give in. He said we
mustn't talk any more than we could help, and then talk
mighty low. The lightning showed us the wreck again
just in time, and we fetched the stabboard derrick and
made fast there.

The deck was high out, here. We went sneaking down
the slope of it to labboard in the dark, towards the
texas, feeling our way slow with our feet and spreading
our hands out to fend off the guys, for it was so dark
we couldn't see no sign of them. Pretty soon we struck
the forward end of the skylight and clumb on to it, and
the next step fetched us in front of the captain's door,
which was open, and by Jimminy, away down through
the texas-hall we see a light! and all in the same second
we seem to hear low voices in yonder!

Jim whispered and said he was feeling powerful sick,
and told me to come along. I says, all right, and was
going to start for the raft, but just then I heard a voice
wail out and say:

"Oh, please don't, boys; I swear I won't ever tell!"

Another voice said, pretty loud:

"It's a lie, Jim Turner. You've acted this way before.
You always want more'n your share of the truck and
you've always got it, too, because you've swore 't if you
didn't you'd tell. But this time you've said it jest one
time too many. You're the meanest, treacherousest
hound in this country."

By this time Jim was gone for the raft. I was just
a-biling with curiosity, and I says to myself, Tom Sawyer wouldn't back out now and so I won't either; I'm
a-going to see what's going on here. So I dropped on my
hands and knees in the little passage, and crept aft in
the dark till there warn't but one stateroom betwixt me

and the cross-hall of the texas. Then in there I see a man stretched on the floor and tied hand and foot and two men standing over him, and one of them had a dim lantern in his hand and the other one had a pistol. This one kept pointing the pistol at the man's head on the floor, and saying:

"I'd *like* to! And I orter, too—a mean skunk!"

The man on the floor would shrivel up and say, "Oh, please don't, Bill; I hain't ever goin' to tell."

And every time he said that the man with the lantern would laugh and say:

"'Deed you *ain't!* You never said no truer thing 'n that, you bet you." And once he said: "Hear him beg! and yit if we hadn't got the best of him and tied him he'd 'a' killed us both. And what *for?* Jist for noth'n'. Jist because we stood on our *rights*—that's what for. But I lay you ain't a-goin' to threaten nobody any more, Jim Turner. Put *up* that pistol, Bill."

Bill says:

"I don't want to, Jake Packard. I'm for killin' him— and didn't he kill old Hatfield jist the same way—and don't he deserve it?"

"But I don't *want* him killed, and I've got my reasons for it."

"Bless yo' heart for them words, Jake Packard! I'll never forget you long's I live!" says the man on the floor, sort of blubbering.

Packard didn't take no notice of that but hung up his lantern on a nail and started towards where I was, there in the dark, and motioned Bill to come. I crawfished as fast as I could about two yards, but the boat slanted so that I couldn't make very good time; so to keep from getting run over and catched I crawled into a stateroom on the upper side. The man come a-pawing along in the dark, and when Packard got to my stateroom, he says:

"Here—come in here."

And in he come and Bill after him. But before they got in I was up in the upper berth, cornered, and sorry I come. Then they stood there, with their hands on the ledge of the berth, and talked. I couldn't see them but I could tell where they was by the whisky they'd been having. I was glad I didn't drink whisky, but it wouldn't made such difference anyway, because most of the time they couldn't 'a' treed me because I didn't breathe. I was too scared. And, besides, a body *couldn't* breathe and hear such talk. They talked low and earnest. Bill wanted to kill Turner. He says:

"He's said he'll tell and he will. If we was to give both our shares to him *now* it wouldn't make no differ-ence after the row and the way we've served him. Shore's you're born, he'll turn state's evidence; now you hear *me*. I'm for putting him out of his troubles."

"So'm I," says Packard, very quiet.

"Blame it, I'd sorter begun to think you wasn't. Well, then, that's all right. Le's go and do it."

"Hold on a minute; I hain't had my say yit. You listen to me. Shooting's good but there's quieter ways if the thing's *got* to be done. But what *I* say is this: it ain't good sense to go court'n' around after a halter if you can git at what you're up to in some way that's jist as good and at the same time don't bring you into no resks. Ain't that so?"

"You bet it is. But how you goin' to manage it this time?"

"Well, my idea is this: we'll rustle around and gather up whatever pickin's we've overlooked in the staterooms, and shove for shore and hide the truck. Then we'll wait. Now I say it ain't a-goin' to be more'n two hours befo' this wrack breaks up and washes off down the river. See? He'll be drownded, and won't have nobody to

blame for it but his own self. I reckon that's a considerble sight better'n killin' of him. I'm unfavorable to
killin' a man as long as you can git aroun' it; it ain't good
sense, it ain't good morals. Ain't I right?"

"Yes, I reck'n you are. But s'pose she *don't* break up
and wash off?"

"Well, we can wait the two hours anyway and see,
can't we?"

"All right, then; come along."

So they started, and I lit out, all in a cold sweat, and
scrambled forward. It was dark as pitch there; but I
said, in a kind of a coarse whisper, "Jim!" and he answered up, right at my elbow, with a sort of a moan,
and I says:

"Quick, Jim, it ain't no time for fooling around and
moaning; there's a gang of murderers in yonder, and if
we don't hunt up their boat and set her drifting down
the river so these fellows can't get away from the wreck
there's one of 'em going to be in a bad fix. But if we
find their boat we can put *all* of 'em in a bad fix—for
the sheriff'll get 'em. Quick—hurry! I'll hunt the labboard side, you hunt the stabboard. You start at the
raft, and—"

"Oh, my lordy, lordy! *Raf?* Dey ain' no raf' no mo';
she done broke loose en gone!—en here we is!"

XIII. Honest Loot from the "Walter Scott"

Well, I catched my breath and most fainted. Shut up
on a wreck with such a gang as that! But it warn't no
time to be sentimentering. We'd *got* to find that boat
now—had to have it for ourselves. So we went a-quak-
ing and shaking down the stabboard side, and slow
work it was, too—seemed a week before we got to the

stern. No sign of a boat. Jim said he didn't believe he could go any farther—so scared he hadn't hardly any strength left, he said. But I said, come on, if we get left on this wreck we are in a fix, sure. So on we prowled again. We struck for the stern of the texas and found it, and then scrabbled along forwards on the skylight, hanging on from shutter to shutter, for the edge of the skylight was in the water. When we got pretty close to the cross-hall door there was the skiff, sure enough! I could just barely see her. I felt ever so thankful. In another second I would 'a' been aboard of her, but just then the door opened. One of the men stuck his head out only about a couple of foot from me, and I thought I was gone; but he jerked it in again, and says:

"Heave that blame' lantern out o' sight, Bill!"

He flung a bag of something into the boat, and then got in himself and set down. It was Packard. Then Bill *he* come out and got in. Packard says, in a low voice:

"All ready—shove off!"

I couldn't hardly hang on to the shutters, I was so weak. But Bill says:

"Hold on—'d you go through him?"

"No. Didn't you?"

"No. So he's got his share o' the cash yet."

"Well, then, come along; no use to take truck and leave money."

"Say, won't he suspicion what we're up to?"

"Maybe he won't. But we got to have it anyway. Come along."

So they got out and went in.

The door slammed to because it was on the careened side, and in a half second I was in the boat, and Jim come tumbling after me. I out with my knife and cut the rope, and away we went!

We didn't touch an oar and we didn't speak nor whisper, nor hardly even breathe. We went gliding swift along, dead silent, past the tip of the paddle-box and past the stern; then in a second or two more we was a hundred yards below the wreck and the darkness soaked her up, every last sign of her, and we was safe and knowed it.

When we was three or four hundred yards downstream we see the lantern show like a little spark at the texas door for a second, and we knowed by that that the rascals had missed their boat and was beginning to understand that they was in just as much trouble now as Jim Turner was.

Then Jim manned the oars and we took out after our raft. Now was the first time that I begun to worry about the men—I reckon I hadn't had time to before. I begun to think how dreadful it was, even for murderers, to be in such a fix. I says to myself, there ain't no telling but I might come to be a murderer myself yet, and then how would I like it? So says I to Jim:

"The first light we see we'll land a hundred yards below it or above it, in a place where it's a good hiding-place for you and the skiff, and then I'll go and fix up some kind of a yarn, and get somebody to go for that gang and get them out of their scrape, so they can be hung when their time comes."

But that idea was a failure, for pretty soon it begun to storm again and this time worse than ever. The rain poured down and never a light showed; everybody in bed, I reckon. We boomed along down the river, watching for lights and watching for our raft. After a long time the rain let up but the clouds stayed, and the lightning kept whimpering and by and by a flash showed us a black thing ahead, floating, and we made for it.

It was the raft, and mighty glad was we to get aboard of it again. We seen a light now away down to the right,

on shore. So I said I would go for it. The skiff was half
full of plunder which that gang had stole there on the
wreck. We hustled it onto the raft in a pile, and I told
Jim to float along down, and show a light when he
judged he had gone about two mile and keep it burning
till I come; then I manned my oars and shoved for the
light. As I got down towards it three or four more
showed—upon a hillside. It was a village. I closed in
above the shore light, and laid on my oars and floated.
As I went by I see it was a lantern hanging on the jack-
staff of a double-hull ferryboat. I skimmed around for
the watchman, a-wondering whereabouts he slept; and
by and by I found him roosting on the bitts forward,
with his head down between his knees. I give his shoulder two or three little shoves, and begun to cry.

He stirred up in a kind of startlish way, but when he
see it was only me he took a good gap and stretch, and
then he says:

"Hello, what's up? Don't cry, bub. What's the
trouble?"

I says:

"Pap, and mam, and sis, and—"

Then I broke down. He says:

"Oh, dang it now, *don't* take on so; we all has to have
our troubles, and this'n 'll come out all right. What's the
matter with 'em?"

"They're—they're—are you the watchman of the
boat?"

"Yes," he says, kind of pretty-well-satisfied like. "I'm
the captain and the owner and the mate and the pilot
and watchman and head deck-hand, and sometimes I'm
the freight and passengers. I ain't as rich as old Jim
Hornback, and I can't be so blame' generous and good
to Tom, Dick, and Harry as what he is and slam around
money the way he does, but I've told him a many a time

't I wouldn't trade places with him; for, says I, a sailor's life's the life for me and I'm derned if *I'd* live two mile out o' town, where there ain't nothing ever goin' on, not for all his spondulicks and as much more on top of it. Says I—"

I broke in and says:

"They're in an awful peck of trouble, and—"

"*Who* is?"

"Why, pap and mam and sis and Miss Hooker, and if you'd take your ferryboat and go up there—"

"Up where? Where are they?"

"On the wreck."

"What wreck?"

"Why, there ain't but one."

"What, you don't mean the *Walter Scott?*"

"Yes."

"Good land! what are they doin' *there*, for gracious sakes?"

"Well, they didn't go there a-purpose."

"I bet they didn't! Why, great goodness, there ain't no chance for 'em if they don't git off mighty quick! Why, how in the nation did they ever git into such a scrape?"

"Easy enough. Miss Hooker was a-visiting up there to the town—"

"Yes, Booth's Landing—go on."

"She was a-visiting there at Booth's Landing, and just in the edge of the evening she started over with her nigger woman in the horse-ferry to stay all night at her friend's house, Miss What-you-may-call-her—I disremember her name—and they lost their steering-oar and swung around and went a-floating down, stern first, about two mile, and saddle-baggsed on the wreck, and all lost, but Miss Hooker she made a grab and got aboard the wreck. Well, about an hour after dark we come

along down in our trading-scow, and it was so dark we
didn't notice the wreck till we was right on it; and so *we*
saddle-baggsed, but all of us was saved but Bill Whipple
—and oh, he *was* the best cretur!—I most wisht it had
been me, I do."

"My George! It's the beatenest thing I ever struck.
And *then* what did you all do?"

"Well, we hollered and took on but it's so wide there
we couldn't make nobody hear. So pap said somebody
got to get ashore and get help somehow. I was the only
one that could swim, so I made a dash for it, and Miss
Hooker she said if I didn't strike help sooner, come here
and hunt up her uncle, and he'd fix the thing. I made the
land about a mile below, and been fooling along ever
since, trying to get people to do something, but they
said, 'What, in such a night and such a current? There
ain't no sense in it; go for the steam-ferry.' Now if you'll
go and—"

"By Jackson, I'd *like* to, and, blame it, I don't know
but I will; but who in the dingnation's a-going to *pay* for
it? Do you reckon your pap—"

"Why *that's* all right. Miss Hooker she told me, *particular*, that her uncle Hornback—"

"Great guns; is *he* her uncle? Looky here, you break
for that light over yonder-way, and turn out west when
you git there, and about a quarter of a mile out you'll
come to the tavern; tell 'em to dart you out to Jim Hornback's and he'll foot the bill. And don't you fool around
any, because he'll want to know the news. Tell him I'll
have his niece all safe before he can get to town. Hump
yourself, now; I'm a-going up around the corner here
to roust out my engineer."

I struck for the light, but as soon as he turned the
corner I went back and got into my skiff and bailed her
out, and then pulled up shore in the easy water about

six hundred yards and tucked myself in among some wood-boats; for I couldn't rest easy till I could see the ferryboat start. But take it all around, I was feeling ruther comfortable on accounts of taking all this trouble for that gang, for not many would 'a' done it. I wished the widow knowed about it. I judged she would be proud of me for helping these rapscallions, because rapscallions and dead-beats is the kind the widow and good people takes the most interest in.

Well, before long here comes the wreck, dim and dusky, sliding along down! A kind of cold shiver went through me, and then I struck out for her. She was very deep and I see in a minute there warn't much chance of anybody being alive in her. I pulled all around her and hollered a little, but there wasn't any answer; all dead still. I felt a little bit heavy-hearted about the gang but not much, for I reckoned if they could stand it I could.

Then here comes the ferryboat; so I shoved for the middle of the river on a long down-stream slant; and when I judged I was out of eye-reach I laid on my oars, and looked back and see her go and smell around the wreck for Miss Hooker's remainders, because the captain would know her uncle Hornback would want them, and then pretty soon the ferryboat give it up and went for the shore and I laid into my work and went a-booming down the river.

It did seem a powerful long time before Jim's light showed up, and when it did show it looked like it was a thousand mile off. By the time I got there the sky was beginning to get a little gray in the east; so we struck for an island and hid the raft and sunk the skiff, and turned in and slept like dead people.

By and by, when we got up, we turned over the truck the gang had stole off of the wreck, and found boots and blankets and clothes and all sorts of other things, and a lot of books and a spy-glass and three boxes of seegars. We hadn't ever been this rich before in neither of our lives. The seegars was prime. We laid off all the afternoon in the woods talking, and me reading the books, and having a general good time. I told Jim all about what happened inside the wreck and at the ferry-boat and I said these kinds of things was adventures, but he said he didn't want no more adventures. He said that when I went in the texas and he crawled back to get on the raft and found her gone he nearly died, because he judged it was all up with *him* anyway it could be fixed, for if he didn't get saved he would get drownded, and if he did get saved, whoever saved him would send him back home so as to get the reward, and then Miss Watson would sell him South, sure. Well, he was right; he was most always right; he had an uncommon level head for a nigger.

I read considerable to Jim about kings and dukes and earls and such, and how gaudy they dressed and how much style they put on, and called each other your majesty, and your grace, and your lordship, and so on, 'stead of mister, and Jim's eyes bugged out and he was interested. He says:

"I didn' know dey was so many un um. I hain't hearn 'bout none un um, skasely, but ole King Sollermun, onless you counts dem kings dat's in a pack er k'yards. How much do a king git?"

"Get?" I says; "why, they get a thousand dollars a month if they want it; they can have just as much as they want; everything belongs to them."

"*Ain'* dat gay? En what dey got to do, Huck?"

"*They* don't do nothing! Why, how you talk! They just set around."

"No; is dat so?"

"Of course it is. They just set around—except, maybe, when there's a war; then they go to the war. But other times they just lazy around, or go hawking—just hawking and sp— Sh!—d'you hear a noise?"

We skipped out and looked; but it warn't nothing but the flutter of a steamboat's wheel away down, coming around the point; so we come back.

"Yes," says I, "and other times, when things is dull, they fuss with the parlyment, and if everybody don't go just so he whacks their heads off. But mostly they hang 'round the harem."

"'Roun' de which?"

"Harem."

"What's de harem?"

"The place where he keeps his wives. Don't you know about the harem? Solomon had one; he had about a million wives."

"Why, yes, dat's so; I—I'd done forgot it. A harem's a bo'd'n-house, I reck'n. Mos' likely dey has rackety times in de nussery. En I reck'n de wives quarrels considable, en dat 'crease de racket. Yet dey say Sollermun de wises' man dat ever live'. I doan' take no stock in dat. Bekase why: would a wise man want to live in de mids' er sich a blimblammin' all de time? No—'deed he wouldn't. A wise man 'ud take en buil' a biler-factry, en den he could shet *down* de biler-factry when he want to res'."

"Well, but he *was* the wisest man, anyway, because the widow she told me so, her own self."

"I doan' k'yer what de widder say, he *warn't* no wise man nuther. He had some er de dad-fetchedes' ways

I ever see. Does you know 'bout dat chile dat he 'uz
gwyne to chop in two?"

"Yes, the widow told me all about it."

"*Well*, den! Warn' dat de beatenes' notion in de worl'?
You jes' take en look at it a minute. Dah's de stump,
dah—dat's one er de women; heah's you—dat's de
yuther one; I's Sollermun; en dish yer dollar bill's de
chile. Bofe un you claims it. What does I do? Does I
shin aroun' mongs' de neighbors en fine out which un
you de bill *do* b'long to, en han' it over to de right one,
all safe en soun', de way dat anybody dat had any
gumption would? No; I take en whack de bill in *two*,
en give half un it to you, en de yuther half to de yuther
woman. Dat's de way Sollermun was gwyne to do wid
de chile. Now I want to ast you: what's de use er dat
half a bill?—can't buy noth'n' wid it. En what use is a
half a chile? I wouldn' give a dern for a million un um."

"But hang it, Jim, you've clean missed the point—
blame it, you've missed it a thousand mile."

"Who? Me? Go 'long. Doan' talk to *me* 'bout yo' p'ints.
I reck'n I knows sense when I sees it; en dey ain' no
sense in sich doin's as dat. De 'spute warn't 'bout a half
a chile, de 'spute was 'bout a whole chile, en de man
dat think he kin settle a 'spute 'bout a whole chile wid
a half a chile doan' know enough to come in out'n de
rain. Doan' talk to me 'bout Sollermun, Huck, I knows
him by de back."

"But I tell you you don't get the point."

"Blame de p'int! I reck'n I knows what I knows. En
mine you, de *real* p'int is down furder—it's down deeper.
It lays in de way Sollermun was raised. You take a man
dat's got on'y one er two chillen; is dat man gwyne to
be waseful o' chillen? No, he ain't; he can't 'ford it. *He*
know how to value 'em. But you take a man dat's got
'bout five million chillen runnin' roun' de house, en it's

diffunt. *He* as soon chop a chile in two as a cat. Dey's plenty mo'. A chile er two, mo' er less, warn't no consekens to Sollermun, dad fetch him!"

I never see such a nigger. If he got a notion in his head once, there warn't no getting it out again. He was the most down on Solomon of any nigger I ever see. So I went to talking about other kings, and let Solomon slide. I told about Louis Sixteenth that got his head cut off in France long time ago; and about his little boy the dolphin, that would 'a' been a king, but they took and shut him up in jail and some say he died there.

"Po' little chap."

"But some says he got out and got away, and come to America."

"Dat's good! But he'll be pooty lonesome—dey ain' no kings here, is dey, Huck?"

"No."

"Den he cain't git no situation. What he gwyne to do?"

"Well, I don't know. Some of them gets on the police, and some of them learns people how to talk French."

"Why, Huck, doan' de French people talk de same way we does?"

"*No*, Jim; you couldn't understand a word they said—not a single word."

"Well, now, I be ding-busted! How do dat come?"

"*I* don't know; but it's so. I got some of their jabber out of a book. S'pose a man was to come to you and say Polly-voo-franzy—what would you think?"

"I wouldn' think nuffn; I'd take en bust him over de head—dat is, ef he warn't white. I wouldn't 'low no nigger to call me dat."

"Shucks, it ain't calling you anything. It's only saying, do you know how to talk French?"

"Well, den, why couldn't he say it?"

"Why, he *is* a-saying it. That's a Frenchman's *way* of saying it."

"Well, it's a blame' ridicklous way, en I doan' want to hear no mo' 'bout it. Dey ain' no sense in it."

"Looky here, Jim; does a cat talk like we do?"

"No, a cat don't."

"Well, does a cow?"

"No, a cow don't, nuther."

"Does a cat talk like a cow, or a cow talk like a cat?"

"No, dey don't."

"It's natural and right for 'em to talk different from each other, ain't it?"

"Course."

"And ain't it natural and right for a cat and a cow to talk different from *us?*"

"Why, mos' sholy it is."

"Well, then, why ain't it natural and right for a *Frenchman* to talk different from us? You answer me that."

"Is a cat a man, Huck?"

"No."

"Well, den, dey ain't no sense in a cat talkin' like a man. Is a cow a man?—er is a cow a cat?"

"No, she ain't either of them."

"Well, den, she ain' got no business to talk like either one er the yuther of 'em. Is a Frenchman a man?"

"Yes."

"*Well,* den! Dad blame it, why doan' he *talk* like a man? You answer me *dat!*"

I see it warn't no use wasting words—you can't learn a nigger to argue. So I quit.

We judged that three nights more would fetch us to Cairo, at the bottom of Illinois, where the Ohio River comes in, and that was what we was after. We would sell the raft and get on a steamboat and go way up the Ohio amongst the free states, and then be out of trouble.

Well, the second night a fog begun to come on and we made for a towhead to tie to, for it wouldn't do to try to run in a fog, but when I paddled ahead in the canoe with the line to make fast, there warn't anything but little saplings to tie to. I passed the line around one of them right on the edge of the cut bank, but there was a stiff current and the raft come booming down so lively she tore it out by the roots and away she went. I see the fog closing down, and it made me so sick and scared I couldn't budge for most a half a minute it seemed to me—and then there warn't no raft in sight; you couldn't see twenty yards. I jumped into the canoe and run back to the stern and grabbed the paddle and set her back a stroke. But she didn't come. I was in such a hurry I hadn't untied her. I got up and tried to untie her, but I was so excited my hands shook so I couldn't hardly do anything with them.

As soon as I got started I took out after the raft, hot and heavy, right down the towhead. That was all right as far as it went but the towhead warn't sixty yards long, and the minute I flew by the foot of it I shot out into the solid white fog and hadn't no more idea which way I was going than a dead man.

Thinks I, it won't do to paddle, first I know I'll run into the bank or a towhead or something, I got to set still and float and yet it's mighty fidgety business to have to hold your hands still at such a time. I whooped and listened. Away down there somewheres I hears a small whoop and up comes my spirits. I went tearing after it, listening sharp to hear it again. The next time it come I see I warn't heading for it, but heading away to the right of it. And the next time I was heading away to the left of it—and not gaining on it much either, for I was flying around, this way and that and t'other, but it was going straight ahead all the time.

I did wish the fool would think to beat a tin pan, and beat it all the time but he never did, and it was the still places between the whoops that was making the trouble for me. Well, I fought along, and directly I hears the whoop *behind* me. I was tangled good now. That was somebody else's whoop, or else I was turned around.

I throwed the paddle down. I heard the whoop again; it was behind me yet but in a different place; it kept coming and kept changing its place and I kept answering, till by and by it was in front of me again and I knowed the current had swung the canoe's head downstream and I was all right if that was Jim and not some other raftsman hollering. I couldn't tell nothing about voices in a fog, for nothing don't look natural nor sound natural in a fog.

The whooping went on and in about a minute I come a-booming down on a cut bank with smoky ghosts of big trees on it, and the current throwed me off to the left and shot by amongst a lot of snags that fairly roared, the current was tearing by them so swift.

In another second or two it was solid white and still again. I set perfectly still then, listening to my heart thump, and I reckon I didn't draw a breath while it thumped a hundred.

I just give up then. I knowed what the matter was. That cut bank was an island and Jim had gone down t'other side of it. It warn't no towhead that you could float by in ten minutes. It had the big timber of a regular island; it might be five or six mile long and more than half a mile wide.

I kept quiet, with my ears cocked, about fifteen minutes, I reckon. I was floating along, of course, four or five mile an hour, but you don't ever think of that. No, you *feel* like you are laying dead still on the water, and if a little glimpse of a snag slips by you don't think to yourself how fast *you're* going, but you catch your breath and think, my! how that snag's tearing along. If you think it ain't dismal and lonesome out in a fog that way by yourself in the night, you try it once—you'll see.

Next, for about a half an hour, I whoops now and then; at last I hears the answer a long ways off, and tries to follow it but I couldn't do it, and directly I judged I'd got into a nest of towheads, for I had little dim glimpses of them on both sides of me—sometimes just a narrow channel between, and some that I couldn't see I knowed was there because I'd hear the wash of the current against the old dead brush and trash that hung over the banks. Well, I warn't long losing the whoops down amongst the towheads, and I only tried to chase them a little while, anyway, because it was worse than chasing a Jack-o'-lantern. You never knowed a sound dodge around so and swap places so quick and so much.

I had to claw away from the bank pretty lively four or five times, to keep from knocking the islands out of the river, and so I judged the raft must be butting into the bank every now and then or else it would get further ahead and clear out of hearing—it was floating a little faster than what I was.

Well, I seemed to be in the open river again by and by, but I couldn't hear no sign of a whoop nowheres. I reckoned Jim had fetched up on a snag, maybe, and it was all up with him. I was good and tired, so I laid down in the canoe and said I wouldn't bother no more. I didn't want to go to sleep, of course; but I was so sleepy I couldn't help it; so I thought I would take jest one little cat-nap.

But I reckon it was more than a cat-nap, for when I waked up the stars was shining bright, the fog was all gone, and I was spinning down a big bend stern first. First I didn't know where I was; I thought I was dreaming; and when things begun to come back to me they seemed to come up dim out of last week.

It was a monstrous big river here, with the tallest and the thickest kind of timber on both banks, just a solid wall, as well as I could see by the stars. I looked away down-stream and seen a black speck on the water. I took out after it, but when I got to it it warn't nothing but a couple of saw-logs made fast together. Then I see another speck and chased that; then another, and this time I was right. It was the raft.

When I got to it Jim was setting there with his head down between his knees, asleep, with his right arm hanging over the steering-oar. The other oar was smashed off and the raft was littered up with leaves and branches and dirt. So she'd had a rough time.

I made fast and laid down under Jim's nose on the raft, and begun to gap and stretch my fists out against Jim, and says:

"Hello, Jim, have I been asleep? Why didn't you stir me up?"

"Goodness gracious, is dat you, Huck? En you ain' dead—you ain' drownded—you's back agin? It's too good for true, honey, it's too good for true. Lemme look at you, chile, lemme feel o' you. No, you ain' dead! you's back agin, 'live en soun', jis de same ole Huck—de same ole Huck, thanks to goodness!"

"What's the matter with you, Jim? You been a-drinking?"

"Drinkin'? Has I ben a-drinkin'? Has I had a chance to be a-drinkin'?"

"Well, then, what makes you talk so wild?"

"How does I talk wild?"

"*How?* Why, hain't you been talking about my coming back, and all that stuff, as if I'd been gone away?"

"Huck—Huck Finn, you look me in de eye; look me in de eye. *Hain't* you ben gone away?"

"Gone away? Why, what in the nation do you mean? I hain't been gone anywheres. Where would I go to?"

"Well, looky here, boss, dey's sumfn wrong, dey is. Is I *me*, or who *is* I? Is I heah, or whah *is* I? Now dat's what I wants to know."

"Well, I think you're here, plain enough, but I think you're a tangle-headed old fool, Jim."

"I is, is I? Well, you answer me dis: Didn't you tote out de line in de canoe fer to make fas' to de towhead?"

"No, I didn't. What towhead? I hain't seen no towhead."

"You hain't seen no towhead? Looky here, didn't de line pull loose en de raf' go a-hummin' down de river, en leave you en de canoe behine in de fog?"

"What fog?"

"Why, *de* fog!—de fog dat's ben aroun' all night. En didn't you whoop, en didn't I whoop, tell we got mix' up in de islands en one un us got los' en t'other one was jis' as good as los', 'kase he didn' know whah he wuz? En didn't I bust up agin a lot er dem islands en have a turrible time en mos' git drownded? Now ain' dat so, boss—ain' it so? You answer me dat."

"Well, this is too many for me, Jim. I hain't seen no fog, nor no islands, nor no troubles, nor nothing. I been setting here talking with you all night till you went to

sleep about ten minutes ago, and I reckon I done the
same. You couldn't 'a' got drunk in that time, so of
course you've been dreaming."

"Dad fetch it, how is I gwyne to dream all dat in ten
minutes?"

"Well, hang it all, you did dream it, because there
didn't any of it happen."

"But, Huck, it's all jis' as plain to me as—"

"It don't make no difference how plain it is; there
ain't nothing in it. I know, because I've been here all
the time."

Jim didn't say nothing for about five minutes, but set
there studying over it. Then he says:

"Well, den, I reck'n I did dream it, Huck; but dog
my cats ef it ain't de powerfulest dream I ever see. En
I hain't ever had no dream b'fo' dat's tired me like dis
one."

"Oh, well, that's all right, because a dream does tire
a body like everything sometimes. But this one was a
staving dream; tell me all about it, Jim."

So Jim went to work and told me the whole thing
right through, just as it happened, only he painted it
up considerable. Then he said he must start in and
" 'terpret" it, because it was sent for a warning. He said
the first towhead stood for a man that would try to do
us some good, but the current was another man that
would get us away from him. The whoops was warnings
that would come to us every now and then, and if we
didn't try hard to make out to understand them they'd
just take us into bad luck, 'stead of keeping us out of it.
The lot of towheads was troubles we was going to get
into with quarrelsome people and all kinds of mean
folks, but if we minded our business and didn't talk
back and aggravate them, we would pull through and
get out of the fog and into the big clear river, which

was the free states, and wouldn't have no more trouble.

It had clouded up pretty dark just after I got on to the raft, but it was clearing up again now.

"Oh, well, that's all interpreted well enough as far as it goes, Jim," I says; "but what does *these* things stand for?"

It was the leaves and rubbish on the raft and the smashed oar. You could see them first-rate now.

Jim looked at the trash, and then looked at me, and back at the trash again. He had got the dream fixed so strong in his head that he couldn't seem to shake it loose and get the facts back into its place again right away. But when he did get the thing straightened around he looked at me steady without ever smiling, and says:

"What do dey stan' for? I's gwyne to tell you. When I got all wore out wid work, en wid de callin' for you, en went to sleep, my heart wuz mos' broke bekase you wuz los', en I didn' k'yer no mo' what become er me en de raf'. En when I wake up en fine you back agin, all safe en soun', de tears come, en I could 'a' got down on my knees en kiss yo' foot, I's so thankful. En all you wuz thinkin' 'bout wuz how you could make a fool uv ole Jim wid a lie. Dat truck dah is *trash;* en trash is what people is dat puts dirt on de head er dey fren's en makes 'em ashamed."

Then he got up slow and walked to the wigwam, and went in there without saying anything but that. But that was enough. It made me feel so mean I could almost kissed *his* foot to get him to take it back.

It was fifteen minutes before I could work myself up to go and humble myself to a nigger—but I done it and I warn't ever sorry for it afterward, neither. I didn't do him no more mean tricks, and I wouldn't done that one if I'd 'a' knowed it would make him feel that way.

We slept most all day, and started out at night, a little ways behind a monstrous long raft that was as long going by as a procession. She had four long sweeps at each end, so we judged she carried as many as thirty men, likely. She had five big wigwams aboard, wide apart, and an open camp-fire in the middle and a tall flag-pole at each end. There was a power of style about her. It *amounted* to something being a raftsman on such a craft as that.

We went drifting down into a big bend and the night clouded up and got hot. The river was very wide and was walled with solid timber on both sides; you couldn't see a break in it hardly ever, or a light. We talked about Cairo and wondered whether we would know it when we got to it. I said likely we wouldn't, because I had heard say there warn't but about a dozen houses there and if they didn't happen to have them lit up, how was we going to know we was passing a town? Jim said if the two big rivers joined together there, that would show. But I said maybe we might think we was passing the foot of an island and coming into the same old river again. That disturbed Jim—and me too. So the question was, what to do? I said, paddle ashore the first time a light showed and tell them pap was behind, coming along with a trading-scow, and was a green hand at the business and wanted to know how far it was to Cairo. Jim thought it was a good idea, so we took a smoke on it and waited.[1]

---

[1] *From here to page 307, the famous "raftsmen passage," though originally part of Huckleberry Finn, has actually been printed as a part of it in only one edition before this one. After writing about half the book, Mark Twain laid the manuscript away for some years.*

But you know a young person can't wait very well when he is impatient to find a thing out. We talked it over and by and by Jim said it was such a black night, now, that it wouldn't be no risk to swim down to the big raft and crawl aboard and listen—they would talk about Cairo, because they would be calculating to go ashore there for a spree, maybe, or anyway they would send boats ashore to buy whisky or fresh meat or something. Jim had a wonderful level head, for a nigger: he could most always start a good plan when you wanted one.

I stood up and shook my rags off and jumped into the river and struck out for the raft's light. By and by, when I got down nearly to her, I eased up and went slow and cautious. But everything was all right—nobody at the sweeps. So I swum down along the raft till I was most abreast the camp-fire in the middle, then I crawled aboard and inched along and got in among some bundles of shingles on the weather side of the fire. There was thirteen men there—they was the watch on deck of course. And a mighty rough-looking lot, too. They had a jug and tin cups, and they kept the jug moving. One man was singing—roaring, you may say; and it wasn't a nice song—for a parlor, anyway. He roared through his nose and strung out the last word of every line very long. When he was done they all fetched a

---

Later, he undertook to expand "Old Times on the Mississippi," which had been published in the Atlantic Monthly, and to make a book of it, the book we know as Life on the Mississippi. He lifted the raftsmen passage from his uncompleted manuscript and ran it as a part of Chapter III of Life on the Mississippi. When, still later, he resumed work on Huckleberry Finn and completed it, he restored the passage, only to delete it again because his nephew and publisher, Charles Webster, felt that the manuscript was too long for the book they had in mind and wanted to cut it down to nearer the length of Tom Sawyer.

kind of Injun war-whoop, and then another was sung.
It begun:

> There was a woman in our towdn,
> In our towdn did dwed'l [dwell],
> She loved her husband dear-i-lee,
> But another man twyste as wed'l.
>
> Singing too, riloo, riloo, riloo,
> Ri-too, riloo, rilay - - - e,
> She loved her husband dear-i-lee,
> But another man twyste as wed'l.

And so on—fourteen verses. It was kind of poor and
when he was going to start on the next verse one of
them said it was the tune the old cow died on, and
another one said, "Oh, give us a rest!" And another one
told him to take a walk. They made fun of him till he
got mad and jumped up and begun to cuss the crowd,
and said he could lam any thief in the lot.

They was all about to make a break for him but the
biggest man there jumped up and says:

"Set whar you are, gentlemen. Leave him to me;
he's my meat."

Then he jumped up in the air three times and cracked
his heels together every time. He flung off a buckskin
coat that was all hung with fringes and says, "You lay
thar tell the chawin-up's done," and flung his hat down,
which was all over ribbons, and says, "You lay thar tell
his sufferin's is over."

Then he jumped up in the air and cracked his heels
together again and shouted out:

"Whoo-oop! I'm the old original iron-jawed, brass-
mounted, copper-bellied corpse-maker from the wilds of
Arkansaw! Look at me! I'm the man they call Sudden
Death and General Desolation! Sired by a hurricane,
dam'd by an earthquake, half-brother to the cholera,

nearly related to the smallpox on the mother's side! Look
at me! I take nineteen alligators and a bar'l of whisky
for breakfast when I'm in robust health, and a bushel of
rattlesnakes and a dead body when I'm ailing. I split
the everlasting rocks with my glance, and I squench the
thunder when I speak! Whoo-oop! Stand back and give
me room according to my strength! Blood's my natural
drink and the wails of the dying is music to my ear. Cast
your eye on me, gentlemen! and lay low and hold your
breath, for I'm 'bout to turn myself loose!"

All the time he was getting this off, he was shaking
his head and looking fierce and kind of swelling around
in a little circle, tucking up his wristbands and now and
then straightening up and beating his breast with his
fist, saying, "Look at me, gentlemen!" When he got
through, he jumped up and cracked his heels together
three times and let off a roaring "Whoo-oop! I'm the
bloodiest son of a wildcat that lives!"

Then the man that had started the row tilted his old
slouch hat down over his right eye; then he bent stooping forward, with his back sagged and his south end
sticking out far, and his fists a-shoving out and drawing
in in front of him, and so went around in a little circle
about three times, swelling himself up and breathing
hard. Then he straightened and jumped up and cracked
his heels together three times before he lit again (that
made them cheer), and he began to shout like this:

"Whoo-oop! bow your neck and spread, for the kingdom of sorrow's a-coming! Hold me down to the earth,
for I feel my powers a-working! whoo-oop! I'm a child
of sin, *don't* let me get a start! Smoked glass, here, for
all! Don't attempt to look at me with the naked eye,
gentlemen! When I'm playful I use the meridians of
longitude and parallels of latitude for a seine and drag
the Atlantic Ocean for whales! I scratch my head with

the lightning and purr myself to sleep with the thunder! When I'm cold, I bile the Gulf of Mexico and bathe in it; when I'm hot I fan myself with an equinoctial storm; when I'm thirsty I reach up and suck a cloud dry like a sponge; when I range the earth hungry, famine follows in my tracks! Whoo-oop! Bow your neck and spread! I put my hand on the sun's face and make it night in the earth; I bite a piece out of the moon and hurry the seasons; I shake myself and crumble the mountains! Contemplate me through leather—*don't* use the naked eye! I'm the man with a petrified heart and biler-iron bowels! The massacre of isolated communities is the pastime of my idle moments, the destruction of nationalities the serious business of my life! The boundless vastness of the great American desert is my inclosed property, and I bury my dead on my own premises!" He jumped up and cracked his heels together three times before he lit (they cheered him again), and as he come down he shouted out: "Whoo-oop! bow your neck and spread, for the Pet Child of Calamity's a-coming!"

Then the other one went to swelling around and blowing again—the first one—the one they called Bob; next, the Child of Calamity chipped in again, bigger than ever; then they both got at it at the same time, swelling round and round each other and punching their fists most into each other's faces and whooping and jawing like Injuns; then Bob called the Child names and the Child called him names back again; next, Bob called him a heap rougher names and the Child come back at him with the very worst kind of language; next, Bob knocked the Child's hat off and the Child picked it up and kicked Bob's ribbony hat about six foot; Bob went and got it and said never mind, this warn't going to be the last of this thing, because he was a man that never forgot and never forgive, and so the Child better look

out for there was a time a-coming, just as sure as he was
a living man, that he would have to answer to him with
the best blood in his body. The Child said no man was
willinger than he for that time to come, and he would
give Bob fair warning, *now*, never to cross his path
again, for he could never rest till he had waded in his
blood, for such was his nature, though he was sparing
him now on account of his family, if he had one.

Both of them was edging away in different directions,
growling and shaking their heads and going on about
what they was going to do, but a little black-whiskered
chap skipped up and says:

"Come back here, you couple of chicken-livered
cowards, and I'll thrash the two of ye!"

And he done it, too. He snatched them, he jerked
them this way and that, he booted them around, he
knocked them sprawling faster than they could get up.
Why, it warn't two minutes till they begged like dogs—
and how the other lot did yell and laugh and clap their
hands all the way through and shout, "Sail in, Corpse-
Maker!" "Hi! at him again, Child of Calamity!" "Bully
for you, little Davy!" Well, it was a perfect powwow for
a while. Bob and the Child had red noses and black eyes
when they got through. Little Davy made them own up
that they was sneaks and cowards and not fit to eat with
a dog or drink with a nigger; then Bob and the Child
shook hands with each other, very solemn, and said they
had always respected each other and was willing to let
bygones be bygones. So then they washed their faces in
the river, and just then there was a loud order to stand
by for a crossing, and some of them went forward to
man the sweeps there and the rest went aft to handle the
after sweeps.

I lay still and waited for fifteen minutes and had a
smoke out of a pipe that one of them left in reach; then

the crossing was finished and they stumped back and had a drink around and went to talking and singing again. Next they got out an old fiddle, and one played and another patted juba and the rest turned themselves loose on a regular old-fashioned keelboat breakdown. They couldn't keep that up very long without getting winded, so by and by they settled around the jug again.

They sung "Jolly, Jolly Raftsman's the Life for Me," with a rousing chorus, and then they got to talking about differences betwixt hogs and their different kind of habits; and next about women and their different ways; and next about the best ways to put out houses that was afire; and next about what ought to be done with the Injuns; and next about what a king had to do and how much he got; and next about how to make cats fight; and next about what to do when a man has fits; and next about differences betwixt clear-water rivers and muddy-water ones. The man they called Ed said the muddy Mississippi water was wholesomer to drink than the clear water of the Ohio; he said if you let a pint of this yaller Mississippi water settle, you would have about a half to three-quarters of an inch of mud in the bottom, according to the stage of the river, and then it warn't no better than Ohio water—what you wanted to do was to keep it stirred up—and when the river was low, keep mud on hand to put in and thicken the water up the way it ought to be.

The Child of Calamity said that was so; he said there was nutritiousness in the mud, and a man that drunk Mississippi water could grow corn in his stomach if he wanted to. He says:

"You look at the graveyards; that tells the tale. Trees won't grow worth shucks in a Cincinnati graveyard, but in a Sent Louis graveyard they grow upwards of eight hundred foot high. It's all on account of the water the people drunk before they laid up. A Cincinnati corpse don't richen a soil any."

And they talked about how Ohio water didn't like to mix with Mississippi water. Ed said if you take the Mississippi on a rise when the Ohio is low, you'll find a wide band of clear water all the way down the east side of the Mississippi for a hundred mile or more, and the minute you get out a quarter of a mile from shore and pass the line, it is all thick and yaller the rest of the way across. Then they talked about how to keep tobacco from getting moldy, and from that they went into ghosts and told about a lot that other folks had seen; but Ed says:

"Why don't you tell something that you've seen yourselves? Now let me have a say. Five years ago I was on a raft as big as this, and right along here it was a bright moonshiny night and I was on watch and boss of the stabboard oar forrard, and one of my pards was a man named Dick Allbright, and he come along to where I was sitting, forrard—gaping and stretching, he was—and stooped down on the edge of the raft and washed his face in the river, and come and set down by me and got out his pipe, and had just got it filled when he looks up and says:

" 'Why looky-here,' he says, 'ain't that Buck Miller's place, over yander in the bend?'

" 'Yes,' says I, 'it is—why?' He laid his pipe down and leaned his head on his hand and says:

" 'I thought we'd be furder down.' I says:

" 'I thought it, too, when I went off watch'—we was standing six hours on and six off—'but the boys told me,' I says, 'that the raft didn't seem to hardly move, for the last hour,' says I, 'though she's a-slipping along all right now,' says I. He give a kind of a groan, and says:

" 'I've seed a raft act so before, along here,' he says,

" 'pears to me the current has most quit above the head of this bend durin' the last two years,' he says.

"Well, he raised up two or three times and looked away off and around on the water. That started me at it, too. A body is always doing what he sees somebody else doing, though there mayn't be no sense in it. Pretty soon I see a black something floating on the water away off to stabboard and quartering behind us. I see he was looking at it, too. I says:

" 'What's that?'

"He says, sort of pettish: " 'Tain't nothing but an old empty bar'l.'

" 'An empty bar'l!' says I, 'why,' says I, 'a spy-glass is a fool to *your* eyes. How can you tell it's an empty bar'l?' He says:

" 'I don't know; I reckon it ain't a bar'l but I thought it might be,' says he.

" 'Yes,' I says, 'so it might be and it might be anything else, too; a body can't tell nothing about it, such a distance as that,' I says.

"We hadn't nothing else to do, so we kept on watching it. By and by I says:

" 'Why, looky-here, Dick Allbright, that thing's a-gaining on us, I believe.'

"He never said nothing. The thing gained and gained, and I judged it must be a dog that was about tired out. Well, we swung down into the crossing and the thing floated across the bright streak of the moonshine, and by George, it *was* a bar'l. Says I:

" 'Dick Allbright, what made you think that thing was a bar'l, when it was half a mile off?' says I. Says he:

" 'I don't know.' Says I:

" 'You tell me, Dick Allbright.' Says he:

" 'Well, I knowed it was a bar'l; I've seen it before; lots has seen it; they says it's a ha'nted bar'l.'

"I called the rest of the watch, and they come and stood there and I told them what Dick said. It floated right along abreast, now, and didn't gain any more. It was about twenty foot off. Some was for having it aboard but the rest didn't want to. Dick Allbright said rafts that had fooled with it had got bad luck by it. The captain of the watch said he didn't believe in it. He said he reckoned the bar'l gained on us because it was in a little better current than what we was. He said it would leave by and by.

"So then we went to talking about other things, and we had a song and then a breakdown; and after that the captain of the watch called for another song; but it was clouding up now and the bar'l stuck right thar in the same place, and the song didn't seem to have much warm-up to it, somehow, and so they didn't finish it and there warn't any cheers; but it sort of dropped flat, and nobody said anything for a minute. Then everybody tried to talk at once and one chap got off a joke, but it warn't no use, they didn't laugh, and even the chap that made the joke didn't laugh at it, which ain't usual. We all just settled down glum, and watched the bar'l and was oneasy and oncomfortable. Well, sir, it shut down black and still, and then the wind began to moan around, and next the lightning began to play and the thunder to grumble. And pretty soon there was a regular storm, and in the middle of it a man that was running aft stumbled and fell and sprained his ankle so that he had to lay up. This made the boys shake their heads. And every time the lightning come, there was that bar'l with the blue lights winking around it. We was always on the lookout for it. But by and by, toward dawn, she was gone. When the day come we couldn't see her anywhere, and we warn't sorry, either.

"But next night about half past nine, when there was songs and high jinks going on, here she comes again and took her old roost on the stabboard side. There warn't no more high jinks. Everybody got solemn; nobody talked; you couldn't get anybody to do anything but set around moody and look at the bar'l. It begun to cloud up again. When the watch changed, the off watch stayed up, 'stead of turning in. The storm ripped and roared around all night, and in the middle of it another man tripped and sprained his ankle and had to knock off. The bar'l left toward day and nobody see it go.

"Everybody was sober and down in the mouth all day. I don't mean the kind of sober that comes of leaving liquor alone—not that. They was quiet, but they all drunk more than usual—not together, but each man sidled off and took it private, by himself.

"After dark the off watch didn't turn in; nobody sung, nobody talked; the boys didn't scatter around, neither; they sort of huddled together, forrard; and for two hours they set there, perfectly still, looking steady in the one direction and heaving a sigh once in a while. And then, here comes the bar'l again. She took up her old place. She stayed there all night; nobody turned in. The storm come on again, after midnight. It got awful dark; the rain poured down; hail, too; the thunder boomed and roared and bellowed; the wind blowed a hurricane; and the lightning spread over everything in big sheets of glare and showed the whole raft as plain as day; and the river lashed up white as milk as far as you could see for miles, and there was that bar'l jiggering along, same as ever. The captain ordered the watch to man the after sweeps for a crossing and nobody would go—no more sprained ankles for them, they said. They wouldn't even *walk* aft. Well, then, just then the sky split wide open, with a crash, and the lightning killed two men of the after watch and crippled two more. Crippled them how, say you? Why, *sprained their ankles!*

"The bar'l left in the dark betwixt lightnings, toward dawn. Well, not a body eat a bite at breakfast that morning. After that the men loafed around in twos and threes, and talked low together. But none of them herded with Dick Allbright. They all give him the cold shake. If he come around where any of the men was, they split up and sidled away. They wouldn't man the sweeps with him. The captain had all the skiffs hauled up on the raft, alongside of his wigwam, and wouldn't let the dead men be took ashore to be planted; he didn't believe a man that got ashore would come back, and he was right.

"After night come, you could see pretty plain that there was going to be trouble if that bar'l come again; there was such a muttering going on. A good many wanted to kill Dick Allbright, because he'd seen the bar'l on other trips and that had an ugly look. Some wanted to put him ashore. Some said: 'Let's all go ashore in a pile, if the bar'l comes again.'

"This kind of whispers was still going on, the men being bunched together forrard watching for the bar'l, when lo and behold you! here she comes again. Down she comes, slow and steady, and settles into her old tracks. You could 'a' heard a pin drop. Then up comes the captain, and says:

" 'Boys, don't be a pack of children and fools; I don't want this bar'l to be dogging us all the way to Orleans, and *you* don't: Well, then, how's the best way to stop it? Burn it up—that's the way. I'm going to fetch it aboard,' he says. And before anybody could say a word, in he went.

"He swum to it and as he come pushing it to the raft, the men spread to one side. But the old man got it aboard and busted in the head, and there was a baby in it! Yes, sir; a stark-naked baby. It was Dick Allbright's baby; he owned up and said so.

" 'Yes,' he says, a-leaning over it, 'yes, it is my own lamented darling, my poor lost Charles William All-bright deceased,' says he—for he could curl his tongue around the bulliest words in the language when he was a mind to, and lay them before you without a jint started anywheres. Yes, he said, he used to live up at the head of this bend and one night he choked his child, which was crying, not intending to kill it—which was prob'ly a lie—and then he was scared, and buried it in a bar'l before his wife got home, and off he went and struck the northern trail and went to rafting, and this was the third year that the bar'l had chased him. He said the bad luck always begun light and lasted till four men was killed, and then the bar'l didn't come any more after that. He said if the men would stand it one more night—and was a-going on like that—but the men had got enough. They started to get out a boat to take him ashore and lynch him, but he grabbed the little child all of a sudden and jumped overboard with it, hugged up to his breast and shedding tears, and we never see him again in this life, poor old suffering soul, nor Charles William neither."

"*Who* was shedding tears?" says Bob; "was it All-bright or the baby?"

"Why, Allbright, of course; didn't I tell you the baby was dead? Been dead three years—how could it cry?"

"Well, never mind how it could cry—how could it *keep* all that time?" says Davy. "You answer me that."

"I don't know how it done it," says Ed. "It done it, though—that's all I know about it."

"Say—what did they do with the bar'l?" says the Child of Calamity.

"Why, they hove it overboard and it sunk like a chunk of lead."

"Edward, did the child look like it was choked?" says one.

"Did it have its hair parted?" says another.

"What was the brand on that bar'l, Eddy?" says a fellow they called Bill.

"Have you got the papers for them statistics, Edmund?" says Jimmy.

"Say, Edwin, was you one of the men that was killed by the lightning?" says Davy.

"Him? Oh, no! he was both of 'em," says Bob. Then they all haw-hawed.

"Say, Edward, don't you reckon you'd better take a pill? You look bad—don't you feel pale?" says the Child of Calamity.

"Oh, come, now, Eddy," says Jimmy, "show up; you must 'a' kept part of that bar'l to prove the thing by. Show us the bung-hole—*do*—and we'll all believe you."

"Say, boys," says Bill, "less divide it up. Thar's thirteen of us. I can swaller a thirteenth of the yarn, if you can worry down the rest."

Ed got up mad and said they could all go to some place which he ripped out pretty savage, and then walked off aft, cussing to himself, and they yelling and jeering at him and roaring and laughing so you could hear them a mile.

"Boys, we'll split a watermelon on that," says the Child of Calamity; and he came rummaging around in the dark amongst the shingle bundles where I was, and put his hand on me. I was warm and soft and naked; so he says "Ouch!" and jumped back.

"Fetch a lantern or a chunk of fire here, boys—there's a snake here as big as a cow!"

So they run there with a lantern and crowded up and looked in on me.

"Come out of that, you beggar!" says one.

"Who are you?" says another.

"What are you after here? Speak up prompt, or overboard you go."

"Snake him out, boys. Snatch him out by the heels."

I began to beg and crept out amongst them trembling. They looked me over, wondering, and the Child of Calamity says:

"A cussed thief! Lend a hand and less heave him overboard!"

"No," says Big Bob, "less get out the paint-pot and paint him a sky-blue all over from head to heel, and *then* heave him over."

"Good! that's it. Go for the paint, Jimmy."

When the paint come and Bob took the brush and was just going to begin, the others laughing and rubbing their hands, I begun to cry, and that sort of worked on Davy and he says:

"'Vast there. He's nothing but a cub. I'll paint the man that teches him!"

So I looked around on them, and some of them grumbled and growled and Bob put down the paint, and the others didn't take it up.

"Come here to the fire, and less see what you're up to here," says Davy. "Now set down there and give an account of yourself. How long have you been aboard here?"

"Not over a quarter of a minute, sir," says I.

"How did you get dry so quick?"

"I don't know, sir. I'm always that way, mostly."

"Oh, you are, are you? What's your name?"

I warn't going to tell my name. I didn't know what to say, so I just says:

"Charles William Allbright, sir."

Then they roared—the whole crowd; and I was mighty glad I said that because, maybe, laughing would get them in a better humor.

When they got done laughing, Davy says:

"It won't hardly do, Charles William. You couldn't have growed this much in five year and you was a baby when you come out of the bar'l, you know, and dead at that. Come, now, tell a straight story and nobody'll hurt you, if you ain't up to anything wrong. What *is* your name?"

"Aleck Hopkins, sir. Aleck James Hopkins."

"Well, Aleck, where did you come from, here?"

"From a trading-scow. She lays up the bend yonder. I was born on her. Pap has traded up and down here all his life, and he told me to swim off here, because when you went by he said he would like to get some of you to speak to a Mr. Jonas Turner, in Cairo, and tell him—"

"Oh, come!"

"Yes, sir, it's as true as the world. Pap he says—"

"Oh, your grandmother!"

They all laughed and I tried again to talk, but they broke in on me and stopped me.

"Now, looky-here," says Davy, "you're scared, and so you talk wild. Honest, now, do you live in a scow, or is it a lie?"

"Yes, sir, in a trading-scow. She lays up at the head of the bend. But I warn't born in her. It's our first trip."

"Now you're talking! What did you come aboard here for? To steal?"

"No, sir, I didn't. It was only to get a ride on the raft. All boys does that."

"Well, I know that. But what did you hide for?"

"Sometimes they drive the boys off."

"So they do. They might steal. Looky-here, if we let you off this time, will you keep out of these kind of scrapes hereafter?"

" 'Deed I will, boss. You try me."

"All right, then. You ain't but little ways from shore. Overboard with you and don't you make a fool of yourself another time this way. Blast it, boy, some raftsmen would rawhide you till you were black and blue!"

I didn't wait to kiss good-by, but went overboard and broke for shore. When Jim come along by and by, the big raft was away out of sight around the point. I swum out and got aboard, and was mighty glad to see home again.

There warn't nothing to do now but to look out sharp for the town and not pass it without seeing it. He said he'd be mighty sure to see it because he'd be a free man the minute he seen it, but if he missed it he'd be in a slave country again and no more show for freedom. Every little while he jumps up and says:

"Dah she is!"

But it warn't. It was Jack-o-lanterns or lightning-bugs, so he set down again and went to watching, same as before. Jim said it made him all over trembly and feverish to be so close to freedom. Well, I can tell you it made me all over trembly and feverish, too, to hear him, because I begun to get it through my head that he *was* most free—and who was to blame for it? Why, *me*. I couldn't get that out of my conscience, no how nor no way. It got to troubling me so I couldn't rest; I couldn't stay still in one place. It hadn't ever come home to me before, what this thing was that I was doing. But now it did, and it stayed with me and scorched me more and more. I tried to make out to myself that *I* warn't to blame because *I* didn't run Jim off from his rightful owner, but it warn't no use, conscience up and says, every time, "But you knowed he was running for his freedom, and you could 'a' paddled ashore and told somebody." That was so—I couldn't get around that no way. That was where it pinched. Conscience says to me, "What had poor Miss Watson done to you that you could see her nigger go off right under your eyes and never say one single word? What did that poor old woman do to you that you could treat her so mean? Why, she tried to learn you your book, she tried to learn you your manners, she tried to be good to you every way she knowed how. *That's* what she done."

I got to feeling so mean and so miserable I most wished I was dead. I fidgeted up and down the raft, abusing myself to myself, and Jim was fidgeting up and down past me. We neither of us could keep still. Every time he danced around and says, "Dah's Cairo!" it went through me like a shot, and I thought if it *was* Cairo I reckoned I would die of miserableness.

Jim talked out loud all the time while I was talking to myself. He was saying how the first thing he would do when he got to a free state he would go to saving up money and never spend a single cent, and when he got enough he would buy his wife, which was owned on a farm close to where Miss Watson lived, and then they would both work to buy the two children, and if their master wouldn't sell them, they'd get an Ab'litionist to go and steal them.

It most froze me to hear such talk. He wouldn't ever dared to talk such talk in his life before. Just see what a difference it made in him the minute he judged he was about free. It was according to the old saying, "Give a nigger an inch and he'll take an ell." Thinks I, this is what comes of my not thinking. Here was this nigger, which I had as good as helped to run away, coming right out flat-footed and saying he would steal his children—children that belonged to a man I didn't even know; a man that hadn't ever done me no harm.

I was sorry to hear Jim say that, it was such a lowering of him. My conscience got to stirring me up hotter than ever, until at last I says to it, "Let up on me—it ain't too late yet—I'll paddle ashore at the first light and tell." I felt easy and happy and light as a feather right off. All my troubles was gone. I went to looking out sharp for a light, and sort of singing to myself. By and by one showed. Jim sings out:

"We's safe, Huck, we's safe! Jump up and crack yo' heels! Dat's de good ole Cairo at las', I jis knows it!"

I says:

"I'll take the canoe and go see, Jim. It mightn't be, you know."

He jumped and got the canoe ready and put his old coat in the bottom for me to set on and give me the paddle; and as I shoved off, he says:

"Pooty soon I'll be a-shout'n' for joy, en I'll say, it's all on accounts o' Huck; I's a free man, en I couldn't ever ben free ef it hadn' ben for Huck; Huck done it. Jim won't ever forgit you, Huck; you's de bes' fren' Jim's ever had; en you's de *only* fren' ole Jim's got now."

I was paddling off, all in a sweat to tell on him, but when he says this, it seemed to kind of take the tuck all out of me. I went along slow then, and I warn't right down certain whether I was glad I started or whether I warn't. When I was fifty yards off, Jim says:

"Dah you goes, de ole true Huck; de on'y white genl-man dat ever kep' his promise to ole Jim."

Well, I just felt sick. But I says, I *got* to do it—I can't get *out* of it. Right then along comes a skiff with two men in it with guns, and they stopped and I stopped. One of them says:

"What's that yonder?"

"A piece of a raft," I says.

"Do you belong on it?"

"Yes, sir."

"Any men on it?"

"Only one, sir."

"Well, there's five niggers run off to-night up yonder, above the head of the bend. Is your man white or black?"

I didn't answer up prompt. I tried to, but the words wouldn't come. I tried for a second or two to brace up and out with it, but I warn't man enough—hadn't the spunk of a rabbit. I see I was weakening; so I just give up trying, and up and says:

"He's white."

"I reckon we'll go and see for ourselves."

"I wish you would," says I, "because it's pap that's there, and maybe you'd help me tow the raft ashore where the light is. He's sick—and so is mam and Mary Ann."

"Oh, the devil! we're in a hurry, boy. But I s'pose we've got to. Come, buckle to your paddle, and let's get along."

I buckled to my paddle and they laid to their oars. When we had made a stroke or two, I says:

"Pap'll be mighty much obleeged to you, I can tell you. Everybody goes away when I want them to help me tow the raft ashore, and I can't do it by myself."

"Well, that's infernal mean. Odd, too. Say, boy, what's the matter with your father?"

"It's the—a—the—well, it ain't anything much."

They stopped pulling. It warn't but a mighty little ways to the raft now. One says:

"Boy, that's a lie. What *is* the matter with your pap?
Answer up square now, and it'll be the better for you."

"I will, sir, I will, honest—but don't leave us, please.
It's the—the— Gentlemen, if you'll only pull ahead, and
let me heave you the headline, you won't have to come
a-near the raft—please do."

"Set her back, John, set her back!" says one. They
backed water. "Keep away, boy—keep to looard. Confound it, I just expect the wind has blowed it to us.
Your pap's got the smallpox and you know it precious
well. Why didn't you come out and say so? Do you want
to spread it all over?"

"Well," says I, a-blubbering, "I've told everybody
before, and they just went away and left us."

"Poor devil, there's something in that. We are right
down sorry for you, but we—well, hang it, we don't
want the smallpox, you see. Look here, I'll tell you what
to do. Don't you try to land by yourself, or you'll smash
everything to pieces. You float along down about twenty
miles and you'll come to a town on the left-hand side of
the river. It will be long after sun-up then, and when you
ask for help you tell them your folks are all down with
chills and fever. Don't be a fool again and let people
guess what is the matter. Now we're trying to do you a
kindness; so you just put twenty miles between us, that's
a good boy. It wouldn't do any good to land yonder
where the light is—it's only a wood-yard. Say, I reckon
your father's poor, and I'm bound to say he's in pretty
hard luck. Here, I'll put a twenty-dollar gold piece on
this board, and you get it when it floats by. I feel mighty
mean to leave you, but my kingdom! it won't do to fool
with smallpox, don't you see?"

"Hold on, Parker," says the man, "here's a twenty to
put on the board for me. Good-by, boy; you do as Mr.
Parker told you, and you'll be all right."

"That's so, my boy—good-by, good-by. If you see any runaway niggers you get help and nab them, and you can make some money by it."

"Good-by, sir," says I, "I won't let no runaway niggers get by me if I can help it."

They went off and I got aboard the raft, feeling bad and low because I knowed very well I had done wrong, and I see it warn't no use for me to try to learn to do right; a body that don't get *started* right when he's little ain't got no show—when the pinch comes there ain't nothing to back him up and keep him to his work, and so he gets beat. Then I thought a minute and says to myself, hold on; s'pose you'd 'a' done right and give Jim up, would you felt better than what you do now? No, says I, I'd feel bad—I'd feel just the same way I do now. Well, then, says I, what's the use you learning to do right when it's troublesome to do right and ain't no trouble to do wrong, and the wages is just the same? I was stuck. I couldn't answer that. So I reckoned I wouldn't bother no more about it, but after this always do whichever come handiest at the time.

I went into the wigwam; Jim warn't there. I looked all around; he warn't anywhere. I says:

"Jim!"

"Here I is, Huck. Is dey out o' sight yit? Don't talk loud."

He was in the river under the stern oar, with just his nose out. I told him they was out of sight, so he come aboard. He says:

"I was a-listenin' to all de talk, en I slips into de river en was gwyne to shove for sho' if dey come aboard. Den I was gwyne to swim to de raf' agin when dey was gone. But lawsy, how you did fool 'em, Huck! Dat *wuz* de smartes' dodge! I tell you, chile, I 'spec it save' ole Jim— ole Jim ain't gwyne to forgit you for dat, honey."

Then we talked about the money. It was a pretty good raise—twenty dollars apiece. Jim said we could take deck passage on a steamboat now, and the money would last us as far as we wanted to go in the free states. He said twenty mile more warn't far for the raft to go, but he wished we was already there.

Towards daybreak we tied up, and Jim was mighty particular about hiding the raft good. Then he worked all day fixing things in bundles, and getting all ready to quit rafting.

That night about ten we hove in sight of the lights of a town away down in a left-hand bend.

I went off in the canoe to ask about it. Pretty soon I found a man out in the river with a skiff, setting a trotline. I ranged up and says:

"Mister, is that town Cairo?"

"Cairo? no. You must be a blame' fool."

"What town is it, mister?"

"If you want to know, go and find out. If you stay here botherin' around me for about a half a minute longer you'll get something you won't want."

I paddled to the raft. Jim was awful disappointed, but I said never mind, Cairo would be the next place, I reckoned.

We passed another town before daylight, and I was going out again; but it was high ground, so I didn't go. No high ground about Cairo, Jim said. I had forgot it. We laid up for the day on a towhead tolerable close to the left-hand bank. I begun to suspicion something. So did Jim. I says:

"Maybe we went by Cairo in the fog that night."

He says:

"Doan' le's talk about it, Huck. Po' niggers can't have no luck. I awluz 'spected dat rattlesnake-skin warn't done wid its work."

"I wish I'd never seen that snake-skin, Jim—I do wish I'd never laid eyes on it."

"It ain't yo' fault, Huck; you didn' know. Don't you blame yo'self 'bout it."

When it was daylight, here was the clear Ohio water inshore, sure enough, and outside was the old regular Muddy! So it was all up with Cairo.

We talked it all over. It wouldn't do to take to the shore; we couldn't take the raft up the stream, of course. There warn't no way but to wait for dark and start back in the canoe and take the chances. So we slept all day amongst the cottonwood thicket, so as to be fresh for the work, and when we went back to the raft about dark the canoe was gone!

We didn't say a word for a good while. There warn't anything to say. We both knowed well enough it was some more work of the rattlesnake-skin; so what was the use to talk about it? It would only look like we was finding fault and that would be bound to fetch more bad luck—and keep on fetching it, too, till we knowed enough to keep still.

By and by we talked about what we better do, and found there warn't no way but just to go along down with the raft till we got a chance to buy a canoe to go back in. We warn't going to borrow it when there warn't anybody around, the way pap would do, for that might set people after us.

So we shoved out after dark on the raft.

Anybody that don't believe yet that it's foolishness to handle a snake-skin, after all that that snake-skin done for us, will believe it now if they read on and see what more it done for us.

The place to buy canoes is off of rafts laying up at shore. But we didn't see no rafts laying up; so we went along during three hours and more. Well, the night got

gray and ruther thick, which is the next meanest thing
to fog. You can't tell the shape of the river and you
can't see no distance. It got to be very late and still, and
then along comes a steamboat up the river. We lit the
lantern and judged she would see it. Up-stream boats
didn't generly come close to us; they go out and follow
the bars and hunt for easy water under the reefs; but
nights like this they bull right up the channel against the
whole river.

We could hear her pounding along but we didn't see
her good till she was close. She aimed right for us. Often
they do that and try to see how close they can come
without touching; sometimes the wheel bites off a
sweep, and then the pilot sticks his head out and laughs
and thinks he's mighty smart. Well, here she comes, and
we said she was going to try and shave us, but she didn't
seem to be sheering off a bit. She was a big one and she
was coming in a hurry, too, looking like a black cloud
with rows of glow-worms around it, but all of a sudden
she bulged out, big and scary, with a long row of wide-
open furnace doors shining like red-hot teeth and her
monstrous bows and guards hanging right over us. There
was a yell at us and a jingling of bells to stop the engines, a powwow of cussing, and whistling of steam—
and as Jim went overboard on one side and I on the
other, she come smashing straight through the raft.

I dived—and I aimed to find the bottom, too, for a
thirty-foot wheel had got to go over me, and I wanted
it to have plenty of room. I could always stay under
water a minute; this time I reckon I stayed under a
minute and a half. Then I bounced for the top in a
hurry, for I was nearly busting. I popped out to my armpits and blowed the water out of my nose, and puffed a
bit. Of course there was a booming current, and of
course that boat started her engines again ten seconds

after she stopped them, for they never cared much for raftsmen, so now she was churning along up the river, out of sight in the thick weather, though I could hear her.

I sung out for Jim about a dozen times but I didn't get any answer; so I grabbed a plank that touched me while I was "treading water" and struck out for shore, shoving it ahead of me. But I made out to see that the drift of the current was towards the left-hand shore, which meant that I was in a crossing; so I changed off and went that way.

It was one of these long, slanting, two-mile crossings; so I was a good long time in getting over. I made a safe landing and clumb up the bank. I couldn't see but a little ways but I went poking along over rough ground for a quarter of a mile or more, and then I run across a big old-fashioned double log house before I noticed it. I was going to rush by and get away but a lot of dogs jumped out and went to howling and barking at me, and I knowed better than to move another peg.

XVII. The Grangerfords Take Me In

In about a minute somebody spoke out of a window without putting his head out, and says:

"Be done, boys! Who's there?"

I says:

"It's me."

"Who's me?"

"George Jackson, sir."

"What do you want?"

"I don't want nothing, sir. I only want to go along by, but the dogs won't let me."

"What are you prowling around here this time of night for—hey?"

"I warn't prowling around, sir; I fell overboard off of the steamboat."

"Oh, you did, did you? Strike a light there, somebody. What did you say your name was?"

"George Jackson, sir. I'm only a boy."

"Look here, if you're telling the truth you needn't be afraid—nobody'll hurt you. But don't try to budge; stand right where you are. Rouse out Bob and Tom, some of you, and fetch the guns. George Jackson, is there anybody with you?"

"No, sir, nobody."

I heard the people stirring around in the house now, and see a light. The man sung out:

"Snatch that light away, Betsy, you old fool—ain't you got any sense? Put it on the floor behind the front door. Bob, if you and Tom are ready, take your places."

"All ready."

"Now, George Jackson, do you know the Shepherd-sons?"

"No, sir; I never heard of them."

"Well, that may be so, and it mayn't. Now, all ready. Step forward, George Jackson. And mind, don't you hurry—come mighty slow. If there's anybody with you, let him keep back—if he shows himself he'll be shot. Come along now. Come slow; push the door open your-self—just enough to squeeze in, d'you hear?"

I didn't hurry; I couldn't if I'd a-wanted to. I took one slow step at a time and there warn't a sound, only I thought I could hear my heart. The dogs were as still as the humans but they followed a little behind me. When I got to the three log doorsteps I heard them unlocking and unbarring and unbolting. I put my hand on the door and pushed it a little and a little more till somebody said, "There, that's enough—put your head in." I done it but I judged they would take it off.

The candle was on the floor and there they all was, looking at me, and me at them, for about a quarter of a minute: three big men with guns pointed at me, which made me wince, I tell you; the oldest gray and about sixty, the other two thirty or more—all of them fine and handsome—and the sweetest old gray-headed lady, and back of her two young women which I couldn't see right well. The old gentleman says:

"There; I reckon it's all right. Come in."

As soon as I was in the old gentleman he locked the door and barred and bolted it, and told the young men to come in with their guns, and they all went in a big parlor that had a new rag carpet on the floor, and got together in a corner that was out of range of the front windows—there warn't none on the side. They held the candle, and took a good look at me, and all said, "Why, he ain't a Shepherdson—no, there ain't any Shepherdson about him." Then the old man said he hoped I wouldn't mind being searched for arms, because he didn't mean no harm by it—it was only to make sure. So he didn't pry into my pockets but only felt outside with his hands, and said it was all right. He told me to make myself easy and at home and tell all about myself, but the old lady says:

"Why, bless you, Saul, the poor thing's as wet as he can be, and don't you reckon it may be he's hungry?"

"True for you, Rachel—I forgot."

So the old lady says:

"Betsy" (this was a nigger woman), "you fly around and get him something to eat as quick as you can, poor thing; and one of you girls go and wake up Buck and tell him—oh, here he is himself. Buck, take this little stranger and get the wet clothes off from him and dress him up in some of yours that's dry."

Buck looked about as old as me—thirteen or fourteen or along there, though he was a little bigger than me. He hadn't on anything but a shirt, and he was very frowzy-headed. He came in gaping and digging one fist into his eyes, and he was dragging a gun along with the other one. He says:

"Ain't they no Shepherdsons around?"

They said, no, 'twas a false alarm.

"Well," he says, "if they'd 'a' ben some, I reckon I'd 'a' got one."

They all laughed, and Bob says:

"Why, Buck, they might have scalped us all, you've been so slow in coming."

"Well, nobody come after me, and it ain't right. I'm always kep' down; I don't get no show."

"Never mind, Buck, my boy," says the old man, "you'll have show enough, all in good time, don't you fret about that. Go 'long with you now, and do as your mother told you."

When we got up-stairs to his room he got me a coarse shirt and a roundabout and pants of his, and I put them on. While I was at it he asked me what my name was, but before I could tell him he started to tell me about a bluejay and a young rabbit he had catched in the woods day before yesterday, and he asked me where Moses was when the candle went out. I said I didn't know; I hadn't heard about it before, no way.

"Well, guess," he says.

"How'm I going to guess," says I, "when I never heard tell of it before?"

"But you can guess, can't you? It's just as easy."

"*Which* candle?" I says.

"Why, any candle," he says.

"I don't know where he was," says I, "where was he?"

"Why, he was in the *dark!* That's where he was!"

"Well, if you knowed where he was, what did you ask me for?"

"Why, blame it, it's a riddle, don't you see? Say, how long are you going to stay here? You got to stay always. We can just have booming times—they don't have no school now. Do you own a dog? I've got a dog—and he'll go in the river and bring out chips that you throw in. Do you like to comb up Sundays, and all that kind of foolishness? You bet I don't, but ma she makes me. Confound these ole britches! I reckon I'd better put 'em on, but I'd ruther not, it's so warm. Are you all ready? All right. Come along, old hoss."

Cold corn-pone, cold corn-beef, butter and buttermilk—that is what they had for me down there, and there ain't nothing better that ever I've come across yet. Buck and his ma and all of them smoked cob pipes, except the nigger woman, which was gone, and the two young women. They all smoked and talked, and I eat and talked. The young women had quilts around them and their hair down their backs. They all asked me questions, and I told them how pap and me and all the family was living on a little farm down at the bottom of Arkansaw, and my sister Mary Ann run off and got married and never was heard of no more, and Bill went to hunt them and he warn't heard of no more, and Tom and Mort died, and then there warn't nobody but just me and pap left, and he was just trimmed down to nothing, on account of his troubles; so when he died I took what there was left, because the farm didn't belong to us, and started up the river, deck passage, and fell overboard; and that was how I come to be here. So they said I could have a home there as long as I wanted it. Then

it was most daylight and everybody went to bed, and
I went to bed with Buck, and when I waked up in the
morning, drat it all, I had forgot what my name was. So
I laid there about an hour trying to think, and when
Buck waked up I says:

"Can you spell, Buck?"

"Yes," he says.

"I bet you can't spell my name," says I.

"I bet you what you dare I can," says he.

"All right," says I, "go ahead."

"G-o-r-g-e J-a-x-o-n—there now," he says.

"Well," says I, "you done it, but I didn't think you
could. It ain't no slouch of a name to spell—right off
without studying."

I set it down, private, because somebody might want
me to spell it next, and so I wanted to be handy with it
and rattle it off like I was used to it.

It was a mighty nice family and a mighty nice house,
too. I hadn't seen no house out in the country before
that was so nice and had so much style. It didn't have
an iron latch on the front door nor a wooden one with a
buckskin string, but a brass knob to turn, the same as
houses in town. There warn't no bed in the parlor, nor a
sign of a bed, but heaps of parlors in towns has beds in
them. There was a big fireplace that was bricked on the
bottom, and the bricks was kept clean and red by pouring water on them and scrubbing them with another
brick; sometimes they wash them over with red water-
paint that they call Spanish-brown, same as they do in
town. They had big brass dog-irons that could hold up a
saw-log. There was a clock on the middle of the mantel-
piece, with a picture of a town painted on the bottom
half of the glass front, and a round place in the middle
of it for the sun, and you could see the pendulum swinging behind it. It was beautiful to hear that clock tick,

and sometimes when one of these peddlers had been along and scoured her up and got her in good shape, she would start in and strike a hundred and fifty before she got tuckered out. They wouldn't took any money for her.

Well, there was a big outlandish parrot on each side of the clock, made out of something like chalk and painted up gaudy. By one of the parrots was a cat made of crockery, and a crockery dog by the other; and when you pressed down on them they squeaked but didn't open their mouths nor look different nor interested. They squeaked through underneath. There was a couple of big wild-turkey-wing fans spread out behind those things. On the table in the middle of the room was a kind of a lovely crockery basket that had apples and oranges and peaches and grapes piled up in it, which was much redder and yellower and prettier than real ones is, but they warn't real because you could see where pieces had got chipped off and showed the white chalk, or whatever it was, underneath.

This table had a cover made out of beautiful oilcloth, with a red and blue spread-eagle painted on it and a painted border all around. It come all the way from Philadelphia, they said. There was some books, too, piled up perfectly exact, on each corner of the table. One was a big family Bible full of pictures. One was *Pilgrim's Progress*, about a man that left his family, it didn't say why. I read considerable in it now and then. The statements was interesting but tough. Another was *Friendship's Offering*, full of beautiful stuff and poetry, but I didn't read the poetry. Another was Henry Clay's *Speeches*, and another was Dr. Gunn's *Family Medicine*, which told you all about what to do if a body was sick or dead. There was a hymn-book and a lot of other books. And there was nice split-bottom chairs, and

perfectly sound, too—not bagged down in the middle
and busted, like an old basket.

They had pictures hung on the walls—mainly
Washingtons and Lafayettes, and battles, and Highland
Marys, and one called "Signing the Declaration." There
was some that they called crayons, which one of the
daughters which was dead made her own self when
she was only fifteen years old. They was different from
any pictures I ever see before—blacker, mostly, than
is common. One was a woman in a slim black dress,
belted small under the armpits, with bulges like a
cabbage in the middle of the sleeves, and a large black
scoop-shovel bonnet with a black veil, and white slim
ankles crossed about with black tape and very wee
black slippers, like a chisel, and she was leaning pensive
on a tombstone on her right elbow under a weeping
willow, and her other hand hanging down her side
holding a white handkerchief and a reticule, and underneath the picture it said "Shall I Never See Thee More
Alas." Another one was a young lady with her hair all
combed up straight to the top of her head and knotted
there in front of a comb like a chair-back, and she was
crying into a handkerchief and had a dead bird laying
on its back in her other hand with its heels up, and
underneath the picture it said "I Shall Never Hear Thy
Sweet Chirrup More Alas." There was one where a
young lady was at a window looking up at the moon,
and tears running down her cheeks; and she had an open
letter in one hand with black sealing wax showing on
one edge of it, and she was mashing a locket with a
chain to it against her mouth and underneath the picture
it said "And Art Thou Gone Yes Thou Art Gone Alas."
These was all nice pictures, I reckon, but I didn't somehow seem to take to them, because if ever I was down a
little they always give me the fantods. Everybody was

sorry she died, because she had laid out a lot more of
these pictures to do and a body could see by what she
had done what they had lost. But I reckoned that with
her disposition she was having a better time in the
graveyard. She was at work on what they said was her
greatest picture when she took sick, and every day and
every night it was her prayer to be allowed to live till
she got it done, but she never got the chance. It was a
picture of a young woman in a long white gown, standing on the rail of a bridge all ready to jump off, with
her hair all down her back, and looking up to the moon
with the tears running down her face, and she had two
arms folded across her breast and two arms stretched
out in front and two more reaching up towards the
moon—and the idea was to see which pair would look
best and then scratch out all the other arms; but, as I
was saying, she died before she got her mind made up
and now they kept this picture over the head of the
bed in her room, and every time her birthday come
they hung flowers on it. Other times it was hid with a
little curtain. The young woman in the picture had a
kind of a nice sweet face but there was so many arms
it made her look too spidery, seemed to me.

This young girl kept a scrap-book when she was alive,
and used to paste obituaries and accidents and cases of
patient suffering in it out of the *Presbyterian Observer*,
and write poetry after them out of her own head. It was
very good poetry. This is what she wrote about a boy
by the name of Stephen Dowling Bots that fell down a
well and was drownded:

ODE TO STEPHEN DOWLING BOTS, DEC'D

And did young Stephen sicken,
  And did young Stephen die?
And did the sad hearts thicken,
  And did the mourners cry?

No; such was not the fate of
   Young Stephen Dowling Bots;
Though sad hearts round him thickened,
   'Twas not from sickness' shots.

No whooping-cough did rack his frame,
   Nor measles drear with spots;
Not these impaired the sacred name
   Of Stephen Dowling Bots.

Despised love struck not with woe
   That head of curly knots,
Nor stomach troubles laid him low,
   Young Stephen Dowling Bots.

O no. Then list with tearful eye,
   Whilst I his fate do tell.
His soul did from this cold world fly
   By falling down a well.

They got him out and emptied him;
   Alas it was too late;
His spirit was gone for to sport aloft
   In the realms of the good and great.

If Emmeline Grangerford could make poetry like
that before she was fourteen, there ain't no telling
what she could 'a' done by and by. Buck said she could
rattle off poetry like nothing. She didn't ever have to
stop to think. He said she would slap down a line, and
if she couldn't find anything to rhyme with it she would
just scratch it out and slap down another one and go
ahead. She warn't particular; she could write about
anything you choose to give her to write about just so
it was sadful. Every time a man died or a woman died
or a child died, she would be on hand with her "tribute"
before he was cold. She called them tributes. The
neighbors said it was the doctor first, then Emmeline,
then the undertaker—the undertaker never got in ahead
of Emmeline but once, and then she hung fire on a
rhyme for the dead person's name, which was Whistler.

She warn't ever the same after that; she never complained but she kind of pined away and did not live long. Poor thing, many's the time I made myself go up to the little room that used to be hers and get out her poor old scrap-book and read in it when her pictures had been aggravating me and I had soured on her a little. I liked all that family, dead ones and all, and warn't going to let anything come between us. Poor Emmeline made poetry about all the dead people when she was alive, and it didn't seem right that there warn't nobody to make some about her now she was gone; so I tried to sweat out a verse or two myself but I couldn't seem to make it go somehow. They kept Emmeline's room trim and nice, and all the things fixed in it just the way she liked to have them when she was alive, and nobody ever slept there. The old lady took care of the room herself, though there was plenty of niggers, and she sewed there a good deal and read her Bible there mostly.

Well, as I was saying about the parlor, there was beautiful curtains on the windows: white, with pictures painted on them of castles with vines all down the walls and cattle coming down to drink. There was a little old piano, too, that had tin pans in it, I reckon, and nothing was ever so lovely as to hear the young ladies sing "The Last Link Is Broken" and play "The Battle of Prague" on it. The walls of all the rooms was plastered and most had carpets on the floors, and the whole house was whitewashed on the outside.

It was a double house and the big open place betwixt them was roofed and floored, and sometimes the table was set there in the middle of the day, and it was a cool, comfortable place. Nothing couldn't be better. And warn't the cooking good, and just bushels of it too!

Col. Grangerford was a gentleman, you see. He was a gentleman all over, and so was his family. He was well born, as the saying is, and that's worth as much in a man as it is in a horse, so the Widow Douglas said, and nobody ever denied that she was of the first aristocracy in our town; and pap he always said it, too, though he warn't no more quality than a mudcat himself. Col. Grangerford was very tall and very slim, and had a darkish-paly complexion, not a sign of red in it anywheres; he was clean-shaved every morning all over his thin face, and he had the thinnest kind of lips and the thinnest kind of nostrils, and a high nose and heavy eyebrows, and the blackest kind of eyes, sunk so deep back that they seemed like they was looking out of caverns at you, as you may say. His forehead was high and his hair was gray and straight and hung to his shoulders. His hands was long and thin, and every day of his life he put on a clean shirt and a full suit from head to foot made out of linen so white it hurt your eyes to look at it, and on Sundays he wore a blue tailcoat with brass buttons on it. He carried a mahogany cane with a silver head to it. There warn't no frivolishness about him, not a bit, and he warn't ever loud. He was as kind as he could be—you could feel that, you know, and so you had confidence. Sometimes he smiled and it was good to see, but when he straightened himself up like a liberty pole and the lightning begun to flicker out from under his eyebrows, you wanted to climb a tree first and find out what the matter was afterwards. He didn't ever have to tell anybody to mind their manners—everybody was always good-mannered where he was. Everybody loved to have him around, too; he was sunshine most always—I mean he made it seem like good weather. When he turned into a cloud-bank it was awful dark for half a minute, and that was enough; there wouldn't nothing go wrong again for a week.

When him and the old lady come down in the morning all the family got up out of their chairs and give them good day, and didn't set down again till they had set down. Then Tom and Bob went to the sideboard where the decanters was and mixed a glass of bitters and handed it to him, and he held it in his hand and waited till Tom's and Bob's was mixed, and then they bowed and said, "Our duty to you, sir, and madam," and *they* bowed the least bit in the world and said thank you, and so they drank, all three, and Bob and Tom poured a spoonful of water on the sugar and the mite of whisky or apple-brandy in the bottom of their tumblers and give it to me and Buck, and we drank to the old people too.

Bob was the oldest and Tom next—tall, beautiful men with very broad shoulders and brown faces, and long black hair and black eyes. They dressed in white linen from head to foot, like the old gentleman, and wore broad Panama hats.

Then there was Miss Charlotte; she was twenty-five and tall and proud and grand but as good as she could be when she warn't stirred up, but when she was she had a look that would make you wilt in your tracks, like her father. She was beautiful.

So was her sister, Miss Sophia, but it was a different kind. She was gentle and sweet like a dove and she was only twenty.

Each person had their own nigger to wait on them—Buck too. My nigger had a monstrous easy time, because I warn't used to having anybody do anything for me, but Buck's was on the jump most of the time.

This was all there was of the family now, but there used to be more—three sons; they got killed; and Emmeline that died.

The old gentleman owned a lot of farms and over a hundred niggers. Sometimes a stack of people would come there, horseback, from ten or fifteen mile around, and stay five or six days and have such junketings round about and on the river, and dances and picnics in the woods daytimes, and balls at the house nights. These people was mostly kinfolks of the family. The men brought their guns with them. It was a handsome lot of quality, I tell you.

There was another clan of aristocracy around there— five or six families—mostly of the name of Shepherdson. They was as high-toned and well born and rich and grand as the tribe of Grangerfords. The Shepherdsons and Grangerfords used the same steamboat landing, which was about two mile above our house; so sometimes when I went up there with a lot of our folks I used to see a lot of the Shepherdsons there on their fine horses.

One day Buck and me was away out in the woods hunting and heard a horse coming. We was crossing the road. Buck says:

"Quick! Jump for the woods!"

We done it, and then peeped down the woods through the leaves. Pretty soon a splendid young man come galloping down the road, setting his horse easy and looking like a soldier. He had his gun across his pommel. I had seen him before. It was young Harney Shepherdson. I heard Buck's gun go off at my ear, and Harney's hat tumbled off from his head. He grabbed his gun and rode straight to the place where we was hid. But we didn't wait. We started through the woods on a run. The woods warn't thick, so I looked over my shoulder to dodge the bullet, and twice I seen Harney cover Buck with his gun; and then he rode away the way he come—to get his hat, I reckon, but I couldn't see. We never stopped running till we got home. The old gentleman's eyes blazed a minute—'twas pleasure, mainly, I judged—then his face sort of smoothed down, and he says, kind of gentle:

"I don't like that shooting from behind a bush. Why didn't you step into the road, my boy?"

"The Shepherdsons don't, father. They always take advantage."

Miss Charlotte she held her head up like a queen while Buck was telling his tale, and her nostrils spread and her eyes snapped. The two young men looked dark but never said nothing. Miss Sophia she turned pale, but the color come back when she found the man warn't hurt.

Soon as I could get Buck down by the corn-cribs under the trees by ourselves, I says:

"Did you want to kill him, Buck?"

"Well, I bet I did."

"What did he do to you?"

"Him? He never done nothing to me."

"Well, then, what did you want to kill him for?"

"Why, nothing—only it's on account of the feud."

"What's a feud?"

"Why, where was you raised? Don't you know what a feud is?"

"Never heard of it before—tell me about it."

"Well," says Buck, "a feud is this way: A man has a quarrel with another man, and kills him; then that other man's brother kills *him;* then the other brothers on both sides goes for one another; then the *cousins* chip in— and by and by everybody's killed off and there ain't

no more feud. But it's kind of slow and takes a long
time."

"Has this one been going on long, Buck?"

"Well, I should *reckon!* It started thirty year ago, or
som'ers along there. There was trouble 'bout something and then a lawsuit to settle it, and the suit went
agin one of the men and so he up and shot the man
that won the suit—which he would naturally do, of
course. Anybody would."

"What was the trouble about, Buck?—land?"

"I reckon maybe—I don't know."

"Well, who done the shooting? Was it a Grangerford
or a Shepherdson?"

"Laws, how do *I* know? It was so long ago."

"Don't anybody know?"

"Oh, yes, pa knows, I reckon, and some of the other
old people; but they don't know now what the row was
about in the first place."

"Has there been many killed, Buck?"

"Yes; right smart chance of funerals. But they don't
always kill. Pa's got a few buckshot in him, but he don't
mind it 'cuz he don't weigh much, anyway. Bob's been
carved up some with a bowie and Tom's been hurt
once or twice."

"Has anybody been killed this year, Buck?"

"Yes; we got one and they got one. 'Bout three
months ago my cousin Bud, fourteen year old, was
riding through the woods on t'other side of the river
and didn't have no weapon with him, which was blame'
foolishness, and in a lonesome place he hears a horse
a-coming behind him and sees old Baldy Shepherdson
a-linkin' after him with his gun in his hand and his white
hair a-flying in the wind; and 'stead of jumping off and
taking to the brush, Bud 'lowed he could outrun him;

so they had it nip and tuck for five mile or more, the
old man a-gaining all the time; so at last Bud seen it
warn't any use, so he stopped and faced around so as
to have the bullet holes in front, you know, and the old
man he rode up and shot him down. But he didn't git
much chance to enjoy his luck, for inside of a week our
folks laid *him* out."

"I reckon that old man was a coward, Buck."

"I reckon he *warn't* a coward. Not by a blame' sight.
There ain't a coward amongst them Shepherdsons—
not a one. And there ain't no cowards amongst the
Grangerfords either. Why, that old man kep' up his
end in a fight one day for half an hour against three
Grangerfords, and come out winner. They was all
a-horseback; he lit off of his horse and got behind a
little woodpile and kep' his horse before him to stop
the bullets; but the Grangerfords stayed on their horses
and capered around the old man and peppered away
at him, and he peppered away at them. Him and his
horse both went home pretty leaky and crippled, but
the Grangerfords had to be *fetched* home—and one of
'em was dead and another died the next day. No, sir;
if a body's out hunting for cowards he don't want to
fool away any time amongst them Shepherdsons, becuz
they don't breed any of that *kind*."

Next Sunday we all went to church, about three mile,
everybody a-horseback. The men took their guns along,
so did Buck, and kept them between their knees or
stood them handy against the wall. The Shepherdsons
done the same. It was pretty ornery preaching—all
about brotherly love, and such-like tiresomeness; but
everybody said it was a good sermon and they all talked
it over going home, and had such a powerful lot to say
about faith and good works and free grace and pre-
foreordestination, and I don't know what all, that it did

seem to me to be one of the roughest Sundays I had run
across yet.

About an hour after dinner everybody was dozing
around, some in their chairs and some in their rooms,
and it got to be pretty dull. Buck and a dog was
stretched out on the grass in the sun sound asleep. I
went up to our room, and judged I would take a nap
myself. I found that sweet Miss Sophia standing in her
door, which was next to ours, and she took me in her
room and shut the door very soft and asked me if I
liked her, and I said I did; and she asked me if I would
do something for her and not tell anybody, and I
said I would. Then she said she'd forgot her Testament
and left it in the seat at church between two other
books, and would I slip out quiet and go there and
fetch it to her and not say nothing to nobody. I said I
would. So I slid out and slipped off up the road and
there warn't anybody at the church, except maybe a
hog or two, for there warn't any lock on the door, and
hogs likes a puncheon floor in summer-time because
it's cool. If you notice, most folks don't go to church
only when they've got to; but a hog is different.

Says I to myself, something's up; it ain't natural for
a girl to be in such a sweat about a Testament. So I
give it a shake, and out drops a little piece of paper
with *"Half past two"* wrote on it with a pencil. I ransacked it, but couldn't find anything else. I couldn't
make anything out of that, so I put the paper in the
book again, and when I got home and upstairs there
was Miss Sophia in her door waiting for me. She pulled
me in and shut the door; then she looked in the Testament till she found the paper, and as soon as she read
it she looked glad; and before a body could think she
grabbed me and give me a squeeze, and said I was the
best boy in the world, and not to tell anybody. She

was mighty red in the face for a minute and her eyes lighted up, and it made her powerful pretty. I was a good deal astonished but when I got my breath I asked her what the paper was about, and she asked me if I had read it, and I said no, and she asked me if I could read writing, and I told her "no, only coarse-hand," and then she said the paper warn't anything but a bookmark to keep her place, and I might go and play now.

I went off down to the river, studying over this thing, and pretty soon I noticed that my nigger was following along behind. When we was out of sight of the house he looked back and around a second and then comes a-running, and says:

"Mars Jawge, if you'll come down into de swamp I'll show you a whole stack o' water-moccasins."

Thinks I, that's mighty curious; he said that yesterday. He oughter know a body don't love water-moccasins enough to go around hunting for them. What is he up to, anyway? So I says:

"All right; trot ahead."

I followed a half a mile; then he struck out over the swamp and waded ankle-deep as much as another half-mile. We come to a little flat piece of land which was dry and very thick with trees and bushes and vines, and he says:

"You shove right in dah jist a few steps, Mars Jawge; dah's whah dey is. I's seed 'em befo'; I don't k'yer to see 'em no mo'."

Then he slopped right along and went away, and pretty soon the trees hid him. I poked into the place a ways and come to a little open patch as big as a bedroom all hung around with vines, and found a man laying there asleep—and, by jings, it was my old Jim!

I waked him up and I reckoned it was going to be

a grand surprise to him to see me again, but it warn't.
He nearly cried he was so glad, but he warn't surprised.
Said he swum along behind me that night, and heard
me yell every time, but dasn't answer, because he didn't
want nobody to pick *him* up and take him into slavery
again. Says he:

"I got hurt a little, en couldn't swim fas', so I wuz a
considable ways behine you towards de las'; when you
landed I reck'ned I could ketch up wid you on de lan'
'dout havin' to shout at you, but when I see dat house
I begin to go slow. I 'uz off too fur to hear what dey say
to you—I wuz 'fraid o' de dogs; but when it 'uz all quiet
agin I knowed you's in de house, so I struck out for de
woods to wait for day. Early in de mawnin' some er de
niggers come along, gwyne to de fields, en dey tuck
me en showed me dis place, whah de dogs can't track
me on accounts o' de water, en dey brings me truck to
eat every night, en tells me how you's a-gittin' along."

"Why didn't you tell my Jack to fetch me here sooner,
Jim?"

"Well, 'twarn't no use to 'sturb you, Huck, tell we
could do sumfn—but we's all right now. I ben a-buyin'
pots en pans en vittles, as I got a chanst, en a-patchin'
up de raf' nights when—"

"*What* raft, Jim?"

"Our ole raf'."

"You mean to say our old raft warn't smashed all to
flinders?"

"No, she warn't. She was tore up a good deal—one
en' of her was; but dey warn't no great harm done, on'y
our traps was mos' all los'. Ef we hadn' dive' so deep
en swum so fur under water, en de night hadn' ben so
dark, en we warn't so sk'yerd, en ben sich punkin-heads,
as de sayin' is, we'd a seed de raf'. But it's jis' as well we

didn't, 'kase now she's all fixed up agin mos' as good as new, en we's got a new lot o' stuff, too, in de place o' what 'uz los'."

"Why, how did you get hold of the raft again, Jim—did you catch her?"

"How I gwyne to ketch her en I out in de woods? No; some er de niggers foun' her ketched on a snag along heah in de ben', en dey hid her in a crick 'mongst de willows, en dey wuz so much jawin' 'bout which un 'um she b'long to de mos' dat I come to heah 'bout it pooty soon, so I ups en settles de trouble by tellin' 'um she don't b'long to none uv 'um, but to you en me; en I ast 'm if dey gwyne to grab a young white genlman's propaty, en git a hid'n' for it? Den I gin 'm ten cents apiece, en dey 'uz mighty well satisfied, en wisht some mo' raf's 'ud come along en make 'm rich agin. Dey's mighty good to me, dese niggers is, en whatever I wants 'm to do fur me I doan' have to ast 'm twice, honey. Dat Jack's a good nigger, en pooty smart."

"Yes, he is. He ain't ever told me you was here; told me to come and he'd show me a lot of water-moccasins. If anything happens *he* ain't mixed up in it. He can say he never seen us together, and it'll be the truth."

I don't want to talk much about the next day. I reckon I'll cut it pretty short. I waked up about dawn and was a-going to turn over and go to sleep again when I noticed how still it was—didn't seem to be anybody stirring. That warn't usual. Next I noticed that Buck was up and gone. Well, I gets up, a-wondering, and goes down-stairs—nobody around; everything as still as a mouse. Just the same outside. Thinks I, what does it mean? Down by the woodpile I comes across my Jack, and says:

"What's it all about?"

Says he:

"Don't you know, Mars Jawge?"

"No," says I, "I don't."

"Well, den, Miss Sophia's run off! 'deed she has. She run off in de night some time—nobody don't know jis' when; run off to get married to dat young Harney Shepherdson, you know—leastways, so dey 'spec. De fambly foun' it out 'bout half an hour ago—maybe a little mo'—en' I *tell* you dey warn't no time los'. Sich another hurryin' up guns en hosses *you* never see! De women folks has gone for to stir up de relations, en ole Mars Saul en de boys tuck dey guns en rode up de river road for to try to ketch dat young man en kill him 'fo' he kin git acrost de river wid Miss Sophia. I reck'n dey's gwyne to be mighty rough times."

"Buck went off 'thout waking me up."

"Well, I reck'n he *did!* Dey warn't gwyne to mix you up in it. Mars Buck he loaded up his gun en 'lowed he's gwyne to fetch home a Shepherdson or bust. Well, dey'll be plenty un 'm dah, I reck'n, en you bet you he'll fetch one ef he gits a chanst."

I took up the river road as hard as I could put. By and by I begin to hear guns a good ways off. When I come in sight of the log store and the woodpile where the steamboats lands I worked along under the trees and brush till I got to a good place, and then I clumb up into the forks of a cottonwood that was out of reach, and watched. There was a wood-rank four foot high a little ways in front of the tree, and first I was going to hide behind that; but maybe it was luckier I didn't.

There was four or five men cavorting around on their horses in the open place before the log store, cussing and yelling and trying to get at a couple of young chaps that was behind the wood-rank alongside of the steamboat landing, but they couldn't come it. Every time one of them showed himself on the river side of the woodpile he got shot at. The two boys was squatting back to back behind the pile, so they could watch both ways.

By and by the men stopped cavorting around and yelling. They started riding towards the store; then up gets one of the boys, draws a steady bead over the wood-rank, and drops one of them out of his saddle. All the men jumped off of their horses and grabbed the hurt one and started to carry him to the store; and that minute the two boys started on the run. They got half-way to the tree I was in before the men noticed. Then the men see them and jumped on their horses and took out after them. They gained on the boys but it didn't do no good, the boys had too good a start; they got to the woodpile that was in front of my tree and slipped in behind it, and so they had the bulge on the men again. One of the boys was Buck, and the other was a slim young chap about nineteen years old.

The men ripped around awhile and then rode away. As soon as they was out of sight I sung out to Buck and told him. He didn't know what to make of my voice coming out of the tree at first. He was awful surprised. He told me to watch out sharp and let him know when the men come in sight again; said they was up to some devilment or other—wouldn't be gone long. I wished I was out of that tree but I dasn't come down. Buck begun to cry and rip, and 'lowed that him and his cousin Joe (that was the other young chap) would make up for this day yet. He said his father and his two brothers was killed, and two or three of the enemy. Said the Shepherdsons laid for them in ambush. Buck said his father and brothers ought to waited for their relations—the Shepherdsons was too strong for them. I asked him what was become of young Harney and Miss Sophia. He said they'd got across the river and was safe. I was glad of that, but the way Buck did take on because he didn't manage to kill Harney that day he shot at him—I hain't ever heard anything like it.

All of a sudden, bang! bang! bang! goes three or four guns—the men had slipped around through the woods and come in from behind without their horses! The boys jumped for the river—both of them hurt—and as they swum down the current the men run along the bank shooting at them and singing out, "Kill them, kill them!" It made me so sick I most fell out of the tree. I ain't a-going to tell *all* that happened—it would make me sick again if I was to do that. I wished I hadn't ever come ashore that night to see such things. I ain't ever going to get shut of them—lots of times I dream about them.

I stayed in the tree till it begun to get dark, afraid to come down. Sometimes I heard guns away off in the woods and twice I seen little gangs of men gallop past the log store with guns; so I reckoned the trouble was still a-going on. I was mighty downhearted; so I made up my mind I wouldn't ever go anear that house again, because I reckoned I was to blame, somehow. I judged that that piece of paper meant that Miss Sophia was to meet Harney somewheres at half past two and run off, and I judged I ought to told her father about that paper and the curious way she acted, and then maybe he would 'a' locked her up and this awful mess wouldn't ever happened.

When I got down out of the tree I crept along down the river bank a piece, and found the two bodies laying in the edge of the water, and tugged at them till I got them ashore; then I covered up their faces and got away as quick as I could. I cried a little when I was covering up Buck's face, for he was mighty good to me.

It was just dark now. I never went near the house but struck through the woods and made for the swamp.

Jim warn't on his island, so I tramped off in a hurry
for the crick, and crowded through the willows, red-
hot to jump aboard and get out of that awful country.
The raft was gone! My souls, but I was scared! I couldn't
get my breath for most a minute. Then I raised a yell.
A voice not twenty-five foot from me says:

"Good lan'! is dat you, honey? Doan' make no noise."

It was Jim's voice—nothing ever sounded so good
before. I run along the bank a piece and got aboard
and Jim he grabbed me and hugged me, he was so glad
to see me. He says:

"Laws bless you, chile, I 'uz right down sho' you's
dead agin. Jack's been heah; he say he reck'n you's ben
shot, kase you didn' come home no mo'; so I's jes' dis
minute a-startin' de raf' down towards de mouf er de
crick, so's to be all ready for to shove out en leave soon
as Jack comes agin en tells me for certain you *is* dead.
Lawsy, I's mighty glad to git you back agin, honey."

I says:

"All right—that's mighty good; they won't find me,
and they'll think I've been killed, and floated down the
river—there's something up there that'll help them think
so—so don't you lose no time, Jim, but just shove off
for the big water as fast as ever you can."

I never felt easy till the raft was two mile below
there and out in the middle of the Mississippi. Then we
hung up our signal lantern and judged that we was free
and safe once more. I hadn't had a bite to eat since
yesterday, so Jim he got out some corn-dodgers and
buttermilk, and pork and cabbage and greens—there
ain't nothing in the world so good when it's cooked
right—and whilst I eat my supper we talked and had a
good time. I was powerful glad to get away from the
feuds, and so was Jim to get away from the swamp.
We said there warn't no home like a raft, after all.

Other places do seem so cramped up and smothery, but a raft don't. You feel mighty free and easy and comfortable on a raft.

XIX. The Duke and the Dauphin Come Aboard.

Two or three days and nights went by; I reckon I might say they swum by, they slid along so quiet and smooth and lovely. Here is the way we put in the time. It was a monstrous big river down there—sometimes a mile and a half wide; we run nights and laid up and hid daytimes; soon as night was most gone we stopped navigating and tied up—nearly always in the dead water under a towhead; and then cut young cottonwoods and willows and hid the raft with them. Then we set out the lines. Next we slid into the river and had a swim, so as to freshen up and cool off; then we set down on the sandy bottom where the water was about knee-deep and watched the daylight come. Not a sound anywheres —perfectly still—just like the whole world was asleep, only sometimes the bullfrogs a-cluttering, maybe. The first thing to see, looking away over the water, was a kind of dull line—that was the woods on t'other side; you couldn't make nothing else out; then a pale place in the sky; then more paleness spreading around; then the river softened up away off, and warn't black any more, but gray; you could see little dark spots drifting along ever so far away—trading-scows, and such things; and long black streaks—rafts; sometimes you could hear a sweep screaking; or jumbled-up voices, it was so still, and sounds come so far; and by and by you could see a streak on the water which you know by the look of the streak that there's a snag there in a swift current which breaks on it and makes that streak look that way;

and you see the mist curl up off of the water, and the east reddens up, and the river, and you make out a log cabin in the edge of the woods, away on the bank on t'other side of the river, being a wood-yard, likely, and piled by them cheats so you can throw a dog through it anywheres; then the nice breeze springs up, and comes fanning you from over there, so cool and fresh and sweet to smell on account of the woods and the flowers; but sometimes not that way, because they've left dead fish laying around, gars and such, and they do get pretty rank; and next you've got the full day, and everything smiling in the sun, and the song-birds just going it!

A little smoke couldn't be noticed now, so we would take some fish off of the lines and cook up a hot breakfast. And afterwards we would watch the lonesomeness of the river, and kind of lazy along and by and by lazy off to sleep. Wake up by and by, and look to see what done it, and maybe see a steamboat coughing along up-stream, so far off towards the other side you couldn't tell nothing about her only whether she was a stern-wheel or side-wheel; then for about an hour there wouldn't be nothing to hear nor nothing to see—just solid lonesomeness. Next you'd see a raft sliding by, away off yonder, and maybe a galoot on it chopping, because they're most always doing it on a raft; you'd see the ax flash and come down—you don't hear nothing; you see that ax go up again, and by the time it's above the man's head then you hear the *k'chunk!*— it had took all that time to come over the water. So we would put in the day, lazying around, listening to the stillness. Once there was a thick fog and the rafts and things that went by was beating tin pans so the steamboats wouldn't run over them. A scow or a raft went by so close we could hear them talking and cussing and laughing—heard them plain; but we couldn't see no sign of them; it made you feel crawly; it was like spirits carrying on that way in the air. Jim said he believed it was spirits; but I says:

"No; spirits wouldn't say, 'Dern the dern fog.'"

Soon as it was night out we shoved; when we got her out to about the middle we let her alone and let her float wherever the current wanted her to; then we lit the pipes and dangled our legs in the water, and talked about all kinds of things—we was always naked, day and night, whenever the mosquitoes would let us—the new clothes Buck's folks made for me was too good to be comfortable and besides I didn't go much on clothes, nohow.

Sometimes we'd have that whole river all to ourselves for the longest time. Yonder was the banks and the islands, across the water; and maybe a spark—which was a candle in a cabin window; and sometimes on the water you could see a spark or two—on a raft or a scow, you know; and maybe you could hear a fiddle or a song coming over from one of them crafts. It's lovely to live on a raft. We had the sky up there, all speckled with stars, and we used to lay on our backs and look up at them and discuss about whether they was made or only just happened. Jim he allowed they was made but I allowed they happened; I judged it would have took too long to *make* so many. Jim said the moon could 'a' *laid* them; well, that looked kind of reasonable, so I didn't say nothing against it, because I've seen a frog lay most as many, so of course it could be done. We used to watch the stars that fell, too, and see them streak down. Jim allowed they'd got spoiled and was hove out of the nest.

Once or twice of a night we would see a steamboat slipping along in the dark, and now and then she would belch a whole world of sparks up out of her chimbleys, and they would rain down in the river and look awful pretty; then she would turn a corner and her lights would wink out and her powwow shut off and leave the river still again; and by and by her waves would get to us a long time after she was gone, and joggle the raft a bit, and after that you wouldn't hear nothing for you couldn't tell how long, except maybe frogs or something.

After midnight the people on shore went to bed, and then for two or three hours the shores was black—no more sparks in the cabin windows. These sparks was our clock—the first one that showed again meant morning was coming, so we hunted a place to hide and tie up right away.

One morning about daybreak I found a canoe and crossed over a chute to the main shore—it was only two hundred yards—and paddled about a mile up a crick amongst the cypress woods, to see if I couldn't get some berries. Just as I was passing a place where a kind of a cowpath crossed the crick, here comes a couple of men tearing up the path as tight as they could foot it. I thought I was a goner, for whenever anybody was after anybody I judged it was *me*—or maybe Jim. I was about to dig out from there in a hurry, but they was pretty close to me then and sung out and begged me to save their lives—said they hadn't been doing nothing and was being chased for it—said there was men and dogs a-coming. They wanted to jump right in, but I says:

"Don't you do it. I don't hear the dogs and horses yet; you've got time to crowd through the brush and get up the crick a little ways; then you take to the water and wad down to me and get in—that'll throw the dogs off the scent."

They done it, and soon as they was aboard I lit out

for our towhead and in about five or ten minutes we heard the dogs and the men away off, shouting. We heard them come along towards the crick but couldn't see them; they seemed to stop and fool around awhile; then as we got further and further away all the time, we couldn't hardly hear them at all; by the time we had left a mile of woods behind us and struck the river, everything was quiet, and we paddled over to the towhead and hid in the cottonwoods and was safe.

One of these fellows was about seventy or upwards, and had a bald head and very gray whiskers. He had an old battered-up slouch hat on, and a greasy blue woolen shirt, and ragged old blue jeans britches stuffed into his boot tops, and home-knit galluses—no, he only had one. He had an old long-tailed blue jeans coat with slick brass buttons flung over his arm, and both of them had big, fat, ratty-looking carpet-bags.

The other fellow was about thirty and dressed about as ornery. After breakfast we all laid off and talked, and the first thing that come out was that these chaps didn't know one another.

"What got you into trouble?" says the baldhead to t'other chap.

"Well, I'd been selling an article to take the tartar off the teeth—and it does take it off, too, and generly the enamel along with it—but I stayed about one night longer than I ought to and was just in the act of sliding out when I ran across you on the trail this side of town, and you told me they were coming, and begged me to help you to get off. So I told you I was expecting trouble myself and would scatter out *with* you. That's the whole yarn—what's yourn?"

"Well, I'd ben a-runnin' a little temperance revival thar 'bout a week, and was the pet of the women folks, big and little, for I was makin' it mighty warm for the rummies, I *tell* you, and takin' as much as five or six dollars a night—ten cents a head, children and niggers free—and business a-growin' all the time, when somehow or another a little report got around last night that I had a way of puttin' in my time with a private jug on the sly. A nigger rousted me out this mornin' and told me the people was getherin' on the quiet with their dogs and horses, and they'd be along pretty soon and give me 'bout half an hour's start and then run me down if they could; and if they got me they'd tar and feather me and ride me on a rail, sure. I didn't wait for no breakfast—I warn't hungry."

"Old man," says the young one, "I reckon we might double-team it together; what do you think?"

"I ain't undisposed. What's your line—mainly?"

"Jour printer by trade; do a little in patent medicines; theatre-actor—tragedy, you know; take a turn at mesmerism and phrenology when there's a chance; teach singing-geography school for a change; sling a lecture sometimes—oh, I do lots of things—most anything that comes handy, so it ain't work. What's your lay?"

"I've done considerble in the doctoring way in my time. Layin' on o' hands is my best holt—for cancer and paralysis, and sich things; and I k'n tell a fortune pretty good when I've got somebody along to find out the facts for me. Preachin's my line, too, and workin' camp-meetin's and missionaryin' around."

Nobody never said anything for a while; then the young man hove a sigh and says:

"Alas!"

"What're you alassin' about?" says the baldhead.

"To think I should have lived to be leading such a life and be degraded down into such company." And he begun to wipe the corner of his eye with a rag.

"Dern your skin, ain't the company good enough for you?" says the baldhead, pretty pert and uppish.

"Yes, it *is* good enough for me; it's as good as I deserve; for who fetched me so low when I was so high? *I* did myself. I don't blame *you*, gentlemen—far from it; I don't blame anybody. I deserve it all. Let the cold world do its worst; one thing I know—there's a grave somewhere for me. The world may go on just as it's always done, and take everything from me—loved ones, property, everything; but it can't take that. Some day I'll lie down in it and forget it all, and my poor broken heart will be at rest." He went on a-wiping.

"Drot your pore broken heart," says the baldhead; "what are you heaving your pore broken heart at *us* f'r? *We* hain't done nothing."

"No, I know you haven't. I ain't blaming you, gentlemen. I brought myself down—yes, I did it myself. It's right I should suffer—perfectly right—I don't make any moan."

"Brought you down from whar? Whar was you brought down from?"

"Ah, you would not believe me; the world never believes—let it pass—'tis no matter. The secret of my birth—"

"The secret of your birth! Do you mean to say—"

"Gentlemen," says the young man, very solemn, "I will reveal it to you, for I feel I may have confidence in you. By rights I am a duke!"

Jim's eyes bugged out when he heard that, and I reckon mine did, too. Then the baldhead says: "No! you can't mean it?"

"Yes. My great-grandfather, eldest son of the Duke of Bridgewater, fled to this country about the end of the last century, to breathe the pure air of freedom; married here and died, leaving a son, his own father dying about the same time. The second son of the late duke seized the titles and estates—the infant real duke was ignored. I am the lineal descendant of that infant—I am the rightful Duke of Bridgewater; and here am I, forlorn, torn from my high estate, hunted of men, despised by the cold world, ragged, worn, heartbroken, and degraded to the companionship of felons on a raft!"

Jim pitied him ever so much, and so did I. We tried to comfort him but he said it warn't much use, he couldn't be much comforted; said if we was a mind to acknowledge him, that would do him more good than most anything else; so we said we would, if he would tell us how. He said we ought to bow when we spoke to him and say "Your Grace," or "My Lord," or "Your Lordship"—and he wouldn't mind it if we called him plain "Bridgewater," which, he said, was a title anyway and not a name; and one of us ought to wait on him at dinner and do any little thing for him he wanted done.

Well, that was all easy, so we done it. All through dinner Jim stood around and waited on him, and says, "Will yo' Grace have some o' dis or some o' dat?" and so on, and a body could see it was mighty pleasing to him.

But the old man got pretty silent by and by—didn't have much to say, and didn't look pretty comfortable over all that petting that was going on around that duke. He seemed to have something on his mind. So, along in the afternoon, he says:

"Looky here, Bilgewater," he says, "I'm nation sorry for you, but you ain't the only person that's had troubles like that."

"No?"

"No, you ain't. You ain't the only person that's ben snaked down wrongfully out'n a high place."

"Alas!"

"No, you ain't the only person that's had a secret of his birth." And, by jings, *he* begins to cry.

"Hold! What do you mean?"

"Bilgewater, kin I trust you?" says the old man, still sort of sobbing.

"To the bitter death!" He took the old man by the hand and squeezed it, and says, "The secret of your being: speak!"

"Bilgewater, I am the late Dauphin!"

You bet you, Jim and me stared this time. Then the duke says:

"You are what?"

"Yes, my friend, it is too true—your eyes is lookin' at this very moment on the pore disappeared Dauphin, Looy the Seventeen, son of Looy the Sixteen and Marry Antonette."

"You! At your age! No! You mean you're the late Charlemagne; you must be six or seven hundred years old, at the very least."

"Trouble has done it, Bilgewater, trouble has done it; trouble has brung these gray hairs and this premature balditude. Yes, gentlemen, you see before you, in blue jeans and misery, the wanderin', exiled, trampled-on and sufferin' rightful King of France."

Well, he cried and took on so that me and Jim didn't know hardly what to do, we was so sorry—and so glad and proud we'd got him with us, too. So we set in, like we done before with the duke, and tried to comfort *him*. But he said it warn't no use, nothing but to be dead and done with it all could do him any good; though he said it often made him feel easier and better for a while if people treated him according to his rights and got down on one knee to speak to him and always called him "Your Majesty," and waited on him first at meals, and didn't set down in his presence till he asked them. So Jim and me set to majestying him and doing this and that and t'other for him and standing up till he told us we might set down. This done him heaps of good, and so he got cheerful and comfortable. But the duke kind of soured on him and didn't look a bit satisfied with the way things was going; still, the king acted real friendly towards him and said the duke's great-grandfather and all the other Dukes of Bilgewater was a good deal thought of by *his* father, and was allowed to come to the palace considerable; but the duke stayed huffy a good while, till by and by the king says:

"Like as not we got to be together a blamed long time on this h-yer raft, Bilgewater, and so what's the use o' your bein' sour? It'll only make things oncomfortable. It ain't my fault I warn't born a duke, it ain't your fault you warn't born a king—so what's the use to worry? Make the best o' things the way you find 'em, says I—that's my motto. This ain't no bad thing that we've struck here—plenty grub and an easy life—come, give us your hand, duke, and le's all be friends."

The duke done it and Jim and me was pretty glad to see it. It took away all the uncomfortableness and we felt mighty good over it, because it would 'a' been a miserable business to have any unfriendliness on the raft; for what you want, above all things, on a raft is for everybody to be satisfied and feel right and kind towards the others.

It didn't take me long to make up my mind that these liars warn't no kings nor dukes at all, but just low-down humbugs and frauds. But I never said nothing, never let on; kept it to myself; it's the best way; then you don't have no quarrels and don't get into no trouble. If they wanted us to call them kings and dukes, I hadn't no objections, 'long as it would keep peace in the family; and it warn't no use to tell Jim, so I didn't tell him. If I never learnt nothing else out of pap, I learnt that the best way to get along with his kind of people is to let them have their own way.

xx. What Royalty Did to Pokeville

They asked us considerable many questions; wanted to know what we covered up the raft that way for, and laid by in the daytime instead of running—was Jim a runaway nigger? Says I:

"Goodness sakes! would a runaway nigger run *south?*"

No, they allowed he wouldn't. I had to account for things some way, so I says:

"My folks was living in Pike County in Missouri, where I was born, and they all died off but me and pa and my brother Ike. Pa, he 'lowed he'd break up and go down and live with Uncle Ben, who's got a little one-horse place on the river forty-four mile below Orleans. Pa was pretty poor and had some debts; so when he'd squared up there warn't nothing left but sixteen dollars and our nigger, Jim. That warn't enough to take us fourteen hundred mile, deck passage nor no other way. Well, when the river rose pa had a streak of luck one day; he ketched this piece of a raft; so we reckoned we'd go down to Orleans on it. Pa's luck didn't hold out; a steamboat run over the forrard corner of the raft one night, and we all went overboard and dove under the wheel; Jim and me come up all right, but pa was drunk, and Ike was only four years old, so they never come up no more. Well, for the next day or two we had considerable trouble, because people was always coming out in skiffs and trying to take Jim away from me, saying they believed he was a runaway nigger. We don't run daytimes no more now; nights they don't bother us."

The duke says:

"Leave me alone to cipher out a way so we can run in the daytime if we want to. I'll think the thing over— I'll invent a plan that'll fix it. We'll let it alone for to-day, because of course we don't want to go by that town yonder in daylight—it mightn't be healthy."

Towards night it begun to darken up and look like rain; the heat-lightning was squirting around low down in the sky and the leaves was beginning to shiver—it was going to be pretty ugly, it was easy to see that. So the duke and the king went to overhauling our wigwam, to see what the beds was like. My bed was a straw tick —better than Jim's, which was a corn-shuck tick; there's always cobs around about in a shuck tick and they poke into you and hurt, and when you roll over the dry shucks sound like you was rolling over in a pile of dead leaves; it makes such a rustling that you wake up. Well, the duke allowed he would take my bed; but the king allowed he wouldn't. He says:

"I should 'a' reckoned the difference in rank would 'a' sejested to you that a corn-shuck bed warn't just fitten for me to sleep on. Your Grace'll take the shuck bed yourself."

Jim and me was in a sweat again for a minute, being afraid there was going to be some more trouble amongst them; so we was pretty glad when the duke says:

" 'Tis my fate to be always ground into the mire under the iron heel of oppression. Misfortune has broken my once haughty spirit; I yield, I submit; 'tis my fate. I am alone in the world—let me suffer; I can bear it."

We got away as soon as it was good and dark. The king told us to stand well out towards the middle of the river and not show a light till we got a long ways below the town. We come in sight of the little bunch of lights by and by—that was the town, you know—and slid by

about a half a mile out, all right. When we was three-
quarters of a mile below we hoisted up our signal lantern; and about ten o'clock it come on to rain and blow
and thunder and lighten like everything; so the king
told us to both stay on watch till the weather got better;
then him and the duke crawled into the wigwam and
turned in for the night. It was my watch below till
twelve but I wouldn't 'a' turned in anyway if I'd had a
bed, because a body don't see such a storm as that
every day in the week, not by a long sight. My souls,
how the wind did scream along! And every second or
two there'd come a glare that lit up the white-caps for
a half a mile around, and you'd see the islands looking
dusty through the rain and the trees thrashing around in
the wind; then comes a *h-whack!*—bum! bum! bumble-
umble-um-bum-bum-bum-bum—and the thunder would
go rumbling and grumbling away, and quit—and then
rip comes another flash and another sockdolager. The
waves most washed me off the raft sometimes, but I
hadn't any clothes on and didn't mind. We didn't have
no trouble about snags; the lightning was glaring and
flittering around so constant that we could see them
plenty soon enough to throw her head this way or that
and miss them.

I had the middle watch, you know, but I was pretty
sleepy by that time, so Jim he said he would stand the
first half of it for me; he was always mighty good that
way, Jim was. I crawled into the wigwam, but the king
and the duke had their legs sprawled around so there
warn't no show for me; so I laid outside—I didn't mind
the rain, because it was warm, and the waves warn't
running so high now. About two they come up again,
though, and Jim was going to call me; but he changed
his mind because he reckoned they warn't high enough
yet to do any harm; but he was mistaken about that, for

pretty soon all of a sudden along comes a regular ripper and washed me overboard. It most killed Jim a-laughing. He was the easiest nigger to laugh that ever was, anyway.

I took the watch and Jim he laid down and snored away; and by and by the storm let up for good and all; and the first cabin-light that showed I rousted him out and we slid the raft into hiding-quarters for the day.

The king got out an old ratty deck of cards after breakfast and him and the duke played seven-up awhile, five cents a game. Then they got tired of it, and allowed they would "lay out a campaign," as they called it. The duke went down into his carpet-bag and fetched up a lot of little printed bills and read them out loud. One bill said, "The celebrated Dr. Armand de Montalban, of Paris," would "lecture on the Science of Phrenology" at such and such a place, on the blank day of blank, at ten cents admission, and "furnish charts of character at twenty-five cents apiece." The duke said that was *him*. In another bill he was the "world-renowned Shakespearian tragedian, Garrick the Younger, of Drury Lane, London." In other bills he had a lot of other names and done other wonderful things, like finding water and gold with a "divining-rod," "dissipating witch spells," and so on. By and by he says:

"But the histrionic muse is the darling. Have you ever trod the boards, Royalty?"

"No," says the king.

"You shall, then, before you're three days older, Fallen Grandeur," says the duke. "The first good town we come to we'll hire a hall and do the sword-fight in 'Richard III.' and the balcony scene in 'Romeo and Juliet.' How does that strike you?"

"I'm in up to the hub for anything that will pay, Bilge-water; but, you see, I don't know nothing about play-actin', and hain't ever seen much of it. I was too small when pap used to have 'em at the palace. Do you reckon you can learn me?"

"Easy!"

"All right. I'm jist a-freezin' for something fresh, anyway. Le's commence right away."

So the duke he told him all about who Romeo was and who Juliet was, and said he was used to being Romeo, so the king could be Juliet.

"But if Juliet's such a young gal, duke, my peeled head and my white whiskers is goin' to look oncommon odd on her, maybe."

"No, don't you worry; these country jakes won't ever think of that. Besides, you know, you'll be in costume and that makes all the difference in the world; Juliet's in a balcony, enjoying the moonlight before she goes to bed, and she's got on her nightgown and her ruffled nightcap. Here are the costumes for the parts."

He got out two or three curtain-calico suits, which he said was meedyevil armor for Richard III and t'other chap, and a long white cotton nightshirt and a ruffled nightcap to match. The king was satisfied; so the duke got out his book and read the parts over in the most splendid spread-eagle way, prancing around and acting at the same time, to show how it had got to be done; then he give the book to the king and told him to get his part by heart.

There was a little one-horse town about three mile down the bend, and after dinner the duke said he had ciphered out his idea about how to run in daylight without it being dangersome for Jim; so he allowed he would go down to the town and fix that thing. The king allowed he would go, too, and see if he couldn't strike something. We was out of coffee, so Jim said I better go along with them in the canoe and get some.

When we got there there warn't nobody stirring; streets empty and perfectly dead and still, like Sunday. We found a sick nigger sunning himself in a back yard, and he said everybody that warn't too young or too sick or too old was gone to camp-meeting, about two mile back in the woods. The king got the directions and allowed he'd go and work that camp-meeting for all it was worth, and I might go, too.

The duke said what he was after was a printing-office. We found it; a little bit of a concern up over a carpenter-shop—carpenters and printers all gone to the meeting and no doors locked. It was a dirty, littered-up place, and had ink-marks and handbills with pictures of horses and runaway niggers on them, all over the walls. The duke shed his coat and said he was all right now. So me and the king lit out for the camp-meeting.

We got there in about a half an hour fairly dripping, for it was a most awful hot day. There was as much as a thousand people there from twenty mile around. The woods was full of teams and wagons, hitched every-wheres, feeding out of the wagon-troughs and stomping to keep off the flies. There was sheds made out of poles and roofed over with branches, where they had lemon-ade and gingerbread to sell and piles of watermelons and green corn and such-like truck.

The preaching was going on under the same kinds of sheds, only they was bigger and held crowds of people. The benches was made out of outside slabs of logs, with holes bored in the round side to drive sticks into for legs. They didn't have no backs. The preachers had high platforms to stand on at one end of the sheds. The women had on sun-bonnets and some had linsey-woolsey frocks, some gingham ones, and a few of the young ones had on calico. Some of the young men was bare-footed and some of the children didn't have on any

clothes but just a tow-linen shirt. Some of the old
women was knitting, and some of the young folks was
courting on the sly.

The first shed we come to the preacher was lining out
a hymn. He lined out two lines, everybody sung it, and
it was kind of grand to hear it, there was so many of
them and they done it in such a rousing way; then he
lined out two more for them to sing—and so on. The
people woke up more and more and sung louder and
louder; and towards the end some begun to groan and
some begun to shout. Then the preacher begun to
preach and begun in earnest, too; and went weaving
first to one side of the platform and then the other, and
then a-leaning down over the front of it with his arms
and his body going all the time, and shouting his words
out with all his might; and every now and then he
would hold up his Bible and spread it open and kind of
pass it around this way and that, shouting, "It's the
brazen serpent in the wilderness! Look upon it and live!"
And people would shout out, "Glory!—A-a-*men!*" And
so he went on, and the people groaning and crying and
saying amen:

"Oh, come to the mourners' bench! come, black with
sin! (*amen!*) come, sick and sore! (*amen!*) come, lame
and halt and blind! (*amen!*) come, pore and needy, sunk
in shame! (*a-a-men!*) come, all that's worn and soiled
and suffering!—come with a broken spirit! come with
a contrite heart! come in your rags and sin and dirt!
the waters that cleanse is free, the door of heaven
stands open—oh, enter in and be at rest!" (*a-a-men!
glory, glory hallelujah!*)

And so on. You couldn't make out what the preacher
said any more, on account of the shouting and crying.
Folks got up everywheres in the crowd and worked their
way just by main strength to the mourners' bench, with

the tears running down their faces; and when all the mourners had got up there to the front benches in a crowd, they sung and shouted and flung themselves down on the straw, just crazy and wild.

Well, the first I knowed the king got a-going and you could hear him over everybody; and next he went a-charging up onto the platform and the preacher he begged him to speak to the people, and he done it. He told them he was a pirate—been a pirate for thirty years out in the Indian Ocean—and his crew was thinned out considerable last spring in a fight and he was home now to take out some fresh men, and thanks to goodness he'd been robbed last night and put ashore off of a steamboat without a cent, and he was glad of it; it was the blessedest thing that ever happened to him, because he was a changed man now and happy for the first time in his life; and, poor as he was, he was going to start right off and work his way back to the Indian Ocean and put in the rest of his life trying to turn the pirates into the true path; for he could do it better than anybody else, being acquainted with all the pirate crews in that ocean; and though it would take him a long time to get there without money, he would get there anyway and every time he convinced a pirate he would say to him, "Don't you thank me, don't you give me no credit; it all belongs to them dear people in Pokeville camp-meeting, natural brothers and benefactors of the race, and that dear preacher there, the truest friend a pirate ever had!"

And then he busted into tears, and so did everybody. Then somebody sings out, "Take up a collection for him, take up a collection!" Well, a half a dozen made a jump to do it but somebody sings out, "Let *him* pass the hat around!" Then everybody said it, the preacher too.

So the king went all through the crowd with his hat, swabbing his eyes and blessing the people and praising

them and thanking them for being so good to the poor
pirates away off there; and every little while the prettiest
kind of girls, with the tears running down their cheeks,
would up and ask him would he let them kiss him for to
remember him by; and he always done it; and some of
them he hugged and kissed as many as five or six times
—and he was invited to stay a week; and everybody
wanted him to live in their houses and said they'd think
it was an honor; but he said as this was the last day of
the camp-meeting he couldn't do no good, and besides
he was in a sweat to get to the Indian Ocean right off
and go to work on the pirates.

When we got back to the raft and he come to count
up he found he had collected eighty-seven dollars and
seventy-five cents. And then he had fetched away a
three-gallon jug of whisky, too, that he found under a
wagon when he was starting home through the woods.
The king said, take it all around, it laid over any day
he'd ever put in in the missionarying line. He said it
warn't no use talking, heathens don't amount to shucks
alongside of pirates to work a camp-meeting with.

The duke was thinking *he'd* been doing pretty well
till the king come to show up, but after that he didn't
think so so much. He had set up and printed off two
little jobs for farmers in that printing-office—horse bills
—and took the money, four dollars. And he had got in
ten dollars' worth of advertisements for the paper, which
he said he would put in for four dollars if they would pay
in advance—so they done it. The price of the paper was
two dollars a year but he took in three subscriptions for
half a dollar apiece on condition of them paying him in
advance; they were going to pay in cordwood and
onions as usual but he said he had just bought the concern and knocked down the price as low as he could
afford it and was going to run it for cash. He set up a

little piece of poetry, which he made himself out of his own head—three verses—kind of sweet and saddish—the name of it was, "Yes, crush, cold world, this breaking heart"—and he left that all set up and ready to print in the paper and didn't charge nothing for it. Well, he took in nine dollars and a half and said he'd done a pretty square day's work for it.

Then he showed us another little job he'd printed and hadn't charged for, because it was for us. It had a picture of a runaway nigger with a bundle on a stick over his shoulder, and "$200 reward" under it. The reading was all about Jim and just described him to a dot. It said he run away from St. Jacques's plantation, forty mile below New Orleans, last winter, and likely went north, and whoever would catch him and send him back he could have the reward and expenses.

"Now," says the duke, "after to-night we can run in the daytime if we want to. Whenever we see anybody coming we can tie Jim hand and foot with a rope, and lay him in the wigwam and show this handbill and say we captured him up the river, and were too poor to travel on a steamboat, so we got this little raft on credit from our friends and are going down to get the reward. Handcuffs and chains would look still better on Jim but it wouldn't go well with the story of us being so poor. Too much like jewelry. Ropes are the correct thing—we must preserve the unities, as we say on the boards."

We all said the duke was pretty smart and there couldn't be no trouble about running daytimes. We judged we could make miles enough that night to get out of the reach of the powwow. We reckoned the duke's work in the printing-office was going to make in that little town; then we could boom right along if we wanted to.

·We laid low and kept still and never shoved out till
nearly ten o'clock; then we slid by, pretty wide away
from the town and didn't hoist our lantern till we was
clear out of sight of it.

When Jim called me to take the watch at four in the
morning, he says:

"Huck, does you reck'n we gwyne to run acrost any
mo' kings on dis trip?"

"No," I says, "I reckon not."

"Well," says he, "dat's all right, den. I doan' mine one
er two kings, but dat's. enough. Dis one's powerful
drunk, en de duke ain' much better."

I found Jim had been trying to get him to talk French,
so he could hear what it was like; but he said he had
been in this country so long and had so much trouble,
he'd forgot it.

XXI. AN ARKANSAW DIFFICULTY

It was after sun-up now but we went right on and
didn't tie up. The king and the duke turned out by and
by looking pretty rusty, but after they'd jumped overboard and took a swim it chippered them up a good
deal. After breakfast the king he took a seat on the
corner of the raft and pulled off his boots and rolled up
his britches and let his legs dangle in the water, so as to
be comfortable, and lit his pipe and went to getting his
"Romeo and Juliet" by heart. When he had got it pretty
good him and the duke begun to practise it together.
The duke had to learn him over and over again how to
say every speech, and he made him sigh and put his
hand on his heart, and after a while he said he done it
pretty well, "only," he says, "you mustn't bellow out
Romeo! that way, like a bull—you must say it soft and

sick and languishy, so—R-o-o-meo! that is the idea; for Juliet's a dear sweet mere child of a girl, you know, and she don't bray like a jackass."

Well, next they got out a couple of long swords that the duke made out of oak laths, and begun to practise the sword-fight—the duke called himself Richard III; and the way they laid on and pranced around the raft was grand to see. But by and by the king tripped and fell overboard, and after that they took a rest and had a talk about all kinds of adventures they'd had in other times along the river.

After dinner the duke says:

"Well, Capet, we'll want to make this a first-class show, you know, so I guess we'll add a little more to it. We want a little something to answer encores with, anyway."

"What's onkores, Bilgewater?"

The duke told him, and then says:

"I'll answer by doing the Highland fling or the sailor's hornpipe, and you—well, let me see—oh, I've got it—you can do Hamlet's soliloquy."

"Hamlet's which?"

"Hamlet's soliloquy, you know; the most celebrated thing in Shakespeare. Ah, it's sublime, sublime! Always fetches the house. I haven't got it in the book—I've only got one volume—but I reckon I can piece it out from memory. I'll just walk up and down a minute and see if I can call it back from recollection's vaults."

So he went to marching up and down, thinking, and frowning horrible every now and then; then he would hoist up his eyebrows; next he would squeeze his hand on his forehead and stagger back and kind of moan; next he would sigh and next he'd let on to drop a tear. It was beautiful to see him. By and by he got it. He told us to give attention. Then he strikes a most noble atti-

tude, with one leg shoved forwards and his arms
stretched away up and his head tilted back, looking up
at the sky, and then he begins to rip and rave and grit
his teeth, and after that, all through his speech, he
howled and spread around and swelled up his chest and
just knocked the spots out of any acting ever *I* see before. This is the speech—I learned it easy enough while
he was learning it to the king:

To be, or not to be; that is the bare bodkin
That makes calamity of so long life;
For who would fardels bear, till Birnam Wood do come to
    Dunsinane,
But that the fear of something after death
Murders the innocent sleep,
Great nature's second course,
And makes us rather sling the arrows of outrageous fortune
Than fly to others that we know not of.
There's the respect must give us pause:
Wake Duncan with thy knocking! I would thou couldst;
For who would bear the whips and scorns of time,
The oppressor's wrong, the proud man's contumely,
The law's delay, and the quietus which his pangs might take,
In the dead waste and middle of the night, when churchyards
    yawn
In customary suits of solemn black,
But that the undiscovered country from whose bourne no
    traveler returns,
Breathes forth contagion on the world,
And thus the native hue of resolution, like the poor cat i' the
    adage,
Is sicklied o'er with care,
And all the clouds that lowered o'er our housetops,
With this regard their currents turn awry,
And lose the name of action.
'Tis a consummation devoutly to be wished. But soft you, the
    fair Ophelia:
Ope not thy ponderous and marble jaws,
But get thee to a nunnery—go!

Well, the old man he liked that speech and he mighty
soon got it so he could do it first-rate. It seemed like he

was just born for it, and when he had his hand in and was excited, it was perfectly lovely the way he would rip and tear and rair up behind when he was getting it off.

The first chance we got the duke he had some show bills printed, and after that, for two or three days as we floated along, the raft was a most uncommon lively place, for there warn't nothing but sword-fighting and rehearsing—as the duke called it—going on all the time. One morning when we was pretty well down the state of Arkansaw, we come in sight of a little one-horse town in a big bend; so we tied up about three-quarters of a mile above it in the mouth of a crick which was shut in like a tunnel by the cypress trees, and all of us but Jim took the canoe and went down there to see if there was any chance in that place for our show.

We struck it mighty lucky; there was going to be a circus there that afternoon and the country people was already beginning to come in, in all kinds of old shackly wagons and on horses. The circus would leave before night, so our show would have a pretty good chance. The duke he hired the courthouse and we went around and stuck up our bills. They read like this:

Shakesperean Revival ! ! !
Wonderful Attraction!
For One Night Only!
The world renowned tragedians,
DAVID GARRICK THE YOUNGER, of Drury Lane Theatre, London,
and
EDMUND KEAN THE ELDER, of the Royal Haymarket Theatre,
Whitechapel, Pudding Lane, Piccadilly, London, and the
Royal Continental Theatres, in their sublime
Shakesperean Spectacle entitled
The Balcony Scene
in
ROMEO AND JULIET ! ! !

Romeo...Mr. Garrick
Juliet...Mr. Kean

Assisted by the whole strength of the company!
New costumes, new scenery, new appointments!

Also:

The thrilling, masterly, and blood-curdling
Broad-sword conflict
In Richard III. ! ! !

Richard III......................................Mr. Garrick
Richmond.......................................Mr. Kean

Also:

(by special request)
HAMLET's IMMORTAL SOLILOQUY ! !
By the Illustrious Kean!
Done by him 300 consecutive nights in Paris!
For One Night Only,
On account of imperative European engagements!
Admission 25 cents; children and servants, 10 cents.

Then we went loafing around town. The stores and
houses was most all old, shackly, dried-up frame concerns that hadn't ever been painted; they was set up
three or four foot above ground on stilts, so as to be out
of reach of the water when the river was overflowed.
The houses had little gardens around them but they
didn't seem to raise hardly anything in them but
jimpson-weeds and sunflowers, and ashpiles and old
curled-up boots and shoes and pieces of bottles, and
rags and played-out tinware. The fences was made of
different kinds of boards nailed on at different times,
and they leaned every which way and had gates that
didn't generly have but one hinge—a leather one. Some
of the fences had been whitewashed some time or another but the duke said it was in Columbus's time, like
enough. There was generly hogs in the garden, and
people driving them out.

All the stores was along one street. They had white

domestic awnings in front, and the country people hitched their horses to the awning-posts. There was empty drygoods boxes under the awnings and loafers roosting on them all day long, whittling them with their Barlow knives and chawing tobacco and gaping and yawning and stretching—a mighty ornery lot. They generly had on yellow straw hats most as wide as an umbrella but didn't wear no coats nor waistcoats; they called one another Bill and Buck and Hank and Joe and Andy, and talked lazy and drawly and used considerable many cuss-words. There was as many as one loafer leaning up against every awning-post and he most always had his hands in his britches pockets, except when he fetched them out to lend a chaw of tobacco or scratch. What a body was hearing amongst them all the time was:

"Gimme a chaw 'v tobacker, Hank."

'Cain't; I hain't got but one chaw left. Ask Bill."

Maybe Bill he gives him a chaw, maybe he lies and says he ain't got none. Some of them kinds of loafers never has a cent in the world nor a chaw of tobacco of their own. They get all their chawing by borrowing; they say to a fellow, "I wisht you'd len' me a chaw, Jack, I jist this minute give Ben Thompson the last chaw I had"—which is a lie pretty much every time, it don't fool nobody but a stranger, but Jack ain't no stranger, so he says:

"*You* give him a chaw, did you? So did your sister's cat's grandmother. You pay me back the chaws you've awready borry'd off'n me, Lafe Buckner, then I'll loan you one or two ton of it and won't charge you no back intrust, nuther."

"Well, I *did* pay you back some of it wunst."

"Yes, you did—'bout six chaws. You borry'd store tobacker and paid back nigger-head."

Store tobacco is flat black plug but these fellows mostly chaws the natural leaf twisted. When they borrow a chaw they don't generly cut it off with a knife, but set the plug in between their teeth and gnaw with their teeth and tug at the plug with their hands till they get it in two; then sometimes the one that owns the tobacco looks mournful at it when it's handed back and says, sarcastic:

"Here, gimme the *chaw* and you take the *plug*."

All the streets and lanes was just mud; they warn't nothing else *but* mud—mud as black as tar and nigh about a foot deep in some places, and two or three inches deep in *all* the places. The hogs loafed and grunted around everywheres. You'd see a muddy sow and a litter of pigs come lazying along the street and whollop herself right down in the way, where folks had to walk around her, and she'd stretch out and shut her eyes and wave her ears whilst the pigs was milking her and look as happy as if she was on salary. And pretty soon you'd hear a loafer sing out, "Hi! *so* boy! sick him, Tige!" and away the sow would go, squealing most horrible, with a dog or two swinging to each ear and three or four dozen more a-coming, and then you would see all the loafers get up and watch the thing out of sight and laugh at the fun and look grateful for the noise. Then they'd settle back again till there was a dog-fight. There couldn't anything wake them up all over and make them happy all over, like a dog-fight—unless it might be putting turpentine on a stray dog and setting fire to him, or tying a tin pan to his tail and see him run himself to death.

On the river-front some of the houses was sticking out over the bank, and they was bowed and bent and about ready to tumble in. The people had moved out of them. The bank was caved away under one corner of some others, and that corner was hanging over. People lived in them yet but it was dangersome, because sometimes a strip of land as wide as a house caves in at a time. Sometimes a belt of land a quarter of a mile deep will start in and cave along and cave along till it all caves into the river in one summer. Such a town as that has to be always moving back, and back, and back, because the river's always gnawing at it.

The nearer it got to noon that day the thicker and thicker was the wagons and horses in the streets, and more coming all the time. Families fetched their dinners with them from the country and eat them in the wagons. There was considerable whisky-drinking going on and I seen three fights. By and by somebody sings out:

"Here comes old Boggs!—in from the country for his little old monthly drunk; here he comes, boys!"

All the loafers looked glad; I reckoned they was used to having fun out of Boggs. One of them says:

"Wonder who he's a-gwyne to chaw up this time. If he'd a-chawed up all the men he's ben a-gwyne to chaw up in the last twenty year he'd have considerable ruputation now."

Another one says, "I wisht old Boggs'd threaten me, 'cuz then I'd know I warn't gwyne to die for a thousan' year."

Boggs comes a-tearing along on his horse, whooping and yelling like an Injun and singing out:

"Cler the track, thar. I'm on the waw-path, and the price uv coffins is a-gwyne to raise."

He was drunk and weaving about in his saddle; he was over fifty year old and had a very red face. Everybody yelled at him and laughed at him and sassed him, and he sassed back and said he'd attend to them and lay them out in their regular turns, but he couldn't wait now because he'd come to town to kill old Colonel Sherburn and his motto was, "Meat first and spoon vittles to top off on."

He see me and rode up and says:

"Whar'd you come f'm, boy? You prepared to die?"

Then he rode on. I was scared but a man says:

"He don't mean nothing; he's always a-carryin' on like that when he's drunk. He's the best-naturedest old fool in Arkansaw—never hurt nobody, drunk nor sober."

Boggs rode up before the biggest store in town and bent his head down so he could see under the curtain of the awning and yells:

"Come out here, Sherburn! Come out and meet the man you've swindled. You're the houn' I'm after and I'm a-gwyne to have you, too!"

And so he went on, calling Sherburn everything he could lay his tongue to, and the whole street packed with people listening and laughing and going on. By and by a proud-looking man about fifty-five—and he was a heap the best-dressed man in that town, too—steps out of the store, and the crowd drops back on each side to let him come. He says to Boggs, mighty ca'm and slow —he says:

"I'm tired of this but I'll endure it till one o'clock. Till one o'clock, mind—no longer. If you open your mouth against me only once after that time you can't travel so far but I will find you."

Then he turns and goes in. The crowd looked mighty sober; nobody stirred and there warn't no more laughing. Boggs rode off blackguarding Sherburn as loud as he could yell, all down the street; and pretty soon back he comes and stops before the store, still keeping it up. Some men crowded around him and tried to get him to shut up but he wouldn't; they told him it would be one o'clock in about fifteen minutes, and so he *must* go home —he must go right away. But it didn't do no good. He cussed away with all his might and throwed his hat down in the mud and rode over it, and pretty soon away he went a-raging down the street again with his gray hair a-flying. Everybody that could get a chance at him tried their best to coax him off of his horse so they could lock him up and get him sober; but it warn't no use—up the street he would tear again, and give Sherburn another cussing. By and by somebody says:

"Go for his daughter!—quick, go for his daughter; sometimes he'll listen to her. If anybody can persuade him, she can."

So somebody started on a run. I walked down street a ways and stopped. In about five or ten minutes here comes Boggs again but not on his horse. He was a-reeling across the street towards me, bareheaded, with a friend on both sides of him a-holt of his arms and hurrying him along. He was quiet and looked uneasy and he warn't hanging back any but was doing some of the hurrying himself. Somebody sings out:

"Boggs!"

I looked over there to see who said it, and it was that Colonel Sherburn. He was standing perfectly still in the street and had a pistol raised in his right hand—not aiming it but holding it out with the barrel tilted up towards the sky. The same second I see a young girl coming on the run, and two men with her. Boggs and the men turned round to see who called him, and when they see the pistol the men jumped to one side, and the pistol-barrel come down slow and steady to a level—both barrels cocked. Boggs throws up both of his hands and says, "O Lord, don't shoot!" Bang! goes the first shot and he staggers back, clawing at the air—bang! goes the second one and he tumbles backwards onto the ground, heavy and solid, with his arms spread out. That young girl screamed out and comes rushing, and down she throws herself on her father, crying, and saying, "Oh, he's killed him, he's killed him!" The crowd closed up around them and shouldered and jammed one another, with their necks stretched, trying to see, and people on the inside trying to shove them back and shouting, "Back, back! give him air, give him air!"

Colonel Sherburn he tossed his pistol onto the ground, and turned around on his heels and walked off.

They took Boggs to a little drug store, the crowd pressing around just the same and the whole town following, and I rushed and got a good place at the window, where I was close to him and could see in. They laid him on the floor and put one large Bible under his head, and opened another one and spread it on his breast; but they tore open his shirt first, and I seen where one of the bullets went in. He made about a dozen long gasps, his breast lifting the Bible up when he drawed in his breath, and letting it down again when he breathed it out—and after that he laid still; he was dead. Then they pulled his daughter away from him, screaming and crying, and took her off. She was about sixteen, and very sweet and gentle-looking, but awful pale and scared.

Well, pretty soon the whole town was there, squirming and scrouging and pushing and shoving to get at the window and have a look, but people that had the places wouldn't give them up and folks behind them was saying all the time, "Say, now, you've looked enough, you fellows; 'tain't right and 'tain't fair for you to stay thar all the time, and never give nobody a chance; other folks has their rights as well as you."

There was considerable jawing back, so I slid out, thinking maybe there was going to be trouble. The streets was full, and everybody was excited. Everybody that seen the shooting was telling how it happened, and

there was a big crowd packed around each one of these
fellows, stretching their necks and listening. One long,
lanky man, with long hair and a big white fur stovepipe
hat on the back of his head, and a crooked-handled
cane, marked out the places on the ground where Boggs
stood and where Sherburn stood, and the people following him around from one place to t'other and watching everything he done, and bobbing their heads to show
they understood and stooping a little and resting their
hands on their thighs to watch him mark the places on
the ground with his cane; and then he stood up straight
and stiff where Sherburn had stood, frowning and having his hat-brim down over his eyes, and sung out,
"Boggs!" and then fetched his cane down slow to a level,
and says "Bang!," staggered backwards, says "Bang!"
again, and fell down flat on his back. The people that
had seen the thing said he done it perfect; said it was
just exactly the way it all happened. Then as much as a
dozen people got out their bottles and treated him.

Well, by and by somebody said Sherburn ought to be
lynched. In about a minute everybody was saying it; so
away they went, mad and yelling and snatching down
every clothes-line they come to to do the hanging with.

XXII. WHY THE LYNCHING BEE FAILED

They swarmed up towards Sherburn's house,
a-whooping and raging like Injuns, and everything had
to clear the way or get run over and tromped to mush,
and it was awful to see. Children was heeling it ahead of
the mob, screaming and trying to get out of the way,
and every window along the road was full of women's
heads, and there was nigger boys in every tree and
bucks and wenches looking over every fence, and as

soon as the mob would get nearly to them they would
break and skaddle back out of reach. Lots of the women
and girls was crying and taking on, scared most to
death.

They swarmed up in front of Sherburn's palings as
thick as they could jam together, and you couldn't hear
yourself think for the noise. It was a little twenty-foot
yard. Some sung out "Tear down the fence! tear down
the fence!" Then there was a racket of ripping and tearing and smashing, and down she goes, and the front wall
of the crowd begins to roll in like a wave.

Just then Sherburn steps out onto the roof of his little
front porch with a double-barrel gun in his hand, and
takes his stand perfectly ca'm and deliberate, not saying
a word. The racket stopped and the wave sucked back.

Sherburn never said a word—just stood there, looking down. The stillness was awful creepy and uncomfortable. Sherburn run his eye slow along the crowd,
and wherever it struck the people tried a little to out-
gaze him but they couldn't, they dropped their eyes and
looked sneaky. Then pretty soon Sherburn sort of
laughed; not the pleasant kind but the kind that makes
you feel like when you are eating bread that's got sand
in it.

Then he says, slow and scornful:

"The idea of *you* lynching anybody! it's amusing. The
idea of you thinking you had pluck enough to lynch a
man! Because you're brave enough to tar and feather
poor friendless cast-out women that come along here,
did that make you think you had grit enough to lay your
hands on a *man?* Why, a *man's* safe in the hands of ten
thousand of your kind—as long as it's daytime and
you're not behind him.

"Do I know you? I know you clear through. I was
born and raised in the South and I've lived in the North,

so I know the average all around. The average man's a
coward. In the North he lets anybody walk over him
that wants to, and goes home and prays for a humble
spirit to bear it. In the South one man, all by himself,
has stopped a stage full of men in the daytime and
robbed the lot. Your newspapers call you a brave people
so much that you think you *are* braver than any other
people—whereas you're just *as* brave and no braver.
Why don't your juries hang murderers? Because they're
afraid the man's friends will shoot them in the back in
the dark—and it's just what they *would* do.

"So they always acquit; and then a *man* goes in the
night, with a hundred masked cowards at his back, and
lynches the rascal. Your mistake is that you didn't bring
a man with you; that's one mistake, and the other is
that you didn't come in the dark and fetch your masks.
You brought *part* of a man—Buck Harkness, there—
and if you hadn't had him to start you, you'd 'a' taken it
out in blowing.

"You didn't want to come. The average man don't like
trouble and danger. *You* don't like trouble and danger.
But if only *half* a man—like Buck Harkness there—
shouts 'Lynch him! lynch him!' you're afraid to back
down—afraid you'll be found out to be what you are—
cowards—and so you raise a yell and hang yourselves
onto that half-a-man's coat-tail and come raging up
here, swearing what big things you're going to do. The
pitifulest thing out is a mob; that's what an army is—a
mob; they don't fight with courage that's born in them
but with courage that's borrowed from their mass and
from their officers. But a mob without any *man* at the
head of it is *beneath* pitifulness. Now the thing for *you*
to do is to droop your tails and go home and crawl in a
hole. If any real lynching's going to be done it will be

done in the dark, Southern fashion; and when they come they'll bring their masks, and fetch a *man* along. Now *leave*—and take your half-a-man with you"—tossing his gun up across his left arm and cocking it when he says this.

The crowd washed back sudden, and then broke all apart and went tearing off every which way, and Buck Harkness he heeled it after them, looking tolerable cheap. I could 'a' stayed if I wanted to but I didn't want to.

I went to the circus and loafed around the back side till the watchman went by, and then dived in under the tent. I had my twenty-dollar gold piece and some other money but I reckoned I better save it, because there ain't no telling how soon you are going to need it, away from home and amongst strangers that way. You can't be too careful. I ain't opposed to spending money on circuses when there ain't no other way, but there ain't no use in *wasting* it on them.

It was a real bully circus. It was the splendidest sight that ever was when they all come riding in, two and two, and gentleman and lady, side by side, the men just in their drawers and undershirts, and no shoes nor stirrups, and resting their hands on their thighs easy and comfortable—there must 'a' been twenty of them—and every lady with a lovely complexion, and perfectly beautiful, and looking just like a gang of real sure-enough queens, and dressed in clothes that cost millions of dollars, and just littered with diamonds. It was a powerful fine sight; I never see anything so lovely. And then one by one they got up and stood, and went a-weaving around the ring so gentle and wavy and graceful, the men looking ever so tall and airy and straight, with their heads bobbing and skimming along away up there under the tent-roof, and every lady's rose-leafy dress flapping soft and silky around her hips, and she looking like the most loveliest parasol.

And then faster and faster they went, all of them dancing, first one foot stuck out in the air and then the other, the horses leaning more and more, and the ringmaster going round and round the center pole, cracking his whip and shouting "Hi!—hi!" and the clown cracking jokes behind him; and by and by all hands dropped the reins and every lady put her knuckles on her hips and every gentleman folded his arms, and then how the horses did lean over and hump themselves! And so one after the other they all skipped off into the ring and made the sweetest bow I ever see and then scampered out, and everybody clapped their hands and went just about wild.

Well, all through the circus they done the most astonishing things, and all the time that clown carried on so it most killed the people. The ringmaster couldn't ever say a word to him but he was back at him quick as a wink with the funniest things a body ever said, and how he ever *could* think of so many of them, and so sudden and so pat, was what I couldn't no way understand. Why, I couldn't 'a' thought of them in a year. And by and by a drunk man tried to get into the ring—said he wanted to ride, said he could ride as well as anybody that ever was. They argued and tried to keep him out but he wouldn't listen, and the whole show come to a standstill. Then the people begun to holler at him and make fun of him, and that made him mad and he begun to rip and tear; so that stirred up the people, and a lot of men begun to pile down off of the benches and swarm towards the ring, saying, "Knock him down! throw him out!" and one or two women begun to scream. So, then, the ringmaster he made a little speech and said he hoped there wouldn't be no disturbance, and if the man would promise he wouldn't make no more trouble he would let him ride if he thought he could stay on the horse. So everybody laughed and said all right, and the man got on. The minute he was on, the horse begun to rip and tear and jump and cavort around, with two circus men hanging on to his bridle trying to hold him, and the drunk man hanging on to his neck and his heels flying in the air every jump, and the whole crowd of people standing up shouting and laughing till the tears rolled down. And at last, sure enough, all the circus men could do, the horse broke loose and away he went like the very nation, round and round the ring, with that sot laying down on him and hanging to his neck, with first one leg hanging most to the ground on one side and then t'other one on t'other side, and the people just crazy. It warn't funny to me, though; I was all of a tremble to see his danger. But pretty soon he struggled up astraddle and grabbed the bridle, a-reeling this way and that, and the next minute he sprung up and dropped the bridle and stood! and the horse a-going like a house afire, too. He just stood up there, a-sailing around as easy and comfortable as if he warn't ever drunk in his life—and then he begun to pull off his clothes and sling them. He shed them so thick they kind of clogged up the air, and altogether he shed seventeen suits. And, then, there he was, slim and handsome and dressed the gaudiest and prettiest you ever saw, and he lit into that horse with his whip and made him fairly hum—and finally skipped off, and made his bow and danced off to the dressing-room, and everybody just a-howling with pleasure and astonishment.

Then the ringmaster he see how he had been fooled,

and he *was* the sickest ringmaster you ever see, I reckon. Why, it was one of his own men! He had got up that joke all out of his own head and never let on to nobody. Well, I felt sheepish enough to be took in so, but I wouldn't 'a' been in that ringmaster's place, not for a thousand dollars. I don't know; there may be bullier circuses than what that one was but I never struck them yet. Anyways, it was plenty good enough for *me;* and wherever I run across it, it can have all of *my* custom every time.

Well, that night we had *our* show, but there warn't only about twelve people there—just enough to pay expenses. And they laughed all the time and that made the duke mad; and everybody left, anyway, before the show was over, but one boy which was asleep. So the duke said these Arkansaw lunkheads couldn't come up to Shakespeare, what they wanted was low comedy—and maybe something ruther worse than low comedy, he reckoned. He said he could size their style. So next morning he got some big sheets of wrapping-paper and some black paint, and drawed off some handbills and stuck them up all over the village. The bills said:

At the Court House!
FOR 3 NIGHTS ONLY!
The World-Renowned Tragedians
DAVID GARRICK THE YOUNGER!
AND
EDMUND KEAN THE ELDER!
Of the London and Continental Theatres,
In their Thrilling Tragedy of
THE KING'S CAMELEOPARD,
OR
THE ROYAL NONESUCH! ! !
Admission 50 cents.

Then at the bottom was the biggest line of all, which said:

LADIES AND CHILDREN NOT ADMITTED

"There," says he, "if that line don't fetch them, I don't know Arkansaw!"

XXIII. THE ORNERINESS OF KINGS

Well, all day him and the king was hard at it, rigging up a stage and a curtain and a row of candles for footlights, and that night the house was jam full of men in no time. When the place couldn't hold no more, the duke he quit tending door and went around the back way and come onto the stage and stood up before the curtain and made a little speech, and praised up this tragedy and said it was the most thrillingest one that ever was; and so he went on a-bragging about the tragedy and about Edmund Kean the Elder, which was to play the main principal part in it; and at last when he'd got everybody's expectations up high enough, he rolled up the curtain, and the next minute the king come a-prancing out on all fours, naked; and he was painted all over, ring-streaked-and-striped, all sorts of colors, as splendid as a rainbow. And—but never mind the rest of his outfit; it was just wild but it was awful funny. The people most killed themselves laughing, and when the king got done capering and capered off behind the scenes, they roared and clapped and stormed and hawhawed till he come back and done it over again, and after that they made him do it another time. Well, it would a-made a cow laugh to see the shines that old idiot cut.

Then the duke he lets the curtain down, and bows to the people and says the great tragedy will be performed only two nights more, on accounts of pressing London engagements, where the seats is all sold already for it in Drury Lane; and then he makes them another bow and says if he has succeeded in pleasing them and instructing them, he will be deeply obleeged if they will mention it to their friends and get them to come and see it.

Twenty people sings out:

"What, is it over? Is that *all*?"

The duke says yes. Then there was a fine time. Everybody sings out, "Sold!" and rose up mad, and was a-going for that stage and them tragedians. But a big, fine-looking man jumps up on a bench and shouts:

"Hold on! Just a word, gentlemen." They stopped to listen. "We are sold—mighty badly sold. But we don't want to be the laughing-stock of this whole town, I reckon, and never hear the last of this thing as long as we live. *No.* What we want is to go out of here quiet, and talk this show up, and sell the *rest* of the town! Then we'll all be in the same boat. Ain't that sensible?" ("You bet it is!—the jedge is right!" everybody sings out.) "All right, then—not a word about any sell. Go along home, and advise everybody to come and see the tragedy."

Next day you couldn't hear nothing around that town but how splendid that show was. House was jammed again that night and we sold this crowd the same way. When me and the king and the duke got home to the raft we all had a supper, and by and by, about midnight, they made Jim and me back her out and float her down the middle of the river and fetch her in and hide her about two mile below town.

The third night the house was crammed again—and they warn't new-comers this time but people that was

at the show the other two nights. I stood by the duke at
the door and I see that every man that went in had his
pockets bulging, or something muffled up under his
coat—and I see it warn't no perfumery, neither, not by
a long sight. I smelt sickly eggs by the barrel, and rotten cabbages, and such things; and if I know the signs
of a dead cat being around, and I bet I do, there was
sixty-four of them went in. I shoved in there for a minute, but it was too various for me; I couldn't stand it.
Well, when the place couldn't hold no more people the
duke he give a fellow a quarter and told him to tend
door for him a minute, and then he started around for
the stage door, I after him; but the minute we turned
the corner and was in the dark he says:

"Walk fast now till you get away from the houses,
and then shin for the raft like the dickens was after you!"

I done it and he done the same. We struck the raft at
the same time, and in less than two seconds we was
gliding down-stream, all dark and still, and edging towards the middle of the river, nobody saying a word. I
reckoned the poor king was in for a gaudy time of it
with the audience, but nothing of the sort; pretty soon
he crawls out from under the wigwam and says:

"Well, how'd the old thing pan out this time, duke?"
He hadn't been up-town at all.

We never showed a light till we was about ten mile
below the village. Then we lit up and had a supper,
and the king and the duke fairly laughed their bones
loose over the way they'd served them people. The duke
says:

"Greenhorns, flatheads! *I* knew the first house would
keep mum and let the rest of the town get roped in, and
I knew they'd lay for us the third night and consider it
was *their* turn now. Well, it *is* their turn and I'd give
something to know how much they'd take for it. I *would*

just like to know how they're putting in their opportunity. They can turn it into a picnic if they want to—they brought plenty provisions."

Them rapscallions took in four hundred and sixty-five dollars in that three nights. I never see money hauled in by the wagon-load like that before.

By and by, when they was asleep and snoring, Jim says:

"Don't it s'prise you de way dem kings carries on, Huck?"

"No," I says, "it don't."

"Why don't it, Huck?"

"Well, it don't, because it's in the breed. I reckon they're all alike."

"But, Huck, dese kings o' ourn is reglar rapscallions; dat's jist what dey is; dey's reglar rapscallions."

"Well, that's what I'm a-saying; all kings is mostly rapscallions, as fur as I can make out."

"Is dat so?"

"You read about them once—you'll see. Look at Henry the Eight; this 'n' 's a Sunday-school Superintendent to *him*. And look at Charles Second, and Louis Fourteen, and Louis Fifteen, and James Second, and Edward Second, and Richard Third, and forty more; besides all them Saxon heptarchies that used to rip around so in old times and raise Cain. My, you ought to seen old Henry the Eight when he was in bloom. He *was* a blossom. He used to marry a new wife every day and chop off her head next morning. And he would do it just as indifferent as if he was ordering up eggs. 'Fetch up Nell Gwynn,' he says. They fetch her up. Next morning, 'Chop off her head!' And they chop it off. 'Fetch up Jane Shore,' he says; and up she comes. Next morning, 'Chop off her head'—and they chop it off. 'Ring up Fair Rosamun.' Fair Rosamun answers the bell. Next morning, 'Chop off her head.' And he made every one of them tell him a tale every night, and he kept that up till he had hogged a thousand and one tales that way, and then he put them all in a book and called it Domesday Book—which was a good name and stated the case. You don't know kings, Jim, but I know them; and this old rip of ourn is one of the cleanest I've struck in history. Well, Henry he takes a notion he wants to get up some trouble with this country. How does he go at it— give notice?—give the country a show? No. All of a sudden he heaves all the tea in Boston Harbor overboard and whacks out a declaration of independence and dares them to come on. That was *his* style—he never give anybody a chance. He had suspicions of his father, the Duke of Wellington. Well, what did he do? Ask him to show up? No—drownded him in a butt of mamsey, like a cat. S'pose people left money laying around where he was—what did he do? He collared it. S'pose he contracted to do a thing, and you paid him and didn't set down there and see that he done it— what did he do? He always done the other thing. S'pose he opened his mouth—what then? If he didn't shut it up powerful quick he'd lose a lie every time. That's the kind of a bug Henry was, and if we'd 'a' had him along 'stead of our kings he'd 'a' fooled that town a heap worse than ourn done. I don't say that ourn is lambs, because they ain't when you come right down to the cold facts, but they ain't nothing to *that* old ram, anyway. All I say is, kings is kings, and you got to make allowances. Take them all around, they're a mighty ornery lot. It's the way they're raised."

"But dis one do *smell* so like de nation, Huck."

"Well, they all do, Jim. *We* can't help the way a king smells; history don't tell no way."

"Now de duke, he's a tolerble likely man in some ways."

"Yes, a duke's different. But not very different. This one's a middling hard lot for a duke. When he's drunk there ain't no near-sighted man could tell him from a king."

"Well, anyways, I doan' hanker for no mo' un um, Huck. Dese is all I kin stan'."

"It's the way I feel, too, Jim. But we've got them on our hands and we got to remember what they are, and make allowances. Sometimes I wish we could hear of a country that's out of kings."

What was the use to tell Jim these warn't real kings and dukes? It wouldn't 'a' done no good, and besides, it was just as I said: you couldn't tell them from the real kind.

I went to sleep and Jim didn't call me when it was my turn. He often done that. When I waked up just at daybreak he was sitting there with his head down betwixt his knees, moaning and mourning to himself. I didn't take notice nor let on. I knowed what it was about. He was thinking about his wife and his children, away up yonder, and he was low and homesick; because he hadn't ever been away from home before in his life; and I do believe he cared just as much for his people as white folks does for their'n. It don't seem natural but I reckon it's so. He was often moaning and mourning that way nights, when he judged I was asleep, and saying, "Po' little 'Lizabeth! po' little Johnny! it's mighty hard; I spec' I ain't ever gwyne to see you no mo', no mo'!" He was a mighty good nigger, Jim was.

But this time I somehow got to talking to him about his wife and young ones, and by and by he says:

"What makes me feel so bad dis time 'uz bekase I hear sumpn over yonder on de bank like a whack, er a

slam, while ago, en it mine me er de time I treat my
little 'Lizabeth so ornery. She warn't on'y 'bout fo' year
ole, en she tuck de sk'yarlet fever, en had a powful
rough spell; but she got well, en one day she was
a-stannin' aroun', en I says to her, I says:

" 'Shet de do'.'

"She never done it; jis' stood dah, kiner smilin' up at
me. It make me mad; en I says agin, mighty loud, I says:

" 'Doan' you hear me? Shet de do'!'

"She jis' stood de same way, kiner smilin' up. I was
a-bilin'! I says:

" 'I lay I *make* you mine!'

"En wid dat I fetch' her a slap side de head dat sont
her a-sprawlin'. Den I went into de yuther room, en 'uz
gone 'bout ten minutes; en when I come back dah was
dat do' a-stannin' open *yit*, en dat chile stannin' mos'
right in it, a-lookin' down and mournin', en de tears
runnin' down. My, but I *wuz* mad! I was a-gwyne for
de chile, but jis' den—it was a do' dat open innerds—
jis' den, 'long come de wind en slam it to, behine de
chile, ker-*blam!*—en my lan', de chile never move'! My
breff mos' hop outer me; en I feel so—so—I doan' know
how I feel. I crope out, all a-tremblin', en crope aroun'
en open de do' easy en slow, en poke my head in behine
de chile, sof' en still, en all uv a sudden I says *pow!* jis'
as loud as I could yell. *She never budge!* Oh, Huck, I
bust out a-cryin' en grab her up in my arms, en says,
'Oh, de po' little thing! De Lord God Amighty fo'give
po' ole Jim, kaze he never gwyne to fo'give hisseff as
long's he live!' Oh, she was plumb deef en dumb, Huck,
plumb deef en dumb—en I'd ben a-treat'n' her so!"

Next day, towards night, we laid up under a little willow towhead out in the middle, where there was a village on each side of the river, and the duke and the king begun to lay out a plan for working them towns. Jim he spoke to the duke and said he hoped it wouldn't take but a few hours, because it got mighty heavy and tiresome to him when he had to lay all day in the wigwam tied with the rope. You see, when we left him all alone we had to tie him, because if anybody happened on him all by himself and not tied it wouldn't look much like he was a runaway nigger, you know. So the duke said it *was* kind of hard to have to lay roped all day and he'd cipher out some way to get around it.

He was uncommon bright, the duke was, and he soon struck it. He dressed Jim up in King Lear's outfit—it was a long curtain-calico gown and a white horse-hair wig and whiskers—and then he took his theatre paint and painted Jim's face and hands and ears and neck all over a dead, dull solid blue, like a man that's been drownded nine days. Blamed if he warn't the horriblest-looking outrage I ever see. Then the duke took and wrote out a sign on a shingle so:

Sick Arab—but harmless when not out of his head.

And he nailed that shingle to a lath and stood the lath up four or five foot in front of the wigwam. Jim was satisfied. He said it was a sight better than laying tied a couple of years every day and trembling all over every time there was a sound. The duke told him to make himself free and easy and if anybody ever come meddling around, he must hop out of the wigwam and carry on a little and fetch a howl or two like a wild beast, and he reckoned they would light out and leave him alone.

Which was sound enough judgment; but you take the average man, and he wouldn't wait for him to howl. Why, he didn't only look like he was dead, he looked considerable more than that.

These rapscallions wanted to try the Nonesuch again because there was so much money in it, but they judged it wouldn't be safe, because maybe the news might 'a' worked along down by this time. They couldn't hit no project that suited exactly; so at last the duke said he reckoned he'd lay off and work his brains an hour or two and see if he couldn't put up something on the Arkansaw village; and the king he allowed he would drop over to t'other village without any plan, but just trust in Providence to lead him the profitable way—meaning the devil, I reckon. We had all bought store clothes where we stopped last; and now the king put his'n on, and he told me to put mine on. I done it, of course. The king's duds was all black and he did look real swell and starchy. I never knowed how clothes could change a body before. Why, before, he looked like the orneriest old rip that ever was, but now when he'd take off his new white beaver and make a bow and do a smile, he looked that grand and good and pious that you'd say he had walked right out of the ark, and maybe was old Leviticus himself. Jim cleaned up the canoe and I got my paddle ready. There was a big steamboat laying at the shore away up under the point, about three mile above town—been there a couple of hours, taking on freight. Says the king:

"Seein' how I'm dressed, I reckon maybe I better arrive down from St. Louis or Cincinnati, or some other big place. Go for the steamboat, Huckleberry; we'll come down to the village on her."

I didn't have to be ordered twice to go and take a steamboat ride. I fetched the shore a half a mile above

the village and then went scooting along the bluff bank
in the easy water. Pretty soon we come to a nice innoc-
cent-looking young country jake setting on a log swabbing the sweat off of his face, for it was powerful warm
weather; and he had a couple of big carpet-bags by him.

"Run her nose inshore," says the king. I done it.
"Wher' you bound for, young man?"

"For the steamboat; going to Orleans."

"Git aboard," says the king. "Hold on a minute, my
servant'll he'p you with them bags. Jump out and he'p
the gentleman, Adolphus"—meaning me, I see.

I done so and then we all three started on again. The
young chap was mighty thankful; said it was tough work
toting his baggage such weather. He asked the king
where he was going, and the king told him he'd come
down the river and landed at the other village this morning, and now he was going up a few mile to see an old
friend on a farm up there. The young fellow says:

"When I first see you I says to myself, 'It's Mr. Wilks,
sure, and he come mighty near getting here in time.'
But then I says again, 'No, I reckon it ain't him or else
he wouldn't be paddling up the river.' You *ain't* him,
are you?"

"No, my name's Blodgett—Elexander Blodgett—*Reverend* Elexander Blodgett, I s'pose I must say, as I'm one
o' the Lord's poor servants. But still I'm jist as able to
be sorry for Mr. Wilks for not arriving in time, all the
same, if he's missed anything by it—which I hope he
hasn't."

"Well, he don't miss any property by it, because he'll
get that all right, but he's missed seeing his brother
Peter die—which he mayn't mind, nobody can tell as to
that—but his brother would 'a' give anything in this
world to see *him* before he died; never talked about
nothing else all these three weeks; hadn't seen him since

they was boys together—and hadn't ever seen his
brother William at all—that's the deef and dumb one—
William ain't more than thirty or thirty-five. Peter and
George was the only ones that come out here; George
was the married brother; him and his wife both died
last year. Harvey and William's the only ones that's left
now; and, as I was saying, they haven't got here in
time."

"Did anybody send 'em word?"

"Oh, yes; a month or two ago, when Peter was first
took, because Peter said then that he sorter felt like he
warn't going to get well this time. You see, he was
pretty old and George's g'yirls was too young to be
much company for him, except Mary Jane, the red-
headed one; and so he was kinder lonesome after George
and his wife died and didn't seem to care much to live.
He most desperately wanted to see Harvey—and William, too, for that matter—because he was one of them
kind that can't bear to make a will. He left a letter behind for Harvey, and said he'd told in it where his
money was hid and how he wanted the rest of the property divided up so George's g'yirls would be all right—
for George didn't leave nothing. And that letter was all
they could get him to put a pen to."

"Why do you reckon Harvey don't come? Wher' does
he live?"

"Oh, he lives in England—Sheffield—preaches there
—hasn't ever been in this country. He hasn't had any
too much time—and besides he mightn't 'a' got the letter at all, you know."

"Too bad, too bad he couldn't 'a' lived to see his
brothers, poor soul. You going to Orleans, you say?"

"Yes, but that ain't only a part of it. I'm going in a
ship, next Wednesday, for Ryo Janeero, where my uncle
lives."

"It's a pretty long journey. But it'll be lovely; I wisht I was a-going. Is Mary Jane the oldest? How old is the others?"

"Mary Jane's nineteen, Susan's fifteen, and Joanna's about fourteen—that's the one that gives herself to good works and has a hare-lip."

"Poor things! to be left alone in the cold world so."

"Well, they could be worse off. Old Peter had friends, and they ain't going to let them come to no harm. There's Hobson, the Babtis' preacher; and Deacon Lot Hovey, and Ben Rucker, and Abner Shackleford and Levi Bell, the lawyer; and Dr. Robinson, and their wives, and the widow Bartley, and—well, there's a lot of them; but these are the ones that Peter was thickest with and used to write about sometimes, when he wrote home; so Harvey'll know where to look for friends when he gets here."

Well, the old man he went on asking questions till he just fairly emptied that young fellow. Blamed if he didn't inquire about everybody and everything in that blessed town, and all about the Wilkses; and about Peter's business—which was a tanner; and about George's—which was a carpenter; and about Harvey's —which was a dissentering minister; and so on, and so on. Then he says:

"What did you want to walk all the way up to the steamboat for?"

"Because she's a big Orleans boat and I was afeard she mightn't stop there. When they're deep they won't stop for a hail. A Cincinnati boat will but this is a St. Louis one."

"Was Peter Wilks well off?"

"Oh, yes, pretty well off. He had houses and land, and it's reckoned he left three or four thousand in cash hid up som'ers."

"When did you say he died?"

"I didn't say but it was last night."

"Funeral to-morrow, likely?"

"Yes, 'bout the middle of the day."

"Well, it's all terrible sad, but we've all got to go, one time or another. So what we want to do is to be prepared; then we're all right."

"Yes, sir, it's the best way. Ma used to always say that."

When we struck the boat she was about done loading and pretty soon she got off. The king never said nothing about going aboard, so I lost my ride, after all. When the boat was gone the king made me paddle up another mile to a lonesome place, and then he got ashore and says:

"Now hustle back, right off, and fetch the duke up here, and the new carpet-bags. And if he's gone over to t'other side, go over there and git him. And tell him to git himself up regardless. Shove along, now."

I see what *he* was up to; but I never said nothing, of course. When I got back with the duke we hid the canoe, and then they set down on a log and the king told him everything, just like the young fellow had said it—every last word of it. And all the time he was a-doing it he tried to talk like an Englishman; and he done it pretty well, too, for a slouch. I can't imitate him and so I ain't a-going to try to; but he really done it pretty good. Then he says:

"How are you on the deef and dumb, Bilgewater?"

The duke said, leave him alone for that; said he had played a deef and dumb person on the histeronic boards. So then they waited for a steamboat.

About the middle of the afternoon a couple of little boats come along but they didn't come from high enough up the river, but at last there was a big one and they hailed her. She sent out her yawl and we went aboard, and she was from Cincinnati; and when they found we only wanted to go four or five mile they was booming mad, and give us a cussing and said they wouldn't land us. But the king was ca'm. He says:

"If gentlemen kin afford to pay a dollar a mile apiece to be took on and put off in a yawl, a steamboat kin afford to carry 'em, can't it?"

So they softened down and said it was all right, and when we got to the village they yawled us ashore. About two dozen men flocked down when they see the yawl a-coming, and when the king says: "Kin any of you gentlemen tell me wher' Mr. Peter Wilks lives?" they give a glance at one another and nodded their heads, as much as to say, "What'd I tell you?" Then one of them says, kind of soft and gentile:

"I'm sorry, sir, but the best we can do is tell you where he *did* live yesterday evening."

Sudden as winking the ornery old cretur went all to smash and fell up against the man, and put his chin on his shoulder and cried down his back and says:

"Alas, alas, our poor brother—gone, and we never got to see him; oh, it's too, *too* hard!"

Then he turns around, blubbering, and makes a lot of idiotic signs to the duke on his hands, and blamed if *he* didn't drop a carpet-bag and bust out a-crying. If they warn't the beatenest lot, them two frauds, that ever I struck.

Well, the men gethered around and sympathized with them and said all sorts of kind things to them, and carried their carpet-bags up the hill for them and let them lean on them and cry, and told the king all about his brother's last moments, and the king he told it all over again on his hands to the duke, and both of them took on about that dead tanner like they'd lost the twelve disciples. Well, if ever I struck anything like it, I'm a nigger. It was enough to make a body ashamed of the human race.

XXV. ALL FULL OF TEARS AND FLAPDOODLE

The news was all over town in two minutes and you could see the people tearing down on the run from every which way, some of them putting on their coats as they come. Pretty soon we was in the middle of a crowd, and the noise of the tramping was like a soldier march. The windows and dooryards was full, and every minute somebody would say, over a fence:

"Is it *them?*"

And somebody trotting along with the gang would answer back and say:

"You bet it is."

When we got to the house, the street in front of it was packed and the three girls was standing in the door. Mary Jane *was* red-headed but that don't make no difference, she was most awful beautiful and her face and her eyes was all lit up like glory, she was so glad her uncles was come. The king he spread his arms and Mary Jane she jumped for them, and the hare-lip jumped for the duke, and there they *had* it! Everybody most, leastways women, cried for joy to see them meet again at last and have such good times.

Then the king he hunched the duke private—I see him do it—and then he looked around and see the coffin over in the corner on two chairs; so then him and the duke, with a hand across each other's shoulder, and t'other hand to their eyes, walked slow and solemn over there, everybody dropping back to give them room, and all the talk and noise stopping, people saying " 'Sh!" and all the men taking their hats off and drooping their heads, so you could 'a' heard a pin fall. And when they got there they bent over and looked in the coffin and took one sight, and then they bust out a-crying so you could 'a' heard them to Orleans, most; and then they put their arms around each other's necks and hung their chins over each other's shoulders; and then for three minutes, or maybe four, I never see two men leak the way they done. And, mind you, everybody was doing the same, and the place was that damp I never see anything like it. Then one of them got on one side of the coffin, and t'other on t'other side, and they kneeled down and rested their foreheads on the coffin and let on to pray all to theirselves. Well, when it come to that it worked the crowd like you never see anything like it, and everybody broke down and went to sobbing right out loud—the poor girls, too; and every woman, nearly, went up to the girls without saying a word and kissed them, solemn, on the forehead, and then put their hand on their head and looked up towards the sky, with the tears running down, and then busted out and went off sobbing and swabbing, and give the next woman a show. I never see anything so disgusting.

Well, by and by the king he gets up and comes forward a little and works himself up and slobbers out a speech, all full of tears and flapdoodle, about its being a sore trial for him and his poor brother to lose the diseased, and to miss seeing diseased alive after the long journey of four thousand mile, but it's a trial that's sweetened and sanctified to us by this dear sympathy and these holy tears, and so he thanks them out of his heart and out of his brother's heart, because out of their mouths they can't, words being too weak and cold, and all that kind of rot and slush, till it was just sickening; and then he blubbers out a pious goody-goody Amen, and turns himself loose and goes to crying fit to bust.

And the minute the words was out of his mouth somebody over in the crowd struck up the doxolojer and
everybody joined in with all their might, and it just
warmed you up and made you feel as good as church
letting out. Music *is* a good thing; and after all that
soul-butter and hogwash I never see it freshen up
things so and sound so honest and bully.

Then the king begins to work his jaw again, and says
how him and his nieces would be glad if a few of the
main principal friends of the family would take supper
here with them this evening, and help set up with the
ashes of the diseased; and says if his poor brother laying
yonder could speak he knows who he would name, foi
they was names that was very dear to him, and mentioned often in his letters; and so he will name the
same, to wit, as follows, viz.:—Rev. Mr. Hobson, and
Deacon Lot Hovey, and Mr. Ben Rucker, and Abner
Shackleford, and Levi Bell, and Dr. Robinson, and their
wives, and the widow Bartley.

Rev. Hobson and Dr. Robinson was down to the end
of the town a-hunting together—that is, I mean the doctor was shipping a sick man to t'other world and the
preacher was pinting him right. Lawyer Bell was away
up to Louisville on business. But the rest was on hand,
and so they all come and shook hands with the king and
thanked him and talked to him, and then they shook
hands with the duke and didn't say nothing but just
kept a-smiling and bobbing their heads like a passel of
sapheads whilst he made all sorts of signs with his hands
and said "Goo-goo—goo-goo-goo" all the time, like a
baby that can't talk.

So the king he blatted along and managed to inquire
about pretty much everybody and dog in town, by his
name, and mentioned all sorts of little things that hap-

pened one time or another in the town, or to George's
family, or to Peter. And he always let on that Peter wrote
him the things; but that was a lie: he got every blessed
one of them out of that young flathead that we canoed
up to the steamboat.

Then Mary Jane she fetched the letter her father left
behind, and the king he read it out loud and cried over
it. It give the dwelling-house and three thousand dollars, gold, to the girls; and it give the tanyard (which
was doing a good business), along with some other
houses and land (worth about seven thousand), and
three thousand dollars in gold to Harvey and William,
and told where the six thousand cash was hid down
cellar. So these two frauds said they'd go and fetch it
up, and have everything square and above-board; and
told me to come with a candle. We shut the cellar door
behind us and when they found the bag they spilt it
out on the floor, and it was a lovely sight, all them yaller-
boys. My, the way the king's eyes did shine! He slaps
the duke on the shoulder and says:

"Oh, *this* ain't bully nor noth'n! Oh, no, I reckon not!
Why, Biljy, it beats the Nonesuch, *don't* it?"

The duke allowed it did. They pawed the yaller-boys
and sifted them through their fingers and let them jingle
down on the floor, and the king says:

"It ain't no use talkin'; bein' brothers to a rich dead
man and representatives of furrin heirs that's got left is
the line for you and me, Bilge. Thish yer comes of
trust'n' to Providence. It's the best way, in the long run.
I've tried 'em all, and ther' ain't no better way."

Most everybody would 'a' been satisfied with the pile,
and took it on trust; but no, they must count it. So they
counts it, and it comes out four hundred and fifteen dollars short. Says the king:

"Dern him, I wonder what he done with that four hunderd and fifteen dollars?"

They worried over that awhile, and ransacked all around for it. Then the duke says:

"Well, he was a pretty sick man, and likely he made a mistake—I reckon that's the way of it. The best way's to let it go, and keep still about it. We can spare it."

"Oh, shucks, yes, we can *spare* it. I don't k'yer noth'n 'bout that—it's the *count* I'm thinkin' about. We want to be awful square and open and above-board here, you know. We want to lug this h'yer money up-stairs and count it before everybody—then ther' ain't noth'n' suspicious. But when the dead man says ther's six thous'n dollars, you know, we don't want to—"

"Hold on," says the duke. "Le's make up the deffisit," and he begun to haul out yaller-boys out of his pocket.

"It's a most amaz'n' good idea, duke—you *have* got a rattlin' clever head on you," says the king. "Blest if the old Nonesuch ain't a heppin' us out agin," and *he* begun to haul out yaller-jackets and stack them up.

It most busted them but they made up the six thousand clean and clear.

"Say," says the duke, "I got another idea. Le's go up-stairs and count this money, and then take and *give it to the girls.*"

"Good land, duke, lemme hug you! It's the most dazzling idea 'at ever a man struck. You have cert'nly got the most astonishin' head I ever see. Oh, this is the boss dodge, ther' ain't no mistake 'bout it. Let 'em fetch along their suspicions now if they want to—this'll lay 'em out."

When we got up-stairs everybody gethered around the table, and the king he counted it and stacked it up, three hundred dollars in a pile—twenty elegant little

piles. Everybody looked hungry at it and licked their
chops. Then they raked it into the bag again, and I see
the king begin to swell himself up for another speech.
He says:

"Friends all, my poor brother that lays yonder has
done generous by them that's left behind in the vale of
sorrers. He has done generous by these yer poor little
lambs that he loved and sheltered, and that's left father-
less and motherless. Yes, and we that knowed him knows
that he would 'a' done *more* generous by 'em if he hadn't
ben afeard o' woundin' his dear William and me. Now,
wouldn't he? Ther' ain't no question 'bout it in *my*
mind. Well, then, what kind o' brothers would it be
that'd stand in his way at sech a time? And what kind o'
uncles would it be that'd rob—yes, *rob*—sech poor
sweet lambs as these 'at he loved so at sech a time? If I
know William—and I *think* I do—he—well, I'll jest ask
him." He turns around and begins to make a lot of
signs to the duke with his hands, and the duke he looks
at him stupid and leather-headed awhile; then all of a
sudden he seems to catch his meaning and jumps for
the king, goo-gooing with all his might for joy, and hugs
him about fifteen times before he lets up. Then the king
says, "I knowed it; I reckon *that'll* convince anybody the
way *he* feels about it. Here, Mary Jane, Susan, Joanner,
take the money—take it *all*. It's the gift of him that lays
yonder, cold but joyful."

Mary Jane she went for him, Susan and the hare-lip
went for the duke, and then such another hugging and
kissing I never see yet. And everybody crowded up with
the tears in their eyes and most shook the hands off of
them frauds, saying all the time:

"You *dear* good souls!—how *lovely!*—how *could*
you!"

Well, then, pretty soon all hands got to talking about

the diseased again and how good he was and what a loss
he was, and all that; and before long a big iron-jawed
man worked himself in there from outside, and stood
a-listening and looking and not saying anything; and nobody saying anything to him either, because the king
was talking and they was all busy listening. The king
was saying—in the middle of something he'd started
in on—

"—they bein' partickler friends o' the diseased. That's
why they're invited here this evenin'; but to-morrow we
want *all* to come—everybody; for he respected everybody, he liked everybody, and so it's fitten that his
funeral orgies sh'd be public."

And so he went a-mooning on and on, liking to hear
himself talk, and every little while he fetched in his
funeral orgies again, till the duke he couldn't stand it no
more; so he writes on a little scrap of paper, "*Obsequies,*
you old fool," and folds it up and goes to goo-gooing
and reaching it over people's heads to him. The king he
reads it and puts it in his pocket, and says:

"Poor William, afflicted as he is, his *heart's* aluz right.
Asks me to invite everybody to come to the funeral—
wants me to make 'em all welcome. But he needn't 'a'
worried—it was jest what I was at."

Then he weaves along again, perfectly ca'm, and goes
to dropping in his funeral orgies again every now and
then, just like he done before. And when he done it the
third time he says:

"I say orgies, not because it's the common term, because it ain't—obsequies bein' the common term—but
because orgies is the right term. Obsequies ain't used in
England no more now—it's gone out. We say orgies now
in England. Orgies is better, because it means the thing
you're after more exact. It's a word that's made up out'n
the Greek *orgo*, outside, open, abroad; and the Hebrew

jeesum, to plant, cover up; hence in*ter.* So, you see, funeral orgies is an open er public funeral."

He was the *worst* I ever struck. Well, the iron-jawed man he laughed right in his face. Everybody was shocked. Everybody says, "Why, *doctor!*" and Abner Shackleford says:

"Why, Robinson, hain't you heard the news? This is Harvey Wilks."

The king he smiled eager, and shoved out his flapper, and says:

"*Is* it my poor brother's dear good friend and physician? I—"

"Keep your hands off me!" says the doctor. "*You* talk like an Englishman, *don't* you? It's the worst imitation I ever heard. *You* Peter Wilks's brother! You're a fraud, that's what you are!"

Well, how they all took on! They crowded around the doctor and tried to quiet him down, and tried to explain to him and tell him how Harvey'd showed in forty ways that he *was* Harvey, and knowed everybody by name, and the names of the very dogs, and begged and *begged* him not to hurt Harvey's feelings and the poor girls' feelings, and all that. But it warn't no use; he stormed right along, and said any man that pretended to be an Englishman and couldn't imitate the lingo no better than what he did was a fraud and a liar. The poor girls was hanging to the king and crying; and all of a sudden the doctor ups and turns on *them.* He says:

"I was your father's friend and I'm your friend; and I warn you *as* a friend, and an honest one that wants to protect you and keep you out of harm and trouble, to turn your backs on that scoundrel and have nothing to do with him, the ignorant tramp, with his idiotic Greek and Hebrew, as he calls it. He is the thinnest kind of an impostor—has come here with a lot of empty names and facts which he picked up somewheres; and you take them for *proofs,* and are helped to fool yourselves by these foolish friends here, who ought to know better. Mary Jane Wilks, you know me for your friend, and for your unselfish friend, too. Now listen to me; turn this pitiful rascal out—I *beg* you to do it. Will you?"

Mary Jane straightened herself up, and my, but she was handsome! She says:

"*Here* is my answer." She hove up the bag of money and put it in the king's hands, and says, "Take this six thousand dollars, and invest for me and my sisters any way you want to, and don't give us no receipt for it."

Then she put her arm around the king on one side and Susan and the hare-lip done the same on the other. Everybody clapped their hands and stomped on the floor like a perfect storm, whilst the king held up his head and smiled proud. The doctor says:

"All right; I wash *my* hands of the matter. But I warn you all that a time's coming when you're going to feel sick whenever you think of this day." And away he went.

"All right, doctor," says the king, kinder mocking him, "we'll try and get 'em to send for you"; which made them all laugh and they said it was a prime good hit.

XXVI. I Steal the King's Plunder

Well, when they was all gone the king he asks Mary Jane how they was off for spare rooms, and she said she had one spare room, which would do for Uncle William, and she'd give her own room to Uncle Harvey, which was a little bigger, and she would turn into the room with her sisters and sleep on a cot, and up garret was a little cubby with a pallet in it. The king said the cubby would do for his valley—meaning me.

So Mary Jane took us up and she showed them their

rooms, which was plain but nice. She said she'd have her frocks and a lot of other traps took out of her room if they was in Uncle Harvey's way, but he said they warn't. The frocks was hung along the wall, and before them was a curtain made out of calico that hung down to the floor. There was an old hair trunk in one corner and a guitar-box in another, and all sorts of little knick-knacks and jimcracks around, like girls brisken up a room with. The king said it was all the more homely and more pleasanter for these fixings, and so don't disturb them. The duke's room was pretty small but plenty good enough, and so was my cubby.

That night they had a big supper and all them men and women was there, and I stood behind the king and the duke's chairs and waited on them, and the niggers waited on the rest. Mary Jane she set at the head of the table with Susan alongside of her, and said how bad the biscuits was and how mean the preserves was and how ornery and tough the fried chickens was—and all that kind of rot, the way women always do' for to force out compliments; and the people all knowed everything was tiptop and said so—said "How *do* you get biscuits to brown so nice?" and "Where, for the land's sake, *did* you get these amaz'n' pickles?" and all that kind of humbug talky-talk, just the way people always does at a supper, you know.

And when it was all done me and the hare-lip had supper in the kitchen off of the leavings, whilst the others was helping the niggers clean up the things. The hare-lip she got to pumping me about England, and blest if I didn't think the ice was getting mighty thin sometimes. She says:

"Did you ever see the king?"

"Who? William Fourth? Well, I bet I have—he goes to our church." I knowed he was dead years ago, but I

never let on. So when I says he goes to our church, she
says:

"What—regular?"

"Yes—regular. His pew's right over opposite ourn—
on t'other side the pulpit."

"I thought he lived in London?"

"Well, he does. Where *would* he live?"

"But I thought *you* lived in Sheffield?"

I see I was up a stump. I had to let on to get choked
with a chicken-bone, so as to get time to think how to
get down again. Then I says:

"I mean he goes to our church regular when he's in
Sheffield. That's only in the summer-time, when he
comes there to take the sea baths."

"Why, how you talk—Sheffield ain't on the sea."

"Well, who said it was?"

"Why, you did."

"I *didn't*, nuther."

"You did!"

"I didn't."

"You did."

"I never said nothing of the kind."

"Well, what *did* you say, then?"

"Said he come to take the sea *baths*—that's what I
said."

"Well, then, how's he going to take the sea baths if it
ain't on the sea?"

"Looky here," I says; "did you ever see any Congress-
water?"

"Yes."

"Well, did you have to go to Congress to get it?"

"Why, no."

"Well, neither does William Fourth have to go to the
sea to get a sea bath."

"How does he get it, then?"

"Gets it the way people down here gets Congress-water—in barrels. There in the palace at Sheffield 'they've got furnaces, and he wants his water hot. They can't bile that amount of water away off there at the sea. They haven't got no conveniences for it."

"Oh, I see, now. You might 'a' said that in the first place and saved time."

When she said that I see I was out of the woods again, and so I was comfortable and glad. Next, she says:

"Do you go to church, too?"

"Yes—regular."

"Where do you set?"

"Why, in our pew."

"*Whose* pew?"

"Why, *ourn*—your Uncle Harvey's."

"His'n? What does *he* want with a pew?"

"Wants it to set in. What did you *reckon* he wanted with it?"

"Why, I thought he'd be in the pulpit."

Rot him, I forgot he was a preacher. I see I was up a stump again, so I played another chicken-bone and got another think. Then I says:

"Blame it, do you suppose there ain't but one preacher to a church?"

"Why, what do they want with more?"

"What!—to preach before a king? I never did see such a girl as you. They don't have no less than seventeen."

"Seventeen! My land! Why, I wouldn't set out such a string as that, not if I *never* got to glory. It must take 'em a week."

"Shucks, they don't *all* of 'em preach the same day—only *one* of 'em."

"Well, then, what does the rest of 'em do?"

"Oh, nothing much. Loll around, pass the plate—and one thing or another. But mainly they don't do nothing."

"Well, then, what are they *for?*"

"Why, they're for *style*. Don't you know nothing?"

"Well, I don't *want* to know no such foolishness as that. How is servants treated in England? Do they treat 'em better'n we treat our niggers?"

"*No!* A servant ain't nobody there. They treat them worse than dogs."

"Don't they give 'em holidays, the way we do, Christmas and New Year's week, and Fourth of July?"

"Oh, just listen! A body could tell *you* hain't ever been to England by that. Why, Hare-l—why, Joanno, they never see a holiday from year's end to year's end, never go to the circus, nor theatre, nor nigger shows, nor nowheres."

"Nor church?"

"Nor church."

"But *you* always went to church."

Well, I was gone up again. I forgot I was the old man's servant. But next minute I whirled in on a kind of an explanation how a valley was different from a common servant and *had* to go to church whether he wanted to or not, and set with the family, on account of its being the law. But I didn't do it pretty good, and when I got done I see she warn't satisfied. She says:

"Honest Injun, now, hain't you been telling me a lot of lies?"

"Honest Injun," says I.

"None of it at all?"

"None of it at all. Not a lie in it," says I.

"Lay your hand on this book and say it."

I see it warn't nothing but a dictionary, so I laid my hand on it and said it. So then she looked a little better satisfied, and says:

"Well, then, I'll believe some of it; but I hope to gracious if I'll believe the rest."

"What is it you won't believe, Jo?" says Mary Jane, stepping in with Susan behind her. "It ain't right nor kind for you to talk so to him, and him a stranger and so far from his people. How would you like to be treated so?"

"That's always your way, Maim—always sailing in to help somebody before they're hurt. I hain't done nothing to him. He's told some stretchers, I reckon, and I said I wouldn't swallow it all, and that's every bit and grain I *did* say. I reckon he can stand a little thing like that, can't he?"

"I don't care whether 'twas little or whether 'twas big, he's here in our house and a stranger and it wasn't good of you to say it. If you was in his place it would make you feel ashamed, and so you oughtn't to say a thing to another person that will make *them* feel ashamed."

"Why, Maim, he said—"

"It don't make no difference what he *said*—that ain't the thing. The thing is for you to treat him *kind*, and not be saying things to make him remember he ain't in his own country and amongst his own folks."

I says to myself, *this* is a girl that I'm letting that old reptyle rob her of her money!

Then Susan *she* waltzed in and if you'll believe me, she did give Hare-lip hark from the tomb!

Says I to myself, and this is *another* one that I'm letting him rob her of her money!

Then Mary Jane she took another inning and went in sweet and lovely again—which was her way; but when she got done there warn't hardly anything left o' poor Hare-lip. So she hollered.

"All right, then," says the other girls, "you just ask his pardon."

She done it, too, and she done it beautiful. She done

it so beautiful it was good to hear, and I wished I could
tell her a thousand lies, so she could do it again.

I says to myself, this is *another* one that I'm letting
him rob her of her money. And when she got through
they all jest laid theirselves out to make me feel at home
and know I was amongst friends. I felt so ornery and
low-down and mean that I says to myself, my mind's
made up; I'll hive that money for them or bust.

So then I lit out—for bed, I said, meaning some time
or another. When I got by myself I went to thinking the
thing over. I says to myself, shall I go to that doctor,
private, and blow on these frauds? No—that won't do.
He might tell who told him; then the king and the duke
would make it warm for me. Shall I go, private, and tell
Mary Jane? No—I dasn't do it. Her face would give
them a hint, sure; they've got the money and they'd
slide right out and get away with it. If she was to fetch
in help I'd get mixed up in the business before it was
done with, I judge. No; there ain't no good way but
one. I got to steal that money, somehow, and I got to
steal it some way that they won't suspicion that I done
it. They've got a good thing here and they ain't a-going
to leave till they've played this family and this town for
all they're worth, so I'll find a chance time enough. I'll
steal it and hide it and by and by, when I'm away down
the river, I'll write a letter and tell Mary Jane where it's
hid. But I better hive it to-night if I can, because the
doctor maybe hasn't let up as much as he lets on he has;
he might scare them out of here yet.

So, thinks I, I'll go and search them rooms. Up-stairs
the hall was dark but I found the duke's room, and
started to paw around it with my hands; but I recol-
lected it wouldn't be much like the king to let anybody
else take care of that money but his own self; so then I

went to his room and begun to paw around there. But
I see I couldn't do nothing without a candle and I dasn't
light one, of course. So I judged I'd got to do the other
thing—lay for them and eavesdrop. About that time I
hears their footsteps coming, and was going to skip
under the bed; I reached for it but it wasn't where I
thought it would be; but I touched the curtain that hid
Mary Jane's frocks, so I jumped in behind that and
snuggled in amongst the gowns and stood there perfectly still.

They come in and shut the door, and the first thing
the duke done was to get down and look under the bed.
Then I was glad I hadn't found the bed when I wanted
it. And yet, you know, it's kind of natural to hide under
the bed when you are up to anything private. They sets
down then, and the king says:

"Well, what is it? And cut it middlin' short, because
it's better for us to be down there a-whoopin' up the
mournin' than up here givin' 'em a chance to talk us
over."

"Well, this is it, Capet. I ain't easy; I ain't comfortable. That doctor lays on my mind. I wanted to know
your plans. I've got a notion and I think it's a sound
one."

"What is it, duke?"

"That we better glide out of this before three in the
morning and clip it down the river with what we've got.
Specially, seeing we got it so easy—*given* back to us,
flung at our heads as you may say, when of course we
allowed to have to steal it back. I'm for knocking off
and lighting out."

That made me feel pretty bad. About an hour or two
ago it would 'a' been a little different but now it made
me feel bad and disappointed. The king rips out and
says:

"What! And not sell out the rest o' the property? March off like a passel of fools and leave eight or nine thous'n' dollars' worth o' property layin' around jest sufferin' to be scooped in?—and all good, salable stuff, too."

The duke he grumbled; said the bag of gold was enough and he didn't want to go no deeper—didn't want to rob a lot of orphans of *everything* they had.

"Why, how you talk!" says the king. "We sha'n't rob 'em of nothing at all but jest this money. The people that *buys* the property is the suff'rers; because as soon's it's found out 'at we didn't own it—which won't be long after we've slid—the sale won't be valid, and it'll all go back to the estate. These yer orphans'll git their house back agin, and that's enough for *them;* they're young and spry and k'n easy earn a livin'. *They* ain't a-goin' to suffer. Why, jest think—there's thous'n's and thous'n's that ain't nigh so well off. Bless you, *they* ain't got noth'n' to complain of."

Well, the king he talked him blind; so at last he give in and said all right, but said he believed it was blamed foolishness to stay and that doctor hanging over them. But the king says:

"Cuss the doctor! What do we k'yer for *him?* Hain't we got all the fools in town on our side? And ain't that a big enough majority in any town?"

So they got ready to go down-stairs again. The duke says:

"I don't think we put that money in a good place."

That cheered me up. I'd begun to think I warn't going to get a hint of no kind to help me. The king says: "Why?"

"Because Mary Jane'll be in mourning from this out, and first you know the nigger that does up the rooms will get an order to box these duds up and put 'em away; and do you reckon a nigger can run across money and not borrow some of it?"

"Your head's level agin, duke," says the king; and he come a-fumbling under the curtain two or three foot from where I was. I stuck tight to the wall and kept mighty still, though quivery, and I wondered what them fellows would say to me if they catched me, and I tried to think what I'd better do if they did catch me. But the king he got the bag before I could think more than about a half a thought, and he never suspicioned I was around. They took and shoved the bag through a rip in the straw tick that was under the feather-bed, and crammed it in a foot or two amongst the straw and said it was all right now, because a nigger only makes up the feather-bed and don't turn over the straw tick only about twice a year, and so it warn't in no danger of getting stole now.

But I knowed better. I had it out of there before they was half-way down-stairs. I groped along up to my cubby and hid it there till I could get a chance to do better. I judged I better hide it outside of the house somewheres, because if they missed it they would give the house a good ransacking: I knowed that very well. Then I turned in, with my clothes all on; but I couldn't 'a' gone to sleep if I'd 'a' wanted to, I was in such a sweat to get through with the business. By and by I heard the king and the duke come up; so I rolled off my pallet and laid with my chin at the top of my ladder, and waited to see if anything was going to happen. But nothing did.

So I held on till all the late sounds had quit and the early ones hadn't begun yet, and then I slipped down the ladder.

I crept to their doors and listened; they was snoring. So I tiptoed along and got down-stairs all right. There warn't a sound anywheres. I peeped through a crack of the dining-room door, and see the men that was watching the corpse all sound asleep on their chairs. The door was open into the parlor where the corpse was laying, and there was a candle in both rooms. I passed along, and the parlor door was open; but I see there warn't nobody in there but the remainders of Peter; so I shoved on by; but the front door was locked and the key wasn't there. Just then I heard somebody coming down the stairs, back behind me. I run in the parlor and took a swift look around, and the only place I see to hide the bag was in the coffin. The lid was shoved along about a foot, showing the dead man's face down in there, with a wet cloth over it, and his shroud on. I tucked the money-bag in under the lid, just down beyond where his hands was crossed, which made me creep, they was so cold, and then I run back across the room and in behind the door.

The person coming was Mary Jane. She went to the coffin, very soft, and kneeled down and looked in; then she put up her handkerchief and I see she begun to cry, though I couldn't hear her and her back was to me. I slid out, and as I passed the dining-room I thought I'd make sure them watchers hadn't seen me; so I looked through the crack and everything was all right. They hadn't stirred.

I slipped up to bed, feeling ruther blue, on accounts of the thing playing out that way after I had took so much trouble and run so much resk about it. Says I, if it could stay where it is, all right; because when we get

411

down the river a hundred mile or two I could write back
to Mary Jane, and she could dig him up again and get
it; but that ain't the thing that's going to happen; the
thing that's going to happen is, the money'll be found
when they come to screw on the lid. Then the king'll get
it again, and it'll be a long day before he gives anybody
another chance to smouch it from him. Of course I
wanted to slide down and get it out of there, but I
dasn't try it. Every minute it was getting earlier now,
and pretty soon some of them watchers would begin to
stir and I might get catched—catched with six thousand
dollars in my hands that nobody hadn't hired me to
take care of. I don't wish to be mixed up in no such
business as that, I says to myself.

When I got down-stairs in the morning the parlor was
shut up and the watchers was gone. There warn't nobody around but the family and the widow Bartley and
our tribe. I watched their faces to see if anything had
been happening but I couldn't tell.

Towards the middle of the day the undertaker come
with his man and they set the coffin in the middle of the
room on a couple of chairs, and then set all our chairs in
rows and borrowed more from the neighbors till the hall
and the parlor and the dining-room was full. I see the
coffin lid was the way it was before, but I dasn't go to
look in under it, with folks around.

Then the people begun to flock in, and the beats and
the girls took seats in the front row at the head of the
coffin, and for a half an hour the people filed around
slow in single rank and looked down at the dead man's
face a minute, and some dropped in a tear and it was all
very still and solemn, only the girls and the beats holding handkerchiefs to their eyes and keeping their heads
bent and sobbing a little. There warn't no other sound
but the scraping of the feet on the floor and blowing

noses—because people always blows them more at a
funeral than they do at other places except church.

When the place was packed full the undertaker he
slid around in his black gloves with his softy soothering
ways, putting on the last touches and getting people and
things all ship-shape and comfortable, and making no
more sound than a cat. He never spoke, he moved
people around, he squeezed in late ones, he opened up
passageways, and done it all with nods, and signs with
his hands. Then he took his place over against the wall.
He was the softest, glidingest, stealthiest man I ever
see; and there warn't no more smile to him than there is
to a ham.

They had borrowed a melodeum—a sick one; and
when everything was ready a young woman set down
and worked it, and it was pretty skreeky and colicky,
and everybody joined in and sung, and Peter was the
only one that had a good thing, according to my notion.
Then the Reverend Hobson opened up, slow and
solemn, and begun to talk; and straight off the most outrageous row busted out in the cellar a body ever heard;
it was only one dog, but he made a most powerful
racket, and he kept it up right along; the parson he had
to stand there, over the coffin, and wait—you couldn't
hear yourself think. It was right down awkward, and
nobody didn't seem to know what to do. But pretty soon
they see that long-legged undertaker make a sign to the
preacher as much as to say, "Don't you worry—just depend on me." Then he stooped down and begun to glide
along the wall, just his shoulders showing over the
people's heads. So he glided along, and the powwow
and racket getting more and more outrageous all the
time, and at last when he had gone around two sides of
the room, he disappears down cellar. Then in about two
seconds we heard a whack and the dog he finished up

with a most amazing howl or two, and then everything
was dead still and the parson begun his solemn talk
where he left off. In a minute or two here comes this
undertaker's back and shoulders gliding along the wall
again; and so he glided and glided around three sides of
the room and then rose up and shaded his mouth with
his hands and stretched his neck out towards the
preacher, over the people's heads, and says, in a kind
of a coarse whisper, *"He had a rat!"* Then he drooped
down and glided along the wall again to his place. You
could see it was a great satisfaction to the people, because naturally they wanted to know. A little thing like
that don't cost nothing, and it's just the little things that
makes a man to be looked up to and liked. There warn't
no more popular man in town than what that undertaker
was.

Well, the funeral sermon was very good but pison
long and tiresome, and then the king he shoved in and
got off some of his usual rubbage, and at last the job
was through and the undertaker begun to sneak up on
the coffin with his screw-driver. I was in a sweat then
and watched him pretty keen. But he never meddled at
all, just slid the lid along as soft as mush and screwed it
down tight and fast. So there I was! I didn't know
whether the money was in there or not. So, says I, s'pose
somebody has hogged that bag on the sly?—now how
do *I* know whether to write to Mary Jane or not? S'pose
she dug him up and didn't find nothing, what would she
think of me? Blame it, I says, I might get hunted up
and jailed; I'd better lay low and keep dark, and not
write at all; the thing's awful mixed now; trying to better it, I've worsened it a hundred times and I wish to
goodness I'd just let it alone, dad fetch the whole
business!

They buried him, and we come back home, and I

went to watching faces again—I couldn't help it, and I couldn't rest easy. But nothing come of it; the faces didn't tell me nothing.

The king he visited around in the evening and sweetened everybody up, and made himself ever so friendly and he give out the idea that his congregation over in England would be in a sweat about him, so he must hurry and settle up the estate right away and leave for home. He was very sorry he was so pushed and so was everybody; they wished he could stay longer but they said they could see it couldn't be done. And he said of course him and William would take the girls home with them, and that pleased everybody too, because then the girls would be well fixed and amongst their own relations; and it pleased the girls, too—tickled them so they clean forgot they ever had a trouble in the world; and told him to sell out as quick as he wanted to, they would be ready. Them poor things was that glad and happy it made my heart ache to see them getting fooled and lied to so, but I didn't see no safe way for me to chip in and change the general tune.

Well, blamed if the king didn't bill the house and the niggers and all the property for auction straight off— sale two days after the funeral; but anybody could buy private beforehand if they wanted to.

So the next day after the funeral, along about noontime, the girls' joy got the first jolt. A couple of nigger-traders come along, and the king sold them the niggers reasonable, for three-day drafts as they called it, and away they went, the two sons up the river to Memphis and their mother down the river to Orleans. I thought them poor girls and them niggers would break their hearts for grief; they cried around each other and took on so it most made me down sick to see it. The girls said they hadn't ever dreamed of seeing the family separated or sold away from the town. I can't ever get it out of my memory, the sight of them poor miserable girls and niggers hanging around each other's necks and crying, and I reckon I couldn't 'a' stood it all, but would 'a' had to bust out and tell on our gang if I hadn't knowed the sale warn't no account and the niggers would be back home in a week or two.

The thing made a big stir in the town, too, and a good many come out flatfooted and said it was scandalous to separate the mother and the children that way. It injured the frauds some, but the old fool he bulled right along, spite of all the duke could say or do, and I tell you the duke was powerful uneasy.

Next day was auction day. About broad day in the morning the king and the duke come up in the garret and woke me up, and I see by their look that there was trouble. The king says:

"Was you in my room night before last?"

"No, your majesty"—which was the way I always called him when nobody but our gang warn't around.

"Was you in there yisterday er last night?"

"No, your majesty."

"Honor bright, now—no lies."

"Honor bright, your majesty, I'm telling you the truth. I hain't been a-near your room since Miss Mary Jane took you and the duke and showed it to you."

The duke says:

"Have you seen anybody else go in there?"

"No, your grace, not as I remember, I believe."

"Stop and think."

I studied awhile and see my chance; then I says:

"Well, I see the niggers go in there several times."

Both of them give a little jump and looked like they hadn't ever expected it, and then like they *had*. Then the duke says:

"What, *all* of them?"

"No—leastways, not all at once—that is, I don't think I ever see them all come *out* at once but just one time."

"Hello! When was that?"

"It was the day we had the funeral. In the morning. It warn't early, because I overslept. I was just starting down the ladder and I see them."

"Well, go on, *go* on! What did they do? How'd they act?"

"They didn't do nothing. And they didn't act anyway much, as fur as I see. They tiptoed away; so I seen, easy enough, that they'd shoved in there to do up your majesty's room, or something, s'posing you was up; and found you *warn't* up, and so they was hoping to slide out of the way of trouble without waking you up, if they hadn't already waked you up."

"Great guns, *this* is a go!" says the king, and both of them looked pretty sick and tolerable silly. They stood there a-thinking and scratching their heads a minute, and the duke he bust into a kind of a little raspy chuckle and says:

"It does beat all how neat the niggers played their hand. They let on to be *sorry* they was going out of this region! And I believed they *was* sorry, and so did you and so did everybody. Don't ever tell *me* any more that a nigger ain't got no histeronic talent. Why, the way they played that thing it would fool *anybody*. In my opinion, there's a fortune in 'em. If I had capital and a theatre, I wouldn't want a better lay-out than that—and here we've gone and sold 'em for a song. Yes, and ain't privileged to sing the song yet. Say, where *is* that song —that draft?"

"In the bank for to be collected. Where *would* it be?"

"Well, *that's* all right then, thank goodness."

Says I. kind of timid-like:

"Is something gone wrong?"

The king whirls on me and rips out:

"None o' your business! You keep your head shet and mind y'r own affairs—if you got any. Long as you're in this town don't you forgit *that*—you hear?" Then he says to the duke, "We got to jest swaller it and say noth'n': mum's the word for *us*."

As they was starting down the ladder the duke he chuckles again, and says:

"Quick sales *and* small profits! It's a good business motto—yes."

The king snarls around on him and says:

"I was trying to do for the best in sellin' 'em out so quick. If the profits has turned out to be none, lackin' considerble, and none to carry, is it my fault any more'n it's yourn?"

"Well, *they'd* be in this house yet and we *wouldn't* if I could 'a' got my advice listened to."

The king sassed back as much as was safe for him and then swapped around and lit into *me* again. He give me down the banks for not coming and *telling* him I see the niggers come out of his room acting that way— said any fool would 'a' *knowed* something was up. And then waltzed in and cussed *himself* awhile, and said it all come of him not laying late and taking his natural rest that morning, and he'd be blamed if he'd ever do it again. So they went off a-jawing; and I felt dreadful glad I'd worked it all off onto the niggers, and yet hadn't done the niggers no harm by it.

XXVIII. OVERREACHING DON'T PAY

By and by it was getting-up time. So I come down the ladder and started for down-stairs, but as I come to the

girls' room the door was open and I see Mary Jane setting by her old hair trunk, which was open and she'd
been packing things in it—getting ready to go to England. But she had stopped now with a folded gown in
her lap and had her face in her hands, crying. I felt
awful bad to see it; of course anybody would. I went in
there and says:

"Miss Mary Jane, you can't a-bear to see people in
trouble, and I can't—most always. Tell me about it."

So she done it. And it was the niggers—I just expected it. She said the beautiful trip to England was
most about spoiled for her; she didn't know *how* she
was ever going to be happy there, knowing the mother
and the children warn't ever going to see each other no
more—and then busted out bitterer than ever and flung
up her hands, and says:

"Oh, dear, dear, to think they ain't *ever* going to see
each other any more!"

"But they *will*—and inside of two weeks—and I *know*
it!" says I.

Laws, it was out before I could think! And before I
could budge she throws her arms around my neck and
told me to say it *again*, say it *again*, say it *again!*

I see I had spoke too sudden and said too much, and
was in a close place. I asked her to let me think a minute; and she set there, very impatient and excited and
handsome but looking kind of happy and eased-up, like
a person that's had a tooth pulled out. So I went to
studying it out. I says to myself, I reckon a body that
ups and tells the truth when he is in a tight place is
taking considerable many resks, though I ain't had no
experience and can't say for certain; but it looks so to
me, anyway; and yet here's a case where I'm blest if it
don't look to me like the truth is better and actuly *safer*
than a lie. I must lay it by in my mind and think it over

some time or other, it's so kind of strange and unregular. I never see nothing like it. Well, I says to myself
at last, I'm a-going to chance it; I'll up and tell the
truth this time, though it does seem most like setting
down on a kag of powder and touching it off just to see
where you'll go to. Then I says:

"Miss Mary Jane, is there any place out of town a
little ways where you could go and stay three or four
days?"

"Yes; Mr. Lothrop's. Why?"

"Never mind why yet. If I'll tell you how I know the
niggers will see each other again—inside of two weeks
—here in this house—and *prove* how I know it—will
you go to Mr. Lothrop's and stay four days?"

"Four days!" she says; "I'll stay a year!"

"All right," I says, "I don't want nothing more out of
you than just your word—I druther have it than another
man's kiss-the-Bible." She smiled and reddened up very
sweet, and I says, "If you don't mind it, I'll shut the
door—and bolt it."

Then I come back and set down again, and says:

"Don't you holler. Just set still and take it like a man.
I got to tell the truth, and you want to brace up, Miss
Mary, because it's a bad kind and going to be hard to
take, but there ain't no help for it. These uncles of
yourn ain't no uncles at all; they're a couple of frauds—
regular dead-beats. There, now we're over the worst of
it, you can stand the rest middling easy."

It jolted her up like everything, of course, but I was
over the shoal water now, so I went right along, her eyes
a-blazing higher and higher all the time, and told her
every blame thing from where we first struck that young
fool going up to the steamboat clear through to where
she flung herself onto the king's breast at the front door
and he kissed her sixteen or seventeen times—and then

up she jumps, with her face afire like sunset, and says:

"The brute! Come, don't waste a minute—not a *second*—we'll have them tarred and feathered, and flung in the river!"

Says I:

"Cert'nly. But do you mean *before* you go to Mr. Lothrop's, or—"

"Oh," she says, "what am I *thinking* about!" she says, and set right down again. "Don't mind what I said—please don't—you *won't*, now, *will* you?" Laying her silky hand on mine in that kind of a way that I said I would die first. "I never thought, I was so stirred up," she says, "now go on, and I won't do so any more. You tell me what to do, and whatever you say I'll do it."

"Well," I says, "it's a rough gang, them two frauds, and I'm fixed so I got to travel with them a while longer whether I want to or not—I druther not tell you why; and if you was to blow on them this town would get me out of their claws, and I'd be all right; but there'd be another person that you don't know about who'd be in big trouble. Well, we got to save *him*, hain't we? Of course. Well, then, we won't blow on them."

Saying them words put a good idea in my head. I see how maybe I could get me and Jim rid of the frauds; get them jailed here and then leave. But I didn't want to run the raft in the daytime without anybody aboard to answer questions but me, so I didn't want the plan to begin working till pretty late to-night. I says:

"Miss Mary Jane, I'll tell you what we'll do, and you won't have to stay at Mr. Lothrop's so long, nuther. How fur is it?"

"A little short of four miles—right out in the country, back here."

"Well, that'll answer. Now you go along out there, and lay low till nine or half-past to-night, and then get them to fetch you home again—tell them you've thought of something. If you get here before eleven put a candle in this window, and if I don't turn up wait *till* eleven, and *then* if I don't turn up it means I'm gone, and out of the way, and safe. Then you come out and spread the news around and get these beats jailed."

"Good," she says, "I'll do it."

"And if it just happens so that I don't get away, but get took up along with them, you must up and say I told you the whole thing beforehand, and you must stand by me all you can."

"Stand by you! indeed I will. They sha'n't touch a hair of your head!" she says, and I see her nostrils spread and her eyes snap when she said it, too.

"If I get away I sha'n't be here," I says, "to prove these rapscallions ain't your uncles, and I couldn't do it if I *was* here. I could swear they was beats and bummers, that's all, though that's worth something. Well, there's others can do that better than what I can, and they're people that ain't going to be doubted as quick as I'd be. I'll tell you how to find them. Gimme a pencil and a piece of paper. There—'*Royal Nonesuch, Bricksville.*' Put it away, and don't lose it. When the court wants to find out something about these two, let them send up to Bricksville and say they've got the men that played the 'Royal Nonesuch,' and ask for some witnesses —why, you'll have that entire town down here before you can hardly wink, Miss Mary. And they'll come a-biling, too."

I judged we had got everything fixed about right now. So I says:

"Just let the auction go right along and don't worry. Nobody don't have to pay for the things they buy till a whole day after the auction on accounts of the short notice, and they ain't going out of this till they get that money; and the way we've fixed it the sale ain't going to count and they ain't going to *get* no money. It's just like the way it was with the niggers—it warn't no sale, and the niggers will be back before long. Why, they can't collect the money for the *niggers* yet—they're in the worst kind of a fix, Miss Mary."

"Well," she says, "I'll run down to breakfast now, and then I'll start straight for Mr. Lothrop's."

" 'Deed, *that* ain't the ticket, Miss Mary Jane," I says, "by no manner of means; go *before* breakfast."

"Why?"

"What did you reckon I wanted you to go at all for, Miss Mary?"

"Well, I never thought—and come to think, I don't know. What was it?"

"Why, it's because you ain't one of these leather-face people. I don't want no better book than what your face is. A body can set down and read it off like coarse print. Do you reckon you can go and face your uncles when they come to kiss you good-morning, and never—"

"There, there, don't! Yes, I'll go before breakfast— I'll be glad to. And leave my sisters with them?"

"Yes; never mind about them. They've got to stand it yet awhile. They might suspicion something if all of you was to go. I don't want you to see them, nor your sisters, nor nobody in this town; if a neighbor was to ask how is your uncles this morning your face would tell something. No, you go right along, Miss Mary Jane, and I'll fix it with all of them. I'll tell Miss Susan to give your love to your uncles and say you've went away for a few hours for to get a little rest and change, or to see a friend, and you'll be back to-night or early in the morning."

"Gone to see a friend is all right but I won't have my love given to them."

"Well, then, it sha'n't be." It was well enough to tell

her so—no harm in it. It was only a little thing to do
and no trouble; and it's the little things that smooths
people's roads the most, down here below; it would
make Mary Jane comfortable, and it wouldn't cost nothing. Then I says: "There's one more thing—that bag of
money."

"Well, they've got that; and it makes me feel pretty
silly to think *how* they got it."

"No, you're out, there. They hain't got it."

"Why, who's got it?"

"I wish I knowed, but I don't. I *had* it, because I stole
it from them; and I stole it to give to you; and I know
where I hid it, but I'm afraid it ain't there no more. I'm
awful sorry, Miss Mary Jane, I'm just as sorry as I can
be; but I done the best I could; I did honest. I come
nigh getting caught, and I had to shove it into the first
place I come to, and run—and it warn't a good place."

"Oh, stop blaming yourself—it's too bad to do it, and
I won't allow it—you couldn't help it; it wasn't your
fault. Where did you hide it?"

I didn't want to set her to thinking about her troubles
again; and I couldn't seem to get my mouth to tell her
what would make her see that corpse laying in the coffin
with that bag of money on his stomach. So for a minute
I didn't say nothing; then I says:

"I'd rather not *tell* you where I put it, Miss Mary Jane,
if you don't mind letting me off; but I'll write it for you
on a piece of paper and you can read it along the road to
Mr. Lothrop's, if you want to. Do you reckon that'll do?"

"Oh, yes."

So I wrote: "I put it in the coffin. It was in there when
you was crying there, away in the night. I was behind
the door, and I was mighty sorry for you, Miss Mary
Jane."

It made my eyes water a little to remember her cry-

ing there all by herself in the night, and them devils
laying there right under her own roof, shaming her and
robbing her; and when I folded it up and give it to her
I see the water come into her eyes, too; and she shook
me by the hand, hard, and says:

"*Good*-by. I'm going to do everything just as you've
told me; and if I don't ever see you again, I sha'n't ever
forget you, and I'll think of you a many and a many a
time, and I'll *pray* for you, too!"—and she was gone.

Pray for me! I reckoned if she knowed me she'd take
a job that was more nearer her size. But I bet she done
it, just the same—she was just that kind. She had the
grit to pray for Judus if she took the notion—there
warn't no back-down to her, I judge. You may say what
you want to but in my opinion she had more sand in her
than any girl I ever see; in my opinion she was just full
of sand. It sounds like flattery but it ain't no flattery.
And when it comes to beauty—and goodness, too—she
lays over them all. I hain't ever seen her since that time
that I see her go out of that door; no, I hain't ever seen
her since but I reckon I've thought of her a many and a
many a million times, and of her saying she would pray
for me; and if ever I'd 'a' thought it would do any good
for me to pray for *her*, blamed if I wouldn't 'a' done it or
bust.

Well, Mary Jane she lit out the back way, I reckon;
because nobody see her go. When I struck Susan and
the hare-lip, I says:

"What's the name of them people over on t'other side
of the river that you all goes to see sometimes?"

They says:

"There's several; but it's the Proctors, mainly."

"That's the name," I says; "I most forgot it. Well,
Miss Mary Jane she told me to tell you she's gone over
there in a dreadful hurry—one of them's sick."

"Which one?"

"I don't know; leastways, I kinder forget; but I think it's—"

"Sakes alive, I hope it ain't *Hanner?*"

"I'm sorry to say it," I says, "but Hanner's the very one."

"My goodness, and she so well only last week! Is she took bad?"

"It ain't no name for it. They set up with her all night, Miss Mary Jane said, and they don't think she'll last many hours."

"Only think of that, now! What's the matter with her?"

I couldn't think of anything reasonable, right off that way, so I says:

"Mumps."

"Mumps your granny! They don't set up with people that's got the mumps."

"They don't, don't they? You better bet they do with *these* mumps. These mumps is different. It's a new kind, Miss Mary Jane said."

"How's it a new kind?"

"Because it's mixed up with other things."

"What other things?"

"Well, measles, and whooping-cough, and erysiplas, and consumption, and yaller janders, and brainfever, and I don't know what all."

"My land! And they call it the *mumps?*"

"That's what Miss Mary Jane said."

"Well, what in the nation do they call it the *mumps* for?"

"Why, because it *is* the mumps. That's what it starts with."

"Well, ther' ain't no sense in it. A body might stump his toe, and take pison, and fall down the well, and break his neck, and bust his brains out, and somebody come along and ask what killed him, and some numskull up and say, 'Why, he stumped his *toe.*' Would ther' be any sense in that? *No.* And ther' ain't no sense in *this,* nuther. Is it ketching?"

"Is it *ketching?* Why, how you talk. Is a *harrow* catching—in the dark? If you don't hitch on to one tooth, you're bound to on another, ain't you? And you can't get away with that tooth without fetching the whole harrow along, can you? Well, these kind of mumps is a kind of a harrow, as you may say—and it ain't no slouch of a harrow, nuther, you come to get it hitched on good."

"Well, it's awful, *I* think," says the hare-lip. "I'll go to Uncle Harvey and—"

"Oh, yes," I says, "I *would.* Of *course* I would. I wouldn't lose no time."

"Well, why wouldn't you?"

"Just look at it a minute, and maybe you can see. Hain't your uncles obleeged to get along home to England as fast as they can? And do you reckon they'd be mean enough to go off and leave you to go all that journey by yourselves? *You* know they'll wait for you. So fur, so good. Your Uncle Harvey's a preacher, ain't he? Very well, then; is a *preacher* going to deceive a steamboat clerk? is he going to deceive a *ship clerk?*— so as to get them to let Miss Mary Jane go aboard? Now *you* know he ain't. What *will* he do, then? Why, he'll say, 'It's a great pity, but my church matters has got to get along the best way they can, for my niece has been exposed to the dreadful pluribus-unum mumps and so it's my bounden duty to set down here and wait the three months it takes to show on her if she's got it.' But never mind, if you think it's best to tell your Uncle Harvey—"

"Shucks, and stay fooling around here when we could all be having good times in England whilst we was

waiting to find out whether Mary Jane's got it or not?
Why, you talk like a muggins."

"Well, anyway, maybe you'd better tell some of the
neighbors."

"Listen at that, now. You do beat all for natural
stupidness. Can't you *see* that *they'd* go and tell? Ther'
ain't no way but just to not tell anybody at *all*."

"Well, maybe you're right—yes, I judge you *are*
right."

"But I reckon we ought to tell Uncle Harvey she's
gone out awhile, anyway, so he won't be uneasy about
her?"

"Yes, Miss Mary Jane she wanted you to do that. She
says, 'Tell them to give Uncle Harvey and William my
love and a kiss, and say I've run over the river to see
Mr.'—Mr.—what *is* the name of that rich family your
Uncle Peter used to think so much of?—I mean the one
that—"

"Why, you must mean the Apthorps, ain't it?"

"Of course; bother them kind of names, a body can't
ever seem to remember them half the time, somehow.
Yes, she said, say she has run over for to ask the Apthorps to be sure and come to the auction and buy this
house, because she allowed her Uncle Peter would
ruther they had it than anybody else; and she's going to
stick to them till they say they'll come and then, if she
ain't too tired, she's coming home; and if she is, she'll
be home in the morning anyway. She said, don't say
nothing about the Proctors but only about the Apthorps—which'll be perfectly true, because she *is* going
there to speak about their buying the house; I know it,
because she told me so herself."

"All right," they said, and cleared out to lay for their
uncles, and give them the love and the kisses, and tell
them the message.

Everything was all right now. The girls wouldn't say nothing because they wanted to go to England, and the king and the duke would ruther Mary Jane was off working for the auction than around in reach of Doctor Robinson. I felt very good; I judged I had done it pretty neat—I reckoned Tom Sawyer couldn't 'a' done it no neater himself. Of course he would 'a' throwed more style into it, but I can't do that very handy, not being brung up to it.

Well, they held the auction in the public square, along towards the end of the afternoon, and it strung along and strung along, and the old man he was on hand and looking his level piousest, up there longside of the auctioneer, and chipping in a little Scripture now and then or a little goody-goody saying of some kind, and the duke he was around goo-gooing for sympathy all he knowed how, and just spreading himself generly.

But by and by the thing dragged through, and everything was sold—everything but a little old trifling lot in the graveyard. So they got to work *that* off—I never see such a girafft as the king was for wanting to swallow *everything*. Well, whilst they was at it a steamboat landed, and in about two minutes up comes a crowd a-whooping and yelling and laughing and carrying on, and singing out:

"*Here's* your opposition line! here's your two sets o' heirs to old Peter Wilks—and you pays your money and you takes your choice!"

XXIX. I Light Out in the Storm

They was fetching a very nice-looking old gentleman along and a nice-looking younger one, with his right arm in a sling. And, my souls, how the people yelled and

laughed, and kept it up. But I didn't see no joke about
it, and I judged it would strain the duke and the king
some to see any. I reckoned they'd turn pale. But no,
nary a pale did *they* turn. The duke he never let on he
suspicioned what was up but just went a goo-gooing
around, happy and satisfied, like a jug that's googling
out buttermilk; and as for the king, he just gazed and
gazed down sorrowful on them new-comers like it give
him the stomach-ache in his very heart to think there
could be such frauds and rascals in the world. Oh, he
done it admirable. Lots of the principal people gethered
around the king, to let him see they was on his side. That
old gentleman that had just come looked all puzzled to
death. Pretty soon he begun to speak, and I see straight
off he pronounced *like* an Englishman—not the king's
way, though the king's *was* pretty good for an imitation.
I can't give the old gent's words, nor I can't imitate
him; but he turned around to the crowd and says about
like this:

"This is a surprise to me which I wasn't looking for;
and I'll acknowledge, candid and frank, I ain't very well
fixed to meet it and answer it; for my brother and me has
had misfortunes; he's broke his arm, and our baggage
got put off at a town above here last night in the night
by a mistake. I am Peter Wilks's brother Harvey, and
this is his brother William, which can't hear nor speak
—and can't even make signs to amount to much, now't
he's only got one hand to work them with. We are who
we say we are; and in a day or two, when I get the baggage, I can prove it. But up till then I won't say nothing
more but go to the hotel and wait."

So him and the new dummy started off; and the king
he laughs, and blethers out:

"Broke his arm—*very* likely, *ain't* it?—and very convenient, too, for a fraud that's got to make signs, and

ain't learnt how. Lost their baggage! That's *mighty good!*—and mighty ingenious—under the *circumstances!*"

So he laughed again, and so did everybody else, except three or four, or maybe half a dozen. One of these was that doctor; another one was a sharp-looking gentleman, with a carpet-bag of the old-fashioned kind made out of carpet-stuff, that had just come off of the steamboat and was talking to him in a low voice, and glancing towards the king now and then and nodding their heads —it was Levi Bell, the lawyer that was gone up to Louisville; and another one was a big rough husky that come along and listened to all the old gentleman said, and was listening to the king now. And when the king got done this husky up and says:

"Say, looky here; if you are Harvey Wilks, when'd you come to this town?"

"The day before the funeral, friend," says the king.

"But what time o' day?"

"In the evenin'—'bout an hour er two before sundown."

"How'd you come?"

"I come down on the *Susan Powell* from Cincinnati."

"Well, then, how'd you come to be up at the Pint in the *mornin'*—in a canoe?"

"I warn't up at the Pint in the mornin'."

"It's a lie."

Several of them jumped for him and begged him not to talk that way to an old man and a preacher.

"Preacher be hanged, he's a fraud and a liar. He was up at the Pint that mornin'. I live up there, don't I? Well, I was up there, and he was up there. I *see* him there. He come in a canoe, along with Tim Collins and a boy."

The doctor he up and says:

"Would you know the boy again if you was to see him, Hines?"

"I reckon I would, but I don't know. Why, yonder he is, now. I know him perfectly easy."

It was me he pointed at. The doctor says:

"Neighbors, I don't know whether the new couple is frauds or not; but if *these* two ain't frauds, I am an idiot, that's all. I think it's our duty to see that they don't get away from here till we've looked into this thing. Come along, Hines; come along, the rest of you. We'll take these fellows to the tavern and affront them with t'other couple, and I reckon we'll find out *something* before we get through."

It was nuts for the crowd, though maybe not for the king's friends; so we all started. It was about sundown. The doctor he led me along by the hand, and was plenty kind enough, but he never let *go* my hand.

We all got in a big room in the hotel and lit up some candles and fetched in the new couple. First, the doctor says:

"I don't wish to be too hard on these two men, but *I* think they're frauds, and they may have 'complices that we don't know nothing about. If they have, won't the 'complices get away with that bag of gold Peter Wilks left? It ain't unlikely. If these men ain't frauds, they won't object to sending for that money and letting us keep it till they prove they're all right—ain't that so?"

Everybody agreed to that. So I judged they had our gang in a pretty tight place right at the outstart. But the king he only looked sorrowful, and says:

"Gentlemen, I wish the money was there, for I ain't got no disposition to throw anything in the way of a fair, open, out-and-out investigation o' this misable business; but, alas, the money ain't there; you k'n send and see, if you want to."

"Where is it, then?"

"Well, when my niece give it to me to keep for her I took and hid it inside o' the straw tick o' my bed, not wishin' to bank it for the few days we'd be here, and considerin' the bed a safe place, we not bein' used to niggers, and suppos'n' 'em honest, like servants in England. The niggers stole it the very next mornin' after I had went down-stairs; and when I sold 'em I hadn't missed the money yit, so they got clean away with it. My servant here k'n tell you 'bout it, gentlemen."

The doctor and several said "Shucks!" and I see nobody didn't altogether believe him. One man asked me if I see the niggers steal it. I said no, but I see them sneaking out of the room and hustling away, and I never thought nothing, only I reckoned they was afraid they had waked up my master and was trying to get away before he made trouble with them. That was all they asked me. Then the doctor whirls on me and says:

"Are *you* English, too?"

I says yes; and him and some others laughed and said, "Stuff!"

Well, then they sailed in on the general investigation, and there we had it, up and down, hour in, hour out, and nobody never said a word about supper, nor ever seemed to think about it—and so they kept it up, and kept it up; and it *was* the worst mixed-up thing you ever see. They made the king tell his yarn and they made the old gentleman tell his'n, and anybody but a lot of prejudiced chuckle-heads would 'a' *seen* that the old gentleman was spinning truth and t'other one lies. And by and by they had me up to tell what I knowed. The king he give me a left-handed look out of the corner of his eye, and so I knowed enough to talk on the right side. I begun to tell about Sheffield, and how we lived there, and all about the English Wilkses, and so on; but

I didn't get pretty fur till the doctor begun to laugh; and Levi Bell, the lawyer, says:

"Set down, my boy; I wouldn't strain myself if I was you. I reckon you ain't used to lying, it don't seem to come handy; what you want is practice. You do it pretty awkward."

I didn't care nothing for the compliment but I was glad to be let off, anyway.

The doctor he started to say something, and turns and says:

"If you'd been in town at first, Levi Bell—"

The king broke in and reached out his hand, and says:

"Why, is this my poor dead brother's old friend that he's wrote so often about?"

The lawyer and him shook hands, and the lawyer smiled and looked pleased, and they talked right along awhile, and then got to one side and talked low; and at last the lawyer speaks up and says:

"That'll fix it. I'll take the order and send it, along with your brother's, and then they'll know it's all right."

So they got some paper and a pen, and the king he set down and twisted his head to one side, and chawed his tongue, and scrawled off something; and then they give the pen to the duke—and then for the first time the duke looked sick. But he took the pen and wrote. So then the lawyer turns to the new old gentleman and says:

"You and your brother please write a line or two and sign your names."

The old gentleman wrote, but nobody couldn't read it. The lawyer looked powerful astonished, and says:

"Well, it beats *me*"—and snaked a lot of old letters out of his pocket, and examined them, and then examined the old man's writing, and then *them* again; and then says: "These old letters is from Harvey Wilks; and here's *these* two handwritings, and anybody can see

they didn't write them" (the king and the duke looked
sold and foolish, I tell you, to see how the lawyer had
took them in), "and here's *this* old gentleman's hand-
writing, and anybody can tell, easy enough, *he* didn't
write them—fact is, the scratches he makes ain't properly *writing* at all. Now, here's some letters from—"

The new old gentleman says:

"If you please, let me explain. Nobody can read my
hand but my brother there—so he always copies for me.
It's *his* hand you've got there, not mine."

"*Well!*" says the lawyer, "this *is* a state of things. I've
got some of William's letters, too; so if you'll get him to
write a line or so we can com—"

"He *can't* write with his left hand," says the old gentleman. "If he could use his right hand, you would see
that he wrote his own letters and mine too. Look at both,
please—they're by the same hand."

The lawyer done it, and says:

"I believe it's so—and if it ain't so, there's a heap
stronger resemblance than I'd noticed before, anyway.
Well, well, well! I thought we was right on the track
of a slution, but it's gone to grass, partly. But anyway,
one thing is proved—*these* two ain't either of 'em
Wilkses"—and he wagged his head towards the king
and the duke.

Well, what do you think? That mule-headed old fool
wouldn't give in *then!* Indeed he wouldn't. Said it warn't
no fair test. Said his brother William was the cussedest
joker in the world, and hadn't *tried* to write—he see
William was going to play one of his jokes the minute he
put the pen to paper. And so he warmed up and went
warbling right along till he was actuly beginning to believe what he was saying *himself*, but pretty soon the
new old gentleman broke in and says:

"I've thought of something. Is there anybody here

that helped to lay out my br—helped to lay out the late Peter Wilks for burying?"

"Yes," says somebody, "me and Ab Turner done it. We're both here."

Then the old man turns toward the king, and says:

"Per'aps this gentleman can tell me what was tattooed on his breast?"

Blamed if the king didn't have to brace up mighty quick, or he'd 'a' squshed down like a bluff bank that the river has cut under, it took him so sudden; and, mind you, it was a thing that was calculated to make most *anybody* sqush to get fetched such a solid one as that without any notice, because how was *he* going to know what was tattooed on the man? He whitened a little; he couldn't help it; and it was mighty still in there, and everybody bending a little forwards and gazing at him. Says I to myself, *Now* he'll throw up the sponge—there ain't no more use. Well, did he? A body can't hardly believe it, but he didn't. I reckon he thought he'd keep the thing up till he tired them people out, so they'd thin out, and him and the duke could break loose and get away. Anyway, he set there, and pretty soon he begun to smile, and says:

"Mf! It's a *very* tough question, *ain't* it! *Yes*, sir, I k'n tell you what's tattooed on his breast. It's jest a small, thin, blue arrow—that's what it is; and if you don't look clost, you can't see it. *Now* what do you say—hey?"

Well, *I* never see anything like that old blister for clean out-and-out cheek.

The new old gentleman turns brisk towards Ab Turner and his pard, and his eye lights up like he judged he'd got the king *this* time, and says:

"There—you've heard what he said! Was there any such mark on Peter Wilks's breast?"

Both of them spoke up and says:

"We didn't see no such mark."

"Good!" says the old gentleman. "Now, what you *did* see on his breast was a small dim P, and a B (which is an initial he dropped when he was young), and a W, and dashes between them, so: P—B—W"—and he marked them that way on a piece of paper. "Come, ain't that what you saw?"

Both of them spoke up again and says:

"No, we *didn't*. We never seen any marks at all."

Well, everybody *was* in a state of mind now, and they sings out:

"The whole *bilin'* of 'em's frauds! Le's duck 'em! le's drown 'em! le's ride 'em on a rail!" and everybody was whooping at once, and there was a rattling powwow. But the lawyer he jumps on the table and yells, and says:

"Gentlemen—gentle*men!* Hear me just a word—just a *single* word—if you PLEASE! There's one way yet—let's go and dig up the corpse and look."

That took them.

"Hooray!" they all shouted, and was starting right off; but the lawyer and the doctor sung out:

"Hold on, hold on! Collar all these four men and the boy, and fetch *them* along, too!"

"We'll do it!" they all shouted; "and if we don't find them marks we'll lynch the whole gang!"

I *was* scared, now, I tell you. But there warn't no getting away, you know. They gripped us all, and marched us right along, straight for the graveyard, which was a mile and a half down the river, and the whole town at our heels, for we made noise enough, and it was only nine in the evening.

As we went by our house I wished I hadn't sent Mary Jane out of town; because now if I could tip her the wink she'd light out and save me, and blow on our dead-beats.

Well, we swarmed along down the river road, just carrying on like wildcats; and to make it more scary the sky was darking up, and the lightning beginning to wink and flitter, and the wind to shiver amongst the leaves. This was the most awful trouble and most dangersome I ever was in, and I was kinder stunned; everything was going so different from what I had allowed for; 'stead of being fixed so I could take my own time if I wanted to and see all the fun and have Mary Jane at my back to save me and set me free when the close-fit come, here was nothing in the world betwixt me and sudden death but just them tattoo-marks. If they didn't find them—

I couldn't bear to think about it, and yet somehow I couldn't think about nothing else. It got darker and darker, and it was a beautiful time to give the crowd the slip, but that big husky had me by the wrist—Hines— and a body might as well try to give Goliar the slip. He dragged me right along, he was so excited, and I had to run to keep up.

When they got there they swarmed into the grave-yard and washed over it like an overflow. And when they got to the grave they found they had about a hundred times as many shovels as they wanted, but nobody hadn't thought to fetch a lantern. But they sailed into digging anyway by the flicker of the lightning and sent a man to the nearest house, a half a mile off, to borrow one.

So they dug and dug like everything; and it got awful dark and the rain started and the wind swished and swushed along, and the lightning come brisker and brisker and the thunder boomed; but them people never took no notice of it, they was so full of this business; and one minute you could see everything and every face in that big crowd, and the shovelfuls of dirt sailing up out of the grave, and the next second the dark wiped it all out, and you couldn't see nothing at all.

At last they got out the coffin and begun to unscrew the lid, and then such another crowding and shouldering and shoving as there was, to scrouge in and get a sight, you never see; and in the dark, that way, it was awful. Hines he hurt my wrist dreadful pulling and tugging so and I reckon he clean forgot I was in the world, he was so excited and panting.

All of a sudden the lightning let go a perfect sluice of white glare, and somebody sings out:

"By the living jingo, here's the bag of gold on his breast!"

Hines let out a whoop, like everybody else, and dropped my wrist and give a big surge to bust his way in and get a look, and the way I lit out and shinned for the road in the dark there ain't nobody can tell.

I had the road all to myself and I fairly flew—least-ways, I had it all to myself except the solid dark and the now-and-then glares, and the buzzing of the rain and the thrashing of the wind and the splitting of the thunder; and sure as you are born I did clip it along!

When I struck the town I see there warn't nobody out in the storm, so I never hunted for no back streets but humped it straight through the main one, and when I begun to get towards our house I aimed my eye and set it. No light there; the house all dark—which made me feel sorry and disappointed, I didn't know why. But at last, just as I was sailing by, *flash* comes the light in Mary Jane's window! and my heart swelled up sudden, like to bust; and the same second the house and all was behind me in the dark and wasn't ever going to be before me no more in this world. She *was* the best girl I ever see, and had the most sand.

The minute I was far enough above the town to see I could make the towhead, I begun to look sharp for a boat to borrow, and the first time the lightning showed me one that wasn't chained I snatched it and shoved. It was a canoe and warn't fastened with nothing but a rope. The towhead was a rattling big distance off, away out there in the middle of the river, but I didn't lose no time; and when I struck the raft at last I was so fagged I would 'a' just laid down to blow and gasp if I could afforded it. But I didn't. As I sprung aboard I sung out:

"Out with you, Jim, and set her loose! Glory be to goodness, we're shut of them!"

Jim lit out and was a-coming for me with both arms spread, he was so full of joy, but when I glimpsed him in the lightning my heart shot up in my mouth and I went overboard backwards, for I forgot he was old King Lear and a drownded A-rab all in one and it most scared the livers and lights out of me. But Jim fished me out and was going to hug me and bless me and so on, he was so glad I was back and we was shut of the king and the duke, but I says:

"Not now; have it for breakfast, have it for breakfast! Cut loose and let her slide!"

So in two seconds away we went a-sliding down the river, and it *did* seem so good to be free again and all by ourselves on the big river and nobody to bother us. I had to skip around a bit and jump up and crack my heels a few times—I couldn't help it, but about the third crack I noticed a sound that I knowed mighty well and held my breath and listened and waited, and sure enough, when the next flash busted out over the water, here they come!—and just a-laying to their oars and making their skiff hum! It was the king and the duke.

So I wilted right down onto the planks then and give up, and it was all I could do to keep from crying.

When they got aboard the king went for me and shook me by the collar, and says:

"Tryin' to give us the slip, was ye, you pup! Tired of our company, hey?"

I says:

"No, your majesty, we warn't—*please* don't, your majesty!"

"Quick, then, and tell us what *was* your idea, or I'll shake the insides out o' you!"

"Honest, I'll tell you everything just as it happened, your majesty. The man that had a-holt of me was very good to me and kept saying he had a boy about as big as me that died last year, and he was sorry to see a boy in such a dangerous fix; and when they was all took by surprise by finding the gold and made a rush for the coffin, he lets go of me and whispers, 'Heel it now, or they'll hang ye, sure!' and I lit out. It didn't seem no good for *me* to stay—*I* couldn't do nothing and I didn't want to be hung if I could get away. So I never stopped running till I found the canoe, and when I got here I told Jim to hurry or they'd catch me and hang me yet, and said I was afeard you and the duke wasn't alive now and I was awful sorry, and so was Jim, and was awful glad when we see you coming; you may ask Jim if I didn't."

Jim said it was so, and the king told him to shut up and said, "Oh, yes, it's *mighty* likely!" and shook me up again, and said he reckoned he'd drownd me. But the duke says:

"Leggo the boy, you old idiot! Would *you* 'a' done any different? Did you inquire around for *him* when you got loose? *I* don't remember it."

So the king let go of me and begun to cuss that town and everybody in it. But the duke says:

"You better a blame' sight give *yourself* a good cussing, for you're the one that's entitled to it most. You hain't done a thing from the start that had any sense in it, except coming out so cool and cheeky with that imaginary blue-arrow mark. That *was* bright—it was downright bully; and it was the thing that saved us. For if it hadn't been for that they'd 'a' jailed us till them Englishmen's baggage come—and then—the penitentiary, you bet! But that trick took 'em to the graveyard, and the gold done us a still bigger kindness; for if the excited fools hadn't let go all holts and made that rush to get a look we'd 'a' slept in our cravats to-night— cravats warranted to *wear*, too—longer than *we'd* need 'em.'"

They was still a minute—thinking; then the king says, kind of absent-minded like:

"Mf! And we reckoned the *niggers* stole it!"

That made me squirm!

"Yes," says the duke, kinder slow and deliberate and sarcastic, "*we* did."

After about a half a minute the king drawls out:

"Leastways, *I* did."

The duke says, the same way:

"On the contrary, *I* did."

The king kind of ruffles up, and says:

"Looky here, Bilgewater, what'r you referrin' to?"

The duke says, pretty brisk:

"When it comes to that, maybe you'll let me ask what was *you* referring to?"

"Shucks!" says the king, very sarcastic; "but *I* don't know—maybe you was asleep, and didn't know what you was about."

The duke bristles up now, and says:

"Oh, let *up* on this cussed nonsense; do you take me for a blame' fool? Don't you reckon *I* know who hid that money in that coffin?"

"*Yes*, sir! I know you *do* know, because you done it yourself!"

"It's a lie!"—and the duke went for him. The king sings out:

"Take y'r hands off!—leggo my throat!—I take it all back!"

The duke says:

"Well, you just own up first that you *did* hide that money there, intending to give me the slip one of these days and come back and dig it up and have it all to yourself."

"Wait jest a minute, duke—answer me this one question, honest and fair; if you didn't put the money there, say it, and I'll b'lieve you, and take back everything I said."

"You old scoundrel, I didn't, and you know I didn't. There, now!"

"Well, then, I b'lieve you. But answer me only jest this one more—now *don't* git mad; didn't you have it in your *mind* to hook the money and hide it?"

The duke never said nothing for a little bit; then he says:

"Well, I don't care if I *did*, I didn't *do* it, anyway. But you not only had it in mind to do it, but you *done* it."

"I wisht I may never die if I done it, duke, and that's honest. I won't say I warn't *goin'* to do it, because I *was;* but you—I mean somebody—got in ahead o' me."

"It's a lie! You done it, and you got to *say* you done it, or—"

The king begun to gurgle, and then he gasps out:

"'Nough!—*I own up!*"

I was very glad to hear him say that; it made me feel much more easier than what I was feeling before. So the duke took his hands off and says:

"If you ever deny it again I'll drown you. It's *well* for you to set there and blubber like a baby—it's fitten for you, after the way you've acted. I never see such an old ostrich for wanting to gobble everything—and I a-trusting you all the time, like you was my own father. You ought to been ashamed of yourself to stand by and hear it saddled on to a lot of poor niggers, and you never say a word for 'em. It makes me feel ridiculous to think I was soft enough to *believe* that rubbage. Cuss you, I can see now why you was so anxious to make up the deffersit—you wanted to get what money I'd got out of the 'Nonesuch' and one thing or another, and scoop it *all!*"

The king says, timid and still a-snuffling:

"Why, duke, it was you that said make up the deffersit; it warn't me."

"Dry up! I don't want to hear no more *out* of you!" says the duke. "And *now* you see what you *got* by it. They've got all their own money back, and all of *ourn* but a shekel or two *besides*. G'long to bed, and don't you deffersit *me* no more deffersits, long's *you* live!"

So the king sneaked into the wigwam and took to his bottle for comfort and before long the duke tackled *his* bottle, and so in about a half an hour they was as thick as thieves again, and the tighter they got the lovinger they got, and went off a-snoring in each other's arms. They both got powerful mellow but I noticed the king didn't get mellow enough to forget to remember to not deny about hiding the money-bag again. That made me feel easy and satisfied. Of course when they got to snoring we had a long gabble and I told Jim everything.

We dasn't stop again at any town for days and days;
kept right along down the river. We was down south in
the warm weather now, and a mighty long ways from
home. We begun to come to trees with Spanish moss on
them, hanging down from the limbs like long, gray
beards. It was the first I ever see it growing and it made
the woods look solemn and dismal. So now the frauds
reckoned they was out of danger, and they begun to
work the villages again.

First they done a lecture on temperance, but they
didn't make enough for them both to get drunk on. Then
in another village they started a dancing-school, but they
didn't know no more how to dance than a kangaroo does,
so the first prance they made the general public jumped
in and pranced them out of town. Another time they
tried a go at yellocution, but they didn't yellocute long
till the audience got up and give them a solid good
cussing, and made them skip out. They tackled missionarying and mesmerizing and doctoring and telling
fortunes, and a little of everything, but they couldn't
seem to have no luck. So at last they got just about dead
broke, and laid around the raft as she floated along,
thinking and thinking, and never saying nothing, by the
half a day at a time, and dreadful blue and desperate.

And at last they took a change and begun to lay their
heads together in the wigwam and talk low and con-
fidential two or three hours at a time. Jim and me got
uneasy. We didn't like the look of it. We judged they
was studying up some kind of worse deviltry than ever.
We turned it over and over, and at last we made up our
minds they was going to break into somebody's house or
store, or was going into the counterfeit-money business,

445

or something. So then we was pretty scared and made up an agreement that we wouldn't have nothing in the world to do with such actions, and if we ever got the least show we would give them the cold shake and clear out and leave them behind. Well, early one morning we hid the raft in a good, safe place about two mile below a little bit of a shabby village named Pikesville, and the king he went ashore and told us all to stay hid whilst he went up to town and smelt around to see if anybody had got any wind of the "Royal Nonesuch" there yet. ("House to rob, you *mean*," says I to myself; "and when you get through robbing it you'll come back here and wonder what has become of me and Jim and the raft— and you'll have to take it out in wondering.") And he said if he warn't back by midday the duke and me would know it was all right, and we was to come along.

So we stayed where we was. The duke he fretted and sweated around, and was in a mighty sour way. He scolded us for everything, and we couldn't seem to do nothing right; he found fault with every little thing. Something was a-brewing, sure. I was good and glad when midday come and no king; we could have a change, anyway—and maybe a chance for *the* change on top of it. So me and the duke went up to the village and hunted around there for the king, and by and by we found him in the back room of a little low doggery, very tight, and a lot of loafers bully-ragging him for sport, and he a-cussing and a-threatening with all his might, and so tight he couldn't walk and couldn't do nothing to them. The duke he begun to abuse him for an old fool, and the king begun to sass back, and the minute they was fairly at it I lit out and shook the reefs out of my hind legs, and spun down the river road like a deer, for I see our chance; and I made up my mind that it would be a long day before they ever see me and Jim again. I got down there all out of breath but loaded up with joy, and sung out:

"Set her loose, Jim; we're all right now!"

But there warn't no answer, and nobody come out of the wigwam. Jim was gone! I set up a shout—and then another—and then another one; and run this way and that in the woods, whooping and screeching; but it warn't no use—old Jim was gone. Then I set down and cried; I couldn't help it. But I couldn't set still long. Pretty soon I went out on the road, trying to think what I better do, and I run across a boy walking, and asked him if he'd seen a strange nigger dressed so and so, and he says:

"Yes."

"Whereabouts?" says I.

"Down to Silas Phelps's place, two mile below here. He's a runaway nigger and they've got him. Was you looking for him?"

"You bet I ain't! I run across him in the woods about an hour or two ago, and he said if I hollered he'd cut my livers out—and told me to lay down and stay where I was; and I done it. Been there ever since; afeard to come out."

"Well," he says, "you needn't be afeard no more, becuz they've got him. He run off f'm down South, som'ers."

"It's a good job they got him."

"Well, I *reckon!* There's two hundred dollars' reward on him. It's like picking up money out'n the road."

"Yes, it is—and *I* could 'a' had it if I'd been big enough; I see him *first.* Who nailed him?"

"It was an old feller—a stranger—and he sold out his chance in him for forty dollars, becuz he's got to go up the river and can't wait. Think o' that, now! You bet *I'd* wait, if it was seven year."

"That's me, every time," says I. "But maybe his chance ain't worth no more than that, if he'll sell it so cheap. Maybe there's something ain't straight about it."

"But it *is*, though—straight as a string. I see the handbill myself. It tells all about him, to a dot—paints him like a picture, and tells the plantation he's frum, below Newr*leans*. No-sirree-*bob*, they ain't no trouble 'bout *that* speculation, you bet you. Say, gimme a chaw tobacker, won't ye?"

I didn't have none, so he left. I went to the raft, and set down in the wigwam to think. But I couldn't come to nothing. I thought till I wore my head sore, but I couldn't see no way out of the trouble. After all this long journey and after all we'd done for them scoundrels, here it was all come to nothing, everything all busted up and ruined, because they could have the heart to serve Jim such a trick as that and make him a slave again all his life, and amongst strangers, too, for forty dirty dollars.

Once I said to myself it would be a thousand times better for Jim to be a slave at home where his family was, as long as he'd *got* to be a slave, and so I'd better write a letter to Tom Sawyer and tell him to tell Miss Watson where he was. But I soon give up that notion for two things: she'd be mad and disgusted at his rascality and ungratefulness for leaving her, and so she'd sell him straight down the river again; and if she didn't, everybody naturally despises an ungrateful nigger and they'd make Jim feel it all the time, and so he'd feel ornery and disgraced. And then think of *me!* It would get all around that Huck Finn helped a nigger to get his freedom, and if I was to ever see anybody from that town again I'd be ready to get down and lick his boots for shame. That's just the way: a person does a low-down thing, and then he don't want to take no consequences of it. Thinks as long as he can hide it, it ain't no disgrace. That was my fix exackly. The more I studied about this the more my conscience went to grinding me, and the more wicked and low-down and ornery I got to feeling. And at last, when it hit me all of a sudden that here was the plain hand of Providence slapping me in the face and letting me know my wickedness was being watched all the time from up there in heaven, whilst I was stealing a poor old woman's nigger that hadn't ever done me no harm, and now was showing me there's One that's always on the lookout and ain't a-going to allow no such miserable doings to go only just so fur and no further, I most dropped in my tracks I was so scared. Well, I tried the best I could to kinder soften it up somehow for myself by saying I was brung up wicked and so I warn't so much to blame, but something inside of me kept saying, "There was the Sunday-school, you could 'a' gone to it; and if you'd 'a' done it they'd 'a' learnt you there that people that acts as I'd been acting about that nigger goes to everlasting fire."

It made me shiver. And I about made up my mind to pray and see if I couldn't try to quit being the kind of a boy I was and be better. So I kneeled down. But the words wouldn't come. Why wouldn't they? It warn't no use to try and hide it from Him. Nor from *me*, neither. I knowed very well why they wouldn't come. It was because my heart warn't right, it was because I warn't square, it was because I was playing double. I was letting *on* to give up sin but away inside of me I was holding on to the biggest one of all. I was trying to make my mouth *say* I would do the right thing and the clean thing, and go and write to that nigger's owner and tell where he was, but deep down in me I knowed it was a lie, and He knowed it. You can't pray a lie—I found that out.

So I was full of trouble, full as I could be; and didn't know what to do. At last I had an idea; and I says, I'll go and write the letter—and *then* see if I can pray. Why, it was astonishing, the way I felt as light as a feather right straight off and my troubles all gone. So I got a piece of paper and a pencil, all glad and excited, and set down and wrote:

Miss Watson, your runaway nigger Jim is down here two mile below Pikesville, and Mr. Phelps has got him and he will give him up for the reward if you send.

HUCK FINN.

I felt good and all washed clean of sin for the first time I had ever felt so in my life, and I knowed I could pray now. But I didn't do it straight off but laid the paper down and set there thinking—thinking how good it was all this happened so, and how near I come to being lost and going to hell. And went on thinking. And got to thinking over our trip down the river; and I see Jim before me all the time: in the day and in the night-time, sometimes moonlight, sometimes storms, and we a-floating along, talking and singing and laughing. But somehow I couldn't seem to strike no places to harden me against him, but only the other kind. I'd see him standing my watch on top of his'n, 'stead of calling me, so I could go on sleeping; and see how glad he was when I come back out of the fog; and when I come to him again in the swamp, up there where the feud was; and such-like times; and would always call me honey and pet me and do everything he could think of for me, and how good he always was; and at last I struck the time I saved him by telling the men we had smallpox aboard, and he was so grateful, and said I was the best friend old Jim ever had in the world and the *only* one he's got now;

and then I happened to look around and see that paper.

It was a close place. I took it up, and held it in my hand. I was a-trembling, because I'd got to decide, forever, betwixt two things, and I knowed it. I studied a minute, sort of holding my breath, and then says to myself:

"All right, then, I'll *go* to hell"—and tore it up.

It was awful thoughts and awful words but they was said. And I let them stay said; and never thought no more about reforming. I shoved the whole thing out of my head and said I would take up wickedness again, which was in my line, being brung up to it, and the other warn't. And for a starter I would go to work and steal Jim out of slavery again; and if I could think up anything worse, I would do that, too; because as long as I was in and in for good, I might as well go the whole hog.

Then I set to thinking over how to get at it and turned over considerable many ways in my mind, and at last fixed up a plan that suited me. So then I took the bearings of a woody island that was down the river a piece, and as soon as it was fairly dark I crept out with my raft and went for it and hid it there, and then turned in. I slept the night through and got up before it was light, and had my breakfast, and put on my store clothes and tied up some others and one thing or another in a bundle, and took the canoe and cleared for shore. I landed below where I judged was Phelps's place, and hid my bundle in the woods, and then filled up the canoe with water, and loaded rocks into her and sunk her where I could find her again when I wanted her, about a quarter of a mile below a little steam-sawmill that was on the bank.

Then I struck up the road, and when I passed the mill I see a sign on it, "Phelps's Sawmill," and when I

come to the farm-houses, two or three hundred yards
further along, I kept my eyes peeled but didn't see nobody around, though it was good daylight now. But I
didn't mind because I didn't want to see nobody just
yet—I only wanted to get the lay of the land. According
to my plan, I was going to turn up there from the
village, not from below. So I just took a look, and shoved
along, straight for town. Well, the very first man I see
when I got there was the duke. He was sticking up a
bill for the "Royal Nonesuch"—three-night performance
—like that other time. *They* had the cheek, them frauds!
I was right on him before I could shirk. He looked astonished, and says:

"Hel-*lo!* Where'd *you* come from?" Then he says,
kind of glad and eager, "Where's the raft?—got her in
a good place?"

I says:

"Why, that's just what I was a-going to ask your
grace."

Then he didn't look so joyful, and says:

"What was your idea for asking *me?*" he says.

"Well," I says, "when I see the king in that doggery
yesterday I says to myself, we can't get him home for
hours, till he's soberer; so I went a-loafing around
town to put in the time and wait. A man up and offered
me ten cents to help him pull a skiff over the river and
back to fetch a sheep, and so I went along; but when we
was dragging him to the boat, and the man left me
a-holt of the rope and went behind him to shove him
along, he was too strong for me and jerked loose and
run, and we after him. We didn't have no dog and so
we had to chase him all over the country till we tired
him out. We never got him till dark; then we fetched
him over and I started down for the raft. When I got
there and see it was gone, I says to myself, 'They've

got into trouble and had to leave; and they've took my nigger, which is the only nigger I've got in the world, and now I'm in a strange country, and ain't got no property no more, nor nothing, and no way to make my living'; so I set down and cried. I slept in the woods all night. But what *did* become of the raft, then?—and Jim—poor Jim!"

"Blamed if *I* know—that is, what's become of the raft. That old fool had made a trade and got fourty dollars, and when we found him in the doggery the loafers had matched half-dollars with him and got every cent but what he'd spent for whisky; and when I got him home late last night and found the raft gone, we said, 'That little rascal has stole our raft and shook us, and run off down the river.'"

"I wouldn't shake my *nigger*, would I?—the only nigger I had in the world, and the only property."

"We never thought of that. Fact is, I reckon we'd come to consider him *our* nigger; yes, we did consider him so—goodness knows we had trouble enough for him. So when we see the raft was gone and we flat broke, there warn't anything for it but to try the 'Royal Nonesuch' another shake. And I've pegged along ever since, dry as a powderhorn. Where's that ten cents? Give it here."

I had considerable money, so I give him ten cents, but begged him to spend it for something to eat and give me some, because it was all the money I had and I hadn't had nothing to eat since yesterday. He never said nothing. The next minute he whirls on me and says:

"Do you reckon that nigger would blow on us? We'd skin him if he done that!"

"How can he blow? Hain't he run off?"

"No! That old fool sold him, and never divided with me, and the money's gone."

"*Sold* him?" I says, and begun to cry; "why, he was *my* nigger, and that was my money. Where is he?—I want my nigger."

"Well, you can't *get* your nigger, that's all—so dry up your blubbering. Looky here—do you think *you'd* venture to blow on us? Blamed if I think I'd trust you. Why, if you *was* to blow on us—"

He stopped but I never see the duke look so ugly out of his eyes before. I went on a-whimpering, and says:

"I don't want to blow on nobody; and I ain't got no time to blow, nohow; I got to turn out and find my nigger."

He looked kinder bothered, and stood there with his bills fluttering on his arm, thinking, and wrinkling up his forehead. At last he says:

"I'll tell you something. We got to be here three days. If you'll promise you won't blow, and won't let the nigger blow, I'll tell you where to find him."

So I promised, and he says:

"A farmer by the name of Silas Ph—" and then he stopped. You see, he started to tell me the truth, but when he stopped that way and begun to study and think again, I reckoned he was changing his mind. And so he was. He wouldn't trust me; he wanted to make sure of having me out of the way the whole three days. So pretty soon he says:

"The man that bought him is named Abram Foster— Abram G. Foster—and he lives forty mile back here in the country, on the road to Lafayette."

"All right," I says, "I can walk it in three days. And I'll start this very afternoon."

"No you won't, you'll start *now*; and don't you lose no time about it, neither, nor do any gabbling by the way. Just keep a tight tongue in your head and move right

along, and then you won't get into trouble with *us*, d'ye
hear?"

That was the order I wanted, and that was the one I
played for. I wanted to be left free to work my plans.

"So clear out," he says; "and you can tell Mr. Foster
whatever you want to. Maybe you can get him to believe
that Jim *is* your nigger—some idiots don't require docu-
ments—leastways I've heard there's such down South
here. And when you tell him the handbill and the reward's bogus, maybe he'll believe you when you explain
to him what the idea was for getting 'em out. Go 'long
now, and tell him anything you want to; but mind you
don't work your jaw any *between* here and there."

So I left, and struck for the back country. I didn't look
around but I kinder felt like he was watching me. But I
knowed I could tire him out at that. I went straight out
in the country as much as a mile before I stopped; then
I doubled back through the woods towards Phelps's. I
reckoned I better start in on my plan straight off without fooling around, because I wanted to stop Jim's
mouth till these fellows could get away. I didn't want no
trouble with their kind. I'd seen all I wanted to of them
and wanted to get entirely shut of them.

XXXII. I HAVE A NEW NAME

When I got there it was all still and Sunday-like, and
hot and sunshiny; the hands was gone to the fields; and
there was them kind of faint dronings of bugs and flies
in the air that makes it seem so lonesome and like everybody's dead and gone; and if a breeze fans along and
quivers the leaves it makes you feel mournful, because
you feel like it's spirits whispering—spirits that's been

dead ever so many years—and you always think they're talking about *you.* As a general thing it makes a body wish *he* was dead, too, and done with it all.

Phelps's was one of these little one-horse cotton plantations and they all look alike. A rail fence round a two-acre yard; a stile made out of logs sawed off and up-ended in steps, like barrels of a different length, to climb over the fence with and for the women to stand on when they are going to jump onto a horse; some sickly grass-patches in the big yard, but mostly it was bare and smooth like an old hat with the nap rubbed off; big double log house for the white folks—hewed logs with the chinks stopped up with mud or mortar, and these mud-stripes been whitewashed some time or another; round-log kitchen with a big broad, open but roofed passage joining it to the house; log smokehouse back of the kitchen; three little log nigger cabins in a row t'other side the smokehouse; one little hut all by itself away down against the back fence, and some outbuildings down a piece the other side; ash-hopper and big kettle to bile soap in by the little hut; bench by the kitchen door, with bucket of water and a gourd; hound asleep there in the sun; more hounds asleep round about; about three shade trees away off in a corner; some currant bushes and gooseberry bushes in one place by the fence; outside of the fence a garden and a watermelon patch; then the cotton-fields begins, and after the fields the woods.

I went around and clumb over the back stile by the ash-hopper and started for the kitchen. When I got a little ways I heard the dim hum of a spinning-wheel wailing along up and sinking along down again; and then I knowed for certain I wished I was dead—for that *is* the lonesomest sound in the whole world.

I went right along, not fixing up any particular plan

but just trusting to Providence to put the right words in
my mouth when the time come; for I'd noticed that
Providence always did put the right words in my mouth
if I left it alone.

When I got half-way, first one hound and then another got up and went for me, and of course I stopped
and faced them and kept still. And such another powwow as they made! In a quarter of a minute I was a
kind of a hub of a wheel, as you may say—spokes made
out of dogs—circle of fifteen of them packed together
around me, with their necks and noses stretched up towards me, a-barking and howling; and more a-coming;
you could see them sailing over fences and around
corners from everywheres.

A nigger woman come tearing out of the kitchen with
a rolling-pin in her hand, singing out, "Begone! *you*
Tige! you Spot! begone sah!" and she fetched first one
and then another of them a clip and sent them howling,
and then the rest followed; and the next second half of
them come back, wagging their tails around me, and
making friends with me. There ain't no harm in a hound,
nohow.

And behind the woman comes a little nigger girl and
two little nigger boys without anything on but tow-linen
shirts, and they hung on to their mother's gown and
peeped out from behind her at me, bashful, the way they
always do. And here comes the white woman running
from the house, about forty-five or fifty year old, bareheaded, and her spinning-stick in her hand; and behind
her comes her little white children, acting the same way
the little niggers was doing. She was smiling all over so
she could hardly stand—and says:

"It's *you*, at last!—*ain't* it?"

I out with a "Yes'm" before I thought.

She grabbed me and hugged me tight, and then

gripped me by both hands and shook and shook, and the
tears come in her eyes and run down over, and she
couldn't seem to hug and shake enough and kept saying, "You don't look as much like your mother as I reckoned you would; but law sakes, I don't care for that, I'm
so glad to see you! Dear, dear, it does seem like I could
eat you up! Childern, it's your cousin Tom!—tell him
howdy."

But they ducked their heads and put their fingers in
their mouths and hid behind her. So she run on:

"Lize, hurry up and get him a hot breakfast right
away—or did you get your breakfast on the boat?"

I said I had got it on the boat. So then she started for
the house, leading me by the hand, and the children tag-
ging after. When we got there she set me down in a
split-bottomed chair and set herself down on a little
low stool in front of me, holding both of my hands, and
says:

"Now I can have a *good* look at you; and, laws-a-me,
I've been hungry for it a many and a many a time, all
these long years, and it's come at last! We been expecting you a couple of days and more. What kep' you?
—boat get aground?"

"Yes'm—she—"

"Don't say yes'm—say Aunt Sally. Where'd she get
aground?"

I didn't rightly know what to say, because I didn't
know whether the boat would be coming up the river
or down. But I go a good deal on instinct, and my instinct said she would be coming up—from down towards
Orleans. That didn't help me much, though, for I didn't
know the names of bars down that way. I see I'd got to
invent a bar or forget the name of the one we got
aground on—or— Now I struck an idea, and fetched
it out:

"It warn't the grounding—that didn't keep us back but a little. We blowed out a cylinder-head."

"Good gracious! anybody hurt?"

"No'm. Killed a nigger."

"Well, it's lucky; because sometimes people do get hurt. Two years ago last Christmas your Uncle Silas was coming up from Newrleans on the old *Lally Rook,* and she blowed out a cylinder-head and crippled a man. And I think he died afterwards. He was a Babtist. Your Uncle Silas knowed a family in Baton Rouge that knowed his people very well. Yes, I remember now, he *did* die. Mortification set in, and they had to amputate him. But it didn't save him. Yes, it was mortification—that was it. He turned blue all over and died in the hope of a glorious resurrection. They say he was a sight to look at. Your uncle's been up to the town every day to fetch you. And he's gone again, not more'n an hour ago; he'll be back any minute now. You must 'a' met him on the road, didn't you?—oldish man, with a—"

"No, I didn't see nobody, Aunt Sally. The boat landed just at daylight, and I left my baggage on the wharf-boat and went looking around the town and out a piece in the country, to put in the time and not get here too soon; and so I come down the back way."

"Who'd you give the baggage to?"

"Nobody."

"Why, child, it'll be stole!"

"Not where *I* hid it I reckon it won't," I says.

"How'd you get your breakfast so early on the boat?"

It was kinder thin ice, but I says:

"The captain see me standing around and told me I better have something to eat before I went ashore, so he took me in the texas to the officers' lunch and give me all I wanted."

I was getting so uneasy I couldn't listen good. I had

my mind on the children all the time; I wanted to get them out to one side and pump them a little and find out who I was. But I couldn't get no show, Mrs. Phelps kept it up and run on so. Pretty soon she made the cold chills streak all down my back, because she says:

"But here we're a-running on this way, and you hain't told me a word about Sis, nor any of them. Now I'll rest my works a little and you start up yourn; just tell me *everything*—tell me all about 'em all—every one of 'em; and how they are and what they're doing and what they told you to tell me, and every last thing you can think of."

Well, I see I was up a stump—and up it good. Providence had stood by me this fur all right but I was hard and tight aground now. I see it warn't a bit of use to try to go ahead—I'd *got* to throw up my hand. So I says to myself, here's another place where I got to resk the truth. I opened my mouth to begin, but she grabbed me and hustled me in behind the bed, and says:

"Here he comes! Stick your head down lower—there, that'll do; you can't be seen now. Don't you let on you're here. I'll play a joke on him. Childern, don't you say a word."

I see I was in a fix now. But it warn't no use to worry; there warn't nothing to do but just hold still and try and be ready to stand from under when the lightning struck.

I had just one little glimpse of the old gentleman when he come in; then the bed hid him. Mrs. Phelps she jumps for him, and says:

"Has he come?"

"No," says her husband.

"Good-*ness* gracious!" she says, "what in the world *can* have become of him?"

"I can't imagine," says the old gentleman; "and I must say it makes me dreadful uneasy."

"Uneasy!" she says; "I'm ready to go distracted! He *must* 'a' come; and you've missed him along the road. I *know* it's so—something *tells* me so."

"Why, Sally, I *couldn't* miss him along the road—*you* know that."

"But oh, dear, dear, what *will* Sis say! He must 'a' come! You must 'a' missed him. He—"

"Oh, don't distress me any more'n I'm already distressed. I don't know what in the world to make of it. I'm at my wit's end and I don't mind acknowledging 't I'm right down scared. But there's no hope that he's come, for he *couldn't* come and me miss him. Sally, it's terrible—just terrible—something's happened to the boat, sure!"

"Why, Silas! Look yonder!—up the road!—ain't that somebody coming?"

He sprung to the window at the head of the bed, and that give Mrs. Phelps the chance she wanted. She stooped down quick at the foot of the bed and give me a pull and out I come, and when he turned back from the window there she stood, a-beaming and a-smiling like a house afire, and I standing pretty meek and sweaty alongside. The old gentleman stared, and says:

"Why, who's that?"

"Who do you reckon 'tis?"

"I hain't no idea. Who *is* it?"

"It's *Tom Sawyer!*"

By jings, I most slumped through the floor! But there warn't no time to swap knives; the old man grabbed me by the hand and shook and kept on shaking; and all the time how the woman did dance around and laugh and cry; and then how they both did fire off questions about Sid and Mary and the rest of the tribe.

But if they was joyful, it warn't nothing to what I was; for it was like being born again, I was so glad to find out who I was. Well, they froze to me for two hours; and at last, when my chin was so tired it couldn't hardly go any more, I had told them more about my family—I mean the Sawyer family—than ever happened to any six Sawyer families. And I explained all about how we blowed out a cylinder-head at the mouth of White River and it took us three days to fix it. Which was all right and worked first-rate, because *they* didn't know but what it would take three days to fix it. If I'd 'a' called it a bolt-head it would 'a' done just as well.

Now I was feeling pretty comfortable all down one side and pretty uncomfortable all up the other. Being Tom Sawyer was easy and comfortable, and it stayed easy and comfortable till by and by I hear a steamboat coughing along down the river. Then I says to myself, s'pose Tom Sawyer comes down on that boat? And s'pose he steps in here any minute, and sings out my name before I can throw him a wink to keep quiet?

Well, I couldn't *have* it that way; it wouldn't do at all. I must go up the road and waylay him. So I told the folks I reckoned I would go up to the town and fetch down my baggage. The old gentleman was for going along with me, but I said no, I could drive the horse myself and I druther he wouldn't take no trouble about me.

XXXIII. The Pitiful Ending of Royalty

So I started for town in the wagon and when I was half-way I see a wagon coming, and sure enough it was Tom Sawyer, and I stopped and waited till he come along. I says "Hold on!" and it stopped alongside, and his mouth opened up like a trunk and stayed so; and he

swallowed two or three times like a person that's got a
dry throat and then says:

"I hain't ever done you no harm. You know that. So,
then, what you want to come back and ha'nt *me* for?"

I says:

"I hain't come back—I hain't been *gone*."

When he heard my voice it righted him up some but
he warn't quite satisfied yet. He says:

"Don't you play nothing on me, because I wouldn't
on you. Honest Injun, you ain't a ghost?"

"Honest Injun, I ain't," I says.

"Well—I—I—well, that ought to settle it, of course;
but I can't somehow seem to understand it no way.
Looky here, warn't you ever murdered *at all?*"

"No. I warn't ever murdered at all—I played it on
them. You come in here and feel of me if you don't believe me."

So he done it, and it satisfied him, and he was that
glad to see me again he didn't know what to do. And he
wanted to know all about it right off, because it was a
grand adventure, and mysterious, and so it hit him
where he lived. But I said, leave it alone till by and by,
and told his driver to wait, and we drove off a little
piece and I told him the kind of a fix I was in, and what
did he reckon we better do? He said, let him alone a
minute and don't disturb him. So he thought and
thought, and pretty soon he says:

"It's all right; I've got it. Take my trunk in your wagon
and let on it's yourn, and you turn back and fool along
slow, so as to get to the house about the time you ought
to; and I'll go towards town a piece and take a fresh
start, and get there a quarter or a half an hour after
you; and you needn't let on to know me at first."

I says:

"All right; but wait a minute. There's one more thing —a thing that *nobody* don't know but me. And that is, there's a nigger here that I'm a-trying to steal out of slavery, and his name is *Jim*—old Miss Watson's Jim."

He says:

"What! Why, Jim is—"

He stopped and went to studying. I says:

"*I* know what you'll say. You'll say it's dirty, low-down business; but what if it is? *I'm* low-down; and I'm a-going to steal him, and I want you to keep mum and not let on. Will you?"

His eye lit up, and he says:

"I'll *help* you steal him!"

Well, I let go all holts then, like I was shot. It was the most astonishing speech I ever heard—and I'm bound to say Tom Sawyer fell considerable in my estimation. Only I couldn't believe it. Tom Sawyer a *nigger-stealer!*

"Oh, shucks!" I says; "you're joking."

"I ain't joking, either."

"Well, then," I says, "joking or no joking, if you hear anything said about a runaway nigger, don't forget to remember that *you* don't know nothing about him, and *I* don't know nothing about him."

Then we took the trunk and put it in my wagon, and he drove off his way and I drove mine. But of course I forgot all about driving slow on accounts of being glad and full of thinking; so I got home a heap too quick for that length of a trip. The old gentleman was at the door, and he says:

"Why, this is wonderful! Whoever would 'a' thought it was in that mare to do it! I wish we'd 'a' timed her. And she hain't sweated a hair—not a hair. It's wonderful. Why, I wouldn't take a hunderd dollars for that horse now—I wouldn't, honest; and yet I'd 'a' sold her for fifteen before, and thought 'twas all she was worth."

That's all he said. He was the innocentest, best old
soul I ever see. But it warn't surprising, because he
warn't only just a farmer, he was a preacher, too, and
had a little one-horse log church down back of the plantation, which he built it himself at his own expense for
a church and schoolhouse, and never charged nothing
for his preaching, and it was worth it, too. There was
plenty other farmer-preachers like that, and done the
same way, down South.

In about half an hour Tom's wagon drove up to the
front stile and Aunt Sally she see it through the window,
because it was only about fifty yards, and says:

"Why, there's somebody come! I wonder who 'tis?
Why, I do believe it's a stranger. Jimmy" (that's one of
the children), "run and tell Lize to put on another plate
for dinner."

Everybody made a rush for the front door, because,
of course, a stranger don't come *every* year, and so he
lays over the yaller-fever, for interest, when he does
come. Tom was over the stile and starting for the house,
the wagon was spinning up the road for the village, and
we was all bunched in the front door. Tom had his store
clothes on, and an audience—and that was always nuts
for Tom Sawyer. In them circumstances it warn't no
trouble to him to throw in an amount of style that was
suitable. He warn't a boy to meeky along up that yard
like a sheep; no, he come ca'm and important, like the
ram. When he got a-front of us he lifts his hat ever so
gracious and dainty, like it was the lid of a box that had
butterflies asleep in it and he didn't want to disturb
them, and says:

"Mr. Archibald Nichols, I presume?"

"No, my boy," says the old gentleman, "I'm sorry to
say 't your driver has deceived you; Nichols's place is
down a matter of three mile more. Come in, come in."

Tom he took a look back over his shoulder, and says, "Too late—he's out of sight."

"Yes, he's gone, my son, and you must come in and eat your dinner with us; and then we'll hitch up and take you down to Nichols's."

"Oh, I *can't* make you so much trouble; I couldn't think of it. I'll walk—I don't mind the distance."

"But we won't *let* you walk—it wouldn't be Southern hospitality to do it. Come right in."

"Oh, *do*," says Aunt Sally; "it ain't a bit of trouble to us, not a bit in the world. You *must* stay. It's a long, dusty three mile, and we *can't* let you walk. And, besides, I've already told 'em to put on another plate when I see you coming, so you mustn't disappoint us. Come right in and make yourself at home."

So Tom he thanked them very hearty and handsome, and let himself be persuaded, and come in; and when he was in he said he was a stranger from Hicksville, Ohio, and his name was William Thompson—and he made another bow.

Well, he run on and on and on, making up stuff about Hicksville and everybody in it he could invent, and I getting a little nervous and wondering how this was going to help me out of my scrape; and at last, still talking along, he reached over and kissed Aunt Sally right on the mouth and then settled back again in his chair comfortable, and was going on talking; but she jumped up and wiped it off with the back of her hand, and says:

"You owdacious puppy!"

He looked kind of hurt, and says:

"I'm surprised at you, m'am."

"You're s'rp— Why, what do you reckon *I* am? I've a good notion to take and— Say, what do you mean by kissing me?"

He looked kind of humble, and says:

"I didn't mean nothing, m'am. I didn't mean no harm. I—I—thought you'd like it."

"Why, you born fool!" She took up the spinning-stick, and it looked like it was all she could do to keep from giving him a crack with it. "What made you think I'd like it?"

"Well, I don't know. Only, they—they—told me you would."

"*They* told you I would. Whoever told you's *another* lunatic. I never heard the beat of it. Who's *they?*"

"Why, everybody. They all said so, m'am."

It was all she could do to hold in, and her eyes snapped, and her fingers worked like she wanted to scratch him, and she says:

"Who's 'everybody'? Out with their names, or ther'll be an idiot short."

He got up and looked distressed, and fumbled his hat, and says:

"I'm sorry, and I warn't expecting it. They told me to. They all told me to. They all said, kiss her; and said she'd like it. They all said it—every one of them. But I'm sorry, m'am, and I won't do it no more—I won't, honest."

"You won't, won't you? Well, I sh'd *reckon* you won't!"

"No'm, I'm honest about it; I won't ever do it again—till you ask me."

"Till I *ask* you! Well, I never see the beat of it in my born days! I lay you'll be the Methusalem-numskull of creation before ever *I* ask you—or the likes of you."

"Well," he says, "it does surprise me so. I can't make it out, somehow. They said you would, and I thought you would. But—" He stopped and looked around slow,

like he wished he could run across a friendly eye somewheres, and fetched up on the old gentleman's, and says,
"Didn't *you* think she'd like me to kiss her, sir?"

"Why, no; I—I—well, no, I b'lieve I didn't."

Then he looks on around the same way to me, and
says:

"Tom, didn't *you* think Aunt Sally'd open out her arms
and say, 'Sid Sawyer—'"

"My land!" she says, breaking in and jumping for him,
"you impudent young rascal, to fool a body so—" and
was going to hug him but he fended her off, and says:

"No, not till you've asked me first."

So she didn't lose no time but asked him and hugged
him and kissed him over and over again, and then
turned him over to the old man and he took what was
left. And after they got a little quiet again she says:

"Why, dear me, I never see such a surprise. We
warn't looking for *you* at all, but only Tom. Sis never
wrote to me about anybody coming but him."

"It's because it warn't *intended* for any of us to come
but Tom," he says; "but I begged and begged, and at
the last minute she let me come, too; so, coming down
the river, me and Tom thought it would be a first-rate
surprise for him to come here to the house first, and for
me to by and by tag along and drop in and let on to be a
stranger. But it was a mistake, Aunt Sally. This ain't no
healthy place for a stranger to come."

"No—not impudent whelps, Sid. You ought to had
your jaws boxed; I hain't been so put out since I don't
know when. But I don't care, I don't mind the terms—
I'd be willing to stand a thousand such jokes to have you
here. Well, to think of that performance! I don't deny it,
I was most putrified with astonishment when you give
me that smack."

We had dinner out in that broad open passage betwixt

the house and the kitchen; and there was things enough
on that table for seven families—and all hot, too, none
of your flabby, tough meat that's laid in a cubboard in a
damp cellar all night and tastes like a hunk of old cold
cannibal in the morning. Uncle Silas he asked a pretty
long blessing over it, but it was worth it; and it didn't
cool it a bit, neither, the way I've seen them kind of in-
terruptions do lots of times.

There was a considerable good deal of talk all the
afternoon, and me and Tom was on the lookout all the
time; but it warn't no use, they didn't happen to say
nothing about any runaway nigger and we was afraid to
try to work up to it. But at supper, at night, one of the
little boys says:

"Pa, mayn't Tom and Sid and me go to the show?"

"No," says the old man, "I reckon there ain't going to
be any; and you couldn't go if there was; because the
runaway nigger told Burton and me all about that scandalous show, and Burton said he would tell the people;
so I reckon they've drove the owdacious loafers out of
town before this time."

So there it was!—but I couldn't help it. Tom and me
was to sleep in the same room and bed; so, being tired,
we bid good-night and went up to bed right after supper and clumb out of the window and down the lightning-rod, and shoved for the town; for I didn't believe
anybody was going to give the king and the duke a hint,
and so if I didn't hurry up and give them one they'd get
into trouble sure.

On the road Tom he told me all about how it was
reckoned I was murdered, and how pap disappeared
pretty soon and didn't come back no more, and what a
stir there was when Jim run away; and I told Tom all
about our "Royal Nonesuch" rapscallions and as much of
the raft voyage as I had time to; and as we struck into

the town and up through the middle of it—it was as
much as half after eight then—here comes a raging
rush of people with torches, and an awful whooping
and yelling and banging tin pans and blowing horns;
and we jumped to one side to let them go by; and as
they went by I see they had the king and the duke
a-straddle of a rail—that is, I knowed it *was* the king and
the duke, though they was all over tar and feathers and
didn't look like nothing in the world that was human—
just looked like a couple of monstrous big soldier-
plumes. Well, it made me sick to see it, and I was sorry
for them poor pitiful rascals, it seemed like I couldn't
ever feel any hardness against them any more in the
world. It was a dreadful thing to see. Human beings *can*
be awful cruel to one another.

We see we was too late—couldn't do no good. We
asked some stragglers about it and they said everybody
went to the show looking very innocent, and laid low
and kept dark till the poor old king was in the middle of
his cavortings on the stage, then somebody give a signal
and the house rose up and went for them.

So we poked along back home and I warn't feeling so
brash as I was before, but kind of ornery and humble,
and to blame, somehow—though *I* hadn't done nothing.
But that's always the way; it don't make no difference
whether you do right or wrong, a person's conscience
ain't got no sense and just goes for him *anyway*. If I
had a yaller dog that didn't know no more than a person's conscience does I would pison him. It takes up
more room than all the rest of a person's insides and yet
ain't no good, nohow. Tom Sawyer he says the same.

We stopped talking, and got to thinking. By and by Tom says:

"Looky here, Huck, what fools we are to not think of it before! I bet I know where Jim is."

"No! Where?"

"In that hut down by the ash-hopper. Why, looky here. When we was at dinner, didn't you see a nigger man go in there with some vittles?"

"Yes."

"What did you think the vittles was for?"

"For a dog."

"So'd I. Well, it wasn't for a dog."

"Why?"

"Because part of it was watermelon."

"So it was—I noticed it. Well, it does beat all that I never thought about a dog not eating watermelon. It shows how a body can see and not see at the same time."

"Well, the nigger unlocked the padlock when he went in and he locked it again when he came out. He fetched Uncle a key about the time we got up from table—same key, I bet. Watermelon shows man, lock shows prisoner; and it ain't likely there's two prisoners on such a little plantation, and where the people's all so kind and good. Jim's the prisoner. All right—I'm glad we found it out detective fashion; I wouldn't give shucks for any other way. Now you work your mind, and study out a plan to steal Jim, and I will study out one, too; and we'll take the one we like the best."

What a head for just a boy to have! If I had Tom Sawyer's head I wouldn't trade it off to be a duke, nor mate of a steamboat, nor clown in a circus, nor nothing I can think of. I went to thinking out a plan, but only just to be doing something; I knowed very well where the right plan was going to come from. Pretty soon Tom says:

"Ready?"

"Yes," I says.

"All right—bring it out."

"My plan is this," I says. "We can easy find out if it s Jim in there. Then get up my canoe to-morrow night, and fetch my raft over from the island. Then the first dark night that comes steal the key out of the old man's britches after he goes to bed, and shove off down the river on the raft with Jim, hiding daytimes and running nights, the way me and Jim used to do before. Wouldn't that plan work?"

"*Work?* Why, cert'nly it would work, like rats a-fighting. But it's too blame' simple; there ain't nothing *to* it. What's the good of a plan that ain't no more trouble than that? It's as mild as goose-milk. Why, Huck, it wouldn't make no more talk than breaking into a soap factory."

I never said nothing because I warn't expecting nothing different, but I knowed mighty well that whenever he got *his* plan ready it wouldn't have none of them objections to it.

And it didn't. He told me what it was and I see in a minute it was worth fifteen of mine for style, and would make Jim just as free a man as mine would, and maybe get us all killed besides. So I was satisfied and said we would waltz in on it. I needn't tell what it was here, because I knowed it wouldn't stay the way it was. I knowed he would be changing it around every which way as we went along, and heaving in new bullinesses wherever he got a chance. And that is what he done.

Well, one thing was dead sure and that was that Tom Sawyer was in earnest and was actly going to help steal that nigger out of slavery. That was the thing that was

too many for me. Here was a boy that was respectable
and well brung up; and had a character to lose; and
folks at home that had characters; and he was bright
and not leather-headed; and knowing and not ignorant;
and not mean but kind; and yet here he was, without
any more pride or rightness or feeling than to stoop to
this business, and make himself a shame and his family
a shame before everybody. I *couldn't* understand it no
way at all. It was outrageous and I knowed I ought to
just up and tell him so, and so be his true friend and let
him quit the thing right where he was and save himself.
And I *did* start to tell him, but he shut me up, and says:

"Don't you reckon I know what I'm about? Don't I
generly know what I'm about?"

"Yes."

"Didn't I *say* I was going to help steal the nigger?"

"Yes."

"*Well*, then."

That's all he said and that's all I said. It warn't no use
to say any more; because when he said he'd do a thing,
he always done it. But *I* couldn't make out how he was
willing to go into this thing; so I just let it go, and never
bothered no more about it. If he was bound to have it
so, *I* couldn't help it.

When we got home the house was all dark and still;
so we went on down to the hut by the ash-hopper for to
examine it. We went through the yard so as to see what
the hounds would do. They knowed us, and didn't make
no more noise than country dogs is always doing when
anything comes by in the night. When we got to the
cabin we took a look at the front and the two sides, and
on the side I warn't acquainted with—which was the
north side—we found a square window-hole, up tolerable high, with just one stout board nailed across it. I
says:

"Here's the ticket. This hole's big enough for Jim to get through if we wrench off the board."

Tom says:

"It's as simple as tit-tat-toe, three-in-a-row, and as easy as playing hooky. I should *hope* we can find a way that's a little more complicated than *that*, Huck Finn."

"Well, then," I says, "how'll it do to saw him out, the way I done before I was murdered that time?"

"That's more *like*," he says. "It's real mysterious, and troublesome, and good," he says; "but I bet we can find a way that's twice as long. There ain't no hurry; le's keep on looking around."

Betwixt the hut and the fence, on the back side, was a lean-to that joined the hut at the eaves and was made out of plank. It was as long as the hut but narrow—only about six foot wide. The door to it was at the south end and was padlocked. Tom he went to the soap-kettle and searched around, and fetched back the iron thing they lift the lid with; so he took it and prized out one of the staples. The chain fell down and we opened the door and went in and shut it and struck a match, and see the shed was only built against the cabin and hadn't no connection with it; and there warn't no floor to the shed, nor nothing in it but some old rusty played-out hoes and spades and picks and a crippled plow. The match went out, and so did we, and shoved in the staple again and the door was locked as good as ever. Tom was joyful. He says:

"Now we're all right. We'll *dig* him out. It'll take about a week!"

Then we started for the house and I went in the back door—you only have to pull a buckskin latchstring, they don't fasten the doors—but that warn't romantical enough for Tom Sawyer; no way would do him but he must climb up the lightning-rod. But after he got up half-way about three times and missed fire and fell every time, and the last time most busted his brains out, he thought he'd got to give it up; but after he was rested he allowed he would give her one more turn for luck and this time he made the trip.

In the morning we was up at break of day, and down to the nigger cabins to pet the dogs and make friends with the nigger that fed Jim—if it *was* Jim that was being fed. The niggers was just getting through breakfast and starting for the fields, and Jim's nigger was piling up a tin pan with bread and meat and things; and whilst the others was leaving, the key come from the house.

This nigger had a good-natured, chuckle-headed face and his wool was all tied up in little bunches with thread. That was to keep witches off. He said the witches was pestering him awful these nights, and making him see all kinds of strange things and hear all kinds of strange words and noises, and he didn't believe he was ever witched so long before in his life. He got so worked up and got to running on so about his troubles, he forgot all about what he'd been a-going to do. So Tom says:

"What's the vittles for? Going to feed the dogs?"

The nigger kind of smiled around graduly over his face, like when you heave a brickbat in a mud-puddle, and he says:

"Yes, Mars Sid, *a* dog. Cur'us dog, too. Does you want to go en look at 'im?"

"Yes."

I hunched Tom, and whispers:

"You going, right here in the daybreak? *That* warn't the plan."

"No, it warn't; but it's the plan *now*."

So, drat him, we went along but I didn't like it much. When we got in we couldn't hardly see anything, it was so dark; but Jim was there, sure enough, and could see us; and he sings out:

"Why, *Huck!* En good *lan'!* ain' dat Misto Tom?"

I just knowed how it would be; I just expected it. *I* didn't know nothing to do; and if I had I couldn't 'a' done it, because that nigger busted in and says:

"Why, de gracious sakes! do he know you genlmen?"

We could see pretty well now. Tom he looked at the nigger, steady and kind of wondering, and says:

"Does *who* know us?"

"Why, dis-yer runaway nigger."

"I don't reckon he does; but what put that into your head?"

"What *put* it dar? Didn' he jis' dis minute sing out like he knowed you?"

Tom says, in a puzzled-up kind of way:

"Well, that's mighty curious. *Who* sung out? *When* did he sing out? *What* did he sing out?" And turns to me, perfectly ca'm, and says, "Did *you* hear anybody sing out?"

Of course there warn't nothing to be said but the one thing; so I says:

"No; *I* ain't heard nobody say nothing."

Then he turns to Jim and looks him over like he never see him before and says:

"Did you sing out?"

"No, sah," says Jim; "*I* hain't said nothing, sah."

"Not a word?"

"No, sah, I hain't said a word."

"Did you ever see us before?"

"No, sah; not as *I* knows on."

So Tom turns to the nigger, which was looking wild and distressed, and says, kind of severe:

"What do you reckon's the matter with you, anyway? What made you think somebody sung out?"

"Oh, it's de dad-blame' witches, sah, en I wisht I was
dead, I do. Dey's awluz at it, sah, en dey do mos' kill
me, dey sk'yers me so. Please to don't tell nobody 'bout
it, sah, er ole Mars Silas he'll scole me; 'kase he say dey
ain't no witches. I jis' wish to goodness he was heah
now—*den* what would he say! I jis' bet he couldn' fine
no way to git aroun' it *dis* time. But it's awluz jis' so;
people dat's *sot,* stays sot; dey won't look into noth'n'
en fine it out f'r deyselves, en when *you* fine it out en
tell um 'bout it, dey doan' b'lieve you."

Tom give him a dime and said we wouldn't tell nobody, and told him to buy some more thread to tie up his
wool with, and then looks at Jim and says:

"I wonder if Uncle Silas is going to hang this nigger.
If I was to catch a nigger that was ungrateful enough to
run away, *I* wouldn't give him up, I'd hang him." And
whilst the nigger stepped to the door to look at the
dime and bite it to see if it was good, he whispers to
Jim and says:

"Don't ever let on to know us. And if you hear any
digging going on nights, it's us; we're going to set you
free."

Jim only had time to grab us by the hand and squeeze
it; then the nigger come back and we said we'd come
again some time if the nigger wanted us to; and he said
he would, more particular if it was dark, because the
witches went for him mostly in the dark and it was good
to have folks around then.

xxxv. Dark, Deep-laid Plans

It would be most an hour yet till breakfast, so we left
and struck down into the woods; because Tom said we
got to have *some* light to see how to dig by, and a lan-

tern makes too much and might get us into trouble; what we must have was a lot of them rotten chunks that's called fox-fire and just makes a soft kind of a glow when you lay them in a dark place. We fetched an armful and hid it in the weeds and set down to rest, and Tom says, kind of dissatisfied:

"Blame it, this whole thing is just as easy and awkward as it can be. And so it makes it so rotten difficult to get up a difficult plan. There ain't no watchman to be drugged—now there *ought* to be a watchman. There ain't even a dog to give a sleeping-mixture to. And there's Jim chained by one leg with a ten-foot chain, to the leg of his bed: why, all you got to do is to lift up the bedstead and slip off the chain. And Uncle Silas he trusts everybody; sends the key to the punkin-headed nigger and don't send nobody to watch the nigger. Jim could 'a' got out of that window-hole before this, only there wouldn't be no use trying to travel with a ten-foot chain on his leg. Why, drat it, Huck, it's the stupidest arrangement I ever see. You got to invent *all* the difficulties. Well, we can't help it; we got to do the best we can with the materials we've got. Anyhow, there's one thing—there's more honor in getting him out through a lot of difficulties and dangers, where there warn't one of them furnished to you by the people who it was their duty to furnish them, and you had to contrive them all out of your own head. Now look at just that one thing of the lantern. When you come down to the cold facts, we simply got to *let on* that a lantern's resky. Why, we could work with a torchlight procession if we wanted to, *I* believe. Now, whilst I think of it, we got to hunt up something to make a saw out of the first chance we get."

"What do we want of a saw?"

"What do we *want* of a saw? Hain't we got to saw the leg of Jim's bed off, so as to get the chain loose?"

"Why, you just said a body could lift up the bed-stead and slip the chain off."

"Well, if that ain't just like you, Huck Finn. You *can* get up the infant-schooliest ways of going at a thing. Why, hain't you ever read any books at all?—Baron Trenck, nor Casanova, nor Benvenuto Chelleeny, nor Henri IV, nor none of them heroes? Who ever heard of getting a prisoner loose in such an old-maidy way as that? No; the way all the best authorities does is to saw the bed-leg in two and leave it just so, and swallow the sawdust, so it can't be found, and put some dirt and grease around the sawed place so the very keenest seneskal can't see no sign of its being sawed and thinks the bed-leg is perfectly sound. Then, the night you're ready, fetch the leg a kick, down she goes, slip off your chain, and there you are. Nothing to do but hitch your rope ladder to the battlements, shin down it, break your leg in the moat—because a rope ladder is nineteen foot too short, you know—and there's your horses and your trusty vassles, and they scoop you up and fling you across a saddle, and away you go to your native Langu-doc or Navarre, or wherever it is. It's gaudy, Huck. I wish there was a moat to this cabin. If we get time, the night of the escape, we'll dig one."

I says:

"What do we want of a moat when we're going to snake him out from under the cabin?"

But he never heard me. He had forgot me and every-thing else. He had his chin in his hand, thinking. Pretty soon he sighs and shakes his head, then sighs again and says:

"No, it wouldn't do—there ain't necessity enough for it."

"For what?" I says.

"Why, to saw Jim's leg off," he says.

"Good land!" I says; "why, there ain't *no* necessity for it. And what would you want to saw his leg off for, anyway?"

"Well, some of the best authorities has done it. They couldn't get the chain off, so they just cut their hand off and shoved. And a leg would be better still. But we got to let that go. There ain't necessity enough in this case; and besides, Jim's a nigger and wouldn't understand the reasons for it, and how it's the custom in Europe; so we'll let it go. But there's one thing—he can have a rope ladder, we can tear up our sheets and make him a rope ladder easy enough. And we can send it to him in a pie; it's mostly done that way. And I've et worse pies."

"Why, Tom Sawyer, how you talk," I says; "Jim ain't got no use for a rope ladder."

"He *has* got use for it. How *you* talk, you better say; you don't know nothing about it. He's *got* to have a rope ladder; they all do."

"What in the nation can he *do* with it?"

"*Do* with it? He can hide it in his bed, can't he? That's what they all do and *he's* got to, too. Huck, you don't ever seem to want to do anything that's regular; you want to be starting something fresh all the time. S'pose he *don't* do nothing with it? ain't it there in his bed for a clue, after he's gone? and don't you reckon they'll want clues? Of course they will. And you wouldn't leave them any? That would be a *pretty* howdy-do, *wouldn't* it! I never heard of such a thing."

"Well," I says, "if it's in the regulations and he's got to have it, all right, let him have it; because I don't wish to go back on no regulations; but there's one thing, Tom Sawyer—if we go to tearing up our sheets to make Jim a rope ladder, we're going to get into trouble with Aunt Sally, just as sure as you're born. Now, the way I look at it, a hick'ry-bark ladder don't cost nothing and don't waste nothing, and is just as good to load up a pie with and hide in a straw tick, as any rag ladder you can start; and as for Jim, he ain't had no experience and so *he* don't care what kind of a—"

"Oh, shucks, Huck Finn, if I was as ignorant as you I'd keep still—that's what *I'd* do. Who ever heard of a state prisoner escaping by a hick'ry-bark ladder? Why, it's perfectly ridiculous."

"Well, all right, Tom, fix it your own way; but if you'll take my advice, you'll let me borrow a sheet off of the clothes-line."

He said that would do. And that gave him another idea, and he says:

"Borrow a shirt, too."

"What do we want of a shirt, Tom?"

"Want it for Jim to keep a journal on."

"Journal your granny—*Jim* can't write."

"S'pose he *can't* write—he can make marks on the shirt, can't he, if we make him a pen out of an old pewter spoon or a piece of an old iron barrel-hoop?"

"Why, Tom, we can pull a feather out of a goose and make him a better one; and quicker, too."

"*Prisoners* don't have geese running around the don-jonkeep to pull pens out of, you muggins. They *always* make their pens out of the hardest, toughest, trouble-somest piece of old brass candlestick or something like that they can get their hands on, and it takes them weeks and weeks and months and months to file it out, too, because they've got to do it by rubbing it on the wall. *They* wouldn't use a goose-quill if they had it. It ain't regular."

"Well, then, what'll we make him the ink out of?"

"Many makes it out of iron-rust and tears; but that's the common sort and women; the best authorities uses their own blood. Jim can do that, and when he wants to

send any little common ordinary mysterious message to
let the world know where he's captivated, he can write
it on the bottom of a tin plate with a fork and throw it
out of the window. The Iron Mask always done that and
it's a blame' good way, too."

"Jim ain't got no tin plates. They feed him in a pan."

"That ain't nothing; we can get him some."

"Can't nobody *read* his plates."

"That ain't got nothing to *do* with it, Huck Finn. All
he's got to do is to write on the plate and throw it out.
You don't *have* to be able to read it. Why, half the time
you can't read anything a prisoner writes on a tin plate,
or anywhere else."

"Well, then, what's the sense in wasting the plates?"

"Why, blame it all, it ain't the *prisoner's* plates."

"But it's *somebody's* plates, ain't it?"

"Well, spos'n it is? What does the *prisoner* care
whose—"

He broke off there, because we heard the breakfast-
horn blowing. So we cleared out for the house.

Along during the morning I borrowed a sheet and a
white shirt off of the clothes-line, and I found an old sack
and put them in it, and we went down and got the fox-
fire and put that in too. I called it borrowing because
that was what pap always called it, but Tom said it
warn't borrowing, it was stealing. He said we was representing prisoners and prisoners don't care how they get
a thing so they get it, and nobody don't blame them for
it, either. It ain't no crime in a prisoner to steal the thing
he needs to get away with, Tom said, it's his right; and
so, as long as we was representing a prisoner, we had a
perfect right to steal anything on this place we had the
least use for to get ourselves out of prison with. He said
if we warn't prisoners it would be a very different thing,
and nobody but a mean, ornery person would steal

when he warn't a prisoner. So we allowed we would steal everything there was that come handy. And yet he made a mighty fuss, one day after that, when I stole a watermelon out of the nigger patch and eat it, and he made me go and give the niggers a dime without telling them what it was for. Tom said that what he meant was, we could steal anything we *needed*. Well, I says, I needed the watermelon. But he said I didn't need it to get out of prison with, there's where the difference was. He said if I'd 'a' wanted it to hide a knife in and smuggle it to Jim to kill the seneskal with, it would 'a' been all right. So I let it go at that, though I couldn't see no advantage in my representing a prisoner if I got to set down and chaw over a lot of gold-leaf distinctions like that every time I see a chance to hog a watermelon.

Well, as I was saying, we waited that morning till everybody was settled down to business and nobody in sight around the yard; then Tom he carried the sack into the lean-to whilst I stood off a piece to keep watch. By and by he come out and we went and set down on the woodpile to talk. He says:

"Everything's all right now except tools; and that's easy fixed."

"Tools?" I says.

"Yes."

"Tools for what?"

"Why, to dig with. We ain't a-going to *gnaw* him out, are we?"

"Ain't them old crippled picks and things in there good enough to dig a nigger out with?" I says.

He turns on me, looking pitying enough to make a body cry, and says:

"Huck Finn, did you *ever* hear of a prisoner having picks and shovels and all the modern conveniences in his wardrobe to dig himself out with? Now I want to

ask you—if you got any reasonableness in you at all—
what kind of a show would *that* give him to be a hero?
Why, they might as well lend him the key and done with
it. Picks and shovels—why, they wouldn't furnish 'em to
a king."

"Well, then," I says, "if we don't want the picks and
shovels, what do we want?"

"A couple of case-knives."

"To dig the foundations out from under that cabin
with?"

"Yes."

"Confound it, it's foolish, Tom."

"It don't make no difference how foolish it is, it's the
right way—and it's the regular way. And there ain't no
other way, that ever *I* heard of, and I've read all the
books that gives any information about these things.
They always dig out with a case-knife—and not through
dirt, mind you, generly it's through solid rock. And it
takes them weeks and weeks and weeks, and for ever
and ever. Why, look at one of them prisoners in the
bottom dungeon of the Castle Deef, in the harbor of
Marseilles, that dug himself out that way—how long
was *he* at it, you reckon?"

"I don't know."

"Well, guess."

"I don't know. A month and a half."

"*Thirty-seven year*—and he come out in China. *That's*
the kind. I wish the bottom of *this* fortress was solid
rock."

"*Jim* don't know nobody in China."

"What's *that* got to do with it? Neither did that other
fellow. But you're always a-wandering off on a side
issue. Why can't you stick to the main point?"

"All right—*I* don't care where he comes out, so he

comes out; and Jim don't, either, I reckon. But there's
one thing, anyway—Jim's too old to be dug out with a
case-knife. He won't last."

"Yes he will *last*, too. You don't reckon it's going to
take thirty-seven years to dig out through a *dirt* foundation, do you?"

"How long will it take, Tom?"

"Well, we can't resk being as long as we ought to, because it mayn't take very long for Uncle Silas to hear
from down there by New Orleans. He'll hear Jim ain't
from there. Then his next move will be to advertise Jim,
or something like that. So we can't resk being as long
digging him out as we ought to. By rights I reckon we
ought to be a couple of years; but we can't. Things
being so uncertain, what I recommend is this: that we
really dig right in as quick as we can; and after that, we
can *let* on, to ourselves, that we was at it thirty-seven
years. Then we can snatch him out and rush him away
the first time there's an alarm. Yes, I reckon that'll be
the best way."

"Now, there's *sense* in that," I says. "Letting on don't
cost nothing; letting on ain't no trouble; and if it's any
object, I don't mind letting on we was at it a hundred
and fifty year. It wouldn't strain me none after I got my
hand in. So I'll mosey along now and smouch a couple
of case-knives."

"Smouch three," he says; "we want one to make a saw
out of."

"Tom, if it ain't unregular and irreligious to sejest it,"
I says, "there's an old rusty saw-blade around yonder
sticking under the weather-boarding behind the smoke-
house."

He looked kind of weary and discouraged-like, and
says:

"It ain't no use to try to learn you nothing, Huck. Run along and smouch the knives—three of them." So I done it.

XXXVI. TRYING TO HELP JIM

As soon as we reckoned everybody was asleep that night we went down the lightning-rod and shut ourselves up in the lean-to, and got out our pile of fox-fire and went to work. We cleared everything out of the way, about four or five foot along the middle of the bottom log. Tom said we was right behind Jim's bed now and we'd dig in under it, and when we got through there couldn't nobody in the cabin ever know there was any hole there, because Jim's counterpin hung down most to the ground and you'd have to raise it up and look under to see the hole. So we dug and dug with the case-knives till most midnight, and then we was dog-tired and our hands was blistered, and yet you couldn't see we'd done anything hardly. At last I says:

"This ain't no thirty-seven-year job; this is a thirty-eight-year job, Tom Sawyer."

He never said nothing. But he sighed and pretty soon he stopped digging, and then for a good little while I knowed he was thinking. Then he says:

"It ain't no use, Huck, it ain't a-going to work. If we was prisoners it would, because then we'd have as many years as we wanted, and no hurry; and we wouldn't get but a few minutes to dig, every day, while they was changing watches, and so our hands wouldn't get blistered and we could keep it up right along, year in and year out, and do it right and the way it ought to be done. But *we* can't fool along; we got to rush; we ain't got no time to spare. If we was to put in another night this way we'd have to knock off for a week to let our hands get well—couldn't touch a case-knife with them sooner."

"Well, then, what we going to do, Tom?"

"I'll tell you. It ain't right and it ain't moral and I wouldn't like it to get out, but there ain't only just the one way: we got to dig him out with the picks and *let on* it's case-knives."

"*Now* you're *talking!*" I says; "your head gets leveler and leveler all the time, Tom Sawyer," I says. "Picks is the thing, moral or no moral; and as for me, I don't care shucks for the morality of it, nohow. When I start in to steal a nigger or a watermelon or a Sunday-school book, I ain't no ways particular how it's done so it's done. What I want is my nigger, or what I want is my water-melon, or what I want is my Sunday-school book; and if a pick's the handiest thing, that's the thing I'm a-going to dig that nigger or that watermelon or that Sunday-school book out with, and I don't give a dead rat what the authorities thinks about it nuther."

"Well," he says, "there's excuse for picks and letting on in a case like this; if it warn't so, I wouldn't approve of it, nor I wouldn't stand by and see the rules broke—because right is right, and wrong is wrong, and a body ain't got no business doing wrong when he ain't ignorant and knows better. It might answer for *you* to dig Jim out with a pick *without* any letting on, because you don't know no better, but it wouldn't for me, because I do know better. Gimme a case-knife."

He had his own by him but I handed him mine. He flung it down, and says:

"Gimme a *case-knife.*"

I didn't know just what to do—but then I thought. I scratched around amongst the old tools and got a pickax and give it to him, and he took it and went to work and never said a word.

He was always just that particular. Full of principle.

So then I got a shovel and then we picked and shoveled, turn about, and made the fur fly. We stuck to it about a half an hour, which was as long as we could stand up, but we had a good deal of a hole to show for it. When I got up-stairs I looked out at the window and see Tom doing his level best with the lightning-rod but he couldn't come it, his hands was so sore. At last he says:

"It ain't no use, it can't be done. What you reckon I better do? Can't you think of no way?"

"Yes," I says, "but I reckon it ain't regular. Come up the stairs, and let on it's a lightning-rod."

So he done it.

Next day Tom stole a pewter spoon and a brass candle-stick in the house, for to make some pens for Jim out of, and six tallow candles; and I hung around the nigger cabins and laid for a chance and stole three tin plates. Tom said it wasn't enough, but I said nobody wouldn't ever see the plates that Jim throwed out, because they'd fall in the dog-fennel and jimpson weeds under the window-hole—then we could tote them back and he could use them over again. So Tom was satisfied. Then he says:

"Now, the thing to study out is, how to get the things to Jim."

"Take them in through the hole," I says, "when we get it done."

He only just looked scornful and said something about nobody ever heard of such an idiotic idea, and then he went to studying. By and by he said he had ciphered out two or three ways but there warn't no need to decide on any of them yet. Said we'd got to post Jim first.

That night we went down the lightning-rod a little after ten and took one of the candles along, and listened under the window-hole and heard Jim snoring; so we pitched it in and it didn't wake him. Then we whirled in with the pick and shovel, and in about two hours and a half the job was done. We crept in under Jim's bed and into the cabin, and pawed around and found the candle and lit it and stood over Jim awhile and found him looking hearty and healthy, and then we woke him up gentle and gradual. He was so glad to see us he most cried, and called us honey and all the pet names he could think of, and was for having us hunt up a cold-chisel to cut the chain off of his leg with right away and clearing out without losing any time. But Tom he showed him how unregular it would be, and set down and told him all about our plans and how we could alter them in a minute any time there was an alarm, and not to be the least afraid because we would see he got away, *sure*. So Jim he said it was all right and we set there and talked over old times awhile, and then Tom asked a lot of questions and when Jim told him Uncle Silas come in every day or two to pray with him and Aunt Sally come in to see if he was comfortable and had plenty to eat, and both of them was kind as they could be, Tom says:

"*Now* I know how to fix it. We'll send you some things by them."

I said, "Don't do nothing of the kind, it's one of the most jackass ideas I ever struck," but he never paid no attention to me; went right on. It was his way when he'd got his plans set.

So he told Jim how we'd have to smuggle in the rope-ladder pie and other large things by Nat, the nigger that fed him, and he must be on the lookout and not be surprised and not let Nat see him open them, and we would put small things in Uncle's coat pockets and he must steal them out, and we would tie things to Aunt's apron-strings or put them in her apron pocket, if we got a chance, and told him what they would be and what they was for. And told him how to keep a journal on the shirt with his blood, and all that. He told him everything. Jim he couldn't see no sense in the most of it but he allowed we was white folks and knowed better than him, so he was satisfied and said he would do it all just as Tom said.

Jim had plenty corn-cob pipes and tobacco, so we had a right down good sociable time; then we crawled out through the hole, and so home to bed, with hands that looked like they'd been chawed. Tom was in high spirits. He said it was the best fun he ever had in his life, and the most intellectural, and said if he only could see his way to it we would keep it up all the rest of our lives and leave Jim to our children to get out, for he believed Jim would come to like it better and better the more he got used to it. He said that in that way it could be strung out to as much as eighty year, and would be the best time on record. And he said it would make us all celebrated that had a hand in it.

In the morning we went out to the woodpile and chopped up the brass candlestick into handy sizes, and Tom put them and the pewter spoon in his pocket. Then we went to the nigger cabins and while I got Nat's notice off, Tom shoved a piece of candlestick into the middle of a corn-pone that was in Jim's pan, and we went along with Nat to see how it would work and it just worked noble; when Jim bit into it it most mashed all his teeth out, and there warn't ever anything could 'a' worked better. Tom said so himself. Jim he never let on but what it was only just a piece of rock or something like that that's always getting into bread, you know, but after that he never bit into nothing but what he jabbed his fork into it in three or four places first.

And whilst we was a-standing there in the dimmish light, here comes a couple of the hounds bulging in from under Jim's bed, and they kept on piling in till there was eleven of them and there warn't hardly room in there to get your breath. By jings, we forgot to fasten that lean-to door! The nigger Nat he only just hollered "Witches!" once, and keeled over onto the floor amongst the dogs and begun to groan like he was dying. Tom jerked the door open and flung out a slab of Jim's meat and the dogs went for it, and in two seconds he was out himself and back again and shut the door, and I knowed he'd fixed the other door too. Then he went to work on the nigger, coaxing him and petting him and asking him if he'd been imagining he saw something again. He raised up, and blinked his eyes around, and says:

"Mars Sid, you'll say I's a fool, but if I didn't b'lieve I see most a million dogs, er devils, or some'n, I wisht I may die right heah in dese tracks. I did, mos' sholy. Mars Sid, I *felt* um—I *felt* um, sah; dey was all over me. Dad fetch it, I jis' wisht I could git my han's on one er dem witches jis' wunst—on'y jis' wunst—it's all I'd ast. But mos'ly I wisht dey'd lemme 'lone, I does."

Tom says:

"Well, I tell you what *I* think. What makes them come here just at this runaway nigger's breakfast-time? It's because they're hungry; that's the reason. You make them a witch-pie—that's the thing for *you* to do."

"But my lan', Mars Sid, how's I gwyne to make 'm a witch-pie? I doan' know how to make it. I hain't ever hearn er sich a thing b'fo'."

"Well, then, I'll have to make it myself."

"Will you do it, honey?—will you? I'll wusshup de groun' und' yo' foot, I will!"

"All right, I'll do it, seeing it's you, and you've been good to us and showed us the runaway nigger. But you got to be mighty careful. When we come around, you turn your back; and then whatever we've put in the pan, don't you let on you see it at all. And don't you look when Jim unloads the pan—something might happen, I don't know what. And above all, don't you *handle* the witch things."

"*Hannel* 'm, Mars Sid? What *is* you a-talkin' 'bout? I wouldn' lay de weight er my finger on um, not f'r ten hund'd thous'n billion dollars, I wouldn't."

XXXVII. JIM GETS HIS WITCH-PIE

That was all fixed. So then we went away and went to the rubbage-pile in the back yard, where they keep the old boots and rags and pieces of bottles and wore-out tin things, and all such truck, and scratched around and found an old tin washpan and stopped up the holes as well as we could, to bake the pie in, and took it down cellar and stole it full of flour and started for breakfast, and found a couple of shingle-nails that Tom said would be handy for a prisoner to scrabble his name and sorrows on the dungeon walls with, and dropped one of them in Aunt Sally's apron pocket which was hanging on a chair, and t'other we stuck in the band of Uncle Silas's hat, which was on the bureau, because we heard the children say their pa and ma was going to the runaway nigger's house this morning, and then went to breakfast, and Tom dropped the pewter spoon in Uncle Silas's coat pocket, and Aunt Sally wasn't come yet, so we had to wait a little while.

And when she come she was hot and red and cross, and couldn't hardly wait for the blessing, and then she went to sluicing out coffee with one hand and cracking the handiest child's head with her thimble with the other, and says:

"I've hunted high and I've hunted low, and it does beat all what *has* become of your other shirt."

My heart fell down amongst my lungs and livers and things, and a hard piece of corn-crust started down my throat after it and got met on the road with a cough, and was shot across the table and took one of the children in the eye and curled him up like a fishing-worm, and let a cry out of him the size of a war-whoop, and Tom he turned kinder blue around the gills, and it all amounted to a considerable state of things for about a quarter of a minute or as much as that, and I would 'a' sold out for half price if there was a bidder. But after that we was all right again—it was the sudden surprise of it that knocked us so kind of cold. Uncle Silas he says:

"It's most uncommon curious, I can't understand it. I know perfectly well I took it *off*, because—"

"Because you hain't got but one *on*. Just *listen* at the man! *I* know you took it off, and know it by a better way than your wool-gethering memory, too, because it was on the clo's-line yesterday—I see it there myself. But it's gone, that's the long and the short of it, and you'll just have to change to a red flann'l one till I can get time to make a new one. And it'll be the third I've made in two years. It just keeps a body on the jump to keep you in shirts, and whatever you do manage to *do* with 'm all is more'n *I* can make out. A body'd think you *would* learn to take some sort of care of 'em at your time of life."

"I know it, Sally, and I do try all I can. But it oughtn't to be altogether my fault, because, you know, I don't see them nor have nothing to do with them except when they're on me, and I don't believe I've ever lost one of them *off* of me."

"Well, it ain't *your* fault if you haven't, Silas; you'd 'a' done it if you could, I reckon. And the shirt ain't all that's gone, nuther. Ther's a spoon gone, and *that* ain't all. There was ten and now ther's only nine. The calf got the shirt, I reckon, but the calf never took the spoon, *that's* certain."

"Why, what else is gone, Sally?"

"Ther's six *candles* gone—that's what. The rats could 'a' got the candles, and I reckon they did; I wonder they don't walk off with the whole place, the way you're always going to stop their holes and don't do it, and if they warn't fools they'd sleep in your hair, Silas—*you'd* never find it out; but you can't lay the *spoon* on the rats, and that I *know*."

"Well, Sally, I'm in fault, and I acknowledge it; I've been remiss; but I won't let to-morrow go by without stopping up them holes."

"Oh, I wouldn't hurry; next year'll do. Matilda Angelina Araminta *Phelps!*"

Whack comes the thimble, and the child snatches her claws out of the sugar-bowl without fooling around any. Just then the nigger woman steps onto the passage, and says:

"Missus, dey's a sheet gone."

"A *sheet* gone! Well, for the land's sake!"

"I'll stop up them holes to-day," says Uncle Silas, looking sorrowful.

"Oh, *do* shet up!—s'pose the rats took the *sheet?* *Where's* it gone, Lize?"

"Clah to goodness I hain't no notion, Miss' Sally. She wuz on de clo's-line yistiddy but she done gone, she ain' dah no mo' now."

"I reckon the world *is* coming to an end. I *never* see the beat of it in all my born days. A shirt, and a sheet, and a spoon, and six can—"

"Missus," comes a young yaller wench, "dey's a brass cannelstick miss'n'."

"Cler out from here, you hussy, er I'll take a skillet to ye!"

Well, she was just a-biling. I begun to lay for a chance, I reckoned I would sneak out and go for the woods till the weather moderated. She kept a-raging right along, running her insurrection all by herself, and everybody else mighty meek and quiet, and at last Uncle Silas, looking kind of foolish, fishes up that spoon out of his pocket. She stopped, with her mouth open and her hands up, and as for me, I wished I was in Jeruslem or somewheres. But not long, because she says:

"It's *just* as I expected. So you had it in your pocket all the time, and like as not you've got the other things there, too. How'd it get there?"

"I reely don't know, Sally," he says, kind of apologizing, "or you know I would tell. I was a-studying over my text in Acts Seventeen before breakfast, and I reckon I put it in there, not noticing, meaning to put my Testament in, and it must be so, because my Testament ain't in—but I'll go and see, and if the Testament is where I had it, I'll know I didn't put it in, and that will show that I laid the Testament down and took up the spoon, and—"

"Oh, for the land's sake! Give a body a rest! Go 'long now, the whole kit and biling of ye, and don't come nigh me again till I've got back my peace of mind."

I'd 'a' heard her if she'd 'a' said it to herself, let alone speaking it out, and I'd 'a' got up and obeyed her if I'd 'a' been dead. As we was passing through the setting-room the old man he took up his hat, and the shingle-nail fell out on the floor, and he just merely picked it up and laid it on the mantel-shelf and never said nothing and went out. Tom see him do it and remembered about the spoon, and says:

"Well, it ain't no use to send things by *him* no more, he ain't reliable." Then he says: "But he done us a good turn with the spoon, anyway, without knowing it, and so we'll go and do him one without *him* knowing it—stop up his rat-holes."

There was a noble good lot of them down cellar, and it took us a whole hour, but we done the job tight and good and shipshape. Then we heard steps on the stairs, and blowed out our light and hid, and here comes the old man with a candle in one hand and a bundle of stuff in t'other, looking as absent-minded as year before last. He went a-mooning around, first to one rat-hole and then another, till he'd been to them all. Then he stood about five minutes, picking tallow-drip off of his candle and thinking. Then he turns off slow and dreamy towards the stairs, saying:

"Well, for the life of me I can't remember when I done it. I could show her now that I warn't to blame on account of the rats. But never mind—let it go. I reckon it wouldn't do no good."

And so he went on a-mumbling up-stairs and then we left. He was a mighty nice old man. And always is.

Tom was a good deal bothered about what to do for a spoon but he said we'd got to have it, so he took a think. When he had ciphered it out he told me how we was to do, then we went and waited around the spoon-basket till we see Aunt Sally coming, and then Tom went to counting the spoons and laying them out to one side, and I slid one of them up my sleeve, and Tom says:

"Why, Aunt Sally, there ain't but nine spoons *yet*."

She says:

"Go 'long to your play, and don't bother me. I know better, I counted 'm myself."

"Well, I've counted them twice, Aunty, and I can't make but nine."

She looked out of all patience but of course she come to count—anybody would.

"I declare to gracious ther' *ain't* but nine!" she says. "Why, what in the world—plague *take* the things, I'll count 'm again."

So I slipped back the one I had and when she got done counting, she says:

"Hang the troublesome rubbage, ther's *ten* now!" and she looked huffy and bothered both. But Tom says:

"Why, Aunty, *I* don't think there's ten."

"You numskull, didn't you see me *count* 'm?"

"I know, but—"

"Well, I'll count 'm *again*."

So I smouched one and they come out nine, same as the other time. Well, she *was* in a tearing way—just a-trembling all over, she was so mad. But she counted and counted till she got that addled she'd start to count in the *basket* for a spoon sometimes, and so three times they come out right and three times they come out wrong. Then she grabbed up the basket and slammed it across the house and knocked the cat galley-west, and she said cler out and let her have some peace, and if we come bothering around her again betwixt that and dinner she'd skin us. So we had the odd spoon and dropped it in her apron pocket whilst she was a-giving us our sailing orders, and Jim got it all right, along with her shingle-nail, before noon. We was very well satisfied with this business, and Tom allowed it was worth twice the trouble it took, because he said *now* she couldn't ever count them spoons twice alike again to save her life, and wouldn't believe she'd counted them right if she *did*, and said that after she'd about counted her head off for the next three days he judged she'd give it up and offer to kill anybody that wanted her to ever count them any more.

So we put the sheet back on the line that night and stole one out of her closet, and kept on putting it back and stealing it again for a couple of days till she didn't know how many sheets she had any more, and said she didn't *care* and warn't a-going to bullyrag the rest of her soul out about it and wouldn't count them again not to save her life, she druther die first.

So we was all right now, as to the shirt and the sheet and the spoon and the candles, by the help of the calf and the rats and the mixed-up counting, and as to the candlestick, it warn't no consequence, it would blow over by and by.

But that pie was a job; we had no end of trouble with that pie. We fixed it up away down in the woods and cooked it there, and we got it done at last, and very satisfactory, too, but not all in one day, and we had to use up three washpans full of flour before we got through, and we got burnt pretty much all over, in places, and eyes put out with the smoke; because, you see, we didn't want nothing but a crust, and we couldn't prop it up right and she would always cave in. But of course we thought of the right way at last—which was to cook the ladder, too, in the pie. So then we laid in with Jim the second night, and tore up the sheet all in little strings and twisted them together, and long before daylight we had a lovely rope that you could 'a' hung a person with. We let on it took nine months to make it.

And in the forenoon we took it down to the woods but it wouldn't go into the pie. Being made of a whole sheet, that way, there was rope enough for forty pies if we'd 'a' wanted them, and plenty left over for soup or sausage or anything you choose. We could 'a' had a whole dinner.

But we didn't need it. All we needed was just enough
for the pie and so we throwed the rest away. We didn't
cook none of the pies in the washpan—afraid the solder
would melt; but Uncle Silas he had a noble brass warming-pan which he thought considerable of, because it belonged to one of his ancesters with a long wooden handle
that come over from England with William the Conqueror in the *Mayflower* or one of them early ships and
was hid away up garret with a lot of other old pots and
things that was valuable, not on account of being any
account, because they warn't, but on account of them
being relicts, you know, and we snaked her out, private,
and took her down there, but she failed on the first pies
because we didn't know how, but she come up smiling
on the last one. We took and lined her with dough and
set her in the coals, and loaded her up with rag rope
and put on a dough roof and shut down the lid, and
put hot embers on top and stood off five foot, with the
long handle, cool and comfortable, and in fifteen minutes she turned out a pie that was a satisfaction to look
at. But the person that et it would want to fetch a couple
of kags of toothpicks along, for if that rope ladder
wouldn't cramp him down to business I don't know nothing what I'm talking about, and lay him in enough
stomach-ache to last him till next time, too.

Nat didn't look when we put the witch-pie in Jim's
pan, and we put the three tin plates in the bottom of the
pan under the vittles, and so Jim got everything all right
and as soon as he was by himself he busted into the pie
and hid the rope ladder inside of his straw tick, and
scratched some marks on a tin plate and throwed it out
of the window-hole.

Making them pens was a distressid tough job and so
was the saw, and Jim allowed the inscription was going
to be the toughest at all. That's the one which the prisoner has to scrabble on the wall. But he had to have it;
Tom said he'd *got* to, there warn't no case of a state
prisoner not scrabbling his inscription to leave behind,
and his coat of arms.

"Look at Lady Jane Grey," he says; "look at Gilford
Dudley; look at old Northumberland! Why, Huck, s'pose
it *is* considerble trouble?—what you going to do?—how
you going to get around it? Jim's *got* to do his inscription and coat of arms. They all do."

Jim says:

"Why, Mars Tom, I hain't got no coat o' arm; I hain't
got nuffn but dish yer ole shirt, en you knows I got to
keep de journal on dat."

"Oh, you don't understand, Jim, a coat of arms is
very different."

"Well," I says, "Jim's right, anyway, when he says he
hain't got no coat of arms, because he hain't."

"I reckon *I* knowed that," Tom says, "but you bet
he'll have one before he goes out of this—because he's
going out *right,* and there ain't going to be no flaws in
his record."

So whilst me and Jim filed away at the pens on a
brick-bat apiece, Jim a-making his'n out of the brass and
I making mine out of the spoon, Tom set to work to
think out the coat of arms. By and by he said he'd struck
so many good ones he didn't hardly know which to take,
but there was one which he reckoned he'd decide on.
He says:

"On the scutcheon we'll have a bend *or* in the dexter
base, a saltire *murrey* in the fess, with a dog, couchant,

for common charge, and under his foot a chain em-
battled, for slavery, with a chevron *vert* in a chief en-
grailed, and three invected lines on a field *azure*, with
the nombril points rampant on a dancette indented;
crest, a runaway nigger, *sable*, with his bundle over his
shoulder on a bar sinister; and a couple of gules for
supporters, which is you and me; motto, *Maggiore fretta,
minore atto.* Got it out of a book—means the more haste
the less speed."

"Geewhillikins," I says, "but what does the rest of it
mean?"

"We ain't got no time to bother over that," he says,
"we got to dig in like all git-out."

"Well, anyway," I says, "what's *some* of it? What's a
fess?"

"A fess—a fess is—*you* don't need to know what a
fess is. I'll show him how to make it when he gets to it."

"Shucks, Tom," I says, "I think you might tell a person. What's a bar sinister?"

"Oh, *I* don't know. But he's got to have it. All the
nobility does."

That was just his way. If it didn't suit him to explain
a thing to you, he wouldn't do it. You might pump at
him a week, it wouldn't make no difference.

He'd got all that coat-of-arms business fixed, so now
he started in to finish up the rest of that part of the
work, which was to plan out a mournful inscription—
said Jim got to have one, like they all done. He made up
a lot, and wrote them out on a paper, and read them
off, so:

1. *Here a captive heart busted.*

2. *Here a poor prisoner, forsook by the world and
friends, fretted out his sorrowful life.*

3. *Here a lonely heart broke, and a worn spirit went
to its rest, after thirty-seven years of solitary captivity.*

4. *Here, homeless and friendless, after thirty-seven*
years of bitter captivity, perished a noble stranger, natu-
ral son of Louis XIV.

Tom's voice trembled whilst he was reading them,
and he most broke down. When he got done he couldn't
no way make up his mind which one for Jim to scrabble
onto the wall, they was all so good, but at last he allowed he would let him scrabble them all on. Jim said
it would take him a year to scrabble such a lot of truck
onto the logs with a nail and he didn't know how to
make letters, besides, but Tom said he would block them
out for him and then he wouldn't have nothing to do but
just follow the lines. Then pretty soon he says:

"Come to think, the logs ain't a-going to do, they don't
have log walls in a dungeon—we got to dig the inscriptions into a rock. We'll fetch a rock."

Jim said the rock was worse than the logs; he said it
would take him such a pison long time to dig them into
a rock he wouldn't ever get out. But Tom said he would
let me help him do it. Then he took a look to see how me
and Jim was getting along with the pens. It was most
pesky tedious hard work and slow, and didn't give my
hands no show to get well of the sores, and we didn't
seem to make no headway, hardly; so Tom says:

"I know how to fix it. We got to have a rock for the
coat of arms and mournful inscriptions, and we can kill
two birds with that same rock. There's a gaudy big
grindstone down at the mill, and we'll smouch it, and
carve the things on it, and file out the pens and the saw
on it, too."

It warn't no slouch of an idea and it warn't no slouch
of a grindstone nuther, but we allowed we'd tackle it. It
warn't quite midnight yet, so we cleared out for the
mill, leaving Jim at work. We smouched the grindstone
and set out to roll her home, but it was a most nation

tough job. Sometimes, do what we could, we couldn't keep her from falling over, and she come mighty near mashing us every time. Tom said she was going to get one of us, sure, before we got through. We got her half-way, and then we was plumb played out and most drownded with sweat. We see it warn't no use, we got to go and fetch Jim. So he raised up his bed and slid the chain off of the bed-leg and wrapt it round and round his neck, and we crawled out through our hole and down there, and Jim and me laid into that grindstone and walked her along like nothing, and Tom superintended. He could out-superintend any boy I ever see. He knowed how to do everything.

Our hole was pretty big but it warn't big enough to get the grindstone through, but Jim he took the pick and soon made it big enough. Then Tom marked out them things on it with the nail, and set Jim to work on them with the nail for a chisel and an iron bolt from the rub-bage in the lean-to for a hammer, and told him to work till the rest of his candle quit on him and then he could go to bed, and hide the grindstone under his straw tick and sleep on it. Then we helped him fix his chain back on the bed-leg, and was ready for bed ourselves. But Tom thought of something and says:

"You got any spiders in here, Jim?"

"No, sah, thanks to goodness I hain't, Mars Tom."

"All right, we'll get you some."

"But bless you, honey, I doan' *want* none. I's afeard un um. I jis' 's soon have a rattlesnake aroun'."

Tom thought a minute or two, and says:

"It's a good idea. And I reckon it's been done. It *must* 'a' been done; it stands to reason. Yes, it's a prime good idea. Where could you keep it?"

"Keep what, Mars Tom?"

"Why, a rattlesnake."

"De goodness gracious alive, Mars Tom! Why, if dey was a rattlesnake to come in heah I'd take en bust right out thoo dat log wall, I would, wid my head."

"Why, Jim, you wouldn't be afraid of it after a little. You could tame it."

"*Tame* it!"

"Yes—easy enough. Every animal is grateful for kindness and petting, and they wouldn't *think* of hurting a person that pets them. Any book will tell you that. You try—that's all I ask, just try for two or three days. Why, you can get him so in a little while that he'll love you and sleep with you, and won't stay away from you a minute, and will let you wrap him round your neck and put his head in your mouth."

"*Please*, Mars Tom—*doan'* talk so! I can't *stan'* it! He'd *let* me shove his head in my mouf—fer a favor, hain't it? I lay he'd wait a pow'ful long time 'fo' I *ast* him. En mo' en dat, I doan' *want* him to sleep wid me."

"Jim, don't act so foolish. A prisoner's *got* to have some kind of a dumb pet, and if a rattlesnake hain't ever been tried, why, there's more glory to be gained in you being the first to ever try it than any other way you could ever think of to save your life."

"Why, Mars Tom, I doan' *want* no sich glory. Snake take 'n bite Jim's chin off, den *whah* is de glory? No, sah, I doan' want no sich doin's."

"Blame it, can't you *try?* I only *want* you to try—you needn't keep it up if it don't work."

"But de trouble all *done* ef de snake bite me while I's a-tryin' him. Mars Tom, I's willin' to tackle mos' anything 'at ain't onreasonable, but ef you en Huck fetches a rattlesnake in heah for me to tame, I's gwyne to *leave*, dat's *shore*."

"Well, then, let it go, let it go, if you're so bullheaded about it. We can get you some garter-snakes, and you can tie some buttons on their tails and let on they're rattlesnakes, and I reckon that'll have to do."

"I k'n stan' *dem*, Mars Tom, but blame' 'f I couldn' git along widout um, I tell you dat. I never knowed b'fo' 'twas so much bother and trouble to be a prisoner."

"Well, it *always* is when it's done right. You got any rats around here?"

"No, sah, I hain't seed none."

"Well, we'll get you some rats."

"Why, Mars Tom, I doan' *want* no rats. Dey's de dad-blamedest creturs to 'sturb a body, en rustle roun' over 'im, en bite his feet, when he's tryin' to sleep, I ever see. No, sah, gimme g'yarter-snakes, 'f I's got to have 'm, but doan' gimme no rats; I hain' got no use f'r um, skasely."

"But, Jim, you *got* to have 'em—they all do. So don't make no more fuss about it. Prisoners ain't ever without rats. There ain't no instance of it. And they train them and pet them and learn them tricks, and they get to be as sociable as flies. But you got to play music to them. You got anything to play music on?"

"I ain't got nuffn but a coase comb en a piece o' paper, en a juice-harp, but I reck'n dey wouldn' take no stock in a juice-harp."

"Yes they would. *They* don't care what kind of music 'tis. A jew's-harp's plenty good enough for a rat. All animals like music—in a prison they dote on it. Specially, painful music; and you can't get no other kind out of a jew's-harp. It always interests them; they come out to see what's the matter with you. Yes, you're all right; you're fixed very well. You want to set on your bed nights before you go to sleep, and early in the mornings, and play your jew's-harp; play 'The Last Link Is Broken'—that's the thing that'll scoop a rat quicker'n anything else; and when you've played about two minutes you'll see all the rats and the snakes and spiders and things begin to feel worried about you, and come. And they'll just fairly swarm over you and have a noble good time."

"Yes, *dey* will, I reck'n, Mars Tom, but what kine er time is *Jim* havin'? Blest if I kin see de pint. But I'll do it ef I got to. I reck'n I better keep de animals satisfied, en not have no trouble in de house."

Tom waited to think it over and see if there wasn't nothing else, and pretty soon he says:

"Oh, there's one thing I forgot. Could you raise a flower here, do you reckon?"

"I doan' know but maybe I could, Mars Tom; but it's tolable dark in heah, en I ain' got no use f'r no flower, nohow, en she'd be a pow'ful sight o' trouble."

"Well, you try it, anyway. Some other prisoners has done it."

"One er dem big cat-tail-lookin' mullen-stalks would grow in heah, Mars Tom, I reck'n, but she wouldn' be wuth half de trouble she'd coss."

"Don't you believe it. We'll fetch you a little one and you plant it in the corner over there, and raise it. And don't call it mullen, call it Pitchiola—that's its right name when it's in a prison. And you want to water it with your tears."

"Why, I got plenty spring water, Mars Tom."

"You don't *want* spring water; you want to water it with your tears. It's the way they always do."

"Why, Mars Tom, I lay I kin raise one er dem mullen-stalks twyste wid spring water whiles another man's a-*start'n'* one wid tears."

"That ain't the idea. You *got* to do it with tears."

"She'll die on my han's, Mars Tom, she sholy will, kase I doan' skasely ever cry."

So Tom was stumped. But he studied it over and then

said Jim would have to worry along the best he could with an onion. He promised he would go to the nigger cabins and drop one, private, in Jim's coffee-pot, in the morning. Jim said he would "jis' 's soon have tobacker in his coffee," and found so much fault with it, and with the work and bother of raising the mullen, and jew's-harping the rats and petting and flattering up the snakes and spiders and things, on top of all the other work he had to do on pens and inscriptions and journals and things, which made it more trouble and worry and re-sponsibility to be a prisoner than anything he ever undertook, that Tom most lost all patience with him and said he was just loadened down with more gaudier chances than a prisoner ever had in the world to make a name for himself, and yet he didn't know enough to ap-preciate them and they was just about wasted on him. So Jim he was sorry, and said he wouldn't behave so no more, and then me and Tom shoved for bed.

XXXIX. TOM WRITES NONNAMOUS LETTERS

In the morning we went up to the village and bought a wire rat-trap and fetched it down and unstopped the best rat-hole, and in about an hour we had fifteen of the bulliest kind of ones and then we took it and put it in a safe place under Aunt Sally's bed. But while we was gone for spiders little Thomas Franklin Benjamin Jefferson Elexander Phelps found it there, and opened the door of it to see if the rats would come out, and they did; and Aunt Sally she come in, and when we got back she was a-standing on top of the bed raising Cain, and the rats was doing what they could to keep off the dull times for her. So she took and dusted us both with the hickry and we was as much as two hours catching another fifteen or sixteen, drat that meddlesome cub, and they warn't the likeliest, nuther, because the first haul was the pick of the flock. I never see a likelier lot of rats than what that first haul was.

We got a splendid stock of sorted spiders and bugs and frogs and caterpillars and one thing or another, and we like to got a hornet's nest, but we didn't. The family was at home. We didn't give it right up but stayed with them as long as we could, because we allowed we'd tire them out or they'd got to tire us out, and they done it. Then we got allycumpain and rubbed on the places and was pretty near all right again, but couldn't set down convenient. And so we went for the snakes and grabbed a couple of dozen garters and house-snakes, and put them in a bag and put it in our room, and by that time it was supper-time, and a rattling good honest day's work; and hungry?—oh, no, I reckon not! And there warn't a blessed snake up there when we went back— we didn't half tie the sack and they worked out somehow, and left. But it didn't matter much, because they was still on the premises somewheres. So we judged we could get some of them again. No, there warn't no real scarcity of snakes about the house for a considerable spell. You'd see them dripping from the rafters and places every now and then, and they generly landed in your plate or down the back of your neck, and most of the time where you didn't want them. Well, they was handsome and striped and there warn't no harm in a million of them, but that never made no difference to Aunt Sally; she despised snakes, be the breed what they might, and she couldn't stand them no way you could fix it, and every time one of them flopped down on her, it didn't make no difference what she was doing, she would just lay that work down and light out. I never see such a woman. And you could hear her whoop to

Jericho. You couldn't get her to take a-holt of one of
them with the tongs. And if she turned over and found
one in bed she would scramble out and lift a howl
that you would think the house was afire. She disturbed
the old man so that he said he could most wish there
hadn't been no snakes created. Why, after every last
snake had been gone clear out of the house for as
much as a week Aunt Sally warn't over it yet, she warn't
near over it; when she was setting thinking about something you could touch her on the back of her neck with
a feather and she would jump right out of her stockings.
It was very curious. But Tom said all women was just
so. He said they was made that way for some reason or
other.

We got a licking every time one of our snakes come
in her way, and she allowed these lickings warn't nothing to what she would do if we ever loaded up the
place again with them. I didn't mind the lickings because they didn't amount to nothing, but I minded the
trouble we had to lay in another lot. But we got them
laid in, and all the other things, and you never see a
cabin as blithesome as Jim's was when they'd all swarm
out for music and go for him. Jim didn't like the spiders
and the spiders didn't like Jim, and so they'd lay for
him and make it mighty warm for him. And he said
that between the rats and the snakes and the grindstone there warn't no room in bed for him, skasely; and
when there was, a body couldn't sleep, it was so lively,
and it was always lively, he said, because *they* never
all slept at one time but took turn about, so when the
snakes was asleep the rats was on deck, and when the
rats turned in the snakes come on watch, so he always
had one gang under him, in his way, and t'other gang
having a circus over him, and if he got up to hunt a
new place the spiders would take a chance at him as

he crossed over. He said if he ever got out this time he wouldn't ever be a prisoner again, not for a salary.

Well, by the end of three weeks everything was in pretty good shape. The shirt was sent in early, in a pie, and every time a rat bit Jim he would get up and write a line in his journal whilst the ink was fresh; the pens was made, the inscriptions and so on was all carved on the grindstone, the bed-leg was sawed in two, and we had et up the sawdust and it give us a most amazing stomach-ache. We reckoned we was all going to die, but didn't. It was the most undigestible sawdust I ever see, and Tom said the same. But as I was saying, we'd got all the work done now, at last, and we was all pretty much fagged out, too, but mainly Jim. The old man had wrote a couple of times to the plantation below Orleans to come and get their runaway nigger but hadn't got no answer, because there warn't no such plantation; so he allowed he would advertise Jim in the St. Louis and New Orleans papers, and when he mentioned the St. Louis ones it give me the cold shivers and I see we hadn't no time to lose. So Tom said, now for the non-namous letters.

"What's them?" I says.

"Warnings to the people that something is up. Sometimes it's done one way, sometimes another. But there's always somebody spying around that gives notice to the governor of the castle. When Louis XVI was going to light out of the Tooleries a servant-girl done it. It's a very good way, and so is the nonnamous letters. We'll use them both. And it's usual for the prisoner's mother to change clothes with him, and she stays in and he slides out in her clothes. We'll do that, too."

"But looky here, Tom, what do we want to *warn* anybody for that something's up? Let them find it out for themselves—it's their lookout."

"Yes, I know, but you can't depend on them. It's the way they've acted from the very start—left us to do *everything*. They're so confiding and mullet-headed they don't take notice of nothing at all. So we don't *give* them notice there won't be nobody nor nothing to interfere with us, and so after all our hard work and trouble this escape'll go off perfectly flat; won't amount to nothing—won't be nothing *to* it."

"Well, as for me, Tom, that's the way I'd like."

"Shucks!" he says, and looked disgusted. So I says:

"But I ain't going to make no complaint. Any way that suits you suits me. What you going to do about the servant-girl?"

"You'll be her. You slide in, in the middle of the night, and hook that yaller girl's frock."

"Why, Tom, that'll make trouble next morning; because, of course, she prob'bly hain't got any but that one."

"I know, but you don't want it but fifteen minutes, to carry the nonnamous letter and shove it under the front door."

"All right, then, I'll do it, but I could carry it just as handy in my own togs."

"You wouldn't look like a servant-girl *then*, would you?"

"No, but there won't be nobody to see what I look like, *anyway*."

"That ain't got nothing to do with it. The thing for us to do is just to do our *duty*, and not worry about whether anybody *sees* us do it or not. Hain't you got no principle at all?"

"All right, I ain't saying nothing; I'm the servant-girl. Who's Jim's mother?"

"I'm his mother. I'll hook a gown from Aunt Sally."

"Well, then, you'll have to stay in the cabin when me and Jim leaves."

"Not much. I'll stuff Jim's clothes full of straw and lay it on his bed to represent his mother in disguise, and Jim'll take Aunt Sally's gown off of me and wear it and we'll all evade together. When a prisoner of style escapes it's called an evasion. It's always called so when a king escapes, f'rinstance. And the same with a king's son, it don't make no difference whether he's a natural one or an unnatural one."

So Tom he wrote the nonnamous letter and I smouched the yaller wench's frock that night and put it on, and shoved it under the front door, the way Tom told me to. It said:

Beware. Trouble is brewing. Keep a sharp lookout.
                                                     UNKNOWN FRIEND

Next night we stuck a picture, which Tom drawed in blood, of a skull and crossbones on the front door, and next night another one of a coffin on the back door. I never see a family in such a sweat. They couldn't 'a' been worse scared if the place had 'a' been full of ghosts laying for them behind everything and under the beds and shivering through the air. If a door banged, Aunt Sally she jumped and said "ouch!"; if anything fell, she jumped and said "ouch!"; if you happened to touch her when she warn't noticing, she done the same; she couldn't face no way and be satisfied, because she allowed there was something behind her every time—so she was always a-whirling around sudden, and saying "ouch," and before she'd got two-thirds around she'd whirl back again and say it again, and she was afraid to go to bed but she dasn't set up. So the thing was working very well, Tom said; he said he never see a thing work more satisfactory. He said it showed it was done right.

So he said, now for the grand bulge! So the very next morning at the streak of dawn we got another letter ready, and was wondering what we better do with it, because we heard them say at supper they was going to have a nigger on watch at both doors all night. Tom he went down the lightning-rod to spy around, and the nigger at the back door was asleep, and he stuck it in the back of his neck and come back. This letter said:

Don't betray me, I wish to be your friend. There is a desprate gang of cutthroats from over in the Ingeun Territory going to steal your runaway nigger to-night, and they have been trying to scare you so as you will stay in the house and not bother them. I am one of the gang, but have got religgion and wish to quit it and lead an honest life again, and will betray the helish design. They will sneak down from northards, along the fence, at midnight exact, with a false key, and go in the nigger's cabin to get him. I am to be off a piece and blow a tin horn if I see any danger; but stead of that I will BA *like a sheep soon as they get in and not blow at all; then whilst they are getting his chains loose, you slip there and lock them in, and can kill them at your leisure. Don't do anything but just the way I am telling you; if you do they will suspicion something and raise whoop-jamboree- hoo. I do not wish any reward but to know I have done the right thing.*

UNKNOWN FRIEND

XL. A MIXED-UP AND SPLENDID RESCUE

We was feeling pretty good after breakfast and took my canoe and went over the river a-fishing, with a lunch, and had a good time, and took a look at the raft and found her all right, and got home late to supper and found them in such a sweat and worry they didn't

know which end they was standing on, and made us go
right off to bed the minute we was done supper and
wouldn't tell us what the trouble was, and never let on
a word about the new letter, but didn't need to, because
we knowed as much about it as anybody did, and as
soon as we was half up-stairs and her back was turned
we slid for the cellar cubboard and loaded up a good
lunch and took it up to our room and went to bed, and
got up about half past eleven, and Tom put on Aunt
Sally's dress that he stole and was going to start with
the lunch, but says:

"Where's the butter?"

"I laid out a hunk of it," I says, "on a piece of a corn-
pone."

"Well, you *left* it laid out, then—it ain't here."

"We can get along without it," I says.

"We can get along *with* it, too," he says; "just you
slide down cellar and fetch it. And then mosey right
down the lightning-rod and come along. I'll go and stuff
the straw into Jim's clothes to represent his mother in
disguise, and be ready to *ba* like a sheep and shove
soon as you get there."

So out he went and down cellar went I. The hunk of
butter, big as a person's fist, was where I had left it, so
I took up the slab of corn-pone with it on and blowed
out my light and started up-stairs very stealthy, and got
up to the main floor all right, but here comes Aunt Sally
with a candle, and I clapped the truck in my hat and
clapped my hat on my head, and the next second she see
me, and she says:

"You been down cellar?"

"Yes'm."

"What you been doing down there?"

"Noth'n."

"*Noth'n!*"

"No'm."

"Well, then, what possessed you to go down there this time of night?"

"I don't know 'm'."

"You don't *know?* Don't answer me that way. Tom, I want to know what you been *doing* down there."

"I hain't been doing a single thing, Aunt Sally, I hope to gracious if I have."

I reckoned she'd let me go now, and as a generl thing she would, but I s'pose there was so many strange things going on she was just in a sweat about every little thing that warn't yard-stick straight; so she says, very decided:

"You just march into that settin'-room and stay there till I come. You been up to something you no business to, and I lay I'll find out what it is before *I'm* done with you."

So she went away as I opened the door and walked into the setting-room. My, but there was a crowd there! Fifteen farmers, and every one of them had a gun. I was most powerful sick, and slunk to a chair and set down. They was setting around, some of them talking a little in a low voice, and all of them fidgety and uneasy but trying to look like they warn't, but I knowed they was, because they was always taking off their hats and putting them on, and scratching their heads and changing their seats, and fumbling with their buttons. I warn't easy myself but I didn't take my hat off, all the same.

I did wish Aunt Sally would come and get done with me, and lick me, if she wanted to, and let me get away and tell Tom how we'd overdone this thing, and what a thundering hornet's nest we'd got ourselves into, so we could stop fooling around straight off, and clear out with Jim before these rips got out of patience and come for us.

At last she come and begun to ask me questions, but
I *couldn't* answer them straight, I didn't know which
end of me was up, because these men was in such a
fidget now that some was wanting to start right *now*
and lay for them desperadoes, and saying it warn't but
a few minutes to midnight, and others was trying to get
them to hold on and wait for the sheep-signal, and here
was Aunty pegging away at the questions, and me
a-shaking all over and ready to sink down in my tracks
I was that scared; and the place getting hotter and
hotter, and the butter beginning to melt and run down
my neck and behind my ears, and pretty soon, when one
of them says, "*I'm* for going and getting in the cabin
first and right *now*, and catching them when they come,"
I most dropped, and a streak of butter come a-trickling
down my forehead, and Aunt Sally she see it and turns
white as a sheet and says:

"For the land's sake, what *is* the matter with the
child? He's got the brain-fever as shore as you're born,
and they're oozing out!"

And everybody runs to see, and she snatches off my
hat and out comes the bread and what was left of the
butter, and she grabbed me and hugged me, and says:

"Oh, what a turn you did give me! and how glad and
grateful I am it ain't no worse; for luck's against us,
and it never rains but it pours, and when I see that truck
I thought we'd lost you, for I knowed by the color and
all it was just like your brains would be if— Dear, dear,
whyd'nt you *tell* me that was what you'd been down
there for, *I* wouldn't 'a' cared. Now cler out to bed, and
don't lemme see no more of you till morning!"

I was up-stairs in a second and down the lightning-
rod in another one, and shinning through the dark for
the lean-to. I couldn't hardly get my words out, I was
so anxious; but I told Tom as quick as I could we must

jump for it now, and not a minute to lose—the house
full of men, yonder, with guns!

His eyes just blazed; and he says:

"No!—is that so? *Ain't* it bully! Why, Huck, if it was
to do over again, I bet I could fetch two hundred! If we
could put it off till—"

"Hurry! *hurry!*" I says. "Where's Jim?"

"Right at your elbow; if you reach out your arm you
can touch him. He's dressed and everything's ready.
Now we'll slide out and give the sheep-signal."

But then we heard the tramp of men coming to the
door, and heard them begin to fumble with the padlock,
and heard a man say:

"I *told* you we'd be too soon; they haven't come—the
door is locked. Here, I'll lock some of you into the
cabin, and you lay for 'em in the dark and kill 'em when
they come; and the rest scatter around a piece and
listen if you can hear 'em coming."

So in they come, but couldn't see us in the dark, and
most trod on us whilst we was hustling to get under the
bed. But we got under all right, and out through the
hole, swift but soft—Jim first, me next, and Tom last,
which was according to Tom's orders. Now we was in
the lean-to, and heard trampings close by outside. So
we crept to the door and Tom stopped us there and put
his eye to the crack, but couldn't make out nothing, it
was so dark; and whispered and said he would listen
for the steps to get further, and when he nudged us Jim
must glide out first, and him last. So he set his ear to the
crack and listened, and listened, and listened, and the
steps a-scraping around out there all the time; and at
last he nudged us, and we slid out and stooped down,
not breathing and not making the least noise, and
slipped stealthy towards the fence in Injun file, and got
to it all right, and me and Jim over it; but Tom's britches

catched fast on a splinter on the top rail, and then he hear the steps coming so he had to pull lose, which snapped the splinter and made a noise, and as he dropped in our tracks and started somebody sings out:

"Who's that? Answer or I'll shoot!"

But we didn't answer; we just unfurled our heels and shoved. Then there was a rush, and a *bang, bang, bang!* and the bullets fairly whizzed around us! We heard them sing out:

"Here they are! They've broke for the river! After 'em, boys, and turn loose the dogs!"

So here they come, full tilt. We could hear them because they wore boots and yelled, but we didn't wear no boots and didn't yell. We was in the path to the mill, and when they got pretty close onto us we dodged into the bush and let them go by, and then dropped in behind them. They'd had all the dogs shut up, so they wouldn't scare off the robbers, but by this time somebody had let them loose and here they come, making powwow enough for a million; but they was our dogs, so we stopped in our tracks till they catched up; and when they see it warn't nobody but us, and no excitement to offer them, they only just said howdy and tore right ahead towards the shouting and clattering; and then we up-stream again and whizzed along after them till we was nearly to the mill, and then struck up through the bush to where my canoe was tied, and hopped in and pulled for dear life towards the middle of the river, but didn't make no more noise than we was obleeged to. Then we struck out, easy and comfortable, for the island where my raft was, and we could hear them yelling and barking at each other all up and down the bank, till we was so far away the sounds got dim and died out. And when we stepped onto the raft I says:

"*Now,* old Jim, you're a free man *again,* and I bet you won't ever be a slave no more."

"En a mighty good job it wuz, too, Huck. It 'uz planned beautiful, en it 'uz *done* beautiful, en dey ain't *nobody* kin git up a plan dat's mo' mixed up en splendid den what dat one wuz."

We was all glad as we could be, but Tom was the gladdest of all because he had a bullet in the calf of his leg.

When me and Jim heard that we didn't feel as brash as what we did before. It was hurting him considerable and bleeding, so we laid him in the wigwam and tore up one of the duke's shirts for to bandage him, but he says:

"Gimme the rags; I can do it myself. Don't stop now; don't fool around here, and the evasion booming along so handsome; man the sweeps, and set her loose! Boys, we done it elegant!—'deed we did. I wish *we'd* 'a' had the handling of Louis XVI, there wouldn't 'a' been no 'Son of Saint Louis, ascend to heaven!' wrote down in *his* biography; no, sir, we'd 'a' whooped him over the *border*—that's what we'd 'a' done with *him*—and done it just as slick as nothing at all, too. Man the sweeps—man the sweeps!"

But me and Jim was consulting—and thinking. And after we'd thought a minute, I says:

"Say it, Jim."

So he says:

"Well, den, dis is de way it look to me, Huck. Ef it wuz *him* dat 'uz dein' sot free, en one er de boys wuz to git shot, would he say, 'Go on en save me, nemmine 'bout a doctor f'r to save dis one'? Is dat like Mars Tom Sawyer? Would he say dat? You *bet* he wouldn't! *Well,* den, is *Jim* gwyne to say it? No, sah—I doan' budge a

step out'n dis place 'dout a *doctor;* not if it's forty
year!"

I knowed he was white inside and I reckoned he'd
say what he did say—so it was all right now, and I told
Tom I was a-going for a doctor. He raised considerable
row about it but me and Jim stuck to it and wouldn't
budge, so he was for crawling out and setting the raft
loose himself, but we wouldn't let him. Then he give us
a piece of his mind but it didn't do no good.

So when he sees me getting the canoe ready, he says:

"Well, then, if you're bound to go, I'll tell you the way
to do when you get to the village. Shut the door and
blindfold the doctor tight and fast and make him swear
to be silent as the grave, and put a purse full of gold in
his hand and then take and lead him all around the
back alleys and everywheres in the dark, and then
fetch him here in the canoe in a roundabout way
amongst the islands, and search him and take his chalk
away from him and don't give it back to him till you
get him back to the village, or else he will chalk this
raft so he can find it again. It's the way they all do."

So I said I would and left, and Jim was to hide in the
woods when he see the doctor coming till he was gone
again.

XLI. "MUST 'A' BEEN SPERITS"

The doctor was an old man, a very nice, kind-look-
ing old man, when I got him up. I told him me and my
brother was over on Spanish Island hunting yesterday
afternoon and camped on a piece of a raft we found,
and about midnight he must 'a' kicked his gun in his
dreams, for it went off and shot him in the leg, and we
wanted him to go over there and fix it and not say

nothing about it, nor let anybody know, because we wanted to come home this evening and surprise the folks.

"Who is your folks?" he says.

"The Phelpses, down yonder."

"Oh," he says. And after a minute, he says:

"How'd you say he got shot?"

"He had a dream," I says, "and it shot him."

"Singular dream," he says.

So he lit up his lantern and got his saddle-bags, and we started. But when he see the canoe he didn't like the look of her—said she was big enough for one, but didn't look pretty safe for two. I says:

"Oh, you needn't be afeard, sir, she carried the three of us easy enough."

"What three?"

"Why, me and Sid, and—and—and *the guns;* that's what I mean."

"Oh," he says.

But he put his foot on the gunnel and rocked her, and shook his head, and said he reckoned he'd look around for a bigger one. But they was all locked and chained, so he took my canoe, and said for me to wait till he come back, or I could hunt around further, or maybe I better go down home and get them ready for the surprise if I wanted to. But I said I didn't; so I told him just how to find the raf', and then he started.

I struck an idea pretty soon. I says to myself, spos'n he can't fix that leg just in three shakes of a sheep's tail, as the saying is? spos'n it takes him three or four days? What are we going to do?—lay around there till he lets the cat out of the bag? No, sir; I know what I'll do. I'll wait, and when he comes back if he says he's got to go any more I'll get down there, too, if I swim; and we'll take and tie him and keep him and shove out down the

river, and when Tom's done with him we'll give him
what it's worth, or all we got, and then let him get
ashore.

So then I crept into a lumber-pile to get some sleep,
and next time I waked up the sun was away up over
my head! I shot out and went for the doctor's house,
but they told me he'd gone away in the night some time
or other and warn't back yet. Well, thinks I, that looks
powerful bad for Tom, and I'll dig out for the island
right off. So away I shoved and turned the corner, and
nearly rammed my head into Uncle Silas's stomach! He
says:

"Why, *Tom!* Where you been all this time, you
rascal?"

"*I* hain't been nowheres," I says, "only just hunting for
the runaway nigger—me and Sid."

"Why, where ever did you go?" he says. "Your aunt's
been mighty uneasy."

"She needn't," I says, "because we was all right. We
followed the men and the dogs but they outrun us and
we lost them, but we thought we heard them on the
water, so we got a canoe and took out after them and
crossed over but couldn't find nothing of them, so we
cruised along up-shore till we got kind of tired and beat
out, and tied up the canoe and went to sleep, and never
waked up till about an hour ago; then we paddle over
here to hear the news and Sid's at the post-office to see
what he can hear, and I'm a-branching out to get something to eat for us, and then we're going home."

So then we went to the post-office to get "Sid"; but
just as I suspicioned, he warn't there; so the old man
he got a letter out of the office and we waited awhile
longer, but Sid didn't come; so the old man said, come
along, let Sid foot it home or canoe it, when he got done
fooling around—but we would ride. I couldn't get him

to let me stay and wait for Sid and he said there warn't
no use in it, and I must come along and let Aunt Sally
see we was all right.

When we got home Aunt Sally was that glad to see
me she laughed and cried both, and hugged me and
give me one of them lickings of hern that don't amount
to shucks, and said she'd serve Sid the same when he
come.

And the place was plum full of farmers and farmers'
wives, to dinner, and such another clack a body never
heard. Old Mrs. Hotchkiss was the worse; her tongue
was a-going all the time. She says:

"Well, Sister Phelps, I've ransacked that-air cabin
over, an' I b'lieve the nigger was crazy. I says so to
Sister Damrell—didn't I, Sister Damrell?—s'I, he's
crazy, s'I—them's the very words I said. You all hearn
me: he's crazy, s'I, everything shows it, s'I. Look at
that-air grindstone, s'I; want to tell *me't* any cretur't's in
his right mind's a-goin' to scrabble all them crazy things
onto a grindstone? s'I. Here sich 'n' sich a person busted
his heart, 'n' here so 'n' so pegged along for thirty-seven
year, 'n' all that—natcherl son o' Louis somebody, 'n'
sich everlast'n' rubbage. He's plumb crazy, s'I; it's what
I says in the fust place, it's what I says in the middle,
'n' it's what I says last 'n' all the time—the nigger's
crazy—crazy's Nebokoodneezer, s'I."

"An' look at that-air ladder made out'n rags, Sister
Hotchkiss," says old Mrs. Damrell; "what in the name o'
goodness *could* he ever want of—"

"The very words I was a-sayin' no longer ago th'n
this minute to Sister Utterback, 'n' she'll tell you so herself. Sh-she, look at that-air rag ladder, sh-she; 'n' s'I,
yes, *look* at it, s'I—what *could* he 'a' wanted of it? s'I.
Sh-she, Sister Hotchkiss, sh-she—"

"But how in the nation'd they ever *git* that grindstone

in there, *anyway?* 'n' who dug that-air *hole?* 'n' who—"

"My very *words,* Brer Penrod! I was a-sayin'—pass
that-air sasser o' m'lasses, won't ye?—I was a-sayin' to
Sister Dunlap, jist this minute, how *did* they git that
grindstone in there? s'I. Without *help,* mind you—'thout
help! Thar's where 'tis. Don't tell *me,* s'I; there *wuz*
help, s'I; 'n' ther' wuz a *plenty* help, too, s'I; ther's ben
a *dozen* a-helpin' that nigger, 'n' I lay I'd skin every last
nigger on this place but *I'd* find out who done it, s'I; 'n'
moreover, s'I—"

"A *dozen* says you!—*forty* couldn't 'a' done everything
that's ben done. Look at them case-knife saws and
things, how tedious they've ben made; look at that bed-
leg sawed off with 'm, a week's work for six men: look
at that nigger made out'n straw on the bed, and look
at—"

"You may *well* say it, Brer Hightower! It's jist as I was
a-sayin' to Brer Phelps, his own self. S'e, what do *you*
think of it, Sister Hotchkiss? s'e. Think o' what, Brer
Phelps? s'I. Think o' that bed-leg sawed off that a way?
s'e. *Think* of it? s'I. I lay it never sawed *itself* off, s'I—
somebody *sawed* it, s'I; that's my opinion, take it or
leave it, it mayn't be no 'count, s'I, but sich as 'tis, it's my
opinion, s'I, 'n' if anybody k'n start a better one, s'I,
let him *do* it, s'I, that's all. I says to Sister Dunlap, s'I—"

"Why, dog my cats, they must 'a' ben a house-full o'
niggers in there every night for four weeks to 'a' done
all that work, Sister Phelps. Look at that shirt—every
last inch of it kivered over with secret African writ'n'
done with blood! Must 'a' ben a raft uv 'm at it right
along, all the time, amost. Why, I'd give two dollars to
have it read to me; 'n' as for the niggers that wrote it, I
'low I'd take 'n' lash 'm t'll—"

"People to *help* him, Brother Marples! Well, I reckon
you'd *think* so if you'd 'a' been in this house for a while

back. Why, they've stole everything they could lay their
hands on—and we a-watching all the time, mind you.
They stole that shirt right off o' the line! and as for that
sheet they made the rag ladder out of, ther' ain't no
telling how many times they *didn't* steal that; and flour
and candles and candlesticks and spoons and the old
warming-pan, and most a thousand things that I disremember now, and my new calico dress; and me and
Silas and my Sid and Tom on the constant watch day
and night, as I was a-telling you, and not a one of us
could catch hide nor hair nor sight nor sound of them;
and here at the last minute, lo and behold you, they
slides right in under our noses and fools us, and not
only fools *us* but the Injun Territory robbers too, and
actuly gets *away* with that nigger safe and sound, and
that with sixteen men and twenty-two dogs right on their
very heels at that very time! I tell you, it just bangs anything I ever *heard* of. Why, *sperits* couldn't 'a' done
better and been no smarter. And I reckon they must 'a'
been sperits—because, *you* know our dogs, and ther'
ain't no better; well, them dogs never even got on the
track of 'm once! You explain *that* to me if you can!—
any of you!"

"Well, it does beat—"

"Laws alive, I never—"

"So help me, I wouldn't 'a' be—"

"*House*-thieves as well as—"

"Goodnessgracioussakes, I'd 'a' ben afeard to *live* in
sich a—"

"'Fraid to *live!*—why, I was that scared I dasn't
hardly go to bed, or get up, or lay down, or *set* down,
Sister Ridgeway. Why, they'd steal the very—why,
goodness sakes, you can guess what kind of a fluster *I*
was in by the time midnight come last night. I hope to
gracious if I warn't afraid they'd steal some o' the family!

I was just to that pass I didn't have no reasoning faculties no more. It looks foolish enough *now,* in the daytime, but I says to myself, there's my two poor boys
asleep, 'way up-stairs in that lonesome room, and I
declare to goodness I was that uneasy 't I crep' up there
and locked 'em in! I *did.* And anybody would. Because,
you know, when you get scared that way, and it keeps
running on and getting worse and worse all the time,
and your wits gets to addling, and you get to doing all
sorts o' wild things, and by and by you think to yourself,
spos'n *I* was a boy, and was away up there, and the
door ain't locked, and you—" She stopped, looking kind
of wondering, and then she turned her head around slow
and when her eye lit on me—I got up and took a walk.

Says I to myself, I can explain better how we come to
not be in that room this morning if I go out to one side
and study over it a little. So I done it. But I dasn't go
fur or she'd 'a' sent for me. And when it was late in the
day the people all went, and then I come in and told
her the noise and shooting waked up me and "Sid," and
the door was locked, and we wanted to see the fun, so
we went down the lightning-rod, and both of us got
hurt a little, and we didn't never want to try *that* no
more. And then I went on and told her all what I told
Uncle Silas before, and then she said she'd forgive us,
and maybe it was all right enough anyway and about
what a body might expect of boys, for all boys was a
pretty harum-scarum lot as fur as she could see; and so,
as long as no harm hadn't come of it, she judged she
better put in her time being grateful we was alive and
well and she had us still, stead of fretting over what was
past and done. So then she kissed me, and patted me on
the head, and dropped into a kind of a brown-study,
and pretty soon jumps up and says:

"Why, lawsamercy, it's most night, and Sid not come yet! What *has* become of that boy?"

I see my chance; so I skips up and says:

"I'll run right up to town and get him," I says.

"No you won't," she says. "You'll stay right wher' you are; *one's* enough to be lost at a time. If he ain't here to supper, your uncle'll go."

Well, he warn't there to supper, so right after supper Uncle went.

He come back about ten a little bit uneasy; hadn't run across Tom's track. Aunt Sally was a good *deal* uneasy, but Uncle Silas he said there warn't no occasion to be—boys will be boys, he said, and you'll see this one turn up in the morning all sound and right. So she had to be satisfied. But she said she'd set up for him awhile anyway, and keep a light burning so he could see it.

And then when I went up to bed she come up with me and fetched her candle and tucked me in, and mothered me so good I felt mean and like I couldn't look her in the face, and she set down on the bed and talked with me a long time and said what a splendid boy Sid was, and didn't seem to want to ever stop talking about him, and kept asking me every now and then if I reckoned he could 'a' got lost or hurt or maybe drownded, and might be laying at this minute somewheres suffering or dead, and she not by him to help him, and so the tears would drip down silent, and I would tell her that Sid was all right and would be home in the morning, sure; and she would squeeze my hand or maybe kiss me, and tell me to say it again and keep on saying it, because it done her good, and she was in so much trouble. And when she was going away she looked down in my eyes so steady and gentle, and says:

"The door ain't going to be locked, Tom, and there's

the window and the rod; but you'll be good, *won't* you?
And you won't go? For *my* sake."

Laws knows I *wanted* to go bad enough to see about
Tom, and was all intending to go, but after that I
wouldn't 'a' went, not for kingdoms.

But she was on my mind and Tom was on my mind,
so I slept very restless. And twice I went down the rod
away in the night, and slipped around front and see her
setting there by her candle in the window with her eyes
towards the road and the tears in them, and I wished I
could do something for her, but I couldn't, only to swear
that I wouldn't never do nothing to grieve her any more.
And the third time I waked up at dawn and slid down,
and she was there yet and her candle was most out, and
her old gray head was resting on her hand, and she was
asleep.

XLII. WHY THEY DIDN'T HANG JIM

The old man was up-town again before breakfast but
couldn't get no track of Tom, and both of them set at
the table thinking and not saying nothing, and looking
mournful, and their coffee getting cold, and not eating
anything. And by and by the old man says:

"Did I give you the letter?"

"What letter?"

"The one I got yesterday out of the post-office."

"No, you didn't give me no letter."

"Well, I must 'a' forgot it."

So he rummaged his pockets and then went off somewheres where he had laid it down, and fetched it and
give it to her. She says:

"Why, it's from St. Petersburg—it's from Sis."

I allowed another walk would do me good, but I
couldn't stir. But before she could break it open she

dropped it and run—for she see something. And so did I. It was Tom Sawyer on a mattress, and that old doctor, and Jim, in *her* calico dress with his hands tied behind him, and a lot of people. I hid the letter behind the first thing that come handy, and rushed. She flung herself at Tom, crying, and says:

"Oh, he's dead, he's dead, I know he's dead!"

And Tom he turned his head a little and muttered something or other, which showed he warn't in his right mind; then she flung up her hands and says:

"He's alive, thank God! And that's enough!" and she snatched a kiss of him, and flew for the house to get the bed ready, and scattering orders right and left at the niggers and everybody else as fast as her tongue could go, every jump of the way.

I followed the men to see what they was going to do with Jim, and the old doctor and Uncle Silas followed after Tom into the house. The men was very huffy and some of them wanted to hang Jim for an example to all the other niggers around there, so they wouldn't be trying to run away like Jim done, and making such a raft of trouble and keeping a whole family scared most to death for days and nights. But the others said, don't do it, it wouldn't answer at all; he ain't our nigger and his owner would turn up and make us pay for him, sure. So that cooled them down a little, because the people that's always the most anxious for to hang a nigger that hain't done just right is always the very ones that ain't the most anxious to pay for him when they've got their satisfaction out of him.

They cussed Jim considerble, though, and give him a cuff or two side the head once in a while, but Jim never said nothing and he never let on to know me, and they took him to the same cabin and put his own clothes on him and chained him again, and not to no bed-leg this time but to a big staple drove into the bottom log, and chained his hands, too, and both legs, and said he warn't to have nothing but bread and water to eat after this till his owner come, or he was sold at auction because he didn't come in a certain length of time, and filled up our hole, and said a couple of farmers with guns must stand watch around about the cabin every night, and a bulldog tied to the door in the day-time; and about this time they was through with the job and was tapering off with a kind of genrl good-by cussing, and then the old doctor comes and takes a look and says:

"Don't be no rougher on him than you're obleeged to, because he ain't a bad nigger. When I got to where I found the boy I see I couldn't cut the bullet out without some help, and he warn't in no condition for me to leave to go and get help; and he got a little worse and a little worse, and after a long time he went out of his head and wouldn't let me come a-nigh him any more, and said if I chalked his raft he'd kill me, and no end of wild foolishness like that, and I see I couldn't do anything at all with him; so I says, I got to have *help* somehow; and the minute I says it out crawls this nigger from somewheres and says he'll help, and he done it, too, and done it very well. Of course I judged he must be a runaway nigger, and there I *was!* and there I had to stick right straight along all the rest of the day and all night. It was a fix, I tell you! I had a couple of patients with the chills, and of course I'd of liked to run up to town and see them, but I dasn't, because the nigger might get away, and then I'd be to blame; and yet never a skiff come close enough for me to hail. So there I had to stick plumb until daylight this morning; and I never see a nigger that was a better nuss or faithfuler, and yet he was resking his freedom to do it, and was all tired out, too, and I see plain enough he'd been worked main hard lately. I liked

the nigger for that; I tell you, gentlemen, a nigger like
that is worth a thousand dollars—and kind treatment,
too. I had everything I needed, and the boy was doing
as well there as he would 'a' done at home, better,
maybe, because it was so quiet; but there I *was*, with
both of 'm on my hands, and there I had to stick till
about dawn this morning; then some men in a skiff
come by, and as good luck would have it the nigger was
setting by the pallet with his head propped on his knees
sound asleep; so I motioned them in quiet, and they
slipped up on him and grabbed him and tied him before
he knowed what he was about, and we never had no
trouble. And the boy being in a kind of a flighty sleep,
too, we muffled the oars and hitched the raft on, and
towed her over very nice and quiet, and the nigger never
made the least row nor said a word from the start. He
ain't no bad nigger, gentlemen; that's what I think about
him."

Somebody says:

"Well, it sounds very good, doctor, I'm obleeged to
say."

Then the others softened up a little, too, and I was
mighty thankful to that old doctor for doing Jim that
good turn; and I was glad it was according to my judgment of him, too; because I thought he had a good heart
in him and was a good man the first time I see him.
Then they all agreed that Jim had acted very well, and
was deserving to have some notice took of it, and reward. So every one of them promised, right out and
hearty, that they wouldn't cuss him no more.

Then they come out and locked him up. I hoped they
was going to say he could have one or two of the chains
took off, because they was rotten heavy, or could have
meat and greens with his bread and water; but they
didn't think of it and I reckoned it warn't best for me to

mix in, but I judged I'd get the doctor's yarn to Aunt
Sally somehow or other as soon as I'd got through the
breakers that was laying just ahead of me—explana-
tions, I mean, of how I forgot to mention about Sid being
shot when I was telling how him and me put in that
dratted night paddling around hunting the runaway
nigger.

But I had plenty time. Aunt Sally she stuck to the
sick-room all day and all night, and every time I see
Uncle Silas mooning around I dodged him.

Next morning I heard Tom was a good deal better and
they said Aunt Sally was gone to get a nap. So I slips to
the sick-room, and if I found him awake I reckoned we
could put up a yarn for the family that would wash. But
he was sleeping, and sleeping very peaceful, too, and
pale, not fire-faced the way he was when he come. So I
set down and laid for him to wake. In about half an
hour Aunt Sally comes gliding in, and there I was, up a
stump again! She motioned me to be still, and set down
by me and begun to whisper, and said we could all be
joyful now, because all the symptoms was first-rate, and
he'd been sleeping like that for ever so long and looking
better and peacefuler all the time, and ten to one he'd
wake up in his right mind.

So we set there watching, and by and by he stirs a bit
and opens his eyes very natural and takes a look, and
says:

"Hello!—why, I'm at *home!* How's that? Where's the
raft?"

"It's all right," I says.

"And *Jim?*"

"The same," I says, but couldn't say it pretty brash.
But he never noticed, but says:

"Good! Splendid! *Now* we're all right and safe! Did
you tell Aunty?"

I was going to say yes; but she chipped in and says:
"About what, Sid?"

"Why, about the way the whole thing was done."

"What whole thing?"

"Why, *the* whole thing. There ain't but one; how we set the runaway nigger free—me and Tom."

"Good land! Set the run— What *is* the child talking about! Dear, dear, out of his head again!"

"*No*, I ain't out of my HEAD; I know all what I'm talking about. We *did* set him free—me and Tom. We laid out to do it and we *done* it. And we done it elegant, too." He'd got a start and she never checked him up, just set and stared and stared, and let him clip along, and I see it warn't no use for *me* to put in. "Why, Aunty, it cost us a power of work—weeks of it—hours and hours, every night, whilst you was all asleep. And we had to steal candles and the sheet and the shirt and your dress, and spoons and tin plates and case-knives, and the warming-pan and the grindstone and flour, and just no end of things, and you can't think what work it was to make the saws and pens and inscriptions and one thing or another, and you can't think *half* the fun it was. And we had to make up the pictures of coffins and things and nonnamous letters from the robbers, and get up and down the lightning-rod, and dig the hole into the cabin and make the rope ladder and send it in cooked up in a pie, and send in spoons and things to work with in your apron pocket—"

"Mercy sakes!"

"—and load up the cabin with rats and snakes and so on, for company for Jim; and then you kept Tom here so long with the butter in his hat that you come near spiling the whole business, because the men come before we was out of the cabin, and we had to rush, and they heard us and let drive at us, and I got my share, and we dodged out of the path and let them go by, and when the dogs come they warn't interested in us but went for the most noise, and we got our canoe and made for the raft, and was all safe, and Jim was a free man, and we done it all by ourselves, and *wasn't* it bully, Aunty!"

"Well, I never heard the likes of it in all my born days! So it was *you*, you little rapscallions, that's been making all this trouble, and turned everybody's wits clean inside out and scared us all most to death. I've as good a notion as ever I had in my life to take it out o' you this very minute. To think, here I've been, night after night, a—*you* just get well once, you young scamp, and I lay I'll tan the Old Harry out o' both o' ye!"

But Tom, he *was* so proud and joyful, he just *couldn't* hold in, and his tongue just *went* it—she a-chipping in and spitting fire all along, and both of them going it at once, like a cat convention, and she says:

"*Well*, you get all the enjoyment you can out of it *now*, for mind I tell you if I catch you meddling with him again—"

"Meddling with *who*?" Tom says, dropping his smile and looking surprised.

"With *who*? Why, the runaway nigger, of course. Who'd you reckon?"

Tom looks at me very grave, and says:

"Tom, didn't you just tell me he was all right? Hasn't he got away?"

"*Him*?" says Aunt Sally; "the runaway nigger? 'Deed he hasn't. They've got him back, safe and sound, and he's in that cabin again, on bread and water and loaded down with chains, till he's claimed or sold!"

Tom rose square up in bed, with his eye hot, and his nostrils opening and shutting like gills, and sings out to me:

"They hain't no *right* to shut him up! *Shove!*—and don't you lose a minute. Turn him loose! he ain't no slave. He's as free as any cretur that walks this earth!"

"What *does* the child mean?"

"I mean every word I *say*, Aunt Sally, and if somebody don't go, *I'll* go. I've knowed him all his life and so has Tom, there. Old Miss Watson died two months ago, and she was ashamed she ever was going to sell him down the river, and *said* so; and she set him free in her will."

Then what on earth did *you* want to set him free for, seeing he was already free?"

"Well, that *is* a question, I must say; and *just* like women! Why, I wanted the *adventure* of it, and I'd 'a' waded neck-deep in blood to—goodness alive, AUNT POLLY!"

If she warn't standing right there, just inside the door, looking as sweet and contented as an angel half full of pie, I wish I may never!

Aunt Sally jumped for her and most hugged the head off of her and cried over her, and I found a good enough place for me under the bed, for it was getting pretty sultry for *us*, seemed to me. And I peeped out, and in a little while Tom's Aunt Polly shook herself loose and stood there looking across at Tom over her spectacles—kind of grinding him into the earth, you know. And then she says:

"Yes, you *better* turn y'r head away—I would if I was you, Tom."

"Oh, deary me!" says Aunt Sally; "*is* he changed so? Why, that ain't *Tom*, it's Sid; Tom's—Tom's—why, where is Tom? He was here a minute ago."

"You mean where's Huck *Finn*—that's what you mean! I reckon I hain't raised such a scamp as my Tom all these years not to know him when I *see* him. That *would* be a pretty howdy-do. Come out from under that bed, Huck Finn."

So I done it. But not feeling brash.

Aunt Sally she was one of the mixed-upest-looking persons I ever see—except one, and that was Uncle Silas, when he come in and they told it all to him. It kind of made him drunk, as you may say, and he didn't know nothing at all the rest of the day, and preached a prayer-meeting sermon that night that gave him a rattling ruputation, because the oldest man in the world couldn't 'a' understood it. So Tom's Aunt Polly she told all about who I was, and what; and I had to up and tell how I was in such a tight place that when Mrs. Phelps took me for Tom Sawyer—she chipped in and says, "Oh, go on and call me Aunt Sally, I'm used to it now, and 'tain't no need to change"—that when Aunt Sally took me for Tom Sawyer I had to stand it—there warn't no other way and I knowed he wouldn't mind, because it would be nuts for him, being a mystery, and he'd make an adventure out of it and be perfectly satisfied. And so it turned out, and he let on to be Sid and made things as soft as he could for me.

And his Aunt Polly she said Tom was right about old Miss Watson setting Jim free in her will; and so, sure enough, Tom Sawyer had gone and took all that trouble and bother to set a free nigger free! and I couldn't ever understand before, until that minute and that talk, how he *could* help a body set a nigger free with his bringing-up.

Well, Aunt Polly she said that when Aunt Sally wrote to her that Tom and *Sid* had come all right and safe, she says to herself:

"Look at that, now! I might have expected it, letting him go off that way without anybody to watch him. So now I got to go and trapse all the way down the river, eleven hundred mile, and find out what that creetur's up to *this* time, as long as I couldn't seem to get any answer out of you about it."

"Why, I never heard nothing from you," says Aunt Sally.

"Well, I wonder! Why, I wrote you twice to ask you what you could mean by Sid being here."

"Well, I never got 'em, Sis."

Aunt Polly she turns around slow and severe, and says:

"You, Tom!"

"Well—*what?*" he says, kind of pettish.

"Don't you what *me*, you impudent thing—hand out them letters."

"What letters?"

"*Them* letters. I be bound, if I have to take a-holt of you I'll—"

"They're in the trunk. There, now. And they're just the same as they was when I got them out of the office. I hain't looked into them, I hain't touched them. But I knowed they'd make trouble, and I thought if you warn't in no hurry, I'd—"

"Well, you *do* need skinning, there ain't no mistake about it. And I wrote another one to tell you I was coming; and I s'pose he—"

"No, it come yesterday; I hain't read it yet but *it's* all right, I've got that one."

I wanted to offer to bet two dollars she hadn't, but I reckoned maybe it was just as safe to not to. So I never said nothing.

The first time I catched Tom private I asked him what was his idea, time of the evasion?—what it was he'd planned to do if the evasion worked all right and he managed to set a nigger free that was already free before? And he said, what he had planned in his head from the start, if we got Jim out all safe, was for us to run him down the river on the raft and have adventures plumb to the mouth of the river, and then tell him about his being free and take him back up home on a steamboat in style, and pay him for his lost time, and write word ahead and get out all the niggers around and have them waltz him into town with a torchlight procession and a brass-band, and then he would be a hero, and so would we. But I reckoned it was about as well the way it was.

We had Jim out of the chains in no time, and when Aunt Polly and Uncle Silas and Aunt Sally found out how good he helped the doctor nurse Tom, they made a heap of fuss over him and fixed him up prime, and give him all he wanted to eat and a good time and nothing to do. And we had him up to the sick-room and had a high talk; and Tom give Jim forty dollars for being prisoner for us so patient, and doing it up so good, and Jim was pleased most to death and busted out and says:

"*Dah*, now, Huck, what I tell you?—what I tell you up dah on Jackson Islan'? I *tole* you I got a hairy breas', en what's de sign un it; en I *tole* you I ben rich wunst, en gwineter to be rich *agin;* en it's come true; en heah she *is! Dah,* now! doan' talk to *me*—signs is *signs,* mine I tell you; en I knowed jis' 's well 'at I 'uz gwineter be rich agin as I's a-stannin' heah dis minute!"

And then Tom he talked along and talked along, and says, le's all three slide out of here one of these nights

and get an outfit and go for howling adventures amongst
the Injuns, over in the Territory, for a couple of weeks
or two; and I says, all right, that suits me, but I ain't
got no money for to buy the outfit and I reckon I
couldn't get none from home, because it's likely pap's
been back before now and got it all away from Judge
Thatcher and drunk it up.

"No, he hain't," Tom says, "it's all there yet—six
thousand dollars and more; and your pap hain't ever
been back since. Hadn't when I come away, anyhow."

Jim says, kind of solemn:

"He ain't a-comin' back no mo', Huck."

I says:

"Why, Jim?"

"Nemmine why, Huck—but he ain't comin' back no
mo'."

But I kept at him, so at last he says:

"Doan' you 'member de house dat was float'n' down
de river, en dey wuz a man in dah, kivered up, en I
went in en unkivered him and didn' let you come in?
Well, den, you kin git yo' money when you wants it, kase
dat wuz him."

Tom's most well now, and got his bullet around his
neck on a watch-guard for a watch, and is always seeing
what time it is, and so there ain't nothing more to write
about, and I am rotten glad of it, because if I'd 'a'
knowed what a trouble it was to make a book I wouldn't
'a' tackled it, and ain't a-going to no more. But I reckon
I got to light out for the Territory ahead of the rest, because Aunt Sally she's going to adopt me and sivilize
me, and I can't stand it. I been there before.

Fenimore Cooper's Literary Offenses

The Pathfinder and *The Deerslayer* stand at the head of Cooper's novels as artistic creations. There are others of his works which contain parts as perfect as are to be found in these, and scenes even more thrilling. Not one can be compared with either of them as a finished whole.

The defects in both of these tales are comparatively slight. They were pure works of art.—*Prof. Lounsbury.*

The five tales reveal an extraordinary fullness of invention.
. . . One of the very greatest characters in fiction, Natty Bumppo. . . .

The craft of the woodsman, the tricks of the trapper, all the delicate art of the forest, were familiar to Cooper from his youth up.—*Prof. Brander Matthews.*

Cooper is the greatest artist in the domain of romantic fiction yet produced by America.—*Wilkie Collins.*

IT SEEMS to me that it was far from right for the Professor of English Literature in Yale, the Professor of English Literature in Columbia, and Wilkie Collins to deliver opinions on Cooper's literature without having read some of it. It would have been much more decorous to keep silent and let persons talk who have read Cooper.

Cooper's art has some defects. In one place in *Deerslayer,* and in the restricted space of two-thirds of a page, Cooper has scored 114 offenses against literary art out of a possible 115. It breaks the record.

There are nineteen rules governing literary art in the domain of romantic fiction—some say twenty-two. In

Deerslayer Cooper violated eighteen of them. These eighteen require:

1. That a tale shall accomplish something and arrive somewhere. But the *Deerslayer* tale accomplishes nothing and arrives in the air.

2. They require that the episodes of a tale shall be necessary parts of the tale and shall help to develop it. But as the *Deerslayer* tale is not a tale and accomplishes nothing and arrives nowhere, the episodes have no rightful place in the work, since there was nothing for them to develop.

3. They require that the personages in a tale shall be alive, except in the case of corpses, and that always the reader shall be able to tell the corpses from the others. But this detail has often been overlooked in the *Deerslayer* tale.

4. They require that the personages in a tale, both dead and alive, shall exhibit a sufficient excuse for being there. But this detail also has been overlooked in the *Deerslayer* tale.

5. They require that when the personages of a tale deal in conversation, the talk shall sound like human talk, and be talk such as human beings would be likely to talk in the given circumstances, and have a discoverable meaning, also a discoverable purpose and a show of relevancy, and remain in the neighborhood of the subject in hand, and be interesting to the reader, and help out the tale, and stop when the people cannot think of anything more to say. But this requirement has been ignored from the beginning of the *Deerslayer* tale to the end of it.

6. They require that when the author describes the character of a personage in his tale, the conduct and conversation of that personage shall justify said descrip-

tion. But this law gets little or no attention in the *Deer-slayer* tale, as Natty Bumppo's case will amply prove.

7. They require that when a personage talks like an illustrated, gilt-edged, tree-calf, hand-tooled, seven-dollar Friendship's Offering in the beginning of a paragraph, he shall not talk like a Negro minstrel in the end of it. But this rule is flung down and danced upon in the *Deerslayer* tale.

8. They require that crass stupidities shall not be played upon the reader as "the craft of the woodsman, the delicate art of the forest," by either the author or the people in the tale. But this rule is persistently violated in the *Deerslayer* tale.

9. They require that the personages of a tale shall confine themselves to possibilities and let miracles alone; or, if they venture a miracle, the author must so plausibly set it forth as to make it look possible and reasonable. But these rules are not respected in the *Deerslayer* tale.

10. They require that the author shall make the reader feel a deep interest in the personages of his tale and in their fate, and that he shall make the reader love the good people in the tale and hate the bad ones. But the reader of the *Deerslayer* tale dislikes the good people in it, is indifferent to the others, and wishes they would all get drowned together.

11. They require that the characters in a tale shall be so clearly defined that the reader can tell beforehand what each will do in a given emergency. But in the *Deerslayer* tale this rule is vacated.

In addition to these large rules there are some little ones. These require that the author shall

12. *Say* what he is proposing to say, not merely come near it.

13. Use the right word, not its second cousin.
14. Eschew surplusage.
15. Not omit necessary details.
16. Avoid slovenliness of form.
17. Use good grammar.
18. Employ a simple and straightforward style.

Even these seven are coldly and persistently violated in the *Deerslayer* tale.

Cooper's gift in the way of invention was not a rich endowment but such as it was he liked to work it, he was pleased with the effects, and indeed he did some quite sweet things with it. In his little box of stage-properties he kept six or eight cunning devices, tricks, artifices for his savages and woodsmen to deceive and circumvent each other with, and he was never so happy as when he was working these innocent things and seeing them go. A favorite one was to make a moccasined person tread in the tracks of the moccasined enemy, and thus hide his own trail. Cooper wore out barrels and barrels of moccasins in working that trick. Another stage-property that he pulled out of his box pretty frequently was his broken twig. He prized his broken twig above all the rest of his effects, and worked it the hardest. It is a restful chapter in any book of his when somebody doesn't step on a dry twig and alarm all the reds and whites for two hundred yards around. Every time a Cooper person is in peril and absolute silence is worth four dollars a minute, he is sure to step on a dry twig. There may be a hundred handier things to step on but that wouldn't satisfy Cooper. Cooper requires him to turn out and find a dry twig, and if he can't do it, go and borrow one. In fact, the Leatherstocking Series ought to have been called the Broken Twig Series.

I am sorry there is not room to put in a few dozen instances of the delicate art of the forest, as practised by Natty Bumppo and some of the other Cooperian experts. Perhaps we may venture two or three samples. Cooper was a sailor, a naval officer; yet he gravely tells us how a vessel, driving toward a lee shore in a gale, is steered for a particular spot by her skipper because he knows of an *undertow* there which will hold her back against the gale and save her. For just pure woodcraft, or sailorcraft, or whatever it is, isn't that neat? For several years Cooper was daily in the society of artillery and he ought to have noticed that when a cannon-ball strikes the ground it either buries itself or skips a hundred feet or so, skips again a hundred feet or so, and so on till finally it gets tired and rolls. Now in one place he loses some "females"—as he always calls women—in the edge of a wood near a plain at night in a fog, on purpose to give Bumppo a chance to show off the delicate art of the forest before the reader. These mislaid people are hunting for a fort. They hear a cannon-blast, and a cannon-ball presently comes rolling into the wood and stops at their feet. To the females this suggests nothing. The case is very different with the admirable Bumppo. I wish I may never know peace again if he doesn't strike out promptly and *follow the track* of that cannon-ball across the plain through the dense fog and find the fort. Isn't it a daisy? If Cooper had any real knowledge of Nature's ways of doing things, he had a most delicate art in concealing the fact. For instance: one of his acute Indian experts, Chingachgook (pronounced Chicago, I think), has lost the trail of a person he is tracking through the forest. Apparently that trail is hopelessly lost. Neither you nor I could ever have guessed out the way to find it. It was very different with Chicago. Chicago was not stumped for long. He turned a running stream out of its course and there, in the slush in its old bed, were that person's moccasin tracks. The current did not wash them away, as it would have done in all other like cases—no, even the eternal laws of Nature have to vacate when Cooper wants to put up a delicate job of woodcraft on the reader.

We must be a little wary when Brander Matthews tells us that Cooper's books "reveal an extraordinary fullness of invention." As a rule, I am quite willing to accept Brander Matthews's literary judgments and applaud his lucid and graceful phrasing of them, but that particular statement needs to be taken with a few tons of salt. Bless your heart, Cooper hadn't any more invention than a horse, and I don't mean a high-class horse, either, I mean a clothes-horse. It would be very difficult to find a really clever "situation" in Cooper's books, and still more difficult to find one of any kind which he has failed to render absurd by his handling of it. Look at the episodes of "the caves"; and at the celebrated scuffle between Maqua and those others on the table-land a few days later; and at Hurry Harry's queer water-transit from the castle to the ark; and at Deerslayer's half-hour with his first corpse; and at the quarrel between Hurry Harry and Deerslayer later; and at— But choose for yourself, you can't go amiss.

If Cooper had been an observer his inventive faculty would have worked better: not more interestingly but more rationally, more plausibly. Cooper's proudest creations in the way of "situations" suffer noticeably from the absence of the observer's protecting gift. Cooper's eye was splendidly inaccurate. Cooper seldom saw anything correctly. He saw nearly all things as through a glass eye, darkly. Of course a man who cannot see the commonest little every-day matters accurately is working at a disadvantage when he is constructing a "situation." In the *Deerslayer* tale Cooper has a stream which is fifty feet wide where it flows out of a lake; it presently narrows to twenty as it meanders along for no given reason, and yet when a stream acts like that it ought to be required to explain itself. Fourteen pages later the width of the brook's outlet from the lake has suddenly shrunk thirty feet and become "the narrowest part of the stream." This shrinkage is not accounted for. The stream has bends in it, a sure indication that it has alluvial banks and cuts them, yet these bends are only thirty and fifty feet long. If Cooper had been a nice and punctilious observer he would have noticed that the bends were oftener nine hundred feet long than short of it.

Cooper made the exit of that stream fifty feet wide in the first place for no particular reason; in the second place, he narrowed it to less than twenty to accommodate some Indians. He bends a "sapling" to the form of an arch over this narrow passage and conceals six Indians in its foliage. They are "laying" for a settler's scow or ark which is coming up the stream on its way to the lake; it is being hauled against the stiff current by a rope whose stationary end is anchored in the lake; its rate of progress cannot be more than a mile an hour. Cooper describes the ark, but pretty obscurely. In the matter of dimensions "it was little more than a modern canal-boat." Let us guess, then, that it was about one hundred and forty feet long. It was of "greater breadth than common." Let us guess, then, that it was about sixteen feet wide. This leviathan had been prowling down bends which were but a third as long as itself and scraping between banks where it had only two feet of space to spare on each side. We cannot too much admire this miracle. A low-roofed log dwelling occupies "two-thirds of the ark's length"—a dwelling ninety feet long and sixteen feet wide, let us say, a kind of vestibule train. The dwelling has two rooms, each forty-five feet long and sixteen feet wide, let us guess. One of them is the bedroom of the Hutter girls, Judith and Hetty; the other is the parlor in the daytime, at night it is papa's bed-chamber. The ark is arriving at the stream's exit now, whose width has been reduced to less than twenty feet to accommodate the Indians—say to eighteen. There is a foot to spare on each side of the boat. Did the Indians notice that there was going to be a tight squeeze there? Did they notice that they could make money by climbing down out of that arched sapling and just stepping aboard when the ark scraped by? No, other Indians would have noticed these things but Cooper's Indians never notice anything. Cooper thinks they are marvelous creatures for noticing but he was almost always in error about his Indians. There was seldom a sane one among them.

The ark is one hundred and forty feet long; the dwelling is ninety feet long. The idea of the Indians is to drop softly and secretly from the arched sapling to the dwelling as the ark creeps along under it at the rate of a mile an hour, and butcher the family. It will take the ark a minute and a half to pass under. It will take the ninety-foot dwelling a minute to pass under. Now, then, what did the six Indians do? It would take you thirty years to guess and even then you would have to give up, I believe. Therefore, I will tell you what the Indians did. Their chief, a person of quite extraordinary intellect for a Cooper Indian, warily watched the canal-boat as it squeezed along under him and when he had got his calculations fined down to exactly the right shade, as he judged, he let go and dropped. And *missed the house!* That is actually what he did. He missed the house and landed in the stern of the scow. It was not much of a fall, yet it knocked him silly. He lay there unconscious. If the house had been ninety-seven feet long he would

have made the trip. The fault was Cooper's, not his.
The error lay in the construction of the house. Cooper
was no architect.

There still remained in the roost five Indians. The
boat has passed under and is now out of their reach.
Let me explain what the five did—you would not be
able to reason it out for yourself. No. 1 jumped for the
boat but fell in the water astern of it. Then No. 2 jumped
for the boat but fell in the water still farther astern of
it. Then No. 3 jumped for the boat and fell a good
way astern of it. Then No. 4 jumped for the boat and
fell in the water *away* astern. Then even No. 5 made a
jump for the boat—for he was a Cooper Indian. In the
matter of intellect, the difference between a Cooper
Indian and the Indian that stands in front of the cigar-
shop is not spacious. The scow episode is really a sublime burst of invention but it does not thrill, because the
inaccuracy of the details throws a sort of air of fictitious-
ness and general improbability over it. This comes of
Cooper's inadequacy as an observer.

The reader will find some examples of Cooper's high
talent for inaccurate observation in the account of the
shooting-match in *The Pathfinder*.

A common wrought nail was driven lightly into the target,
its head having been first touched with paint.

The color of the paint is not stated—an important
omission, but Cooper deals freely in important omis-
sions. No, after all, it was not an important omission,
for this nail-head is *a hundred yards from* the marksmen and could not be seen by them at that distance, no
matter what its color might be. How far can the best
eyes see a common house-fly? A hundred yards? It is
quite impossible. Very well, eyes that cannot see a
house-fly that is a hundred yards away cannot see an

ordinary nail-head at that distance, for the size of the two objects is the same. It takes a keen eye to see a fly or a nail-head at fifty yards—one hundred and fifty feet. Can the reader do it?

The nail was lightly driven, its head painted, and game called. Then the Cooper miracles began. The bullet of the first marksman chipped an edge of the nail-head; the next man's bullet drove the nail a little way into the target—and removed all the paint. Haven't the miracles gone far enough now? Not to suit Cooper, for the purpose of this whole scheme is to show off his prodigy, Deerslayer-Hawkeye-Long-Rifle-Leatherstocking-Pathfinder-Bumppo before the ladies.

"Be all ready to clench it, boys!" cried out Pathfinder, stepping into his friend's tracks the instant they were vacant. "Never mind a new nail; I can see that, though the paint is gone, and what I can see I can hit at a hundred yards, though it were only a mosquito's eye. Be ready to clench!"

The rifle cracked, the bullet sped its way, and the head of the nail was buried in the wood, covered by the piece of flattened lead.

There, you see, is a man who could hunt flies with a rifle, and command a ducal salary in a Wild West show today if we had him back with us.

The recorded feat is certainly surprising just as it stands, but it is not surprising enough for Cooper. Cooper adds a touch. He has made Pathfinder do this miracle with another man's rifle; and not only that, but Pathfinder did not have even the advantage of loading it himself. He had everything against him, and yet he made that impossible shot, and not only made it but did it with absolute confidence, saying, "Be ready to clench." Now a person like that would have undertaken the same feat with a brickbat, and with Cooper to help he would have achieved it, too.

Pathfinder showed off handsomely that day before the ladies. His very first feat was a thing which no Wild West show can touch. He was standing with the group of marksmen, observing—a hundred yards from the target, mind; one Jasper raised his rifle and drove the center of the bull's-eye. Then the Quartermaster fired. The target exhibited no result this time. There was a laugh. "It's a dead miss," said Major Lundie. Pathfinder waited an impressive moment or two, then said in that calm, indifferent, know-it-all way of his, "No, Major, he has covered Jasper's bullet, as will be seen if anyone will take the trouble to examine the target."

Wasn't it remarkable! How *could* he see that little pellet fly through the air and enter that distant bullet-hole? Yet that is what he did, for nothing is impossible to a Cooper person. Did any of those people have any deep-seated doubts about this thing? No; for that would imply sanity and these were all Cooper people.

The respect for Pathfinder's skill and for his *quickness and accuracy of sight* [the italics are mine] was so profound and general, that the instant he made this declaration the spectators began to distrust their own opinions, and a dozen rushed to the target in order to ascertain the fact. There, sure enough, it was found that the Quartermaster's bullet had gone through the hole made by Jasper's, and that, too, so accurately as to require a minute examination to be certain of the circumstance, which, however, was soon clearly established by discovering one bullet over the other in the stump against which the target was placed.

They made a "minute" examination; but never mind, how could they know that there were two bullets in that hole without digging the latest one out? for neither probe nor eyesight could prove the presence of any more than one bullet. Did they dig? No; as we shall see. It is the Pathfinder's turn now; he steps out before the ladies, takes aim, and fires.

But, alas! here is a disappointment, an incredible, an unimaginable disappointment—for the target's aspect is unchanged; there is nothing there but that same old bullet-hole!

"If one dared to hint at such a thing," cried Major Duncan, "I should say that the Pathfinder has also missed the target!"

As nobody had missed it yet, the "also" was not necessary, but never mind about that for the Pathfinder is going to speak.

"No, no, Major," said he, confidently, "that *would* be a risky declaration. I didn't load the piece, and can't say what was in it; but if it was lead, you will find the bullet driving down those of the Quartermaster and Jasper, else is not my name Pathfinder."

A shout from the target announced the truth of this assertion.

Is the miracle sufficient as it stands? Not for Cooper. The Pathfinder speaks again, as he "now slowly advances toward the stage occupied by the females":

"That's not all, boys, that's not all; if you find the target touched at all, I'll own to a miss. The Quartermaster cut the wood, but you'll find no wood cut by that last messenger."

The miracle is at last complete. He knew—doubtless *saw*—at the distance of a hundred yards—that his bullet had passed into the hole *without fraying the edges*. There were now three bullets in that one hole, three bullets embedded processionally in the body of the stump back of the target. Everybody knew this, somehow or other, and yet nobody had dug any of them out to make sure. Cooper is not a close observer but he is interesting. He is certainly always that, no matter what happens. And he is more interesting when he is not noticing what he is about than when he is. This is a considerable merit.

The conversations in the Cooper books have a curious sound in our modern ears. To believe that such talk really ever came out of people's mouths would be to believe that there was a time when time was of no value to a person who thought he had something to say, when it was the custom to spread a two-minute remark out to ten, when a man's mouth was a rolling-mill and busied itself all day long in turning four-foot pigs of thought into thirty-foot bars of conversational railroad iron by attenuation, when subjects were seldom faithfully stuck to but the talk wandered all around and arrived nowhere, when conversations consisted mainly of irrelevancies with here and there a relevancy, a relevancy with an embarrassed look, as not being able to explain how it got there.

Cooper was certainly not a master in the construction of dialogue. Inaccurate observation defeated him here as it defeated him in so many other enterprises of his. He even failed to notice that the man who talks corrupt English six days in the week must and will talk it on the seventh, and can't help himself. In the *Deerslayer* story he lets Deerslayer talk the showiest kind of book-talk sometimes, and at other times the basest of base dialects. For instance, when some one asks him if he has a sweetheart, and if so where she abides, this is his majestic answer:

"She's in the forest—hanging from the boughs of the trees, in a soft rain—in the dew on the open grass—the clouds that float about in the blue heavens—the birds that sing in the woods—the sweet springs where I slake my thirst—and in all the other glorious gifts that come from God's Providence!"

And he preceded that, a little before, with this:

"It consarns me as all things that touches a fri'nd consarns a fri'nd."

And this is another of his remarks:

"If I was Injin born, now, I might tell of this, or carry in
the scalp and boast of the expl'ite afore the whole tribe; or if
my inimy had only been a bear"—[and so on].

We cannot imagine such a thing as a veteran Scotch
Commander-in-Chief comporting himself in the field
like a windy melodramatic actor, but Cooper could. On
one occasion Alice and Cora were being chased by the
French through a fog in the neighborhood of their
father's fort:

"*Point de quartier aux coquins!*" cried an eager pursuer,
who seemed to direct the operations of the enemy.

"Stand firm and be ready, my gallant 60ths!" suddenly exclaimed a voice above them; "wait to see the enemy; fire low,
and sweep the glacis."

"Father! father," exclaimed a piercing cry from out the
mist; "it is I! Alice! thy own Elsie! spare, O! save your
daughters!"

"Hold!" shouted the former speaker, in the awful tones of
parental agony, the sound reaching even to the woods, and
rolling back in solemn echo. " 'Tis she! God has restored me
my children! Throw open the sally-port; to the field, 60ths,
to the field! pull not a trigger, lest ye kill my lambs! Drive off
these dogs of France with your steel!"

Cooper's word-sense was singularly dull. When a
person has a poor ear for music he will flat and sharp
right along without knowing it. He keeps near the tune,
but it is *not* the tune. When a person has a poor ear for
words, the result is a literary flatting and sharping; you
perceive what he is intending to say but you also perceive that he doesn't *say* it. This is Cooper. He was not
a word-musician. His ear was satisfied with the *approxi-
mate* word. I will furnish some circumstantial evidence
in support of this charge. My instances are gathered
from half a dozen pages of the tale called *Deerslayer*.

He uses "verbal" for "oral"; "precision" for "facility"; "phenomena" for "marvels"; "necessary" for "predetermined"; "unsophisticated" for "primitive"; "preparation" for "expectancy"; "rebuked" for "subdued"; "dependent on" for "resulting from"; "fact" for "condition"; "fact" for "conjecture"; "precaution" for "caution"; "explain" for "determine"; "mortified" for "disappointed"; "meretricious" for "factitious"; "materially" for "considerably"; "decreasing" for "deepening"; "increasing" for "disappearing"; "embedded" for "inclosed"; "treacherous" for "hostile"; "stood" for "stooped"; "softened" for "replaced"; "rejoined" for "remarked"; "situation" for "condition"; "different" for "differing"; "insensible" for "unsentient"; "brevity" for "celerity"; "distrusted" for "suspicious"; "mental imbecility" for "imbecility"; "eyes" for "sight"; "counteracting" for "opposing"; "funeral obsequies" for "obsequies."

There have been daring people in the world who claimed that Cooper could write English but they are all dead now—all dead but Lounsbury. I don't remember that Lounsbury makes the claim in so many words, still he makes it for he says that *Deerslayer* is a "pure work of art." Pure, in that connection, means faultless—faultless in all details—and language is a detail. If Mr. Lounsbury had only compared Cooper's English with the English which he writes himself—but it is plain that he didn't, and so it is likely that he imagines until this day that Cooper's is as clean and compact as his own. Now I feel sure, deep down in my heart, that Cooper wrote about the poorest English that exists in our language and that the English of *Deerslayer* is the very worst that even Cooper ever wrote.

I may be mistaken, but it does seem to me that *Deerslayer* is not a work of art in any sense; it does seem to me that it is destitute of every detail that goes to the making of a work of art; in truth, it seems to me that *Deerslayer* is just simply a literary *delirium tremens.*

A work of art? It has no invention; it has no order, system, sequence, or result; it has no lifelikeness, no thrill, no stir, no seeming of reality; its characters are confusedly drawn and by their acts and words they prove that they are not the sort of people the author claims that they are; its humor is pathetic; its pathos is funny; its conversations are—oh! indescribable; its love-scenes odious; its English a crime against the language.

Counting these out, what is left is Art. I think we must all admit that.

FROM PUDD'NHEAD WILSON'S CALENDAR

THERE is no character, howsoever good and fine, but it can be destroyed by ridicule, howsoever poor and witless. Observe the ass, for instance: his character is about perfect, he is the choicest spirit among all the humbler animals, yet see what ridicule has brought him to. Instead of feeling complimented when we are called an ass, we are left in doubt.

Tell the truth or trump—but get the trick.

Adam was but human—this explains it all. He did not want the apple for the apple's sake, he wanted it only because it was forbidden. The mistake was in not forbidding the serpent; then he would have eaten the serpent.

Whoever has lived long enough to find out what life is, knows how deep a debt of gratitude we owe to Adam, the first great benefactor of our race. He brought death into the world.

Adam and Eve had many advantages, but the principal one was that they escaped teething.

There is this trouble about special providences—namely, there is so often a doubt as to which party was intended to be the beneficiary. In the case of the children, the bears, and the prophet, the bears got more real satisfaction out of the episode than the prophet did, because they got the children.

Training is everything. The peach was once a bitter almond; cauliflower is nothing but cabbage with a college education.

Let us endeavor so to live that when we come to die even the undertaker will be sorry.

Habit is habit and not to be flung out of the window by any man but coaxed down-stairs a step at a time.

One of the most striking differences between a cat and a lie is that a cat has only nine lives.

The holy passion of Friendship is of so sweet and steady and loyal and enduring a nature that it will last through a whole lifetime, if not asked to lend money.

Consider well the proportions of things. It is better to be a young June-bug than an old bird of paradise.

Why is it that we rejoice at a birth and grieve at a funeral? It is because we are not the person involved.

It is easy to find fault, if one has that disposition. There was once a man who, not being able to find any other fault with his coal, complained that there were too many prehistoric toads in it.

All say, "How hard it is that we have to die"—a strange complaint to come from the mouths of people who have had to live.

When angry, count four; when very angry, swear.

There are three infallible ways of pleasing an author and the three form a rising scale of compliment: 1, to tell him you have read one of his books; 2, to tell him you have read all of his books; 3, to ask him to let you read the manuscript of his forthcoming book. No. 1 admits you to his respect; No. 2 admits you to his admiration; No. 3 carries you clear into his heart.

As to the Adjective: when in doubt, strike it out.

Courage is resistance to fear, mastery of fear—not absence of fear. Except a creature be part coward it is not a compliment to say it is brave; it is merely a loose misapplication of the word. Consider the flea!—incomparably the bravest of all the creatures of God, if ignorance of fear were courage. Whether you are asleep or awake he will attack you, caring nothing for the fact that in bulk and strength you are to him as are the massed armies of the earth to a sucking child; he lives both day and night and all days and nights in the very lap of peril and the immediate presence of death, and yet is no more afraid than is the man who walks the streets of a city that was threatened by an earthquake ten centuries before. When we speak of Clive, Nelson, and Putnam as men who "didn't know what fear was," we ought always to add the flea—and put him at the head of the procession.

When I reflect upon the number of disagreeable people who I know have gone to a better world, I am moved to lead a different life.

The true Southern watermelon is a boon apart and not to be mentioned with commoner things. It is chief of this world's luxuries, king by the grace of God over all the fruits of the earth. When one has tasted it, he knows what the angels eat. It was not a Southern watermelon that Eve took; we know it because she repented.

Nothing so needs reforming as other people's habits.

Behold, the fool saith, "Put not all thine eggs in the one basket"—which is but a manner of saying, "Scatter your money and your attention"; but the wise man saith, "Put all your eggs in the one basket and— WATCH THAT BASKET."

If you pick up a starving dog and make him prosperous, he will not bite you. This is the principal difference between a dog and a man.

We know all about the habits of the ant, we know all about the habits of the bee, but we know nothing at all about the habits of the oyster. It seems almost certain that we have been choosing the wrong time for studying the oyster.

Even popularity can be overdone. In Rome, along at first, you are full of regrets that Michelangelo died, but by and by you only regret that you didn't see him do it.

July 4. Statistics show that we lose more fools on this day than in all the other days of the year put together. This proves, by the number left in stock, that one Fourth of July per year is now inadequate, the country has grown so.

Gratitude and treachery are merely the two extremities of the same procession. You have seen all of it that is worth staying for when the band and the gaudy officials have gone by.

Thanksgiving Day. Let all give humble, hearty, and sincere thanks, now, but the turkeys. In the island of Fiji they do not use turkeys; they use plumbers. It does not become you and me to sneer at Fiji.

Few things are harder to put up with than the annoyance of a good example.

It were not best that we should all think alike; it is difference of opinion that makes horse-races.

Even the clearest and most perfect circumstantial evidence is likely to be at fault, after all, and therefore ought to be received with great caution. Take the case of any pencil sharpened by any woman: if you have witnesses you will find she did it with a knife, but if you take simply the aspect of the pencil you will say she did it with her teeth.

He is useless on top of the ground; he ought to be under it, inspiring the cabbages.

April 1. This is the day upon which we are reminded of what we are on the other three hundred and sixty-four.

It is often the case that the man who can't tell a lie thinks he is the best judge of one.

FROM PUDD'NHEAD WILSON'S NEW CALENDAR

A man may have no bad habits and have worse.

When in doubt, tell the truth.

It is more trouble to make a maxim than it is to do right.

A dozen direct censures are easier to bear than one morganatic compliment.

Noise proves nothing. Often a hen who has merely laid an egg cackles as if she had laid an asteroid.

He was as shy as a newspaper is when referring to its own merits.

Truth is the most valuable thing we have. Let us economize it.

It could probably be shown by facts and figures that there is no distinctly native American criminal class except Congress.

It is your human environment that makes climate.

Everything human is pathetic. The secret source of Humor itself is not joy but sorrow. There is no humor in heaven.

We should be careful to get out of an experience only the wisdom that is in it—and stop there; lest we be like the cat that sits down on a hot stove-lid. She will never sit down on a hot stove-lid again, and that is well; but also she will never sit down on a cold one any more.

There are those who scoff at the school-boy, calling him frivolous and shallow. Yet it was the school-boy who said, "Faith is believing what you know ain't so."

The timid man yearns for full value and demands a tenth. The bold man strikes for double value and compromises on par.

We can secure other people's approval if we do right and try hard, but our own is worth a hundred of it and no way has been found out of securing that.

Truth is stranger than Fiction, but it is because Fiction is obliged to stick to possibilities; Truth isn't.

There is a Moral Sense and there is an Immoral Sense. History shows us that the Moral Sense enables us to perceive morality and how to avoid it, and that the Immoral Sense enables us to perceive immorality and how to enjoy it.

The English are mentioned in the Bible: Blessed are the meek, for they shall inherit the earth.

It is easier to stay out than get out.

Pity is for the living, envy is for the dead.

It is by the goodness of God that in our country we have those three unspeakably precious things: freedom of speech, freedom of conscience, and the prudence never to practise either of them.

Man will do many things to get himself loved, he will do all things to get himself envied.

Be careless in your dress if you must but keep a tidy soul.

There is no such thing as "the Queen's English." The property has gone into the hands of a joint stock company and we own the bulk of the shares.

"*Classic.*" A book which people praise and don't read.

There are people who can do all fine and heroic things but one: keep from telling their happinesses to the unhappy.

Man is the Only Animal that blushes. Or needs to.

The universal brotherhood of man is our most precious possession, what there is of it.

Let us be thankful for the fools. But for them the rest of us could not succeed.

When people do not respect us we are sharply offended; yet deep down in his private heart no man much respects himself.

Nature makes the locust with an appetite for crops; man would have made him with an appetite for sand.

The spirit of wrath—not the words—is the sin; and the spirit of wrath is cursing. We begin to swear before we can talk.

The man with a new idea is a Crank until the idea succeeds.

Let us be grateful to Adam our benefactor. He cut us out of the "blessing" of idleness and won for us the "curse" of labor.

The Autocrat of Russia possesses more power than any other man in the earth, but he cannot stop a sneeze.

There are several good protections against temptations but the surest is cowardice.

To succeed in the other trades, capacity must be shown; in the law, concealment of it will do.

Prosperity is the best protector of principle.

By trying we can easily learn to endure adversity. Another man's, I mean.

Few of us can stand prosperity. Another man's, I mean.

There is an old-time toast which is golden for its beauty, "When you ascend the hill of prosperity may you not meet a friend."

Each person is born to one possession which outvalues all his others—his last breath.

Hunger is the handmaid of genius.

The old saw says, "Let a sleeping dog lie." Right. Still, when there is much at stake it is better to get a newspaper to do it.

It takes your enemy and your friend, working together, to hurt you to the heart, the one to slander you and the other to get the news to you.

If the desire to kill and the opportunity to kill came always together, who would escape hanging?

Simple rules for saving money: To save half, when you are fired by an eager impulse to contribute to a charity, wait and count forty. To save three-quarters, count sixty. To save it all, county sixty-five.

Grief can take care of itself, but to get the full value of a joy you must have somebody to divide it with.

He had had much experience of physicians, and said "the only way to keep your health is to eat what you don't want, drink what you don't like, and do what you'd druther not."

The man who is ostentatious of his modesty is twin to the statue that wears a fig-leaf.

Let me make the superstitions of a nation and I care not who makes its laws or its songs either.

True irreverence is disrespect for another man's god.

Do not undervalue the headache. While it is at its sharpest it seems a bad investment, but when relief begins the unexpired remainder is worth four dollars a minute.

There are eight hundred and sixty-nine different forms of lying, but only one of them has been squarely forbidden. Thou shalt not bear false witness against thy neighbor.

There are two times in a man's life when he should not speculate: when he can't afford it and when he can.

She was not quite what you would call refined. She was not quite what you would call unrefined. She was the kind of person that keeps a parrot.

Make it a point to do something every day that you don't want to do. This is the golden rule for acquiring the habit of doing your duty without pain.

Don't part with your illusions. When they are gone you may still exist but you have ceased to live.

Often, the surest way to convey misinformation is to tell the strict truth.

SATAN (impatiently) to NEW-COMER. The trouble with you Chicago people is that you think you are the best people down here, whereas you are merely the most numerous.

In the first place God made idiots. This was for practice. Then He made School Boards.

When your watch gets out of order you have choice of two things to do: throw it in the fire or take it to the watch-tinker. The former is the quickest.

In statesmanship get the formalities right, never mind about the moralities.

Every one is a moon and has a dark side which he never shows to anybody.

First catch your Boer, then kick him.

The very ink with which all history is written is merely fluid prejudice.

There isn't a Parallel of Latitude but thinks it would have been the Equator if it had had its rights.

I have traveled more than any one else and I have noticed that even the angels speak English with an accent.

PURCHASING CIVIC VIRTUE

THE human race was always interesting and we know by its past that it will always continue so. Monotonously. It is always the same; it never changes. Its circumstances change from time to time, for better or worse, but the race's *character* is permanent and never changes. In the course of the ages it has built up several great and worshipful civilizations and has seen unlooked-for circumstances slily emerge bearing deadly gifts which looked like benefits and were welcomed, whereupon the decay and destruction of each of these stately civilizations has followed.

It is not worth while to try to keep history from repeating itself, for man's character will always make the preventing of the repetitions impossible. Whenever man makes a large stride in material prosperity and progress he is sure to think that *he* has progressed, whereas he has not advanced an inch, nothing has progressed but his circumstances. *He* stands where he stood before. He knows more than his forebears knew but his intellect is no better than theirs and never will be. He is richer than his forebears but his character is no improvement upon theirs. Riches and education are not a permanent possession; they will pass away, as in the case of Rome and Greece and Egypt and Babylon, and a moral and mental midnight will follow—with a dull long sleep and a slow reawakening. From time to time he makes what looks like a change in his character but it is not a real change, and it is only transitory anyway. He cannot even invent a religion and keep it intact; circumstances are stronger than he and all his works. Circumstances and conditions are always changing, and they always compel him to modify his religions to harmonize with the new situation.

For twenty-five or thirty years I have squandered a deal of my time—too much of it perhaps—in trying to guess what is going to be the process which will turn our republic into a monarchy and how far off that event might be. Every man is a master and also a servant, a vassal. There is always someone who looks up to him and admires and envies him; there is always someone to whom he looks up and whom he admires and envies. This is his nature; this is his character; and it is unchangeable, indestructible; therefore republics and democracies are not for such as he; they cannot satisfy the requirements of his nature. The inspirations of his character will always breed circumstances and conditions which must in time furnish him a king and an aristocracy to look up to and worship. In a democracy he will try—and honestly—to keep the crown away, but Circumstance is a powerful master and will eventually defeat him.

Republics have lived long but monarchy lives forever. By our teaching we learn that vast material prosperity always brings in its train conditions which debase the morals and enervate the manhood of a nation— then the country's liberties come into the market and are bought, sold, squandered, thrown away, and a popular idol is carried to the throne upon the shields or shoulders of the worshiping people and planted there in permanency. We are always being taught—no, formerly we were always being taught—to look at Rome and beware. The teacher pointed to Rome's stern virtue, incorruptibility, love of liberty, and all-sacrificing patriotism—this when she was young and poor; then he pointed to her later days when her sunbursts of material prosperity and spreading dominion came and were exultingly welcomed by the people, they not suspecting that these were not fortunate glories, happy benefits, but were a disease and freighted with death.

The teacher reminded us that Rome's liberties were not auctioned off in a day, but were bought slowly, gradually, furtively, little by little; first with a little corn and oil for the exceedingly poor and wretched, later with corn and oil for voters who were not quite so poor, later still with corn and oil for pretty much every man that had a vote to sell—exactly our own history over again. At first we granted deserved pensions, righteously and with a clean and honorable motive, to the disabled soldiers of the Civil War. The clean motive began and ended there. We have made many and amazing additions to the pension list but with a motive which dishonors the uniform and the Congresses which have voted the additions, the sole purpose back of the additions being the purchase of votes. It is corn and oil over again, and promises to do its full share in the eventual subversion of the republic and the substitution of monarchy in its place. The monarchy would come anyhow, without this, but this has a peculiar interest for us in that it prodigiously hastens the day. We have the two Roman conditions: stupendous wealth with its inevitable corruptions and moral blight, and the corn and oil pensions—that is to say, vote bribes, which have taken away the pride of thousands of tempted men and turned them into willing alms receivers and unashamed.

It is curious—curious that physical courage should be so common in the world and moral courage so rare. A year or two ago a veteran of the Civil War asked me if I did not sometimes have a longing to attend the an-nual great Convention of the Grand Army of the Re-public and make a speech. I was obliged to confess that I wouldn't have the necessary moral courage for the venture, for I would want to reproach the old soldiers for not rising up in indignant protest against our gov-ernment's vote-purchasing additions to the pension list, which is making of the remnant of their brave lives one long blush. I might try to say the words but would lack the guts and would fail. It would be one tottering moral coward trying to rebuke a houseful of like breed—men nearly as timid as himself but not any more so.

Well, there it is—I am a moral coward like the rest; and yet it is amazing to me that out of the hundreds of thousands of physically dauntless men who faced death without a quiver of the nerves on a hundred bloody fields, not one solitary individual of them all has had courage enough to rise up and bravely curse the Con-gresses which have degraded him to the level of the bounty-jumper and the bastards of the same. Every-body laughs at the grotesque-est of them all, the most shameless of them all, the most transparent of them all, the only frankly lawless one of them all—the immortal Executive Order 78. Everybody laughs—privately; everybody scoffs—privately; everybody is indignant—privately; everybody is ashamed to look a real soldier in the face—but none of them exposes his feelings publicly. This is perfectly natural and wholly in-evitable, for it is the nature of man to hate to say the disagreeable thing. It is his character, his nature; it has always been so; his character cannot change; while he continues to exist it will never change by a shade.

Europe and Elsewhere

CORN-PONE OPINIONS

FIFTY years ago, when I was a boy of fifteen and helping to inhabit a Missourian village on the banks of the Mississippi, I had a friend whose society was very dear to me because I was forbidden by my mother to partake of it. He was a gay and impudent and satirical and delightful young black man—a slave —who daily preached sermons from the top of his master's woodpile, with me for sole audience. He imitated the pulpit style of the several clergymen of the village, and did it well and with fine passion and energy. To me he was a wonder. I believed he was the greatest orator in the United States and would some day be heard from. But it did not happen; in the distribution of rewards he was overlooked. It is the way, in this world.

He interrupted his preaching now and then to saw a stick of wood, but the sawing was a pretense—he did it with his mouth, exactly imitating the sound the buck-saw makes in shrieking its way through the wood. But it served its purpose, it kept his master from coming out to see how the work was getting along. I listened to the sermons from the open window of a lumber room at the back of the house. One of his texts was this:

"You tell me whar a man gits his corn pone, en I'll tell you what his 'pinions is."

I can never forget it. It was deeply impressed upon

me. By my mother. Not upon my memory, but else-where. She had slipped in upon me while I was absorbed and not watching. The black philosopher's idea was that a man is not independent and cannot afford views which might interfere with his bread and butter. If he would prosper, he must train with the majority; in matters of large moment, like politics and religion, he must think and feel with the bulk of his neighbors or suffer dam-age in his social standing and in his business prosperities. He must restrict himself to corn-pone opinions—at least on the surface. He must get his opinions from other people, he must reason out none for himself, he must have no first-hand views.

I think Jerry was right, in the main, but I think he did not go far enough.

1. It was his idea that a man conforms to the major-ity view of his locality by calculation and intention.

This happens, but I think it is not the rule.

2. It was his idea that there is such a thing as a first-hand opinion, an original opinion, an opinion which is coldly reasoned out in a man's head by a searching analysis of the facts involved, with the heart uncon-sulted and the jury room closed against outside in-fluences. It may be that such an opinion has been born somewhere at some time or other, but I suppose it got away before they could catch it and stuff it and put it in the museum.

I am persuaded that a coldly-thought-out and inde-pendent verdict upon a fashion in clothes, or manners, or literature, or politics, or religion, or any other matter that is projected into the field of our notice and interest is a most rare thing—if it has indeed ever existed.

A new thing in costume appears—the flaring hoop-skirt, for example—and the passers-by are shocked, and the irreverent laugh. Six months later everybody is reconciled; the fashion has established itself; it is admired now and no one laughs. Public opinion resented it before, public opinion accepts it now and is happy in it. Why? Was the resentment reasoned out? Was the acceptance reasoned out? No. The instinct that moves to conformity did the work. It is our nature to conform; it is a force which not many can successfully resist. What is its seat? The inborn requirement of self-approval. We all have to bow to that; there are no exceptions. Even the woman who refuses from first to last to wear the hoopskirt comes under that law and is its slave; she could not wear the skirt and have her own approval, and that she *must* have, she cannot help herself. But as a rule our self-approval has its source in but one place and not elsewhere—the approval of other people. A person of vast consequences can introduce any kind of novelty in dress and the general world will presently adopt it—moved to do it in the first place by the natural instinct to passively yield to that vague something recognized as authority, and in the second place by the human instinct to train with the multitude and have its approval. An empress introduced the hoopskirt and we know the result. A nobody introduced the bloomer and we know the result. If Eve should come again in her ripe renown, and re-introduce her quaint styles—well, we know what would happen. And we should be cruelly embarrassed, along at first.

The hoopskirt runs its course and disappears. Nobody reasons about it. One woman abandons the fashion, her neighbor notices this and follows her lead, this influences the next woman and so on and so on, and presently the skirt has vanished out of the world, no one knows how nor why; nor cares, for that matter. It will come again by and by, and in due course will go again.

Twenty-five years ago in England, six or eight wine

glasses stood grouped by each person's plate at a dinner party, and they were used, not left idle and empty; to-day there are but three or four in the group and the average guest sparingly uses about two of them. We have not adopted this new fashion yet, but we shall do it presently. We shall not think it out, we shall merely conform and let it go at that. We get our notions and habits and opinions from outside influences; we do not have to study them out.

Our table manners and company manners and street manners change from time to time, but the changes are not reasoned out; we merely notice and conform. We are creatures of outside influences; as a rule we do not think, we only imitate. We cannot invent standards that will stick; what we mistake for standards are only fashions, and perishable. We may continue to admire them but we drop the use of them. We notice this in literature. Shakespeare is a standard, and fifty years ago we used to write tragedies which we couldn't tell from—from somebody else's, but we don't do it any more now. Our prose standard three quarters of a century ago was ornate and diffuse; some authority or other changed it in the direction of compactness and simplicity, and conformity followed without argument. The historical novel starts up suddenly and sweeps the land. Everybody writes one and the nation is glad. We had historical novels before; but nobody read them and the rest of us conformed—without reasoning it out. We are conforming in the other way now, because it is another case of everybody.

The outside influences are always pouring in upon us and we are always obeying their orders and accepting their verdicts. The Smiths like the new play, the Joneses go to see it and they copy the Smith verdict. Morals, religions, politics, get their following from sur-

rounding influences and atmospheres almost entirely;
not from study, not from thinking. A man must and will
have his own approval first of all, in each and every moment and circumstance of his life—even if he must re-
pent of a self-approved act the moment after its commission in order to get his self-approval *again:* but
speaking in general terms, a man's self-approval in the
large concerns of life has its source in the approval of
the peoples about him, and not in a searching personal
examination of the matter. Mohammedans are Mohammedans because they are born and reared among
that sect, not because they have thought it out and can
furnish sound reasons for being Mohammedans; we
know why Catholics are Catholics, why Presbyterians
are Presbyterians, why Baptists are Baptists, why Mormons are Mormons, why thieves are thieves, why
monarchists are monarchists, why Republicans are Republicans and Democrats, Democrats. We know it is a
matter of association and sympathy, not reasoning and
examination; that hardly a man in the world has an
opinion upon morals, politics, or religion which he got
otherwise than through his associations and sympathies.
Broadly speaking, there are none but corn-pone opinions. And broadly speaking, corn-pone stands for self-
approval. Self-approval is acquired mainly from the
approval of other people. The result is conformity.
Sometimes conformity has a sordid business interest—
the bread-and-butter interest—but not in most cases, I
think. I think that in the majority of cases it is unconscious and not calculated, that it is born of the human
being's natural yearning to stand well with his fellows
and have their inspiring approval and praise—a yearning which is commonly so strong and so insistent that
it cannot be effectually resisted and must have its way.

A political emergency brings out the corn-pone opin-

ion in fine force in its two chief varieties—the pocket-
book variety, which has its origin in self-interest, and
the bigger variety, the sentimental variety—the one
which can't bear to be outside the pale; can't bear to be
in disfavor, can't endure the averted face and the cold
shoulder, wants to stand well with his friends, wants to
be smiled upon, wants to be welcome, wants to hear
the precious words, "*He's* on the right track!" Uttered
perhaps by an ass, but still an ass of high degree, an
ass whose approval is gold and diamonds to a smaller
ass, and confers glory and honor and happiness and
membership in the herd. For these gauds many a man
will dump his life-long principles into the street, and his
conscience along with them. We have seen it happen.
In some millions of instances.

Men think they think upon great political questions,
and they do; but they think with their party, not inde-
pendently; they read its literature but not that of the
other side; they arrive at convictions but they are drawn
from a partial view of the matter in hand and are of
no particular value. They swarm with their party, they
feel with their party, they are happy in their party's
approval; and where the party leads they will follow,
whether for right and honor or through blood and dirt
and a mush of mutilated morals.

In our late canvass half of the nation passionately
believed that in silver lay salvation, the other half as
passionately believed that that way lay destruction. Do
you believe that a tenth part of the people on either
side had any rational excuse for having an opinion about
the matter at all? I studied that mighty question to the
bottom—came out empty. Half of our people passionately believe in high tariff, the other half believe
otherwise. Does this mean study and examination or only
feeling? The latter, I think. I have deeply studied that

question, too—and didn't arrive. We all do no end of
feeling and we mistake it for thinking. And out of it we
get an aggregation which we consider a boon. Its name
is Public Opinion. It is held in reverence. It settles
everything. Some think it the Voice of God.

Europe and Elsewhere

THE WAR PRAYER

IT WAS a time of great and exalting excitement. The country was up in arms, the war was on, in every breast burned the holy fire of patriotism; the drums were beating, the bands playing, the toy pistols popping, the bunched firecrackers hissing and spluttering; on every hand and far down the receding and fading spread of roofs and balconies a fluttering wilderness of flags flashed in the sun; daily the young volunteers marched down the wide avenue gay and fine in their new uniforms, the proud fathers and mothers and sisters and sweethearts cheering them with voices choked with happy emotion as they swung by; nightly the packed mass meetings listened, panting, to patriot oratory which stirred the deepest deeps of their hearts and which they interrupted at briefest intervals with cyclones of applause, the tears running down their cheeks the while; in the churches the pastors preached devotion to flag and country and invoked the God of Battles, beseeching His aid in our good cause in outpouring of fervid eloquence which moved every listener. It was indeed a glad and gracious time, and the half-dozen rash spirits that ventured to disapprove of the war and cast a doubt upon its righteousness straightway got such a stern and angry warning that for their personal safety's sake they quickly shrank out of sight and offended no more in that way.

Sunday morning came—next day the battalions would

leave for the front; the church was filled; the volunteers were there, their young faces alight with martial dreams —visions of the stern advance, the gathering momentum, the rushing charge, the flashing sabers, the flight of the foe, the tumult, the enveloping smoke, the fierce pursuit, the surrender!—then home from the war, bronzed heroes, welcomed, adored, submerged in golden seas of glory! With the volunteers sat their dear ones, proud, happy, and envied by the neighbors and friends who had no sons and brothers to send forth to the field of honor, there to win for the flag or, failing, die the noblest of noble deaths. The service proceeded; a war chapter from the Old Testament was read; the first prayer was said; it was followed by an organ burst that shook the building, and with one impulse the house rose, with glowing eyes and beating hearts, and poured out that tremendous invocation—

"God the all-terrible! Thou who ordainest,
Thunder thy clarion and lightning thy sword!"

Then came the "long" prayer. None could remember the like of it for passionate pleading and moving and beautiful language. The burden of its supplication was that an ever-merciful and benignant Father of us all would watch over our noble young soldiers and aid, comfort, and encourage them in their patriotic work; bless them, shield them in the day of battle and the hour of peril, bear them in His mighty hand, make them strong and confident, invincible in the bloody onset; help them to crush the foe, grant to them and to their flag and country imperishable honor and glory—

An aged stranger entered and moved with slow and noiseless step up the main aisle, his eyes fixed upon the minister, his long body clothed in a robe that reached to his feet, his head bare, his white hair descending in a frothy cataract to his shoulders, his seamy face unnaturally pale, pale even to ghastliness. With all eyes following him and wondering, he made his silent way; without pausing, he ascended to the preacher's side and stood there, waiting. With shut lids the preacher, unconscious of his presence, continued his moving prayer, and at last finished it with the words, uttered in fervent appeal, "Bless our arms, grant us the victory, O Lord our God, Father and Protector of our land and flag!"

The stranger touched his arm, motioned him to step aside—which the startled minister did—and took his place. During some moments he surveyed the spellbound audience with solemn eyes in which burned an uncanny light; then in a deep voice he said:

"I come from the Throne—bearing a message from Almighty God!" The words smote the house with a shock; if the stranger perceived it he gave no attention. "He has heard the prayer of His servant your shepherd and will grant it if such shall be your desire after I, His messenger, shall have explained to you its import—that is to say, its full import. For it is like unto many of the prayers of men, in that it asks for more than he who utters it is aware of—except he pause and think.

"God's servant and yours has prayed his prayer. Has he paused and taken thought? Is it one prayer? No, it is two—one uttered, the other not. Both have reached the ear of Him Who heareth all supplications, the spoken and the unspoken. Ponder this—keep it in mind. If you would beseech a blessing upon yourself, beware! lest without intent you invoke a curse upon a neighbor at the same time. If you pray for the blessing of rain upon your crop which needs it, by that act you are possibly praying for a curse upon some neighbor's crop which may not need rain and can be injured by it.

"You have heard your servant's prayer—the uttered

part of it. I am commissioned of God to put into words
the other part of it—that part which the pastor, and
also you in your hearts, fervently prayed silently. And
ignorantly and unthinkingly? God grant that it was so!
You heard these words: 'Grant us the victory, O Lord
our God!' That is sufficient. The *whole* of the uttered
prayer is compact into those pregnant words. Elabora-
tions were not necessary. When you have prayed for
victory you have prayed for many unmentioned results
which follow victory—*must* follow it, cannot help but
follow it. Upon the listening spirit of God the Father fell
also the unspoken part of the prayer. He commandeth
me to put it into words. Listen!

"O Lord our Father, our young patriots, idols of our
hearts, go forth to battle—be Thou near them! With
them, in spirit, we also go forth from the sweet peace
of our beloved firesides to smite the foe. O Lord our
God, help us to tear their soldiers to bloody shreds with
our shells; help us to cover their smiling fields with the
pale forms of their patriot dead; help us to drown the
thunder of the guns with the shrieks of their wounded,
writhing in pain; help us to lay waste their humble
homes with a hurricane of fire; help us to wring the
hearts of their unoffending widows with unavailing
grief; help us to turn them out roofless with their little
children to wander unfriended the wastes of their deso-
lated land in rags and hunger and thirst, sports of the
sun flames of summer and the icy winds of winter,
broken in spirit, worn with travail, imploring Thee for
the refuge of the grave and denied it—for our sakes who
adore Thee, Lord, blast their hopes, blight their lives,
protract their bitter pilgrimage, make heavy their steps,
water their way with their tears, stain the white snow
with the blood of their wounded feet! We ask it, in the
spirit of love, of Him Who is the Source of Love, and

Who is the ever-faithful refuge and friend of all that are sore beset and seek His aid with humble and contrite hearts. Amen.

(*After a pause*) "Ye have prayed it; if ye still desire it, speak! The messenger of the Most High waits."

It was believed afterward that the man was a lunatic, because there was no sense in what he said.

Europe and Elsewhere

THE UNITED STATES
OF LYNCHERDOM

AND so Missouri has fallen, that great state! Certain of her children have joined the lynchers and the smirch is upon the rest of us. That handful of her children have given us a character and labeled us with a name, and to the dwellers in the four quarters of the earth we are "lynchers" now, and ever shall be. For the world will not stop and think—it never does, it is not its way; its way is to generalize from a single sample. It will not say, "Those Missourians have been busy eighty years in building an honorable good name for themselves; these hundred lynchers down in the corner of the state are not real Missourians, they are renegades." No, that truth will not enter its mind; it will generalize from the one or two misleading samples and say, "The Missourians are lynchers." It has no reflection, no logic, no sense of proportion. With it, figures go for nothing; to it, figures reveal nothing, it cannot reason upon them rationally; it would say, for instance, that China is being swiftly and surely Christianized, since nine Chinese Christians are being made every day; and it would fail, with him, to notice that the fact that 33,000 pagans are *born* there every day damages the argument. It would say, "There are a hundred lynchers there, therefore, the Missourians are lynchers"; the considerable fact that there are two and a half million Missourians who **are** *not* lynchers would not affect their verdict.

II

Oh, Missouri!

The tragedy occurred near Pierce City, down in the southwestern corner of the state. On a Sunday afternoon a young white woman who had started alone from church was found murdered. For there are churches there; in my time religion was more general, more pervasive, in the South than it was in the North, and more virile and earnest too, I think; I have some reason to believe that this is still the case. The young woman was found murdered. Although it was a region of churches and schools the people rose, lynched three Negroes— two of them very aged ones—burned out five Negro households, and drove thirty Negro families into the woods.

I do not dwell upon the provocation which moved the people to these crimes, for that has nothing to do with the matter; the only question is, does the assassin *take the law into his own hands?* It is very simple and very just. If the assassin be proved to have usurped the law's prerogative in righting his wrongs, that ends the matter; a thousand provocations are no defense. The Pierce City people had bitter provocation—indeed, as revealed by certain of the particulars, the bitterest of all provocations —but no matter, they took the law into their own hands when by the terms of their statutes their victim would certainly hang if the law had been allowed to take its course, for there are but few Negroes in that region and they are without authority and without influence in overawing juries.

Why has lynching, with various barbaric accompaniments, become a favorite regulator in cases of "the usual crime" in several parts of the country? Is it because men think a lurid and terrible punishment a more forcible object lesson and a more effective deterrent than a sober and colorless hanging done privately in a jail would be? Surely sane men do not think that. Even the average child should know better. It should know that any strange and much-talked-of event is always followed by imitations, the world being so well supplied with excitable people who only need a little stirring up to make them lose what is left of their heads and do mad things which they would not have thought of ordinarily. It should know that if a man jump off Brooklyn Bridge another will imitate him; that if a person venture down Niagara Whirlpool in a barrel another will imitate him; that if a Jack the Ripper make notoriety by slaughtering women in dark alleys he will be imitated; that if a man attempt a king's life and the newspapers carry the noise of it around the globe, regicides will crop up all around. The child should know that one much-talked-of outrage and murder committed by a Negro will upset the disturbed intellects of several other negroes and produce a series of the very tragedies the community would so strenuously wish to prevent; that each of these crimes will produce another series, and year by year steadily increase the tale of these disasters instead of diminishing it; that, in a word, the lynchers are themselves the worst enemies of their women. The child should also know that by a law of our make, communities as well as individuals are imitators, and that a much-talked-of lynching will infallibly produce other lynchings here and there and yonder, and that in time these will breed a mania, a fashion; a fashion which will spread wide and wider, year by year, covering state after state, as with an advancing disease. Lynching has reached Colorado, it has reached California, it has reached Indiana—and now Missouri! I may live to see a Negro burned in Union Square, New York, with fifty thousand people present and not a sheriff visible, not a governor, not a constable, not a colonel, not a clergy-man, not a law-and-order representative of any sort.

Increase in Lynching.—In 1900 there were eight more cases than in 1899, and probably this year there will be more than there were last year. The year is little more than half gone, and yet there are eighty-eight cases as compared with one hundred and fifteen for all of last year. The four Southern states, Alabama, Georgia, Louisiana, and Mississippi are the worst offenders. Last year there were eight cases in Alabama, sixteen in Georgia, twenty in Louisiana, and twenty in Mississippi—over one-half the total. This year to date there have been nine in Alabama, twelve in Georgia, eleven in Louisiana, and thirteen in Mississippi—again more than one-half the total number in the whole United States.—Chicago *Tribune.*

It must be that the increase comes of the inborn human instinct to imitate—that and man's commonest weakness, his aversion to being unpleasantly conspicuous, pointed at, shunned, as being on the unpopular side. Its other name is Moral Cowardice, and is the commanding feature of the make-up of 9,999 men in the 10,000. I am not offering this as a discovery; privately the dullest of us knows it to be true. History will not allow us to forget or ignore this supreme trait of our character. It persistently and sardonically reminds us that from the beginning of the world no revolt against a public infamy or oppression has ever been begun but by the one daring man in the 10,000, the rest timidly waiting, and slowly and reluctantly joining under the influence of that man and his fellows from the other ten thousands. The abolitionists remember. Privately the public feeling was with them early, but each man was afraid to speak out until he got some hint that his neighbor was privately feeling as he privately felt himself. Then the boom followed. It always does. It will occur in New York some day, and even in Pennsylvania.

It has been supposed—and said—that the people at a

lynching enjoy the spectacle and are glad of a chance
to see it. It cannot be true; all experience is against it.
The people in the South are made like the people in the
North, the vast majority of whom are right-hearted and
compassionate and would be cruelly pained by such a
spectacle—and *would attend it* and let on to be pleased
with it, if the public approval seemed to require it. We
are made like that and we cannot help it. The other animals are not so but we cannot help that, either. They
lack the Moral Sense; we have no way of trading ours
off for a nickel or some other thing above its value. The
Moral Sense teaches us what is right, and how to avoid
it—when unpopular.

It is thought, as I have said, that a lynching crowd
enjoys a lynching. It certainly is not true; it is impossible
of belief. It is freely asserted—you have seen it in print
many times of late—that the lynching impulse has been
misinterpreted, that it is *not* the outcome of a spirit of
revenge but of a "mere atrocious hunger *to look upon
human suffering.*" If that were so, the crowds that saw
the Windsor Hotel burn down would have enjoyed the
horrors that fell under their eyes. Did they? No one will
think that of them, no one will make that charge. Many
risked their lives to save the men and women who were
in peril. Why did they do that? Because *none would
disapprove.* There was no restraint; they could follow
their natural impulse. Why does a crowd of the same
kind of people in Texas, Colorado, Indiana, stand by,
smitten to the heart and miserable, and by ostentatious
outward signs pretend to enjoy a lynching? Why does it
lift no hand or voice in protest? Only because it would
be unpopular to do it, I think; each man is afraid of his
neighbor's disapproval, a thing which, to the general
run of the race, is more dreaded than wounds and death.
When there is to be a lynching the people hitch up and

come miles to see it, bringing their wives and children.
Really to see it? No—they come only because they are
afraid to stay at home, lest it be noticed and offensively
commented upon. We may believe this, for we all know
how *we* feel about such spectacles—also, how we would
act under the like pressure. We are not any better nor
any braver than anybody else and we must not try to
creep out of it.

A Savonarola can quell and scatter a mob of lynchers
with a mere glance of his eye: so can a Merrill[1] or a
Beloat.[2] For no mob has any sand in the presence of a
man known to be splendidly brave. Besides, a lynching
mob would *like* to be scattered, for of a certainty there
are never ten men in it who would not prefer to be
somewhere else—and would be if they but had the
courage to go. When I was a boy I saw a brave gentleman deride and insult a mob and drive it away, and
afterward in Nevada I saw a noted desperado make two
hundred men sit still, with the house burning under
them, until he gave them permission to retire. A plucky
man can rob a whole passenger train by himself, and the
half of a brave man can hold up a stagecoach and strip
its occupants.

Then perhaps the remedy for lynchings comes to
this: station a brave man in each affected community
to encourage, support, and bring to light the deep disapproval of lynching hidden in the secret places of its
heart—for it is there, beyond question. Then those communities will find something better to imitate—of
course, being human, they must imitate something.
Where shall these brave men be found? That is indeed

[1] Sheriff of Carroll County, Georgia.
[2] Sheriff, Princeton, Indiana. By that formidable power which
lies in an established reputation for cold pluck they faced lynching
mobs and securely held the field against them.

a difficulty; there are not three hundred of them in the earth. If merely *physically* brave men would do, then it were easy; they could be furnished by the cargo. When Hobson called for seven volunteers to go with him to what promised to be certain death, four thousand men responded, the whole fleet in fact. Because *all the world would approve*. They knew that; but if Hobson's project had been charged with the scoffs and jeers of the friends and associates whose good opinion and approval the sailors valued, he could not have got his seven.

No, upon reflection, the scheme will not work. There are not enough morally brave men in stock. We are out of moral-courage material; we are in a condition of profound poverty. We have those two sheriffs down South who—but never mind, it is not enough to go around; they have to stay and take care of their own communities.

But if we only *could* have three or four more sheriffs of that great breed! Would it help? I think so. For we are all imitators: other brave sheriffs would follow; to be a dauntless sheriff would come to be recognized as the correct and only thing and the dreaded disapproval would fall to the share of the other kind; courage in this office would become custom, the absence of it a dishonor, just as courage presently replaces the timidity of the new soldier; then the mobs and the lynchings would disappear, and—

However. It can never be done without some starters, and where are we to get the starters? Advertise? Very well, then, let us advertise.

In the meantime, there is another plan. Let us import American missionaries from China and send them into the lynching field. With 1,511 of them out there converting two Chinamen apiece per annum against an uphill birth rate of 33,000 pagans per day, it will take upward of a million years to make the conversions balance the output and bring the Christianizing of the country in sight to the naked eye; therefore if we can offer our missionaries as rich a field at home at lighter expense and quite satisfactory in the matter of danger, why shouldn't they find it fair and right to come back and give us a trial? The Chinese are universally conceded to be excellent people, honest, honorable, industrious, trustworthy, kind-hearted, and all that—leave them alone, they are plenty good enough just as they are; and besides, almost every convert runs a risk of catching our civilization. We ought to be careful. We ought to think twice before we encourage a risk like that, for *once civilized, China can never be uncivilized again.* We have not been thinking of that. Very well, we ought to think of it now. Our missionaries will find that we have a field for them—and not only for the 1,511, but for 15,011. Let them look at the following telegram and see if they have anything in China that is more appetizing. It is from Texas:

The Negro was taken to a tree and swung in the air. Wood and fodder were piled beneath his body and a hot fire was made. *Then it was suggested that the man ought not to die too quickly, and he was let down to the ground while a party went to Dexter, about two miles distant, to procure coal oil.* This was thrown on the flames and the work completed.

We implore them to come back and help us in our need. Patriotism imposes this duty on them. Our country is worse off than China; they are our countrymen, their motherland supplicates their aid in this her hour of deep distress. They are competent; our people are not. They are used to scoffs, sneers, revilings, danger; our people are not. They have the martyr spirit; nothing but the martyr spirit can brave a lynching mob and cow it and scatter it. They can save their country, we beseech them to come home and do it. We ask them to read that telegram again and yet again, and picture the scene in their minds, and soberly ponder it; then multiply it by 115, add 88; place the 203 in a row, allowing 600 feet of space for each human torch, so that there may be viewing room around it for 5,000 Christian American men, women, and children, youths and maidens; make it night, for grim effect; have the show in a gradually rising plain and let the course of the stakes be uphill; the eye can then take in the whole line of twenty-four miles of blood-and-flesh bonfires unbroken, whereas if it occupied level ground the ends of the line would bend down and be hidden from view by the curvature of the earth. All being ready now, and the darkness opaque, the stillness impressive—for there should be no sound but the soft moaning of the night wind and the muffled sobbing of the sacrifices—let all the far stretch of kerosened pyres be touched off simultaneously and the glare and the shrieks and the agonies burst heavenward to the Throne.

There are more than a million persons present; the light from the fires flushes into vague outline against the night the spires of five thousand churches. O kind missionary, O compassionate missionary, leave China! come home and convert these Christians!

I believe that if anything can stop this epidemic of bloody insanities it is martial personalities that can face mobs without flinching; and as such personalities are developed only by familiarity with danger and by the training and seasoning which come of resisting it, the likeliest place to find them must be among the missionaries who have been under tuition in China during the past year or two. We have abundance of work for them and for hundreds and thousands more, and the field is daily growing and spreading. Shall we find them? We can try. In 75,000,000 there must be other Merrills and Beloats; and it is the law of our make that each example shall wake up drowsing chevaliers of the same great knighthood and bring them to the front.

TO THE PERSON
SITTING IN DARKNESS

Christmas will dawn in the United States over a people full
of hope and aspiration and good cheer. Such a condition
means contentment and happiness. The carping grumbler
who may here and there go forth will find few to listen to
him. The majority will wonder what is the matter with him
and pass on.—New York *Tribune,* on Christmas Eve.

From the *Sun,* of New York:

The purpose of this article is not to describe the terrible
offenses against humanity committed in the name of Politics
in some of the most notorious East Side districts. *They could
not be described, even verbally.* But it is the intention to let
the great mass of more or less careless citizens of this beautiful
metropolis of the New World get some conception of the
havoc and ruin wrought to man, woman, and child in the
most densely populated and least-known section of the city.
Name, date, and place can be supplied to those of little faith
—or to any man who feels himself aggrieved. It is a plain
statement of record and observation, written without license
and without garnish.

Imagine, if you can, a section of the city territory completely dominated by one man, without whose permission
neither legitimate nor illegitimate business can be conducted;
*where illegitimate business is encouraged and legitimate busi-
ness discouraged;* where the respectable residents have to
fasten their doors and windows summer nights and sit in their
rooms with asphyxiating air and 100-degree temperature,
rather than try to catch the faint whiff of breeze in their
natural breathing places, the stoops of their homes; *where
naked women dance by night in the streets, and unsexed men
prowl like vultures through the darkness on "business" not*
only permitted but encouraged by the police; *where the education of infants begins with the knowledge of prostitution*

and the training of little girls is training in the arts of Phryne; where *American* girls brought up with the refinements of *American* homes are imported from small towns up-state, Massachusetts, Connecticut, and New Jersey, and kept as virtually prisoners as if they were locked up behind jail bars until they have lost all semblance of womanhood; *where small boys are taught to solicit for the women of disorderly houses;* where there is an organized society of young men *whose sole business in life is to corrupt young girls and turn them over to bawdy houses;* where men walking with their wives along the street are openly insulted; *where children that have adult diseases are the chief patrons of the hospitals and dispensaries;* where it is the rule, rather than the exception, that *murder, rape, robbery, and theft go unpunished*—in short where the Premium of the most awful forms of Vice is the Profit of the politicians.

The following news from China appeared in the *Sun,* of New York, on Christmas Eve. The italics are mine:

The Rev. Mr. Ament, of the American Board of Foreign Missions, has returned from a trip which he made for the purpose of collecting indemnities for damages done by Boxers. *Everywhere he went he compelled the Chinese to pay.* He says that all his native Christians are now provided for. He had 700 of them under his charge, and 300 were killed. He has *collected 300 taels for each* of these murders, and has *compelled full payment for all the property belonging to Christians* that was destroyed. He also assessed *fines* amounting to THIRTEEN TIMES the amount of the indemnity. *This money will be used for the propagation of the Gospel.*

Mr. Ament declares that the compensation he has collected is *moderate* when compared with the amount secured by the Catholics, who demand, in addition to money, *head for head.* They collect 500 taels for each murder of a Catholic. In the Wenchiu country, 680 Catholics were killed, and for this the European Catholics here demand 750,000 strings of cash and 680 *heads.*

In the course of a conversation, Mr. Ament referred to the attitude of the missionaries toward the Chinese. He said:

"I deny emphatically that the missionaries are *vindictive,* that they *generally* looted, or that they have done anything *since* the siege that *the circumstances did not demand.* I criticize the Americans. *The soft hand of the Americans is not as good as the mailed fist of the Germans.* If you deal with the Chinese with a soft hand they will take advantage of it.

"The statement that the French government will return the loot taken by the French soldiers is the source of the greatest amusement here. The French soldiers were more systematic looters than the Germans, and it is a fact that to-day *Catholic Christians,* carrying French flags and armed with modern guns, *are looting villages* in the Province of Chili."

By happy luck, we get all these glad tidings on Christmas Eve—just in time enable us to celebrate the day with proper gaiety and enthusiasm. Our spirits soar, and we find we can even make jokes: Taels, I win, Heads you lose.

Our Reverend Ament is the right man in the right place. What we want of our missionaries out there is, not that they shall merely represent in their acts and persons the grace and gentleness and charity and loving-kindness of our religion, but that they shall also represent the American spirit. The oldest Americans are the Pawnees. Macallum's *History* says:

When a white Boxer kills a Pawnee and destroys his property, the other Pawnees do not trouble to seek *him* out, they kill any white person that comes along; also, they make some white village pay deceased's heirs the full cash value of deceased, together with full cash value of the property destroyed; they also make the village pay, in addition, *thirteen times* the value of that property into a fund for the dissemination of the Pawnee religion, which they regard as the best of all religions for the softening and humanizing of the heart of man. It is their idea that it is only fair and right that the innocent should be made to suffer for the guilty, and that it is better that ninety and nine innocent should suffer than that one guilty person should escape.

Our Reverend Ament is justifiably jealous of those enterprising Catholics who not only get big money for each lost convert but get "head for head" besides. But

he should soothe himself with the reflections that the
entirety of their exactions are for their own pockets,
whereas he, less selfishly, devotes only 300 taels per
head to that service, and gives the whole vast thirteen
repetitions of the property-indemnity to the service of
propagating the Gospel. His magnanimity has won him
the approval of his nation and will get him a monument.
Let him be content with these rewards. We all hold him
dear for manfully defending his fellow missionaries
from exaggerated charges which were beginning to distress us, but which his testimony has so considerably
modified that we can now contemplate them without
noticeable pain. For now we know that, even before the
siege, the missionaries were not "generally" out looting,
and that "since the siege" they have acted quite handsomely, except when "circumstances" crowded them. I
am arranging for the monument. Subscriptions for it can
be sent to the American Board, designs for it can be
sent to me. Designs must allegorically set forth the
Thirteen Reduplications of the Indemnity and the Object for which they were exacted; as Ornaments the designs must exhibit 680 Heads, so disposed as to give a
pleasing and pretty effect, for the Catholics have done
nicely, and are entitled to notice in the monument.
Mottoes may be suggested, if any shall be discovered
that will satisfactorily cover the ground.

Mr. Ament's financial feat of squeezing a thirteen-
fold indemnity out of the pauper peasants to square
other people's offenses, thus condemning them and their
women and innocent little children to inevitable starvation and lingering death, in order that the blood money
so acquired might be *used for the propagation of the
Gospel,*" does not flutter my serenity; although the act
and the words, taken together, concrete a blasphemy
so hideous and so colossal that without doubt its mate

is not findable in the history of this or of any other age. Yet if a layman had done that thing and justified it with those words, I should have shuddered, I know. Or if I had done the thing and said the words myself— However, the thought is unthinkable, irreverent as some imperfectly informed people think me. Sometimes an ordained minister sets out to be blasphemous. When this happens the layman is out of the running; he stands no chance.

We have Mr. Ament's impassioned assurance that the missionaries are not "vindictive." Let us hope and pray that they will never become so, but will remain in the almost morbidly fair and just and gentle temper which is affording so much satisfaction to their brother and champion today.

The following is from the New York *Tribune* of Christmas Eve. It comes from that journal's Tokyo correspondent. It has a strange and impudent sound, but the Japanese are but partially civilized as yet. When they become wholly civilized they will not talk so:

The missionary question, of course, occupies a foremost place in the discussion. It is now felt as essential that the Western Powers take cognizance of the sentiment here, that religious invasions of Oriental countries by powerful Western organizations are tantamount to filibustering expeditions, and should not only be discountenanced, but that stern measures should be adopted for their suppression. The feeling here is that the missionary organizations constitute a constant menace to peaceful international relations.

Shall we? That is, shall we go on conferring our Civilization upon the peoples that sit in darkness, or shall we give those poor things a rest? Shall we bang right ahead in our old-time, loud, pious way, and commit the new century to the game; or shall we sober up and sit down and think it over first? Would it not be prudent to get our Civilization tools together and see how much stock is left on hand in the way of Glass Beads and Theology, and Maxim Guns and Hymn Books, and Trade Gin and Torches of Progress and Enlightenment (patent adjustable ones, good to fire villages with, upon occasion), and balance the books and arrive at the profit and loss, so that we may intelligently decide whether to continue the business or sell out the property and start a new Civilization Scheme on the proceeds?

Extending the Blessings of Civilization to our Brother who Sits in Darkness has been a good trade and has paid well, on the whole; and there is money in it yet, if carefully worked—but not enough, in my judgment, to make any considerable risk advisable. The People that Sit in Darkness are getting to be too scarce—too scarce and too shy. And such darkness as is now left is really of but an indifferent quality, and not dark enough for the game. The most of those People that Sit in Darkness have been furnished with more light than was good for them or profitable for us. We have been injudicious.

The Blessings-of-Civilization Trust, wisely and cautiously administered, is a Daisy. There is more money in it, more territory, more sovereignty and other kinds of emolument, than there is in any other game that is played. But Christendom has been playing it badly of late years and must certainly suffer by it, in my opinion. She has been so eager to get every stake that appeared on the green cloth that the People who Sit in Darkness have noticed it—they have noticed it and have begun to show alarm. They have become suspicious of the Blessings of Civilization. More—they have begun to examine them. This is not well. The Blessings of Civilization are all right, and a good commercial property; there could not be a better, in a dim light. In the right kind of a light and at a proper distance, with the goods

a little out of focus, they furnish this desirable exhibit
to the Gentlemen who Sit in Darkness:

Love	Law and Order
Justice	Liberty
Gentleness	Equality
Christianity	Honorable Deal-
Protection to the	ing
Weak	Mercy
Temperance	Education

—and so on.

There. Is it good? Sir, it is pie. It will bring into camp
any idiot that sits in darkness anywhere. But not if we
adulterate it. It is proper to be emphatic upon that
point. This brand is strictly for Export—apparently.
Apparently. Privately and confidentially, it is nothing of
the kind. Privately and confidentially, it is merely an
outside cover, gay and pretty and attractive, displaying
the special patterns of our Civilization which we reserve for Home Consumption, while *inside* the bale is
the Actual Thing that the Customer Sitting in Darkness
buys with his blood and tears and land and liberty.
That Actual Thing is indeed Civilization, but it is only
for Export. Is there a difference between the two
brands? In some of the details, yes.

We all know that the Business is being ruined. The
reason is not far to seek. It is because our Mr. McKinley,
and Mr. Chamberlain, and the Kaiser and the Tsar and
the French have been exporting the Actual Thing *with
the outside cover left off*. This is bad for the Game. It
shows that these new players of it are not sufficiently
acquainted with it.

It is a distress to look on and note the mismoves, they
are so strange and so awkward. Mr. Chamberlain manu-

factures a war out of materials so inadequate and so fanciful that they make the boxes grieve and the gallery laugh, and he tries hard to persuade himself that it isn't purely a private raid for cash but has a sort of dim, vague respectability about it somewhere, if he could only find the spot; and that by and by he can scour the flag clean again after he has finished dragging it through the mud, and make it shine and flash in the vault of heaven once more as it had shone and flashed there a thousand years in the world's respect until he laid his unfaithful hand upon it. It is bad play—bad. For it exposes the Actual Thing to Them that Sit in Darkness, and they say: "What! Christian against Christian? And only for money? Is *this* a case of magnanimity, forbearance, love, gentleness, mercy, protection of the weak—this strange and overshowy onslaught of an elephant upon a nest of field mice, on the pretext that the mice had squeaked an insolence at him—conduct which 'no self-respecting government could allow to pass' unavenged'? as Mr. Chamberlain said. Was that a good pretext in a small case, when it had not been a good pretext in a large one?—for only recently Russia had affronted the elephant three times and survived alive and unsmitten. Is this Civilization and Progress? Is it something better than we already possess? These harryings and burnings and desert-makings in the Transvaal —is this an improvement on our darkness? Is it, perhaps, possible that there are two kinds of Civilization— one for home consumption and one for the heathen market?"

Then They that Sit in Darkness are troubled, and shake their heads, and they read this extract from a letter of a British private, recounting his exploits in one of Methuen's victories some days before the affair of Magersfontein, and they are troubled again:

We tore up the hill and into the intrenchments, and the Boers saw we had them; so they dropped their guns and went down on their knees and put up their hands clasped, and begged for mercy. And we gave it them—*with the long spoon.*

The long spoon is the bayonet. See *Lloyd's Weekly,* London, of those days. The same number—and the same column—contained some quite unconscious satire in the form of shocked and bitter upbraidings of the Boers for their brutalities and inhumanities!

Next, to our heavy damage, the Kaiser went to playing the game without first mastering it. He lost a couple of missionaries in a riot in Shantung, and in his account he made an overcharge for them. China had to pay a hundred thousand dollars apiece for them in money; twelve miles of territory, containing several millions of inhabitants and worth twenty million dollars; and to build a monument and also a Christian church; whereas the people of China could have been depended upon to remember the missionaries without the help of these expensive memorials. This was all bad play. Bad, because it would not, and could not, and will not now or ever, deceive the Person Sitting in Darkness. He knows that it was an overcharge. He knows that a missionary is like any other man: he is worth merely what you can supply his place for and no more. He is useful, but so is a doctor, so is a sheriff, so is an editor; but a just Emperor does not charge war prices for such. A diligent, intelligent, but obscure missionary, and a diligent, intelligent country editor are worth much, and we know it; but they are not worth the earth. We esteem such an editor and we are sorry to see him go, but when he goes, we should consider twelve miles of territory and a church and a fortune overcompensation for his loss. I mean, if he was a Chinese editor and we had to settle for him. It is no proper figure for an editor or a missionary; one can get shop-worn kings for less. It was bad play on the Kaiser's part. It got this property, true; but it *produced the Chinese revolt*, the indignant uprising of China's traduced patriots, the Boxers. The results have been expensive to Germany and to the other Disseminators of Progress and the Blessings of Civilization.

The Kaiser's claim was paid, yet it was bad play, for it could not fail to have an evil effect upon Persons Sitting in Darkness in China. They would muse upon the event and be likely to say: "Civilization is gracious and beautiful, for such is its reputation, but can we afford it? There are rich Chinamen, perhaps they can afford it; but this tax is not laid upon them, it is laid upon the peasants of Shantung; it is they that must pay this mighty sum and their wages are but four cents a day. Is this a better civilization than ours, and holier and higher and nobler? Is not this rapacity? Is not this extortion? Would Germany charge America two hundred thousand dollars for two missionaries, and shake the mailed fist in her face and send warships and send soldiers, and say, 'Seize twelve miles of territory, worth twenty millions of dollars, as additional pay for the missionaries, and make those peasants build a monument to the missionaries, and a costly Christian church to remember them by?' And later would Germany say to her soldiers, 'March through America and slay, *giving no quarter;* make the German face there, as has been our Hun-face here, a terror for a thousand years; march through the Great Republic and slay, slay, slay, carving a road for our offended religion through its heart and bowels?' Would Germany do like this to America, to England, to France, to Russia? Or only to China, the helpless— imitating the elephant's assault upon the field mice? Had we better invest in this Civilization—this Civilization which called Napoleon a buccaneer for carrying off

Venice's bronze horses, but which steals our ancient
astronomical instruments from our walls and goes looting like common bandits—that is, all the alien soldiers
except America's; and (Americans again excepted)
storms frightened villages and cables the result to glad
journals at home every day: 'Chinese losses, 450 killed;
ours, *one officer and two men wounded.* Shall proceed
against neighboring village tomorrow, where a *massacre*
is reported.' Can we afford Civilization?"

And next Russia must go and play the game inju-
diciously. She affronts England once or twice—with the
Person Sitting in Darkness observing and noting; by
moral assistance of France and Germany, she robs Japan
of her hard-earned spoil, all swimming in Chinese blood
—Port Arthur—with the Person again observing and
noting; then she seizes Manchuria, raids its villages, and
chokes its great river with the swollen corpses of countless massacred peasants—that astonished Person still
observing and noting. And perhaps he is saying to himself, "It is yet *another* Civilized Power, with its banner
of the Prince of Peace in one hand and its loot basket
and its butcher knife in the other. Is there no salvation
for us but to adopt Civilization and lift ourselves down
to its level?"

And by and by comes America, and our Master of
the Game plays it badly—plays it as Mr. Chamberlain
was playing it in South Africa. It was a mistake to do
that; also, it was one which was quite unlooked for in a
Master who was playing it so well in Cuba. In Cuba,
he was playing the usual and regular *American* game
and it was winning, for there is no way to beat it. The
Master, contemplating Cuba, said, "Here is an oppressed
and friendless little nation which is willing to fight to be
free; we go partners, and put up the strength of seventy

million sympathizers and the resources of the United
States: play!" Nothing but Europe combined could call
that hand, and Europe cannot combine on anything.
There in Cuba he was following our great traditions in
a way which made us very proud of him, and proud of
the deep dissatisfaction which his play was provoking in
continental Europe. Moved by a high inspiration, he
threw out those stirring words which proclaimed that
forcible annexation would be "criminal aggression," and
in that utterance fired another "shot heard round the
world." The memory of that fine saying will be outlived
by the remembrance of no act of his but one—that he
forgot it within the twelvemonth, and its honorable
gospel along with it.

For presently came the Philippine temptation. It was
strong, it was too strong, and he made that bad mistake:
he played the European game, the Chamberlain game.
It was a pity, it was a great pity, that error—that one
grievous error, that irrevocable error. For it was the very
place and time to play the American game again. And at
no cost. Rich winnings to be gathered in, too, rich and
permanent, indestructible, a fortune transmissible forever to the children of the flag. Not land, not money,
not dominion—no, something worth many times more
than that dross: our share, the spectacle of a nation of
long harassed and persecuted slaves set free through
our influence; our posterity's share, the golden memory
of that fair deed. The game was in our hands. If it had
been played according to the American rules, Dewey
would have sailed away from Manila as soon as he had
destroyed the Spanish fleet—after putting up a sign on
shore guaranteeing foreign property and life against
damage by the Filipinos, and warning the Powers that
interference with the emancipated patriots would be

regarded as an act unfriendly to the United States. The Powers cannot combine in even a bad cause, and the sign would not have been molested.

Dewey could have gone about his affairs elsewhere and left the competent Filipino army to starve out the little Spanish garrison and send it home, and the Filipino citizens to set up the form of government they might prefer and deal with the friars and their doubtful acquisitions according to Filipino ideas of fairness and justice —ideas which have since been tested and found to be of as high an order as any that prevail in Europe or America.

But we played the Chamberlain game and lost the chance to add another Cuba and another honorable deed to our good record.

The more we examine the mistake, the more clearly we perceive that it is going to be bad for the Business. The Person Sitting in Darkness is almost sure to say, "There is something curious about this—curious and unaccountable. There must be two Americas, one that sets the captive free, and one that takes a once-captive's new freedom away from him, and picks a quarrel with him with nothing to found it on, then kills him to get his land."

The truth is, the Person Sitting in Darkness *is* saying things like that, and for the sake of the Business we must persuade him to look at the Philippine matter in another and healthier way. We must arrange his opinions for him. I believe it can be done, for Mr. Chamberlain has arranged England's opinion of the South African matter and done it most cleverly and successfully. He presented the facts—some of the facts—and showed those confiding people what the facts meant. He did it statistically, which is a good way. He used the formula:

"Twice 2 are 14, and 2 from 9 leaves 35." Figures are effective; figures will convince the elect.

Now, my plan is a still bolder one than Mr. Chamberlain's, though apparently a copy of it. Let us be franker than Mr. Chamberlain; let us audaciously present the whole of the facts, shirking none, then explain them according to Mr. Chamberlain's formula. This daring truthfulness will astonish and dazzle the Person Sitting in Darkness, and he will take the Explanation down before his mental vision has had time to get back into focus. Let us say to him:

"Our case is simple. On the first of May, Dewey destroyed the Spanish fleet. This left the Archipelago in the hands of its proper and rightful owners, the Filipino nation. Their army numbered 30,000 men and they were competent to whip out or starve out the little Spanish garrison; then the people could set up a government of their own devising. Our traditions required that Dewey should now set up his warning sign and go away. But the Master of the Game happened to think of another plan—the European plan. He acted upon it. This was to send out an army—ostensibly to help the native patriots put the finishing touch upon their long and plucky struggle for independence, but really to take their land away from them and keep it. That is, in the interest of Progress and Civilization. The plan developed stage by stage, and quite satisfactorily. We entered into a military alliance with the trusting Filipinos and they hemmed in Manila on the land side, and by their valuable help the place, with its garrison of 8,000 or 10,000 Spaniards, was captured—a thing which we could not have accomplished unaided at that time. We got their help by—by ingenuity. We knew they were fighting for their independence and that they had been at it for two years. We knew they supposed that we also were fighting in their worthy cause—just as we had helped the Cubans fight for Cuban independence—and we allowed them to go on thinking so. *Until Manila was ours and we could get along without them.* Then we showed our hand. Of course, they were surprised—that was natural, surprised and disappointed, disappointed and grieved. To them it looked un-American, uncharacteristic, foreign to our established traditions. And this was natural, too, for we were only playing the American Game in public—in private it was the European. It was neatly done, very neatly, and it bewildered them. They could not understand it, for we had been so friendly— so affectionate, even—with those simple-minded patriots! We, our own selves, had brought back out of exile their leader, their hero, their hope, their Washington—Aguinaldo; brought him in a warship, in high honor, under the sacred shelter and hospitality of the flag; brought him back and restored him to his people and got their moving and eloquent gratitude for it. Yes, we had been so friendly to them and had heartened them up in so many ways! We had lent them guns and ammunition; advised with them; exchanged pleasant courtesies with them; placed our sick and wounded in their kindly care; intrusted our Spanish prisoners to their humane and honest hands; fought shoulder to shoulder with them against "the common enemy" (our own phrase); praised their courage, praised their gallantry, praised their mercifulness, praised their fine and honorable conduct; borrowed their trenches, borrowed strong positions which they had previously captured from the Spaniards; petted them, lied to them—officially proclaiming that our land and naval forces came to give them their freedom and displace the bad Spanish Government—fooled them, used them until we needed them no longer, then derided the sucked orange and threw it away. We kept the positions which we had beguiled them of, by and by we moved a force forward and overlapped patriot ground—a clever thought, for we needed trouble and this would produce it. A Filipino soldier, crossing the ground, where no one had a right to forbid him, was shot by our sentry. The badgered patriots resented this with arms, without waiting to know whether Aguinaldo, who was absent, would approve or not. Aguinaldo did not approve, but that availed nothing. What we wanted in the interest of Progress and Civilization was the Archipelago, unencumbered by patriots struggling for independence; and War was what we needed. We clinched our opportunity. It is Mr. Chamberlain's case over again—at least in its motive and intention; and we played the game as adroitly as he played it himself."

At this point in our frank statement of fact to the Person Sitting in Darkness, we should throw in a little trade taffy about the Blessings of Civilization—for a change, and for the refreshment of his spirit—then go on with our tale:

"We and the patriots having captured Manila, Spain's ownership of the Archipelago and her sovereignty over it were at an end—obliterated—annihilated—not a rag or shred of either remaining behind. It was then that we conceived the divinely humorous idea of *buying* both of these specters from Spain! [It is quite safe to confess this to the Person Sitting in Darkness, since neither he nor any other sane person will believe it.] In buying those ghosts for twenty millions, we also contracted to take care of the friars and their accumulations. I think we also agreed to propagate leprosy and smallpox, but as to this there is doubt. But it is not important, persons afflicted with the friars do not mind other diseases.

"With our Treaty ratified, Manila subdued, and our Ghosts secured, we had no further use for Aguinaldo and the owners of the Archipelago. We forced a war and we have been hunting America's guest and ally through the woods and swamps ever since."

At this point in the tale, it will be well to boast a little of our war work and our heroisms in the field, so as to make our performance look as fine as England's in South Africa, but I believe it will not be best to emphasize this too much. We must be cautious. Of course, we must read the war telegrams to the Person, in order to keep up our frankness, but we can throw an air of humorousness over them and that will modify their grim eloquence a little, and their rather indiscreet exhibitions of gory exultation. Before reading to him the following display heads of the dispatches of November 18, 1900, it will be well to practice on them in private first, so as to get the right tang of lightness and gayety into them:

"ADMINISTRATION WEARY OF PROTRACTED HOSTILITIES!"

"REAL WAR AHEAD FOR FILIPINO REBELS!" [1]

"WILL SHOW NO MERCY!"

"KITCHENER'S PLAN ADOPTED!"

Kitchener knows how to handle disagreeable people who are fighting for their homes and their liberties, and we must let on that we are merely imitating Kitchener and have no national interest in the matter, further than to get ourselves admired by the Great Family of Na-

---

[1] "Rebels!" Mumble that funny word—don't let the Person catch it distinctly.

tions, in which august company our Master of the Game
has bought a place for us in the back row.

Of course, we must not venture to ignore our General
MacArthur's reports—oh, why do they keep on printing
those embarrassing things?—we must drop them trip-
pingly from the tongue and take the chances:

> During the last ten months our losses have been 268 killed
> and 750 wounded; Filipino loss, *three thousand two hundred
> and twenty-seven killed,* and 694 wounded.

We must stand ready to grab the Person Sitting in
Darkness, for he will swoon away at this confession,
saying, "Good God! those 'niggers' spare their wounded,
and the Americans massacre theirs!"

We must bring him to and coax him and coddle him,
and assure him that the ways of Providence are best
and that it would not become us to find fault with them;
and then, to show him that we are only imitators, not
originators, we must read the following passage from
the letter of an American soldier lad in the Philippines
to his mother, published in *Public Opinion,* of Decorah,
Iowa, describing the finish of a victorious battle:

> "WE NEVER LEFT ONE ALIVE. IF ONE WAS WOUNDED,
> WE WOULD RUN OUR BAYONETS THROUGH HIM."

Having now laid all the historical facts before the
Person Sitting in Darkness, we should bring him to
again and explain them to him. We should say to him:
"They look doubtful but in reality they are not. There
have been lies, yes, but they were told in a good cause.
We have been treacherous, but that was only in order
that real good might come out of apparent evil. True,
we have crushed a deceived and confiding people; we
have turned against the weak and the friendless who

trusted us; we have stamped out a just and intelligent and well-ordered republic; we have stabbed an ally in the back and slapped the face of a guest; we have bought a Shadow from an enemy that hadn't it to sell; we have robbed a trusting friend of his land and his liberty; we have invited our clean young men to shoulder a discredited musket and do bandits' work under a flag which bandits have been accustomed to fear, not to follow; we have debauched America's honor and blackened her face before the world; but each detail was for the best. We know this. The Head of every State and Sovereignty in Christendom and 90 per cent of every legislative body in Christendom, including our Congress and our fifty state legislatures, are members not only of the church but also of the Blessings-of-Civilization Trust. This world-girdling accumulation of trained morals, high principles, and justice cannot do an unright thing, an unfair thing, an ungenerous thing, an unclean thing. It knows what it is about. Give yourself no uneasiness; it is all right."

Now then, that will convince the Person. You will see. It will restore the Business. Also, it will elect the Master of the Game to the vacant place in the Trinity of our national gods, and there on their high thrones the Three will sit, age after age, in the people's sight, each bearing the Emblem of his service: Washington, the Sword of the Liberator; Lincoln, the Slave's Broken Chains; the Master, the Chains Repaired.

It will give the Business a splendid new start. You will see.

Everything is prosperous, now; everything is just as we should wish it. We have got the Archipelago, and we shall never give it up. Also, we have every reason to hope that we shall have an opportunity before very long to slip out of our congressional contract with Cuba and give her something better in the place of it. It is a rich country and many of us are already beginning to see that the contract was a sentimental mistake. But now—right now—is the best time to do some profitable rehabilitating work—work that will set us up and make us comfortable, and discourage gossip. We cannot conceal from ourselves that, privately, we are a little troubled about our uniform. It is one of our prides, it is acquainted with honor, it is familiar with great deeds and noble, we love it, we revere it, and so this errand it is on makes us uneasy. And our flag—another pride of ours, our chiefest! We have worshiped it so, and when we have seen it in far lands—glimpsing it unexpectedly in that strange sky, waving its welcome and benediction to us—we have caught our breaths and uncovered our heads and couldn't speak for a moment, for the thought of what it was to us and the great ideals it stood for. Indeed, we *must* do something about these things; it is easily managed. We can have a special one —our states do it: we can have just our usual flag, with the white stripes painted black and the stars replaced by the skull and crossbones.

And we do not need that Civil Commission out there. Having no powers, it has to invent them, and that kind of work cannot be effectively done by just anybody; an expert is required. Mr. Croker can be spared. We do not want the United States represented there, but only the Game.

By help of these suggested amendments, Progress and Civilization in that country can have a boom, and it will take in the Persons who are Sitting in Darkness, and we can resume Business at the old stand.

Mark Twain's Autobiography

MY UNCLE, John A. Quarles, was a farmer and his place was in the country four miles from Florida. He had eight children and fifteen or twenty Negroes and was also fortunate in other ways, particularly in his character. I have not come across a better man than he was. I was his guest for two or three months every year, from the fourth year after we removed to Hannibal till I was eleven or twelve years old. I have never consciously used him or his wife in a book, but his farm has come very handy to me in literature once or twice. In *Huck Finn* and in *Tom Sawyer, Detective* I moved it down to Arkansas. It was all of six hundred miles but it was no trouble; it was not a very large farm, five hundred acres perhaps, but I could have done it if it had been twice as large. And as for the morality of it, I cared nothing for that; I would move a state if the exigencies of literature required it.

It was a heavenly place for a boy, that farm of my uncle John's. The house was a double log one with a spacious floor (roofed in) connecting it with the kitchen. In the summer the table was set in the middle of that shady and breezy floor, and the sumptuous meals— well, it makes me cry to think of them. Fried chicken, roast pig, wild and tame turkeys, ducks and geese, venison just killed, squirrels, rabbits, pheasants, partridges, prairie-chickens, biscuits, hot batter-cakes, hot buckwheat cakes, hot "wheat bread," hot rolls, hot corn pone; fresh corn boiled on the ear, succotash, butter-beans, string-beans, tomatoes, peas, Irish potatoes, sweet potatoes; buttermilk, sweet milk; "clabber"; watermel-ons, muskmelons, cantaloupes—all fresh from the gar-den—apple pie, peach pie, pumpkin pie, apple dump-lings, peach cobbler—I can't remember the rest. The way that the things were cooked was perhaps the main splendor, particularly a certain few of the dishes. For instance the corn bread, the hot biscuits and wheat bread, and the fried chicken. These things have never been properly cooked in the North—in fact no one there is able to learn the art, so far as my experience goes. The North thinks it knows how to make corn bread but this is mere superstition. Perhaps no bread in the world is quite so good as Southern corn bread, and perhaps no bread in the world is quite so bad as the Northern imitation of it. The North seldom tries to fry chicken and this is well; the art cannot be learned north of the line of Mason and Dixon, nor anywhere in Europe. This is not hearsay; it is experience that is speaking. In Europe it is imagined that the custom of serving various kinds of bread blazing hot is "American" but that is too broad a spread; it is custom in the South but is much less than that in the North. In the North and in Europe hot bread is considered unhealthy. This is probably an-other fussy superstition, like the European superstition that ice-water is unhealthy. Europe does not need ice-water and does not drink it; and yet notwithstanding this its word for it is better than ours, because it de-scribes it, whereas ours doesn't. Europe calls it "iced" water. Our word describes water made from melted ice —a drink which has a characterless taste and which we have but little acquaintance with.

It seems a pity that the world should throw away so

many good things merely because they are unwholesome. I doubt if God has given us any refreshment which, taken in moderation, is unwholesome, except microbes. Yet there are people who strictly deprive themselves of each and every eatable, drinkable, and smokable which has in anyway acquired a shady reputation. They pay this price for health. And health is all they get for it. How strange it is. It is like paying out your whole fortune for a cow that has gone dry.

The farm-house stood in the middle of a very large yard and the yard was fenced on three sides with rails and on the rear side with high palings; against these stood the smoke-house; beyond the palings was the orchard; beyond the orchard were the Negro quarter and the tobacco fields. The front yard was entered over a stile made of sawed-off logs of graduated heights; I do not remember any gate. In a corner of the front yard were a dozen lofty hickory trees and a dozen black walnuts, and in the nutting season riches were to be gathered there.

Down a piece, abreast the house, stood a little log cabin against the rail fence; and there the woody hill fell sharply away, past the barns, the corn-crib, the stables, and the tobacco-curing house, to a limpid brook which sang along over its gravelly bed and curved and frisked in and out and here and there and yonder in the deep shade of overhanging foliage and vines—a divine place for wading, and it had swimming-pools too, which were forbidden to us and therefore much frequented by us. For we were little Christian children and had early been taught the value of forbidden fruit.

In the little log cabin lived a bedridden white-headed slave woman whom we visited daily and looked upon with awe, for we believed she was upward of a thousand years old and had talked with Moses. The younger Negroes credited these statistics and had furnished them to us in good faith. We accommodated all the details which came to us about her, and so we believed that she had lost her health in the long desert trip coming out of Egypt and had never been able to get it back again. She had a round bald place on the crown of her head, and we used to creep around and gaze at it in reverent silence and reflect that it was caused by fright through seeing Pharaoh drowned. We called her "Aunt" Hannah, Southern fashion. She was superstitious, like the other Negroes; also, like them, she was deeply religious. Like them, she had great faith in prayer and employed it in all ordinary exigencies, but not in cases where a dead certainty of result was urgent. Whenever witches were around she tied up the remnant of her wool in little tufts with white thread, and this promptly made the witches impotent.

All the Negroes were friends of ours and with those of our own age we were in effect comrades. I say in effect, using the phrase as a modification. We were comrades and yet not comrades; color and condition interposed a subtle line which both parties were conscious of and which rendered complete fusion impossible. We had a faithful and affectionate good friend, ally, and adviser in "Uncle Dan'l," a middle-aged slave whose head was the best one in the Negro quarter, whose sympathies were wide and warm, and whose heart was honest and simple and knew no guile. He has served me well these many, many years. I have not seen him for more than half a century, and yet spiritually I have had his welcome company a good part of that time and have staged him in books under his own name and as Jim and carted him all around, to Hannibal, down the Mississippi on a raft, and even across the Desert of Sahara in a balloon —and he has endured it all with the patience and friendliness and loyalty which were his birthright. It was on the farm that I got my strong liking for his race and my appreciation of certain of its fine qualities. This feeling and this estimate have stood the test of sixty years and more, and have suffered no impairment. The black face is as welcome to me now as it was then.

In my school-boy days I had no aversion to slavery. I was not aware that there was anything wrong about it. No one arraigned it in my hearing; the local papers said nothing against it; the local pulpit taught us that God approved it, that it was a holy thing, and that the doubter need only look in the Bible if he wished to settle his mind—and then the texts were read aloud to us to make the matter sure; if the slaves themselves had an aversion to slavery, they were wise and said nothing. In Hannibal we seldom saw a slave misused; on the farm, never.

There was, however, one small incident of my boyhood days which touched this matter and it must have meant a good deal to me or it would not have stayed in my memory, clear and sharp, vivid and shadowless, all these slow-drifting years. We had a little slave boy whom we had hired from some one, there in Hannibal. He was from the Eastern Shore of Maryland and had been brought away from his family and his friends, halfway across the American continent, and sold. He was a cheery spirit, innocent and gentle, and the noisiest creature that ever was perhaps. All day long he was singing, whistling, yelling, whooping, laughing—it was maddening, devastating, unendurable. At last, one day, I lost all my temper and went raging to my mother and said Sandy had been singing for an hour without a single break, and I couldn't stand it, and *wouldn't* she please shut him up. The tears came into her eyes and her lip trembled, and she said something like this:

"Poor thing, when he sings it shows that he is not remembering, and that comforts me; but when he is still I am afraid he is thinking and I cannot bear it. He will never see his mother again; if he can sing, I must not hinder it but be thankful for it. If you were older, you would understand me; then that friendless child's noise would make you glad."

It was a simple speech and made up of small words but it went home, and Sandy's noise was not a trouble to me any more. She never used large words but she had a natural gift for making small ones do effective work. She lived to reach the neighborhood of ninety years and was capable with her tongue to the last, especially when a meanness or an injustice roused her spirit. She has come handy to me several times in my books, where she figures as Tom Sawyer's Aunt Polly. I fitted her out with a dialect and tried to think up other improvements for her, but did not find any. I used Sandy once, also; it was in *Tom Sawyer*. I tried to get him to whitewash the fence but it did not work. I do not remember what name I called him by in the book.

I can see the farm yet with perfect clearness. I can see all its belongings, all its details: the family room of the house with a "trundle" bed in one corner and a spinning-wheel in another, a wheel whose rising and falling wail, heard from a distance, was the mournfulest of all sounds to me and made me homesick and low-spirited and filled my atmosphere with the wandering spirits of the dead; the vast fireplace, piled high on winter nights with flaming hickory logs from whose ends a sugary sap bubbled out but did not go to waste, for we scraped it off and ate it; the lazy cat spread out on the rough hearth-stones; the drowsy dogs braced against the jambs and blinking; my aunt in one chimney corner, knitting; my uncle in the other, smoking his corn-cob pipe; the slick and carpetless oak floor faintly mirroring the dancing flame-tongues and freckled with black indentations where fire-coals had popped out and died a leisurely death; half a dozen children romping in the background twilight; split-bottomed chairs here and there, some with rockers; a cradle, out of service but waiting with confidence; in the early cold mornings a snuggle of children in shirts and chemises occupying the hearth-stone and procrastinating—they could not bear to leave that comfortable place and go out on the wind-swept floor-space between the house and kitchen where the general tin basin stood, and wash.

Along outside of the front fence ran the country road, dusty in the summertime and a good place for snakes—they liked to lie in it and sun themselves; when they were rattlesnakes or puff adders, we killed them; when they were black snakes or racers or belonged to the fabled "hoop" breed, we fled, without shame; when they were "house-snakes" or "garters" we carried them home and put them in Aunt Patsy's work-basket for a surprise; for she was prejudiced against snakes and always when she took the basket in her lap and they began to climb out of it, it disordered her mind. She never could seem to get used to them, her opportunities went for nothing. And she was always cold toward bats, too, and could not bear them; and yet I think a bat is as friendly a bird as there is. My mother was Aunt Patsy's sister and had the same wild superstitions. A bat is beautifully soft and silky; I do not know any creature that is pleasanter to the touch or is more grateful for caressings, if offered in the right spirit. I know all about these coleoptera because our great cave, three miles below Hannibal, was multitudinously stocked with them and often I brought them home to amuse my mother with. It was easy to manage if it was a school-day, because then I had ostensibly been to school and hadn't any bats. She was not a suspicious person but full of trust and confidence, and when I said, "There's something in my coat-pocket for you," she would put her hand in. But she always took it out again, herself; I didn't have to tell her. It was remarkable, the way she couldn't learn to like private bats. The more experience she had, the more she could not change her views.

I think she was never in the cave in her life; but everybody else went there. Many excursion parties came from considerable distances up and down the river to visit the cave. It was miles in extent and was a tangled wilderness of narrow and lofty clefts and passages. It was an easy place to get lost in; anybody could do it, including the bats. I got lost in it myself, along with a lady, and our last candle burned down to almost nothing before we glimpsed the search-party's lights winding about in the distance.

"Injun Joe," the half-breed, got lost in there once and would have starved to death if the bats had run short. But there was no chance of that, there were myriads of them. He told me all his story. In the book called *Tom Sawyer* I starved him entirely to death in the cave but that was in the interest of art: it never happened. "General" Gaines, who was our first town drunkard before Jimmy Finn got the place, was lost in there for the space of a week and finally pushed his handkerchief out of a hole in a hilltop near Saverton, several miles down the river from the cave's mouth, and somebody saw it and dug him out. There is nothing the matter with his statistics except the handkerchief. I knew him for years and he hadn't any. But it could have been his nose. That would attract attention.

The cave was an uncanny place for it contained a corpse, the corpse of a young girl of fourteen. It was in a

glass cylinder inclosed in a copper one which was suspended from a rail which bridged a narrow passage.
The body was preserved in alcohol, and it was said that
loafers and rowdies used to drag it up by the hair and
look at the dead face. The girl was the daughter of a
St. Louis surgeon of extraordinary ability and wide
celebrity. He was an eccentric man and did many
strange things. He put the poor thing in that forlorn
place himself.

II

Beyond the road where the snakes sunned themselves
was a dense young thicket, and through it a dim-lighted
path led a quarter of a mile; then out of the dimness
one emerged abruptly upon a level great prairie which
was covered with wild strawberry plants, vividly starred
with prairie pinks, and walled in on all sides by forests.
The strawberries were fragrant and fine and in the
season we were generally there in the crisp freshness
of the early morning, while the dew-beads still sparkled
upon the grass and the woods were ringing with the
first songs of the birds.

Down the forest-slopes to the left were the swings.
They were made of bark stripped from hickory saplings.
When they became dry they were dangerous. They usually broke when a child was forty feet in the air, and
this was why so many bones had to be mended every
year. I had no ill luck myself, but none of my cousins
escaped. There were eight of them and at one time and
another they broke fourteen arms among them. But it
cost next to nothing, for the doctor worked by the year
—twenty-five dollars for the whole family. I remember
two of the Florida doctors, Chowning and Meredith.
They not only tended an entire family for twenty-five

dollars a year but furnished the medicines themselves.
Good measure, too. Only the largest persons could hold
a whole dose. Castor oil was the principal beverage. The
dose was half a dipperful, with half a dipperful of New
Orleans molasses added to help it down and make it
taste good, which it never did. The next standby was
calomel, the next rhubarb, and the next jalap. Then they
bled the patient and put mustard plasters on him. It
was a dreadful system and yet the death-rate was not
heavy. The calomel was nearly sure to salivate the
patient and cost him some of his teeth. There were no
dentists. When teeth became touched with decay or
were otherwise ailing, the doctor knew of but one thing
to do: he fetched his tongs and dragged them out. If
the jaw remained, it was not his fault. Doctors were not
called in cases of ordinary illness; the family grandmother attended to those. Every old woman was a doctor and gathered her own medicines in the woods, and
knew how to compound doses that would stir the vitals
of a cast-iron dog. And then there was the "Indian doctor," a grave savage, remnant of his tribe, deeply read
in the mysteries of nature and the secret properties of
herbs; and most backwoodsmen had high faith in his
powers and could tell of wonderful cures achieved by
him. In Mauritius, away off yonder in the solitudes of
the Indian Ocean, there is a person who answers to our
Indian doctor of the old times. He is a Negro and has
had no teaching as a doctor, yet there is one disease
which he is master of and can cure and the doctors
can't. They send for him when they have a case. It is a
child's disease of a strange and deadly sort, and the
Negro cures it with an herb-medicine which he makes
himself, from a prescription which has come down to
him from his father and grandfather. He will not let
anyone see it. He keeps the secret of its components to

himself, and it is feared that he will die without divulging it; then there will be consternation in Mauritius. I was told these things by the people there, in 1896.

We had the "faith doctor" too, in those early days, a woman. Her specialty was toothache. She was a farmer's old wife and lived five miles from Hannibal. She would lay her hand on the patient's jaw and say, "Believe!" and the cure was prompt. Mrs. Utterback. I remember her very well. Twice I rode out there behind my mother, horseback, and saw the cure performed. My mother was the patient.

Dr. Meredith removed to Hannibal by and by, and was our family physician there, and saved my life several times. Still, he was a good man and meant well. Let it go.

I was always told that I was a sickly and precarious and tiresome and uncertain child, and lived mainly on allopathic medicines during the first seven years of my life. I asked my mother about this in her old age—she was in her eighty-eighth year—and said:

"I suppose that during all that time you were uneasy about me?"

"Yes, the whole time."

"Afraid I wouldn't live?"

After a reflective pause, ostensibly to think out the facts, "No—afraid you would."

The country school-house was three miles from my uncle's farm. It stood in a clearing in the woods and would hold about twenty-five boys and girls. We attended the school with more or less regularity once or twice a week in summer, walking to it in the cool of the morning by the forest paths and back in the gloaming at the end of the day. All the pupils brought their dinners in baskets—corn dodger, buttermilk, and other good things—and sat in the shade of the trees at noon

and ate them. It is the part of my education which I
look back upon with the most satisfaction. My first visit
to the school was when I was seven. A strapping girl
of fifteen, in the customary sunbonnet and calico dress,
asked me if I "used tobacco," meaning did I chew it. I
said no. It roused her scorn. She reported me to all the
crowd, and said:

"Here is a boy seven years old who can't chew
tobacco."

By the looks and comments which this produced I
realized that I was a degraded object, and was cruelly
ashamed of myself. I determined to reform. But I only
made myself sick; I was not able to learn to chew tobacco. I learned to smoke fairly well but that did not
conciliate anybody and I remained a poor thing, and
characterless. I longed to be respected but I never was
able to rise. Children have but little charity for each
other's defects.

As I have said, I spent some part of every year at the
farm until I was twelve or thirteen years old. The life
which I led there with my cousins was full of charm and
so is the memory of it yet. I can call back the solemn
twilight and mystery of the deep woods, the earthy
smells, the faint odors of the wild flowers, the sheen of
rain-washed foliage, the rattling clatter of drops when
the wind shook the trees, the far-off hammering of
woodpeckers and the muffled drumming of wood-
pheasants in the remoteness of the forest, the snapshot
glimpses of disturbed wild creatures scurrying through
the grass—I can call it all back and make it as real as it
ever was, and as blessed. I can call back the prairie,
and its loneliness and peace, and a vast hawk hanging
motionless in the sky with his wings spread wide and
the blue of the vault showing through the fringe of their
end-feathers. I can see the woods in their autumn dress,

the oaks purple, the hickories washed with gold, the maples and the sumachs luminous with crimson fires, and I can hear the rustle made by the fallen leaves as we plowed through them. I can see the blue clusters of wild grapes hanging amongst the foliage of the saplings, and I remember the taste of them and the smell. I know how the wild blackberries looked and how they tasted; and the same with the pawpaws, the hazelnuts, and the persimmons; and I can feel the thumping rain upon my head of hickory-nuts and walnuts when we were out in the frosty dawn to scramble for them with the pigs, and the gusts of wind loosed them and sent them down. I know the stain of blackberries and how pretty it is, and I know the stain of walnut hulls and how little it minds soap and water, also what grudged experience it had of either of them. I know the taste of maple sap and when to gather it, and how to arrange the troughs and the delivery tubes, and how to boil down the juice, and how to hook the sugar after it is made; also how much better hooked sugar tastes than any that is honestly come by, let bigots say what they will.

I know how a prize watermelon looks when it is sunning its fat rotundity among pumpkin vines and "simblins"; I know how to tell when it is ripe without "plugging" it. I know how inviting it looks when it is cooling itself in a tub of water under the bed, waiting; I know how it looks when it lies on the table in the sheltered great floor-space between house and kitchen, and the children gathered for the sacrifice and their mouths watering. I know the crackling sound it makes when the carving knife enters its end and I can see the split fly along in front of the blade as the knife cleaves its way to the other end; I can see its halves fall apart and display the rich red meat and the black seeds, and the heart standing up, a luxury fit for the elect. I know how a boy looks behind a yard-long slice of that melon and I know how he feels, for I have been there. I know the taste of the watermelon which has been honestly come by and I know the taste of the watermelon which has been acquired by art. Both taste good but the experienced know which tastes best.

I know the look of green apples and peaches and pears on the trees, and I know how entertaining they are when they are inside of a person. I know how ripe ones look when they are piled in pyramids under the trees, and how pretty they are and how vivid their colors. I know how a frozen apple looks in a barrel down cellar in the wintertime, and how hard it is to bite and how the frost makes the teeth ache, and yet how good it is notwithstanding. I know the disposition of elderly people to select the specked apples for the children and I once knew ways to beat the game. I know the look of an apple that is roasting and sizzling on a hearth on a winter's evening, and I know the comfort that comes of eating it hot, along with some sugar and a drench of cream. I know the delicate art and mystery of so cracking hickory-nuts and walnuts on a flatiron with a hammer that the kernels will be delivered whole, and I know how the nuts, taken in conjunction with winter apples, cider, and doughnuts, make old people's old tales and old jokes sound fresh and crisp and enchanting, and juggle an evening away before you know what went with the time. I know the look of Uncle Dan'l's kitchen as it was on privileged nights when I was a child, and I can see the white and black children grouped on the hearth, with the firelight playing on their faces and the shadows flickering upon the walls clear back toward the cavernous gloom of the rear, and I can hear Uncle Dan'l telling the immortal tales which Uncle Remus Harris was to gather into his book and charm the world with, by and by. And I can feel again the creepy joy which quivered through me when the time for the ghost story was reached—and the sense of regret too which came over me, for it was always the last story of the evening and there was nothing between it and the unwelcome bed.

I can remember the bare wooden stairway in my uncle's house and the turn to the left above the landing, and the rafters and the slanting roof over my bed, and the squares of moonlight on the floor and the white cold world of snow outside, seen through the curtainless window. I can remember the howling of the wind and the quaking of the house on stormy nights, and how snug and cozy one felt under the blankets, listening; and how the powdery snow used to sift in around the sashes and lie in little ridges on the floor, and make the place look chilly in the morning and curb the wild desire to get up —in case there was any. I can remember how very dark that room was in the dark of the moon, and how packed it was with ghostly stillness when one woke up by accident away in the night, and forgotten sins came flocking out of the secret chambers of the memory and wanted a hearing; and how ill-chosen the time seemed for this kind of business and how dismal was the hoo-hooing of the owl and the wailing of the wolf, sent mourning by on the night wind.

I remember the raging of the rain on that roof, summer nights, and how pleasant it was to lie and listen to it and enjoy the white splendor of the lightning and the majestic booming and crashing of the thunder. It was a very satisfactory room, and there was a lightning rod which was reachable from the window, an adorable and skittish thing to climb up and down, summer nights when there were duties on hand of a sort to make privacy desirable.

I remember the 'coon and 'possum hunts, nights, with the Negroes, and the long marches through the black gloom of the woods and the excitement which fired everybody when the distant bay of an experienced dog announced that the game was treed; then the wild scramblings and stumblings through briers and bushes and over roots to get to the spot; then the lighting of a fire and the felling of the tree, the joyful frenzy of the dogs and the negroes, and the weird picture it all made in the red glare—I remember it all well, and the delight that everyone got out of it, except the 'coon.

I remember the pigeon seasons, when the birds would come in millions and cover the trees and by their weight break down the branches. They were clubbed to death with sticks; guns were not necessary and were not used. I remember the squirrel hunts and prairie-chicken hunts and wild-turkey hunts, and all that; and how we turned out, mornings, while it was still dark to go on these expeditions, and how chilly and dismal it was and how often I regretted that I was well enough to go. A toot on a tin horn brought twice as many dogs as were needed, and in their happiness they raced and scampered about and knocked small people down and made no end of unnecessary noise. At the word, they vanished away toward the woods and we drifted silently after them in the melancholy gloom. But presently the gray dawn stole over the world, the birds piped up, then the sun rose and poured light and comfort all around, everything was fresh and dewy and fragrant, and life was a boon again. After three hours of tramping we arrived back wholesomely tired, overladen with game, very hungry, and just in time for breakfast.

THE
Mysterious Stranger

Chapter I

IT WAS in 1590—winter. Austria was far away from the world, and asleep; it was still the Middle Ages in Austria and promised to remain so forever. Some even set it away back centuries upon centuries and said that by the mental and spiritual clock it was still the Age of Belief in Austria. But they meant it as a compliment, not a slur, and it was so taken and we were all proud of it. I remember it well, although I was only a boy; and I remember, too, the pleasure it gave me.

Yes, Austria was far from the world, and asleep, and our village was in the middle of that sleep, being in the middle of Austria. It drowsed in peace in the deep privacy of a hilly and woodsy solitude where news from the world hardly ever came to disturb its dreams, and was infinitely content. At its front flowed the tranquil river, its surface painted with cloud-forms and the reflections of drifting arks and stone-boats; behind it rose the woody steeps to the base of the lofty precipice; from the top of the precipice frowned a vast castle, its long stretch of towers and bastions mailed in vines; beyond the river, a league to the left, was a tumbled expanse of forest-clothed hills cloven by winding gorges where the sun never penetrated; and to the right a precipice overlooked the river, and between it and the hills just spoken

of lay a far-reaching plain dotted with little homesteads
nested among orchards and shade trees.

The whole region for leagues around was the heredi-
tary property of a prince, whose servants kept the castle
always in perfect condition for occupancy, but neither
he nor his family came there oftener than once in five
years. When they came it was as if the lord of the world
had arrived and had brought all the glories of its kingdoms along, and when they went they left a calm behind
which was like the deep sleep which follows an orgy

Eseldorf was a paradise for us boys. We were not
overmuch pestered with schooling. Mainly we were
trained to be good Christians, to revere the Virgin, the
Church, and the saints above everything. Beyond these
matters we were not required to know much; and, in
fact, not allowed to. Knowledge was not good for the
common people and could make them discontented with
the lot which God had appointed for them, and God
would not endure discontentment with His plans. We
had two priests. One of them, Father Adolf, was a very
zealous and strenuous priest, much considered.

There may have been better priests in some ways than
Father Adolf, but there was never one in our commune
who was held in more solemn and awful respect. This
was because he had absolutely no fear of the Devil. He
was the only Christian I have ever known of whom that
could be truly said. People stood in deep dread of him
on that account, for they thought that there must be
something supernatural about him, else he could not be
so bold and so confident. All men speak in bitter disapproval of the Devil but they do it reverently, not flip-
pantly, but Father Adolf's way was very different; he
called him by every name he could lay his tongue to
and it made everyone shudder that heard him; and often
he would even speak of him scornfully and scoffingly;

then the people crossed themselves and went quickly out of his presence, fearing that something fearful might happen.

Father Adolf had actually met Satan face to face more than once, and defied him. This was known to be so. Father Adolf said it himself. He never made any secret of it, but spoke it right out. And that he was speaking true there was proof in at least one instance, for on that occasion he quarreled with the enemy and intrepidly threw his bottle at him, and there, upon the wall of his study, was the ruddy splotch where it struck and broke.

But it was Father Peter, the other priest, that we all loved best and were sorriest for. Some people charged him with talking around in conversation that God was all goodness and would find a way to save all his poor human children. It was a horrible thing to say but there was never any absolute proof that Father Peter said it, and it was out of character for him to say it too, for he was always good and gentle and truthful. He wasn't charged with saying it in the pulpit, where all the congregation could hear and testify, but only outside, in talk, and it is easy for enemies to manufacture *that*. Father Peter had an enemy and a very powerful one, the astrologer who lived in a tumbled old tower up the valley and put in his nights studying the stars. Every one knew he could foretell wars and famines, though that was not so hard, for there was always a war and generally a famine somewhere. But he could also read any man's life through the stars in a big book he had, and find lost property, and every one in the village except Father Peter stood in awe of him. Even Father Adolf, who had defied the Devil, had a wholesome respect for the astrologer when he came through our village wearing his tall, pointed hat and his long, flowing robe with stars on it, carrying his big book and a staff which was known to have magic power. The bishop himself sometimes listened to the astrologer, it was said, for besides studying the stars and prophesying the astrologer made a great show of piety, which would impress the bishop of course.

But Father Peter took no stock in the astrologer. He denounced him openly as a charlatan—a fraud with no valuable knowledge of any kind or powers beyond those of an ordinary and rather inferior human being, which naturally made the astrologer hate Father Peter and wish to ruin him. It was the astrologer, as we all believed, who originated the story about Father Peter's shocking remark and carried it to the bishop. It was said that Father Peter had made the remark to his niece, Marget, though Marget denied it and implored the bishop to believe her and spare her old uncle from poverty and disgrace. But the bishop wouldn't listen. He suspended Father Peter indefinitely, though he wouldn't go so far as to excommunicate him on the evidence of only one witness, and now Father Peter had been out a couple of years and our other priest, Father Adolf, had his flock.

Those had been hard years for the old priest and Marget. They had been favorites but of course that changed when they came under the shadow of the bishop's frown. Many of their friends fell away entirely, and the rest became cool and distant. Marget was a lovely girl of eighteen when the trouble came and she had the best head in the village, and the most in it. She taught the harp and earned all her clothes and pocket money by her own industry. But her scholars fell off one by one now, she was forgotten when there were dances and parties among the youth of the village, the young fellows stopped coming to the house, all except Wilhelm Meidling—and he could have been spared; she and her uncle were sad and forlorn in their neglect and disgrace, and the sunshine was gone out of their lives. Matters went worse and worse, all through the two years. Clothes were wearing out, bread was harder and harder to get. And now, at last, the very end was come. Solomon Isaacs had lent all the money he was willing to put on the house and gave notice that to-morrow he would foreclose.

Chapter II

Three of us boys were always together and had been so from the cradle, being fond of one another from the beginning, and this affection deepened as the years went on—Nikolaus Bauman, son of the principal judge of the local court, Seppi Wohlmeyer, son of the keeper of the principal inn, the "Golden Stag," which had a nice garden with shade trees reaching down to the riverside, and pleasure boats for hire, and I was the third—Theodor Fischer, son of the church organist, who was also leader of the village musicians, teacher of the violin, composer, tax-collector of the commune, sexton, and in other ways a useful citizen and respected by all. We knew the hills and the woods as well as the birds knew them, for we were always roaming them when we had leisure—at least, when we were not swimming or boating or fishing, or playing on the ice or sliding down hill.

And we had the run of the castle park and very few had that. It was because we were pets of the oldest servingman in the castle, Felix Brandt, and often we went there nights, to hear him talk about old times and strange things and to smoke with him (he taught us that) and to drink coffee, for he had served in the wars and was at the siege of Vienna; and there, when the Turks were defeated and driven away, among the cap-

tured things were bags of coffee, and the Turkish prisoners explained the character of it and how to make a
pleasant drink out of it, and now he always kept coffee
by him, to drink himself and also to astonish the ignorant
with. When it stormed he kept us all night; and while it
thundered and lightened outside he told us about ghosts
and horrors of every kind, and of battles and murders
and mutilations and such things, and made it pleasant
and cozy inside; and he told these things from his own
experience largely. He had seen many ghosts in his time,
and witches and enchanters, and once he was lost in a
fierce storm at midnight in the mountains, and by the
glare of the lightning had seen the Wild Huntsman rage
on the blast with his specter dogs chasing after him
through the driving cloud-rack. Also he had seen an
incubus once, and several times he had seen the great
bat that sucks the blood from the necks of people while
they are asleep, fanning them softly with its wings and
so keeping them drowsy till they die.

He encouraged us not to fear supernatural things,
such as ghosts, and said they did no harm but only
wandered about because they were lonely and distressed
and wanted kindly notice and compassion, and in time
we learned not to be afraid, and even went down with
him in the night to the haunted chamber in the dun-
geons of the castle. The ghost appeared only once, and it
went by very dim to the sight and floated noiseless
through the air and then disappeared, and we scarcely
trembled, he had taught us so well. He said it came up
sometimes in the night and woke him by passing its
clammy hand over his face but it did him no hurt, it
only wanted sympathy and notice. But the strangest
thing was that he had seen angels—actual angels out of
heaven—and had talked with them. They had no wings,
and wore clothes, and talked and looked and acted just

like any natural person, and you would never know them for angels except for the wonderful things they did which a mortal could not do, and the way they suddenly disappeared while you were talking with them, which was also a thing which no mortal could do. And he said 'they were pleasant and cheerful, not gloomy and melancholy, like ghosts.

It was after that kind of a talk one May night that we got up next morning and had a good breakfast with him and then went down and crossed the bridge and went away up into the hills on the left to a woody hill-top which was a favorite place of ours, and there we stretched out on the grass in the shade to rest and smoke and talk over these strange things, for they were in our minds yet and impressing us. But we couldn't smoke, because we had been heedless and left our flint and steel behind.

Soon there came a youth strolling toward us through the trees, and he sat down and began to talk in a friendly way, just as if he knew us. But we did not answer him, for he was a stranger and we were not used to strangers and were shy of them. He had new and good clothes on, and was handsome and had a winning face and a pleasant voice, and was easy and graceful and unembarrassed, not slouchy and awkward and diffident, like other boys. We wanted to be friendly with him but didn't know how to begin. Then I thought of the pipe and wondered if it would be taken as kindly meant if I offered it to him. But I remembered that we had no fire, so I was sorry and disappointed. But he looked up bright and pleased, and said:

"Fire? Oh, that is easy; I will furnish it."

I was so astonished I couldn't speak, for I had not said anything. He took the pipe and blew his breath on it, and the tobacco glowed red and spirals of blue smoke rose up. We jumped up and were going to run, for that was natural; and we did run a few steps, although he was yearningly pleading for us to stay and giving us his word that he would not do us any harm, but only wanted to be friends with us and have company. So we stopped and stood, and wanted to go back, being full of curiosity and wonder, but afraid to venture. He went on coaxing in his soft, persuasive way, and when we saw that the pipe did not blow up and nothing happened, our confidence returned by little and little, and presently our curiosity got to be stronger than our fear, and we ventured back—but slowly and ready to fly at any alarm.

He was bent on putting us at ease and he had the right art; one could not remain doubtful and timorous where a person was so earnest and simple and gentle and talked so alluringly as he did; no, he won us over, and it was not long before we were content and comfortable and chatty, and glad we had found this new friend. When the feeling of constraint was all gone we asked him how he had learned to do that strange thing, and he said he hadn't learned it at all; it came natural to him—like other things—other curious things.

"What ones?"

"Oh, a number; I don't know how many."

"Will you let us see you do them?"

"Do—please!" the others said.

"You won't run away again?"

"No—indeed we won't. Please do. Won't you?"

"Yes, with pleasure; but you mustn't forget your promise, you know."

We said we wouldn't, and he went to a puddle and came back with water in a cup which he had made out of a leaf, and blew upon it and threw it out, and it was a lump of ice the shape of the cup. We were astonished and charmed but not afraid any more; we were very glad to be there and asked him to go on and do some more things. And he did. He said he would give us any kind of fruit we liked, whether it was in season or not. We all spoke at once:

"Orange!"

"Apple!"

"Grapes!"

"They are in your pockets," he said, and it was true. And they were of the best, too, and we ate them and wished we had more, though none of us said so.

"You will find them where those came from," he said, "and everything else your appetites call for; and you need not name the thing you wish; as long as I am with you, you have only to wish and find."

And he said true. There was never anything so wonderful and so interesting. Bread, cakes, sweets, nuts—whatever one wanted, it was there. He ate nothing himself, but sat and chatted and did one curious thing after another to amuse us. He made a tiny toy squirrel out of clay, and it ran up a tree and sat on a limb overhead and barked down at us. Then he made a dog that was not much larger than a mouse, and it treed the squirrel and danced about the tree, excited and barking, and was as alive as any dog could be. It frightened the squirrel from tree to tree and followed it up until both were out of sight in the forest. He made birds out of clay and set them free, and they flew away, singing.

At last I made bold to ask him to tell us who he was.

"An angel," he said, quite simply, and set another bird free and clapped his hands and made it fly away.

A kind of awe fell upon us when we heard him say that and we were afraid again, but he said we need not be troubled, there was no occasion for us to be afraid of an angel, and he liked us, anyway. He went on chatting as simply and unaffectedly as ever, and while he talked he made a crowd of little men and women the size of your finger, and they went diligently to work and cleared and leveled off a space a couple of yards square in the grass and began to build a cunning little castle in it, the women mixing the mortar and carrying it up the scaffoldings in pails on their heads, just as our work-women have always done, and the men laying the courses of masonry—five hundred of these toy people swarming briskly about and working diligently and wiping the sweat off their faces as natural as life. In the absorbing interest of watching those five hundred little people make the castle grow step by step and course by course, and take shape and symmetry, that feeling and awe soon passed away and we were quite comfortable and at home again. We asked if we might make some people and he said yes, and told Seppi to make some cannon for the walls, and told Nikolaus to make some halberdiers with breastplates and greaves and helmets, and I was to make some cavalry, with horses, and in allotting these tasks he called us by our names but did not say how he knew them. Then Seppi asked him what his own name was, and he said, tranquilly, "Satan," and held out a chip and caught a little woman on it who was falling from the scaffolding and put her back where she belonged, and said, "She is an idiot to step backward like that and not notice what she is about."

It caught us suddenly, that name did, and our work dropped out of our hands and broke to pieces—a cannon, a halberdier, and a horse. Satan laughed, and asked what was the matter. I said, "Nothing, only it seemed a strange name for an angel." He asked why.

"Because it's—it's—well, it's his name, you know."

"Yes—he is my uncle."

He said it placidly but it took our breath for a moment and made our hearts beat. He did not seem to notice that, but mended our halberdiers and things with a touch, handing them to us finished, and said, "Don't you remember?—he was an angel himself, once."

"Yes—it's true," said Seppi, "I didn't think of that."

"Before the Fall he was blameless."

"Yes," said Nikolaus, "he was without sin."

"It is a good family—ours," said Satan; "there is not a better. He is the only member of it that has ever sinned."

I should not be able to make any one understand how exciting it all was. You know that kind of quiver that trembles around through you when you are seeing something so strange and enchanting and wonderful that it is just a fearful joy to be alive and look at it, and you know how you gaze, and your lips turn dry and your breath comes short, but you wouldn't be anywhere but there, not for the world. I was bursting to ask one question—I had it on my tongue's end and could hardly hold it back—but I was ashamed to ask it; it might be a rudeness. Satan set an ox down that he had been making and smiled up at me and said:

"It wouldn't be a rudeness and I should forgive it if it was. Have I seen him? Millions of times. From the time that I was a little child a thousand years old I was his second favorite among the nursery angels of our blood and lineage—to use a human phrase—yes, from that time until the Fall, eight thousand years, measured as you count time."

"Eight—thousand!"

"Yes." He turned to Seppi and went on as if answering something that was in Seppi's mind, "Why, naturally I look like a boy, for that is what I am. With us what you call time is a spacious thing; it takes a long stretch of it to grow an angel to full age." There was a question in my mind, and he turned to me and answered it, "I am

sixteen thousand years old—counting as you count."
Then he turned to Nikolaus and said: "No, the Fall did
not affect me nor the rest of the relationship. It was only
he that I was named for who ate of the fruit of the tree
and then beguiled the man and the woman with it. We
others are still ignorant of sin; we are not able to commit
it; we are without blemish, and shall abide in that estate
always. We—" Two of the little workmen were quar-
reling, and in buzzing little bumblebee voices they were
cursing and swearing at each other; now came blows
and blood; then they locked themselves together in a
life-and-death struggle. Satan reached out his hand and
crushed the life out of them with his fingers, threw them
away, wiped the red from his fingers on his handkerchief, and went on talking where he had left off: "We
cannot do wrong; neither have we any disposition to do
it, for we do not know what it is."

It seemed a strange speech, in the circumstances, but
we barely noticed that, we were so shocked and grieved
at the wanton murder he had committed—for murder it
was, that was its true name and it was without palliation
or excuse, for the men had not wronged him in any way.
It made us miserable, for we loved him, and had thought
him so noble and so beautiful and gracious and had
honestly believed he was an angel, and to have him do
this cruel thing—ah, it lowered him so, and we had had
such pride in him. He went right on talking just as if
nothing had happened, telling about his travels and the
interesting things he had seen in the big worlds of our
solar systems and of other solar systems far away in the
remotenesses of space, and about the customs of the
immortals that inhabit them, somehow fascinating us,
enchanting us, charming us in spite of the pitiful scene
that was now under our eyes, for the wives of the little
dead men had found the crushed and shapeless bodies

and were crying over them and sobbing and lamenting, and a priest was kneeling there with his hands crossed upon his breast, praying; and crowds and crowds of pitying friends were massed about them, reverently uncovered, with their bare heads bowed and many with the tears running down—a scene which Satan paid no attention to until the small noise of the weeping and praying began to annoy them, then he reached out and took the heavy board seat out of our swing and brought it down and mashed all those people into the earth just as if they had been flies, and went on talking just the same.

An angel, and kill a priest! An angel who did not know how to do wrong and yet destroys in cold blood hundreds of helpless poor men and women who had never done him any harm! It made us sick to see that awful deed and to think that none of those poor creatures was prepared except the priest, for none of them had ever heard a mass or seen a church. And we were witnesses, we had seen these murders done and it was our duty to tell, and let the law take its course.

But he went on talking right along, and worked his enchantments upon us again with that fatal music of his voice. He made us forget everything; we could only listen to him and love him and be his slaves, to do with us as he would. He made us drunk with the joy of being with him and of looking into the heaven of his eyes, and of feeling the ecstasy that thrilled along our veins from the touch of his hand.

Chapter III

The Stranger had seen everything, he had been everywhere, he knew everything, and he forgot nothing. What another must study, he learned at a glance; there were no difficulties for him. And he made things live before you when he told about them. He saw the world made; he saw Adam created; he saw Samson surge against the pillars and bring the temple down in ruins about him; he saw Cæsar's death; he told of the daily life in heaven; he had seen the damned writhing in the red waves of hell; and he made us see all these things, and it was as if we were on the spot and looking at them with our own eyes. And we felt them too, but there was no sign that they were anything to him beyond mere entertainments. Those visions of hell, those poor babes and women and girls and lads and men shrieking and supplicating in anguish—why, we could hardly bear it, but he was as bland about it as if it had been so many imitation rats in an artificial fire.

And always when he was talking about men and women here on the earth and their doings—even their grandest and sublimest—we were secretly ashamed, for his manner showed that to him they and their doings were of paltry poor consequence; often you would think he was talking about flies, if you didn't know. Once he even said in so many words that our people down here were quite interesting to him, notwithstanding they were so dull and ignorant and trivial and conceited, and so diseased and rickety and such a shabby, poor, worthless lot all around. He said it in a quite matter-of-course way and without bitterness, just as a person might talk about bricks or manure or any other thing that was of no consequence and hadn't feelings. I could see he meant no offense but in my thoughts I set it down as not very good manners.

"Manners!" he said. "Why, it is merely the truth, and truth is good manners; manners are a fiction. The castle is done. Do you like it?"

Any one would have been obliged to like it. It was

lovely to look at, it was so shapely and fine and so cunningly perfect in all its particulars, even to the little flags waving from the turrets. Satan said we must put the artillery in place now and station the halberdiers and display the cavalry. Our men and horses were a spectacle to see, they were so little like what they were intended for; for, of course, we had no art in making such things. Satan said they were the worst he had seen, and when he touched them and made them alive, it was just ridiculous the way they acted, on account of their legs not being of uniform lengths. They reeled and sprawled around as if they were drunk and endangered everybody's lives around them, and finally fell over and lay helpless and kicking. It made us all laugh, though it was a shameful thing to see. The guns were charged with dirt, to fire a salute, but they were so crooked and so badly made that they all burst when they went off, and killed some of the gunners and crippled the others. Satan said we would have a storm now, and an earthquake if we liked, but we must stand off a piece, out of danger. We wanted to call the people away, too, but he said never mind them; they were of no consequence and we could make more, some time or other, if we needed them.

A small storm-cloud began to settle down black over the castle and the miniature lightning and thunder began to play, and the ground to quiver, and the wind to pipe and wheeze, and the rain to fall, and all the people flocked into the castle for shelter. The cloud settled down blacker and blacker and one could see the castle only dimly through it; the lightning blazed out flash upon flash and pierced the castle and set it on fire, and the flames shone out red and fierce through the cloud, and the people came flying out, shrieking, but Satan brushed them back, paying no attention to our begging and crying and imploring; and in the midst of the howling of the wind and volleying of the thunder the magazine blew up, the earthquake rent the ground wide, and the castle's wreck and ruin tumbled into the chasm, which swallowed it from sight, and closed upon it, with all that innocent life, not one of the five hundred poor creatures escaping. Our hearts were broken; we could not keep from crying.

'Don't cry," Satan said; "they were of no value."

"But they are gone to hell!"

"Oh, it is no matter; we can make plenty more."

It was of no use to try to move him; evidently he was wholly without feeling and could not understand. He was full of bubbling spirits and as gay as if this were a wedding instead of a fiendish massacre. And he was bent on making us feel as he did, and of course his magic accomplished his desire. It was no trouble to him; he did whatever he pleased with us. In a little while we were dancing on that grave and he was playing to us on a strange, sweet instrument which he took out of his pocket; and the music—but there is no music like that, unless perhaps in heaven, and that was where he brought it from, he said. It made one mad, for pleasure; and we could not take our eyes from him, and the looks that went out of our eyes came from our hearts and their dumb speech was worship. He brought the dance from heaven, too, and the bliss of paradise was in it.

Presently he said he must go away on an errand. But we could not bear the thought of it and clung to him, and pleaded with him to stay; and that pleased him and he said so, and said he would not go yet but would wait a little while and we would sit down and talk a few minutes longer; and he told us Satan was only his real name and he was to be known by it to us alone, but he had chosen another one to be called by in the presence

of others; just a common one, such as people have—
Philip Traum.

It sounded so odd and mean for such a being! But it
was his decision and we said nothing; his decision was
sufficient.

We had seen wonders this day; and my thoughts began to run on the pleasure it would be to tell them when
I got home, but he noticed those thoughts and said:

"No, all these matters are a secret among us four. I do
not mind your trying to tell them, if you like, but I will
protect your tongues and nothing of the secret will escape from them."

It was a disappointment but it couldn't be helped,
and it cost us a sigh or two. We talked pleasantly along
and he was always reading our thoughts and responding
to them, and it seemed to me that this was the most
wonderful of all the things he did, but he interrupted
my musings and said:

"No, it would be wonderful for you but it is not wonderful for me. I am not limited like you. I am not subject to human conditions. I can measure and understand
your human weaknesses, for I have studied them, but I
have none of them. My flesh is not real, although it
would seem firm to your touch; my clothes are not real;
I am a spirit. Father Peter is coming." We looked
around, but did not see any one. "He is not in sight yet,
but you will see him presently."

"Do you know him, Satan?"

"No."

"Won't you talk with him when he comes? He is not
ignorant and dull like us, and he would so like to talk
with you. Will you?"

"Another time, yes, but not now. I must go on my
errand after a little. There he is now; you can see him.
Sit still, and don't say anything."

We looked up and saw Father Peter approaching through the chestnuts. We three were sitting together in the grass, and Satan sat in front of us in the path. Father Peter came slowly along with his head down, thinking, and stopped within a couple of yards of us and took off his hat and got out his silk handkerchief, and stood there mopping his face and looking as if he were going to speak to us, but he didn't. Presently he muttered, "I can't think what brought me here; it seems as if I were in my study a minute ago—but I suppose I have been dreaming along for an hour and have come all this stretch without noticing; for I am not myself in these troubled days." Then he went mumbling along to himself and walked straight through Satan, just as if nothing were there. It made us catch our breath to see it. We had the impulse to cry out, the way you nearly always do when a startling thing happens, but something mysteriously restrained us and we remained quiet, only breathing fast. Then the trees hid Father Peter after a little, and Satan said:

"It is as I told you—I am only a spirit."

"Yes, one perceives it now," said Nikolaus, "but we are not spirits. It is plain he did not see you, but were we invisible, too? He looked at us, but he didn't seem to see us."

"No, none of us was visible to him, for I wished it so."

It seemed almost too good to be true, that we were actually seeing these romantic and wonderful things, and that it was not a dream. And there he sat, looking just like anybody—so natural and simple and charming, and chatting along again the same as ever, and—well, words cannot make you understand what we felt. It was an ecstasy; and an ecstasy is a thing that will not go into words; it feels like music, and one cannot tell about music so that another person can get the feeling of it.

He was back in the old ages once more now, and making them live before us. He had seen so much, so much! It was just a wonder to look at him and try to think how it must seem to have such experience behind one.

But it made you seem sorrowfully trivial, and the creature of a day, and such a short and paltry day, too. And he didn't say anything to raise up your drooping pride—no, not a word. He always spoke of men in the same old indifferent way—just as one speaks of bricks and manure-piles and such things; you could see that they were of no consequence to him, one way or the other. He didn't mean to hurt us, you could see that; just as we don't mean to insult a brick when we disparage it; a brick's emotions are nothing to us; it never occurs to us to think whether it has any or not.

Once when he was bunching the most illustrious kings and conquerors and poets and prophets and pirates and beggars together—just a brick-pile—I was shamed into putting in a word for man, and asked him why he made so much difference between men and himself. He had to struggle with that a moment; he didn't seem to understand how I could ask such a strange question. Then he said:

"The difference between man and me? The difference between a mortal and an immortal? between a cloud and a spirit?" He picked up a wood-louse that was creeping along a piece of bark: "What is the difference between Cæsar and this?"

I said, "One cannot compare things which by their nature and by the interval between them are not comparable."

"You have answered your own question," he said. "I will expand it. Man is made of dirt—I saw him made. I am not made of dirt. Man is a museum of diseases, a home of impurities; he comes today and is gone to-morrow; he begins as dirt and departs as stench; I am of the aristocracy of the Imperishables. And man has the *Moral Sense*. You understand? He has the *Moral Sense*. That would seem to be difference enough between us, all by itself."

He stopped there, as if that settled the matter. I was sorry, for at that time I had but a dim idea of what the Moral Sense was. I merely knew that we were proud of having it, and when he talked like that about it, it wounded me and I felt as a girl feels who thinks her dearest finery is being admired and then overhears strangers making fun of it. For a while we were all silent and I, for one, was depressed. Then Satan began to chat again, and soon he was sparkling along in such a cheerful and vivacious vein that my spirits rose once more. He told some very cunning things that put us in a gale of laughter; and when he was telling about the time that Samson tied the torches to the foxes' tails and set them loose in the Philistines' corn, and Samson sitting on the fence slapping his thighs and laughing, with the tears running down his cheeks, and lost his balance and fell off the fence, the memory of that picture got him to laughing, too, and we did have a most lovely and jolly time. By and by he said:

"I am going on my errand now."

"Don't!" we all said. "Don't go; stay with us. You won't come back."

"Yes, I will; I give you my word."

"When? To-night? Say when."

"It won't be long. You will see."

"We like you."

"And I you. And as a proof of it I will show you something fine to see. Usually when I go I merely vanish, but now I will dissolve myself and let you see me do it."

He stood up and it was quickly finished. He thinned

away and thinned away until he was a soap-bubble, except that he kept his shape. You could see the bushes through him as clearly as you see things through a soap-bubble, and all over him played and flashed the delicate iridescent colors of the bubble, and along with them was that thing shaped like a window-sash which you always see on the globe of the bubble You have seen a bubble strike the carpet and lightly bound along two or three times before it bursts. He did that. He sprang— touched the grass—bounded—floated along—touched again—and so on, and presently exploded—puff! and in his place was vacancy.

It was a strange and beautiful thing to see. We did not say anything but sat wondering and dreaming and blinking, and finally Seppi roused up and said, mournfully sighing:

"I suppose none of it has happened."

Nikolaus sighed and said about the same.

I was miserable to hear them say it, for it was the same cold fear that was in my own mind. Then we saw poor old Father Peter wandering along back, with his head bent down, searching the ground. When he was pretty close to us he looked up and saw us, and said, "How long have you been here, boys?"

"A little while, Father."

"Then it is since I came by, and maybe you can help me. Did you come up by the path?"

"Yes, Father."

"That is good. I came the same way. I have lost my wallet. There wasn't much in it, but a very little is much to me, for it was all I had. I suppose you haven't seen anything of it?"

"No, Father, but we will help you hunt."

"It is what I was going to ask you. Why, here it is!"

We hadn't noticed it; yet there it lay, right where

Satan stood when he began to melt—if he did melt and it wasn't a delusion. Father Peter picked it up and looked very much surprised.

"It is mine," he said, "but not the contents. This is fat, mine was flat; mine was light, this is heavy." He opened it; it was stuffed as full as it could hold with gold coins. He let us gaze our fill; and of course we did gaze, for we had never seen so much money at one time before. All our mouths came open to say "Satan did it!" but nothing came out. There it was, you see—we couldn't tell what Satan didn't want told; he had said so himself.

"Boys, did you do this?"

It made us laugh. And it made him laugh, too, as soon as he thought what a foolish question it was.

"Who has been here?"

Our mouths came open to answer but stood so for a moment, because we couldn't say "Nobody," for it wouldn't be true, and the right word didn't seem to come; then I thought of the right one, and said it:

"Not a human being."

"That is so," said the others, and let their mouths go shut.

"It is not so," said Father Peter, and looked at us very severely. "I came by here a while ago and there was no one here, but that is nothing; some one has been here since. I don't mean to say that the person didn't pass here before you came, and I don't mean to say that you saw him, but some one did pass, that I know. On your honor—you saw no one?"

"Not a human being."

"That is sufficient; I know you are telling me the truth."

He began to count the money on the path, we on our knees eagerly helping to stack it in little piles.

"It's eleven hundred ducats odd!" he said. "Oh dear! if it were only mine—and I need it so!" and his voice broke and his lips quivered.

"It is yours, sir!" we all cried out at once, "every heller!"

"No—it isn't mine. Only four ducats are mine; the rest . . . !" He fell to dreaming, poor old soul, and caressing some of the coins in his hands, and forgot where he was, sitting there on his heels with his old gray head bare; it was pitiful to see. "No," he said, waking up, "it isn't mine. I can't account for it. I think some enemy . . . it must be a trap."

Nikolaus said: "Father Peter, with the exception of the astrologer you haven't a real enemy in the village—nor Marget, either. And not even a half-enemy that's rich enough to chance eleven hundred ducats to do you a mean turn. I'll ask you if that's so or not?"

He couldn't get around that argument and it cheered him up. "But it isn't mine, you see—it isn't mine, in any case."

He said it in a wistful way, like a person that wouldn't be sorry, but glad, if anybody would contradict him.

"It is yours, Father Peter, and we are witness to it. Aren't we, boys?"

"Yes, we are—and we'll stand by it, too."

"Bless your hearts, you do almost persuade me; you do, indeed. If I had only a hundred-odd ducats of it! The house is mortgaged for it, and we've no home for our heads if we don't pay to-morrow. And that four ducats is all we've got in the—"

"It's yours, every bit of it, and you've got to take it—we are bail that it's all right. Aren't we, Theodor? Aren't we, Seppi?"

We two said yes, and Nikolaus stuffed the money back into the shabby old wallet and made the owner take it. So he said he would use two hundred of it, for his house was good enough security for that, and would put the rest at interest till the rightful owner came for it, and on our side we must sign a paper showing how he got the money—a paper to show to the villagers as proof that he had not got out of his troubles dishonestly.

Chapter IV

It made immense talk next day, when Father Peter paid Solomon Isaacs in gold and left the rest of the money with him at interest. Also, there was a pleasant change; many people called at the house to congratulate him and a number of cool old friends became kind and friendly again, and to top all, Marget was invited to a party.

And there was no mystery; Father Peter told the whole circumstance just as it happened and said he could not account for it, only it was the plain hand of Providence, so far as he could see.

One or two shook their heads and said privately it looked more like the hand of Satan; and really that seemed a surprisingly good guess for ignorant people like that. Some came slyly buzzing around and tried to coax us boys to come out and "tell the truth," and promised they wouldn't ever tell but only wanted to know for their own satisfaction, because the whole thing was so curious. They even wanted to buy the secret and pay money for it, and if we could have invented something that would answer—but we couldn't, we hadn't the ingenuity, so we had to let the chance go by, and it was a pity.

We carried that secret around without any trouble, but the other one, the big one, the splendid one, burned the very vitals of us, it was so hot to get out and we so hot to let it out and astonish people with it. But we had to keep it in; in fact, it kept itself in. Satan said it would, and it did. We went off every day and got to ourselves in the woods so that we could talk about Satan, and really that was the only subject we thought of or cared anything about, and day and night we watched for him and hoped he would come, and we got more and more impatient all the time. We hadn't any interest in the other boys any more and wouldn't take part in their games and enterprises. They seemed so tame, after Satan, and their doings so trifling and commonplace after his adventures in antiquity and the constellations, and his miracles and meltings and explosions and all that.

During the first day we were in a state of anxiety on account of one thing, and we kept going to Father Peter's house on one pretext or another to keep track of it. That was the gold coin; we were afraid it would crumble and turn to dust, like fairy money. If it did— But it didn't. At the end of the day no complaint had been made about it, so after that we were satisfied that it was real gold and dropped the anxiety out of our minds.

There was a question which we wanted to ask Father Peter, and finally we went there the second evening, a little diffidently, after drawing straws, and I asked it as casually as I could, though it did not sound as casual as I wanted, because I didn't know how:

"What is the Moral Sense, sir?"

He looked down, surprised, over his great spectacles, and said, "Why, it is the faculty which enables us to distinguish good from evil."

It threw some light but not a glare, and I was a little

disappointed, also to some degree embarrassed. He was waiting for me to go on, so, in default of anything else to say, I asked, "Is it valuable?"

"Valuable? Heavens! lad, it is the one thing that lifts man above the beasts that perish and makes him heir to immortality!"

This did not remind me of anything further to say, so I got out, with the other boys, and we went away with that indefinite sense you have often had of being filled but not fatted. They wanted me to explain but I was tired.

We passed out through the parlor, and there was Marget at the spinnet teaching Marie Lueger. So one of the deserting pupils was back, and an influential one too; the others would follow. Marget jumped up and ran and thanked us again with tears in her eyes—this was the third time—for saving her and her uncle from being turned into the street, and we told her again we hadn't done it; but that was her way, she never could be grateful enough for anything a person did for her so we let her have her say. And as we passed through the garden, there was Wilhelm Meidling sitting there waiting, for it was getting toward the edge of the evening, and he would be asking Marget to take a walk along the river with him when she was done with the lesson. He was a young lawyer and succeeding fairly well and working his way along, little by little. He was very fond of Marget and she of him. He had not deserted along with the others but had stood his ground all through. His faithfulness was not lost on Marget and her uncle. He hadn't so very much talent but he was handsome and good, and these are a kind of talents themselves and help along. He asked us how the lesson was getting along and we told him it was about done. And maybe it was so; we didn't know anything about it but we judged it would please him, and it did, and didn't cost us anything.

Chapter V

On the fourth day comes the astrologer from his crumbling old tower up the valley, where he had heard the news, I reckon. He had a private talk with us, and we told him what we could, for we were mightily in dread of him. He sat there studying and studying awhile to himself; then he asked:

"How many ducats did you say?"

"Eleven hundred and seven, sir."

Then he said, as if he were talking to himself: "It is ver-y singular. Yes . . . very strange. A curious coincidence." Then he began to ask questions, and went over the whole ground from the beginning, we answering. By and by he said: "Eleven hundred and six ducats. It is a large sum."

"Seven," said Seppi, correcting him.

"Oh, seven, was it? Of course a ducat more or less isn't of consequence, but you said eleven hundred and six before."

It would not have been safe for us to say he was mistaken but we knew he was. Nikolaus said, "We ask pardon for the mistake, but we meant to say seven."

"Oh, it is no matter, lad; it was merely that I noticed the discrepancy. It is several days, and you cannot be expected to remember precisely. One is apt to be inexact when there is no particular circumstance to impress the count upon the memory."

"But there was one, sir," said Seppi, eagerly.

"What was it, my son?" asked the astrologer, indifferently.

"First, we all counted the piles of coin, each in turn,

and all made it the same—eleven hundred and six. But I had slipped one out for fun, when the count began, and now I slipped it back and said, 'I think there is a mistake—there are eleven hundred and seven; let us count again.' We did, and of course I was right. They were astonished; then I told how it came about."

The astrologer asked us if this was so, and we said it was.

"That settles it," he said. "I know the thief now. Lads, the money was stolen."

Then he went away, leaving us very much troubled, and wondering what he could mean. In about an hour we found out, for by that time it was all over the village that Father Peter had been arrested for stealing a great sum of money from the astrologer. Everybody's tongue was loose and going. Many said it was not in Father Peter's character and must be a mistake, but the others shook their heads and said misery and want could drive a suffering man to almost anything. About one detail there were no differences; all agreed that Father Peter's account of how the money came into his hands was just about unbelievable—it had such an impossible look. They said it might have come into the astrologer's hands in some such way, but into Father Peter's, never! Our characters began to suffer now. We were Father Peter's only witnesses; how much did he probably pay us to back up his fantastic tale? People talked that kind of talk to us pretty freely and frankly, and were full of scoffings when we begged them to believe really we had told only the truth. Our parents were harder on us than any one else. Our fathers said we were disgracing our families, and they commanded us to purge ourselves of our lie, and there was no limit to their anger when we continued to say we had spoken true. Our mothers cried over us and begged us to give back our bribe and get back our honest names and save our families from shame, and come out and honorably confess. And at last we were so worried and harassed that we tried to tell the whole thing, Satan and all—but no, it wouldn't come out. We were hoping and longing all the time that Satan would come and help us out of our trouble, but there was no sign of him.

Within an hour after the astrologer's talk with us, Father Peter was in prison and the money sealed up and in the hands of the officers of the law. The money was in a bag, and Solomon Isaacs said he had not touched it since he had counted it; his oath was taken that it was the same money, and that the amount was eleven hundred and seven ducats. Father Peter claimed trial by the ecclesiastical court, but our other priest, Father Adolf, said an ecclesiastical court hadn't jurisdiction over a suspended priest. The bishop upheld him. That settled it; the case would go to trial in the civil court. The court would not sit for some time to come. Wilhelm Meidling would be Father Peter's lawyer and do the best he could, of course, but he told us privately that a weak case on his side and all the power and prejudice on the other made the outlook bad.

So Marget's new happiness died a quick death. No friends came to condole with her and none were expected; an unsigned note withdrew her invitation to the party. There would be no scholars to take lessons. How could she support herself? She could remain in the house, for the mortgage was paid off, though the government and not poor Solomon Isaacs had the mortgage-money in its grip for the present. Old Ursula, who was cook, chambermaid, housekeeper, laundress, and everything else for Father Peter and had been Marget's nurse in earlier years, said God would provide. But she said that from habit, for she was a good Christian. She meant to help in the providing, to make sure, if she could find a way.

We boys wanted to go and see Marget and show friendliness for her, but our parents were afraid of offending the community and wouldn't let us. The astrologer was going around inflaming everybody against Father Peter, and saying he was an abandoned thief and had stolen eleven hundred and seven gold ducats from him. He said he knew he was a thief from that fact, for it was exactly the sum he had lost and which Father Peter pretended he had "found."

In the afternoon of the fourth day after the catastrophe old Ursula appeared at our house and asked for some washing to do, and begged my mother to keep this secret, to save Marget's pride, who would stop this project if she found it out, yet Marget had not enough to eat and was growing weak. Ursula was growing weak herself and showed it, and she ate of the food that was offered her like a starving person but could not be persuaded to carry any home, for Marget would not eat charity food. She took some clothes down to the stream to wash them, but we saw from the window that handling the bat was too much for her strength; so she was called back and a trifle of money offered her, which she was afraid to take lest Marget should suspect; then she took it, saying she would explain that she found it in the road. To keep it from being a lie and damning her soul, she got me to drop it while she watched; then she went along by there and found it and exclaimed with surprise and joy, and picked it up and went her way. Like the rest of the village, she could tell every-day lies fast enough and without taking any precautions against fire and brimstone on their account, but this was a new kind of lie and it had a dangerous look because she hadn't had any practice in it. After a week's practice it wouldn't have given her any trouble. It is the way we are made.

I was in trouble, for how would Marget live? Ursula could not find a coin in the road every day—perhaps not even a second one. And I was ashamed too, for not having been near Marget, and she so in need of friends; but that was my parents' fault, not mine, and I couldn't help it.

I was walking along the path, feeling very downhearted, when a most cheery and tingling freshening-up sensation went rippling through me and I was too glad for any words, for I knew by that sign that Satan was by. I had noticed it before. Next moment he was alongside of me and I was telling him all my trouble and what had been happening to Marget and her uncle. While we were talking we turned a curve and saw old Ursula resting in the shade of a tree, and she had a lean stray kitten in her lap and was petting it. I asked her where she got it and she said it came out of the woods and followed her, and she said it probably hadn't any mother or any friends and she was going to take it home and take care of it. Satan said:

"I understand you are very poor. Why do you want to add another mouth to feed? Why don't you give it to some rich person?"

Ursula bridled at this and said: "Perhaps you would like to have it. You must be rich, with your fine clothes and quality airs." Then she sniffed and said: "Give it to the rich—the idea! The rich don't care for anybody but themselves; it's only the poor that have feeling for the poor, and help them. The poor and God. God will provide for this kitten."

"What makes you think so?"

Ursula's eyes snapped with anger. "Because I know it!" she said. "Not a sparrow falls to the ground without His seeing it."

"But it falls, just the same. What good is seeing it fall?"

Old Ursula's jaws worked but she could not get any word out for the moment, she was so horrified. When she got her tongue she stormed out, "Go about your business, you puppy, or I will take a stick to you!"

I could not speak, I was so scared. I knew that with his notions about the human race Satan would consider it a matter of no consequence to strike her dead, there being "plenty more," but my tongue stood still, I could give her no warning. But nothing happened; Satan remained tranquil—tranquil and indifferent. I suppose he could not be insulted by Ursula any more than the king could be insulted by a tumble-bug. The old woman jumped to her feet when she made her remark, and did it as briskly as a young girl. It had been many years since she had done the like of that. That was Satan's influence; he was a fresh breeze to the weak and the sick, wherever he came. His presence affected even the lean kitten, and it skipped to the ground and began to chase a leaf. This surprised Ursula and she stood looking at the creature and nodding her head wonderingly, her anger quite forgotten.

"What's come over it?" she said. "Awhile ago it could hardly walk."

"You have not seen a kitten of that breed before," said Satan.

Ursula was not proposing to be friendly with the mocking stranger, and she gave him an ungentle look and retorted: "Who asked you to come here and pester me, I'd like to know? And what do you know about what I've seen and what I haven't seen?"

"You haven't seen a kitten with the hair-spines on its tongue pointing to the front, have you?"

"No—nor you, either."

"Well, examine this one and see."

Ursula was become pretty spry but the kitten was spryer and she could not catch it, and had to give it up Then Satan said:

"Give it a name, and maybe it will come."

Ursula tried several names but the kitten was not interested.

"Call it Agnes. Try that."

The creature answered to the name and came. Ursula examined its tongue. "Upon my word, it's true!" she said. "I have not seen this kind of a cat before. Is it yours?"

"No."

"Then how did you know its name so pat?"

"Because all cats of that breed are named Agnes; they will not answer to any other."

Ursula was impressed. "It is the most wonderful thing!" Then a shadow of trouble came into her face, for her superstitions were aroused and she reluctantly put the creature down, saying: "I suppose I must let it go; I am not afraid—no, not exactly that, though the priest—well, I've heard people—indeed, many people . . . And, besides, it is quite well now and can take care of itself." She sighed, and turned to go, murmuring: "It is such a pretty one too, and would be such company—and the house is so sad and lonesome these troubled days . . . Miss Marget so mournful and just a shadow, and the old master shut up in jail."

"It seems a pity not to keep it," said Satan.

Ursula turned quickly—just as if she were hoping some one would encourage her.

"Why?" she asked, wistfully.

"Because this breed brings luck."

"Does it? Is it true? Young man, do you know it to be true? How does it bring luck?"

"Well, it brings money, anyway."

Ursula looked disappointed. "Money? A cat bring money? The idea! You could never sell it here; people do not buy cats here; one can't even give them away." She turned to go.

"I don't mean sell it. I mean have an income from it. This kind is called the Lucky Cat. Its owner finds four silver groschen in his pocket every morning."

I saw the indignation rising in the old woman's face. She was insulted. This boy was making fun of her. That was her thought. She thrust her hands into her pockets and straightened up to give him a piece of her mind. Her temper was all up, and hot. Her mouth came open and let out three words of a bitter sentence, . . . then it fell silent, and the anger in her face turned to surprise or wonder or fear, or something, and she slowly brought out her hands from her pockets and opened them and held them so. In one was my piece of money, in the other lay four silver groschen. She gazed a little while, perhaps to see if the groschen would vanish away; then she said, fervently:

"It's true—it's true—and I'm ashamed and beg forgiveness, O dear master and benefactor!" And she ran to Satan and kissed his hand, over and over again, according to the Austrian custom.

In her heart she probably believed it was a witch-cat and an agent of the Devil; but no matter, it was all the more certain to be able to keep its contract and furnish a daily good living for the family, for in matters of finance even the piousest of our peasants would have more confidence in an arrangement with the Devil than with an archangel. Ursula started homeward with Agnes in her arms, and I said I wished I had her privilege of seeing Marget.

Then I caught my breath, for we were there. There in the parlor, and Marget standing looking at us, astonished. She was feeble and pale, but I knew that those conditions would not last in Satan's atmosphere, and it turned out so. I introduced Satan—that is, Philip Traum —and we sat down and talked. There was no constraint. We were simple folk in our village, and when a stranger was a pleasant person we were soon friends. Marget wondered how we got in without her hearing us. Traum said the door was open and we walked in and waited until she should turn around and greet us. This was not true; no door was open; we entered through the walls or the roof or down the chimney, or somehow; but no matter, what Satan wished a person to believe, the person was sure to believe, and so Marget was quite satisfied with that explanation. And then the main part of her mind was on Traum, anyway; she couldn't keep her eyes off him, he was so beautiful. That gratified me, and made me proud. I hoped he would show off some, but he didn't. He seemed only interested in being friendly and telling lies. He said he was an orphan. That made Marget pity him. The water came into her eyes. He said he had never known his mamma, she passed away while he was a young thing, and said his papa was in shattered health and had no property to speak of—in fact, none of any earthly value—but he had an uncle in business down in the tropics and he was very well off and had a monopoly, and it was from this uncle that he drew his support. The very mention of a kind uncle was enough to remind Marget of her own, and her eyes filled again. She said she hoped their two uncles would meet, some day. It made me shudder. Philip said he hoped so, too; and that made me shudder again.

"Maybe they will," said Marget. "Does your uncle travel much?"

"Oh yes, he goes all about; he has business everywhere."

And so they went on chatting, and poor Marget forgot her sorrow for one little while, anyway. It was probably the only really bright and cheery hour she had known lately. I saw she liked Philip, and I knew she would. And when he told her he was studying for the ministry I could see that she liked him better than ever. And then, when he promised to get her admitted to the jail so that she could see her uncle, that was the capstone. He said he would give the guards a little present, and she must always go in the evening after dark and say nothing "but just show this paper and pass in, and show it again when you come out"—and he scribbled some queer marks on the paper and gave it to her, and she was ever so thankful, and right away was in a fever for the sun to go down; for in that old, cruel time prisoners were not allowed to see their friends, and sometimes they spent years in the jails without ever seeing a friendly face. I judged that the marks on the paper were an enchantment and that the guards would not know what they were doing, nor have any memory of it afterward; and that was indeed the way of it. Ursula put her head in at the door now and said:

"Supper's ready, miss." Then she saw us and looked frightened, and motioned me to come to her, which I did, and she asked if we had told about the cat. I said no, and she was relieved and said please don't, for if Miss Marget knew, she would think it was an unholy cat and would send for a priest and have its gifts all purified out of it, and then there wouldn't be any more dividends. So I said we wouldn't tell and she was satisfied. Then I was beginning to say good-by to Marget, but Satan interrupted and said, ever so politely—well, I don't remember just the words, but anyway he as good as invited himself to supper, and me, too. Of course Marget was miserably embarrassed, for she had no reason to suppose there would be half enough for a sick bird. Ursula heard him, and she came straight into the room, not a bit pleased. At first she was astonished to see Marget looking so fresh and rosy, and said so; then she spoke up in her native tongue, which was Bohemian, and said—as I learned afterward—"Send him away, Miss Marget; there's not victuals enough."

Before Marget could speak, Satan had the word, and was talking back to Ursula in her own language— which was a surprise to her, and for her mistress, too. He said, "Didn't I see you down the road awhile ago?"

"Yes, sir."

"Ah, that pleases me; I see you remember me." He stepped to her and whispered: "I told you it is a Lucky Cat. Don't be troubled; it will provide."

That sponged the slate of Ursula's feelings clean of its anxieties and a deep, financial joy shone in her eyes. The cat's value was augmenting. It was getting full time for Marget to take some sort of notice of Satan's invitation, and she did it in the best way, the honest way that was natural to her. She said she had little to offer but that we were welcome if we would share it with her.

We had supper in the kitchen and Ursula waited at table. A small fish was in the frying-pan, crisp and brown and tempting, and one could see that Marget was not expecting such respectable food as this. Ursula brought it and Marget divided it between Satan and me, declining to take any of it herself, and was beginning to say she did not care for fish to-day, but she did not finish the remark. It was because she noticed that another fish had appeared in the pan. She looked surprised, but did not say anything. She probably meant to inquire of Ursula about this later. There were other surprises: flesh and game and wines and fruits—things which had been strangers in that house lately; but Marget made no exclamations and now even looked unsurprised, which was Satan's influence of course. Satan talked right along and was entertaining, and made the time pass pleasantly and cheerfully, and although he told a good many lies, it was no harm in him, for he was only an angel and did not know any better. They do not know right from wrong; I knew this, because I remembered what he had said about it. He got on the good side of Ursula. He praised her to Marget confidentially, but speaking just loud enough for Ursula to hear. He said she was a fine woman and he hoped some day to bring her and his uncle together. Very soon Ursula was mincing and simpering around in a ridiculous girly way, and smoothing out her gown and prinking at herself like a foolish old hen, and all the time pretending she was not hearing what Satan was saying. I was ashamed, for it showed us to be what Satan considered us, a silly race and trivial. Satan said his uncle entertained a great deal, and to have a clever woman presiding over the festivities would double the attractions of the place.

"But your uncle is a gentleman, isn't he?" asked Marget.

"Yes," said Satan indifferently; "some even call him a Prince, out of compliment, but he is not bigoted; to him personal merit is everything, rank nothing."

My hand was hanging down by my chair; Agnes came along and licked it; by this act a secret was revealed. I started to say, "It is all a mistake; this is just a common, ordinary cat; the hair-needles on her tongue point inward, not outward." But the words did not come, because they couldn't. Satan smiled upon me and I understood.

When it was dark Marget took food and wine and fruit in a basket and hurried away to the jail, and Satan and I walked toward my home. I was thinking to myself that I should like to see what the inside of the jail was like; Satan overheard the thought and the next moment we were in the jail. We were in the torture-chamber, Satan said. The rack was there, and the other instruments, and there was a smoky lantern or two hanging on the walls and helping to make the place look dim and dreadful. There were people there—and executioners— but as they took no notice of us, it meant that we were invisible. A young man lay bound, and Satan said he was suspected of being a heretic, and the executioners were about to inquire into it. They asked the man to confess to the charge, and he said he could not, for it was not true. Then they drove splinter after splinter under his nails and he shrieked with the pain. Satan was not disturbed but I could not endure it, and had to be whisked out of there. I was faint and sick but the fresh air revived me and we walked toward my home. I said it was a brutal thing.

"No, it was a human thing. You should not insult the brutes by such a misuse of that word; they have not deserved it," and he went on talking like that. "It is like your paltry race—always lying, always claiming virtues which it hasn't got, always denying them to the higher animals, which alone possess them. No brute ever does a cruel thing—that is the monopoly of those with the Moral Sense. When a brute inflicts pain he does it innocently; it is not wrong; for him there is no such thing as wrong. And he does not inflict pain for the pleasure of inflicting it—only man does that. Inspired by that mongrel Moral Sense of his! A sense whose function is to distinguish between right and wrong, with liberty to choose which of them he will do. Now what advantage can he get out of that? He is always choosing, and in nine cases out of ten he prefers the wrong. There shouldn't be any wrong; and without the Moral Sense there couldn't be any. And yet he is such an unreasoning creature that he is not able to perceive that the Moral Sense degrades him to the bottom layer of animated beings and is a shameful possession. Are you feeling better? Let me show you something."

Chapter VI

In a moment we were in a French village. We walked through a great factory of some sort, where men and women and little children were toiling in heat and dirt and a fog of dust; and they were clothed in rags and drooped at their work, for they were worn and half starved, and weak and drowsy. Satan said:

"It is some more Moral Sense. The proprietors are rich and very holy, but the wage they pay to these poor brothers and sisters of theirs is only enough to keep them from dropping dead with hunger. The work-hours are fourteen per day, winter and summer—from six in the morning till eight at night—little children and all. And they walk to and from the pigsties which they inhabit, four miles each way, through mud and slush, rain, snow, sleet, and storm, daily, year in and year out. They get four hours of sleep. They kennel together, three families in a room, in unimaginable filth and stench; and disease comes, and they die off like flies. Have they committed a crime, these mangy things? No. What have they done, that they are punished so? Nothing at all, except getting themselves born into your foolish race. You have seen how they treat a misdoer there in the jail; now you see how they treat the innocent and the worthy. Is your race logical? Are these ill-smelling innocents better off than that heretic? Indeed, no; his punishment is trivial compared with theirs. They broke him on the wheel and smashed him to rags and pulp after we left, and he is dead now and free of your precious race, but these poor slaves here—why, they have been dying for years and some of them will not escape from life for years to come. It is the Moral Sense which teaches the factory proprietors the difference between right and wrong—you perceive the result. They think themselves better than dogs. Ah, you are such an illogical, unreasoning race! And paltry—oh, unspeakably!"

Then he dropped all seriousness and just overstrained himself making fun of us and deriding our pride in our warlike deeds, our great heroes, our imperishable fames, our mighty kings, our ancient aristocracies, our venerable history—and laughed and laughed till it was enough to make a person sick to hear him; and finally he sobered a little and said, "But, after all, it is not all ridiculous; there is a sort of pathos about it when one remembers how few are your days, how childish your pomps, and what shadows you are!"

Presently all things vanished suddenly from my sight and I knew what it meant. The next moment we were walking along in our village, and down toward the river I saw the twinkling lights of the Golden Stag. Then in the dark I heard a joyful cry:

"He's come again!"

It was Seppi Wohlmeyer. He had felt his blood leap and his spirits rise in a way that could mean only one thing and he knew Satan was near, although it was too dark to see him. He came to us and we walked along together, and Seppi poured out his gladness like water.

It was as if he were a lover and had found his sweetheart who had been lost. Seppi was a smart and animated boy, and had enthusiasm and expression, and was a contrast to Nikolaus and me. He was full of the last new mystery, now—the disappearance of Hans Oppert, the village loafer. People were beginning to be curious about it, he said. He did not say anxious—curious was the right word, and strong enough. No one had seen Hans for a couple of days.

"Not since he did that brutal thing, you know," he said.

"What brutal thing?" It was Satan that asked.

"Well, he is always clubbing his dog, which is a good dog and his only friend, and is faithful and loves him, and does no one any harm; and two days ago he was at it again, just for nothing—just for pleasure—and the dog was howling and begging, and Theodor and I begged too, but he threatened us and struck the dog again with all his might and knocked one of his eyes out, and he said to us, 'There, I hope you are satisfied now; that's what you have got for him by your damned meddling'—and he laughed, the heartless brute." Seppi's voice trembled with pity and anger. I guessed what Satan would say, and he said it.

"There is that misused word again—that shabby slander. Brutes do not act like that, but only men."

"Well, it was inhuman, anyway."

"No, it wasn't, Seppi; it was human—quite distinctly human. It is not pleasant to hear you libel the higher animals by attributing to them dispositions which they are free from and which are found nowhere but in the human heart. None of the higher animals is tainted with the disease called the Moral Sense. Purify your language, Seppi; drop those lying phrases out of it."

He spoke pretty sternly—for him—and I was sorry I

hadn't warned Seppi to be more particular about the word he used. I knew how he was feeling. He would not want to offend Satan; he would rather offend all his kin. There was an uncomfortable silence but relief soon came, for that poor dog came along now, with his eye hanging down, and went straight to Satan and began to moan and mutter brokenly, and Satan began to answer in the same way, and it was plain that they were talking together in the dog language. We all sat down in the grass in the moonlight, for the clouds were breaking away now, and Satan took the dog's head in his lap and put the eye back in its place, and the dog was comfortable and he wagged his tail and licked Satan's hand, and looked thankful and said the same; I knew he was saying it, though I did not understand the words. Then the two talked together a bit, and Satan said:

"He says his master was drunk."

"Yes, he was," said we.

"And an hour later he fell over the precipice there beyond the Cliff Pasture."

"We know the place; it is three miles from here."

"And the dog has been often to the village, begging people to go there, but he was only driven away and not listened to."

We remembered it, but hadn't understood what he wanted.

"He only wanted help for the man who had misused him, and he thought only of that and has had no food nor sought any. He has watched by his master two nights. What do you think of your race? Is heaven reserved for it and this dog ruled out, as your teachers tell you? Can your race add anything to this dog's stock of morals and magnanimities?" He spoke to the creature, who jumped up, eager and happy, and apparently ready for orders and impatient to execute them. "Get some men; go with the dog—he will show you that carrion; and take a priest along to arrange about insurance, for death is near."

With the last word he vanished, to our sorrow and disappointment. We got the men and Father Adolf, and we saw the man die. Nobody cared but the dog; he mourned and grieved and licked the dead face, and could not be comforted. We buried him where he was and without a coffin, for he had no money and no friend but the dog. If we had been an hour earlier the priest would have been in time to send that poor creature to heaven, but now he was gone down into the awful fires, to burn forever. It seemed such a pity that in a world where so many people have difficulty to put in their time, one little hour could not have been spared for this poor creature who needed it so much, and to whom it would have made the difference between eternal joy and eternal pain. It gave an appalling idea of the value of an hour, and I thought I could never waste one again without remorse and terror. Seppi was depressed and grieved, and said it must be so much better to be a dog and not run such awful risks. We took this one home with us and kept him for our own. Seppi had a very good thought as we were walking along, and it cheered us up and made us feel much better. He said the dog had forgiven the man that had wronged him so, and maybe God would accept that absolution.

There was a very dull week now, for Satan did not come, nothing much was going on, and we boys could not venture to go and see Marget, because the nights were moonlit and our parents might find us out if we tried. But we came across Ursula a couple of times taking a walk in the meadows beyond the river to air the cat, and we learned from her that things were going well. She had natty new clothes on and bore a pros-

perous look. The four groschen a day were arriving without a break, but were not being spent for food and wine
and such things—the cat attended to all that.

Marget was enduring her forsakenness and isolation
fairly well, all things considered, and was cheerful, by
help of Wilhelm Meidling. She spent an hour or two
every night in the jail with her uncle and had fattened
him up with the cat's contributions. But she was curious
to know more about Philip Traum, and hoped I would
bring him again. Ursula was curious about him herself
and asked a good many questions about his uncle. It
made the boys laugh, for I had told them the nonsense
Satan had been stuffing her with. She got no satisfaction out of us, our tongues being tied.

Ursula gave us a small item of information: money
being plenty now, she had taken on a servant to help
about the house and run errands. She tried to tell it in
a commonplace, matter-of-course way, but she was so
set up by it and so vain of it that her pride in it leaked
out pretty plainly. It was beautiful to see her veiled delight in this grandeur, poor old thing, but when we
heard the name of the servant we wondered if she had
been altogether wise; for although we were young, and
often thoughtless, we had fairly good perception on
some matters. This boy was Gottfried Narr, a dull, good
creature, with no harm in him and nothing against him
personally; still, he was under a cloud, and properly so,
for it had not been six months since a social blight
had mildewed the family—his grandmother had been
burned as a witch. When that kind of a malady is in the
blood it does not always come out with just one burning.
Just now was not a good time for Ursula and Marget
to be having dealings with a member of such a family,
for the witch-terror had risen higher during the past
year than it had ever reached in the memory of the

oldest villagers. The mere mention of a witch was almost
enough to frighten us out of our wits. This was natural
enough, because of late years there were more kinds of
witches than there used to be; in old times it had been
only old women but of late years they were of all ages
—even children of eight and nine; it was getting so that
anybody might turn out to be a familiar of the Devil—
age and sex hadn't anything to do with it. In our little
region we had tried to extirpate the witches but the
more of them we burned the more of the breed rose up
in their places.

Once, in a school for girls only ten miles away the
teachers found that the back of one of the girls was all
red and inflamed, and they were greatly frightened, believing it to be the Devil's marks. The girl was scared
and begged them not to denounce her, and said it was
only fleas; but of course it would not do to let the matter
rest there. All the girls were examined and eleven out
of the fifty were badly marked, the rest less so. A commission was appointed but the eleven only cried for
their mothers and would not confess. Then they were
shut up, each by herself, in the dark and put on black
bread and water for ten days and nights; and by that
time they were haggard and wild, and their eyes were
dry and they did not cry any more, but only sat and
mumbled and would not take the food. Then one of
them confessed and said they had often ridden through
the air on broomsticks to the witches' Sabbath, and in a
bleak place high up in the mountains had danced and
drunk and caroused with several hundred other witches
and the Evil One, and all had conducted themselves in
a scandalous way and had reviled the priests and blas-
phemed God. That is what she said—not in narrative
form, for she was not able to remember any of the details without having them called to her mind one after

the other; but the commission did that, for they knew just what questions to ask, they being all written down for the use of witch-commissioners two centuries before. They asked, "Did you do so and so?" and she always said yes and looked weary and tired, and took no interest in it. And so when the other ten heard that this one confessed, they confessed too, and answered yes to the questions. Then they were burned at the stake all together, which was just and right; and everybody went from all the countryside to see it. I went, too; but when I saw that one of them was a bonny, sweet girl I used to play with and looked so pitiful there chained to the stake, and her mother crying over her and devouring her with kisses and clinging around her neck, and saying, "Oh, my God! oh, my God!" it was too dreadful, and I went away.

It was bitter cold weather when Gottfried's grandmother was burned. It was charged that she had cured bad headaches by kneading the person's head and neck with her fingers, as she said, but really by the Devil's help, as everybody knew. They were going to examine her but she stopped them and confessed straight off that her power was from the Devil. So they appointed to burn her next morning, early, in our market-square. The officer who was to prepare the fire was there first, and prepared it. She was there next—brought by the constables, who left her and went to fetch another witch. Her family did not come with her. They might be reviled, maybe stoned, if the people were excited. I came and gave her an apple. She was squatting at the fire, warming herself and waiting; and her old lips and hands were blue with the cold. A stranger came next. He was a traveler, passing through; and he spoke to her gently and, seeing nobody but me there to hear, said he was sorry for her. And he asked if what she confessed was true and she said no. He looked surprised and still more sorry then, and asked her:

"Then why did you confess?"

"I am old and very poor," she said, "and I work for my living. There was no way but to confess. If I hadn't they might have set me free. That would ruin me, for no one would forget that I had been suspected of being a witch, and so I would get no more work and wherever I went they would set the dogs on me. In a little while I would starve. The fire is best; it is soon over. You have been good to me, you two, and I thank you."

She snuggled closer to the fire and put out her hands to warm them, the snow-flakes descending soft and still on her old gray head and making it white and whiter. The crowd was gathering now and an egg came flying and struck her in the eye, and broke and ran down her face. There was a laugh at that.

I told Satan all about the eleven girls and the old woman, once, but it did not affect him. He only said it was the human race, and what the human race did was of no consequence. And he said he had seen it made, and it was not made of clay; it was made of mud—part of it was, anyway. I knew what he meant by that—the Moral Sense. He saw the thought in my head and it tickled him and made him laugh. Then he called a bullock out of a pasture and petted it and talked with it, and said:

"There—he wouldn't drive children mad with hunger and fright and loneliness, and then burn them for confessing to things invented for them which had never happened. And neither would he break the hearts of innocent, poor old women and make them afraid to trust themselves among their own race, and he would not insult them in their death-agony. For he is not besmirched with the Moral Sense, but is as the angels are, and knows no wrong, and never does it."

Lovely as he was, Satan could be cruelly offensive when he chose, and he always chose when the human race was brought to his attention. He always turned up his nose at it and never had a kind word for it.

Well, as I was saying, we boys doubted if it was a good time for Ursula to be hiring a member of the Narr family. We were right. When the people found it out they were naturally indignant. And, moreover, since Marget and Ursula hadn't enough to eat themselves, where was the money coming from to feed another mouth? That is what they wanted to know, and in order to find out they stopped avoiding Gottfried and began to seek his society and have sociable conversations with him. He was pleased—not thinking any harm and not seeing the trap—and so he talked innocently along, and was no discreeter than a cow.

"Money!" he said; "they've got plenty of it. They pay me two groschen a week, besides my keep. And they live on the fat of the land, I can tell you; the prince himself can't beat their table."

This astonishing statement was conveyed by the astrologer to Father Adolf on a Sunday morning when he was returning from mass. He was deeply moved, and said:

"This must be looked into."

He said there must be witchcraft at the bottom of it, and told the villagers to resume relations with Marget and Ursula in a private and unostentatious way and keep both eyes open. They were told to keep their own counsel and not rouse the suspicions of the household. The villagers were at first a bit reluctant to enter such a dreadful place, but the priest said they would be under his protection while there and no harm could come to them, particularly if they carried a trifle of holy water along and kept their beads and crosses handy. This satisfied them and made them willing to go; envy and malice made the baser sort even eager to go.

And so poor Marget began to have company again, and was as pleased as a cat. She was like 'most anybody else—just human and happy in her prosperities and not averse from showing them off a little, and she was humanly grateful to have the warm shoulder turned to her and be smiled upon by her friends and the village again; for of all the hard things to bear, to be cut by your neighbors and left in contemptuous solitude is maybe the hardest.

The bars were down and we could all go there now and we did—our parents and all—day after day. The cat began to strain herself. She provided the top of everything for those companies, and in abundance— among them many a dish and many a wine which they had not tasted before and which they had not even heard of except at second-hand from the prince's servants. And the tableware was much above ordinary, too.

Marget was troubled at times and pursued Ursula with questions to an uncomfortable degree, but Ursula stood her ground and stuck to it that it was Providence and said no word about the cat. Marget knew that nothing was impossible to Providence but she could not help having doubts that this effort was from there, though she was afraid to say so, lest disaster come of it. Witchcraft occurred to her but she put the thought aside, for this was before Gottfried joined the household and she knew Ursula was pious and a bitter hater of witches. By the time Gottfried arrived Providence was established, unshakably intrenched, and getting all the gratitude.

The cat made no murmur but went on composedly improving in style and prodigality by experience.

In any community, big or little, there is always a fair proportion of people who are not malicious or unkind by nature and who never do unkind things except when they are overmastered by fear, or when their self-interest is greatly in danger, or some such matter as that. Eseldorf had its proportion of such people, and ordinarily their good and gentle influence was felt, but these were not ordinary times—on account of the witch-dread —and so we did not seem to have any gentle and compassionate hearts left, to speak of. Every person was frightened at the unaccountable state of things at Marget's house, not doubting that witchcraft was at the bottom of it, and fright frenzied their reason. Naturally there were some who pitied Marget and Ursula for the danger that was gathering about them but naturally they did not say so; it would not have been safe. So the others had it all their own way and there was none to advise the ignorant girl and the foolish woman and warn them to modify their doings. We boys wanted to warn them but we backed down when it came to the pinch, being afraid. We found that we were not manly enough nor brave enough to do a generous action when there was a chance that it could get us into trouble. Neither of us confessed this poor spirit to the others but did as other people would have done—dropped the subject and talked about something else. And I knew we all felt mean, eating and drinking Marget's fine things along with those companies of spies and petting her and complimenting her with the rest, and seeing with self-reproach how foolishly happy she was and never saying a word to put her on her guard. And, indeed, she was happy and as proud as a princess, and so grateful to have friends again. And all the time these people were watching with all their eyes and reporting all they saw to Father Adolf.

But he couldn't make head or tail of the situation. There must be an enchanter somewhere on the premises but who was it? Marget was not seen to do any jugglery, nor was Ursula, nor yet Gottfried, and still the wines and dainties never ran short, and a guest could not call for a thing and not get it. To produce these effects was usual enough with witches and enchanters—that part of it was not new, but to do it without any incantations or even any rumblings or earthquakes or lightnings or apparitions—that was new, novel, wholly irregular. There was nothing in the books like this. Enchanted things were always unreal. Gold turned to dirt in an unenchanted atmosphere, food withered away and vanished. But this test failed in the present case. The spies brought samples: Father Adolf prayed over them, exorcised them, but it did no good; they remained sound and real, they yielded to natural decay only and took the usual time to do it.

Father Adolf was not merely puzzled, he was also exasperated; for these evidences very nearly convinced him—privately—that there was no witchcraft in the matter. It did not wholly convince him, for this could be a new kind of witchcraft. There was a way to find out as to this: if this prodigal abundance of provender was not brought in from the outside, but produced on the premises, there was witchcraft, sure.

Chapter VII

Marget announced a party and invited forty people; the date for it was seven days away. This was a fine opportunity. Marget's house stood by itself, and it could be easily watched. All the week it was watched night and day. Marget's household went out and in as usual but they carried nothing in their hands, and neither they nor others brought anything to the house. This was ascertained. Evidently rations for forty people were not being fetched. If they were furnished any sustenance it would have to be made on the premises. It was true that Marget went out with a basket every evening, but the spies ascertained that she always brought it back empty.

The guests arrived at noon and filled the place. Father Adolf followed; also, after a little, the astrologer, without invitation. The spies had informed him that neither at the back nor the front had any parcels been brought in. He entered and found the eating and drinking going on finely, and everything progressing in a lively and festive way. He glanced around and perceived that many of the cooked delicacies and all of the native and foreign fruits were of a perishable character, and he also recognized that these were fresh and perfect. No apparitions, no incantations, no thunder. That settled it. This was witchcraft. And not only that but of a new kind, a kind never dreamed of before. It was a prodigious power, an illustrious power; he resolved to discover its secret. The announcement of it would resound throughout the world, penetrate to the remotest lands, paralyze all the nations with amazement—and carry his name with it, and make him renowned forever. It was a wonderful piece of luck, a splendid piece of luck; the glory of it made him dizzy.

All the house made room for him; Marget politely seated him; Ursula ordered Gottfried to bring a special table for him. Then she decked it and furnished it, and asked for his orders.

"Bring me what you will," he said.

The two servants brought supplies from the pantry,

together with white wine and red—a bottle of each.
The astrologer, who very likely had never seen such
delicacies before, poured out a beaker of red wine,
drank it off, poured another, then began to eat with a
grand appetite.

I was not expecting Satan, for it was more than a week
since I had seen or heard of him but now he came in—
I knew it by the feel, though people were in the way and
I could not see him. I heard him apologizing for intruding, and he was going away but Marget urged him
to stay, and he thanked her and stayed. She brought him
along, introducing him to the girls and to Meidling and
to some of the elders, and there was quite a rustle of
whispers: "It's the young stranger we hear so much
about and can't get sight of, he is away so much."
"Dear, dear, but he is beautiful—what is his name?"
"Philip Traum." "Ah, it fits him!" (You see, "Traum" is
German for "Dream.") "What does he do?" "Studying
for the ministry, they say." "His face is his fortune—
he'll be a cardinal some day." "Where is his home?"
"Away down somewhere in the tropics, they say—has a
rich uncle down there." And so on. He made his way at
once; everybody was anxious to know him and talk with
him. Everybody noticed how cool and fresh it was all
of a sudden, and wondered at it, for they could see that
the sun was beating down the same as before outside,
and the sky was clear of clouds, but no one guessed the
reason, of course.

The astrologer had drunk his second beaker; he
poured out a third. He set the bottle down, and by accident overturned it. He seized it before much was spilled,
and held it up to the light, saying, "What a pity—it is
royal wine." Then his face lighted with joy or triumph,
or something, and he said, "Quick! Bring a bowl."

It was brought—a four-quart one. He took up that

two-pint bottle and began to pour; went on pouring, the red liquor gurgling and gushing into the white bowl and rising higher and higher up its sides, everybody staring and holding their breath—and presently the bowl was full to the brim.

"Look at the bottle," he said, holding it up, "it is full yet!" I glanced at Satan, and in that moment he vanished. Then Father Adolf rose up, flushed and excited, crossed himself, and began to thunder in his great voice, "This house is bewitched and accursed!" People began to cry and shriek and crowd toward the door. "I summon this detected household to—"

His words were cut off short. His face became red, then purple, but he could not utter another sound. Then I saw Satan, a transparent film, melt into the astrologer's body; then the astrologer put up his hand, and apparently in his own voice said, "Wait—remain where you are." All stopped where they stood. "Bring a funnel!" Ursula brought it, trembling and scared, and he stuck it in the bottle and took up the great bowl and began to pour the wine back, the people gazing and dazed with astonishment, for they knew the bottle was already full before he began. He emptied the whole of the bowl into the bottle, then smiled out over the room, chuckled, and said, indifferently, "It is nothing—anybody can do it! With my powers I can even do much more."

A frightened cry burst out everywhere. "Oh, my God, he is possessed!" and there was a tumultuous rush for the door which swiftly emptied the house of all who did not belong in it except us boys and Meidling. We boys knew the secret, and would have told it if we could, but we couldn't. We were very thankful to Satan for furnishing that good help at the needful time.

Marget was pale and crying; Meidling looked kind of petrified; Ursula the same; but Gottfried was the worst

—he couldn't stand, he was so weak and scared. For he was of a witch family, you know, and it would be bad for him to be suspected. Agnes came loafing in, looking pious and unaware, and wanted to rub up against Ursula and be petted, but Ursula was afraid of her and shrank away from her, but pretending she was not meaning any incivility, for she knew very well it wouldn't answer to have strained relations with that kind of a cat. But we boys took Agnes and petted her, for Satan would not have befriended her if he had not had a good opinion of her, and that was indorsement enough for us. He seemed to trust anything that hadn't the Moral Sense.

Outside, the guests, panic-stricken, scattered in every direction and fled in a pitiable state of terror; and such a tumult as they made with their running and sobbing and shrieking and shouting that soon all the village came flocking from their houses to see what had happened, and they thronged the street and shouldered and jostled one another in excitement and fright; and then Father Adolf appeared, and they fell apart in two walls like the cloven Red Sea, and presently down this lane the astrologer came striding and mumbling, and where he passed the lanes surged back in packed masses and fell silent with awe, and their eyes stared and their breasts heaved and several women fainted; and when he was gone by the crowd swarmed together and followed him at a distance, talking excitedly and asking questions and finding out the facts. Finding out the facts and passing them on to others, with improvements—improvements which soon enlarged the bowl of wine to a barrel, and made the one bottle hold it all and yet remain empty to the last.

When the astrologer reached the market-square he went straight to a juggler, fantastically dressed, who was keeping three brass balls in the air, and took them from him and faced around upon the approaching crowd and said: "This poor clown is ignorant of his art. Come forward and see an expert perform."

So saying, he tossed the balls up one after another and set them whirling in a slender bright oval in the air, and added another, then another and another, and soon—no one seeing whence he got them—adding, adding, adding, the oval lengthening all the time, his hands moving so swiftly that they were just a web or a blur and not distinguishable as hands; and such as counted said there were now a hundred balls in the air. The spinning great oval reached up twenty feet in the air and was a shining and glinting and wonderful sight. Then he folded his arms and told the balls to go on spinning without his help—and they did it. After a couple of minutes he said, "There, that will do," and the oval broke and came crashing down, and the balls scattered abroad and rolled every whither. And wherever one of them came the people fell back in dread and no one would touch it. It made him laugh, and he scoffed at the people and called them cowards and old women. Then he turned and saw the tight-rope, and said foolish people were daily wasting their money to see a clumsy and ignorant varlet degrade that beautiful art; now they should see the work of a master. With that he made a spring into the air and lit firm on his feet on the rope. Then he hopped the whole length of it back and forth on one foot, with his hands clasped over his eyes; and next he began to throw somersaults, both backward and forward, and threw twenty-seven.

The people murmured, for the astrologer was old and always before had been halting of movement and at times even lame, but he was nimble enough now and went on with his antics in the liveliest manner. Finally he sprang lightly down and walked away and passed up the road and around the corner and disappeared. Then that great, pale, silent, solid crowd drew a deep breath and looked into one another's faces as if they said: "Was it real? Did you see it, or was it only I—and I was dreaming?" Then they broke into a low murmur of talking, and fell apart in couples and moved toward their homes, still talking in that awed way, with faces close together and laying a hand on an arm and making other such gestures as people make when they have been deeply impressed by something.

We boys followed behind our fathers and listened, catching all we could of what they said, and when they sat down in our house and continued their talk they still had us for company. They were in a sad mood, for it was certain, they said, that disaster for the village must follow this awful visitation of witches and devils. Then my father remembered that Father Adolf had been struck dumb at the moment of his denunciation.

"They have not ventured to lay their hands upon an anointed servant of God before," he said; "and how they could have dared it this time I cannot make out, for he wore his crucifix. Isn't it so?"

"Yes," said the others, "we saw it."

"It is serious, friends, it is very serious. Always before, we had a protection. It has failed."

The others shook, as with a sort of chill, and muttered those words over—"It has failed." "God has forsaken us."

"It is true," said Seppi Wohlmeyer's father; "there is nowhere to look for help."

"The people will realize this," said Nikolaus's father, the judge, "and despair will take away their courage and their energies. We have indeed fallen upon evil times."

He sighed, and Wohlmeyer said in a troubled voice, "The report of it all will go about the country, and our village will be shunned as being under the displeasure of God. The Golden Stag will know hard times."

"True, neighbor," said my father, "all of us will suffer—all in repute, many in estate. And, good God!—"

"What is it?"

"That can come—to finish us!"

"Name it—um Gottes Willen!"

"The Interdict!"

It smote like a thunderclap and they were like to swoon with the terror of it. Then the dread of this calamity roused their energies, and they stopped brooding and began to consider ways to avert it. They discussed this, that, and the other way, and talked till the afternoon was far spent, then confessed that at present they could arrive at no decision. So they parted sorrowfully, with oppressed hearts which were filled with bodings.

While they were saying their parting words I slipped out and set my course for Marget's house to see what was happening there. I met many people, but none of them greeted me. It ought to have been surprising but it was not, for they were so distraught with fear and dread that they were not in their right minds, I think; they were white and haggard and walked like persons in a dream, their eyes open but seeing nothing, their lips moving but uttering nothing, and worriedly clasping and unclasping their hands without knowing it.

At Marget's it was like a funeral. She and Wilhelm sat together on the sofa, but said nothing, and not even holding hands. Both were steeped in gloom and Marget's eyes were red from the crying she had been doing. She said:

"I have been begging him to go and come no more, and so save himself alive. I cannot bear to be his murderer. This house is bewitched and no inmate will escape the fire. But he will not go, and he will be lost with the rest."

Wilhelm said he would not go; if there was danger for her, his place was by her and there he would remain. Then she began to cry again and it was all so mournful that I wished I had stayed away. There was a knock, now, and Satan came in, fresh and cheery and beautiful, and brought that winy atmosphere of his and changed the whole thing. He never said a word about what had been happening nor about the awful fears which were freezing the blood in the hearts of the community, but began to talk and rattle on about all manner of gay and pleasant things: and next about music—an artful stroke which cleared away the remnant of Marget's depression and brought her spirits and her interests broad awake. She had not heard any one talk so well and so knowingly on that subject before, and she was so uplifted by it and so charmed that what she was feeling lit up her face and came out in her words, and Wilhelm noticed it and did not look as pleased as he ought to have done. And next Satan branched off into poetry and recited some and did it well, and Marget was charmed again; and again Wilhelm was not as pleased as he ought to have been, and this time Marget noticed it and was remorseful.

I fell asleep to pleasant music that night—the patter of rain upon the panes and the dull growling of distant thunder. Away in the night Satan came and roused me and said: "Come with me. Where shall we go?"

"Anywhere—so it is with you."

Then there was a fierce glare of sunlight, and he said, "This is China."

That was a grand surprise and made me sort of drunk with vanity and gladness to think I had come so far—so much, much farther than anybody else in our village, including Bartel Sperling who had such a great opinion of his travels. We buzzed around over that empire for more than half an hour and saw the whole of it. It was wonderful, the spectacles we saw; and some were beautiful, others too horrible to think. For instance—However, I may go into that by and by and also why Satan chose China for this excursion instead of another place; it would interrupt my tale to do it now. Finally we stopped flitting and lit.

We sat upon a mountain commanding a vast landscape of mountain-range and gorge and valley and plain and river, with cities and villages slumbering in the sunlight and a glimpse of blue sea on the farther verge. It was a tranquil and dreamy picture, beautiful to the eye and restful to the spirit. If we could only make a change like that whenever we wanted to, the world would be easier to live in than it is, for change of scene shifts the mind's burdens to the other shoulder and banishes old, shop-worn wearinesses from mind and body both.

We talked together, and I had the idea of trying to reform Satan and persuade him to lead a better life. I told him about all those things he had been doing, and begged him to be more considerate and stop making people unhappy. I said I knew he did not mean any harm but that he ought to stop and consider the possible consequences of a thing before launching it in that impulsive and random way of his, then he would not make so much trouble. He was not hurt by this plain speech; he only looked amused and surprised, and said:

"What? I do random things? Indeed, I never do. I stop and consider possible consequences? Where is the need? I know what the consequences are going to be—always."

"Oh, Satan, then how could you do these things?"

"Well, I will tell you, and you must understand if you can. You belong to a singular race. Every man is a suffering-machine and a happiness-machine combined. The two functions work together harmoniously, with a fine and delicate precision, on the give-and-take principle. For every happiness turned out in the one department the other stands ready to modify it with a sorrow or a pain—maybe a dozen. In most cases the man's life is about equally divided between happiness and unhappiness. When this is not the case the unhappiness predominates—always, never the other. Sometimes a man's make and disposition are such that his misery-machine is able to do nearly all the business. Such a man goes through life almost ignorant of what happiness is. Everything he touches, everything he does, brings a misfortune upon him. You have seen such people? To that kind of a person life is not an advantage, is it? It is only a disaster. Sometimes for an hour's happiness a man's machinery makes him pay years of misery. Don't you know that? It happens every now and then. I will give you a case or two presently. Now the people of your village are nothing to me—you know that, don't you?"

I did not like to speak out too flatly, so I said I had suspected it.

"Well, it is true that they are nothing to me. It is not possible that they should be. The difference between them and me is abysmal, immeasurable. They have no intellect."

"No intellect?"

"Nothing that resembles it. At a future time I will examine what man calls his mind and give you the details of that chaos, then you will see and understand. Men have nothing in common with me—there is no point of contact; they have foolish little feelings and foolish little vanities and impertinences and ambitions; their foolish little life is but a laugh, a sigh, and extinction; and they have no sense. Only the Moral Sense. I will show you what I mean. Here is a red spider, not so big as a pin's head. Can you imagine an elephant being interested in him—caring whether he is happy or isn't, or whether he is wealthy or poor, or whether his sweetheart returns his love or not, or whether his mother is sick or well, or whether he is looked up to in society or not, or whether his enemies will smite him or his friends desert him, or whether his hopes will suffer blight or his political ambitions fail, or whether he shall die in the bosom of his family or neglected and despised in a foreign land? These things can never be important to the elephant, they are nothing to him, he cannot shrink his sympathies to the microscopic size of them. Man is to me as the red spider is to the elephant. The elephant has nothing against the spider—he cannot get down to that remote level; I have nothing against man. The elephant is indifferent; I am indifferent. The elephant would not take the trouble to do the spider an ill turn; if he took the notion he might do him a good turn, if it came in his way and cost nothing. I have done men good service but no ill turns.

"The elephant lives a century, the red spider a day; in power, intellect, and dignity the one creature is separated from the other by a distance which is simply astronomical. Yet in these, as in all qualities, man is immeasurably further below me than is the wee spider below the elephant.

"Man's mind clumsily and tediously and laboriously patches little trivialities together and gets a result—such as it is. My mind creates! Do you get the force of that? Creates anything it desires—and in a moment. Creates without material. Creates fluids, solids, colors—

anything, everything—out of the airy nothing which is called Thought. A man imagines a silk thread, imagines a machine to make it, imagines a picture, then by weeks of labor embroiders it on canvas with the thread. I think the whole thing, and in a moment it is before you—created.

"I think a poem, music, the record of a game of chess—anything—and it is there. This is the immortal mind—nothing is beyond its reach. Nothing can obstruct my vision; the rocks are transparent to me and darkness is daylight. I do not need to open a book, I take the whole of its contents into my mind at a single glance, through the cover; and in a million years I could not forget a single word of it, or its place in the volume. Nothing goes on in the skull of man, bird, fish, insect, or other creature which can be hidden from me. I pierce the learned man's brain with a single glance, and the treasures which cost him threescore years to accumulate are mine; he can forget and he does forget, but I retain.

"Now, then, I perceive by your thoughts that you are understanding me fairly well. Let us proceed. Circumstances might so fall out that the elephant could like the spider—supposing he can see it—but he could not love it. His love is for his own kind—for his equals. An angel's love is sublime, adorable, divine, beyond the imagination of man—infinitely beyond it! But it is limited to his own august order. If it fell upon one of your race for only an instant, it would consume its object to ashes. No, we cannot love men but we can be harmlessly indifferent to them; we can also like them, sometimes. I like you and the boys, I like Father Peter, and for your sakes I am doing all these things for the villagers."

He saw that I was thinking a sarcasm and he explained his position.

"I have wrought well for the villagers, though it does not look like it on the surface. Your race never know good fortune from ill. They are always mistaking the one for the other. It is because they cannot see into the future. What I am doing for the villagers will bear good fruit some day, in some cases to themselves, in others to unborn generations of men. No one will ever know that I was the cause but it will be none the less true, for all that. Among you boys you have a game: you stand a row of bricks on end a few inches apart, you push a brick, it knocks its neighbor over, the neighbor knocks over the next brick—and so on till all the row is prostrate. That is human life. A child's first act knocks over the initial brick and the rest will follow inexorably. If you could see into the future as I can, you would see everything that was going to happen to that creature, for nothing can change the order of its life after the first event has determined it. That is, nothing will change it, because each act unfailingly begets an act, that act begets another, and so on to the end, and the seer can look forward down the line and see just when each act is to have birth, from cradle to grave."

"Does God order the career?"

"Foreordain it? No. The man's circumstances and environment order it. His first act determines the second and all that follow after. But suppose, for argument's sake, that the man should skip one of these acts, an apparently trifling one, for instance; suppose that it had been appointed that on a certain day, at a certain hour and minute and second and fraction of a second he should go to the well, and he didn't go. That man's career would change utterly from that moment; thence to the grave it would be wholly different from the career which his first act as a child had arranged for him. Indeed, it might be that if he had gone to the well he would have ended his career on a throne, and that omitting to do it would set him upon a career that would lead to beggary and a pauper's grave. For instance: if at any time—say in boyhood—Columbus had skipped the triflingest little link in the chain of acts projected and made inevitable by his first childish act, it would have changed his whole subsequent life, and he would have become a priest and died obscure in an Italian village, and America would not have been discovered for two centuries afterward. I know this. To skip any one of the billion acts in Columbus's chain would have wholly changed his life. I have examined his billion of possible careers and in only one of them occurs the discovery of America. You people do not suspect that all of your acts are of one size and importance, but it is true; to snatch at an appointed fly is as big with fate for you as in any other appointed act—"

"As the conquering of a continent, for instance?"

"Yes. Now, then, no man ever does drop a link—the thing has never happened! Even when he is trying to make up his mind as to whether he will do a thing or not, that itself is a link, an act, and has its proper place in his chain; and when he finally decides an act, that also was the thing which he was absolutely certain to do. You see now that a man will never drop a link in his chain. He cannot. If he made up his mind to try, that project would itself be an unavoidable link—a thought bound to occur to him at that precise moment, and made certain by the first act of his babyhood."

It seemed so dismal!

"He is a prisoner for life," I said sorrowfully, "and cannot get free."

"No, of himself he cannot get away from the consequences of his first childish act. But I can free him."

I looked up wistfully.

"I have changed the careers of a number of your villagers."

I tried to thank him but found it difficult, and let it drop.

"I shall make some other changes. You know that little Lisa Brandt?"

"Oh yes, everybody does. My mother says she is so sweet and so lovely that she is not like any other child. She says she will be the pride of the village when she grows up, and its idol too, just as she is now."

"I shall change her future."

"Make it better?" I asked.

"Yes. And I will change the future of Nikolaus."

I was glad this time, and said, "I don't need to ask about his case; you will be sure to do generously by him."

"It is my intention."

Straight off I was building that great future of Nicky's in my imagination, and had already made a renowned general of him and hofmeister at the court, when I noticed that Satan was waiting for me to get ready to listen again. I was ashamed of having exposed my cheap imaginings to him and was expecting some sarcasms, but it did not happen. He proceeded with his subject:

"Nicky's appointed life is sixty-two years."

"That's grand!" I said.

"Lisa's, thirty-six. But, as I told you, I shall change their lives and those ages. Two minutes and a quarter from now Nikolaus will wake out of his sleep and find the rain blowing in. It was appointed that he should turn over and go to sleep again. But I have appointed that he shall get up and close the window first. That trifle will change his career entirely. He will rise in the morning two minutes later than the chain of his life had appointed him to rise. By consequence, thenceforth nothing will ever happen to him in accordance with the details of the old chain." He took out his watch and sat looking at it a few moments, then said: "Nikolaus has risen to close the window. His life is changed, his new career has begun. There will be consequences."

It made me feel creepy; it was uncanny.

"But for this change certain things would happen twelve days from now. For instance, Nikolaus would save Lisa from drowning. He would arrive on the scene at exactly the right moment—four minutes past ten, the long-ago appointed instant of time—and the water would be shoal, the achievement easy and certain. But he will arrive some seconds too late, now; Lisa will have struggled into deeper water. He will do his best but both will drown."

"Oh, Satan! oh, dear Satan!" I cried, with the tears rising in my eyes, "save them! Don't let it happen. I can't bear to lose Nikolaus, he is my loving playmate and friend; and think of Lisa's poor mother!"

I clung to him and begged and pleaded but he was not moved. He made me sit down again and told me I must hear him out.

"I have changed Nikolaus's life and this has changed Lisa's. If I had not done this, Nikolaus would save Lisa, then he would catch cold from his drenching; one of your race's fantastic and desolating scarlet fevers would follow, with pathetic after-effects; for forty-six years he would lie in his bed a paralytic log, deaf, dumb, blind, and praying night and day for the blessed relief of death. Shall I change his life back?"

"Oh no! Oh, not for the world! In charity and pity leave it as it is."

"It is best so. I could not have changed any other link in his life and done him so good a service. He had a billion possible careers but not one of them was worth living; they were charged full with miseries and disasters. But for my intervention he would do his brave deed twelve days from now—a deed begun and ended in six minutes—and get for all reward those forty-six years of sorrow and suffering I told you of. It is one of the cases I was thinking of awhile ago when I said that sometimes an act which brings the actor an hour's happiness and self-satisfaction is paid for—or punished—by years of suffering."

I wondered what poor little Lisa's early death would save her from. He answered the thought:

"From ten years of pain and slow recovery from an accident, and then from nineteen years' pollution, shame, depravity, crime, ending with death at the hands of the executioner. Twelve days hence she will die; her mother would save her life if she could. Am I not kinder than her mother?"

"Yes—oh, indeed yes, and wiser."

"Father Peter's case is coming on presently. He will be acquitted, through unassailable proofs of his innocence."

"Why, Satan, how can that be? Do you really think it?"

"Indeed, I know it. His good name will be restored and the rest of his life will be happy."

"I can believe it. To restore his good name will have that effect."

"His happiness will not proceed from that cause. I shall change his life that day, for his good. He will never know his good name has been restored."

In my mind—and modestly—I asked for particulars but Satan paid no attention to my thought. Next my mind wandered to the astrologer, and I wondered where he might be.

"In the moon," said Satan, with a fleeting sound which I believed was a chuckle. "I've got him on the cold side of it, too. He doesn't know where he is and is not having a pleasant time; still, it is good enough for him, a good place for his star studies. I shall need him presently; then I shall bring him back and possess him again. He has a long and cruel and odious life before him but I will change that, for I have no feeling against him and am quite willing to do him a kindness. I think I shall get him burned."

He had such strange notions of kindness! But angels are made so and do not know any better. Their ways are not like our ways, and besides, human beings are nothing to them; they think they are only freaks. It seems to me odd that he should put the astrologer so far away; he could have dumped him in Germany just as well, where he would be handy.

"Far away?" said Satan. "To me no place is far away; distance does not exist for me. The sun is less than a hundred million miles from here and the light that is falling upon us has taken eight minutes to come, but I can make that flight, or any other, in a fraction of time so minute that it cannot be measured by a watch. I have but to think the journey and it is accomplished."

I held out my hand and said, "The light lies upon it; think it into a glass of wine, Satan."

He did it. I drank the wine.

"Break the glass," he said.

I broke it.

"There—you see it is real. The villagers thought the brass balls were magic stuff and as perishable as smoke. They were afraid to touch them. You are a curious lot—your race. But come along; I have business. I will put you to bed." Said and done. Then he was gone, but his voice came back to me through the rain and darkness saying, "Yes, tell Seppi, but no other."

It was the answer to my thought.

Chapter VIII

Sleep would not come. It was not because I was proud of my travels and excited about having been around the big world to China, and feeling contemptuous of Bartel Sperling, "the traveler," as he called himself, and looked down upon us others because he had been to Vienna once and was the only Eseldorf boy who had made such a journey and seen the world's wonders. At another time that would have kept me awake but it did not affect me now. No, my mind was filled with Nikolaus, my thoughts ran upon him only, and the good days we had seen together at romps and frolics in the woods and the fields and the river in the long summer days, and skating and sliding in the winter when our parents thought we were in school. And now he was going out of this young life, and the summers and winters would come and go, and we others would rove and play as before, but his place would be vacant; we should see him no more. To-morrow he would not suspect but would be as he had always been, and it would shock me to hear him laugh and see him do lightsome and frivolous things, for to me he would be a corpse, with waxen hands and dull eyes, and I should see the shroud around his face; and next day he would not suspect, nor the next, and all the time his handful of days would be wasting swiftly away and that awful thing coming nearer and nearer, his fate closing steadily around him and no one knowing it but Seppi and me. Twelve days—only twelve days. It was awful to think of. I noticed that in my thoughts I was not calling him by his familiar names, Nick and Nicky, but was speaking of him by his full name, and reverently, as one speaks of the dead. Also, as incident after incident of our comradeship came thronging into my mind out of the past, I noticed that they were mainly cases where I had wronged him or hurt him, and they rebuked me and reproached me and my heart was wrung with remorse, just as it is when we remember our unkindnesses to friends who have passed beyond the veil and we wish we could have them back again, if only for a moment, so that we could go on our knees to them and say, "Have pity and forgive."

Once when we were nine years old he went a long errand of nearly two miles for the fruiterer, who gave him a splendid big apple for reward, and he was flying home with it, almost beside himself with astonishment and delight, and I met him, and he let me look at the apple, not thinking of treachery, and I ran off with it, eating it as I ran, he following me and begging, and when he overtook me I offered him the core, which was all that was left, and I laughed. Then he turned away, crying, and said he had meant to give it to his little sister. That smote me, for she was slowly getting well of a sickness and it would have been a proud moment for him, to see her joy and surprise and have her caresses. But I was ashamed to say I was ashamed and only said something rude and mean, to pretend I did not care, and he made no reply in words but there was a wounded look in his face as he turned away toward his home which rose before me many times in after years, in the night, and reproached me and made me ashamed again. It had grown dim in my mind, by and by, then it disappeared; but it was back now, and not dim.

Once at school, when we were eleven, I upset my ink and spoiled four copy-books and was in danger of severe punishment, but I put it upon him and he got the whipping.

And only last year I had cheated him in a trade, giving him a large fish-hook which was partly broken through for three small sound ones. The first fish he caught broke the hook, but he did not know I was blamable and he refused to take back one of the small hooks which my conscience forced me to offer him, but said, "A trade is a trade; the hook was bad but that was not your fault."

No, I could not sleep. These little shabby wrongs upbraided me and tortured me, and with a pain much sharper than one feels when the wrongs have been done to the living. Nikolaus was living but no matter; he was to me as one already dead. The wind was still moaning about the eaves, the rain still pattering upon the panes.

In the morning I sought out Seppi and told him. It was down by the river. His lips moved but he did not say anything, he only looked dazed and stunned, and his face turned very white. He stood like that a few moments, the tears welling into his eyes, then he turned away and I locked my arm in his and we walked along thinking, but not speaking. We crossed the bridge and wandered through the meadows and up among the hills and the woods, and at last the talk came and flowed freely, and it was all about Nikolaus and was a recalling of the life we had lived with him. And every now and then Seppi said, as if to himself:

"Twelve days!—less than twelve days."

We said we must be with him all the time; we must have all of him we could; the days were precious now. Yet we did not go to seek him. It would be like meeting the dead and we were afraid. We did not say it but that was what we were feeling. And so it gave us a shock when we turned a curve and came upon Nikolaus face to face. He shouted, gaily:

"Hi-hi! What is the matter? Have you seen a ghost?"

We couldn't speak but there was no occasion; he was willing to talk for us all, for he had just seen Satan and was in high spirits about it. Satan had told him about

our trip to China, and he had begged Satan to take him
a journey and Satan had promised. It was to be a far
journey, and wonderful and beautiful, and Nikolaus had
begged him to take us too, but he said no, he would take
us some day, maybe, but not now. Satan would come for
him on the 13th and Nikolaus was already counting the
hours, he was so impatient.

That was the fatal day. We were already counting the
hours, too.

We wandered many a mile, always following paths
which had been our favorites from the days when we
were little, and always we talked about the old times.
All the blitheness was with Nikolaus; we others could
not shake off our depression. Our tone toward Nikolaus
was so strangely gentle and tender and yearning that he
noticed it and was pleased, and we were constantly doing him deferential little offices of courtesy and saying,
"Wait, let me do that for you," and that pleased him,
too. I gave him seven fish-hooks—all I had—and made
him take them, and Seppi gave him his new knife and a
humming-top painted red and yellow—atonements for
swindles practiced upon him formerly, as I learned later,
and probably no longer remembered by Nikolaus now.
These things touched him and he could not have believed that we loved him so, and his pride in it and
gratefulness for it cut us to the heart, we were so undeserving of them. When we parted at last he was radiant,
and said he had never had such a happy day.

As we walked along homeward, Seppi said, "We always prized him but never so much as now, when we
are going to lose him."

Next day and every day we spent all of our spare time
with Nikolaus, and also added to it time which we (and
he) stole from work and other duties, and this cost the
three of us some sharp scoldings and some threats of

punishment. Every morning two of us woke with a start and a shudder, saying as the days flew along, "Only ten days left;" "only nine days left;" "only eight;" "only seven." Always it was narrowing. Always Nikolaus was gay and happy and always puzzled because we were not. He wore his invention to the bone trying to invent ways to cheer us up but it was only a hollow success; he could see that our jollity had no heart in it and that the laughs we broke into came up against some obstruction or other and suffered damage and decayed into a sigh. He tried to find out what the matter was, so that he could help us out of our trouble or make it lighter by sharing it with us; so we had to tell many lies to deceive him and appease him.

But the most distressing thing of all was that he was always making plans and often they went beyond the 13th! Whenever that happened it made us groan in spirit. All his mind was fixed upon finding some way to conquer our depression and cheer us up; and at last, when he had but three days to live he fell upon the right idea and was jubilant over it—a boys-and-girls' frolic and dance in the woods, up there where we first met Satan, and this was to occur on the 14th. It was ghastly, for that was his funeral day. We couldn't venture to protest; it would only have brought a "Why?" which we could not answer. He wanted us to help him invite his guests and we did it—one can refuse nothing to a dying friend. But it was dreadful, for really we were inviting them to his funeral.

It was an awful eleven days; and yet, with a lifetime stretching back between today and then, they are still a grateful memory to me, and beautiful. In effect they were days of companionship with one's sacred dead and I have known no comradeship that was so close or so precious. We clung to the hours and the minutes, counting them as they wasted away and parting with them with that pain and bereavement which a miser feels who sees his hoard filched from him coin by coin by robbers and is helpless to prevent it.

When the evening of the last day came we stayed out too long; Seppi and I were in fault for that; we could not bear to part with Nikolaus; so it was very late when we left him at his door. We lingered near awhile, listening and that happened which we were fearing. His father gave him the promised punishment and we heard his shrieks. But we listened only a moment, then hurried away remorseful for this thing which we had caused. And sorry for the father, too, our thought being, "If he only knew—if he only knew!"

In the morning Nikolaus did not meet us at the appointed place, so we went to his home to see what the matter was. His mother said:

"His father is out of all patience with these goings-on and will not have any more of it. Half the time when Nick is needed he is not to be found; then it turns out that he has been gadding around with you two. His father gave him a flogging last night. It always grieved me before and many's the time I have begged him off and saved him, but this time he appealed to me in vain, for I was out of patience myself."

"I wish you had saved him just this one time," I said, my voice trembling a little, "it would ease a pain in your heart to remember it some day."

She was ironing at the time and her back was partly toward me. She turned about with a startled or wondering look in her face and said, "What do you mean by that?"

I was not prepared and didn't know anything to say; so it was awkward, for she kept looking at me; but Seppi was alert and spoke up:

"Why, of course it would be pleasant to remember, for the very reason we were out so late was that Nikolaus got to telling how good you are to him and how he never got whipped when you were by to save him, and he was so full of it and we were so full of the interest of it that none of us noticed how late it was getting."

"Did he say that? Did he?" and she put her apron to her eyes.

"You can ask Theodor—he will tell you the same."

"It is a dear, good lad, my Nick," she said. "I am sorry I let him get whipped; I will never do it again. To think —all the time I was sitting here last night, fretting and angry at him, he was loving me and praising me! Dear, dear, if we could only know! Then we shouldn't ever go wrong, but we are only poor, dumb beasts groping around and making mistakes. I sha'n't ever think of last night without a pang."

She was like all the rest; it seemed as if nobody could open a mouth in these wretched days without saying something that made us shiver. They were "groping around," and did not know what true, sorrowfully true things they were saying by accident.

Seppi asked if Nikolaus might go out with us.

"I am sorry," she answered, "but he can't. To punish him further, his father doesn't allow him to go out of the house today."

We had a great hope! I saw it in Seppi's eyes. We thought, "If he cannot leave the house, he cannot be drowned." Seppi asked, to make sure:

"Must he stay in all day or only the morning?"

"All day. It's such a pity, too; it's a beautiful day and he is so unused to being shut up. But he is busy planning his party and maybe that is company for him. I do hope he isn't too lonesome."

Seppi saw that in her eye which emboldened him to ask if we might go up and help him pass his time.

"And welcome!" she said, right heartily. "Now I call that real friendship, when you might be abroad in the fields and the woods, having a happy time. You are good boys, I'll allow that, though you don't always find satisfactory ways of improving it. Take these cakes—for yourselves—and give him this one, from his mother."

The first thing we noticed when we entered Nikolaus's room was the time—a quarter to 10. Could that be correct? Only such a few minutes to live! I felt a contraction at my heart. Nikolaus jumped up and gave us a glad welcome. He was in good spirits over his plannings for his party and had not been lonesome.

"Sit down," he said, "and look at what I've been doing. And I've finished a kite that you will say is a beauty. It's drying in the kitchen; I'll fetch it."

He had been spending his penny savings in fanciful trifles of various kinds, to go as prizes in the games, and they were marshaled with fine and showy effect upon the table. He said:

"Examine them at your leisure while I get mother to touch up the kite with her iron if it isn't dry enough yet."

Then he tripped out and went clattering down-stairs, whistling.

We did not look at the things; we couldn't take any interest in anything but the clock. We sat staring at it in silence, listening to the ticking, and every time the minute-hand jumped we nodded recognition—one minute fewer to cover in the race for life or for death. Finally Seppi drew a deep breath and said:

"Two minutes to ten. Seven minutes more and he will pass the death-point. Theodor, he is going to be saved! He's going to—"

"Hush! I'm on needles. Watch the clock and keep still."

Five minutes more. We were panting with the strain and the excitement. Another three minutes, and there was a footstep on the stair.

"Saved!" And we jumped up and faced the door.

The old mother entered, bringing the kite. "Isn't it a beauty?" she said. "And, dear me, how he has slaved over it—ever since daylight, I think, and only finished it awhile before you came." She stood it against the wall and stepped back to take a view of it. "He drew the pictures his own self, and I think they are very good. The church isn't so very good, I'll have to admit, but look at the bridge—any one can recognize the bridge in a minute. He asked me to bring it up. . . . Dear me! it's seven minutes past ten, and I—"

"But where is he?"

"He? Oh, he'll be here soon; he's gone out a minute."

"Gone out?"

"Yes. Just as he came down-stairs little Lisa's mother came in and said the child had wandered off somewhere, and as she was a little uneasy I told Nikolaus to never mind about his father's orders—go and look her up. . . . Why, how white you two do look! I do believe you are sick. Sit down; I'll fetch something. That cake has disagreed with you. It is a little heavy but I thought—"

She disappeared without finishing her sentence, and we hurried at once to the back window and looked toward the river. There was a great crowd at the other end of the bridge and people were flying toward that point from every direction.

"Oh, it is all over—poor Nikolaus! Why, oh, why did she let him get out of the house!"

"Come away," said Seppi, half sobbing, "come quick

—we can't bear to meet her; in five minutes she will know."

But we were not to escape. She came upon us at the foot of the stairs, with her cordials in her hands, and made us come in and sit down and take the medicine. Then she watched the effect and it did not satisfy her; so she made us wait longer, and kept upbraiding herself for giving us the unwholesome cake.

Presently the thing happened which we were dreading. There was a sound of tramping and scraping outside and a crowd came solemnly in, with heads uncovered, and laid the two drowned bodies on the bed.

"Oh, my God!" that poor mother cried out, and fell on her knees, and put her arms about her dead boy and began to cover the wet face with kisses. "Oh, it was I that sent him, and I have been his death. If I had obeyed and kept him in the house, this would not have happened. And I am rightly punished; I was cruel to him last night, and him begging me, his own mother, to be his friend."

And so she went on and on, and all the women cried and pitied her, and tried to comfort her, but she could not forgive herself and could not be comforted, and kept on saying if she had not sent him out he would be alive and well now, and she was the cause of his death.

It shows how foolish people are when they blame themselves for anything they have done. Satan knows, and he said nothing happens that your first act hasn't arranged to happen and made inevitable, and so of your own motion you can't ever alter the scheme or do a thing that will break a link. Next we heard screams, and Frau Brandt came wildly plowing and plunging through the crowd with her dress in disorder and hair flying loose, and flung herself upon her dead child with moans and kisses and pleadings and endearments; and by and by she rose up almost exhausted with her outpourings of passionate emotion, and clenched her fist and lifted it toward the sky and her tear-drenched face grew hard and resentful, and she said:

"For nearly two weeks I have had dreams and presentiments and warnings that death was going to strike what was most precious to me, and day and night and night and day I have groveled in the dirt before Him praying Him to have pity on my innocent child and save it from harm—and here is His answer!"

Why, He had saved it from harm—but she did not know.

She wiped the tears from her eyes and cheeks, and stood awhile gazing down at the child and caressing its face and its hair with her hands; then she spoke again in that bitter tone, "But in His hard heart is no compassion. I will never pray again."

She gathered her dead child to her bosom and strode away, the crowd falling back to let her pass and smitten dumb by the awful words they had heard. Ah, that poor woman! It is as Satan said, we do not know good fortune from bad and are always mistaking the one for the other. Many a time since I have heard people pray to God to spare the life of sick persons, but I have never done it.

Both funerals took place at the same time in our little church next day. Everybody was there, including the party guests. Satan was there too; which was proper, for it was on account of his efforts that the funerals had happened. Nikolaus had departed this life without absolution and a collection was taken up for masses, to get him out of purgatory. Only two-thirds of the required money was gathered and the parents were going to try to borrow the rest, but Satan furnished it. He told us privately that there was no purgatory but he had contributed in order that Nikolaus's parents and their friends might be saved from worry and distress. We thought it very good of him but he said money did not cost him anything.

At the graveyard the body of little Lisa was seized for debt by a carpenter to whom the mother owed fifty groschen for work done the year before. She had never been able to pay this and was not able now. The carpenter took the corpse home and kept it four days in his cellar, the mother weeping and imploring about his house all the time; then he buried it in his brother's cattle-yard without religious ceremonies. It drove the mother wild with grief and shame and she forsook her work and went daily about the town, cursing the carpenter and blaspheming the laws of the emperor and the church, and it was pitiful to see. Seppi asked Satan to interfere but he said the carpenter and the rest were members of the human race and were acting quite neatly for that species of animal. He would interfere if he found a horse acting in such a way, and we must inform him when we came across that kind of horse doing that kind of a human thing, so that he could stop it. We believed this was sarcasm, for of course there wasn't any such horse.

But after a few days we found that we could not abide that poor woman's distress, so we begged Satan to examine her several possible careers and see if he could not change her, to her profit, to a new one. He said the longest of her careers as they now stood gave her forty-two years to live and her shortest one twenty-nine, and that both were charged with grief and hunger and cold and pain. The only improvement he could make would be to enable her to skip a certain three minutes from now, and he asked us if he should do it. This was such a short time to decide in that we went to pieces with nervous excitement and before we could pull ourselves together and ask for particulars he said the time would be up in a few more seconds; so then we gasped out, "Do it!"

"It is done," he said, "she was going around a corner; I have turned her back; it has changed her career."

"Then what will happen, Satan?"

"It is happening now. She is having words with Fischer, the weaver. In his anger Fischer will straightway do what he would not have done but for this accident. He was present when she stood over her child's body and uttered those blasphemies."

"What will he do?"

"He is doing it now—betraying her. In three days she will go to the stake."

We could not speak; we were frozen with horror, for if we had not meddled with her career she would have been spared this awful fate. Satan noticed these thoughts, and said:

"What you are thinking is strictly human-like—that is to say, foolish. The woman is advantaged. Die when she might, she would go to heaven. By this prompt death she gets twenty-nine years more of heaven than she is entitled to and escapes twenty-nine years of misery here."

A moment before we were bitterly making up our minds that we would ask no more favors of Satan for friends of ours, for he did not seem to know any way to do a person a kindness but by killing him, but the whole aspect of the case was changed now and we were glad of what we had done and full of happiness in the thought of it.

After a little I began to feel troubled about Fischer, and asked, timidly, "Does this episode change Fischer's life-scheme, Satan?"

"Change it? Why, certainly. And radically. If he had

not met Frau Brandt awhile ago he would die next year, thirty-four years of age. Now he will live to be ninety and have a pretty prosperous and comfortable life of it, as human lives go."

We felt a great joy and pride in what we had done for Fischer and were expecting Satan to sympathize with this feeling, but he showed no sign and this made us uneasy. We waited for him to speak but he didn't; so, to assuage our solicitude we had to ask him if there was any defect in Fischer's good luck. Satan considered the question a moment, then said, with some hesitation:

"Well, the fact is, it is a delicate point. Under his several former possible life-careers he was going to heaven."

We were aghast. "Oh, Satan! and under this one—"

"There, don't be so distressed. You were sincerely trying to do him a kindness; let that comfort you."

"Oh, dear, dear, that cannot comfort us. You ought to have told us what we were doing, then we wouldn't have acted so."

But it made no impression on him. He had never felt a pain or a sorrow and did not know what they were, in any really informing way. He had no knowledge of them except theoretically—that is to say, intellectually. And of course that is no good. One can never get any but a loose and ignorant notion of such things except by experience. We tried our best to make him comprehend the awful thing that had been done and how we were compromised by it, but he couldn't seem to get hold of it. He said he did not think it important where Fischer went to; in heaven he would not be missed, there were "plenty there." We tried to make him see that he was missing the point entirely, that Fischer, and not other people, was the proper one to decide about the importance of it, but it all went for nothing; he said he did not care for Fischer—there were plenty more Fischers.

The next minute Fischer went by on the other side of the way and it made us sick and faint to see him, remembering the doom that was upon him, and we the cause of it. And how unconscious he was that anything had happened to him! You could see by his elastic step and his alert manner that he was well satisfied with himself for doing that hard turn for poor Frau Brandt. He kept glancing back over his shoulder expectantly. And, sure enough, pretty soon Frau Brandt followed after, in charge of the officers and wearing jingling chains. A mob was in her wake, jeering and shouting, "Blasphemer and heretic!" and some among them were neighbors and friends of her happier days. Some were trying to strike her, and the officers were not taking as much trouble as they might to keep them from it.

"Oh, stop them, Satan!" It was out before we remembered that he could not interrupt them for a moment without changing their whole after-lives. He puffed a little puff toward them with his lips and they began to reel and stagger and grab at the empty air; then they broke apart and fled in every direction, shrieking, as if in intolerable pain. He had crushed a rib of each of them with that little puff. We could not help asking if their life-chart was changed.

"Yes, entirely. Some have gained years, some have lost them. Some few will profit in various ways by the change, but only that few."

We did not ask if we had brought poor Fischer's luck to any of them. We did not wish to know. We fully believed in Satan's desire to do us kindnesses but we were losing confidence in his judgment. It was at this time that our growing anxiety to have him look over our life-charts and suggest improvements began to fade out and give place to other interests.

For a day or two the whole village was a chattering

turmoil over Frau Brandt's case and over the mysterious calamity that had overtaken the mob, and at her trial the place was crowded. She was easily convicted of her blasphemies, for she uttered those terrible words again and said she would not take them back. When warned that she was imperiling her life, she said they could take it in welcome, she did not want it, she would rather live with the professional devils in perdition than with these imitators in the village. They accused her of breaking all those ribs by witchcraft, and asked her if she was not a witch? She answered scornfully:

"No. If I had that power would any of you holy hypocrites be alive five minutes? No; I would strike you all dead. Pronounce your sentence and let me go; I am tired of your society."

So they found her guilty and she was excommunicated and cut off from the joys of heaven and doomed to the fires of hell; then she was clothed in a coarse robe and delivered to the secular arm, and conducted to the market-place, the bell solemnly tolling the while. We saw her chained to the stake and saw the first film of blue smoke rise on the still air. Then her hard face softened and she looked upon the packed crowd in front of her and said, with gentleness:

"We played together once, in long-agone days when we were innocent little creatures. For the sake of that, I forgive you."

We went away then and did not see the fires consume her, but we heard the shrieks, although we put our fingers in our ears. When they ceased we knew she was in heaven, notwithstanding the excommunication, and we were glad of her death and not sorry that we had brought it about.

One day, a little while after this, Satan appeared again. We were always watching out for him, for life was never very stagnant when he was by. He came upon us at that place in the woods where we had first met him. Being boys, we wanted to be entertained; we asked him to do a show for us.

"Very well," he said, "would you like to see a history of the progress of the human race?—its development of that product which it calls civilization?"

We said we should.

So, with a thought, he turned the place into the Garden of Eden, and we saw Abel praying by his altar; then Cain came walking toward him with his club, and did not seem to see us, and would have stepped on my foot if I had not drawn it in. He spoke to his brother in a language which we did not understand; then he grew violent and threatening, and we knew what was going to happen and turned away our heads for the moment; but we heard the crash of the blows and heard the shrieks and the groans; then there was silence and we saw Abel lying in his blood and gasping out his life, and Cain standing over him and looking down at him, vengeful and unrepentant.

Then the vision vanished and was followed by a long series of unknown wars, murders, and massacres. Next we had the Flood, and the Ark tossing around in the stormy waters, with lofty mountains in the distance showing veiled and dim through the rain. Satan said:

"The progress of your race was not satisfactory. It is to have another chance now."

The scene changed and we saw Noah overcome with wine.

Next, we had Sodom and Gomorrah, and "the attempt to discover two or three respectable persons there," as Satan described it. Next, Lot and his daughters in the cave.

Next came the Hebraic wars, and we saw the victors

massacre the survivors and their cattle, and save the young girls alive and distribute them around.

Next we had Jael, and saw her slip into the tent and drive the nail into the temple of her sleeping guest, and we were so close that when the blood gushed out it trickled in a little, red stream to our feet, and we could have stained our hands in it if we had wanted to.

Next we had Egyptian wars, Greek wars, Roman wars, hideous drenchings of the earth with blood, and we saw the treacheries of the Romans toward the Carthaginians, and the sickening spectacle of the massacre of those brave people. Also we saw Cæsar invade Britain—"not that those barbarians had done him any harm, but because he wanted their land, and desired to confer the blessings of civilization upon their widows and orphans," as Satan explained.

Next, Christianity was born. Then ages of Europe passed in review before us and we saw Christianity and Civilization march hand in hand through those ages, "leaving famine and death and desolation in their wake, and other signs of the progress of the human race," as Satan observed.

And always we had wars, and more wars, and still other wars—all over Europe, all over the world. "Sometimes in the private interest of royal families," Satan said, "sometimes to crush a weak nation; but never a war started by the aggressor for any clean purpose—there is no such war in the history of the race."

"Now," said Satan, "you have seen your progress down to the present, and you must confess that it is wonderful—in its way. We must now exhibit the future."

He showed us slaughters more terrible in their destruction of life, more devastating in their engines of war, than any we had seen.

"You perceive," he said, "that you have made continual progress. Cain did his murder with a club; the Hebrews did their murders with javelins and swords; the Greeks and Romans added protective armor and the fine arts of military organization and generalship; the Christian has added guns and gunpowder; a few centuries from now he will have so greatly improved the deadly effectiveness of his weapons of slaughter that all men will confess that without Christian civilization war must have remained a poor and trifling thing to the end of time."

Then he began to laugh in the most unfeeling way, and make fun of the human race, although he knew that what he had been saying shamed us and wounded us. No one but an angel could have acted so; but suffering is nothing to them, they do not know what it is, except by hearsay.

More than once Seppi and I had tried in a humble and diffident way to convert him, and as he had remained silent we had taken his silence as a sort of encouragement; necessarily, then, this talk of his was a disappointment to us, for it showed that we had made no deep impression upon him. The thought made us sad and we knew then how the missionary must feel when he has been cherishing a glad hope and has seen it blighted. We kept our grief to ourselves, knowing that this was not the time to continue our work.

Satan laughed his unkind laugh to a finish; then he said: "It is a remarkable progress. In five or six thousand years five or six high civilizations have risen, flourished, commanded the wonder of the world, then faded out and disappeared, and not one of them except the latest ever invented any sweeping and adequate way to kill people. They all did their best—to kill being the chiefest ambition of the human race and the earliest incident in its history—but only the Christian civilization has scored a trumph to be proud of. Two or three centuries from now it will be recognized that all the competent killers are Christians; then the pagan world will go to school to the Christian—not to acquire his religion, but his guns. The Turk and the Chinaman will buy those to kill missionaries and converts with."

By this time his theater was at work again, and before our eyes nation after nation drifted by, during two or three centuries, a mighty procession, an endless procession, raging, struggling, wallowing through seas of blood, smothered in battle-smoke through which the flags glinted and the red jets from the cannon darted, and always we heard the thunder of the guns and the cries of the dying.

"And what does it amount to?" said Satan, with his evil chuckle. "Nothing at all. You gain nothing; you always come out where you went in. For a million years the race has gone on monotonously propagating itself and monotonously reperforming this dull nonsense—to what end? No wisdom can guess! Who gets a profit out of it? Nobody but a parcel of usurping little monarchs and nobilities who despise you; would feel defiled if you touched them; would shut the door in your face if you proposed to call; whom you slave for, fight for, die for, and are not ashamed of it but proud; whose existence is a perpetual insult to you and you are afraid to resent it; who are mendicants supported by your alms, yet assume toward you the airs of benefactor toward beggar; who address you in the language of master to slave and are answered in the language of slave to master; who are worshiped by you with your mouth, while in your heart—if you have one—you despise yourselves for it. The first man was a hypocrite and a coward, qualities which have not yet failed in his line; it is the foundation upon which all civilizations have been built. Drink to their perpetuation! Drink to their augmentation! Drink to—" Then he saw by our faces how much we were hurt and he cut his sentence short and stopped chuckling, and his manner changed. He said, gently: "No, we will drink one another's health, and let civilization go. The wine which has flown to our hands out of space by desire is earthly, and good enough for that other toast; but throw away the glasses, we will drink this one in wine which has not visited this world before."

We obeyed, and reached up and received the new cups as they descended. They were shapely and beautiful goblets but they were not made of any material that we were acquainted with. They seemed to be in motion, they seemed to be alive, and certainly the colors in them were in motion. They were very brilliant and sparkling and of every tint, and they were never still, but flowed to and fro in rich tides which met and broke and flashed out dainty explosions of enchanting color. I think it was most like opals washing about in waves and flashing out their splendid fires. But there is nothing to compare the wine with. We drank it, and felt a strange and witching ecstasy as of heaven go stealing through us, and Seppi's eyes filled and he said worshipingly:

"We shall be there some day, and then—"

He glanced furtively at Satan, and I think he hoped Satan would say, "Yes, you will be there some day," but Satan seemed to be thinking about something else and said nothing. This made me feel ghastly, for I knew he had heard; nothing, spoken or unspoken, ever escaped him. Poor Seppi looked distressed and did not finish his remark. The goblets rose and clove their way into the sky, a triplet of radiant sundogs, and disappeared. Why didn't they stay? It seemed a bad sign, and depressed me. Should I ever see mine again? Would Seppi ever see his?

Chapter IX

It was wonderful, the mastery Satan had over time and distance. For him they did not exist. He called them human inventions and said they were artificialities. We often went to the most distant parts of the globe with him and stayed weeks and months, and yet were gone only a fraction of a second, as a rule. You could prove it by the clock. One day when our people were in such awful distress because the witch commission were afraid to proceed against the astrologer and Father Peter's household, or against any, indeed, but the poor and the friendless, they lost patience and took to witch-hunting on their own score, and began to chase a born lady who was known to have the habit of curing people by devilish arts, such as bathing them, washing them, and nourishing them instead of bleeding them and purging them through the ministrations of a barber-surgeon in the proper way. She came flying down, with the howling and cursing mob after her, and tried to take refuge in houses, but the doors were shut in her face. They chased her more than half an hour, we following to see it, and at last she was exhausted and fell and they caught her. They dragged her to a tree and threw a rope over the limb, and began to make a noose in it, some holding her, meantime, and she crying and begging and her young daughter looking on and weeping, but afraid to say or do anything.

They hanged the lady and I threw a stone at her, although in my heart I was sorry for her, but all were throwing stones and each was watching his neighbor, and if I had not done as the others did it would have been noticed and spoken of. Satan burst out laughing.

All that were near by turned upon him, astonished and not pleased. It was an ill time to laugh, for his free and scoffing ways and his supernatural music had brought him under suspicion all over the town and turned many privately against him. The big blacksmith called attention to him now, raising his voice so that all should hear, and said:

"What are you laughing at? Answer! Moreover, please explain to the company why you threw no stone."

"Are you sure I did not throw a stone?"

"Yes. You needn't try to get out of it; I had my eye on you."

"And I—I noticed you!" shouted two others.

"Three witnesses," said Satan: "Mueller, the blacksmith; Klein, the butcher's man; Pfeiffer, the weaver's journeyman. Three very ordinary liars. Are there any more?"

"Never mind whether there are others or not, and never mind about what you consider us—three's enough to settle your matter for you. You'll prove that you threw a stone or it shall go hard with you."

"That's so!" shouted the crowd, and surged up as closely as they could to the center of interest.

"And first you will answer that other question," cried the blacksmith, pleased with himself for being mouthpiece to the public and hero of the occasion. "What are you laughing at?"

Satan smiled and answered, pleasantly: "To see three cowards stoning a dying lady when they were so near death themselves."

You could see the superstitious crowd shrink and catch their breath, under the sudden shock. The blacksmith, with a show of bravado, said:

"Pooh! What do you know about it?"

"I? Everything. By profession I am a fortune-teller and I read the hands of you three—and some others— when you lifted them to stone the woman. One of you will die to-morrow week; another of you will die to-night; the third has but five minutes to live—and yonder is the clock!"

It made a sensation. The faces of the crowd blanched, and turned mechanically toward the clock. The butcher and the weaver seemed smitten with an illness but the blacksmith braced up and said, with spirit:

"It is not long to wait for prediction number one. If it fails, young master, you will not live a whole minute after, I promise you that."

No one said anything; all watched the clock in a deep stillness which was impressive. When four and a half minutes were gone the blacksmith gave a sudden gasp and clapped his hands upon his heart, saying, "Give me breath! Give me room!" and began to sink down. The crowd surged back, no one offering to support him, and he fell lumbering to the ground and was dead. The people stared at him, then at Satan, then at one another, and their lips moved but no words came. Then Satan said:

"Three saw that I threw no stone. Perhaps there are others; let them speak."

It struck a kind of panic into them and, although no one answered him, many began to violently accuse one another, saying, "You said he didn't throw," and getting for reply, "It is a lie, and I will make you eat it!" And so in a moment they were in a raging and noisy turmoil, and beating and banging one another, and in the midst was the only indifferent one—the dead lady hanging from her rope, her troubles forgotten, her spirit at peace.

So we walked away, and I was not at ease but was saying to myself, "He told them he was laughing at them but it was a lie—he was laughing at me."

That made him laugh again, and he said, "Yes, I was laughing at you, because, in fear of what others might report about you, you stoned the woman when your heart revolted at the act—but I was laughing at the others, too."

"Why?"

"Because their case was yours."

"How is that?"

"Well, there were sixty-eight people there, and sixty-two of them had no more desire to throw a stone than you had."

"Satan!"

"Oh, it's true. I know your race. It is made up of sheep. It is governed by minorities, seldom or never by majorities. It suppresses its feelings and its beliefs and follows the handful that makes the most noise. Sometimes the noisy handful is right, sometimes wrong; but no matter, the crowd follows it. The vast majority of the race, whether savage or civilized, are secretly kind-hearted and shrink from inflicting pain, but in the presence of the aggressive and pitiless minority they don't dare to assert themselves. Think of it! One kind-hearted creature spies upon another, and sees to it that he loyally helps in iniquities which revolt both of them. Speaking as an expert, I know that ninety-nine out of a hundred of your race were strongly against the killing of witches when that foolishness was first agitated by a handful of pious lunatics in the long ago. And I know that even to-day, after ages of transmitted prejudice and silly teaching, only one person in twenty puts any real heart into the harrying of a witch. And yet apparently everybody hates witches and wants them killed. Some day a handful will rise up on the other side and make the most noise—perhaps even a single daring man with a big voice and a determined front will do it—and in a week all the sheep will wheel and follow him, and witch-hunting will come to a sudden end.

"Monarchies, aristocracies, and religions are all based upon that large defect in your race—the individual's distrust of his neighbor, and his desire, for safety's or comfort's sake, to stand well in his neighbor's eye. These institutions will always remain and always flourish, and always oppress you, affront you, and degrade you, because you will always be and remain slaves of minorities. There was never a country where the majority of the people were in their secret hearts loyal to any of these institutions."

I did not like to hear our race called sheep and said I did not think they were.

"Still, it is true, lamb," said Satan. "Look at you in war—what mutton you are, and how ridiculous!"

"In war? How?"

"There has never been a just one, never an honorable one—on the part of the instigator of the war. I can see a million years ahead and this rule will never change in so many as half a dozen instances. The loud little handful—as usual—will shout for the war. The pulpit will—warily and cautiously—object—at first; the great, big, dull bulk of the nation will rub its sleepy eyes and try to make out why there should be a war and will say, earnestly and indignantly, "It is unjust and dishonorable and there is no necessity for it." Then the handful will shout louder. A few fair men on the other side will argue and reason against the war with speech and pen, and at first will have a hearing and be applauded, but it will not last long; those others will outshout them, and presently the anti-war audiences will thin out and lose popularity. Before long you will see this curious thing: the speakers stoned from the platform, and free speech strangled by hordes of furious men who in their secret hearts are still at one with those stoned speakers—as earlier—but do not dare to say so. And now the whole nation—pulpit and all—will take up the war-cry and shout itself hoarse, and mob any honest man who ventures to open his mouth, and presently such mouths will cease to open. Next the statesmen will invent cheap lies, putting the blame upon the nation that is attacked, and every man will be glad of those conscience-soothing falsities and will diligently study them, and refuse to examine any refutations of them, and thus he will by and by convince himself that the war is just and will thank God for the better sleep he enjoys after this process of grotesque self-deception."

Chapter X

Days and days went by now, and no Satan. It was dull without him. But the astrologer, who had returned from his excursion to the moon went about the village, braving public opinion and getting a stone in the middle of his back now and then when some witch-hater got a safe chance to throw it and dodge out of sight. Meantime two influences had been working well for Marget. That Satan, who was quite indifferent to her, had stopped going to her house after a visit or two had hurt her pride, and she had set herself the task of banishing him from her heart. Reports of Wilhelm Meidling's dissipation brought to her from time to time by old Ursula had touched her with remorse, jealousy of Satan being the cause of it; and so now, these two matters working upon her together, she was getting a good profit out of the combination—her interest in Satan was steadily

cooling, her interest in Wilhelm as steadily warming. All
that was needed to complete her conversion was that
Wilhelm should brace up and do something that should
cause favorable talk and incline the public toward him
again.

The opportunity came now. Marget sent and asked
him to defend her uncle in the approaching trial, and
he was greatly pleased and stopped drinking and began
his preparations with diligence. With more diligence
than hope, in fact, for it was not a promising case. He
had many interviews in his office with Seppi and me
and threshed out our testimony pretty thoroughly, thinking to find some valuable grains among the chaff, but
the harvest was poor, of course.

If Satan would only come! That was my constant
thought. He could invent some way to win the case,
for he had said it would be won, so he necessarily knew
how it could be done. But the days dragged on and still
he did not come. Of course I did not doubt that it would
win and that Father Peter would be happy for the rest
of his life, since Satan had said so; yet I knew I should
be much more comfortable if he would come and tell us
how to manage it. It was getting high time for Father
Peter to have a saving change toward happiness, for by
general report he was worn out with his imprisonment
and the ignominy that was burdening him, and was like
to die of his miseries unless he got relief soon.

At last the trial came on and the people gathered
from all around to witness it, among them many strangers from considerable distances. Yes, everybody was
there except the accused. He was too feeble in body for
the strain. But Marget was present, and keeping up her
hope and her spirit the best she could. The money was
present, too. It was emptied on the table, and was

handled and caressed and examined by such as were privileged.

The astrologer was put in the witness-box. He had on his best hat and robe for the occasion.

Question. You claim that this money is yours?

Answer. I do.

Q. How did you come by it?

A. I found the bag in the road when I was returning from a journey.

Q. When?

A. More than two years ago.

Q. What did you do with it?

A. I brought it home and hid it in a secret place in my observatory, intending to find the owner if I could.

Q. You endeavored to find him?

A. I made diligent inquiry during several months, but nothing came of it.

Q. And then?

A. I thought it not worth while to look further, and was minded to use the money in finishing the wing of the foundling-asylum connected with the priory and nunnery. So I took it out of its hiding-place and counted it to see if any of it was missing. And then—

Q. Why do you stop? Proceed.

A. I am sorry to have to say this but just as I had finished and was restoring the bag to its place, I looked up and there stood Father Peter behind me.

Several murmured, "That looks bad," but others answered, "Ah, but he is such a liar!"

Q. That made you uneasy?

A. No, I thought nothing of it at the time, for Father Peter often came to me unannounced to ask for a little help in his need.

Marget blushed crimson at hearing her uncle falsely

and impudently charged with begging, especially from one he had always denounced as a fraud, and was going to speak but remembered herself in time and held her peace.

Q. Proceed.

A. In the end I was afraid to contribute the money to the foundling-asylum, but elected to wait yet another year and continue my inquiries. When I heard of Father Peter's find I was glad and no suspicion entered my mind; when I came home a day or two later and discovered that my own money was gone I still did not suspect until three circumstances connected with Father Peter's good fortune struck me as being singular coincidences.

Q. Pray name them.

A. Father Peter had found his money in a path—I had found mine in a road. Father Peter's find consisted exclusively of gold ducats—mine also. Father Peter found eleven hundred and seven ducats—I exactly the same.

This closed his evidence, and certainly it made a strong impression on the house; one could see that.

Wilhelm Meidling asked him some questions, then called us boys, and we told our tale. It made the people laugh, and we were ashamed. We were feeling pretty badly, anyhow, because Wilhelm was hopeless, and showed it. He was doing as well as he could, poor young fellow, but nothing was in his favor, and such sympathy as there was was now plainly not with his client. It might be difficult for court and people to believe the astrologer's story, considering his character, but it was almost impossible to believe Father Peter's. We were already feeling badly enough, but when the astrologer's lawyer said he believed he would not ask us any questions—for our story was a little delicate and it would be cruel for him to put any strain upon it—everybody tit tered and it was almost more than we could bear. Then he made a sarcastic little speech and got so much fun out of our tale, and it seemed so ridiculous and childish and every way impossible and foolish, that it made everybody laugh till the tears came; and at last Marget could not keep up her courage any longer but broke down and cried, and I was so sorry for her.

Now I noticed something that braced me up. It was Satan standing alongside of Wilhelm! And there was such a contrast!—Satan looked so confident, had such a spirit in his eyes and face and Wilhelm looked so depressed and despondent. We two were comfortable now, and judged that he would testify and persuade the bench and the people that black was white and white black, or any other color he wanted it. We glanced around to see what the strangers in the house thought of him, for he was beautiful, you know—stunning, in fact—but no one was noticing him; so we knew by that that he was invisible.

The lawyer was saying his last words; and while he was saying them Satan began to melt into Wilhelm. He melted into him and disappeared; and then there was a change, when his spirit began to look out of Wilhelm's eyes.

That lawyer finished quite seriously, and with dignity. He pointed to the money and said:

"The love of it is the root of all evil. There it lies, the ancient tempter, newly red with the shame of its latest victory—the dishonor of a priest of God and his two poor juvenile helpers in crime. If it could but speak, let us hope that it would be constrained to confess that of all its conquests this was the basest and the most pathetic."

He sat down. Wilhelm rose and said:

"From the testimony of the accuser I gather that he

found this money in a road more than two years ago. Correct me, sir, if I misunderstood you."

The astrologer said his understanding of it was correct.

"And the money so found was never out of his hands thenceforth up to a certain definite date—the last day of last year. Correct me, sir, if I am wrong."

The astrologer nodded his head. Wilhelm turned to the bench and said:

"If I prove that this money here was not that money, then it is not his?"

"Certainly not; but this is irregular. If you had such a witness it was your duty to give proper notice of it and have him here to—" He broke off and began to consult with the other judges. Meantime that other lawyer got up excited and began to protest against allowing new witnesses to be brought into the case at this late stage.

The judges decided that his contention was just and must be allowed.

"But this is not a new witness," said Wilhelm. "It has already been partly examined. I speak of the coin."

"The coin? What can the coin say?"

"It can say it is not the coin that the astrologer once possessed. It can say it was not in existence last December. By its date it can say this."

And it was so! There was the greatest excitement in the court while that lawyer and the judges were reaching for coins and examining them and exclaiming. And everybody was full of admiration of Wilhelm's brightness in happening to think of that neat idea. At last order was called and the court said:

"All of the coins but four are of the date of the present year. The court tenders its sincere sympathy to the accused, and its deep regret that he, an innocent man, through an unfortunate mistake, has suffered the undeserved humiliation of imprisonment and trial. The case is dismissed."

So the money could speak, after all, though that lawyer thought it couldn't. The court rose and almost everybody came forward to shake hands with Marget and congratulate her, and then to shake with Wilhelm and praise him; and Satan had stepped out of Wilhelm and was standing around looking on full of interest, and people walking through him every which way, not knowing he was there. And Wilhelm could not explain why he only thought of the date on the coins at the last moment, instead of earlier; he said it just occurred to him all of a sudden, like an inspiration, and he brought it right out without any hesitation, for, although he didn't examine the coins, he seemed, somehow, to know it was true. That was honest of him, and like him; another would have pretended he had thought of it earlier and was keeping it back for a surprise.

He had dulled down a little now; not much, but still you could notice that he hadn't that luminous look in his eyes that he had while Satan was in him. He nearly got it back, though, for a moment when Marget came and praised him and thanked him and couldn't keep him from seeing how proud she was of him. The astrologer went off dissatisfied and cursing, and Solomon Isaacs gathered up the money and carried it away. It was Father Peter's for good and all, now.

Satan was gone. I judged that he had spirited himself away to the jail to tell the prisoner the news, and in this I was right. Marget and the rest of us hurried thither at our best speed, in a great state of rejoicing.

Well, what Satan had done was this: he had appeared before that poor prisoner, exclaiming, "The trial is over, and you stand forever disgraced as a thief—by verdict of the court!"

The shock unseated the old man's reason. When we arrived, ten minutes later, he was parading pompously up and down and delivering commands to this and that and the other constable or jailer, and calling them Grand Chamberlain, and Prince This and Prince That, and Admiral of the Fleet, Field Marshal in Command, and all such fustian, and was as happy as a bird. He thought he was Emperor!

Marget flung herself on his breast and cried, and indeed everybody was moved almost to heartbreak. He recognized Marget but could not understand why she should cry. He patted her on the shoulder and said:

"Don't do it, dear; remember, there are witnesses, and it is not becoming in the Crown Princess. Tell me your trouble—it shall be mended; there is nothing the Emperor cannot do." Then he looked around and saw old Ursula with her apron to her eyes. He was puzzled at that, and said, "And what is the matter with you?"

Through her sobs she got out words explaining that she was distressed to see him—"so." He reflected over that a moment, then muttered, as if to himself, "A singular old thing, the Dowager Duchess—means well, but is always snuffling and never able to tell what it is about. It is because she doesn't know." His eyes fell on Wilhelm. "Prince of India," he said, "I divine that it is you that the Crown Princess is concerned about. Her tears shall be dried; I will no longer stand between you; she shall share your throne; and between you you shall inherit mine. There, little lady, have I done well? You can smile now—isn't it so?"

He petted Marget and kissed her, and was so contented with himself and with everybody that he could not do enough for us all but began to give away kingdoms and such things right and left, and the least that any of us got was a principality. And so at last, being persuaded to go home, he marched in imposing state; and when the crowds along the way saw how it gratified him to be hurrahed at, they humored him to the top of his desire, and he responded with condescending bows and gracious smiles and often stretched out a hand and said, "Bless you, my people!"

As pitiful a sight as ever I saw. And Marget, and old Ursula crying all the way.

On my road home I came upon Satan and reproached him with deceiving me with that lie. He was not embarrassed but said, quite simply and composedly:

"Ah, you mistake; it was the truth. I said he would be happy the rest of his days and he will, for he will always think he is the Emperor and his pride in it and his joy in it will endure to the end. He is now, and will remain, the one utterly happy person in this empire."

"But the method of it, Satan, the method! Couldn't you have done it without depriving him of his reason?"

It was difficult to irritate Satan but that accomplished it.

"What an ass you are!" he said. "Are you so unobservant as not to have found out that sanity and happiness are an impossible combination? No sane man can be happy, for to him life is real and he sees what a fearful thing it is. Only the mad can be happy, and not many of those. The few that imagine themselves kings or gods are happy, the rest are no happier than the sane. Of course, no man is entirely in his right mind at any time but I have been referring to the extreme cases. I have taken from this man that trumpery thing which the race regards as a Mind, I have replaced his tin life with a silver gilt fiction; you see the result—and you criticize! I said I would make him permanently happy and I have done it. I have made him happy by the only means possible to his race—and you are not satisfied!" He heaved a discouraged sigh, and said, "It seems to me that this race is hard to please."

There it was, you see. He didn't seem to know any way to do a person a favor except by killing him or making a lunatic out of him. I apologized, as well as I could, but privately I did not think much of his processes —at that time.

Satan was accustomed to say that our race lived a life of continuous and uninterrupted self-deception. It duped itself from cradle to grave with shams and delusions which it mistook for realities, and this made its entire life a sham. Of the score of fine qualities which it imagined it had and was vain of, it really possessed hardly one. It regarded itself as gold, and was only brass. One day when he was in this vein he mentioned a detail—the sense of humor. I cheered up then, and took issue. I said we possessed it.

"There spoke the race!" he said, "always ready to claim what it hasn't got and mistake its ounce of brass filings for a ton of gold-dust. You have a mongrel perception of humor, nothing more; a multitude of you possess that. This multitude see the comic side of a thousand low-grade and trivial things—broad incongruities, mainly; grotesqueries, absurdities, evokers of the horse-laugh. The ten thousand high-grade comicalities which exist in the world are sealed from their dull vision. Will a day come when the race will detect the funniness of these juvenilities and laugh at them—and by laughing at them destroy them? For your race, in its poverty, has unquestionably one really effective weapon —laughter. Power, money, persuasion, supplication, persecution—these can lift at a colossal humbug—push it a little—weaken it a little, century by century, but only laughter can blow it to rags and atoms at a blast.

Against the assault of laughter nothing can stand. You are always fussing and fighting with your other weapons. Do you ever use that one? No, you leave it lying rusting. As a race, do you ever use it at all? No, you lack sense and the courage."

We were traveling at the time and stopped at a little city in India and looked on while a juggler did his tricks before a group of natives. They were wonderful but I knew Satan could beat that game, and I begged him to show off a little and he said he would. He changed himself into a native in turban and breech-cloth, and very considerately conferred on me a temporary knowledge of the language.

The juggler exhibited a seed, covered it with earth in a small flower-pot, then put a rag over the pot; after a minute the rag began to rise; in ten minutes it had risen a foot; then the rag was removed and a little tree was exposed, with leaves upon it and ripe fruit. We ate the fruit and it was good. But Satan said:

"Why do you cover the pot? Can't you grow the tree in the sunlight?"

"No," said the juggler, "no one can do that."

"You are only an apprentice; you don't know your trade. Give me the seed. I will show you." He took the seed and said, "What shall I raise from it?"

"It is a cherry seed; of course you will raise a cherry."

"Oh no; that is a trifle; any novice can do that. Shall I raise an orange-tree from it?"

"Oh yes!" and the juggler laughed.

"And shall I make it bear other fruits as well as oranges?"

"If God wills!" and they all laughed.

Satan put the seed in the ground, put a handful of dust on it, and said, "Rise!"

A tiny stem shot up and began to grow, and grew so fast that in five minutes it was a great tree, and we were sitting in the shade of it. There was a murmur of wonder, then all looked up and saw a strange and pretty sight, for the branches were heavy with fruits of many kinds and colors—oranges, grapes, bananas, peaches, cherries, apricots, and so on. Baskets were brought and the unlading of the tree began, and the people crowded around Satan and kissed his hand and praised him, calling him the prince of jugglers. The news went about the town and everybody came running to see the wonder—and they remembered to bring baskets, too. But the tree was equal to the occasion; it put out new fruits as fast as any were removed; baskets were filled by the score and by the hundred, but always the supply remained undiminished. At last a foreigner in white linen and sun-helmet arrived and exclaimed, angrily:

"Away from here! Clear out, you dogs; the tree is on my lands and is my property."

The natives put down their baskets and made humble obeisance. Satan made humble obeisance, too, with his fingers to his forehead, in the native way, and said:

"Please let them have their pleasure for an hour, sir—only that, and no longer. Afterward you may forbid them, and you will still have more fruit than you and the state together can consume in a year."

This made the foreigner very angry and he cried out, "Who are you, you vagabond, to tell your betters what they may do and what they mayn't!" and he struck Satan with his cane and followed this error with a kick.

The fruits rotted on the branches, and the leaves withered and fell. The foreigner gazed at the bare limbs with the look of one who is surprised, and not gratified. Satan said:

"Take good care of the tree, for its health and yours are bound together. It will never bear again but if you tend it well it will live long. Water its roots once in each hour every night—and do it yourself; it must not be done by proxy, and to do it in daylight will not answer. If you fail only once in any night, the tree will die, and you likewise. Do not go home to your own country any more—you would not reach there; make no business or pleasure engagements which require you to go outside your gate at night—you cannot afford the risk; do not rent or sell this place—it would be injudicious."

The foreigner was proud and wouldn't beg but I thought he looked as if he would like to. While he stood gazing at Satan we vanished away and landed in Ceylon.

I was sorry for that man; sorry Satan hadn't been his customary self and killed him or made him a lunatic. It would have been a mercy. Satan overheard the thought, and said:

"I would have done it but for his wife, who has not offended me. She is coming to him presently from their native land, Portugal. She is well but has not long to live and has been yearning to see him and persuade him to go back with her next year. She will die without knowing he can't leave that place?"

"He won't tell her?"

"He? He will not trust that secret with any one; he will reflect that it could be revealed in sleep, in the hearing of some Portuguese guest's servant some time or other."

"Did none of those natives understand what you said to him?"

"None of them understood but he will always be afraid that some of them did. That fear will be torture to him, for he has been a harsh master to them. In his dreams he will imagine them chopping his tree down. That will make his days uncomfortable—I have already arranged for his nights."

It grieved me, though not sharply, to see him take such a malicious satisfaction in his plans for this foreigner.

"Does he believe what you told him, Satan?"

"He thought he didn't but our vanishing helped. The tree where there had been no tree before—that helped. The insane and uncanny variety of fruits—the sudden withering—all these things are helps. Let him think as he may, reason as he may, one thing is certain, he will water the tree. But between this and night he will begin his changed career with a very natural precaution—for him."

"What is that?"

"He will fetch a priest to cast out the tree's devil. You are such a humorous race—and don't suspect it."

"Will he tell the priest?"

"No. He will say a juggler from Bombay created it and that he wants the juggler's devil driven out of it, so that it will thrive and be fruitful again. The priest's incantations will fail; then the Portuguese will give up that scheme and get his watering-pot ready."

"But the priest will burn the tree. I know it; he will not allow it to remain."

"Yes, and anywhere in Europe he would burn the man, too. But in India the people are civilized and these things will not happen. The man will drive the priest away and take care of the tree."

I reflected a little, then said, "Satan, you have given him a hard life, I think."

"Comparatively. It must not be mistaken for a holiday."

We flitted from place to place around the world as we had done before, Satan showing me a hundred wonders, most of them reflecting in some way the weakness and triviality of our race. He did this now every few days—not out of malice—I am sure of that—it only seemed to amuse and interest him, just as a naturalist might be amused and interested by a collection of ants.

Chapter XI

For as much as a year Satan continued these visits but at last he came less often, and then for a long time he did not come at all. This always made me lonely and melancholy. I felt that he was losing interest in our tiny world and might at any time abandon his visits entirely. When one day he finally came to me I was overjoyed, but only for a little while. He had come to say good-by, he told me, and for the last time. He had investigations and undertakings in other corners of the universe, he said, that would keep him busy for a longer period than I could wait for his return.

"And you are going away, and will not come back any more?"

"Yes," he said. "We have comraded long together, and it has been pleasant—pleasant for both; but I must go now, and we shall not see each other any more."

"In this life, Satan, but in another? We shall meet in another, surely?"

Then, all tranquilly and soberly, he made the strange answer, *"There is no other."*

A subtle influence blew upon my spirit from his, bringing with it a vague, dim, but blessed and hopeful feeling that the incredible words might be true—even *must* be true.

"Have you never suspected this, Theodor?"

"No. How could I? But if it can only be true—"

"It is true."

A gust of thankfulness rose in my breast but a doubt checked it before it could issue in words, and I said, "But—but—we have seen that future life—seen it in its actuality, and so—"

"It was a vision—it had no existence."

I could hardly breathe for the great hope that was struggling in me. "A vision?—a vi—"

"*Life itself is only a vision, a dream.*"

It was electrical. By God! I had had that very thought a thousand times in my musings!

"*Nothing* exists; all is a dream. God—man—the world —the sun, the moon, the wilderness of stars—a dream, all a dream; they have no existence. *Nothing exists save empty space—and you!*"

"I!"

"And you are not you—you have no body, no blood, no bones, you are but a *thought*. I myself have no existence; I am but a dream—your dream, creature of your imagination. In a moment you will have realized this, then you will banish me from your visions and I shall dissolve into the nothingness out of which you made me. . . .

"I am perishing already—I am failing—I am passing away. In a little while you will be alone in shoreless space, to wander its limitless solitudes without friend or comrade forever—for you will remain a *thought*, the only existent thought, and by your nature inextinguishable, indestructible. But I, your poor servant, have revealed you to yourself and set you free. Dream other dreams, and better!

"Strange! that you should not have suspected years

ago—centuries, ages, eons, ago!—for you have existed, companionless, through all the eternities. Strange, indeed, that you should not have suspected that your universe and its contents were only dreams, visions, fiction! Strange, because they are so frankly and hysterically insane—like all dreams: a God who could make good children as easily as bad, yet preferred to make bad ones; who could have made every one of them happy, yet never made a single happy one; who made them prize their bitter life, yet stingily cut it short; who gave his angels eternal happiness unearned, yet required his other children to earn it; who gave his angels painless lives, yet cursed his other children with biting miseries and maladies of mind and body; who mouths justice and invented hell—mouths mercy and invented hell—mouths Golden Rules, and forgiveness multiplied by seventy times seven, and invented hell; who mouths morals to other people and has none himself; who frowns upon crimes, yet commits them all; who created man without invitation, then tries to shuffle the responsibility for man's acts upon man, instead of honorably placing it where it belongs, upon himself; and finally, with altogether divine obtuseness, invites this poor, abused slave to worship him! . . .

"You perceive, *now*, that these things are all impossible except in a dream. You perceive that they are pure and puerile insanities, the silly creations of an imagination that is not conscious of its freaks—in a word, that they are a dream, and you the maker of it. The dream-marks are all present; you should have recognized them earlier.

"It is true, that which I have revealed to you; there is no God, no universe, no human race, no earthly life, no heaven, no hell. It is all a dream—a grotesque and fool ish dream. Nothing exists but you. And you are but a *thought*—a vagrant thought, a useless thought, a homeless thought, wandering forlorn among the empty eternities!"

He vanished and left me appalled, for I knew, and realized, that all he had said was true.

Letters

To Thomas Bailey Aldrich

Buffalo, January 28, 1871.

DEAR MR. ALDRICH:

. . . But I did hate to be accused of plagiarizing Bret
Harte, who trimmed and trained and schooled me patiently until he changed me from an awkward utterer of
coarse grotesquenesses to a writer of paragraphs and
chapters that have found a certain favor in the eyes of
even some of the very decentest people in the land—
and this grateful remembrance of mine ought to be
worth its face, seeing that Bret broke our long friendship a year ago without any cause or provocation that
I am aware of.

Well it *is* funny, the reminiscences that glare out from
murky corners of one's memory, now and then, without
warning. Just at this moment a picture flits before me:
Scene—private room in Barnum's Restaurant, Virginia,
Nevada; present, Artemus Ward, Joseph T. Goodman
(editor and proprietor Daily "Enterprise"), and "Dan
de Quille" and myself, reporters for same; remnants of
the feast thin and scattering, but *such* tautology and
repetition of empty bottles everywhere visible as to be
offensive to the sensitive eye; time, 2.30 A.M., Artemus
thickly reciting a poem about a certain infant you wot
of,[1] and interrupting himself and *being* interrupted
every few lines by poundings of the table and shouts of
"Splennid, by Shorghe!" Finally, a long, vociferous,

---

[1] "Baby Bell," by Aldrich.—Ed.

745

poundiferous and vitreous jingling of applause announces the conclusion, and then Artemus: "Let every man 'at loves his fellow man and 'preciates a poet 'at loves *his* fellow-man, stan' up!—stan' up and drink health and long life to Thomas Bailey Aldrich!—and drink it *stanning!*" (On all hands fervent, enthusiastic, and sincerely honest attempts to comply.) Then Artemus: "Well—*consider* it stanning, and drink it just as ye are!" Which was done.

You must excuse all this stuff from a stranger, for the present, and when I see you I will apologize in full.

Do you know the prettiest fancy and the neatest that ever shot through Harte's brain? It was this: When they were trying to decide upon a vignette for the cover of the *Overland,* a grizzly bear (of the arms of the State of California) was chosen. Nahl Bros. carved him and the page was printed, with him in it looking thus: [Rude sketch of a grizzly bear.]

As a bear, he was a success—he was a good bear.— But then it was objected that he was an *objectless* bear —a bear that *meant* nothing in particular, signified nothing,—simply stood there snarling over his shoulder at nothing—and was painfully and manifestly a boorish and ill-natured intruder upon the fair page. All hands said that—none were satisfied. They hated badly to give him up, and yet they hated as much to have him there when there was no *point* to him. But presently Harte took a pencil and drew these two simple lines under his feet and behold he was a magnificent success!—the ancient symbol of Californian savagery snarling at the approaching type of high and progressive Civilization, the first Overland locomotive!: [Sketch of a small section of railway track.] . . .

Yrs Truly
SAML. L. CLEMENS

To William Dean Howells

MY DEAR HOWELLS:

I left No. 3 (Miss. chapter) in my eldest's reach, and it may have gone to the postman and it likewise may have gone into the fire. I confess to a dread that the latter is the case and that that stack of MS will have to be written over again. If so, O for the return of the lamented Herod!

You and Aldrich have made one woman deeply and sincerely grateful—Mrs. Clemens. For months—I may even say years—she had shown unaccountable animosity toward my neck-tie, even getting up in the night to take it with the tongs and blackguard it—sometimes also going so far as to threaten it.

When I said you and Aldrich had given me two *new* neck-ties and that they were in a paper in my overcoat pocket, she was in a fever of happiness until she found I was going to frame them; then all the venom in her nature gathered itself together—insomuch that I, being near to a door, went without, perceiving danger. . . .

Yrs ever,

S. L. CLEMENS

P.S.—John Hay of his own free will and accord, volunteers me a letter which is so gratifying in its nature that I am obliged to copy it for you to read. I was born and reared at Hannibal, and John Hay at Warsaw, 40 miles higher up, on the river (one of the Keokuk packet ports):

"Dear Clemens—I have just read with delight your article in the *Atlantic*.[1] It is perfect—no more nor less. I don't see how you do it. I knew all that, every word of it—passed as much time on the levee as you ever did,

---

[1] *First installment of "Old Times on the Mississippi."—Ed.*

knew the same crowd and saw the same scenes—but I could not have remembered one word of it all. You have the two greatest gifts of the writer, memory and imagination. I congratulate you."

Now isn't that outspoken and hearty and just like that splendid John Hay?

S L C

To William Dean Howells

Hartford, November 23, 1875.

MY DEAR HOWELLS:

Herewith is the proof. In spite of myself, how awkwardly I do jumble words together and how often I do use three words where one would answer—a thing I am always trying to guard against. I shall become as slovenly a writer as Charles Francis Adams if I don't look out. (That is said in jest, because of course I do not seriously fear getting so bad as that. I never shall drop so far toward his and Bret Harte's level as to catch myself saying, "It must have been wiser to have believed that he might have accomplished it if he could have felt that he would have been supported by those who should have etc. etc. etc.") The reference to Bret Harte reminds me that I often accuse him of being a deliberate imitator of Dickens, and this in turn reminds me that I have charged unconscious plagiarism upon Charley Warner, and *this* in turn reminds me that I have been delighting my soul for two weeks over a bran' new and ingenious way of beginning a novel—and behold, all at once it flashes upon me that *Charley Warner* originated the idea 3 years ago and told me about it! Aha! So much for self-righteousness! I am well repaid. Here are 108 pages of MS, new and clean, lying disgraced in the waste paper basket, and I am beginning the novel over again in an unstolen way. I would not wonder if I am the worst literary thief in the world, without knowing it.

It is glorious news that you like *Tom Sawyer* so well. I mean to see to it that your review of it shall have plenty of time to appear before the other notices. Mrs. Clemens decides with you that the book should issue as a book for boys, pure and simple—and so do I. It is surely the correct idea. As to that last chapter, I think of just leaving it off and adding nothing in its place. Something told me that the book was done when I got to that point—and so the strong temptation to put Huck's life at the Widow's into detail, instead of generalizing it in a paragraph, was resisted. Just send *Sawyer* to me by express—I enclose money for it. If it should get lost it will be no great matter.

Company interfered last night and so "Private Theatricals" goes over till this evening, to be read aloud. Mrs. Clemens is mad but the story will take *that* all out. This is going to be a splendid winter night for fireside reading, anyway.

I am almost at a dead stand-still with my new story, on account of the misery of having to do it all over again.

We-all send love to you-all.

Yrs ever

MARK

To J. H. Burrough of Cape Girardeau, Missouri

[Corrected text of a published letter]

Hartford, November 1, 1876.

MY DEAR BURROUGH:

As you describe me I can picture myself as I was 22

years ago. The portrait is correct. You think I have grown some; upon my word there was room for it. You have described a callow fool, a self-sufficient ass, a mere human tumble-bug, stern in air, heaving at his bit of dung and imagining he is re-molding the world and is entirely capable of doing it right. Ignorance, intolerance, egotism, self-assertion, opaque perception, dense and pitiful chuckle-headedness—and an almost pathetic unconsciousness of it all. That is what I was at 19-20, and that is what the average Southerner is at 60 today. Northerners too, of a certain grade. It is of children like this that voters are made. And such is the primal source of our government! A man hardly knows whether to swear or cry over it.

I think I comprehend their position there—perfect freedom to vote just as you choose, provided you choose to vote as *other people* think, social ostracism otherwise. The same thing exists here among the Irish. An Irish Republican is a pariah among his people. Yet that race find fault with the same spirit in Know-Nothingism.

Fortunately a good deal of experience of men enabled me to choose my residence wisely. I live in the freest corner of the country. There are no social disabilities between me and my democratic personal friends. We break the bread and eat the salt of hospitality freely together and never dream of such a thing as offering impertinent interference in each other's political opinions. . . .

Yes, Will Bowen and I have exchanged letters now and then for several years but I suspect that I made him mad with my last—shortly after you saw him in St. Louis, I judge. There is one thing which I can't stand, and *won't* stand from many people. That is sham senti-

mentality—the kind a school-girl puts into her graduating composition; the sort that makes up the Original
Poetry column of a country newspaper; the rot that
deals in "the happy days of yore," "the sweet yet melancholy past," with its "blighted hopes" and its "vanished dreams"—and all that sort of drivel. Will's were
always of this stamp. I stood it years. When I get a letter like that from a grown man and he a widower with a
family, it gives me the bowel complaint. And I just told
Will Bowen so, last summer. I told him to stop being
16 at 40; told him to stop drooling about the sweet yet
melancholy past and take a pill. I said there was but one
solitary thing about the past worth remembering and
that was the fact that it *is* the past—can't be restored.
Well, I exaggerated some of these truths a little—but
only a little—but my idea was to kill his nasty sham
sentimentality once and forever and so make a good
fellow of him again. I went to the unheard of trouble
of re-writing the letter and saying the same harsh things
softly, so as to sugar-coat the anguish and make it a
little more endurable, and I asked him to write and
thank me honestly for doing him the best and kindliest
favor that any friend ever *had* done him—but he hasn't
done it yet. Maybe he will some time. I am grateful to
God that I got that letter off before he was married (I
get that news from you), else he would just have slob-
bered all over me and drowned me when that event
happened.

I enclose photograph for the young ladies. I will remark that I do not wear seal-skin for grandeur but because I found, when I used to lecture in the winter,
that nothing else was able to keep a man warm sometimes, in these high latitudes. I wish you had sent pictures of yourself and family—I'll trade picture for pic-

ture with you, straight through, if you are commercially inclined.

Your old friend
SAML L. CLEMENS

To William Dean Howells

[Published here for the first time]

Heidelberg, June 27, 1878.

MY DEAR HOWELLS:

What do the newspapers say about Harte's appointment? Billiardly-speaking, the President scored 400 points on each when he appointed [James Russell] Lowell and [Bayard] Taylor—but when he appointed Harte he simply pocketed his own ball. Now just take a realizing sense of what this fellow is when one names things by their plain dictionary names—to wit: Harte is a liar, a thief, a swindler, a snob, a sot, a sponge, a coward, a Jeremy Diddler, he is brim full of treachery, and he conceals his Jewish birth as carefully as if he considered it a disgrace. How do I know? By the best of all evidence, personal observation. With one exception: I don't know him, myself, to be a thief, but John Carmany, publisher of the *Overland Monthly*, charges him with stealing money delivered to him to be paid to contributors, and the defrauded contributors back Mr. Carmany. I think Charley Stoddard said Harte had never ventured to deny this in print, though W. A. Kendall, who published the charge in the San Francisco *Chronicle*, not only invited him to deny it but dared him to do it. O, the loveliness of putting Harte into the public service, after removing Geo. H. Butler from it for lack of character! If he had only been made a home official, I think I could stand it; but to send this nasty creature to puke upon the American name in a foreign land is too much.

I don't deny that I feel personally snubbed, for it seems only fair that after the letter I wrote last summer the President should not have silently ignored my testimony, but should have given me a chance to prove what I had said against Harte. I think I could have piled up facts enough to show that Harte was fitted for the highest office in the gift of the city of New York.

Now there's one thing that *shan't* happen. Harte shan't swindle the Germans if I can help it. Tell me what German town he is to filthify with his presence; then I will write the authorities there that he is a persistent borrower who never pays. They need not believe it unless they choose—that is their affair, not mine.

Have you heard any literary men express an opinion about the appointment? Who were they—and what said they?

Ah, don't I wish I could venture to write for the *Atlantic!* The only thing in the way is Canada. If Mr. Houghton can copyright my stuff in Canada and hold it *himself*, and will prosecute and stop any infringement, I shall be glad enough to write but I can't trust any more Canadians after my late experience. I suppose they are all born pirates. I do not know that I have any printable stuff just now, separatable stuff that is, but I shall have by and by. It is very gratifying to hear that it is wanted by anybody. I stand always prepared to hear the reverse and am constantly surprised that it is delayed so long. Consequently it is not going to astonish me when it comes.

Mrs. Clemens, who even reads note-books in her hunger for culture, was rather startled to run across this paragraph in mine, last night:

"Have all sorts of heavens—have a gate for each sort. Wakeman visits these various heavens. One gate where they receive a bar-keeper with artillery salutes, swarms of angels in the sky, and a noble torch-light procession. *He* thinks he is *the* lion of Heaven. Procession over, he drops at once into solid obscurity. But the roughest part of it is that he has to do 30 weeks' penance —day and night he must carry a torch and shout himself hoarse to do honor to some poor scrub whom he wishes had gone to hell."

I wish I was writing that Wakeman book, but I suppose I shan't get at it again before next year.

Privately, I have some good news to tell you. That is, I believe it will gratify you—in fact I am sure it will— though I am not acquainted with a great many people whom it would please. It is this: *we've quit feeling poor!* Isn't that splendid? You know that for two years we have been coming to want, every little while, and have straightway gone to economizing. Yesterday we fell to figuring and discovered that we have more than income enough from investments to live in Hartford on a generous scale. Well, now that we are fixed at last, of course the communists and the asinine government will go to work and smash it all. No matter, we have resolved to quit feeling poor for a little while, anyway. This thing was so gratifying to me that my first impulse was to run to you with it.

Drat this German tongue, I never shall be able to learn it. I think I could learn a little conversational stuff maybe if I could attend to it, but I found I couldn't spare the time. I took lessons two weeks and got so I could understand the talk going on around me, and even answer back after a fashion. But I neither talk nor listen now, so I can't even understand the language any more. Mrs. Clemens is getting along fast and Miss Spaulding and our little Susie talk the devilish tongue without difficulty. But the Bay [Clara Clemens] scorns the language. The nurse and the governess blandish around her in vain. She maintains the calm and persistent attitude of not caring a damn for German. There is a good deal of character in the Bay—such as it is.

Look here, Howells, when I choose to gratify my passions by writing great long letters to you, you are not to consider anything but the briefest answers necessary —and not even those when you have got things to do. Don't forget that. A lengthy letter from you is a great prize and a welcome, but it gives me a reproach because I seem to have robbed a busy man of time which he ought not to have spared.

Well, good bye and good luck attend you. We both send love to you and yours.

As Ever
MARK

All day to-day I have been having an experience— and it results in this maxim:

To man all things are possible but one—he cannot have a hole in the seat of his breeches and keep his fingers out of it.

A man does seem to feel more distress and more persistent and distracting solicitude about such a thing than he could about a sick child that was threatening to grow worse every time he took his attention away from it.

(Mrs. Clemens said you wouldn't understand the maxim unless I explained it!)

To the Reverend J. H. Twichell

Munich, January 26, 1879.

DEAR OLD JOE:

Sunday. Your delicious letter arrived exactly at the right time. It was laid by my plate as I was finishing breakfast at 12 noon. Livy and Clara [Spaulding] arrived from church 5 minutes later; I took a pipe and spread myself out on the sofa and Livy sat by and read, and I warmed to that butcher the moment he began to swear. There is more than one way of praying and I like the butcher's way because the petitioner is so apt to be in earnest. I was peculiarly alive to his performance just at this time for another reason, to wit: Last night I awoke at 3 this morning and after raging to myself for 2 interminable hours, I gave it up. I rose, assumed a catlike stealthiness, to keep from waking Livy, and proceeded to dress in the pitch dark. Slowly but surely I got on garment after garment—all down to one sock; I had one slipper on and the other in my hand. Well, on my hands and knees I crept softly around, pawing and feeling and scooping along the carpet and among chair-legs for that missing sock; I kept that up;—and still kept it up and *kept* it up. At first I only said to myself "Blame that sock," but that soon ceased to answer; my expletives grew steadily stronger and stronger and at last, when I found I was *lost*, I had to sit flat down on the floor and take hold of something to keep from lifting the roof off with the profane explosion that was trying to get out of me. I could see the dim blur of the window, but of course it was in the wrong place and could give me no information as to where I was. But I had one comfort, I had not waked Livy; I believed I could find that sock in silence if the night lasted long enough. So I started again and softly pawed

756

all over the place, and sure enough at the end of half
an hour I laid my hand on the missing article. I rose
joyfully up and butted the wash-bowl and pitcher off
the stand and simply raised —— so to speak. Livy
screamed. then said, "Who is that? what *is* the matter?"
I said "There ain't anything the matter—I'm hunting
for my sock." She said, "Are you hunting for it with a
club?". . .

To William Dean Howells

[*Full text of a letter previously published only in part*]

Hartford, November 17, 1879.

MY DEAR HOWELLS:

Just got home from Chicago at 2.30 this morning,
after a solid week of unparalleled dissipation. I was up
all night Monday, Tuesday, Wednesday and Thursday
nights and was in bed only four and five hours a day
during three of those days—the first (Monday) I was
up at 6 AM and did not go to bed till 7 the next morning. Still, I have not at any time felt tired and hardly
even drowsy. But of course the fatigue is in me somewhere and will begin to come to the surface now.

I wish you had gone out there—you would have been
glad all your life. I doubt if America has ever seen anything quite equal to it; I am well satisfied I shall not
live to see its equal again. How pale those speeches are
in print—but how radiant, how full of color, how blinding they were in the delivery! Bob Ingersoll's speech was
sadly crippled by the proof-readers but its music will
sing through my memory always as the divinest that ever
enchanted my ears. And I shall always see him as he
stood that night on a dinner table, under the flash of
lights and banners, in the midst of seven hundred frantic

shouters, the most beautiful human creature that ever lived. "They fought that a mother might own her child" —the words look like any other print but Lord bless me, he borrowed the very accent of the angel of Mercy to say them in, and you should have seen that vast house rise to its feet, and you should have heard the hurricane that followed. That's the *only* test!—people may shout, clap their hands, stamp, wave their napkins, but none but the master can make them *get up on their feet*.

I heard four speeches which carried away all my wits and made me drunk with enthusiasm. When I look at them in print they don't seem the same—their still sentences seem rather the prone dead forms of a host whom I had lately seen moving to the assault in the fire and smoke and tumult of battle, with flags flying and drums beating and the clarion voice of command ringing out above the thunder of the guns. Lord, there's nothing like the human organ to make words live and throb and lift the bearer to the full altitudes of their meaning.

But—what I set out to say was, I can't talk before those ladies because I'm not going to have the time. If I had the time, and *could* talk about the wonders I saw in Chicago, and those ladies cared for anything so uninstructive, I'd do that; but I couldn't, for I choke up with the mere memory of it—to talk of it would simply be impossible. Imagine what it was like, to see a bullet-shredded old battle-flag reverently unfolded to the gaze of a thousand middle-aged soldiers most of whom hadn't seen it since they saw it advancing over victorious fields when they were in their prime. And imagine what it was like when Grant, their first commander, stepped into view while they were still going mad over the flag—and then right in the midst of it all, somebody struck up

"When We Were Marching through Georgia." Well, you should have heard the thousand voices lift that chorus and seen the tears stream down. If I live a hundred years I shan't ever forget these things—nor be able to talk about them. I shan't ever forget that I saw Phil Sheridan, with martial cloak and plumed chapeau, riding his big black horse in the midst of his own cannon—by all odds the superbest figure of a soldier *I* ever looked upon.

Grand times, my boy, grand times. Gen. Grant sat at the banquet like a statue of iron and listened without the faintest suggestion of emotion to fourteen speeches which tore other people all to shreds, but when I lit in with the fifteenth and last his time was come! I shook him up like dynamite and he sat there fifteen minutes and laughed and cried like the mortalest of mortals. But bless you I had measured this unconquerable conqueror and went at my work with the confidence of conviction, for I knew I could lick him. He told me he had shaken hands with 15,000 people that day and come out of it without an ache or pain, but that my truths had racked all the bones of his body apart. General Sherman said— well, no matter what he said, but it was mighty hearty and flattering and most admirably worded, for he knows how to handle English.

But this postscript is extending itself too much. Its object is—now that I seem to have got down to it—to wail over the fact that my proof sheets have begun to pile in on me at last, and *that* means, the dozen closing chapters of my book have got to be tackled now and stuck to without interruption till they are all written and completed—and this bars me out of the Holmes breakfast and my visit with you; and I just can't bear to think of it. I've been imagining that visit and the lovely talks in the lovely new house and the delightful times we should have—and now it is all "up." But you've got to extend the time and allow me to come as soon as my confinement with this book is over and I'm able to be around again.

Yrs ever
MARK

To an Unidentified Person

[Published here for the first time]

Hartford, September 19, 1883.

DEAR SIRS:

You have a contract with Mr. Will Gillette; and I am aware that you are trying (as usual with you) to sneak out of the performance of its conditions. I am personally interested in the matter; therefore I suggest to you couple of piety-mouthing, hypocritical thieves and liars that you change your customary policy this time.

Truly Yours
S. L. CLEMENS

To William Dean Howells

[Published here for the first time]

May 24, 1884.

DEAR HOWELLS:

Good land, have you seen the "poems" of that South Carolinian idiot, "Belton O'Neall Townsend, A B. and Attorney at Law?"—and above all, the dedication of them to you?

If you *did* write him what he says you did, you richly deserve hanging; and if you didn't, *he* deserves hanging.

But he deserves hanging anyway and in any and all cases—no, boiling, gutting, brazing in a mortar—no, no, there *is* no death that can meet his case. Now think of this literary louse dedicating his garbage to you, and quoting encouraging compliments from you and poor dead Longfellow. Let us hope there is a hell, for this poet's sake, who carries his bowels in his skull and when they operate works the discharge into rhyme and prints it.

Ah, if he had only dedicated this diarrhea to Aldrich, I could just howl with delight; but the joke is lost on you—just about wasted.

Ys Ever
MARK

To William Dean Howells

Philadelphia, February 27, 1885.

MY DEAR HOWELLS:

To-night in Baltimore, to-morrow afternoon and night in Washington, and my four-months platform campaign is ended at last. It has been a curious experience. It has taught me that Cable's[1] gifts of mind are greater and higher than I had suspected. But—

That "But" is pointing toward his religion. You will never, never know, never divine, guess, imagine, how loathsome a thing the Christian religion can be made until you come to know and study Cable daily and hourly. Mind you, I like him; he is pleasant company; I rage and swear at him sometimes, but we do not quarrel; we get along mighty happily together; but in him and his person I have learned to hate all religions. He

---

[1] George Washington Cable.—Ed.

has taught me to abhor and detest the Sabbath-day and hunt up new and troublesome ways to dishonor it. . . .

Ys Ever

MARK

To Frank A. Nichols, Secretary, Concord Free Trade Club

[Previously published only in part]

Hartford, March, 1885.

DEAR SIR:

I am in receipt of your favor of the 24th inst., conveying the gratifying intelligence that I have been made an honorary member of the Free Trade Club of Concord, Massachusetts, and I desire to express to the Club, through you, my grateful sense of the high compliment thus paid me.

It does look as if Massachusetts were in a fair way to embarrass me with kindnesses this year. In the first place a Massachusetts Judge has just decided in open court that a Boston publisher may sell not only his own property in a free and unfettered way, but may also as freely sell property which does not belong to him but to me— property which he has not bought and which I have not sold. Under this ruling I am now advertising that judge's homestead for sale; and if I make as good a sum out of it as I expect I shall go on and sell the rest of his property.

In the next place, a committee of the public library of your town has condemned and excommunicated my last book,[1] and doubled its sale. This generous action of theirs must necessarily benefit me in one or two addi-

---

[1] *Adventures of Huckleberry Finn.*—Ed.

tional ways. For instance, it will deter other libraries from buying the book and you are doubtless aware that one book in a public library prevents the sale of a sure ten and a possible hundred of its mates. And secondly it will cause the purchasers of the book to read it, out of curiosity, instead of merely intending to do so after the usual way of the world and library committees; and then they will discover, to my great advantage and their own indignant disappointment, that there is nothing objectionable in the book, after all.

And finally, the Free Trade Club of Concord comes forward and adds to the splendid burden of obligations already conferred upon me by the Commonwealth of Massachusetts, an honorary membership which is more worth than all the rest since it endorses me as worthy to associate with certain gentlemen whom even the moral icebergs of the Concord library committee are bound to respect.

May the great Commonwealth of Massachusetts endure forever, is the heartfelt prayer of one who, long a recipient of her mere general good will, is proud to realize that he is at last become her pet.

Thanking you again, dear sir and gentlemen, I remain

Your obliged servant

S. L. CLEMENS

(known to the Concord Winter School of Philosophy as "Mark Twain.")

To an Unidentified Person

[Perhaps as an autograph]

November 6, 1886.

When the Lord finished the world, he pronounced it good. That is what I said about my first work, too. But

Time, I tell you, Time takes the confidence out of these incautious early opinions. It is more than likely that He thinks about the world, now, pretty much as I think about the *Innocents Abroad.* The fact is, there is a trifle too much water in both.

Truly Yours

S. L. CLEMENS

MARK TWAIN

To Jeannette Gilder

[Not mailed]

Hartford, May 14, 1887.

MY DEAR MISS GILDER:

We shall spend the summer at the same old place— the remote farm called "Rest-and-be-Thankful" on top of the hills three miles from Elmira, N. Y. Your other question is harder to answer. It is my habit to keep four or five books in process of erection all the time and every summer add a few courses of bricks to two or three of them, but I cannot forecast which of the two or three it is going to be. It takes seven years to complete a book by this method but still it is a good method: gives the public a rest. I have been accused of "rushing into print" prematurely, moved thereto by greediness for money, but in truth I have never done that. Do you care for trifles of information? Well, then, *Tom Sawyer* and *The Prince and the Pauper* were each on the stocks two or three years, and "Old Times on the Mississippi" eight.[1] One of my unfinished books has been on the stocks sixteen years, another seventeen. This latter book could have been finished in a day, at any time

---

[1] *Rather, Life on the Mississippi.—Ed.*

during the past five years. But as in the first of these
two narratives all the action takes place in Noah's ark,
and as in the other the action takes place in heaven,
there seemed to be no hurry and so I have not hurried.
Tales of stirring adventure in those localities do not need
to be rushed to publication lest they get stale by waiting.
In twenty-one years, with all my time at my free dis-
posal, I have written and completed only eleven books,
whereas with half the labor that a journalist does I could
have written sixty in that time. I do not greatly mind
being accused of a proclivity for rushing into print but
at the same time I don't believe that the charge is really
well founded. Suppose I did write eleven books, have
you nothing to be grateful for? Go to—remember the
forty-nine which I didn't write.

Truly Yours

S. L. CLEMENS

NOTES [ADDED TWENTY-TWO YEARS LATER]:
Stormfield, April 30, 1909. It seems the letter was not
sent. I probably feared she might print it and I couldn't
find a way to say so without running a risk of hurting
her. No one would hurt Jeannette Gilder purposely and
no one would want to run the risk of doing it uninten-
tionally. She is my neighbor, six miles away now, and I
must ask her about this ancient letter.

I note with pride and pleasure that I told no untruths
in my unsent answer. I still have the habit of keeping
unfinished books lying around years and years, waiting.
I have four or five novels on hand at present in a half-
finished condition and it is more than three years since I
have looked at any of them. I have no intention of
finishing them. I could complete all of them in less than
a year, if the impulse should come powerfully upon me.
Long, long ago money-*necessity* furnished that impulse

once, (*Following the Equator*), but mere desire for money has never furnished it so far as I remember. Not even money-necessity was able to overcome me on a couple of occasions when perhaps I ought to have allowed it to succeed. While I was a bankrupt and in debt two offers were made me for weekly literary contributions to continue during a year and they would have made a debtless man of me, but I declined them, with my wife's full approval, for I had known of no instance where a man had pumped himself out once a week and failed to run "emptyings" before the year was finished.

As to that "Noah's Ark" book, I began it in Edinburgh in 1873; I don't know where the manuscript is now. It was a Diary, which professed to be the work of Shem but wasn't. I began it again several months ago, but only for recreation; I hadn't any intention of carrying it to a finish—or even to the end of the first chapter, in fact.

As to the book whose action "takes place in Heaven." That was a small thing, *Captain Stormfield's Visit to Heaven*. It lay in my pigeon-holes 40 years, then I took it out and printed it in *Harper's Monthly* last year.

S. L. C.

To William Dean Howells

Elmira, August 22, 1887.

MY DEAR HOWELLS:

. . . How stunning are the changes which age makes in a man while he sleeps. When I finished Carlyle's *French Revolution* in 1871 I was a Girondin; every time I have read it since I have read it differently—being influenced and changed, little by little, by life and environment (and Taine and St. Simon): and now I lay the book down once more, and recognize that I am a Sansculotte! And not a pale, characterless Sansculotte but a Marat. Carlyle teaches no such gospel: so the change is in *me*—in my vision of the evidences.

People pretend that the Bible means the same to them at 50 that it did at all former milestones in their journey. I wonder how they can lie so. It comes of practice, no doubt. They would not say that of Dickens's or Scott's books. *Nothing* remains the same. When a man goes back to look at the house of his childhood, it has always *shrunk:* there is no instance of such a house being as big as the picture in memory and imagination calls for. Shrunk how? Why, to its correct dimensions: the house hasn't altered, this is the first time it has been in focus.

Well, that's loss. To have house and Bible shrink so under the disillusioning corrected angle is loss—for a moment. But there are compensations. You tilt the tube skyward and bring planets and comets and corona flames a hundred and fifty thousand miles high into the field. Which I see you have done, and found Tolstoi. I haven't got him in focus yet but I've got Browning. . . .

Ys Ever
Mark

To Orion Clemens

November 29, 1888.

Jesus *Christ!* It is perilous to write such a man. You can go crazy on less material than anybody that ever lived. What in hell has produced all these maniacal imaginings? You told me you *had* hired an attendant for ma. Now hire one instantly, and stop this nonsense of wearing Mollie and yourself out trying to do that nursing yourselves. Hire the attendant and tell me her

cost so that I can instruct Webster & Co. to add it every
month to what they already send. Don't fool away any
more time about this. And don't write me any more
damned rot about "storms" and inability to pay trivial
sums of money and—and—hell and *damnation!* You
see I've read only the first page of your letter; I wouldn't
read the rest for a million dollars.

Yr SAM

P.S. Don't imagine that I have lost my temper, because I swear. I swear all day, but I do not lose my
temper. And don't imagine that I am on my way to the
poor house, for I am not; or that I am uneasy, for I am
not; or that I am uncomfortable or unhappy—for I *never
am.* I don't know what it is to be unhappy or uneasy,
and I am not going to try to learn how at this late day.

SAM

To Orion Clemens

Hartford, January 5, 1889.

DEAR ORION:

At 12.20 this afternoon a line of movable types was
spaced and justified by machinery for the first time in
the history of the world! And I was there to see. It was
done *automatically*—instantly—perfectly. This is indeed
the first line of movable types that ever *was* perfectly
spaced and perfectly justified on this earth.

This was the last function that remained to be tested
—and so by long odds the most amazing and extraordinary invention ever born of the brain of man stands
completed and perfect. Livy is down stairs celebrating.

But it's a cunning devil, is that machine!—and knows
more than any man that ever lived. You shall see. We

made the test in this way. We set up a lot of random letters in a stick—three-fourths of a line; then filled out the line with quads representing 14 spaces, each space to be 35-1000 of an inch thick. Then we threw aside the quads and put the letters into the machine and formed them into 15 two-letter words, leaving the words separated by two-inch vacancies. Then we started up the machine slowly, by hand, and fastened our eyes on the space-selecting pins. The first pin-block projected its third pin as the first word came traveling along the raceway; second block did the same; but the third block projected its *second* pin!

"Oh, hell! stop the machine—something wrong—it's going to set a 30-1000 space!"

General consternation. "A foreign substance has got into the spacing plates." This from the head mathematician.

"Yes, that is the trouble," assented the foreman.

Paige examined. "No—look in, and you can see that there's nothing of the kind." Further examination. "*Now* I know what it is—what it *must* be: one of those plates projects and binds. It's too bad—the first test is a failure." A *pause*. "Well, boys, no use to cry. Get to work—take the machine down.—No—Hold on! don't touch a thing! Go right ahead! We are fools, the machine isn't. The machine knows what it's about. There is a *speck of dirt* on one of those types and the machine is putting in a thinner space to *allow* for it!"

That was just it. The machine went right ahead, spaced the line, justified it to a hair, and shoved it into the galley complete and perfect! We took it out and examined it with a glass. You could not tell by your eye that the third space was thinner than the others, but the glass and the calipers showed the difference. Paige had always said that the machine would measure invisible particles of dirt and allow for them, but even he had forgotten that vast fact for the moment.

All the witnesses made written record of the immense historical birth—the first justification of a line of movable type by machinery—and also set down the hour and the minute. Nobody had drank anything and yet everybody seemed drunk. Well—dizzy, stupefied, stunned.

All the other wonderful inventions of the human brain sink pretty nearly into commonplace contrasted with this awful mechanical miracle. Telephones, telegraphs, locomotives, cotton gins, sewing machines, Babbage calculators, Jacquard looms, perfecting presses, Arkwright's frames—all mere toys, simplicities! The Paige Compositor marches alone and far in the lead of human inventions.

In two or three weeks we shall work the stiffness out of her joints and have her performing as smoothly and softly as human muscles, and then we shall speak out the big secret and let the world come and gaze.

Return me this letter when you have read it.

SAM

To Andrew Lang

[Early 1890]

. . . The little child is permitted to label its drawings "This is a cow—this is a horse" and so on. This protects the child. It saves it from the sorrow and wrong of hearing its cows and its horses criticised as kangaroos and work-benches. A man who is whitewashing a fence is doing a useful thing, so also is the man who is adorning a rich man's house with costly frescoes; and all of us are sane enough to judge these performances by standards proper to each. Now then, to be fair an author ought to be allowed to put upon his book an explanatory line: "This is written for the Belly and the Members." And the critic ought to hold himself in honor bound to put away from him his ancient habit of judging all books by one standard and thenceforth follow a fairer course.

The critic assumes every time that if a book doesn't meet the cultivated-class standard, it isn't valuable. Let us apply his law all around: for if it is sound in the case of novels, narratives, pictures, and such things, it is certainly sound and applicable to all the steps which lead up to culture and make culture possible. It condemns the spelling book, for a spelling book is of no use to a person of culture; it condemns all school books and all schools which lie between the child's primer and Greek, and between the infant school and the university; it condemns all the rounds of art which lie between the cheap terra cotta groups and the Venus de Medici, and between the chromo and the Transfiguration; it requires Whitcomb Riley to sing no more till he can sing like Shakspeare, and it forbids all amateur music and will grant its sanction to nothing below the "classic."

Is this an extravagant statement? No, it is a mere statement of fact. It is the fact itself that is extravagant and grotesque. And what is the result? This, and it is sufficiently curious: the critic has actually imposed upon the world the superstition that a painting by Raphael is more valuable to the civilizations of the earth than is a chromo; and the august opera than the hurdy-gurdy and the villagers' singing society; and Homer than the little everybody's-poet whose rhymes are in all mouths to-day and will be in nobody's mouth next generation; and the Latin classics than Kipling's far-reaching bugle-note; and Jonathan Edwards than the Salvation Army; and the Venus di Medici than the plaster-cast peddler; the superstition, in a word, that the vast and awful comet that trails its cold lustre through the remote abysses of space once a century and interests and instructs a cultivated handful of astronomers is worth more to the world than the sun which warms and cheers all the nations every day and makes the crops to grow.

If a critic should start a religion it would not have any object but to convert angels, and they wouldn't need it. The thin top crust of humanity—the cultivated—are worth pacifying, worth pleasing, worth coddling, worth nourishing and preserving with dainties and delicacies, it is true; but to be caterer to that little faction is no very dignified or valuable occupation, it seems to me; it is merely feeding the over-fed and there must be small satisfaction in that. It is not that little minority who are already saved that are best worth lifting at, I should think, but the mighty mass of the uncultivated who are underneath. That mass will never see the Old Masters— that sight is for the few; but the chromo maker can lift them all one step upward toward appreciation of art; they cannot have the opera, but the hurdy-gurdy and the singing class lift them a little way toward that far height; they will never know Homer, but the passing rhymester of their day leaves them higher than he found them; they may never even hear of the Latin classics but they will strike step with Kipling's drum-beat, and they will march; for all Jonathan Edwards's help they would die in their slums, but the Salvation Army will beguile some of them up to pure air and a cleaner life; they know no sculpture, the Venus is not even a name to them, but they are a grade higher in the scale of civilization by the ministrations of the plaster-cast than they were before it took its place upon their mantel and made it beautiful to their unexacting eyes.

Indeed I have been misjudged from the very first. I

have never tried in even one single little instance to help cultivate the cultivated classes. I was not equipped for it, either by native gifts or training. And I never had any ambition in that direction, but always hunted for bigger game—the masses. I have seldom deliberately tried to instruct them but have done my best to entertain them. To simply amuse them would have satisfied my dearest ambition at any time; for they could get instruction elsewhere and I had two chances to help to the teacher's one: for amusement is a good preparation for study and a good healer of fatigue after it. My audience is dumb, it has no voice in print, and so I cannot know whether I have won its approbation or only got its censure.

Yes, you see, I have always catered for the Belly and the Members but have been served like the others—criticized from the culture-standard—to my sorrow and pain; because, honestly, I never cared what became of the cultured classes; they could go to the theatre and the opera, they had no use for me and the melodeon.

And now at last I arrive at my object and tender my petition, making supplication to this effect: that the critics adopt a rule recognizing the Belly and the Members and formulate a standard whereby work done for them shall be judged. Help me, Mr. Lang; no voice can reach further than yours in a case of this kind, or carry greater weight of authority.

To an Unidentified Person

1890

. . . Your surmise is correct, sharply and exactly so—that I confine myself to life with which I am familiar, when pretending to portray life. But I confined myself to the boy-life out on the Mississippi because that had a peculiar charm for me and not because I was not familiar with other phases of life. I was a *soldier* two weeks once in the beginning of the war, and was hunted like a rat the whole time. Familiar? My splendid Kipling himself hasn't a more burnt-in, hard-baked and unforgetable familiarity with that death-on-the-pale-horse-with-hell-following-after which is a raw soldier's first fortnight in the field—and which, without any doubt, is the most tremendous fortnight and the vividest he is ever going to see.

Yes and I have shoveled silver tailings in a quartz mill a couple of weeks, and acquired the last possibilities of culture in *that* direction. And I've done "pocket-mining" during three months in the one little patch of ground in the whole globe where Nature conceals gold in pockets—or *did*, before we robbed all of those pockets and exhausted, obliterated, annihilated the most curious freak Nature ever indulged in. There are not thirty men left alive who, being told there was a pocket hidden on the broad slope of a mountain, would know how to go and find it or have even the faintest idea of how to set about it—but I am one of the possible 20 or 30 who possess the secret and I could go and put my hand on that hidden treasure with a most deadly precision.

And I've been a prospector and know pay rock from poor when I find it—just with a touch of the tongue. And I've been a silver *miner* and know how to dig and shovel and drill, and put in a blast. And so I know the mines and the miners interiorly as well as Bret Harte knows them exteriorly and superficially.

And I was a newspaper reporter four years in cities, and so saw the inside of many things; and was reporter in a legislature two sessions and the same in Congress one session—and thus learned to know personally three sample-bodies of the smallest minds and the selfishest souls and the cowardliest hearts that God makes.

And I was some years a Mississippi pilot and familiarly knew all the different kinds of steamboatmen—a race apart and not like other folk.

And I was for some years a traveling "jour" printer, and wandered from city to city—and so I *know* that sect familiarly.

And I was a lecturer on the public platform a number of seasons and was a responder to toasts at all the different kinds of banquets—and so I know a great many secrets about audiences—secrets not to be got out of books but only acquirable by experience.

And I watched over one dear project of mine five years, spent a fortune on it, and failed to make it go— and the history of that would make a large book in which a million men would see themselves as in a mirror; and they would testify and say, Verily this is not imagination, this fellow has been there—and after would they cast dust upon their heads, cursing and blaspheming.

And I am a publisher and did pay to one author's widow [General Grant's] the largest copyright checks this world has seen—aggregating more than £80,000 in the first year.

And I have been an author for 20 years and an ass for 55.

Now then: as the most valuable capital, or culture, or education usable in the building of novels is personal experience, I ought to be well equipped for that trade. I surely have the equipment, a wide culture and all of it real, none of it artificial, for I don't know anything about books.

To the Gas Company

Hartford, February 12, 1891.

DEAR SIRS:

Some day you will move me almost to the verge of irritation by your chuckle-headed Goddamned fashion of shutting your Goddamned gas off without giving any notice to your Goddamned parishioners. Several times you have come within an ace of smothering half of this household in their beds and blowing up the other half by this idiotic, not to say criminal, custom of yours. And it has happened again to-day. Haven't you a telephone?

Ys

S L CLEMENS

To the Reverend J. H. Twichell

May, 1892.

DEAR JOE:

. . . The dogs of the Campagna (they watch sheep without human assistance) are big and warlike, and are terrible creatures to meet in those lonely expanses. Two young Englishmen—one of them a friend of mine—were away out there yesterday, with a peasant guide of the region who is a simple-hearted and very devout Roman Catholic. At one point the guide stopped and said they were now approaching a spot where two especially ferocious dogs were accustomed to herd sheep: that it would be well to go cautiously and be prepared to retreat if they saw the dogs. So then they started on but presently came suddenly upon the dogs. The immense brutes came straight for them, with death in their eyes. The guide said in a voice of horror, "Turn your backs, but for God's sake don't stir—I will pray—I will pray the Virgin to do a miracle and save us; she will hear me, oh, my God she surely will." And straightway he began to pray. The Englishmen stood quaking with fright, and wholly without faith in the man's prayer. But all at once the furious snarling of the dogs ceased—at three steps distant—and there was dead silence. After a moment my friend, who could no longer endure the awful suspense, turned—and there was the miracle, sure enough: the gentleman dog had mounted the lady dog and both had forgotten their solemn duty in the ecstasy of a higher interest!

The strangers were saved and they retired from that place with thankful hearts. The guide was in a frenzy of pious gratitude and exultation, and praised and glorified the Virgin without stint; and finally wound up with, "But you—you are Protestants; she would not have done it for you; she did it for me—only me—praised be she for evermore! and I will hang a picture of it in the church and it shall be another proof that her loving care is still with her children who humbly believe and adore."

By the time the dogs got unattached the men were five miles from there.

To William Dean Howells

Vienna, January 22, 1898.

DEAR HOWELLS:

Look at those ghastly figures. I used to write it "Hartford, 1871." There was no Susy then—there is no Susy now. And how much lies between—one long lovely stretch of scented fields, and meadows, and shady woodlands; and suddenly Sahara! You speak of the glorious days of that old time—and they were. It is my quarrel—that traps like that are set. Susy and Winnie given us, in miserable sport, and then taken away.

About the last time I saw you I described to you the culminating disaster in a book I was going to write (and will yet, when the stroke is further away)—a man's dead daughter brought to him when he had been through all other possible misfortunes—and I said it couldn't be done as it ought to be done except by a man who had lived it—it must be written with the blood out of a man's heart. I couldn't know, then, how soon I was to be made competent. I have thought of it many a time since. If.you were here I think we could cry down each other's necks, as in your dream. For we *are* a pair of old derelicts drifting around, now, with some of our passengers gone and the sunniness of the others in eclipse.

I couldn't get along without work now. I bury myself in it up to the ears. Long hours—8 and 9 on a stretch, sometimes. And all the days, Sundays included. It isn't all for print, by any means, for much of it fails to suit me; 50,000 words of it in the past year. It was because of the deadness which invaded me when Susy died. . . .

MARK

To H. H. Rogers

Rouen, October, 1894.

DEAR MR. ROGERS:

Yours of the 24th Sept. has arrived filled with pleasantness and peace. I would God I were in my room in the new house in Fairhaven, so'st I could have one good solid night's sleep. I might have had one last night if I hadn't lost my temper, for I was loaded up high with fatigue; but at two this morning I had a W.C. call and jumped up in the dark and ran in my night-shirt and without a candle—for I believed I knew my way. This hotel d'Angleterre must be a congeries of old dwellings —if it isn't, it is built up in a series of water-tight compartments, like the American liners, that go clear to the top. You can't get out of your own compartment. There is only your one hall; it has four rooms on each side of it and a staircase in the midst; would you think a person could get lost in such a place? I assure you it is possible; for a person of talent.

We are on the second floor from the ground. There's a W.C. on the floor *above* us and one on the floor *below* us. Halls pitch dark. I groped my way and found the upper W.C. Starting to return, I went up stairs instead of down, and went to what I supposed was my room, but I could not make out the number in the dark and was afraid to enter it. Then I remembered that I—no, my mind lost confidence and began to wander. I was no longer sure as to what floor I was on, and the minute I realized that, the rest of my mind went. One cannot stand still in a dark hall at two in the morning, lost, and be content. One must move and go on moving, even at the risk of getting worse lost. I groped up and down a couple of those flights over and over again, cursing to myself. And every time I thought I heard somebody coming, I shrank together like one of those toy balloons when it collapses. You see, I was between two fires; I could not grope to the top floor and start fresh and count down to my own, for it was all occupied by young ladies and a dangerous place to get caught in, clothed as I was clothed, and not in my right mind. I could not grope down to the ground floor and count *up*, for there was a ball down there. A ball, and young ladies likely to be starting up to bed about this time. And so they were. I saw the glow of their distant candle, I felt the chill of their distant cackle. I did not know whether I was on a W.C. floor or not but I had to take a risk. I groped to the door that ought to be it—right where you turn down the stairs; and it was it. I entered it grateful, and stood in its dark shelter with a beating heart and thought how happy I should be to live there always, in that humble cot, and go out no more among life's troubles and dangers. Several of the young ladies applied for admission but I was not receiving. Thursdays being my day. I meant to freeze out the ball if it took a week. And I did. When the drone and burr of its music had ceased for twenty minutes and the house was solidly dead and dark, I groped down to the ground floor, then turned and counted my way up home, all right.

Then straightway my temper went up to 180 in the shade and I began to put it into form. Presently an admiring voice said—"When you are through with your prayers, I would like to ask where you have been all night."

To William Dean Howells

London, January 25, 1900.

DEAR HOWELLS:

If you got half as much as Pond prophesied, be content and praise God—it has not happened to another. But I am sorry he didn't go with you, for it is marvelous to hear him yarn. He is good company, cheery and hearty, and his mill is never idle. Your doing a lecture tour was heroic. It was the highest order of grit and you have a right to be proud of yourself. No amount of applause or money or both could save it from being a hell to a man constituted as you are. It is that even to me, who am made of coarser stuff.

I knew the audiences would come forward and shake hands with you—that one infallible sign of sincere approval. In all my life, wherever it failed me I left the hall sick and ashamed, knowing what it meant.

Privately speaking, this is a sordid and criminal war

and in every way shameful and excuseless. Every day I
write (in my head) bitter magazine articles about it
but I have to stop with that. For England must not fall;
it would mean an inundation of Russian and German
political degradations which would envelop the globe
and steep it in a sort of Middle-Age night and slavery
which would last till Christ comes again. Even wrong—
and she is wrong—England must be upheld. He is an
enemy of the human race who shall speak against her
now. Why *was* the human race created? Or at least why
wasn't something creditable created in place of it? God
had his opportunity. He could have made a reputation.
But no, He must commit this grotesque folly—a lark
which must have cost him a regret or two when He
came to think it over and observe effects. For a giddy
and unbecoming caprice there has been nothing like it
till this war. I talk the war with both sides—always
waiting until the other man introduces the topic. Then
I say "My head is with the Briton but my heart and such
rags of morals as I have are with the Boer—now we
will talk, unembarrassed and without prejudice." And
so we discuss, and have no trouble.

January 26.

It was my intention to make some disparaging remarks about the human race and so I kept this letter
open for that purpose, and for the purpose of telling
my dream, wherein the Trinity were trying to guess a
conundrum, but I can do better—for I can snip out of
the *Times* various samples and side-lights which bring
the race down to date and expose it as of yesterday. If
you will notice, there is seldom a telegram in a paper
which fails to show up one or more members and bene-
ficiaries of our Civilization as promenading in his shirt-
tail, with the rest of his regalia in the wash.

I love to see the holy ones air their smug pieties and admire them and smirk over them, and at the same moment frankly and publicly show their contempt for the pieties of the Boer—confidently expecting the approval of the country and the pulpit, and getting it.

I notice that God is on both sides in this war; thus history repeats itself. But I am the only person who has noticed this; everybody here thinks He is playing the game for this side, and for this side only.

With great love to you all

MARK

To Andrew Carnegie

DEAR SIR AND FRIEND:

You seem to be in prosperity. Could you lend an admirer $1.50 to buy a hymn-book with? God will bless you. I feel it; I know it. So will I.

N.B.—If there should be other applications, this one not to count.

Yours,

MARK

P.S.—Don't send the hymn-book; send the money; I want to make the selection myself.

M.

To William Dean Howells

[Published here for the first time]

Riverdale, February 13, 1903.

DEAR HOWELLS:

I am infinitely sorry. I was lying awake at the time and felt sure I heard voices; so sure that I put on a dressing-gown and went down to inquire into the matter but you were already gone. I encountered Sam coming up as I turned the lower corner of the house and he said it was a stranger, who insisted on seeing me—"a stumpy little gray man with furtive ways and an evil face."

"What did he say his name was?"

"He didn't say. He offered his card but I didn't take it."

"That was stupid. Describe him again—and more in detail."

He did it.

"I can't seem to locate him—I wish you had taken his card. Why didn't you?"

"I didn't like his manners."

"Why? What did he do?"

"He called me a quadrilateral astronomical incandescent son of a bitch."

"Oh, that was Howells. Is *that* what annoyed you! What is the matter with it? Is that a thing to distort into an offense, when you couldn't possibly know but that he meant it as a compliment? And it *is* a compliment, too."

"I don't think so, it only just sounds so. I am not finding any fault with the main phrase, which is hallowed to me by memories of childhood's happy days, now vanished never to return, on account of its being my sainted mother's diminutive for me, but I did not like those adverbs. I have an aversion for adverbs. I will not take adverbs from a stranger."

"Very well," I said coldly. "Such being your theology, you can get your money after breakfast and seek another place. I know you are honest, I know you are competent, and I am sorry to part with you; you are the best gardener I have ever had but in matters of grammar you are morbid, and this makes you over-sensitive and altogether too god dam particular."

I am sorry and ashamed, Howells, and so is Clara, who is helping write this letter, with expressions she got of her mother, but the like will not happen again on this place, I can assure you.

Yrs Ever
MARK

P.S.—This page had to be re-written and made parlor-mentory, because I found Mrs. Clemens had given orders that the letter be brought under her blue pencil before mailing. But I knew 2 of the pages would pass.

M. T.

"Very well," I said, coldly. "Such being your theology, you can get your money after breakfast and seek another place. I know you are honest, I know you are competent, and I am sorry to part with you; you are the best gardener I have ever had, but in matters of grammar you are morbid, and this makes you over-sensitive and altogether too amsterdam particular."

I am sorry and ashamed, Howells, and so are Clara and Mrs. Clemens, who blame me for allowing it to happen, but the like will not happen again on this place, I can assure you.

Ys Ever
MARK

To the Editor of the New York Times

[Published here for the first time]

October 4, 1907.

TO THE EDITOR:

I would like to know what kind of a goddam govment this is that discriminates between two common carriers and makes a goddam railroad charge everybody equal

and lets a goddam man charge any goddam price he
wants to for his goddam opera box

                                    W D HOWELLS

Howells it is an outrage the way the govment is acting
so I sent this complaint to N. Y. *Times* with your name
signed because it would have more weight.

                                            MARK

To William Dean Howells

                                    January 18, 1909.

DEAR HOWELLS:
   I have to write a line, lazy as I am, to say how your
Poe article delighted me; and to say that I am in agreement with substantially all you say about his literature.
To me his prose is unreadable—like Jane Austin's [*sic*].
No, there is a difference. I could read his prose on
salary, but not Jane's. Jane is entirely impossible. It
seems a great pity that they allowed her to die a natural death.
   Another thing: you grant that God and circumstances
sinned against Poe but you also grant that he sinned
against himself—a thing which he couldn't do and
didn't do.
   It is lively up here now. I wish you could come.

                                    Yrs ever,
                                        MARK

To J. Wylie Smith, Glasgow, Scotland

[Corrected text of a published letter]

August 7, 1909.

DEAR SIR:

My view of the matter has not changed. To-wit, that Christian Science is valuable; that it has just the same value now that it had when Mrs. Eddy stole it from Quimby; that its healing principle (its most valuable asset) possesses the same force now that it possessed a million years before Quimby was born; that Mrs. Eddy the fraud, the humbug, *organized* that force and is *entitled to high credit for that*. Then with a splendid sagacity she hitched it to the shirt-tail of a religion—the surest of all ways to secure friends for it, and support. In a fine and lofty way—figuratively speaking—it was a tramp stealing a ride on the lightning express. Ah, how did that ignorant village-born peasant woman know the human ass so well? She has no more intellect than a tadpole—until it comes to *business*—then she is a marvel!

Am I sorry I wrote the book? Most certainly not. You say you have 500 in Glasgow. Fifty years from now, your posterity will not count them by the hundred but by the thousand. I feel absolutely sure of this.

Very Truly Yours
S L. CLEMENS

BIBLIOGRAPHY

BY JOHN SEELYE

BIOGRAPHY

*Andrews, Kenneth R., *Nook Farm: Mark Twain's Hartford Circle* (Cambridge, Mass., and London, 1950)

Benson, Ivan, *Mark Twain's Western Years* (Stanford, Calif., and London, 1938)

*Branch, Edgar M., *The Literary Apprenticeship of Mark Twain* (Urbana, Ill., 1950)

*Brashear, Minnie M., *Mark Twain, Son of Missouri* (Chapel Hill, N.C., and London, 1934)

*Brooks, Van Wyck, *The Ordeal of Mark Twain,* rev. ed. (New York, 1933; London, 1934)†

*Canby, Henry Seidel, *Turn West, Turn East* (Boston, 1951)

*De Voto, Bernard, *Mark Twain's America* (Boston, 1932)

Duckett, Margaret, *Mark Twain and Bret Harte* (Norman, Okla., 1964)

Fatout, Paul, *Mark Twain in Virginia City* (Bloomington, Ind., 1964)

————, *Mark Twain on the Lecture Circuit* (Bloomington, Ind., 1960)

*Ferguson, DeLancey, *Mark Twain: Man and Legend* (Indianapolis, Ind., 1943)†

Gillis, William R., *Goldrush Days with Mark Twain* (New York, 1930)

Grant, Douglas, *Mark Twain* (New York and London, 1962)

Hill, Hamlin, *Mark Twain and Elisha Bliss* (Columbia, Mo., 1964)

*Howells, William Dean, *My Mark Twain* (New York and London, 1910)

*Kaplan, Justin, *Mr. Clemens and Mark Twain, a Biography* (New York, 1966; London, 1967)

*Mack, Effie Mona, *Mark Twain in Nevada* (New York, 1947)

Meltzer, Milton, *Mark Twain Himself: A Pictorial Biography* (New York, 1960)

*Paine, Albert Bigelow, *Mark Twain: A Biography,* 3 vols. (New York and London, 1912). [Inclusive, but not always trustworthy]

Salsbury, Edith Colgate, ed., *Susy and Mark Twain: Family Dialogues* (New York, 1965; London, 1966)

Turner, Arlin, *Mark Twain and G. W. Cable: The Record*

of a Literary Friendship (East Lansing, Mich., Sydney, and London, 1960)

*Wagenknecht, Edward, *Mark Twain, The Man and His Work*, rev. ed. (Norman, Okla., 1961)

*Wecter, Dixon, *Sam Clemens of Hannibal*, ed. Elizabeth Wecter (Boston, 1952)†

CRITICISM

*Bellamy, Gladys Carmen, *Mark Twain as a Literary Artist* (Norman, Okla., 1950)

*Blair, Walter, *Mark Twain and Huck Finn* (Berkeley and Los Angeles, Calif., 1960)†

*Branch, Edgar M., *The Literary Apprenticeship of Mark Twain; with Selections from His Apprentice Writing* (Urbana, Ill., 1950)

Budd, Louis J., *Mark Twain: Social Philosopher* (Bloomington, Ind., 1962)

Covici, Pascal, Jr., *Mark Twain's Humor: The Image of a World* (Dallas, Texas, 1962)

Cox, James M., *Mark Twain: The Fate of Humor* (Princeton, N.J., 1966; London, 1967)

Foner, Philip S., *Mark Twain, Social Critic* (New York, 1939)†

French, Bryant M., *Mark Twain and* The Gilded Age: *The Book That Named an Era* (Dallas, 1965)

Harnsberger, Caroline Thomas, *Mark Twain's Views of Religion* (Evanston, Ill., 1961)

Hemminghaus, Edgar H., *Mark Twain in Germany* (New York, 1939)

Liljegren, Sten B., *The Revolt Against Romanticism in American Literature as Evidenced in the Works of S. L. Clemens* (Uppsala, Sweden, 1965)

*Long, E. Hudson, *Mark Twain Handbook* (New York, 1957)

*Lynn, Kenneth S., *Mark Twain and Southwestern Humor* (Boston and London, 1960)

Regan, Robert, *Unpromising Heroes: Mark Twain and His Characters* (Berkeley, Calif., and London, 1966)

Rogers, Franklin R., *Mark Twain's Burlesque Patterns as Seen in the Novels and Narratives, 1855–1885* (Dallas, Texas, 1955)

Salomon, Roger B., *Mark Twain and the Image of History* (New Haven, Conn., and London, 1961)

Smith, Henry Nash, *Mark Twain: The Development of a Writer* (Cambridge, Mass., and London, 1962)

———, *Mark Twain's Fable of Progress: Political and Economic Ideas in* A Connecticut Yankee (New Brunswick, N.J., 1964)

Spengemann, William C., *Mark Twain and the Backwoods Angel: The Matter of Innocence in the Works of Samuel L. Clemens* (Kent, Ohio, 1966)

*Stone, Albert E., *The Innocent Eye: Childhood in Mark Twain's Imagination* (New Haven, Conn., and London, 1961)

Tuckey, John Sutton, *Mark Twain and Little Satan: The Writing of* The Mysterious Stranger (West Lafayette, 1963)

Wiggins, Robert A., *Mark Twain: Jackleg Novelist* (Seattle, Wash., 1964)

LITERARY HISTORY, GENERAL STUDIES, ESSAYS

Blair, Walter, *Horse Sense in American Humor* (Chicago, 1942)

———, *Native American Humor: 1800–1900* (New York, 1937)†

Bradley, Sculley, R. C. Beatty, and E. H. Long, eds., *Adventures of Huckleberry Finn: An Annotated Text, Backgrounds and Sources, Essays in Criticism* (New York, 1962)†

Bridgman, Richard, *The Colloquial Style in America* (New York and London, 1966)

Camp, James E. and X. J. Kennedy, eds., *Mark Twain's Frontier: A Textbook of Primary Source Materials for Student Research and Writing* (New York and London, 1963)†

Cardwell, Guy A., ed., *Discussions of Mark Twain* (Boston, 1963)†

Carter, Everett, *Howells and the Age of Realism* (Philadelphia, 1954; London, 1958)

Chase, Richard, *The American Novel and Its Tradition* (New York, 1957; London, 1958)†

Cowie, Alexander, *The Rise of the American Novel* (New York, 1948; London, 1951)

Fiedler, Leslie A., *Love and Death in the American Novel* (New York, 1960; London, 1961)†

Hoffman, Daniel G., *Form and Fable in American Fiction* (New York and London, 1961)†

Kaul, A. N., *The American Vision: Actual and Ideal Society in Nineteenth-Century Fiction* (New Haven, Conn., and London, 1963)

Leary, Lewis, ed., *A Casebook on Mark Twain's Wound* (New York, 1962)†

Lynn, Kenneth S., ed., *Huckleberry Finn: Text, Sources, and Criticism* (New York, 1961)†

Marks, Barry A., ed., *Mark Twain's Huckleberry Finn* (Boston and London, 1959)†

Marx, Leo, *The Machine in the Garden: Technology and the Pastoral Ideal in America* (New York, 1964; London, 1965)†

Meine, Franklin J., ed., *Tall Tales of the Southwest* (New York, 1946)

Morgan, H. Wayne, *American Writers in Rebellion from Twain to Dreiser* (New York, 1965)†

Parrington, Vernon L., "The Backwash of the Frontier— Mark Twain," *Main Currents in American Thought*, Vol. III (New York, 1927–30)†

Pizer, Donald, *Realism and Naturalism in Nineteenth-Century American Literature* (Carbondale, Ill., 1966)

Rourke, Constance, *American Humor: A Study of the National Character* (New York, 1931)†

Rubin, Louis D., Jr., and John Rees Moore, eds., *The Idea of an American Novel* (New York, 1961)

Scott, Arthur L., ed., *Mark Twain: Selected Criticism* (Dallas, 1955)

Smith, Henry Nash, ed., *Mark Twain: A Collection of Critical Essays* (Englewood Cliffs, N.J. and London, 1963)†

Tanner, Tony, *The Reign of Wonder: Naïvety and Reality in American Literature* (London, 1965)

Wagenknecht, Edward, *Cavalcade of the American Novel* (New York and London, 1952)

Wecter, Dixon, "Mark Twain," *Literary History of the United States*, ed. Robert E. Spiller, Willard Thorpe, *et al*, Vol. II (New York and London, 1948)

INTRODUCTORY STUDIES

Baldanza, Frank, *Mark Twain: An Introduction and Interpretation* (New York, 1961)†

Leary, Lewis, *Mark Twain* ("University of Minnesota Pamphlets on American Writers," No. 5) (Minneapolis, Minn., and London, 1960)†

*Particularly recommended (applies only to "Biography" and "Criticism" and to books published before 1962).

†Available in U.S. in paperback edition.

THE VIKING PORTABLE LIBRARY